The Lost Diary of George Washington

The Revolutionary War Years

Johnny Teague

The Lost Diary of George Washington

The Revolutionary War Years

Addison & Highsmith

Addison & Highsmith Publishers

Las Vegas ◊ Chicago ◊ Palm Beach

Published in the United States of America by
Histria Books
7181 N. Hualapai Way, Ste. 130-86
Las Vegas, NV 89166 USA
HistriaBooks.com

Addison & Highsmith is an imprint of Histria Books. Titles published under the imprints of Histria Books are distributed worldwide.

Library of Congress Control Number: 2023930004

ISBN 978-1-59211-200-5 (hardcover)
ISBN 978-1-59211-262-3 (eBook)
ISBN 978-1-59211-430-6 (softbound)

Contents

Introduction 7

The Year 1775 9

The Year 1776 50

The Year 1777 186

The Year 1778 298

The Year 1779 375

The Year 1780 433

The Year 1781 514

DEDICATION

To the God of all creation,
the Founder of this nation,
and the men and women who worked
and sacrificed in His Name
to make this an exceptional nation.
And, to my wife Lori
and our two daughters Brittany and Kate.

Introduction

To find in my study of George Washington that he had kept a diary throughout his life except during the war years was a surprise. When he resumed his diary in May of 1781, his first entry expressed his regret that he had not kept a diary during those crucial years in the fight for the nation's independence. To this end, I have researched General Washington's writings, letters, and orders, as well as the recollection of others. I have visited the battlefields and campsites to gain a clearer perspective. What you will read in the following pages is the reconstructed diary of the Father of Our Nation. This writing is a paraphrase of the sentiments that he personally wrote. The entries come primarily from his own hand staying true to the events, the challenges, the struggles, the heartbreaks, the victories, and the emotions of America's first Commander-in-Chief. For those who do not want to just learn history, but rather desire to touch and feel it, this lost diary is for you.

The Year 1775

Monday, June 19, 1775 — Philadelphia, Pennsylvania

Mr. Henry made an efficacious appeal to each citizen to decide between the two choices — liberty or death. His rousing speech convicted all in attendance, "Is life so dear, or peace so sweet, as to be purchased at the price of chains and slavery?" The events up to that time had warranted such a question. It was a few days after this, that I put on my uniform of war past — viz — the French and Indian War. I made it obvious that my decision was the same as Mr. Henry's — liberty or death. Many thought I wore my uniform because I was looking to command the army. This was never my intent. My intent was to serve in whatever capacity as called to ensure freedom for Mrs. Washington, the family, and our colonies.

My greatest concern at this moment, even more then the challenge itself, is the well-being of Mrs. Washington. I have been so long away that an assurance expressed was necessary so she would know my preferred and happy station is always with her. After I went to Christ Church yesterday, I dispatched a letter to Mrs. Washington on the subject to let her know that this was not my choice, but my destiny. The responsibility is one I cannot imagine bearing. The whole of the American cause must rest on someone's shoulders. My peers feel it is best rested upon me. I am inadequate for such a duty, but my character and duty demand I accept it, relying on that Providence who has kept me safe thus far. I have asked Mrs. Washington to accept the duties that now fall upon her consequently with faith in that same Providence. My earnest desires are that she will not be lonely and that she will not hold me up to a complaint as to some better alternative which I should have charted for my course. I am confident that I will be seen safely through this whole ordeal and wish my wife to have the same confidence. Sadly, in contradiction to that hope, it was beholden upon me to send to her my Will, which can provide for her should the unexpected occur. I also am sending to her my friends and family to encourage her in the days ahead. I lay this as my brother John's chief responsibility. This will give me peace of mind.

I write these things knowing that life will not be the same for me in the foreseeable future. I have sought to be faithful in the few things. Now it seems I have been appointed to the greater. How I desire that the task be not so ominous. Even the contemplation of the onerous business at-hand causes me to question my ability to succeed. I must command all the forces now formed, raise up more, and provide the instruments of war, as well as the strategy and execution of the plan. I can find comfort in knowing that if I give my best and fail, the fault will not lie with me, but with those who appointed me. I am encouraged that at the onset, Congress has given assurance to supply my needs with two million dollars and a pledge of fifteen thousand fighting men, which they will increase as the war necessitates. My hope and consolation are that they, as honorable men, will do as they say. I am encouraged by the men with whom they have appointed to serve under me — General Ward, General Lee, General Schuyler, General Putnam, and Adjutant-General Gates.

Tuesday, June 20, 1775 — Philadelphia, Pennsylvania

Dined at the City Tavern and spent the evening making plans.

Wednesday, June 21, 1775 — Philadelphia, Pennsylvania

Dined with Mr. Robert Morris and discussed financing matters of war.

Met with Mr. John Adams and his cousin Mr. Samuel Adams to discuss the formation of the army from the various sectors of the colonies. Congress has already begun the recruitment for the provincial army in earnest, raising ten companies from Philadelphia, Maryland, and Virginia, which add to the numbers already formed and fighting in Boston. I found great encouragement as we visited about the recent events in Massachusetts. They relayed how the Minute Men were comprised of liberty-loving men from every corner of society — farmers, merchants, tradesmen, teachers, ministers who all dropped what they were doing in their respective vocations. They traded their stations in life to pick up arms for the cause of freedom. The casualties exacted so far by these mere common men against a well-trained British army have been beyond human explanation. Something about the heart beats in this land. This something is what brought many here. This something is a vision that causes men and women all around to take hold of the plow both in the field and on the battleground.

Thursday, June 22, 1775 — Philadelphia, Pennsylvania

Dined at Dr. Cadwaladers, along with Generals Lee and Schuyler, to make final travel preparations for tomorrow morning's ride.

Tomorrow I leave Philadelphia to assume command of our troops. I find comfort in the two who will ride by my side. General Lee, a seasoned warrior, fought by my side under General Braddock in the previous war. He was a former British officer who has come to the aid of our cause just in time. General Schuyler is a man of great respect, being a successful landowner from New York. He has served with me in the Continental Congress and before that, in the French and Indian War.

I welcome these men to bear my burden as Moses did Aaron and Hur. Their assistance has already been appreciated as we received bad news earlier this evening. Our American soldiers have taken high ground to counter British aggression in Boston. British General Gage (I served with him under Braddock) ordered a bold move under General Howe to dislodge our men. They had failed twice, but on the third attempt, Howe and company found our men out of ammunition. With British bayonets and gunfire, our men were forced to relinquish their position. The good news is our men exacted almost three times the casualties on their British counterparts. If nothing else, the British found we will fight. The bad news is the loss was avoidable. If only we had been prepared and organized. The supplies, I am told, were available, just not delivered.

Friday, June 23, 1775 — Philadelphia, Pennsylvania

Set out this day for Boston with General Lee and General Schuyler. Rain soon fell and our progress has been slowed. I am anxious to get to my station and begin our work. I fear time is of the essence.

Sunday, June 25, 1775 — New York

Arrived in New York this afternoon. I was greatly surprised at the unwarranted crowd of people cheering us as we entered. We can understand this reception to a degree, as their citizenry knows that this city is most strategic. New York will be the goal of the British to win and fortify as a base for all other operations. They could use this city to cut off our people from commerce and support. My plan is to leave General

Schuyler in this place to build its defenses and reduce its vulnerability. I have let Schuyler know that he is to build up the stores and prepare the defenses. He is to keep Congress apprised of his actions. The task assigned to General Schuyler is complicated by a governor here, named Governor Tryon, whose sentiments lie with the British and the Tory party. It may be necessary under the authority and consent of the Continental Congress to remove Tryon from his position. I have also warned Schuyler to beware of the Indians and Canadians in this city who may work against the cause on which we are now invested. I must make an imperative plea on General Schuyler to keep me informed concerning all he does with a monthly report and more often as the need arises. In this endeavor, to have as much information as possible from every corner of the hostilities is necessary. Leaving him here gives me comfort, but also concern as my only communication will be delayed and sometimes challenged. Thus, I will have to rest in his good sense in all matters.

Received a letter written to Congress from the provincial camp in Massachusetts Bay. I am sad to read that they are dangerously low on powder. The gentlemen here in New York had heard this complaint earlier and sent all that they could to assist their brothers in Boston. Sadly, our patriots in Boston have used that in the most needful way and, once again, they are low. New York now joins them in shortage. I have found that New York stands destitute with only four barrels of powder in the entire city to defend themselves against the certain-coming British. I have written a letter immediately requesting Congress to aid this cause by supplying this necessary article speedily and effectually. I am in some anxiety already at the dire circumstances in which we find ourselves but am confident we are together with one mind and resolve.

Monday, June 26, 1775 — New York

I was greeted this morning in my quarters by a delegation from the New York Provincial Congress. They were kind to honor me and give me their best wishes. In drafting my reply, I must keep in mind that this city is diverse. It has devoted Colonists and status-quo Tories. It has Indians and Canadians. And, it has people like me who love our mother country and have served her, but who have seen the objectionable behavior toward us. Britain has treated us as if we are secondary or exiled citizens. They must all know that our goal is not one of separation, but rather of reconciliation, reform if possible. I want them to know that when we assumed the soldier, we did not lay down the citizen. I pray my response will grant them the unifying peace to bring this conflict to a rapid and acceptable close.

Tuesday, June 27, 1775 — New York

Set out for Boston.

Sunday, July 2, 1775 — Cambridge, Massachusetts

Came to the army's camp outside of Boston. The Massachusetts' officers greeted me. After a few opening exchanges, I took my leave to ride around the city to gather a personal view of the condition of the city and the state of fortifications (getting my que from Nehemiah who entered Jerusalem and rode around it in the evening to get a sense of the situation as recorded in the Holy Scriptures). What I found today was the enemy holding Charlestown and entrenched on Bunker Hill. They are making fortifications to remain. I could see in the distance several British ships anchored in the harbor ready to harass. As Boston exists almost as an island, the British station men at the neck to prevent our raw army from invading the remainder of the continent. Our army is divided between two hills a little over a mile from the enemy. A third part of the army was guarding the entrance and exit of Boston, opposite theirs at the neck. The British are in control of the water and can move readily against any directional attack. Our situation is disagreeable to me, but seemingly necessary. Though the enemy is bottled up, our lack of supplies and manpower makes any attack foolish. After my reconnoiter, I have decided it best that we strengthen our positions, train our men, and buy time with the hope that needed supplies will be received before action is required.

One side note, I am greatly impressed by the beauty of this area and the captivating view of the city of Boston. How tragic that we are forced to come to such a place as this to commence a war. I cannot help but think how Mrs. Washington would enjoy this town and the charming landscapes that surround it.

Monday, July 3, 1775 — Cambridge, Massachusetts

Finished introductions with the officers here. As rough and disorganized as these men appear, I am moved by the fact that they have chosen liberty to the point of leaving the enjoyments of domestic life and family. They have chosen to stand at their stations and do the work for the rights of mankind. I look into the faces of these men who stood pat as the British came over their walls at Bunker Hill. They held their fire until they saw the whites of the enemies' eyes and shot as one — bringing fear, devastation, and the spirit of defeat to the greatest trained army in the world. Having been in the fires of battle, many men have fled under less strain. Yet, in these men from Boston, resides a public spirit and a love of our common country that beckons them to sacrifice their own lives for a greater virtue. Whatever their deficiencies, they are brave. They are united. They expect success and shall have it if I can do my part to bring order, discipline, and supplies to their access.

At first blush, it worries me that the army does not have the manpower to match the British. I am told that we have twenty thousand at our disposal, but this does not seem possible. Since no one can give me a solid count of our force, I am sending our officers out immediately for an accurate account. To match personnel with geography, I have drawn a rough map of the troop placements for this army as well as those of the enemy. I am not pleased with its accuracy, so I am also employing Governor Trumbull's son from Connecticut to draw more accurate maps. He comes highly recommended in this art.

Sunday, July 9, 1775 — Cambridge, Massachusetts

Went to Church and fasted all day. I have settled in a gray clapboard house formerly belonging to a Loyalist named John Vassall who has fled in fear of the war. The house overlooks the Charles river and provides a very pleasant view when I have time to glance between our feverish activities. From my quarters, officers have come and gone all day, bringing me insight and information as they deem useful.

From what I can tell, beyond the army being spread thin to cover a wide perimeter, these men have little experience in military life. Often finding myself in prayer, I consider what I have seen of the enemy. They have three floating batteries in the Mystic river near their camp. They have one twenty-gun ship between Boston and Charlestown. They have a battery at Cops Hill on the Boston side. To our favor, the enemy seems hesitant to engage. I can only assume they imagine we match and surpass them in men, supplies, and position. If that is the case, our goal will be to do all we can to allow them to continue to believe this for our own survival.

Seemingly, troubles in every quadrant. The generals are unhappy because of promotions from the Continental Congress and the Provincial Congress. Beyond this petty grievance, I see a greater problem. We lack arms. What good are men without arms? And what good are arms without men? Our regiments are far short of sufficiency, and this provides for the present exigency. Because of the need for troops, any and every man who joins is given great levity in conduct and in following orders. Because we are a volunteer-based army, officers are fearful of demands lest their men abandon this exercise. The lack of character of the men who are now serving, though necessary for numbers, bring great discontent in the entire outfit. We need to recruit more men of character and discipline to enable officers to weed-out those of poor character and those lacking the capacity or skill to fight.

Awaiting such hoped-for levies, I decided a few days ago to issue new guidelines to our troops. Providence has aided me, in that these rough recruits are granting huge swaths of authority to me. This is because they have heard stories of my leadership and character in previous battles from a war that seems so long ago now. They are granting a respect for me that I fear I have not earned. That be as it may, I am seizing that authority while I have it to require that these men clean up, dress neatly, abstain from cursing and drunkenness. We are in a war for life and liberty. They must not forget that. And we are in this for a higher cause. Thus, I am requiring all who are not on duty to attend services every Sabbath and to pray for Divine safety and defense.

Monday, July 10, 1775 — Cambridge, Massachusetts

I am disappointed to log into this record that the soldier count is just now being brought to me. Our numbers of able-bodied men are much less then I was told. No more than nine thousand men from this province are fit for duty. Thankfully, an additional five thousand, five hundred hail from the other colonies of Rhode Island, Connecticut, and New Hampshire.

Swallowing hard at the state of our force, I wonder greatly what the enemy is doing. Seemingly since my arrival, the seriousness of our situation has permeated our ranks. I am assigning men from various vantage points to keep a constant watch on the British. What telescopes we have have been assigned to watchmen, and watchmen assigned on a rotation to be around-the-clock lookouts. We are digging redoubts even as I write this and working hurriedly to throw up lines. Our belief is that, once the British receive fresh troops and have rested a few days, they will soon come for a visit.

Tension now exists in the camp and along our existing lines; such that, we lie down and rise up with little rest for want of not knowing when the attack will come. I am reminded again of Nehemiah in the Scriptures whose men held a sword in one hand and a trowel in the other, where the men half-worked and half-watched, and all were on alert.

Our lack of gunpowder and artillery places us in a dangerous position. I am writing my friend Mr. Richard Henry Lee for his aid with Congress to act in great haste. I am hoping to gain the essentials we need to facilitate this war. In the meantime, we will not retreat from this position of lacking as it will embolden our enemy and dishearten our colony and people.

Tuesday, July 11, 1775 — Cambridge, Massachusetts

I looked back at my previous journals over the years and remember a practice that I always followed during the work by my people on our various lands and projects. The constant refrain, "Rid to Muddy Hole, Doug Run, My Mill, My Harvest Fields" &ca. I often found my overseers working with indifference when my own oversight was absent. I found then that I must be a constant presence at every undertaking so that all responsibilities are being carried forth. This position that I now hold is no different. I constantly ride out over our defenses. I observe firsthand the work and the status of our officers and troops of this United Provinces of North America. Congress has placed them under my care. I must fulfill my assignment. I have given General Lee the same duty as it is impossible for me to do it on my own. We are requiring the same from all our officers, along with a requirement that they report frequently the status of our army.

Wednesday, July 12, 1775 — Cambridge, Massachusetts

In a short time, positive changes have occurred in this army. Our troops are responding. A unity and an effort exists to make this army an equal in state to the British and greater in spirit then they. With our force not being fully fit, I am obliged to tighten up our situation. These men are unaccustomed to being a military unit. To a degree, they have lived life as independents working as detached body parts versus attached body parts functioning in oneness. To improve the general health, proper sanitation is required. To deal with our shortages, a system of distribution has been created. To deal with the continued state of desertions (which every fighting force faces), penalties have been established. Rules and regulations have been drawn up. Punishments have been communicated. Granted, this is a voluntary force, but voluntary or not, a regimen must be followed to secure readiness and success. To strengthen our men and to focus our eyes on the purpose of our very existence, I have instituted prayers every morning before we go about our work.

Friday, July 14, 1775 — Cambridge, Massachusetts

I am in distress over the lack of provisions for this fighting group. My daily rides throughout the ranks have shown this deficiency, confirmed by comparing notes with General Lee. Some were bountifully supplied by their neighbors; others brought the weapons they received, which were passed down through their families. Some of our men had no weapons at all. We have worked to get these weapons post-haste. With this in action, I question if we have the gunpowder sufficient for our cause. It stands to reason that if we are short on guns, we will be short on gunpowder. I am constantly reassured that we have ample powder held in approximately three hundred and eight barrels.

Regardless, Congress and the States must realize our situation and move with immediacy to stock us with all the above. The army is in want of engineers, tools, tents, clothing (especially hunting shirts), ammunition, &ca. Connecticut is an exception compared to the other troops. They are well-provided for under the direction of Governor Trumbull. Not only does he provide for his troops, but he helps others who are in want. For Congress would establish a commissary-general to gather and supply the army's needs would be beneficial. I will recommend that this position be created and nominate Mr. Trumbull to serve in this capacity.

Saturday, July 15, 1775 — Cambridge, Massachusetts

Rode the lines, the redoubts, dined with General Lee and General Putnam.

Sunday, July 16, 1775 — Cambridge, Massachusetts

Had Church in the camp. Clergyman Emerson led the services. Our men were attentive, mostly present, and other than those on duty, enjoyed a day of rest. Fresh food was in great supply. We enjoyed fresh eggs, apples, peaches, warm bread, and coffee for breakfast. For dinner, we had a delightful meal consisting of pork and cabbage.

Tuesday, July 18, 1775 — Cambridge, Massachusetts

A uniform method of training is needed. Different companies from different colonies are doing drills that seem to conflict with one another. Each day, I see something that I did not notice the day before. Perhaps this is because as I deal with one problem, it pulls back the peel of the onion to unveil another problem. The living quarters of these men are quite unique. From one perspective, I am appreciative of this. These men are from different areas, many having acclimated to the surroundings from which they came. This was clear in the construction of their shelters. Some were made of boards, some of cloth, some of stone, some of clay, some of brick, and some of brush. The enlightening thing is that this is a group of soldiers who make do with what they have. In an army of sparsity, this is encouraging. They are survivors. This may benefit them in the days ahead, but I pray not. One group of soldiers from Rhode Island had, what I would call, proper military-grade tents. They were under the leadership of Nathanael Greene. They were aligned like the British encampments in neatly spaced and nicely ordered rows. The enemy surely sees this as they watch us. We watch them as well. I fear our disorder, as seen through their telescopes, will give them confidence in attacking us. Conversely, it could also cause them to underestimate us which would be to our good. Nonetheless, I must work this rough material into a well-functioning competitive combative tribe.

Wednesday, July 19, 1775 — Cambridge, Massachusetts

I was up most of the night considering the state of our provincial army compared to the might and crispness of the professional battle-hardened British army. In a way, I feel like Gideon leading his three hundred men with just jars, candles, and horns against a well-outfitted superior force. The more I struggled on the impossibilities of our lot against this foe, I remembered my time serving on their side as an unofficial lowly British officer. Reminiscence brought courage. Not all that is seen — is what it seems. Upon this subject, I beg to state we are here because we want to be. The British soldiers are here because they have to be. I seek to train and mold our troops for fighting within their own free will. The enemy is drilled incessantly against his. They are forced to daily powder their hair, wear spotless white breeches; and when those become less then spotless, apply pipe clay to hide the stains. This leaves their breeches damp, chafing their legs through the next day's drills. They are poorly paid. Many are forced to be in their units because of illegal press gangs. They are the unemployed and unemployable with no better options. They are the poor, the ex-convicts, and the mentally challenged. Their numbers also consist of those who had the choice — not liberty or death, but military or prison. Their officers are of the "finest of bloodlines." Their position is not through merit but through birthright.

This has to work in our favor. I will drill our men, but I will remind them that they came out by their own free will. They entered a covenant to do this. Though they are free, they came through an oath. I intend for them to keep the oath they willingly signed. To bolster our ranks it would be far easier to have illegal press gangs and kidnappings too. Instead, pleading for our cause is the higher method under Heaven. Our plea is not conquest but patriotism, defense of God-given rights, and freedom from tyrannical rule. I feel our advantage lies in our hearts, but I fear our hearts will be challenged. I appeal to Congress to meet our needs. Their responsibility is to supply; ours is to execute. This is my daily prayer, along with the request for the Hand of Providence to weigh in on our side of the scale.

Thursday, July 20, 1775 — Cambridge, Massachusetts

I received great news today from Governor Trumbull. Connecticut has voted to raise up two regiments of seven hundred men each to join our party here. Rhode Island has made the augmentation for this same purpose. We are also expecting a host of riflemen any day. If the promises hold, these reinforcements will compose an arm sufficient to oppose any foe. Now the task at-hand is to equip these new recruits upon their arrival with order, expectations, and discipline to face any opposition. For a better handling of our army, I wish to divide it into three divisions with a general assigned to lead each one. As our ranks fill, my concern will be the financial provisions. I rely on Congress to procure these, and on our stewardship to disperse frugally and wisely with full accountability.

Friday, July 21, 1775 — Cambridge, Massachusetts

I received a good report today from the area of Boston. Our enemy is sickly and in need of provisions. They have no beef available as we have bottled them in at the neck of Boston, blocking their access to the countryside. I have ordered all stock driven into the country away from their access to pastures by the waterway. Our prayer is for the misery of the enemy and for his soon departure. We will do all we can to harass and make their stay as uncomfortable as possible. This is a better option than face-to-face combat, at least until we are fully supplied, armed, and manned. I am surprised that the British have not ventured in our direction. I am in great wonder about what delays them. We are working to make ready and pray for that day to be delayed further as I want to make us more ready for the eventual conflict.

Saturday, July 22, 1775 — Cambridge, Massachusetts

Rode our line. Inspected our progress. Wrote letters of update.

Sunday, July 23, 1775 — Cambridge, Massachusetts

Attended Church with the troops. Enjoyed a day of rest.

Monday, July 24, 1775 — Cambridge, Massachusetts

Rode our line. Conferred with my generals. Awaiting promised troops. Dined with Officer Nathanael Greene.

Tuesday, July 25, 1775 — Cambridge, Massachusetts

Every day, expectation of attack is present. Through our watchmen, the redcoats seem to be preparing for an immediate initiative. Each day ends with no encounter.

Friday, July 28, 1775 — Cambridge, Massachusetts

As I endeavor to work up these raw materials into a good manufacture, I am in continual enterprise to deal with the discord and confusion. It serves a great encouragement then to me to realize that I am not facing these things uniquely. General

Schuyler is facing the same things in his corner of our Continent. I warned him of the three greatest variables he would face — the Ministerial Governor of New York, the Indians and the one who stirs them, and the Canadians. I am favored with a letter from the General informing me of Colonel Johnson's attempt to stir the Indians and Schuyler's success to circumvent. He had found the Canadians reticent to enter this unnatural contest. The Governor there has been a non-issue (on the surface at least). What I am facing, he is facing. May we bring each other succor in times as these. The one difference between the two. I am facing the enemy. General Schuyler is preparing to face the enemy. May my experience shared be beneficial should his time come. I practice for myself patience and perseverance. May each in their station — General Schuyler, General Lee &ca. do the same.

Monday, July 31, 1775 — Cambridge, Massachusetts

A letter from the speaker of the General Assembly of Massachusetts Bay was received this morning. He is requesting that our army here be spread throughout the Massachusetts Bay area to protect their citizens as the British are branching out, harassing citizens, taking stores, and abusing households. Though this is a legitimate concern beyond the provincial army I lead, the militia still exists in every station. They must muster their force to be a deterrent to such depredations. Though the voices from every town and every part of our seacoast are growing to detach this army to various regions, Congress and the general officers agree that this will not protect, but rather endanger our Nation and our cause. To decline brings no joy, but necessity and the greater good requires such. The burden rests with me both to state and to accept the criticism for any misfortune.

Tuesday, August 1, 1775 — Cambridge, Massachusetts

A week has passed in readiness. The ministerial army postures for attack. Our provincial army braces, but then the enemy reclines. There comes a point that the dread becomes a longing. The efficacy of drills is inestimable without the test of fire. At this point, we need this test. The men want this action. Sitting still wears on those who volunteered for a sacrificial purpose. The collective resolve wanes. To keep busy, I requested a status update on men, arms, and ammunition. To the point of ammunition, no secure answer was given on the available amount. Finally, today, a supply officer came to me with a calculation. The gunpowder amounted to only thirty-six barrels in stock. Divided among the men fit for fighting, this quantity equated to about nine rounds per man. Nine rounds per man! When I heard this, I could not speak. I nodded in disgust and turned to leave rather than express my full displeasure. Providence has been good to us. The redcoats could attack. The men wanted them to attack. Providential sovereignty knew better. The outcome would have equaled that of Bunker Hill with less attempts needed by the British. I have hurriedly and secretly made appeals to remedy this scarcity. I reached out to nearby townships, neighboring colonies, and expedited a letter to Congress. Every pound that can be spared is needed. No quantity, however small, is beneath notice.

Disposed to this cause, it is told that the island of Barbados has ample inventory of powder and is willing to supply. I have written the Governor of Rhode Island to procure one of the armed vessels in his province to sail with the chimerical chance of acquiring a good portion of their magazine. Necessity requires such an enterprise. The salvation of our country is dependent upon every effort to garner the supplies we need. I have been praying and fasting this day. And I am waiting for my petition to be granted.

Friday, August 4, 1775 — Cambridge, Massachusetts

I am favored with a letter received from Governor Trumbull. Connecticut is sending an additional fourteen-hundred men. Confident that these will arrive along with powder, I am required to turn attention to the clothing of the men who are in camp. Many are destitute of the species of uniform. I am sending a letter out today to request the kind Governor to assist Congress in procuring tow cloth for Indian or hunting shirts and that he can engage this cloth for the manufacture of such and the convey-ance to this army as they are available. Provisions were assured to all who joined in this effort. Daily I am reminded of these and am looked to as the deliverer of these promises. How heavy this weighs on me. To lead, strategize, and fight a war is burden enough. To raise the army with which to fight is straining. To clothe and feed that same army and meet its complaints is exhausting. No doubt, criticisms will follow which must be handled too. May Congress remember my confessions of ineptitude at the inception of this assignment and empathize to assist rather than judge.

Saturday, August 5, 1775 — Cambridge, Massachusetts

I am forced to ask the question why. Why has the enemy been inactive in the field of battle? I cannot help from my quarters to consider that they may feel we are stronger than they wish. They may be playing the waiting game with the hope that the troops leave in discouragement, or the Congress recalls many due to the expense of financing a standing army. Perhaps they are waiting for winter to attack when our experience is in wanting. They may rather choose to bombard us and drive us from our present line of defense.

From my own experience, having served in their ranks and now in seeing our own, their waiting may lessen their own strength due to sickness, desertions, and inner squabbles. These have fought and won all over the world, so again my question is, why are they delaying? In my prayer, I cannot help but thank the Author and Finisher of our faith that they do delay. From one aspect, the delay is a hardship, but a mercy on all others as we gain men and necessities. The delay has afforded the further organization of the army, dividing it into three grand divisions. General Ward, General Lee, and General Putnam respectively will be leading.

Sunday, August 6, 1775 — Cambridge, Massachusetts

Went to Church to worship and laid my questions at the feet of Providential Care.

Monday, August 7, 1775 — Cambridge, Massachusetts

The general return was made to me last week. I have found it so in my rides throughout the army. Many are absent from duty. I ordered repeated roll calls per day to lessen the time for departure without notice. The majority are Massachusetts soldiers. This leads me to believe they are going to their respective homes and farms. Some perhaps to take care of duties, others to profiteer as they are paid by the public, while gaining income in their vocation. This is pernicious conduct that cannot be tolerated. I am writing the Council of Massachusetts Bay for aid in finding these men and returning them. I must make an example of them with the desire to discourage such deserting delinquents in the future. To hold an army together when no action binds the parts is difficult.

Tuesday, August 8, 1775 — Cambridge, Massachusetts

As I found succor in shared hardships with General Schuyler, I find additional consolation from the oddest of sources. What I am facing with the absence of a fight is what the British officers are facing within a mile of our lines. The favor we have is food and domestic surroundings. The ministerial troops are on foreign soil lacking food, struggling with camp fever, blighted with desertions, discouragement, and dissatisfaction. With passivity, hope exists for withdrawal due to a lack of will or a lack of justification.

No sooner did I make the above entry; information has been received that fresh provisions were brought into the Boston harbor by some villain seeking to bring about ministerial success and provincial failure. I am writing the Provincial Congress of New York to solicit their exposure of this offender to our common country. This is important to note to those in New York, not only to reduce comfort to the enemy but to let them know that I am starting to think the British are preparing for a fight there and not here. It is the only reasonable explanation I can make for their inaction in these parts.

Wednesday, August 9, 1775 — Cambridge, Massachusetts

Despite some bored Massachusetts men slipping off after a long time of inactivity, more men are showing up every day to join our ranks. They are farmers, artisans, shoemakers, saddlers, carpenters, blacksmiths, tailors, and the like. It dawns on me that every vocation has a purpose. How amazing is Providence to call men and women to the service of others with talent they have strategically been given to meet a need where they land. This is true for this army. The varied backgrounds bring expertise to help solve the multitude of problems.

A talented group of men appeared after riding six hundred miles in the heat of summer. By their count, they averaged thirty miles per day. They were riflemen from Virginia under the command of Captain Daniel Morgan. I could not help but become exhilarated when they demonstrated their marksmanship, hitting targets accurately from 250 yards. I immediately put them to the charge of firing on British sentries, picking them off with shocking accuracy to us and more so to the British. General Washington (I write to myself), you are seeing a formidable army forming from the rawest of means. It is enough to make me fall to my knees for a mid-week Church service of one.

Thursday, August 10, 1775 — Cambridge, Massachusetts

Riding the lines today. The good thing about running my own property before this assignment is that I have acquired the knack of utilizing every resource to improve and strengthen. Gave orders to continue to dig trenches, build redoubts, and laid out guidelines for cleanliness and sanitation. At this point, the enemy we face is sickness and boredom rather than wounds and musket fire.

This Continental army lacks clothing, which is being remedied by the day. With the want of uniformity in dress, it has become needful to develop a way to distinguish officers from the rank- and-file. I have directed that major generals wear a purple ribbon across their chests. Brigadier generals are to wear pink ribbons. Field officers are to wear different-colored cockades in their hats. Sergeants are to tie red cloths on their right shoulders.

I have met with my officers again to remind them to be easy — but not too familiar — with those under them. This is the only way they can maintain respect and felicity to their commands.

Friday, August 11, 1775 — Cambridge, Massachusetts

I have been informed of horrific abuses of our men who find themselves prisoners of war under Lieutenant-General Gage. We, like them, have British prisoners-of-war. We treat them with respect. We care for their needs. We do so as gentlemen. Once having fought on the British side, the kind decorum by which we treated such men of opposing views was done as a favor to humanity. Most differences can be settled on the battlefield, but when it comes to treatment of those captured in war, the only recourse I see is reciprocation. I am writing Gage to let him know that if he continues to treat our men abusively as felons, then the only control I have is to do the same to his. This is greatly disagreeable to me, but it is the only counter at our disposal. Certainly, given this raw remonstration, he will improve his conduct toward those caught in his care.

Sunday, August 20, 1775 — Cambridge, Massachusetts

Went to Church and had much for which to be thankful. Daily, gunpowder is entering our camp from all over these United Colonies. Our land is filled with virtuous
citizens who are sacrificing for the love of our country and the cause of liberty. My
hope is that what is coming in is but the first fruits of a bountiful harvest of more
powder. I am assured that is the case. I will not allow the delays to dampen my ardor.
Faith, hope, and perseverance — I will cling to these.

In honoring the Sabbath and thinking on Providence's Hand, I look at the shortages we suffer and the numerical inequalities we now hold in looking across the lines
at our enemy. It would be easy to be disheartened, but then I am reminded that
America has the greater advantages over the British — the sacred causes of religion,
liberty, and decency. I then see the number of people who crowd our camp daily,
animated with the purest principles of virtue and love of country. I communicate this
to the enemy. I share this with our friends every chance I can. In the realms of darkness, this light emboldens me to move ahead despite all voices that say retreat or
surrender. I cannot help but believe God will look upon America and judge in our
favor. May His Gracious Hand grant us health and success equal to our merit and
wishes. On this, the Lord's Day, I pray.

Sunday, August 27, 1775 — Cambridge, Massachusetts

Engaging in work with one thousand two hundred men all last night and into this
morning digging a trench toward the enemy's line. The enemy responded this morning from their position on Bunker Hill with heavy cannonade throughout the day.
Their fire did not impede our work. The only loss we suffered in this barrage was
four men. Only two were killed due to their fire. Having the lack of ammunition and
powder, we held fire. Though the British now occupy Bunker Hill as a memento of
success, they have learned from that endeavor that sometimes a lack of return is due
to strategy not resources. Much was gained from that lost battle as to weigh the net
result a positive.

We were finally obliged to show some resistance, and to this point, we fired our
nine-pounder which sunk one of their floating batteries. Efficacy over quantity is our

goal. Such action has deterred their approach to this hill on Charleston Neck, a position that is advantageous for our cause. Perhaps the enemy is growing as restless as we are. Nonetheless, restraint is required until we are stocked. The encounter of the day brought excitement in our army and a renewal of purpose for which I am grateful.

Tuesday, August 29, 1775 — Cambridge, Massachusetts

As supplies of powder are arriving daily, I had an inventory taken. We now have one hundred and eighty-four barrels of powder, which equates to twenty-five musket cartridges per man. This is an improvement but is still far short of the supply we need for engagement. Congress expects me to act upon the enemy, but Congress has no thought of the condition of scarcity in which we find ourselves. Prudence says we gather and prepare.

The enemy's delay stymies me. He has all he needs. It can only be the Divine intervention that retards his willingness to act. I think of how birds of prey, gathering in number, circle an animal in decline awaiting the day of stillness for their feast. The British delay, gather their numbers, and I believe are waiting for such a time. Across their line, I see our army — rather than being an animal in decline, we are an animal of new birth slowly gaining use of all appendages, nearing a time when we can stand on our own with full vitality. I dare write this, but I believe their best advantage to attack was a month ago. The longer they hesitate for whatever logic they render, the stronger our Continental force will be. On one hand, my men and I long for the battle. On the other, I rejoice in their delay. If only I can dispense this insight to our men convincingly so that they will see their waiting allows drilling which will lead to success.

Thursday, September 7, 1775 — Cambridge, Massachusetts

We are gaining in strength and position, but the hold in sword to breast contact allows me to plan. I realize the plans of man are dependent upon the All-wise Disposer of events. What He shuts no one can open and what He opens, no one can shut. However, mankind must do his part as no one builds a tower without estimating the cost. The cost of holding this army into the winter months is a monstrous undertaking. There must be wood for fires, clothing for soldiers, blankets for beds, and warm and comfortable barracks for the troops. Depending on the severity of the weather, no fence, house, or orchard will be spared for want of heat. Pressing further on this stark necessity is the fact that enlistments expire on January 1st. With this date approaching more quickly than we care to imagine, each man will consider the time at service weighted against the comforts of home. I fear a mass exodus.

If this war is to continue for our existence, an army must be had and maintained against the enemy line. If troops are leaving, then troops must be entering. Our generals and I cannot wait until one army disbands to recruit another. Training and transition will leave a gap. Common sense would say that a replacement army must now be recruited and trained while the current army stands its ground. This will render a complication. The expense to Congress and this country will far exceed the reserve in paying, in essence, two armies when our United Colonies find it difficult to pay one army and provide the ammunition for that one. Would that this conflict would commence in full and be successfully concluded prior to January 1st. This is my urgent prayer, but should the Disposer choose otherwise, I must meet with our generals to plan. I feel it is the best course to continue in our recruiting, calling on Colonies to dispatch men and material. However, we need to find a way to persuade our current army stay beyond their dates of employment. Their comfort and the sense of value they feel from this Nation can enhance their will to continue in this effort.

Friday, September 8, 1775 — Cambridge, Massachusetts

General Schuyler has been very responsive to my letters. He has been diligent to keep me abreast of all things in New York and to the north. He faces shortages and challenges unique to that region, but I trust his wisdom and the support of that province. He is buffeted by the threats of British loyalist Guy Johnson and British-placed Quebec Governor Carleton. Schuyler intends to send a party to engage the British in the region of Canada and seeks my assistance. I am dispatching Colonel Arnold with a detachment of a thousand troops to his aid with the hope to reduce the northern vulnerability. The risk exists of injuring the delicate balance the neutral Canadians are attending between America and the British. To this end, it is imperative punctual and fair payment be made to the Canadian merchants for any supplies we purchase from them. I am requesting General Schuyler's constant information as to his actions and success.

Sunday, September 10, 1775 — Cambridge, Massachusetts

Just as worship this morning recessed, a deserter came into our camp from Boston. He has let us know (if we can believe him), that the British are suffering great inconveniences from the siege. For this, we can continue to give thanks. As the preacher brought a message on that blessed Psalm 100, we as an army are glad to make a joyful noise unto the Lord in praise and with ample gunfire. The Provider has granted the request for a great quantity of gunpowder for this station in Massachusetts. We have the provisions now to affect a favorable outcome should the British desire to attack.

With this provision, I felt comfortable in sending Colonel Arnold to assist General Schuyler with the goal of a surprise attack on the British at Quebec. I would scarcely have given this order two weeks prior. Now, with enough ammunition to sustain a prolonged defense, I have given Colonel Arnold instructions concerning the attack. I am noting these orders here as evidence and support in advance of any indiscretion. May God bring success as we press with expediency. The winter season aggressively advances. I have warned competent Arnold that if the Canadians take exception to our actions, to cease prosecution of this plan. To this end, our troops are to behave with the greatest courtesy to the inhabitants and their possessions. Our men and officers alike must adhere to the strictest discipline in abstaining from plunder of any kind. We dare not push them to the British side of aggression. My greatest desire is that Arnold's march bring about good will to all the Canadians, convincing them that we come as supporters of their own liberties and in response to abuses they themselves have suffered at British hands. Any impolite act must be severely punished within our own ranks.

Arnold is to gain as much of the King's supplies as possible and gather as much intelligence as he can to assist our prosecution of this war for liberty. I fear Colonel Arnold, an abled yet ambitious soldier, will meet up with General Schuyler and see his purpose as separate or at odds with that of the General. I have made known to him that upon union with General Schuyler, Arnold is to submit to his authority and follow orders as if they were from me. It is honorable to lead, and it is equally honorable to follow. Every station of life has honor of its own. All positions are given so that a man can prove himself in the service of his country. I wish that all men in this army will realize this truth.

In all things, our men must act with kindness and civility. Should any prisoners fall into Arnold's hands, they must be treated with humanity in keeping with the character of America. This includes paying for any supplies needed and received from the Canadian people. I have sent money with Arnold which he is to dispense with great frugality, even more so than if it were his own. I fear Arnold has a taste of the better things in life and may spend beyond value or need. I am particularly concerned about the differences in religion that the Canadians hold to as compared to what we as Americans observe. Arnold is to not say or do anything injurious to the exercise of religion in that country. He should encourage and commend the free exercise thereof to the rights of conscience. I write this acknowledging that as Christians, we will look upon their errors without insulting them, leaving it to God, the Judge of all men, to deal with their failings and misunderstandings. To do more is beyond this expedition under Arnold.

Monday, September 11, 1775 — Cambridge, Massachusetts

As gratifying as it is to make a move against the British in Canada, downcast resides in the hearts of those who remain here in a bed of inactivity. Restlessness abounds. Since our men cannot fight the enemy, they expend their energies attacking each other. A mutiny broke out among the Pennsylvania riflemen after many of their rabble-rousers had been confined to the guardhouse. General Greene and his men had to put the mutiny down, but a sense of unease pervades the camp. At times, I feel the whole army is coming apart and I the only seam that prevents complete unraveling.

I called the generals together to discuss a plan I had for an all-out amphibious assault on Boston. Sometimes attempting something is better than doing nothing. I am of the belief that great sacrifice is called for when the cause is justified. The offset is enslavement. I have had flat-bottomed boats constructed which can carry fifty men each. With winter coming and the men on the edge of imploding, it would seem beneficial to divert these energies and hostilities toward the real enemy. After ample deliberation concerning the plan, the generals discouraged such a move. Their belief is that this would place our men exactly where the enemy desired and bring about a defeat from which our Nation might not recover. I have acquiesced to their opinions, knowing that in the number of many counselors, wisdom exists. If nothing else, our time encouraged our generals that we are in this together. I still believe in my soul that a decisive stroke is necessary.

Wednesday, September 20, 1775 — Cambridge, Massachusetts

I look across the lines each day and realize the enemy is our neighbor within no more than five hundred yards. I daily make ready our men for defense of our Nation. Supplies, men, training, digging, finances, discipline, and encouraging are never-ending challenges. In addition, I must deal with insults and attacks on my character. I expect it from the disgruntled and welcome it from the Tories, but it is painful when it comes from supporting patriots like Governor Trumbull of Connecticut. He is a great ally and sacrificially supports our cause. He and his colony are under assault from the ministerial troops and want me to dispatch some men to confront their aggression. I would hasten to do this for such a friend, but in doing so, I would have to respond in kind for the other colonies. To do so would cause the dissolution of our army or make it too anemic to stand against the main body of the British forces. I have already reduced my force by dispatching Colonel Arnold to assist General Schuyler. Sometimes the right stand is a lonely one. May God judge my actions and make known to me His Way.

Thursday, September 21, 1775 — Cambridge, Massachusetts

The paymaster called for an urgent meeting today. He has not one single dollar left with which to pay our troops. He is even facing mutiny from his own company because he has called them to join him in doing without to set an example for others. Winter is fast-approaching. Our soldiers are by all standards naked and enlistments are expiring. Lack of pay, lack of provisions, and limited contracts make the dissolving of this army a reasonable recourse. I send letters constantly to Congress. They have dispatched members to observe our situation, and yet we receive nothing. Daily, I look for a rider with a fresh supply of money and provisions, but none appear. In the field just a few months, but aging seems to be overwhelming me as worry is at my every turn.

Tuesday, September 26, 1775 — Cambridge, Massachusetts

Sadness has entered my quarters. Our friend and surgeon general of our army, Dr. Church has been found a spy and a traitor. The Scriptures say in Ecclesiastes that "God will bring every deed into judgment, including every hidden thing, whether it is good or evil." I am sad but grateful that the Almighty has done what He said and brought Dr. Church's deeds so "accidentally" into light. What treachery, not just to me, but to our friends and family across this continent. I grasp, ever so slightly, what our Lord felt when Judas sat at His table already having plotted betrayal, eating bread with our dear Savior as if a close friend. I pray that Church is the only one, but if it can be a man of Church's stature, I wonder how many more are at our table who are not really with us in this righteous endeavor?

Saturday, September 30, 1775 — Cambridge, Massachusetts

I have had the privilege to send Reverend Samuel Kirkland to Congress for assistance. He is a missionary and friend to the Oneidas. I gave him thirty-two pounds lawful money to help him with his expenses and hope that Congress will do the same.

Wednesday, October 4, 1775 — Cambridge, Massachusetts

Colonel Arnold sent me a petition requesting that I deal with Captain Daniel Morgan's refusal to follow his ranking orders. Seemingly, the riflemen under his authority feel themselves exempt from the normal order of command. I am grateful for the contributions of Captain Morgan, but I must take exception to his behavior. Should any group feel exempted, this army will crumble into disorder and disharmony.

We were recipients of a great report regarding another beneficial return from the battle of Bunker Hill. General Gage has been recalled and replaced by General Howe. The king seemed greatly distressed by the casualties and was desirous to make changes in leadership. To the king, Great Britain's stature will be questioned the world over should they lose to provincials such as ourselves.

Thursday, October 5, 1775 — Cambridge, Massachusetts

Received bad news today that General Schuyler is sick and has stepped down from his command on route to Canada and has given General Wooster top rank. Wooster is sheepish in initiatives of military conflict. I fear he will discontinue the mission and leave Colonel Arnold (who was sent to help them) alone at the mercies of the British armies and their Canadian sympathizers.

The enemy in Boston and on the heights of Charlestown are well-fortified to make an attack a suicidal disaster. The hesitance of the enemy or their plans elsewhere has prevented them from attacking our quarters. Daily cannonade is assailed against us but to no real consequence. We return fire on occasion for the sake of obligation. Powder conservation for full engagement is the priority.

Thursday, October 12, 1775 — Cambridge, Massachusetts

To counter the British incursions along the waterways, I have given orders for some armed vessels to intercept the enemy supplies of provisions and ammunition. I have assigned officers from the Continental army who are familiar with the sea to lead additional vessels. Their success will buoy this campaign.

Friday, October 13, 1775 — Cambridge, Massachusetts

It is of great enjoyment that I have a brother in John Augustine Washington. I received a letter from him today bringing news that an effort to raise up a militia and arm the men of that Colony has been ongoing. They realize the need to be equipped and to be ready to wage a defense against the British trespasses. Our neighbors are also engaged in the manufacturing of arms and ammunition for public use. The unanimity and fortitude of our countrymen is a great help to this army and alleviates some of my worries. I would that Governor Trumbull and others will do the same in their respective colonies. How much better for the British to see opposition in every corner. It would detract them from this army I lead and discourage their army under a tentative siege.

Winter is coming. Due to inactivity, we are given the luxury of preparation time. I have ordered ten thousand cords of firewood for the barracks that are in the process of construction. It appears I will not see Mrs. Washington for the winter. My hope is that she is safe, and if possible, able to come to me.

Wednesday, October 25, 1775 — Cambridge, Massachusetts

Reports are coming often now to confirm that four British ships have bombarded the town of Falmouth and that their soldiers are in the process of burning our seaport towns like that one with barbarity and cruelty. They seek revenge on us because we want liberty, because we love our country, and because we want a voice. Their actions are carried on with malice in response to our refusal to be enslaved. I idly sit here facing the main body of the enemy while the Nation bleeds from the destruction of ministerial tentacles. May the winter season slow their injurious assaults upon our people. How I long to hasten a conclusion to their infringement.

Thursday, October 26, 1775 — Cambridge, Massachusetts

If ever I was given a reason to motivate our troops for our cause, it is with this news from Falmouth. I cannot bear the thought that soldiers would willingly leave their posts regardless of enlistment terms when life, liberty, and property are at stake. We are not devoting ourselves to arms to invade another country. We are taking them up to defend our own. The enemy is wantonly shedding blood wherever he sets foot. Our towns are in ashes. Women and children who should be exempted from such aggression by supposed "Christian" British men find themselves beaten and raped as mere collateral and chattel from the fight. Many of these innocents are driven from their homes and forced to live off the charity of strangers. How savage can our home country be? How can men of these colonies step away with good conscience while this occurs?

Already, I am having to have deserters escorted back under allied guns. Others are holding out for reenlistment, bargaining for better terms, more money, and more entitlements. I am serving for free in this man's army. I am away from home just as they are. They can leave. I cannot. How selfish can we be as a Nation and what is our prospect of continuance if this is the sort of people our Nation births? I will not abandon my command, but had I known what would be involved beforehand, I would have run from the appointment.

Sunday, October 29, 1775 — Cambridge, Massachusetts

I prayed today during worship that God Almighty who brings help and hope would relieve my anxiety regarding reenlistments. Even with the current war crimes from our enemy, officers have shared their intentions with me to retire. It seems one-third to one-half plan to do so at the end of their enlistment periods. Because these are leaders of men, they are encouraging their men to join them in exit, harming our prospects for the next campaign. Some close to me recommend that I dismiss each officer the moment they share their intentions to leave to prevent a virus of defection.

I fear that immediate dismissal could prove dangerous and justify exits across the rank-and-file.

I sometimes am filled with worry wondering if I will be the only one left to serve in this army. If I am alone, what does that say about my leadership? I am not a leader if no one follows. I cannot simply will success, but I am striving to lead and live in a way to deserve its fruits. I am finding the absence of my secretary Joseph Reed more distressing today. I understood his need to ride home and tend to urgent family business, but I need his counsel and the company of a confidant.

The traveling Methodist minister Schibler came into our camp. He shared a text to which I cling. Psalm 84, "For the Lord God is a sun and shield: the Lord will give grace and glory: no good thing will He withhold from them that walk uprightly. O Lord of hosts, blessed is the man that trusteth in thee." I need the Lord to be my shield and to give us grace in this hour and glory in this war's outcome. If He will not withhold any good thing from one whose walk is upright, then I will do my best to walk in that way and trust that men will join and stay in this army. Pastor Schibler reminded us to not worry in this hour, but to trust in God.

Sunday, November 5, 1775 — Cambridge, Massachusetts

Received good news today. General Montgomery's progress in Canada goes well. He is moving toward Montreal now with the fall of Fort Chamblee. His success, along with Arnold's determination, moves our campaign to a more favorable position. I have sent six armed vessels to capture supplies from the enemy's store-ships and transports. I pray that work goes unchallenged. Tomorrow, the men return to erecting barracks after their Sabbath rest.

Monday, November 6, 1775 — Cambridge, Massachusetts

I am sending Brigadier-General Sullivan to proceed immediately to Portsmouth, New Hampshire, to complete the defense works there and secure the towns along the Piscataqua river against attacks by the British ships. He is to use fire-ships and fire-rafts to slow the enemy. Because we are short of ammunition and powder, I have ordered him to capture any officers of the crown they find and use them as leverage to halt enemy aggressions. Our usage of hostages can do what our lack of artillery cannot.

I still await news from Colonel Arnold. My hope is that he has arrived with his thousand to Quebec. He has been informed to tell me otherwise. No dispatch from him holds me in suspense. I remain hopeful.

Wednesday, November 8, 1775 — Cambridge, Massachusetts

Where money is lacking, resourcefulness supplies. Our boats trolling the rivers have come upon materials of wine, dry goods, and paper from shipwrecked and confiscated enemy vessels. I have ordered the sale of these so that we might have the money to purchase more useful supplies for our effort.

In this united provincial army, a segmentation of sorts exists. It has come to my attention that the Connecticut corps wants no Massachusetts men. The Massachusetts corps wants no Rhode Islanders. New Hampshire's officers no longer want to serve with New Hampshire as their wants and needs are not gainfully met. This may be our lot for the foreseeable future. Somehow, I must maintain this army and tolerate such objections in view of a greater good.

Friday, November 10, 1775 — Cambridge, Massachusetts

In seeking my advice, Colonel Woodford has written regarding the problems he is facing in command. I have asked of all my officers the same — require nothing unreasonable, respond quickly to their needs, reward and punish per merit and not bias, discourage vice of every form, reinforce the importance of our cause, and drill daily as if the enemy is at-hand and ready to strike. All orders are to be plain and precise. All those under me should do what I do — write down those orders as a ready-reference in times of question or mistakes so that blame may be aptly applied, and lessons learned. The quest of such notation is to avoid repetition of error.

Saturday, November 11, 1775 — Cambridge, Massachusetts

We are gaining provisions through aggressive actions on the rivers. Today, I have received information that we have obtained beef, pork, butter, and more. This is immensely helpful to our cause.

A fear has cropped in my mind as I make this entry. I think back to Dr. Church and his devious acts of betrayal. During his affairs in this army, he was well-aware of our shortages of ammunition and manpower. He had insight into our thoughts and strategies. How much of this has brought aid to the enemy in his own confidence and planning? Perhaps the waiting game is his prime strategy with the objective that our men will slowly go home. Then, the British can bring an easier end to this contest.

I am moving now to reenlist the officers as my top priority. The men under them are hesitant to reenlist until they know the officers they follow will be at their head. I do admire the loyalty these officers have drawn from their men. For the most part, these are the glue at the operational level that will enable this army to move in a concerted way.

I am laboring under the anxiety of mind with regard to our gunpowder. We had surplus enough to engage in an attack or to mount a hardy defense, but, with this damp winter setting in, we are finding that the powder our men have carried has been made of no use due to the moisture. This was driven home to me yesterday. Four or five hundred of the enemy landed at Lechmere's Point. Our men rallied for action. As drilled, they checked their cartouche-boxes to find that the greater part of the ammunition was too damaged to use. Fresh ammunition was given to them from the stores we had. This begs me to question how useful is the supply of powder that is in inventory.

Regarding the attack by the British at the Point, Colonel Thompson met the enemy with his riflemen. Under the gale of rifle fire, the enemy retreated. Our losses were negligible as we lost only ten cows and one man. Two of our men were dangerously wounded, while the enemy lost two men by their count.

Sunday, November 12, 1775 — Cambridge, Massachusetts

On this Lord's Day, we pray for those in Boston who have had every freedom and liberty stripped of their being. General Howe has threatened execution for any who leave that town without his permission. He has restricted not only travel, but what can be carried of their property. He is also forcing many of our own citizens to serve his army, to fire on their own countrymen, or face the deaths of their wives and children. Howe's system is tyrannical and cruel. We are reminded again of why we are in this fight.

Monday, November 13, 1775 — Cambridge, Massachusetts

Stringent measures of the most antiquated kind were found necessary today. We have suspended the morning gun to conserve powder, but further, I have recruited thirty men to agree to bear and use spears to defend our line. David had his mighty men. I have these who are active, bold, and courageous. At first blush, this is retreating to savage times, but if the British boast of their bayonets, we can boast of our spears.

Thursday, November 16, 1775 — Cambridge, Massachusetts

There is a young officer in our camp who is tall, healthy, and carries a booming voice. He is well-read and has an intellect not seen in these parts. His name is Colonel Henry Knox. I have enjoyed his company and find he and Nathanael Green as deserving candidates for promotion. Colonel Knox has reminded me of the guns, cannons, and ammunition abandoned at Fort Ticonderoga. He desires to lead an expedition of men to collect the artillery. This would be beneficial to our cause and a partial answer to our shortages. I firmly believe he is industrious enough to succeed in this ambitious task. Therefore, I am sending him out with orders to gain assistance from Philadelphia and then to proceed to New York to obtain whatever necessaries he identifies. I have given him the warrant to obtain from the paymaster-general a thousand dollars to defray the expenses that will arise from his journey. His mission is of the utmost import. No cost or man should be spared. With this said, full accountability must be documented and given upon return.

Friday, November 17, 1775 — Cambridge, Massachusetts

With the hard winter cold approaching and a thick ice forming, movement will be made easy with no water hedge to protect us from the enemy or the enemy from us. I have met with our generals to make sure they are secure from attack. I also let them know that it has been on my mind to launch an offensive against the British at Castle William. No more than three hundred of the enemy soldiers are there. It would afford us a victory, perhaps even gain some stores and supplies for the coming months. I am leaving it to the generals to decide its merit and opportunity for success.

Sunday, November 19, 1775 — Cambridge, Massachusetts

Congress has sent a letter dated November 10th to establish two battalions of marines — men seasoned with the bilateral ability to fight on the sea and on the shore. While I see the benefit of such a force dealing with an enemy who has superiority on the sea, my anxieties lay with the fact that our force is already thin here at Boston's neck. I am strained to fill this army by some method of retaining expiring enlistments and meld them with hoped-for new recruits. I believe Philadelphia and New York would be more eligible to meet Congress's resolve and raise up this new order of fighters from their pantry of men. In these two areas, sailors are unemployed who, upon recruitment, could find high satisfaction to see their talents engaged in our National defense. I will do what they request until further notice. I long for those Congressmen who have visited our camp to remember the state in which our army exists and the over-weighing burdens I currently bear. Must they add new ones? Must we thin out what we have when the enemy entrenchments practically touch ours?

I dare not complain outwardly, nor give voice to my displeasure except in this private self-correspondence. The state of our forces is waning as people come and go with little forethought of the void they leave. Great hesitancy is present to sign up for the winter months, when the first object they see is lack of wood for warmth. Couple that with next to no pay for the previous two months, the lone incentive of love of country falls wanting. I am writing Congress to keep their obligation to these men. Pay them what is owed. Pay them a month in advance as an additional incentive for them to stay. The nest is bare, but it must have some feather to it.

This is the day of prayer and in it I rejoice. I am finding that every day is a day of prayer in the station from which I kneel.

Monday, November 20, 1775 — Cambridge, Massachusetts

If one were to have liberty to read this prose, I fear depression would overwhelm. They would soon call for a doctor to treat my ailing prospects. My secretary Mr. Reed delays his return. Many are attempting to fill his shoes, but none are able. Speaking of doctors, Dr. Morgan, who directs our hospital, is absent and is sorely needed. Colonel Arnold cannot feel the least different as Colonel Enos has unceremoniously left him and his mission. Enos took with him all but three companies. I dare not consider what Carleton has in store for Arnold if things do not improve in that direction.

I cannot help but flatter the man Colonel Benedict Arnold. Why did Enos leave him? Because the men were out of provisions. They were eating soap and hair grease. They boiled and roasted any article of leather. They ate the dogs that accompanied them. Their clothes were rags. Their feet were covered with raw skins for shoes, yet Arnold marches on. I am reminded of that great chapter of Hebrews 11 detailing the heroes of faith in the Holy Scriptures. It says, "They were stoned, they were sawn asunder, were tempted, were slain with the sword: they wandered about in sheepskins and goatskins; being destitute, afflicted, tormented; Of whom the world was not worthy: they wandered in deserts, and in mountains, and in dens and caves of the earth. And these all, having obtained a good report through faith." As lofty an opinion Arnold has of himself, I dare say I hold one even more lofty of him.

The good news is, Mrs. Washington is on her way, along with Mr. Custis, her son. She should be arriving in Philadelphia soon per last report, having traveled over four hundred and fifty miles thus far. I will be appreciative if Mr. Reed, while he is at his home in Philadelphia, will give instruction and advice to help her navigate her way across the Hudson, the bad roads, and the cold weather. As a gentleman and a friend, I would appreciate if Mr. Reed would meet both my petitions and return with her to my aid.

Sunday, November 26, 1775 — Cambridge, Massachusetts

In days of distress, I have found it helpful to give thanks. When I begin to enumerate the bountiful blessings that Heaven has bestowed, my enormous problems of this battle sink to a more tolerable perspective. I can focus on this war knowing that my own possessions, lands, and farms are being well-managed by my brother Lund. Many have no one to look after their properties. They stand a greater risk of loss than me. Providence has bestowed upon me supports for my personal affairs. What the Lord says in Joshua 1:8 is true, that if we follow His Commands, He will make us successful and prosperous. The correspondence from my brother not only lightens my steps but gives me some assurance that my ways are finding some approval with the Almighty. In the spirit of caring for others, I am instructing Lund to help any poor who wander up. I wish no one to go away from my house hungry. If they have need of seed or food, it shall be provided as long as this does not assist them in idleness. In Lund's frugality and economy, I have encouraged him to give up to fifty pounds per year to charity when he thinks it is well-bestowed.

Tuesday, November 28, 1775 — Cambridge, Massachusetts

Colonel Enos has arrived with no good excuse for his reckless retreat from the service of Arnold. He is in gaol. His trial awaits news from Colonel Arnold.

Three hundred men, women, and children of great poverty have left Boston and entered our camp. We will do our best to place them. They inform me that General Howe is aware of our scarcities and will, at some point, make use of that status.

We have a recruitment update. Our new enlistments number two thousand five hundred and forty men. This is egregious, in the face of attack. To compensate, I have thrown up several redoubts and half-moons along the bay. I fear that I will need to call up the militia and minutemen of this country for our assistance should the British take initiative. This adds to distress as such fighting units are wary of orders and at variance to discipline.

Smallpox is now in Boston. Because of my exposure early-on, I have seen the benefit of inoculation, though many are leery of potential complications. Nevertheless, I am taking the necessary steps to prohibit its spread among our men. I have taken a few men at a time, as a precaution to any adverse effects. I also have limited the number treated so that we have the majority of our force healthy to deal with any attack. My method of inoculation is to place a small cut on their skin, rub pus from infected smallpox victims into their cut, and let the body do its part.

I am writing Mr. Reed again to gain his assistance, least while he remains in Philadelphia, to come to our aid for money for our troops. That the Continental bills are so slow in coming is astonishing. I pray for God's mercy that such behavior ceases by those in the employment of government. Their delay and excuses will bring destruction to the army whose existence allows them the freedom to conduct business so causally. I have enlisted now three thousand five hundred men in total. With what I will pay these, I have no conception. Congress needs to supply a sum of no less than two hundred and seventy-five thousand dollars to supply our purpose.

Thursday, November 30, 1775 — Cambridge, Massachusetts

The various enemies that appear at my door cannot steal my joy on this day. Captain John Manley, commanding the schooner Lee, captured a British supply ship called the Nancy off Cape Ann on the northern edge of Boston. Plunder of this ship has provided provisions that Congress has not been able to provide — two thousand five hundred stands of arms, cannon, mortars, flints, forty tons of shot, and two thousand bayonets. If only there had been gunpowder, but I will not complain! No doubt, on this day, I celebrate God's Mighty Hand. I am reminded of Jehoshaphat facing great odds. The Almighty gave him the promise that He would fight for them. He told them to just take their positions and watch. That day the Lord did what He said. The people of Judah gained such plunder that they called that place the Valley of Berachah, the Valley of Blessing. I could call Manley's haul, a valley of blessing too. More and more, I realize that if this contest is to conclude in our favor, it will be by Divine intervention rather than our intention.

Friday, December 1, 1775 — Cambridge, Massachusetts

Another enemy entered the camp today — bored and on-edge soldiery. To blow off steam, an innocent snowball fight erupted between some Virginia riflemen and a few Marblehead area sailors. Before long, it grew into a huge riot, estimated to include a thousand men. As furious as the fight, I found myself the more furious. I rode into the middle of it, jumped off my horse, grabbed two men fighting in the middle and shook them, yelling at them alternatively. Seeing me, the other participants fled to avoid reprisal. The fight soon ended, and the two men at the center of the malaise apologized effusively. The one good thing from it all, I gained in those men a higher respect than I would have anticipated. For this I am grateful.

Saturday, December 2, 1775 — Cambridge, Massachusetts

Tomorrow will be a day of worship, but more a day for prayer in anguish for me. The Connecticut troops have been well-supplied by their State in comparison to the others and had given great assurances that they would remain with the army until ample replacements could be found. With many of the other troops leaving, some deserting, and more than a few sick, I began to bring in three thousand minutemen from the area and called for two thousand more men from New Hampshire province to bulk our ranks. Upon this news, the Connecticut men who vowed to stay, began to leave in vast numbers against their pledge and even before their enlistments end. We pursued them, but many got away with their arms and ammunition that we so desperately need. What about Country? What about this war for liberty? What about a man's word? Do these mean anything?

Sunday, December 3, 1775 — Cambridge, Massachusetts

I find some of my best considerations come on the Lord's Day. It is a time of reflection, of thought, of ideas, and of vertical petitions to my Commander-in-Chief. If Connecticut men are leaving so easily, how soon will the Massachusetts Bay men, the New Hampshire men, and the Rhode Island men follow? We must have a pipeline of men flowing into our ranks to match that flowing out. It is of great necessity that Congress requires a quota of men from every town during this campaign to remedy such deficiencies. It is an endeavor which we as a whole Nation have undertaken. That some bear the burden while others do not isn't right. If this is successful, all will benefit, so all should invest. That I should scramble to fill the need and accept the failures while a Congress resides safely behind the lines legislating is also unfair. A clamor for action arose from my quarter but with lack of men, arms, and powder, such initiative would bring a failed closure to this enterprise as opposed to a successful one. Congress needs to make these shortages their main call to business.

Tuesday, December 5, 1775 — Cambridge, Massachusetts

To look at the good that is going on in this righteous cause is so important. I have the highest satisfaction to write that Colonel Arnold is proving himself daily to be a great leader and patriot. After losing one-third of his troops to desertion and making a long and fatiguing march, he and his men have reached Point Levi in good spirits. A task that is set upon and completed through great resistance often does bring a sense of accomplishment, feeding the spirit of joy. I flatter myself to believe Colonel Arnold will distinguish himself through his prudence and valor and effect greater successes. I am mindful to say that no man can command success, but if it could be done, Arnold would be the man to do it. Arnold is due great laurels for all his heroic toils.

I must encourage General Schuyler in the instant. It has been conveyed that he has mentioned to Congress his inclination to retire. He has been filled with complaints and shortages similar to mine. I understand his claim to dismission. What he does not realize, perhaps, is that his desire to leave causes others to want to do the same. It is a disincentive to his peers and subordinates alike. If only he knew that I am trying my hardest to hold the whole together. He has been an encouragement to me like Arnold. When those I trust and lean on start to falter, it causes a hopelessness inside me. The cause to which we are exerting is just and right. We must rise superior to every obstacle. I must. He must too.

Sunday, December 10, 1775 — Cambridge, Massachusetts

Reverend Leonard, from Connecticut, has been serving ably as our Chaplain. His message this morning spoke of how the Almighty ordains for times like these an intersection of need and His Word. Speaking on Jehoshaphat again, he told how faith is not the absence of fear, but the carrying on of one's duty despite fear. He referred to that precious Psalm 23, where he relayed that we walk in the valley of death. We eat in the presence of our enemies. Following what is right does not prevent our exposure to danger and the wiles of the devil. Jehoshaphat and his men faced long odds. Jehoshaphat led his men in prayer saying that we do not know what to do or what we can do, but our eyes are on You. When the soldiers set out for battle, fear rushed back over them to the point that they wanted to desert. Their wise general Jehoshaphat told them to "have faith in the Lord your God and you will be successful." How the Reverend's words buttressed our men. He gave me support in my heart, and he gave me support in my command. He has become a warm and steady friend to his country. I will pray and seek Providence as Jehoshaphat, and trust for His Divine Hand to fight this battle with us.

Monday, December 11, 1775 — Cambridge, Massachusetts

Today has been a great day after the consideration of all things. News arrived that Captain Manley has won two more prizes. He took the enemy ship Jenny with coal and porter. He also took the brigantine Little Hannah with its cargo. We have dispersed the plunder among the army and navy at this station.

The militia is coming in fast. This province and the province of New Hampshire have provided needed men with alacrity. At this rate, the provision which I requested from these will be met.

The enemy in Boston is tearing down houses and using the wood to warm themselves. They do this also to prevent an outbreak of fire should we begin to bombard them. It is good to see them scramble. This and the effect of smallpox and desertions give us comfort that we are not the only ones to feel the inconveniences of war.

The greatest thing I write today is that Mrs. Washington has arrived with son Jack and his wife Nelly. I know she had to overcome her great fears of long travel and exposure to war. I am consoled that our Nation's people extolled her virtue and our sacrifices as she entered one town after another on her journey. After seven months apart, my joy is incomprehensible. When Mrs. Washington is present, every place feels like home. There was another whose love I longed for in the past, but I realize more today that the one Providence had for me was better than the one I wished for myself. She is here in my arms this day. I give thanks.

Thursday, December 14, 1775 — Cambridge, Massachusetts

Another one hundred and fifty sick have entered our camp from Boston. Many have smallpox. General Howe's initiative to quell this disease is to send these mistreated people to our care as contagions to bolster their defense against us. This gives even greater assurance that we have taken the right steps proactively to inoculate our army. We must always be aware of the enemy in our own camp. In this case, it is disease.

Mrs. Washington is horrified at our conditions. Even out of her element, she has labored to bring comfort to the men, host those who visit, and encourage me. She is often awakened at night by cannon fire and, at times, wishes to leave. I am always supportive of this measure, but she always reaffirms an hour or two later that she is resolved to stay the winter and assist me. I am more and more becoming acquainted with the Heavenly intention of a helpmate.

Friday, December 15, 1775 — Cambridge, Massachusetts

It has been my wish to invite a number of gentlemen to dine with me each evening. I have longed to build goodwill with those in this colony as well as form a relationship and a bond from which to wage war. Sadly, jealousies have arisen because of names I have overlooked, and because of my inability to do this on a regular basis. Entertaining is important for support, but the support of the army and the war is a dire priority which cannot be neglected.

Letters are being published from this camp as well as in Philadelphia without my approbation. Though some are flattering toward me, some are also critical. Neither of these are my focus. What is being printed is a revelation of the army's sparse conditions and tactical planning. For the Tories in Philadelphia and the British sympathizers, these give comfort and aid to the enemy which is tantamount treason.

Money has been promised for the army, which is in much want. Enlistments are going slowly as exits loom. I do believe many will reenlist but are waiting for more favorable incentives. Knowing this does not help because all this is truly unknowable until the day of decision.

Every time I put my finger in a hole of the dike, another hole opens requiring another finger. I am stretching to contain the flood and wish for others' fingers to assist.

Sunday, December 17, 1775 — Cambridge, Massachusetts

Reverend Leonard brought another needed message this morning, but we were disheartened to hear that he may soon depart our ranks. I pray that he will not leave. As I depend on the General Schuylers, Colonel Arnolds, and Colonel Knoxes of this army, I depend on this Chaplain. My prayer is for him to remain.

Monday, December 18, 1775 — Cambridge, Massachusetts

Colonel Ethan Allen was captured in Montreal in September following his great success at Fort Ticonderoga. It has been conveyed that he is being placed in chains and suffers a felon's hardships with no regard to humanity or the rules of war. It is incumbent upon me to attempt to relieve his suffering. General Howe must know that what he does to our men, we must do to his according to all that is right before God and man. I am writing a letter to request kind treatment, appealing to his better nature, and propose a trade of Brigadier Prescott for Allen. I pray for a favorable response.

Captain Manley continues his string of successes manning the waters, though our ship the Washington has been captured and its crew sent to England. Captain Manley has taken the armed sloop Betsy, which was dispatched by Lord Dunmore. We have gained Indian corn, potatoes, and oats. For this we are grateful, but of greater value are the letters confiscated from this prize. Dunmore's letters to General Howe detail the enemy's plans. Upon them, Congress must be apprised and respond. What is expected and dreaded is the British intend to engage the savages against us. It is a fact with which we must contend.

Our work on Lechmere's Hill continues unimpeded. A ship fired on the work there, but our return fire moved the ship out of cannon reach. If work continues as planned and the powder arrives, we should be able to carry out Congress's resolve for Boston. In the meantime, we move closer and closer with each passing day to the enemy lines. Our army numbers seven thousand, one hundred, and forty. It is enhanced by fine-looking men of the militia who go about their work with great alacrity.

Reverend Dr. Wheelock of Dartmouth College has sent intelligence from his vantage point of the movements of General Carleton. I am forwarding this to General Schuyler.

Sunday, December 24, 1775 — Cambridge, Massachusetts

Congress has forwarded extracts and letters written to them from General Schuyler. He has stated to them that he and General Montgomery incline to quit the service. I thought we had taken care of this. I am facing all that they are facing and more. I have written a letter back to Schuyler with my exasperation. When is the time for brave men to exert themselves in the cause of liberty if not now? Should any complication or challenge deter them from their duty? God knows what we are facing. The Savior told us that in this world we would have trouble, but to take heart for He has overcome the world. If the Savior could face all He faced without quitting, and He tells us to follow Him bearing our crosses, how can we quit in this walk that we have been called to take?

To add to my disgust, General Montgomery intends that the military clothing of his men remain in Albany for others to wear who are not in the line of duty. How can he do this when our men suffer for lack of clothing in the service of others? Do not those who remain, who refuse to quit, deserve provision? Questions! Expectations! Duty and Honor! I will continue my solicitation for their continuance despite being told otherwise.

Monday, December 25, 1775 — Cambridge, Massachusetts

It is Christmas. The weather around us will attest to the season. This day, however, is just another day of preparing for war, gaining supplies, and enlisting men to fight. Instructions are being sent artfully concealed — even to the point that false instructions are made more visible to deceive the enemy should the messenger be caught.

We have received the money from Congress after numerous delays. As grateful as I am to receive it, I hesitantly must convey to them that it is short of what we need. We must pay our men for three months of service in arrears and give them one month's pay in advance. We must also allow two dollars for a blanket for each man. Then there is the payment to the men who are leaving their weaponry behind to arm the troops who will arrive. Additionally, there are money demands for the commissary and the quartermaster-generals. I must, therefore, beg for another remittance. Enlistments have increased to eight thousand five hundred men. For this I am grateful, though it creates the need for more funds.

A committee from this province appeared at my door the other day requesting arms for their local defense. If Colonel Knox returns with the arms he was sent for, I may be able to accommodate. However, at this time, I must empathize with a promise based on future supplies. This does not go well with the hearers, but it is the truth.

The people in Rhode Island fear the British ships which have left Great Britain are on their way for Newport. I have sent Major-General Lee to show them how to form a defense.

Tuesday, December 26, 1775 — Cambridge, Massachusetts

As the snow falls outside my window and into our ranks, our lack of powder, wood, and barracks alarms me. What bothers me more is that General Howe is a formidable enemy whose forces are growing like a snowball rolling rapidly downhill. It is hard to be the beggar at times like these. I feel as though I am on an island, unable to reach others or receive from others what is in want. I send letter after letter recounting our plight. I receive letters, not as frequent, bringing intentions and sentiments but little of what we need.

Sunday, December 31, 1775 — Cambridge, Massachusetts

At the close of this year, I have tallied our monthly financial needs. They total a need for two hundred and seventy-five thousand dollars per month. I have passed this on to Congress. This is just for the armies under me. It does not include separate-forming armies in Braintree, Weymouth, and Hingham. To see a fervor in this Nation to serve whether under my command or in defense of the individual provinces is good.

A complication of sorts has arisen. The general officers have decided not to reenlist the free negroes who have served in this army. I disagree. I am going to go against the officers' resolution. These men have served well. I have given license for their enlistment in the provincial army to serve with us. I pray that Congress will agree.

Colonel Gridley, our chief engineer, intends to continue in this army. He has been instrumental in building defenses around Boston. He and the assistant engineers receive such small pay that it is difficult to imagine men of science engaging in this cause. I must convince Congress that a provision for them be made.

A need exists to raise the pay of our chaplains. These men have left their flocks. They are paying parsons to fill in for them in an amount exceeding that which they receive from their country. These are patriots who deserve our Nation's gratitude, expressed through adequate pay. Their lives and their conversations are benefiting this army in ways few would comprehend. They benefit me. If payment is hard pressed, we could assign one chaplain for two regiments cutting their numbers, thereby increasing the pay for those retained.

On the war front, General Montgomery has joined Colonel Arnold's efforts in preparing for an attack on Quebec. Our enlistments here under my command number nine thousand, six hundred, and fifty. Our provisions grow scarcer. The soldiers are having to eat their food raw as little firewood is left for cooking. Fences all around have been cut down as have the trees within a mile around the camp. I overheard one soldier grouse that we have never been so weak. Yet, we will be weaker still when tomorrow comes.

The Year 1776

Monday, January 1, 1776 — Cambridge, Massachusetts

In my mortal attempt to inspire the men, I made a declaration that this new year brings a new army. To represent this, I had a new flag made with the British colors in the canton and thirteen alternating red and white stripes. This canton is to depict that we are British citizens being fired upon. The stripes show that we are thirteen colonies seeking for liberty to live and work as Providence has allowed. I had it raised with a thirteen-gun salute. This representation of individual stripes is appropriate because this new army is truly continental, populated and supported by all thirteen colonies.

We have been serving for most of this conflict under a flag with a pine tree called the "Liberty Tree." The words, "Appeal to Heaven" are written upon it. In the face of tyranny, we have protested and appealed to Heaven for grace, help, and resolution. With the close of 1775, the plethora of dire needs are daunting. We see our spirits and our army at the brink of despair. Our yearning even now is that Heaven will answer our plea.

With every new year, new hope presents that things will be different. Today, I awoke with expectation until I looked out on the camp to see nothing different. I prayed for Divine Favor, for something this day to encourage me and inspire our troops. Heaven brought help from the strangest of places — from King George III. A print of the speech he delivered at the opening of Parliament in October reached our lines this day. In it, he vowed to utterly crush the colonial rebellion. I wonder if the redcoats are expecting our surrender this instant? If they are, I gladly write that they will be sorely disappointed. The proclamation from the king had the most desirous of effects. The spirit of our men rose to a level that I could not have produced. Anger and yelling ensued all around. Our men were reminded of the reason for which we suffer. The soldiers with indignation burned the speech in a public rebuke.

I made plans to inspire the army. God had His Plan to do more than I could ask or think. By His Favor, my plans and His came together in answer to our appeal to Heaven. Men are invigorated. Patriotism swells our ranks. Men who were leaving have decided to stay. Men who were retiring have taken furloughs instead, vowing to return. New recruits have a glow in their hearts with a love for freedom, family, and country. Our trust grows in the only One who can save us against such great odds — The Almighty.

Thursday, January 4, 1776 — Cambridge, Massachusetts

It is not found in the pages of history, the story of an army sitting this close to an opponent for a period of six months without an advance from either side. Beyond this oddity, one army has completely replaced itself in harm's way, while the opponent continues to amass its superior strength. I pray Congress will ascertain that the delay is not want of inclination, but rather a response to circumstances. To act too early would make the devastating status irremediable.

Messengers from Boston report that the British are sending out convoys for aggression upon Long Island. Congress must decide the prudence of sending Jersey troops to New York to prevent an evil which the enemy no doubt has planned at some point.

Saturday, January 6, 1776 — Cambridge, Massachusetts

Governor Cooke of Rhode Island has sent blankets for our men and promised more. His men are making ready for any British attacks near Halifax thanks to General Lee's counsel. Governor Trumbull of Connecticut has won the full support of his colony to our cause — passing acts to raise up troops, provide armed vessels, and produce lead for the Continental army. He has initiated punishment to any who aid the enemy with confiscation of property and imprisonment for up to three years. It is hoped that the other colonies will follow in the effort to preserve our country.

Sunday, January 7, 1776 — Cambridge, Massachusetts

A visiting reverend brought the message today to our troops. Attendance was great. The message came from the Book of Numbers in the tenth chapter. The main text was quoted, "Rise up, Lord, and let Thine enemies be scattered; and let them that hate Thee flee before Thee." This is the appeal of our Nation against our foe. I need the Lord to rise up for me. I am promised many things from men that never come to pass. I go from one difficulty to another. How it will end, only God in His great goodness will direct. I remain His servant above all others and am thankful for the protection that He has given me throughout my life and trust He will continue.

My friend John Adams is in our camp. I invited him for an evening meal to gain his counsel. News has flooded my quarters that the British troops are embarking for some destination southward. I presume it will be New York. Their success in taking New York would be tantamount to commanding the country and all communications. This is no trifling consideration. I let Mr. Adams know that it was imperative to send General Lee in the instant to raise up volunteers. Together, they should repair to the city of New York to defend it with the assistance of forces from New Jersey. I hope Congress will approve of my conduct in this matter. It is easier to prevent an enemy from posting themselves, than to dislodge them after they have gained possession. Mr. Adams approves of this move. He believes all of Congress will approve once he conveys the strategy.

Monday, January 8, 1776 — Cambridge, Massachusetts

I sent General Lee on his way with letters to the governors of the colonies to assist him along the way.

Late this evening, I ordered Major Knowlton to cross upon the mill-dam and set fire to as many of the fourteen houses the redcoat gentry has identified to be pulled down to fuel their fires for the winter cold. If he is successful, the British will be given warmth, but only for a night.

Returns show that eight of the fourteen houses were burned. How many nights of warmth and comfort did that cost them? I pray many.

Tuesday, January 9, 1776 — Cambridge, Massachusetts

I was gratified to learn that while Major Knowlton was burning down houses set aside for fuel, many of the enemy's men were watching a play at our beloved Faneuil Hall, which mocked our efforts in this war. They thought the commotion our men made was part of the play. When the realization came upon the audience of soldiers, they ran out of the building to contend, but found they were too late to interfere. We suffered no harm or losses. Our men took five soldiers and a wife of one as prisoners. One of their men was killed.

Friday, January 12, 1776 — Cambridge, Massachusetts

Colonel Benedict Arnold continues his felicity to this noble cause. His men are near Quebec. I expect him soon to be reporting from within Quebec's walls as the victor. I have encouraged him to send blankets, clothing, and military stores from that city as we are in great want. His success will greatly exhort the united voice of America. Congress is in consideration to raise an army to defend Canada. They may want to build it under the likes of Colonel Arnold and General Montgomery. I know this would be pleasant for both. Selfishly, such a promotion of a man of Arnold's ilk causes me pain as I need more active men like him helping me here.

Sunday, January 14, 1776 — Cambridge, Massachusetts

I received a letter from the good Joseph Reed today. I long for him to return to my aid in this camp. In the meantime, his help with Congress proves invaluable. His letter is what it always is, full of praise of me. He constantly recounts how people in Congress and our Nation respect and honor me. His conveyance of continental gratitude is effusive. Such words are meant to encourage, but when Congress does not respond to my repeated requests for aid, I cannot help but think that there is some matter of objection to my conduct. Based on Reverend Schibler's message on this day from the book of Proverbs in the ninth chapter, I am reminded of the precept, "Reprove not a scorner, lest he hate thee: rebuke a wise man, and he will love thee. Give instruction to a wise man, and he will be yet wiser: teach a just man, and he will increase in learning." I have implored Reed today via dispatched letter that I truly want to know where I stand in the opinion of others and what faults are apparent so that I might correct these errors and make my conduct coincide with the wishes of our countrymen.

I have reiterated in my long discourse what I have twenty times urged Congress. We are in want of money, arms, a brigadier, engineers, tents, clothing, and always powder. The officers in these parts are discontented and rightly so. They place the blame upon me, not realizing that I am their greatest advocate. If I had only known this would be my lot, I would have preferred to take up a musket and join at the shoulder the men who fight this battle.

As in need we are of arms, I am exceedingly in want of sleep. Anxieties cover me while our men lay wrapped in sleep relieved that they have pressed the burden upon me. I am consoled in the prayers I whisper on my pillow and by the warmth of Mrs. Washington's side. It has reached my desk that five regiments from Ireland set sail when a violent storm forced them to a distressed conclusion. They are now unable to continue to this continent in their present condition. I must look beyond our hardships to see the benevolent Hand of Providence guarding us. No other explanation is plausible for why the enemy has not put us out of our misery with one fell swoop. If only they knew our condition. I believe they have been apprised of our state, but it is such a poor report that they can hardly believe it for fear it is a planted falsehood. For these, I give thanks as my appeal to Heaven continues unabated.

Tuesday, January 16, 1776 — Cambridge, Massachusetts

I would not like to think myself a worrier. Rather, I consider myself a hoper. I hope people do as they say. I hope things turn out the way they need to. I hope the enemy does not attack. I hope we have enough provision for this army. I hope this army grows with ample men to continue this fight and for the powder to increase correspondingly. I hope Congress will act to support us with more urgency. I hope Colonel Arnold and General Montgomery achieve success in Canada. I hope that General Schuyler does not quit his post. I hope Colonel Knox makes it from Ticonderoga with the arms and supplies. It is my understanding that a small portion of what he is attempting to bring us has arrived in New York, but great restraints attach to this effort. I hope that the local generals will cease to grant furloughs for troops who most likely will not return. It is better to discharge them disconnecting them from the pay commitments. Currently, officers are furloughing men who are home tending to their business while receiving army pay. They are doing nothing for our defense but profiting from poor stewardship. It is inimical to worry but is hoping ad nauseam any less harmful? Proverbs 13:12 agrees, "Hope deferred maketh the heart sick: but when the desire cometh, it is a tree of life." I am looking for the desire to come soon.

Thursday, January 18, 1776 — Cambridge, Massachusetts

Hope is not lost this day, but it is greatly diminished. News has reached the camp that the attack on Quebec under Colonel Arnold and General Montgomery has been defeated. Colonel Arnold was wounded in the affair. Add death to injury, General Montgomery was killed. I have consulted Mr. John Adams and other members of influence to ascertain what should be done in response to this melancholy affair. They are of the mind to raise up three regiments from the Colonies of Massachusetts, New Hampshire, and Connecticut to dispatch assistance to Colonel Arnold. This would be done with the hopes of keeping what we have gained from General Carleton and, perhaps, gain from him Quebec in the process prior to winter's thickness. I am writing Congress and the three nearest colonies with a request that they raise up the regiments whose enlistments extend to the 1st of January 1777 at the earliest.

Friday, January 19, 1776 — Cambridge, Massachusetts

Congress has sent letters for my review, perusal, insight, and pleasure. One letter written by Nathanael Green to Samuel Ward in Philadelphia especially caught my eye. His words touched me deeply. I venture to rewrite them here for my constant reflection: "Heaven hath decreed that tottering empire Britain to irretrievable ruin and thanks to God, since Providence hath so determined, America must raise an empire of permanent duration, supported upon the grand pillars of Truth, Freedom, and Religion encouraged by the smiles of Justice and defended by her own patriotic sons. . . . Permit me then to recommend from the sincerity of my heart, ready at all times to bleed in my country's cause, a Declaration of

Independence, and call upon the world and the great God who governs it to witness the necessity, propriety, and rectitude thereof." I am not sure if it is independence we seek, though it may be independence we need. Regardless of that
concern, my overall opinion on the letter is the word from that Holy Text —
"Amen" — so let it be.

Saturday, January 20, 1776 — Cambridge, Massachusetts

There is burgeoning in the soul of this continent — a cry for freedom. Many have
understood the things that precipitated this conflict, but the reasoning to justify
its escalation has been lacking. Just when we seemed adrift of all explanations, Mr.
Thomas Paine penned the answer, a drink of cool water to quench our thirst for
why. He has declared that England is not our parent; rather Europe is. That this
continent on which we abide was "the asylum for the persecuted lovers of civil
and religious liberty from every part of Europe who have fled not from the tender
embrace of the mother but from the cruelty of the monster. . . . That same tyranny
which drove the first emigrants from home, pursues their descendants still." He
went on to say that "Until independence is declared, the continent will feel itself
like a man who continues putting off some unpleasant business from day-to-day,
yet knows it must be done, hates to set about it, wishes it over, and is continually
haunted with the thoughts of its necessity." I believe in the heart of every American is this negligence to do what they know must be done. To come to this conclusion took me awhile, but I am arriving at that reality and perhaps arrived earlier
than I even thought, else I would not have endeavored to lead this effort. "Common sense will tell us, that the power which hath endeavored to subdue us, is of
all others the most improper to defend us." I am humored by Paine's tongue-in-
cheek comment that though it may make sense for a continent to protect an island, it makes no sense for an island to rule a continent. Little Britain on that
island seeks to rule an entire continent as if the tail can wag the dog.

Everything that we were feeling but could not express, Mr. Paine has done for
us. His religious reasoning places the proper and Divine period to the argument:
"When a man seriously reflects on the idolatrous homage which is paid to the
persons of kings, he need not wonder that the Almighty, ever jealous of His
Honor, should disapprove of a form of government which so impiously invades

the prerogative of Heaven. . . . Even the distance at which the Almighty hath placed England and America, is a strong and natural proof, that the authority of the one, over the other, was never the design of Heaven."

I have read this over numerous times and find something even more compelling with each pass. I am having this read throughout our camp and am relaying it to every sector of this army so that they can understand the reason we bear arms at this time. As Paine has said, "The cause of America is in great measure the cause of all mankind." Once again, I say, "Amen."

Sunday, January 21, 1776 — Cambridge, Massachusetts

On this Lord's Day, worship and rest occurred. This evening we were visited by thirteen Caughnawaga Indians. Colonel Louis led them to me. We have done our best to entertain them and will continue until they leave so that they may be impressed with sentiments of our friendship and strength. Their kind disposition toward us can at the least prevent them from taking arms against us. At best, it can influence them to fill a gap for us where fighting men are in short supply.

Tuesday, January 23, 1776 — Cambridge, Massachusetts

Our enemies across the Atlantic are building up their strength here in this area. They are on the move southward, most likely to New York. I sent a request for Congress to send two regiments to deal with the Tories on Long Island, our domestic enemies working in concert with the ministerial enemies. Congress countermanded this request. I believe this is largely a case of parsimony. Such frugality seems right to them, but I long for them to understand what is lost to our cause when they miserly extend succor.

Notwithstanding, under the New York Provincial Congress, Colonel McDougall, who is fervent for our cause regardless of personal cost, is raising up four regiments to defend New York. He is a patriot and a leader with great initiative. He has the same zeal for our success in Boston as for his own in New York. I am asking General Lee to press Colonel McDougal to forward shells and powder to me as much as he can spare.

I am writing letters daily from my desk soliciting help and returning correspondence, along with giving orders to those in other sectors. Mr. Joseph Reed served in this capacity so effectually in the past. He has promised time-and-again that he will return to help, but he has of yet appeared. Spending time on the administrative side of war keeps me away from the strategic and fighting side of this effort. I am hopeful and constantly exhorting, even begging, his leave to our aid. He may tire of my requests as I am tiring of my petitions, but if there was another who could fill this spot, I would gladly disembark from these requests.

Wednesday, January 24, 1776 — Cambridge, Massachusetts

Mr. George Washington — Commander-in-Chief of the army, recruiter, secretary, quartermaster, drill instructor, paymaster, accountant, and department of complaints. I am doing all this without a salary. For Congress to point the finger at one man, to excuse any shortages as another's fault, and explain defeats as another's inadequacy must be easy. I accepted the post that was given me with the assurances of full cooperation. At this instant in our need of money and resources, murmurings are ensuing for a full accounting of what has been received. I have recommended with absolute necessity that a proper person would come to settle the accounts of this army and keep a tight recording forthwith. No such person has been provided. I am requesting this again. If only these selectmen would spend a week here on these lines to see all that is done and all that is left undone, perhaps empathy and ready assistance would be given. I am grateful Mr. John Adams has been faithful to come to our side. With each visit, he agrees with my requisitions.

I am longing to make a decisive move on Boston and destroy the British nest there, but until I am equipped with the powder and men, delay is the only wise path. Militia continue to be a bulwark for this army.

Saturday, January 27, 1776 — Cambridge, Massachusetts

Our Caughnawaga Indian visitors are still here. They had signed a neutrality pact with General Schuyler on the ultimo, and now are intimating that they are willing to take up arms on behalf of the United Colonies. They have given an assurance to raise four or five hundred men to join our effort. I am not sure how Schuyler seeks to use them. I am equally unsure what the expense will be to pay them. I am sure that if we do not accede to their demands, the British side will gladly oblige.

Speaking of General Schuyler, I am delighted to hear that he has had a successful expedition into Tryon County. I am praying that the Supreme Dispenser of everything good will grant General Lee the same on Long Island.

Colonel Arnold is on the mend but in grave danger in Canada. The governments of Connecticut and New Hampshire have vowed to raise three regiments to come to Arnold's aid, along with two being raised by Congress from Pennsylvania and the Jerseys. Expediency is required. The possession of Canada is of great importance and can help render the freedom of America secure. May Colonel Arnold hold fast and reengage the fight until he and his men enter that fortress and receive the laurels their bravery and perseverance merit.

Sunday, January 28, 1776 — Cambridge, Massachusetts

Bright spots and brave men dot the landscape of this war. Colonel Arnold is one. General Nathanael Greene is another. General Lee is one. General Daniel Morgan is yet another.

And then there is Commodore John Manley. With little direction from me and no need for encouragement or accommodation, he wages war on the British with relentless fury. He has carried into Plymouth two of the enemy's transports, while engaging an eight-gun schooner. This patriot deserves the thanks of his country. He certainly has mine. He deserves an even stronger vessel of war. I cannot fathom what this commodore could do when equipped with a ship of equal footing to the enemy. Until then, he must continue in the schooner Hancock. He is short of men. I am asking him to complete the complement of forty men to assist his efforts. I am hoping that he can stimulate the captains of our other schooners to follow his example into the fire. Their efforts can be an extended source to satisfy our most evident needs. That we could defeat the redcoat force with their own arms is a justifying thought.

Colonel Henry Knox is cut from the same cloth as Manley. Knox arrived this day after a four-month journey to and from Fort Ticonderoga covering three hundred miles of nothing but trouble. He spent two thousand, five hundred dollars of his own money building sleds, hiring one hundred and sixty teamsters and oxen, and purchasing other articles to deal with the challenge. He faced hardships, tears, discouraged men, high mountains, frozen and thawing terrain, obstinate weather, and even had to retrieve cannons from the freezing rivers when boats sank. There is no quit in Colonel Knox. This twenty-five-year-old former bookseller successfully delivered one hundred and twenty thousand pounds of artillery, including fifty-eight cannons. In King Jehoshaphat's day, God defeated Judah's enemy and the Nation gained great plunder from the defeated army. The victory at Ticonderoga has finally produced the plunder for which we had hoped. Knox is enterprising, resourceful, and committed. In struggles, he is determined not to quit. I am the same.

When I think again of King David's mighty men, I picture a few of them with their miraculous exploits when I consider Greene, Morgan, Arnold, Manley, and Knox. Finally, the war is breaking in our favor. I will not share this with Congress, though I know these miraculous exploits will spread soon enough. Silence on them in my correspondence is necessary to keep the pressure on the colonies and Congress to do what they have committed. I cannot let them rest.

Tuesday, January 30, 1776 — Cambridge, Massachusetts

Even with successes, the truth is we need arms and powder. Though Congress has said that each man who joins must bring his own arms, powder, blanket, and clothing, the vast majority are coming lacking the aforementioned. Our standing army has run short due to usage and weather effects. I have applied to the colonies to supply us, but that has returned void. I have sent out officers with money to purchase supplies from the people around us, but I am not convinced much will be procured this way.

Requests are being received by me for men in other areas endangered. I do not have the men to confront the challenges here. As I am seeking to raise up men to aid our efforts here, I answer all outside requests with the recommendations that they raise up men for themselves from their locations. Facing my own need, I met today again with the Caughnawaga Indians as well as with three of the tribes of St. John's and Passamaquoddy Indians. Holding them neutral or recruiting them to our side is necessary when our manpower is so paltry.

I am convinced that British General Clinton is on an expedition to Long Island with four or five hundred men. General Lee needs to take the arms from the Tories immediately because it is certain they will use those arms on us. There is no doubt who the Tories are. Their allegiance has been publicly proclaimed. In Lee's efforts, I hesitate, but wish he would arrest Governor Tryon who is empowering the Tories there.

I am doing my best to defer to Congress in these decisions. I am keeping them abreast of our situation and the situation around this Nation. I write to them often and give my opinions while submitting myself to their leadership. This does not make my efforts easier. I expect the chain-of-command to be followed under me, so I must model it upward to those to whom I willingly subject myself. All for the sake of our cause.

With this said, I am ready to make a bold move toward Boston. We have equipment and with a portion of the British on the move southward, this may be the best time to make a decisive stroke. The biggest obstacle is moving the artillery and army across the bay. I have gone out the last few days and even jumped up and down on the ice. It still is not sturdy enough at this point, to make our move. All necessary arrangements are being made so that when the moment appears, we will be prepared and ready to move.

Wednesday, January 31, 1776 — Cambridge, Massachusetts

My continued appeal to Joseph Reed to return to help me has brought me to a point of doubt and self-criticism. As much as I want and need him here by my side, I fear that he would come before he is ready. I could even see that my persistent requests could alienate him. He has ventured to raise up a navy using resources that should be coming our way. I am a little provoked by this diverting of needed articles. With the support that Manley and Knox have brought, I have the luxury to be a little more forward in my writings to Reed. My hope is that he will respond. Even though I fear duplicity of sorts in Mr. Reed, he continues to relay kind sentiments toward me and Mrs. Washington. He even had a portrait made of me, though comically I see a hint of terror in my countenance.

Reinforcement of cause and unity of spirit for my countrymen of Virginia is my hope at the news that the British have burned Norfolk. Their crimes against Falmouth and Norfolk add even more to the reasoning behind the pamphlet Mr. Paine wrote called "Common Sense." That spirit is being displayed still in Canada as Arnold is continuing the blockade of Quebec. His ability and perseverance are well-exhibited amidst great difficulties. I hope that this will stimulate other officers to do likewise in their corner of the war.

A move by this army against the British in Boston would lift all sectors for our Nation's cause. This would embolden men everywhere if they can see that a real resistance is on the cusp and that a General is equipped and engaged, no longer willing to stand for ministerial oppression.

Thursday, February 8, 1776 — Cambridge, Massachusetts

It has risen in my mind, that legislating from afar is less than optimal. Every leader who has visited this camp leaves here with agreement as to our needs and how they must be met. Sadly, few have ventured to this quarter to view the circumstances for themselves. I am going to write to Congress in a very direct and descriptive manner, hoping they will take my word along with those who have personally witnessed our obstacles. Want of men contributed to the unnecessary loss of General Montgomery. Had he had sufficient men, capitulation need not to have been inevitable.

Our current method of gaining an army is inadequate. In a coherent and persuasive letter, I will enumerate the realities. Marching men in to replace men leaving and expecting the same results from the new army compared to the seasoned army goes against all logic. With new men in the army, training is needed as well as required discipline and subordination. With short-term enlistments, the officers are at the mercy of the soldiers. They must appease the soldier, cajole the soldier, and befriend the soldier in hopes that he will do what he is told and that he will have a favorable view of all things army to motivate him to serve a second tour. In doing this, discipline and order suffer.

This state of being brings danger to the operation and to the men. Men, trained and familiar with danger, run into it without shrinking. The untrained and unfamiliar to rigors of war, see danger at every corner and avoid it at every measure. I believe three things prompt men to do their duty in a time of action — natural bravery, hope of reward, and fear of punishment. The first two are inherent attributes of the trained and the untrained. The third, fear of punishment, is the lasting motivator for the untrained. If he fears repercussions of death from his own men should he shrink from duty, he will be more apt to face that danger from the enemy than to suffer that certainty from his friends.

To buttress my argument, I need to bring one other thing to Congress's attention. Those who are near to their enlistment expiration become lax in their duties and in the care for their arms, ammunition, utensils, and quarters. Thus, when they phase out, new expenses are to be had in procuring new arms and new or repaired barracks.

With these stated supports, I want to propose longer enlistment periods, consideration of a draft, and raising of pay to incentivize men to stay. I may not present all these at once. We take one bite at a time.

Along with our need for men, a great need presents for firelocks. Currently, we have two thousand men in camp without the access to such. If any hope exists to send the British back across the ocean, it will require this army to have a respectable footing in armaments. We are blessed with the big guns from Ticonderoga, which will greatly loosen the enemy from his hold, but it will take the individual arms to dislodge them one-by-one. I have borrowed twenty-five thousand pounds from the local governments to acquire some necessities and sent officers out to purchase from individuals needed arms and ammunition. I hold little expectation that this will suffice, but it will shore up some deficiencies. I am doing all in my power. I need Congress to do what I cannot. Without men, without arms, without ammunition, without the things that are needed to accommodate a soldier, little can be done to advance this army from our current stead.

Saturday, February 10, 1776 — Cambridge, Massachusetts

What do others think of me? How can I do a better job to commend their accommodation of confidence? Mr. Reed is hesitant to offer honest appraisal. He thinks it would be taken as criticism, but how can a man avoid the shelves and rocks if he has no idea where they lie? I need to know what reflections are cast upon my conduct thus far.

I will continue in this command — not for my ease but for the freedoms of my country. I flatter myself that France may soon send help. Until then, Congress must forward powder from their province to the edge of the battle where it is needed. I am at the point where I must conceal our true condition from the officers around me and surely from the enemy. There is powder by the chimney-corner in Philadelphia, but that does our noble cause little good. Congress demands action, but seldom does anything to furnish the means.

Bunker Hill is continually mentioned as an object of dispatch, but to attack that entrenchment presents the potential of great loss and discouragement. Granted the victory on such a bastion would ingratiate all to this fight for freedom, but the odds lean heavily to a great loss rather than to a great gain. My belief is that an endeavor should be made at Dorchester Hill. Our laborious piece of work at Lechmere's Point should be finished by Sunday.

Sunday, February 11, 1776 — Cambridge, Massachusetts

Today I prayed for the Lord's Hand to be involved in my life, my post, and in this worthy cause. I have searched my heart relentlessly to gauge the reason and explanation of this current conflict. We have suffered long under Great Britain's tyranny and diabolical ministry. As dutiful subjects to this former government across the sea, we made petitions, we waged efforts ardently to seek reconciliation. Each of these proved abortive. The spirit of freedom rose within these colonies, which forbid the continuing station of slavery. We are determined now to shake all connections with this sovereign and stand as clear of their unjust and unnatural intentions. The Sovereign Ruler and all-wise Dispenser of justice is the One on whom we seek to rely. It is in God we will trust. We will not fear what man may do to us.

Wednesday, February 14, 1776 — Cambridge, Massachusetts

Speaking of Dorchester Heights, the enemy made a foray through the Dorchester Neck last night burning some houses which had no value to us. Our men responded, but the British retreated back across before we could engage them.

Sunday, February 18, 1776 — Cambridge, Massachusetts

The militia has arrived at great expense to our Nation. The eyes of the continent are fixed upon this army with expectation of some great event. The irksomeness of our idleness falls upon this whole continent, but what few realize is that I am the one most irked. This compelled me to call for a council of war this day among our officers with the subject of making an attack on Boston before the ministerial reinforcements arrive. With the winter freeze making a strong ice bridge from Dorchester Point to the Boston Neck, and from Roxbury to the Common, I felt it was ideal for an attack. The council, including General Gates and General Putnam, believed such action would be imprudent in consideration of the enemy's position and artillery, and our shortages to contend with complexities which might occur. That they did resolve to have a cannonade and bombardment once powder is sufficient is a relief. They were encouraging in respect to the prospect of taking Dorchester Heights per my suggestion. The council recommended taking Noddle's Island as well if this could be effected. Such agreement commends the opinion that I am not willing to act out of impatience; nor, do I set upon unnecessary hazards. I am sensible of our situation and do believe that the situation demands a change in the status quo.

Monday, February 26, 1776 — Cambridge, Massachusetts

Lechmere's Point is now strong. I am sending heavy cannon to the Point. The platforms for the mortars are prepared. I will set another at Lamb's Dam as we make the necessary disposition to take possession of Dorchester Heights by the end of this week. Strong guards are mounted at Lechmere Point and Cobble Hill. Ten regiments of militia have bolstered our hand for the offensive. I am alerting the Massachusetts Bay council to be ready. They will need to direct their militia to cover the lines contiguous to Dorchester and Roxbury. Finally, action is near for this army. All are alert and waiting for this engagement. We just need the enemy to be so kind as to come out to meet us. Divine Providence will aid in reducing this question to certain success.

A letter from General Lee arrived today, though it has been a long time in coming. I grow more impatient with his hesitancy to keep me apprised of his command in New York. He was said to have been vying for the position of Commander-in-Chief at the onset of this affair. He was disappointed at not receiving the appointment. His rejection was mainly due to fears of his allegiance, as he had left the British army and the nation of his birth for our cause.

The British movements of late signal they are heading for a large-scale attack, most likely in New York. The total of topsail vessels has been readied and watered. They appear to be debarking in earnest. General Lee needs to know this and be prepared with men, arms, cannon, ammunition, and powder. What we have expected here in Boston may be exacted in New York. I am letting Lee know that I will dispatch men and arms to him, even this whole army under my charge if that is the case.

The potential for movement bolsters my activity and confidence. The Almighty has encouraged me not just with circumstances now at our disposal, but by a poem written by the gifted Miss Phillis Wheatley. Her poem to my flattery is much appreciated. I would love for others to read it to appreciate her gifts, but to do so would have incurred the imputation of vanity. I have written her to express my gratitude. I hope to meet her one day in our camp. I read and reread her poem concerning me. It is much needed in the ebb-and-flow of war and self-evaluation.

Tuesday, February 27, 1776 — Cambridge, Massachusetts

This venture in battle entails so much. We must occupy the Heights on a single night before the British can know what we are doing. On one night, the cannons must be hauled up the steep Dorchester Heights. Breastworks must be built without drawing attention to their building. The sight of activity will ruin the surprise and the chances for success.

In deliberating over this, Rufus Putnam, the General's brother, has led our efforts fabricating fortifications away from Dorchester Heights, with the concern of orchestrating their movement up the heights at the same time as the guns. I also have suggested filling barrels with earth to show strength on the Heights and to be a mode of defense. Should the enemy attempt to ascend, they can be rolled down upon them. I had wooden frames filled with hay to align the front of the heights to cover our movements and to guard us from enemy fire. General Thomas has been given the assignment to lead three thousand men in fortifying Dorchester Heights on the night in question. Another four thousand men will be led by General Greene and General Sullivan on the morning for an amphibious attack on Boston. Two thousand militia stand ready to maximize our strength.

All this construction requires noise which the enemy will hear. I have ordered multiple barrages of artillery fire from Roxbury, Cobble Hill, and Lechmere Point to divert the enemy's attention. The army hospital at Cambridge is making ready thousands of bandages and additional beds for the injured. This is the sad point of any military encounter — the dead and wounded. I do not take this lightly; nor, do I deceive myself to think that our men do not consider this outcome. I am calling on our men to prepare themselves and think on how much our Nation depends on our exertions. Such sacrifice will bring great advantages to our Nation, our lives, our families, and our posterity. They need to know that though personal bravery and reward combine as a strong impetus for this activity, cowardice or retreat from the enemy will bring about assured execution to deter others from doing the same.

By all measures of progress, the evening of March 4th has been chosen to instigate this operation. They will be carried into operation on the enemy the morning of March 5th, which coincides Providentially with the anniversary of the Boston Massacre.

Saturday, March 2, 1776 — Cambridge, Massachusetts

I am writing Mr. Reed again regarding my despair of not receiving the equipage needed after multiple requests to Congress. I am sensibly mortified that Congress does not even think it necessary to take the least notice of my application for these things. I continually give them a full accounting of the resources that I receive and those that I raise on my own.

From one hand, I am not getting what is necessary. On the other hand, commitments of resources are made that were not promised or approved. New York is in grave danger with General Clinton sailing in that direction. If he is successful, it will be a capital blow to the interests of America. In response to the alerts that I have dispatched, Captain Sears of Connecticut assures me that one thousand volunteers would be sent to defend the place with no pay required, only provisions. Knowing that New York cannot be depended upon and unable to ascertain if the Jersey troops have the numbers to help, I approved the Connecticut proposition. I later found that Governor Trumbull raised up the troops as promised, but informed the men they would receive Continental pay. This was contrary to my expectation. I had not authorized this, nor was I of the capacity to authorize it. Now I have one thousand troops marching to New York expecting pay. We have no money to pay them at this instant. I am unsure Congress will approve such a large distribution since it was without their consent. My first thought was to recall them, but with New York in such jeopardy, I deemed it too hazardous to countermand their regiments. I am never fond of stretching my powers, but success in this effort is my chief concern. Should Congress rebuke me, I shall do my best not to offend them in this way again. I pray Congress will understand the hard position in which I am placed.

Sunday, March 3, 1776 — Cambridge, Massachusetts

At midnight last night, we began bombardment of the British in Boston from our posts at Cobble Hill, Lechmere's Point, and Lamb's Dam. This scheme effected the desired result as the British fired back creating ample noise to cover the sound of our construction of breastworks, defenses, and wooden frames. All was carried off perfectly except for the bursting of two thirteen-inch and three ten-inch mortars. I am unsure if the mishap was due to defects in the mortars or in the inexperience of the bombardiers. Regardless, we will continue this distraction into the evening as our men are making great progress to the goal we have set.

Monday, March 4, 1776 — Cambridge, Massachusetts

Last night, the bombardment was much heavier between our guns and the British. Everything should be ready by this evening to make the ascent up Dorchester Heights. I am praying all goes well. With the help of Providence, the British will be dislodged or suffer greatly for their unwelcomed stay.

Tuesday, March 5, 1776 — Cambridge, Massachusetts

On the signal of the first sound of our guns yesterday evening, Brigadier-General Thomas with two thousand men silently and quickly crossed the neck. Their movement was cloaked by the hay bales, unnoticed by the enemy. Thomas's men were able to secure the two hills. A guard of eight hundred riflemen spread out across the base of the Heights to address any British incursions. Behind these, one thousand, two hundred men began the arduous work of moving wagons, wooden frames, constructed breastworks, guns, powder, and mortars up the steep Dorchester Heights. They worked in amazing concert. The bombardment carried on covering our movements and placements. We lost only two men, one to a cannonball taking off his leg at the thigh and the other by an explosion of a shell. Four or five others were wounded from that explosion, but minimally. By morning light, our redoubts were ready to defend and twenty of our cannons were on the Heights ready to fire.

I do have to make a special note. For the days of discouragement, it will be important to remember that the Almighty is engaged. He is assisting in ways beyond comprehension. Last night was clear and the moon was bright. It was almost as if God Himself was holding a torch light for our passage. The fear was, that with His Light so bright, surely the enemy would see our endeavors. As the Dispenser of all things would have it, He graced us with a fine mist at a level of a few feet above the bottom of the hill obscuring the enemy's view of our advancements. I have seen His Hand protect me in many battles. I rejoice that His Protection has not left me though I often feel others have.

Wednesday, March 6, 1776 — Dorchester Heights, Massachusetts

At daybreak yesterday morning, we could see the enemy gazing up at us. We have gained the upper hand, literally speaking. Our guns are now able to reach any part of the city, including the harbor where the British ships have moored. They certainly will not dare to sail much closer. The enemy fire up at us but are unable to get the right angle to reach our position. As Boston is laid out below us, our men are ready for battle. We chose this day in earnest, so that all would remember our brethren who fell at Bunker Hill. The men are elated. Finally, a sense of engagement is present, of inflicting toil and suffering on the instigators. During the day, we could see the soldiers being moved to various sectors in what would be a night attack. We have filled barrels with rock and frozen earth ready to roll down on any approach the enemy might make to injure their movement toward us. We will give them a warm reception upon their chosen time of ascent.

As night fell, I am glad to report again the Hand of the Almighty. Just as the enemy were making their move, a storm began to rage with hail, snow, sleet, and extremely heavy winds. We had to continually brace ourselves against the redoubts and use them to block the cold. I thought the wind was heavy because of where we were on the Heights, but as we looked down, it caused hurricane-like havoc below too. As my men and I shivered, we were in awe of what was happening. General Heath verbalized what we all believed, "Kind Heaven has intervened."

I have slipped away for a time of reflection late this morning. As I write this, the wind is still blowing furiously. A hard rain is pounding us and the enemy. We are strengthening our positions, waiting to see if the enemy will attempt such a run up this hill. Our men hope they will. We have never been in a more advantageous position. I cannot help but think to a degree that the heavy storm was a help to the enemy as our forces would have surely exacted heavy losses on their side. Regardless, I know our Redeemer is watching and knows more on the matter than we.

If the enemy makes an attack on Dorchester Heights with a significant number of their men, Boston will be left unprotected. I have four thousand men awaiting my signal to attack Boston embarking on the mouth of the Cambridge river in two divisions under Brigadier-General Sullivan and Brigadier-General Greene. Major-General Putnam will take the lead command for this strike. My wish is for one division to gain possession of Beacon Hill and Mount Horam. The plan is for the second division to take Barton's Point. With success, these can then join the other divisions at the neck leading into Boston. Three floating batteries are to precede and keep up heavy fire to cover the men as they land.

Thursday, March 7, 1776 — Dorchester Heights, Massachusetts

We continue to wait for some initiative by the enemy. Every moment they hesitate gives our men the chance to strengthen this position and to move forward to take post on Nook's Hill and points south of Boston. This contiguity will serve us well against the enemy. I am having mortars furnaced at two locations with great expedition as they are essential to the prosecution of our plans. My hope is they can succeed in providing additional thirteen-inch mortars to enhance our ability to answer the enemy's fire. The local militia have responded admirably with the spirited determination. Freedom is at stake. My resolve is that these measures will provoke the enemy to attack and face great loss — or quit their present possessions altogether.

Saturday, March 9, 1776 — Dorchester Heights, Massachusetts

I have received information from Captain Irvine and other sources that the British intend to disembark from this quarter. It has not been authenticated but all movements seem to corroborate, including their burning of materials which they cannot carry with them. Even so, I am having a battery thrown up on Nook's Hill and Dorchester Point. As much as I desire to inflict damage to the enemy's cause, seemingly no opportunity presents. I am directing Commodore Manley and his little fleet to dog them if they move out. Perchance the enemy leaves, efforts will be made to fortify the entrance into Boston harbor to thwart their return. With this, my men will move to meet the enemy at their next point of consideration.

Sunday, March 10, 1776 — Dorchester Heights, Massachusetts

Last night, an all-out bombardment occurred of our position on Dorchester Heights. I am unsure what Howe's plan was. My only thought was perhaps he was distracting us to move his troops into position to surprise us as we did a week earlier. This morning, we found no great damage from their attempts. We actually gathered seven hundred enemy cannonballs for our arsenal from those that landed short and stuck into the hillside.

In this time of watching and waiting, we assembled at the Lord's behest to thank Him for His Favor over these last few days. I am gratified that the movements of the Continental army of late have made the enemy wary of our strategy, will, and force. I dare to reflect for a moment from the enemy's point of view. They went to bed on Monday evening staring at an empty Dorchester Heights, admiring its naked beauty. They then wake up Tuesday morning to see a fortress standing in its fullness surrounding them on those same Heights. The impossibilities of such a thing happening without their notice, and executed on one single night, is paralyzing. They must be shaking their heads wondering what else this army of ours is capable of doing. I cannot help but think of Elisha's servant waking up from their tent to find the enemy all around. He troubled Elisha with his fear. Elisha prayed that the Lord would open his eyes to see the unseeable. And, in answer to that prayer, he saw an army of angels surrounding their enemy. The chorus that there are more for us than against us naturally ensued. This is what was played out before the enemy's eyes earlier this week. We give thanks to the One who gave us insight, ingenuity, cover, and execution.

Beyond all this, it has been very uplifting to finally confront the enemy in a significant way and see the enemy blink and move away. Our reasons to defend are greater than the ministerial troops' reasons to engage. Confidence is moving through our ranks. The proverb on our side may come to play, "a bad beginning will end well."

Monday, March 11, 1776 — Dorchester Heights, Massachusetts

British embarkation continues with determination. Little doubt exists they are heading to New York. As a result, that city must be fortified. I flatter myself to think that if everywhere the enemy lands, a fortress of colonials awaits, perhaps he will sail from this continent back to warmer seas and let their former country-men resume peaceful and personal pursuits. To this end, I shall dispatch a regiment of riflemen under Brigadier-General Sullivan to repair to New York with all possible expedition. Upon the redcoat departure, I shall send Major-General Putnam to follow. Once my fortifying work is done here, I will move to that southward direction with the remainder of the army.

Due to weather and roads, I am unsure how long it will take our men to get to the next sector. I am sending letters to solicit Governor Trumbull of Connecticut to forward, with the utmost exertions, two thousand men to defend New York. I am requesting that New Jersey send one thousand for the same purpose. I am ordering vessels in Norwich to be ready to transport troops toward New York to expedite their arrival and save the troops the exhaustion that accompanies a march of that distance. This will enable those upon arrival to have the freshness and strength to dig entrenchments and throw up works of defense. New York is of such importance that prudence and policy require every precaution devised be adapted to frustrate the enemy's designs of possessing it.

Thursday, March 14, 1776 — Cambridge, Massachusetts

General Howe is still in Boston, but by all appearances, he is resolved to move out. In the back of my mind, I cannot help but think what a ruse he could deploy. I send men out of here, leaving a skeleton crew, and then he strikes with such force that the entire cause is thrown into doubt. For this reason, I man our posts with a sizeable force to gain an advantage, if need be, to defeat his potential deceptive efforts.

Being double-minded is not the strongest position to hold, but it must be held. It makes strategic sense for General Howe to proceed to New York. If he can gain control of the North river, he will be able to divide the colonies and prevent intercourse of supplies and arms. It may be the fate of America rests on what happens next in New York.

Sunday, March 17, 1776 — Cambridge, Massachusetts

A great Amen was added to our Sabbath as the British have left Boston. We are now in full control of the city that hosted a rousing tea party and a valiant defense of Bunker and Breed's Hill. I have written Governor Cooke to lessen his fears of an attack on Rhode Island, but urge his readiness, nonetheless. I apprehend the ministerial troops are on route for New York. They left in their wake several cannons, a fine iron mortar, and abundant stores. The quartermaster is quantifying our gains and applying them where needed.

Reverend Abiel Leonard of Connecticut delivered a powerful message from Exodus 14 to commemorate the activities of these past few days. The memorable part of that passage summarized what our army had just seen, "And it came to pass, that in the morning watch the Lord looked unto the host of the Egyptians through the pillar of fire and of the cloud, and troubled the host of the Egyptians, And took off their chariot wheels, that they drove them heavily: so that the Egyptians said, Let us flee from the face of Israel; for the Lord fighteth for them against the Egyptians." Indeed, the transpiring events bring such an explanation to consider.

I am issuing strict orders for the soldiers whom we leave for the defense of Boston to take great pains to live in the strictest of peace and amity with the inhabitants of this city. There can be nothing worse than to have an alien army inflicting harm on a town just to be replaced by a friendly army who acts the same. Punishments will be administered severely for any offenses toward these. Our aim is to garner more and more support, not to dwindle that through selfish acts no matter how justified. Our remaining army will serve the role of assisting civil magistrates in the execution of their duties. I leave the expansion of the defense works of Boston to the people of Massachusetts as their civic duty to be prepared in the spirit of personal responsibility.

Monday, March 18, 1776 — Cambridge, Massachusetts

I had the opportunity to ride into Boston to survey the city, witness the stores gained, and assess the damage done by the enemy. I was flattered that the damage was minimal; the supply gains were immense.

After the fact, it is interesting to see what our army would have faced had the enemy laid the bulk of their troops against the Heights. A segment of our men, who were waiting on my signal, would have invaded the city just to find it strongly fortified and virtually impregnable. I still do not doubt our success, but am taking note of how they build their defenses so we can form better strategies to dislodge them.

Tuesday, March 19, 1776 — Cambridge, Massachusetts

The quartermaster-general Mifflin has provided a rough inventory. So far, we have gained five thousand bushels of wheat, one thousand bushels of beans, ten tons of hay, thirty-five thousand feet of good planks, and over one hundred horses. It is like manna from Heaven. We give thanks and will make the efficient use of these provisions.

Wednesday, March 20, 1776 — Cambridge, Massachusetts

I am confused as to why the British have not completely sailed from these parts. They made out like they were. The whole seemed to have set sail, but now I find they have lingered near Nantasket road. They have inflicted some damage to the Castle and the houses belonging to it. We stand ready to do what is necessary. I have thrown up a large and strong work on Fort Hill, which commands the whole harbor. It can greatly annoy any fleet that the enemy may send back. I have also put Boston under Brigadier-General Greene's command for the time being. Once we leave Boston, I will replace him with Artemus Ward, a thorough New England man. I will need Greene and all his skill at-hand for whatever lies ahead in New York.

Sunday, March 24, 1776 — Cambridge, Massachusetts

A slim hope exists regarding news that England is sending Commissioners to propose terms for an accommodation to cease hostile relations. I cannot imagine that after one stand-off, such terms would be sought, especially when the majority of their army is on the sea to the presumed destination of New York. Stranger things have happened. I imagine any terms coming from England this early will be an insult. My belief is they wish for reconciliation and peace without attending to the conditions that fomented this division.

Monday, March 25, 1776 — Cambridge, Massachusetts

The enemy has the best knack for puzzling people. Several British vessels are still in this quarter. What are they doing? Most information coming to me is that they are simply repairing these vessels as they are in too much disorder to sail. This may be the case, but I must plan for the devious. They could desire that once enlistments run out and men leave, we will be in a weakened state for attack. We still have brave men who know little fear. I believe they can withstand any assault. I have worked to effect every advantage of position should the need arise.

I have ordered the quartermaster-general Colonel Mifflin to work in concert with Brigadier-Generals Heath and Sullivan. They are to regulate the embarkation of a large portion of troops and stores from Norwich in Connecticut toward New York. He is to then get to New York and provide barracks for the men, entrenchment tools, and set up houses to serve as hospitals. Because the duty is immense and cannot be detailed, I am trusting him with latitude to meet the needs and placement of provisions. I am giving the same liberty to Major-General Putnam to do what is necessary in coordination with Major-General Lee to secure the East and North rivers. They are also to work to prevent the British from securing communication to Canada by Hudson's river.

Wednesday, March 27, 1776 — Cambridge, Massachusetts

I am preparing to move our operation to New York. General Thomas is taking the lead in Canada and will need artillerists. I am sending some on the march immediately. Jonathan Eddy of Nova Scotia is requesting men sent to their country to discourage the enemy's harassments and to keep the Indians neutral. I have enough on my plate. I am referring this to Congress for their consideration.

Sunday, March 31, 1776 — Cambridge, Massachusetts

The prayer I offer this day is, "May that Being who is powerful to save, and in whose Hands is the fate of nations, look down with an eye of tender pity and compassion upon the whole of the United Colonies. May He continue to smile upon their counsels and arms. May He crown them with success whilst employed in the cause of virtue and mankind."

I have written my dear brother John. I have not had time in a while to write personal letters to family and friends. As busy as I am, I do flatter myself to say that I have written them more than they have written me. In writing my brother, thoughts came to my mind that I must note here. First — those who sympathized with the King grew more aggressive and hateful by the day hiding behind the veil of the King's army, which they felt far superior to that of their countrymen. They felt the British would handily win the day over our cause. Once they saw the Ministerial army pull out, they were caught short-of-breath and absent of courage. They left out as quickly as did the enemy. To their chagrin, their ally, the King's army, had no room for them in their transports. Rather than face the wrath of their own people for their betrayal, they chose to brave the dangers of a tempestuous sea. May they receive the recompense of their actions.

Second, I have faced crisis after hardship in this position and have had to do things once thought unseemly. Our shortages were so great that I dared not let the enemy catch wind of them and be emboldened, nor let our army be aware of the matter and be discouraged. Such secrecy has brought accusations regarding my character. If only those who accuse knew the full account. Thankfully, with the events having transpired as they have, my character has received warm commendations from the citizenry most exposed — those being in the Massachusetts colony.

Third, any time a victory occurs, the people saying they supported the cause come out of the woodwork. By no means is this war won, nor have we inflicted a decisive blow on the enemy, but a positive wind has addressed our sails. My beliefs are reinforced at this moment that it is insufficient for a man to be a passive friend and a well-wisher on the side of the cause. Every person should be active in some department, ignoring personal interests of ease and profit. Inactivity in some people, disaffection in others, and timidity in many more will only hurt our cause and delay a favorable outcome. I would that now, more than ever, our Nation and its people will take up the cause with all vigor and fervor, abandoning all other concerns.

On to New York. I regard General Lee as the first officer in military knowledge and experience. He has zealously abandoned his past celebrity for this cause. He can be fickle and violent in temper, but he has an uncommon share of good sense that I believe will benefit this country.

Monday, April 1, 1776 — Cambridge, Massachusetts

I am sending General Greene with five regiments to New York this day and will follow them soon after. We are still awaiting word of the British commissioners' arrival and their offering of peace. Peace is what I seek, but I dare say reuniting is falling off the table from America's side. Thomas Paine's "Common Sense" is working powerfully to change minds. For a people to detach from royalty known since birth is difficult, but independence is a yeast working its way through the loaf of these colonies.

Wednesday, April 3, 1776 — Cambridge, Massachusetts

Colonel Arnold continues to await recruitments for his work in Canada. He is disappointed in the few who have shown. His problem is one we all face. I never want him to be discouraged, so I hold out hope that his numbers will grow once the lakes are passable. I have dispatched two companies from Colonel Knox's regiment of artillery, along with two mortars and other articles. I doubt I will have more to spare once we reach New York and are engaged. In the slim chance that we are not entangled with the enemy there, I shall send Arnold more as I have quantity.

Thursday, April 4, 1776 — Cambridge, Massachusetts

I am writing Congress today to again solicit arms for this Colonial Army. One would wish, after a stroke of victory in Boston with few shots fired, that things would go smoothly for a while. Unfortunately, the preparations for war and the war itself demand diligent attention in every quadrant. We need arms. I must note this day, that we also need a paymaster-general. Colonel Warren chooses not to travel with this army because of personal affairs in this colony. He cannot effectively implement his role distant from headquarters. Speaking of pay, we need money as well. It is hoped that Congress will expend money for its army on the move, but also for the men who must stay behind to defend the ground gained.

Greediness abounds. Many of the militia regiments are demanding pay from the time they were called upon to make ready to march until the time they were relieved. The truth is, many of these men were called upon to make ready, but were not required to leave their homes for many days later. I do not believe we should pay men to stay home or pay them for army service, while they were at home making money in private enterprise undisturbed. Such profiteering from our countrymen should be unrequited.

With these complaints recorded, I am heading with the remainder of our army, save those left behind to guard this post, for New York.

Saturday, April 6, 1776 — Providence, Rhode Island

Our army is making a good pace toward the next aggression. Riding into Providence, Rhode Island, our army was escorted by two of General Greene's regiments. I was surprised to see the huge crowds turning out to greet us. They seemed to clamor above all to see me. We do want to make a good impression on all who come to see this army so that they might be reinvigorated for our cause and remember our courtesies the next time we need supplies and men. An elegant banquet was prepared for me and our officers last night at Hackers Hall. ·

We have not been distracted. Early this morning, we set out and marched five or six miles before breakfast. We continued and have covered over twenty-five miles this day. The men are unified. They are filled with a patriotic spirit that can offset any damper. All understand that a battle in the field is certain in the days ahead. Almost all believe the British cannot match our courage, strength, or resolve.

Monday, April 8, 1776 — Norwich, Connecticut

Heavy rains fell upon us in our march, which hampered our progress. Nonetheless, we arrived in Norwich late last night.

We set out for New London this morning and arrived even later this evening. I am sending most of our regiments by waterway. This should expedite their travel and ensure their freshness upon arrival in New York. The rest of our men will continue the march to New York.

Tuesday, April 9, 1776 — New London, Connecticut

We set out early this morning. With less men to account for, the march was more rapid. We should arrive in New York earlier than expected despite some wet and muddy roads. We are bringing with us ten heavy brass field pieces.

Saturday, April 13, 1776 — New York

With great relief, our march terminated for the time being as we entered New York. I expected to see General Greene here with the regiments accompanying him, but to this instant, they have not arrived. My understanding is that a severe storm hit as they were embarking and may have thrown them off-course or caused them damage or harm. My prayer is that they are safe and just late.

General Sullivan is here with his division. I am expecting that the whole of the troops will arrive in the course of this week. I am gratified to find new battalions have arrived from Connecticut, New Jersey, and Pennsylvania. We are told to expect more from Maryland and Delaware. I find that the troops we have here are scattered. The majority of them are stationed at Staten Island and Long Island. Many of the defenses that I requested General Schuyler, General Lee, and then General Alexander to build are in the process. Some are finished.

I do see the puzzle of which General Lee spoke when he arrived here. This city is cornered by two navigable rivers and a harbor that can host the largest naval fleet imaginable. The thought of seeing the British ships arrive does pose a great obstacle.

Sunday, April 14, 1776 — New York

Of the overwhelming forces aligned against us, it is appropriate this day to affirm that we will rely on the protection of a kind Providence and the unanimity of all Americans.

This was my thought going into our worship service this morning. I had the opportunity to read a letter from Mr. Joseph Reed this evening while sitting in my quarters. Seemingly, unanimity is not to be counted upon if I am to believe his letter. He has stated there are divisions regarding our cause where he is. A mood is leaning against independence in the Southern colonies. Of all the things I fear — the enemy's strength and naval superiority, the lack of our own manpower and powder, the constant end of enlistments in the face of needed reenlistments and new recruits — disunion is my greatest fear. This will ruin all exertions to this cause. I find myself depending on the only constant — the protection of our gracious Providence. Jehoshaphat was right, we do not know what to do, but our eyes are upon You, Almighty God.

Wednesday, April 17, 1776 — New York

In a time of war, when our ports are shut, our trade destroyed, our property seized, our towns burnt, some of our citizens are taken captive, many more are suffering, it is unbelievable to me that there would be a large number of Tories, Loyalists, and a sell-out Governor dominating this city of New York. Even now, many are on board the enemy's ships of war in intercourse to injure the common cause of these colonies. Our own countrymen of New York are supplying the enemy and providing intelligence to them. Even as I write this, I look out of the window of my headquarters here on Broad street and see a larger-than-life statue of King George III on his horse standing tall on Bowling Green. That it still stands amidst all the depredations brought upon our country is a mystery to me and a revealing token of the character I fear in this city.

I am beseeching the leaders of New York to stop this fraternizing with the enemy immediately. My duty is to remove such evil from this province or face the ruin of our great cause. I am calling on the Committee of Safety in New York to assist in this purpose. The American brethren are watching. The reputation of this colony is in jeopardy. We are fighting for American liberty. May the Lord be judge between us and them.

Thursday, April 18, 1776 — New York

To lean upon God in all that we do is a good thing. We seek His approval above all others. I feel that if I am right with Him, I can take what comes and He will take care of me. That was shown again this day. I am delighted to note that I received a letter of commendation and a medal from Congress thanking me and our army for the successes gained in Boston. I am warmed by the token of appreciation, but more than anything, I desire the esteem of my countrymen in this grand labor to see our rights restored.

Friday, April 19, 1776 — New York

General Schuyler received word from Colonel Hazen in Canada that the Canadians are against our endeavor. We must work as hard as we can to conciliate their affections as well as the savages who will not remain neutral for long. I am calling on Congress to make every effort to employ the Indians on our side. We are in a contest not just of arms, but of minds. We must win the minds of the Indians by taking hold of their confidence and affections. Better to have them on our side, regardless of their contributions, than to have them on the ministerial side dividing our focus.

As it now stands, the citizens of Canada are refusing to provide any supplies. They are even hampering the delivery of supplies to our men. I have dispatched immediately five hundred barrels of provisions. I will also send a company of riflemen, a company of artificers, and two engineers for their plight. We are making constant applications from all quarters for men and ammunition. To supply the armies scattered in other fields while this branch is in great need facing the greater threat of conflict is difficult. I can imagine the generals in other quarters think I am hoarding arms, ammunition, and men. Would that there were any to hoard! Spreading the scarcity is the best I can do at this moment. I take heart that help is on the way.

Sunday, April 21, 1776 — New York

Again, Proverb 13:12 rings in my mind, "Hope deferred makes the heart sick, but a longing fulfilled is a tree of life." I have had many things promised to me during this war and the incessant waiting makes this army sick. When complaints occur in our camp about provisions, the easy answer is to say that they have been promised, that they are on the way, that they are soon to arrive. Tomorrow brings nothing. The day after is the same. A week later, the men ask. My answer is the same. Why? Because that is what I was told. A longing fulfilled is a tree of life. Every time a new group of men show up, we rejoice. Each time a herd of cattle are driven into our camp, we celebrate. We are encouraged when what is told is finally realized.

I write this because General Schuyler needs men for the Canada offensive. I scarce have them to send, but I said that I would. General Schuyler is hoping that I tell the truth. Today, I did what I said. I have sent four regiments designed for Canada under Colonels Greaton, Patterson, Bond, and Poor. In addition, I have sent a company of riflemen, a company of artificers, and two engineers. I write notes so that I can remember what I have said, what I have promised. It is so much easier to keep my promise when I can commit them to letters to ensure that what I say, I do. Keeping my word puts this army in a stressful need of arms. To meet my needs would mean to not help others. To promise and then not to perform after further inventory makes logical sense, but is disastrous to the ones promised. I choose to keep my word and trust that I will be taken care of in the instant.

I find that our New York regiments are poorly supplied. Colonel Ritzema's men are a prime example. His men scarcely have any arms. They cannot fight without the arms. I could send them home, but I am also short of men. Which is easier to gain — arms or men. I dare not let go either that I have. I hope instead that whichever is lacking will be filled to the full measure.

Dealing with the enemy includes more than just dealing with those wearing red coats. The enemy is smallpox. The enemy is lack of arms. The enemy is lack of men. The enemy is the enemy who pretends to be a friend. The enemy is talking too loudly and have a traitor overhear and disclose our plans. The enemy is enlistment expirations and the need to induce men to stay whilst enticing new men to enter. The enemy is the cold-faced with no blankets. The enemy is the undermanned fleet of Commodore Hopkins. The enemy is a paymaster without money to pay. The enemy is an army whose pay is in arrears. The enemy is underpaid men of skill like engineer Baldwin. He is being sent to Canada but demands pay consistent with his knowledge and rank consistent with his merit. I am requesting a raise for him to Congress as well as a promotion to the rank of lieutenant-colonel for which he is deserving.

I look back on my old diaries and realize I never wrote so much. In fact, accounts were just given of where I was, what I did, where I ate, and with whom, along with weather accounts. I should think it odd that now my diary overflows with details, emotions, and the enumeration of needs. I do not doubt that once this war is over and prayerfully won, I will return to a less eventful diary. For now, this enables me to say what cannot be said outwardly other than to Mrs. Washington and the Lord to whom I pray. I find it is helpful to write these things down, to read back over and reflect. It helps me strategize for certain. To be grateful as the Almighty meets the needs as He sees fit also keeps me accountable.

Monday, April 22, 1776 — New York

The extreme affluence of this city of New York is only matched by the extreme degradation I see as I walk the streets. It has been called a city of sin, but I knew such legends are often proved exaggerations by those who are prejudiced for one city over another. As I viewed the Church steeples of every persuasion when I entered the city, I assumed sin city was a bitter moniker of a passing tourist longing for home. I then heard of an area owned by the Trinity Church that was called the Holy Ground. Supposedly, it was anything but holy. Walking in that direction, I was sickened by what I saw. Gin shops, bawdy houses, and hundreds of prostitutes working the streets abounded. They seemed emboldened by the influx of soldiers entering their fair city, feverishly attempting to make up for revenue lost by citizens who had fled for fear of certain conflict. I was saddened to see many of our own men roaming the streets intrigued and enthralled.

New York has given our men shelter which we lacked on the outskirts of Boston. We are sheltered here from the elements at this moment, but we are exposed to worse elements of liquor and whoredom. I have issued orders that no one is to frequent such places in this city. We are here for a high calling. If we are seeking God's Favor, we must be men who merit such.

Tuesday, April 23, 1776 — New York

I can scarcely write this. No sooner did I return and make orders to stay away from the unHoly Ground, I received a report that two of our soldiers were found mutilated in one of the brothels. Now I understand the phrase "righteous indignation." How can our countrymen ever seek to maintain freedom when we surrender to the desires of the flesh? Other armies may allow for this, but this one will not. I issued orders that our men are to stay far clear of such areas of this city. Any who are found there will face penalties commensurate to what we would do to our worst enemies. I am sending out patrols to this area to deal with any soldiers participating in that debauchery. The problem will be that since our men do not have uniforms or identifying markings on their clothing, it is hard to tell who is a citizen and who is a soldier.

Wednesday, April 24, 1776 — New York

The more the concerns of this war and the financial issues weigh on this conflict, the more I am glad I refused pay. It makes it easier for me to ask for money for necessities screened through my leanings to parsimony. I have made huge requirements on one group of people above all others. The Aides-de-camp who serve me and this Continental army are required to be on-hand at all hours on all days. They live with me. They work with me. They tend to their responsibilities not for pay but in sacrifice to our great American call for liberty. Unlike the other officers, they have no time off, no recreation, and no instances to disengage. For this reason, I am asking Congress to increase their pay.

Thursday, April 25, 1776 — New York

A great stipend for the men on our vessels is booty divided. This has worked well for our crews on the water. The major motivation for men to enlist is the added bonus they are promised upon success. To be equitable in meeting the needs of the war whilst rewarding the crews, we have put in place a valuation requirement.

This allows the captors to receive their dividend, but not at the expense of supplying the war effort. I was disappointed to hear that Congress has not dealt with this in a reasonable amount of time. Commodore Manley is doing a great job with his little fleet. The last thing we need is for them to disengage. They run their operation with little drama, except for the British fleet who daily complain of our floating continental nuisances. I am asking Congress to repair this with immediacy.

Idleness removes the focus from what matters. I received another complaint today. The officers of the middle colonies are murmuring that their pay is less than what the regiments from the eastward are receiving. They argue that they do the same work with the same fatigue for five dollars per month, while the eastern regiments receive six and two-thirds dollars per month. I am requesting Congress address this with the goal of equal pay for every soldier and equal pay for every corresponding rank of officer. The British do this with their troops. That America would treat our soldiers with less regard is insulting.

A luxury occurs in having time to gather men and supplies to prepare for battle. The disadvantage is that men have more time to compare and complain. On one hand, I wish for time, but it breeds divisions. On the other hand, I wish for conflict that breeds unity but exposes our lack of readiness.

Friday, April 26, 1776 — New York

Two fronts of battle are a dilemma. The first dilemma is the British. They believe Canada to be of great importance and may send their entire force under General Howe up the river St. Lawrence to relieve Quebec and recover Canada. The men we have in place there are inadequate to defend their designs. The second dilemma is the enemy may choose to exert their whole force here to put this city under their command. To do this, they will seek to secure the Hudson river for navigation so they can deliver men and supplies to any point of conflict. Should this be their choice, our manpower is inadequate to check them. That they could attempt both is not improbable. Only then could we be somewhat suited to hold them at bay and perhaps gain an advantage. So then, do I send men to Canada for its defense or do I leave men here for New York's defense? Or do I spread the men out and hope for a dual engagement?

Our general officers feel we should keep the greater number of our men here. It would be easier to send them to Canada for whatever befalls there than to hope men could be sent from Canada to here. Many impediments present moving from that direction. The advantage we have here over our position in Canada is that our army in Canada has no source for men but from us. Our army here in New York can draw from the militia in our time of need. In considering the options, I have with good counsel sent six regiments more to Canada under General Sullivan to join forces with General Thomas. I have ordered General Dayton to take his regiment from New Jersey to be one of those six. I am hoping that Congress will provide the rest of the needs for Canada from Pennsylvania.

These deployments leave our army here in New York far short of what is necessary to defend it. Should the enemy attack us in this State, I fear alarming and fatal consequences. I am alerting dependable Governor Trumbull to have his militia ready. I am also urging New Jersey, along with the New York colony, to have their militias on-call and ready at the appearance of the enemy. Such timely succor could prevent destruction and even bring about the most salutary end.

Monday, April 29, 1776 — New York

The King's ships have moved down to the Hook about thirty miles from this place. Their embarkation was in response to the works we have constructed, which place us within pistol-shot of the wharves. The Committee of Safety is helping restrict intercourse between the inhabitants of this colony and the enemy.

I am greatly lifted by the presence of Mrs. Washington who is still here. I am hoping she gains the courage to be vaccinated for the smallpox. Mr. and Mrs. Custis will soon be leaving for Maryland. I know Mrs. Washington has mixed emotions concerning this. She fears for their safety here, but longs for their presence when they are away. War brings sacrifice, unease, and calamities. I pray our countrymen, especially in this colony, will appreciate which army is the cause of such things and act affectionately toward the army trying to stop these.

Tuesday, April 30, 1776 — New York

My last correspondence to the Committee of Safety of New York has given them umbrage for which I did not intend. I feel as though I am walking on eggshells with this colony. It has strong ministerial feelings and devotions to the King, yet it is the key center of commerce for these Colonies and is well-represented in Congress. As a result, I take special care not to exert authority that is not mine, nor to delegate or dictate as if I am the replacement for the King or their local government. When they raised up four regiments for their defense, I was unsure by their language if they were under their governance or mine. To understand their intent, I sent a letter requesting clarification. They responded tersely, but respectfully that they had no intentions of undermining the Continental General. Rather, they are seeking to assist and support the men they send. In reading the various letters of correspondence past, I wonder if I am just too much in a hurry and am too overwhelmed by demands on my attention. As a result, I may cloud the meanings I wish to convey. This is something that I must continually be aware of. At times like these, I wish even more that Joseph Reed would come back to our camp to assist me in these things. He would have surely brought clarity and prevented any hurt or misunderstanding.

Governor Cooke of Rhode Island has requested Continental army support for their defense. That they have a long seacoast and great harbors from which our shipping and vessels sail is true. Because of their role in our sea-going activities, they are susceptible to enemy ravages. I am asking that colony to do its best to raise up a defense for themselves. Though they may not have pay, a local militia invested in its own survival should meet a large part of their need. I will request that Congress do what it can to provide for such militia and perhaps send some men and pay to assist on that front.

Saturday, May 4, 1776 — New York

I have been reviewing the plans of defense that General Lee has proposed. He believes that to defend New York, battle placements must be built on Long Island. The bluff that I see jutting up on the other side of the East river is called Brooklyn Heights or Noble Heights. Lee has suggested building a large bastion there and place at least eight cannons at that location. Additionally, he suggested that we build batteries along the New York shore of the Hudson to address any British ships coming in from that direction. I am placing General Greene in command of the work on Long Island and am sending him with a Pennsylvania rifle company to station near Brooklyn. I felt it necessary to build three more forts on the eastern side of Brooklyn just in case the British come ashore on the broad beaches west of Gravesend. The logistics of this work are complex. The time in which we have to complete them is unknown. I do know that with the time we have, a system of entrenchments is needed. We must clear trees to provide a clean line for cannon fire. I have given orders for the works to begin immediately

Sunday, May 5, 1776 — New York

Complaints. Complaints. Complaints. Complaints are to be heard because often they are warranted. Our recruiting officers have been promised ten shillings for every man they enlist. Many of these officers have let me know that they have not received the promised rewards. It could be that Congress issued this incentive in answer to my request for more men. The recruiters are asking when does the incentive accrue — from the time the resolve was received or from the time the resolve was issued? The question also arises by these officers (who have not received any compensation), was the resolve for all recruiting officers in general or for those in areas where troops are in greater need? Such matters seem trivial, but to the men working tirelessly to fill our ranks, who also have families to feed and needs to meet, ten shillings make a difference. I pray that Congress will make them generally available and distribute them in a timely manner.

The situation in Canada is of a nature that requires men and supplies without hesitation. I am apprehensive that General Thompson and General Sullivan with their men will not reach their destination with the expedition desired. Such delays can be excused due to the inability to get teams and provender of cattle necessary to carry their baggage or the number of bateaux needed to carry them across the Lakes. No excuse regardless of legitimacy will console an army that has been overrun. My apprehension is multiplied by the fact that I receive little or no reports from the officers in the different districts. Things could be fine, but I do not know it. Things could be terrible, and I have no report on which to react. I am the

Commander-in-Chief of this Continental army, but it seems officers are content to let a member of Congress know and bypass my notification. If I am to lead, supply, plan, and act, information will be my greatest resource. Otherwise, I am left to conjecture. This never produces good strategy. I am requesting that Congress place a directive that monthly returns to me become a military propriety for all officers in every station.

Monday, May 6, 1776 — New York

At our council of officers this morning, I made inquiries as to the conduct of our men since the events of the 22nd ultimo. Though a remnant of soldiers is frequenting the unHoly Ground, a large share is acting with the utmost integrity. General Alexander relayed an article brought to his attention yesterday from a local paper. It told how our men are well-behaved and that the civility of our men to the inhabitants of this city "is very commendable." He said the article went on to boast that our camps have prayers at dawn and dusk every day and that our men make it their practice to be in the Lord's House each Sunday for worship. I am flattered to hear such returns. I have sought to instill the reverence of God in the men as it will be most advantageous if we are to receive a favorable outcome in this war.

Tuesday, May 7, 1776 — New York

Our work is going well for the defenses of New York. I noticed that Governor's Island would be a strategic location for earthworks and gun emplacements. Orders were sent to begin this. We are throwing up barricades in the city even as I write, looking out near King George's statue. We have placed guns along the banks of the Hudson river, heavy cannon at old Fort George and at Whitehall dock. I would like to think we are making this place impenetrable and deadly to any assault. To our disadvantage, the British ability to avail themselves of so many opportunities make no plan undefeatable. We have placed one hundred and twenty cannons in the city area. Finally, we have a sufficient quantity of ammunition, but we are short of guns. We are placing those without arms into training to be artillerymen.

Thursday, May 9, 1776 — New York

Major-General Ward has been dutiful to keep me abreast of the progress of the defense works in Boston. If the rumors are correct that Hessian and Hanoverian troops are moving toward that province with the eye of regaining a footing, it is of prime importance that they be completed.

Friday, May 10, 1776 — New York

Like other soldiers, personal obligations must be addressed regardless of where I lay my head. When I was blessed to marry Mrs. Washington, it was incumbent upon me to oversee the estate of Patsy and Jacky Custis. With Patsy's passing, her moiety of their fortune was to go to Mr. Custis. He is due a final settlement. I am not in a place to liquidate their accounts and make this, so I am trusting George Mason and my cousin Lund Washington to handle this for me. My attendance in Congress and now as commander of this army have delayed my ability to carry out this errand. I have done my utmost to care for Jacky's estate and have refused any reimbursement for expenses incurred in so doing. I dare not delay closing out this business as it adds to the load I must bear; not to mention, give fodder for any who would question my stewardship should it be postponed any longer.

Saturday, May 11, 1776 — New York

I must address a logistical complexity with Congress as I have numerous times before. With regard to prisoners of war, it is discerning to have a person or persons appointed to manage the whole of the prisoners now in our custody and to plan and care for those who will come. Having this centralized to one department of responsibility will save the colonies money and infuse security for the American population. Beyond this, confinement away from the trafficked areas will reduce opportunities of escape; and more so, prevent the dissemination of their pernicious intrigues. Such transmission of their opinions among our citizenry could bring a wavering of American resolve and paint virtue on the British actions. Remote locations will also be beneficial should the enemy attack. A ready manpower would be available to them if they are able to get to the places where the enemy soldiers are housed. I am hopeful Congress will give guidance on this matter and issue a resolve for every colony to consider.

To sleep is difficult when thoughts flood my mind of things that are occurring, things that need to occur, and ideas of how to offset things that might occur. Some point in the night, it occurred to me that if the British are sending German troops as I have heard, might it be advisable to raise some companies of Germans from our faithful countrymen? They could be sent to infiltrate the British German ranks to excite a spirit of disaffection and desertion. Afterall, these German troops that the British have employed have no enmity toward us nor any emotional tie to this argument between us. I am raising this consideration to Congress as well.

Wednesday, May 15, 1776 — New York

Fox hunting was great delight for me before the war. The unknowns of the chase are exhilarating. Though a common pattern is present, each chase is unique. Hounds, horses, and men work in concert to force the cagey pest to go to ground. It is then ferreted out of its den and summarily removed. The Committee of Long Island has brought good news of their own version of fox hunting in their apprehension of sundry Tories. These abominable pests pose a much greater danger to society and its possessions than any fox could inflict. The Committee's actions have reduced my concerns as to their commitment to America. Many of these Tories have been their neighbors for years and have supped with them in their homes. Fraternity is good, but fidelity to principle requires a breaking of old bonds and a forming of new ones. This is perhaps more difficult here with Governor Tryon continuing his treacherous influence on behalf of the enemy. I long for the citizens of this province to realize that their new fellowships can be stronger when formed with those who meet the criteria of nobleness rather than sentiment.

Thursday, May 16, 1776 — New York

The Continental Congress has ordered that this Friday be a day of fasting, humiliation, and prayer to supplicate the mercy of Almighty God, that He might pardon our sins, prosper our arms, and bring peace and freedom to America. May this incline our Lord to fight on our side and to prosper our activities. Congress can make no better request than this. We have no hope unless the Giver of all good things gives us victory that defies all logic and expectations. Our men will follow this decree with the utmost solicitude.

Friday, May 17, 1776 — New York

The Day of Atonement was the only day the Almighty required His children to fast in seeking atonement for sin. The day was somber then. The day is a somber day now. On this day, a view is present of all our personal defeats and the reasonings behind them. It is a day to look to the Lord and realize that only He can atone for our sins. Only He can make us right and give us a fresh start and a new direction always leading to Himself.

People may speak of coincidence or chance. I do not believe in either. The Hands of God lead. He is the Author and the Active Participant in all that goes on below. He is not a clock maker who builds the clock and then lets it run without any intervention. Truly, the clock left to its own will drag slowly or run fast or stop completely. The clock maker sets it, corrects it, fixes it, and restarts it. Deists say God is indifferent to mankind's state and divorced from any effort be it good or bad. I am not of that ilk. I have seen God's Hand in manifold instances in my life and in this Nation. We saw His Work on Dorchester Heights. We see His solemn work on this day. It is no accident that Congress called for a day of fasting and prayer when on this day, I receive a letter from General Schuyler informing me that victory is not to be had in Canada. Our men are in retreat with great loss of cannon, firearms, and powder. Schuyler has directed General Sullivan to halt his brigade and for all troops to remain in Albany to prevent further loss. He will make every attempt to stop others who have not received his orders from nearing the enemy lines.

On this day of fasting and prayer, I am encouraging him not to despair. A manly and spirited opposition can still ensure success under the Hand to Whom we pray. That it is on this of all days that we would humble ourselves, repent, and seek God's Face is timely.

Saturday, May 18, 1776 — New York

We had quite an alarm today. Some thought they saw the sails of the British ships of war coming our way. The alert was not founded, but we realize that any day those sails will appear. We must be ready. As it was in Boston, so it is in New York. We must keep one hand on the sword and the other hand on the trowel, one eye on the work and another eye on the harbor. I am grateful for the precaution made earlier to put in place a signal system between Long Island, Staten Island, and New York.

To increase our state of readiness, I am having the men stay current with their marksmanship, and practice moving in and out of our entrenchments to be familiar with them for the day the British come. No doubt exists the British will come. The only question is to when.

Sunday, May 19, 1776 — New York

So many things to cover with Congress. Some things which are new and some things which have gone unanswered or unremedied for sundry reasons. I am sending General Gates with matters that need to be considered. Having him there will ensure reply and give Congress the ability to converse, with no delay, their concerns and questions. General Gates will be able to answer as to the conditions here. He will also be able to subjoin items to apprehend material. His personal interview will accomplish more than a volume of letters. In this crisis, military necessary measures can be agreed upon, supplied for, and executed.

Monday, May 20, 1776 — New York

No sooner do I dispatch General Gates, I receive a letter from Mr. Hancock requesting my attendance in Philadelphia. Though busy, this may be the opportune time to meet with Congress before British vessels arrive and the conflict ensues. I will do my best to settle some matters here and then be on my way to meet with Congress. It is too late to recall General Gates. Hopefully, he will understand that this was Congress's express wish and not my lack of confidence in his representation.

I do have misgivings about leaving my command. My anxieties are that no sooner do I get a good distance away, the enemy will come. To rest my concerns, I have ordered fast horses to be held at different stations along the way for the event that I must make a quick return.

Tuesday, May 21, 1776 — New York

I received a dispatch this morning accusing General Schuyler of abhorrent acts on behalf of the enemy and with which he has been dealing duplicitously. Not only was this sent to me, but it is my understanding a copy was sent to Congress and to other generals in our army. I know General Schuyler. I have the utmost confidence in his integrity. His attachment to our cause is incontestable. I am sending him a letter to let him know of the accusations before he hears word of it from other quarters. I do not want him to worry that I doubt his commitment. These actions are nothing more than insidious schemes to bring dissension among us.

Not only does General Schuyler need to be aware of what the enemy is doing, he must also hold skepticism any time a Tory or a loyalist or a lukewarm friend treats him well. With injurious motivations, they will often bring requests in the guise of human decency. Recently, some men of that sort passed through this way with permits from General Schuyler. He trusted them. I do not. I believe these used their request as a ruse to tend to personal affairs. I fear more than that, they desire to inspect our lines and measure our defenses. They can then provide intelligence to our enemy. I am going to warn the General not to allow such permits again, regardless of how sincere the requests may seem.

As I will soon be leaving for Philadelphia, I am putting Major-General Putnam in charge in my stead. I am expectant of a decision soon by the Provincial Congress to have the army seize the principal Tories and disaffected persons of Long Island and the country nearby. I am going to have he and General Greene to concert measures with any who come from Congress to execute this plan in secrecy, but with utmost decency and good order.

Tuesday, May 28, 1776 — Philadelphia, Pennsylvania

I am concerned over the distress of our troops in Canada. My understanding from General Thomas is that they are unable to make a stand at Dechambeau. Our hope of reducing the whole of Canada to our control was blasted. This is a sad shock to our schemes. I am now focusing on getting that part of our army to secure a post as low down the river as possible. This will allow for an easier retreat if necessity dictates it. It will also allow easier access for them to gain needed provisions. We must continue to do all we can to supply that venture. Losses of any form are detrimental to our plans, but with vigorous exertions we can repair our fortune and move forward. I will write as much to General Thomas in Canada so that he knows a countermove exists for every move the enemy makes. He and his men must discipline themselves to hold on and do all that is in their power to advance our country's cause.

Friday, May 31, 1776 — Philadelphia, Pennsylvania

Mrs. Washington and I arrived in Philadelphia a few days ago. She has been thirteen days under the inoculation. I expect she will have a light case of smallpox and a favorable recovery. She has very few pustules but is being cautious as not to spread it to anyone else. She is even so careful as to not write a letter to anyone for fear she may convey the infection in that manner.

I am disappointed to find in this city that the will of Congress to win this war has been diluted by the contemplation of some unrepentant appeal from Great Britain for reconciliation. It is this faint hope longed for that prevents Congress from the resolve to exert every effort to attain victory. Clearly, from my standpoint, we have only one of two choices now — to conquer or to submit to unconditional surrender leading to our imprisonment, hanging, and accepting every kind of punishment exacted upon the backs of those who dare to be free.

North Carolina and the south are facing the encroachment of British forces. The numbers they comprise are hard to calculate. I have sent General Lee to rebuff any interlude. If the enemy has come with a small force of five thousand, as many believe, they must be counting on support from loyalists, Indians, and individuals who believe their livelihoods will be enhanced from across the sea. I still expect a bloody summer in New York and Canada as I presume these will be where the grand efforts of the enemy are expended. I am emboldened by the certainty that our cause is just, and because it is, I believe Providence will give us aid as He has done so faithfully to this date.

To this end, I am heartened to see that our Virginia colony has set in motion their decision to write their own constitution for governance. My brother John is actively involved in this process. We have learned what bad government is like. We have struggled under our own inadequate government. Time, study, and patience is necessary to draft a government which shall render the millions under its authority happy.

Monday, June 3, 1776 — Philadelphia, Pennsylvania

I am pressing Congress to augment the army in Canada. Some believe we should send some of our men from New York up to Canada. This would be detrimental as I expect very soon a need for every man in our ranks and thousands more to contest the British's vigorous attempt to make an impress in New York. Congress has responded by sending General Gates to Canada to see if he can remedy that situation. I am glad to report that with much argument, Joseph Reed has agreed to return to my side and help me in New York to replace Gates. He is being promoted to the rank of Colonel. I will never be able to express my relief at his assistance.

I have just sent a letter to Major-General Putnam to employ carpenters immediately to construct gondolas and fire-rafts to prevent the men-of-war and enemy ships from entering New York Bay or the Narrows. I am sending a person from here to superintend that work. He should make it in a day or two. Would that more men of this skill-level were available. Every time King David or King Solomon wanted to build something, it seemed they would always go to Hiram, King of Tyre. His men were skilled in all kinds of construction and design. What I would not give to have a King of Tyre allied with us to send engineers, builders, and overseers.

Thursday, June 6, 1776 — New York

My return to New York from Philadelphia today brought an unexpected surprise. The men were waiting for me in total. Drum rolls occurred and even five regiments had a parade through Broadway and around the King George statue. I was not sure as to why the big reception. Later, I was told that a rumor had spread that I had gone to Philadelphia suddenly after sending General Gates because my frustrations had driven me to resign. How little do my men know me? I have fought to keep a distance from them in an effort to maintain authority, but no resignation resides in my soul. I pray that my return will embolden the rest to stay at the plow and do the work without looking back.

Friday, June 7, 1776 — New York

The situation in Canada grows worse. General Thomas has smallpox. General Arnold has been defeated. Montreal is lost. Congress has resolved to reinforce the army in Canada with quotas given to each colony to raise for that quarter. Also, Congress has given General Schuyler the resolution to enlist up to two thousand Indians to bring assistance. I know Schuyler is skeptical of this latter effort as the Indians tend to fight on the side they feel is strongest, where pay is greatest, and where their own personal risk is minimized. Nevertheless, to attempt their alliance is better than to simply surrender their savagery for the enemy's line.

All seems well at the camp. Before I left, I gave orders. Seemingly, every one of them has been prosecuted with diligence and dispatch. The man I sent from Philadelphia to oversee construction of the gondolas has arrived. He is making proper channel for facilitating the work as desired. We are needing guns to go with these gondolas. I had hoped to receive some from Commodore Hopkins, but as of my report to Congress this day, none have been received. The greatest battle I seem to face is the battle to get ready for battle.

Saturday, June 8, 1776 — New York

General Schuyler has received Congress's blessing and mine to pursue and arrest Sir John Johnson. After being imprisoned for aiding the enemy, Johnson was released with the promise to desist from such activity. Now it is reported that he has violated his parole. He has resumed his heinous acts against liberty, building a coalition of Indians to suppress our efforts. May he be rounded up or stopped by any means necessary.

Sunday, June 9, 1776 — New York

The Commissioners called on me today. They surprised me with an explicit account of the defeat of Colonel Bedel and Major Sherburne and their party at the Cedars. I should never be treated to such surprises. To be the last to know what goes on in the army of my command is humiliating. My generals conduct the war as if I am ancillary to the effort. They give me few troop counts, no report on stores, and little information on their efforts in the field; yet they cry continually for assistance. My exhortations for reporting from the various sectors seem to come to deaf ears. If it has not become too inveterate, I must do all I can to require timely and detailed reports with the cost of demotion for noncompliance. Pride makes me want to withhold any help of men and arms unless reports are received, but then I realize this would just hurt our cause and bring further division.

The situation in Canada is truly alarming and more so with each report that I do receive. I am convinced that their defeat lies at the feet of a deficiency of troops and the lack of training for the inadequate number there. I am desirous for a liberal allowance to be expended for reenlistments. Thus, we can build upon their experience and discipline. A new and inexperienced army every few months jeopardizes our effort and also frustrates those who stay.

Moreover, Congress must possess the propriety to keep our military chests supplied with money, so our troops are paid in a timely manner and rewarded further as merit dictates. This will prevent them from becoming restless and impatient. They have enough to worry about without having to worry about pay. In the spirit of efficiency, I am requesting Congress to appoint adjunct and quartermaster-generals for here and for Canada. Colonel Reed needs their assistance in augmenting this army. They will come at an expense, but a shilling saved in pay may cause a pound to be lost by mismanagement. If only they can think in these terms.

Monday, June 10, 1776 — New York

General Greene and Colonel Knox conferred with me today about the progress of our defense works. In their daily patrol, they felt that the upper highest point of York Island was ideal for another major post to keep the British from coming up the Hudson river. They want to call it Fort Washington. On the opposite side of the Hudson, they desire to build another fort. I am grateful for such industrious patriotic men. I think one good consequence to be gained from the horrors of war other than liberty, freedom, and righting injustice, is the blessing of fraternity. My absence from these men while in Philadelphia has cemented that opinion as they were greatly missed.

A ruckus is being heard all about that the British troops have left Halifax and are on the waters with the destination New York. Governor Tryon of New York is stirring as a result, seeking to secure unified support of all loyalists and Tories in our midst. Though our entrenchments are strong and face the harbor of pending combat, our danger is expanded for we have no idea how many of the enemy will come from behind the barriers of our own traitorous countrymen. With such affronts looming, I question the desire of Congress to keep troops under Colonels Shee and Magaw at Philadelphia. Every man armed for battle will be needed for this Goliath assault.

We are at a critical conjuncture of affairs. We need men. We have weakened our forces here to succor those in Canada. I am writing ever-zealous Governor Trumbull to send battalion after battalion of men to this front. No time is left to gather them together as a complement and send them whole. We need them in part as they are formed to embark to this vulnerable destination. New York is of the utmost importance to this country. Should this colony be lost, the present controversy may be decided against our preference and our posterity.

Wednesday, June 12, 1776 — New York

Seldom is there a day that I am not thankful that Mrs. Washington is here by my side. This is one of the few days that I wish she were somewhere else. An assassination plot was discovered in the city. It was to be orchestrated by a number of loyalists. A dozen men from several occupations were arrested giving us an idea of how widespread the descension was. Mayor David Matthews and two soldiers of my own Life Guard were involved. The mayor's complicity is not a surprise, but two of my own men is disturbing indeed. A mob of patriots took to the streets to do what I had been wanting. They hunted down Loyalists and Tories and seized them. They proceeded to tar and feather many. They made a few ride the rail which may be a punishment deserved but too harsh in my estimation. I have moved my headquarters to City Hall for stronger confines. I have requested Mrs. Washington to remain outside the city for her safety.

I wish not to dwell on this. I have advised a conference to be held forthwith by General Schuyler to venture an alliance with the Six Nations tribe. We could use two thousand of their Indians to reinforce our defenses. Sir John Johnson is expected to come down the Mohawk river with Mohawk Indians that he has enlisted to disrupt our supplies of men and provisions. Concomitantly, I have advised Schuyler to employ Colonel Dayton's regiment in this intention to oppose Sir John. General Schuyler has recommended fortification of a post opposite of Ticonderoga. My wish is that he strengthens Fort Ticonderoga in addition.

Thursday, June 13, 1776 — New York

Local merchants are exporting pork and beef from this area. I have requested that the Provincial Congress restrain this trade as these stores could be intercepted and provide food for the enemy. In addition, it will bring scarcity for our army bringing additional discomfort and suffering to usward.

I am saddened to hear that General Thomas has died of smallpox in Sorel. I have selected General Sullivan to take over command in Canada. The enemy of smallpox is an inimical and impartial foe that afflicts both armies. I am thankful to have survived this ailment and have been taught the way to combat it. Our determination to inoculate is an advantage over the enemy we wish to maintain.

I am in hopes that General Sullivan can turn the melancholy state-of-affairs in Canada from chaos to order. It will be an arduous task, but with the direction of a gracious Providence, victory can still be attained. To reduce my anxieties, my only request to him personally is to faithfully send returns on the state of the army there, its military stores, and to apprise me of any military occurrences. Information next to Providence is my best friend.

Saturday, June 15, 1776 — New York

Though an immense lack of reporting from other quadrants of this war exists, those that do come in are usually requests. Others are of resignations, frustrations, and complaints. A rare report reached me today telling of heroic valor. One of Commodore Manley's men, Captain Mugford and two of his schooners (one named the Lady Washington) were attacked by twelve or thirteen boats full of British troops. The seven or eight men on those two schooners killed sixty or seventy of the enemy and sank many of their vessels. Captain Mugford was killed in the action, which is a great loss to our cause. His bravery and ferocious defense are to be heralded [Pennsylvania Evening Post, June 1, 1776]. Our Continental Navy continues to be a bright spot for our side. They have captured one of the transports with a company of Highlanders on board. Boston is to be well-defensed with notable acts as these.

Sunday, June 16, 1776 — New York

More good news arrived by dispatch, and from the unlikeliest of places — Canada. Brigadier-General Sullivan reports the Canadians are more favorable to our cause than at first thought. With so many misfortunes, I had considered this expedition a loss. I have believed many of the misfortunes in that country were primarily due to lack of discipline and training of the soldiery. Perhaps General Sullivan is changing that. I pray his influence will also win the minds of our soldiers and the people in Canada. With a few victories, he believes more will join our cause as they see defeat is uncertain and victory is possible. If General Thompson brings success at Three rivers to the British chagrin, their schemes may be disconcerted. General Sullivan's eyes must then be directed downward to the lowest points toward the United Colonies. We need more security for that army and make supplying them efficient. The Canadians are an ingenious people, capable of finesse and cunning. Our army is to speak of trust with them but never lean on that trust. We must guard against any treacherous conduct made by them.

I am giving all generals the same advice. We must maintain a good understanding and free communication with the field-officers. Nothing can produce greater benefits than this. History evinces the fatal consequences, which have resulted from distrust, jealousy, and disagreement within the ranks.

Monday, June 17, 1776 — New York

I was unable to get much sleep last night. I was able to lay down at my usual hour, but the thoughts of General Sullivan plague me. I sent him a letter giving him my confidence in his initiatives because I find myself grasping at any good news to the north of us. I then remember that General Gates has been sent to Canada to do what he can to rectify the situation. I fear my letter to General Sullivan may bring a conflict of command. Beyond this, the more I think on Sullivan, the more I realize he has his strengths and he has his foibles. He has a tincture of vanity and a pressing desire to be popular. He takes what limited experience he has had in war and believes he can graft that over a larger scale. Though strategic genius may be innate to his character and the ability to lead men, something of his nature at birth, overconfidence and undue risk could lead to his downfall and ours. I am sending Congress a letter to gain their sentiments regarding this officer and his command.

Congress has authorized the Committee of Safety for Pennsylvania to build a redoubt at Billingsport and to throw obstructions across the Delaware to oppose the approach of any enemy ships. To achieve these constructions for defense, they have requested an engineer to assist them. I do not have one to spare. I have made Congress aware of this need on several occasions. Prayerfully, the committee will understand that I am not holding out on them, but am facing certain attack. The one engineer that I rely on is needed at this location.

Tuesday, June 18, 1776 — New York

I am delighted to record that Congress has approved the appointment of a war-office. The goal is to lessen my burden and to increase our efficiency. This body will keep up with the officers and their ranks, see about recruitment for every venture engaged by Congress, and assure that money, arms, and supplies are delivered with all punctuality. They will also take responsibility for all prisoners-of-war. Though I admit freely that the first formation and activities of such a group will be done with defects, over time, those may be remedied. The war-office, through experience, will grow into a huge contribution to this effort.

Thursday, June 20, 1776 — New York

Every time I mention the word "necessity," I am sadly reminded of my first military encounter and surrender of Fort Necessity during the last war. I think one terrible taste of defeat drives me to do all in my power to never see it repeated. God works all things for good. This may be the good that I can look back on should this present conflict come to a successful close. I digress. In the mode of necessity to somehow trouble our enemy while enlisting the ever-present dilemma of savages in our midst, Congress has agreed to my request that we pay the Indians one hundred dollars for every commissioned officer and thirty dollars for every soldier of the King's troops they capture. This is a great incentive to keep them neutral at worst and helpful at best. It is far better the enemy has more to worry about than we.

Sunday, June 23, 1776 — New York

On this Lord's Day, it is good to give thanks even when things do not turn out the way we planned. I have received letters from Generals Schuyler, Sullivan, and Arnold. They have informed me that General Thompson was repulsed at Three rivers. He has been taken prisoner by General Burgoyne along with others of our men. By all reports, Burgoyne's army is considerable in size. I fear our misfortunes there are not over. I am in prayer that they will at least make a successful retreat to avoid the great calamity of complete destruction of our army in that quarter.

General Gates has yet to leave for Canada, but he should be leaving tomorrow with all possible dispatch. I am in great pains over the potential loss of this important area to our cause. I flatter myself that General Gates can rectify the situation with utmost exertions. I am ordering General Gates to appoint a deputy adjutant-general, a deputy quartermaster-general, a deputy mustermaster-general, and any other officers needed. He is to secure the means and lines of supply. He is to consult with Colonel Knox regarding artillery and with General Schuyler regarding provisions and stores. Any soldiers whose enlistments are up must not be allowed to leave until they surrender their arms, clothing, ammunition, and accoutrements. If they go before, it will further increase our scarcities. Above all else, I have communicated with him verbally and in writing that he must make an accurate return of where his army stands and remit frequent correspondence to assist my decision making.

Monday, June 24, 1776 — New York

I am apprehensive to hear what greater calamity has befallen our army in the quarter of Canada. General Sullivan is dispirited by the situation. General Arnold confirms the facts to be so. My hope is that this army can be saved through retreat. Retreat is not a favorable desire but compared to being imprisoned or killed, it is a sort of victory of its own accord. Any army that successfully retreats enables its usage on a more favorable exercise. The men saved by evacuation maintain troop levels and reduce the necessary training of new ones. Beyond this, an army that falls back is wiser for the next engagement. It has taken this conflict to make me appreciate the manifold values of retreat. In the days ahead, this may be my cup as well. People will question retreat and see it as defeat. From the position where I command, I see better and deeper than any who sit by as spectators and second-guessers.

We must make ready for the advancement of any victorious British armies that move down into our colonies. The goal to defeat them in Canada was a cushion of safety that I fear we have lost. I am having General Schuyler in Albany make ready his army and militia for the defense of the country there.

Thursday, June 27, 1776 — New York

Per General Arnold's desires, Congress has requested that I send carpenters to Canada to assist in building gondolas and galleys for them. I understand that work would benefit our army there, but whereas their situation is in a melancholy state, ours is in direct threat of enemy landing. It would not be wise to withdraw the carpenters from the needed work of these vessels here and allow the enemy vessels simply to pass by without rebuttal. The goal is to harass the enemy, to stop the enemy, and to sink as many of their weapons and men as possible.

I am disappointed from a letter that I received from Joseph Hawley of Massachusetts dated of the 21st instant. He has informed me that the majority in the House are newcomers. They are slow to make decisions, calling for everything to be substantiated before acting. Such delays put our whole campaign in jeopardy. They should be moving with the utmost dispatch. He believes not a single company will be engaged here or in Canada before snowfalls. Seemingly, Congress desires more troops in Boston which is safe and removed now from conflict. That is not the case here in New York where reports say the British are expected any moment. May the Lord help us and move them expeditiously. I am praying that the British delay their actions.

Friday, June 28, 1776 — New York

A plot has been discovered. Many of the disaffected have grouped together to aid the British once they arrive to our detriment. Governor Tryon is instrumental in this. He was using the mayor of New York as a conduit. Thankfully, as I noted earlier, the mayor and some citizens assisting him have been placed in confinement. Some of this army and even of my personal guard were involved. Beyond their plans to assassinate me and others of my generals, they planned to fire upon their own countrymen from behind. One such collaborator was my guard Thomas Hickey. He has been arrested, tried for mutiny, sedition, and treachery. He was sentenced to die. He was hanged this morning at eleven o'clock. It is a sad turn of events and I am continually revisited with doubts of those closest to me. I pray that his punishment will deter others considering such betrayal.

I am writing General Schuyler to take the post at Fort Stanwix post haste. He is to reinforce several garrisons and communications at the different passes. Naturally, the enemy will strain every nerve to damage this campaign and injure us wherever possible.

Saturday, June 29, 1776 — New York

For the last few days, reports came of British ships arriving. I have received confirmation that forty-five have arrived today at the Lower Bay of Sandy Hook. I suppose their whole fleet will be in shortly. The city is panicked. Warning guns are firing as trained. Troops are running to their posts. Everything is in a state of controlled chaos. We have not wasted one minute to prepare for this, yet we need more minutes and days. Regardless, our men have been trained in what to do and how to do it, even carrying out drills to familiarize themselves for this moment.

Our troops are few and spread over a vast area, but I will make the most of what I have to prevent destruction. I received a letter today from Mr. Hancock letting me know that Congress has been alarmed by the victory of General Burgoyne. They are concerned knowing his history of quick aggression. They have resolved to augment the northern department by four thousand men and to give each soldier financial incentives to sign for three years. They are also raising up four companies of Germans from Pennsylvania and four companies in Maryland. In addition, my understanding is they have enlisted six companies of riflemen to serve for three years to strengthen the three companies already raised here in New York. I am emboldened by this but saddened that it took defeat to get them to act. More responsive action could have prevented collapse in Canada. It would also make victory in this colony more certain. I am hopeful that I will receive these reinforcements before the enemy attacks.

I am ordering Brigadier-General Livingston not to lose a moment's time in sending parts of the militia from Staten Island to this city. I expect that order to bring three companies. I am sending orders also to our men with my expectations that they will behave with coolness and bravery. In the fire of battle, it is important not to waste ammunition or powder. I want the officers to draw a circle with brush around our defenses as a marker that must be crossed before our men fire.

They are to have their pieces loaded with one musket-ball and four or eight buck-shot depending on the capacity of their arms.

I have sent Mrs. Washington, along with Mrs. Knox and Mrs. Greene with their children, out of the city in the company of many citizens.

Sunday, June 30, 1776 — New York

With engagement days away if not sooner, I find great solace from our worship earlier this morning. I have a more perfect reliance on the All-wise and Powerful Supreme Being. I dare say that no other man at this juncture of time needs His Aid nor seeks it more fervently than I do. I am ordering an appointment of a chaplain for each regiment at this instant. Of all the times in our history, the blessings and protections of Heaven are most necessary right now for us on this continent. We face obstacles for this cause that only the Almighty can overcome. My hope is that every officer and man will endeavor to act as a Christian soldier ought. We are in this conflict to defend the rights and liberties of our country, those that our Creator gave us from the very start. As I seek His Guidance with each day on my knees, I pray that this practice of reverence will spread throughout our camps.

More complete reports have arrived. General Greene reports that over one hundred and twenty ships with approximately ten thousand troops on board have arrived. More British ships are said to be near. Colonel Webb expects fifteen-to-twenty thousand more enemy troops to arrive onboard those. I would flatter my-self to say I expected this size, but I would not be truthful. I did believe they would attack New York or Canada or both. Now I feel they have chosen the former. We knew New York to be of prime importance. It appears the British concur. We are outmanned. We are overwhelmed. Our hands are full. Our situation is as Jehosh-aphat's, we do not know what to do, but our eyes are on You O Lord. Please come to our aid.

Tuesday, July 2, 1776 — New York

From where I command, this is the battle we have been waiting for, the one that may well decide the contest. My generals with battle experience are few. We are shorthanded in comparison to the enemy. I must communicate to the men some things to remember as the battle begins. We are to decide whether we will be slave or free. We are to decide the questions, can we own our own lands and homes? Or must we live at the whim of tyranny? The fate of millions of unborn rests upon our courage and conduct as we rest our own fate in the Hands of God. The enemy's unrelenting provocations have pushed us against the wall. We must resolve — resistance or submission, victory or death. I contend that freemen contending for liberty on their own grounds are superior to any collection of slavish mercenaries on earth. This contest will be an experiment for the world to determine if my contention is correct or grossly misled. As the battle soon begins, we will rely upon the goodness of our cause and the help of that Supreme Being in Whose Hands victory rests. He alone can animate us to great and noble actions.

Thursday, July 4, 1776 — New York

The enemy is upon us. They are building works for defense on the north side of Staten Island. The one thing that seems to delay them is the expectation that General Howe's fleet is soon to appear to initiate action. I am calling on Congress to free up the regiments from Boston and the Massachusetts area to come to our assistance. The enemy poses no threat in that quarter. Congress must see that the redcoats are putting all their force here. We must meet them here with all of ours. I am calling on the Flying Camps to be raised and make swift dispatch toward New Jersey. We will have to face the enemy here in New York without the benefit of the New Jersey militia. They are distressed and in need of their own men to repulse any British incursions that are attempted there.

Saturday, July 6, 1776 — New York

New Jersey has many disaffected people. Inveterate enemies have shown themselves inimical. This area is wrought with them. They are ready and willing to help the enemy against this campaign, even when I have been so indulgent with them. Thereby, I am ordering they be apprehended and moved from this quarter to limit their interference.

Congress has acceded to my request that chaplains be established throughout this army with pay. The same is to be provided for regimental surgeons. I am concerned for the body of these men, but I am also concerned for their souls. I do not believe that without our rightness toward God, our cause will succeed. Righteousness exalts a nation, even an infant one.

Monday, July 8, 1776 — New York

Colonel Seymore arrived today from Connecticut. I was glad to see him and his men. Governor Trumbull is a faithful friend to this cause. He responds immediately at every request. I need his militia to be ready to fly to our aid as need warrants. I also need him in Connecticut to help remove all provisions that might be accessible to the British. They are known to take things by brute force. No citizen can resist. The only option we have is to move whatever they would take, far out of their reach. The Governor can do this with all items of supply and livestock. I have been told that the enemy plans to attack by descent on the Jersey side with part of his army and use the remainder of his men as well as his fleet against this city. Feeling this is legitimate, I am requesting Governor Turnbull to dispatch the three row-galleys he has in New London. I am asking him to send as many cannons as he can, along with any additional men that he can spare who have muskets ready to fire.

This city, the hub of the continent with all spokes terminating here, must be the focus of every colony. That is essential for Connecticut, Maryland, Massachusetts, and Philadelphia. Our time is near. Excuses and delays cannot be countenanced at this time of certain collision. In this vein, I am instructing General Putnam that all the arms taken in the Scottish transport be sent hither.

Tuesday, July 9, 1776 — New York

If not for the dire situation we face here, it would have been a joy to have been in Philadelphia a few days prior. I received their Declaration of Independence. I am heartened to read it. Congress has been impelled by necessity to dissolve all connections between Great Britain and the American Colonies. We are declaring that we are Free and Independent States. We are no longer colonies possessed by a nation abroad, nor should we be called as such. I will henceforth refer to our provinces by the appropriate and accurate title "States." Hallelujah! This was the thing that had to be done though it was with great hesitancy and pain that it was finally exercised. It is well past due. History should record this declaration as a notification to every tyrant that their abuses will not be tolerated.

I am instructing the Declaration be read to every regiment so that the men can know where we stand. There is no chance for reunion with Great Britain. We now exist as an independent people defending our sovereignty, unrestrained by a foreign power. We are free men created equal to any in Britain. We are endowed by our Creator with certain unalienable rights. That endowment is what we pray our Creator will aid us to defend. We are free to pursue life, liberty, and happiness. Just as those men who signed that document, this army has shown by example the pledge of our lives, our fortune, and our sacred honor.

As invigorating as this declaration is, it is nothing more than paper unless our actions on the field establish it as so. Should we be defeated, that document will be made infamous throughout the known world. Every servant will have removed from their minds the hope to one day be free. This should provide a fresh incentive to every officer and soldier to act with fidelity and courage.

Congress's resolve in this declaration is the most important statement perhaps any people have ever made. It is in this historic time that we now live and fight. We have no real say in the final verdict of things except to give our all and trust ourselves and our posterity to that Being who controls all things, to bring about His own determinations.

Wednesday, July 10, 1776 — New York

The army has heartily embraced the Declaration. With glee, I observed the statue of King George III toppled with his colossal horse from its stand on Bowling Greene. This, to me, carries strong symbolism that the King and his court have no say in the matters of this independent nation. If my army has anything to say about it, he never will again.

Activity continues with a higher sense of purpose and urgency. Militia are on their way from Maryland, Delaware, and Pennsylvania to form the Flying Camp.

The readiness and alacrity for all involved gives evidence that all regard this supreme quest. They are exerting themselves with zeal and sacrifice. Even with the militias knowing that many cannot be paid for their efforts, they choose to reside and fight.

Thursday, June 11, 1776 — New York

The enemy is prosecuting the war with unexampled severity. They have called upon foreign mercenaries, slaves, and savages to arms against us. We must be willing to adopt every possible expedient ourselves and call upon others to help as well. I am asking the General Court of Massachusetts Bay to engage the St. John's, Nova Scotia, and Penobscot Indians to our side. They can probably be engaged for less pay than the Continental troops, but even if for the same, their enlistment is urgent.

Congress has agreed to send three regiments northward to assist the northern army. Instead of having them partake in a tiresome march, I am having them set sail from Norwich and embark for Albany. I have ordered General Ward to carry this out and to write Mr. Huntington of Norwich to prepare as many vessels as necessary to bring the whole of those troops hence. These, in concert with the militia that is supplied by several States, will join the troops of General Sullivan to repel any invasion that is attempted from that quarter.

General Gates and General Schuyler are in a quandary over who is in command in Canada. I am hoping that harmony and good agreement will subsist between these two men for the good of our cause.

With all the things that I must do in this instant, a need exists to which I have expended no time, though it has fallen as one of my premier responsibilities. That is the accounting for the money sent this way. I am requesting an auditor again from Congress. I have done so on many occasions but without response. I am doing so again. To have an auditor to ensure that every resource given is used for the purpose of this army and not for the personal enrichment of its members is prudent. Beyond this, I need an auditor to protect me from accusations of fraud or profiteering. I have dealt with a few scoundrels in my private business. I have seen the harm their actions have played upon their character and future endeavors.

I wish not to have any such protests made toward me. Rather, I desire a defense to any, which an auditor would provide.

Friday, July 12, 1776 — New York

About half past three o'clock this evening, two of the enemy's ships with tenders left Staten Island. They moved up the harbor in full sail. Our alarm guns sounded in the city and our soldiers rushed to their posts. In the streets, women and children were screaming. We fired at them from Red Hook at Governor's Island. Our men reacted with incessant cannonade. The ships return fire was overwhelming. They sailed up the Hudson river past our batteries with little or no damage from what we can surmise. I am at a loss of what their intent is, perhaps to cut off communication. They may be seeking to supply the Tories behind our lines. What is so disturbing to me is that if two of their ships can pass by so easily and settle up-river, then more may cut off any chance our army has to escape.

I am apprehensive that their design is to seize the passes in the Highlands by land. I am ordering Brigadier-General Clinton to send General Ten Broeck to march down and secure the passes as well as the post where the road runs over Anthony's Nose. I need General Clinton to alert Connecticut that their forces are needed to assist us, even if it is just to keep the Tories in line.

Saturday, July 13, 1776 — New York

I am asking the Secret Committee of the Convention of the State of New York to remove the Tory prisoners, those soldiers who have been convicted of treason, and all those whose sentiments lean toward our enemy. It cannot be calculated the harm their influence and actions might bring. I cannot focus fully forward when I am having to look over my shoulder.

Sunday, July 14, 1776 — New York

While the enemy is in full view and the disaffected are lingering in the shadows, preparations are ongoing. Shortages are being compensated. I am grieved that at a moment when our Nation needs men, Colonel Ritzema is soliciting to resign his commission. He is bitter over the court of inquiry initiated against him by General Stirling. Stirling wrote him up for his tardiness to parade review and for his lax enforcement of discipline and order. I wish this dribble would cease in the face of the enemy. We should be of one accord. Colonel Ritzema should be more concerned for his Nation than his own grievances. It shows me a lot about his character which I may have to address when danger passes.

As the British may be seeking to block off our provisions, I have asked the commissary to update me on the condition of our supplies. He has given me positive news. He forwarded some to Albany sufficient to sustain ten thousand men for a period of four months. He also let me know that we had enough in the city to supply twenty thousand men for three months. This removes one of my great worries.

Monday, July 15, 1776 — New York

I have been stewing over the report telling of General Burgoyne's permissive barbary of our men at the Cedars after our defeat there. The savages were allowed to murder men and heap abuse upon the rest. This is a flagrant violation of Christian principles, humanity, and the respect between nations even at war. I am asking Congress to let the British know on no uncertain terms, that if this practice is repeated, it will be met sadly with reciprocation, regardless of how heinous those acts may be. I am hopeful that this will deter any future offenses.

Wednesday, July 17, 1776 — New York

The Connecticut light-horse regiment was discharged today. They soon will return home. As much as we need them, they refuse fatigue duty and standing guard. This regiment declares themselves exempt from such responsibilities. Had I given them indulgence, this would only have encouraged others to reject orders on similar grounds. For the good of this army, we must have order, discipline, and submission to officers.

To add to my burden of inner squabbles, General Sullivan tendered his resignation from the army because he felt insulted that General Gates would be sent to supersede his command. I am doing the best of my ability to keep all engaged and committed. I hate three things, even four. I hate the character of quitters, the treachery of the Tories, the promises given but not kept, and the selfishness when so much is at stake.

General Schuyler called a general council of officers to discuss abandoning Crown Point on Lake Champlain. Though most agreed to abandon the post, twenty-one inferior officers have written a remonstrance against this action offering alternative ideas. I wish I had a better understanding of that area. I tend to side with the superior officers to honor the authority that we have entrusted to them. I also never want disagreements between superior officers and inferior officers to be appealed to me. This is inefficient and very disheartening to the officers we have placed in command. That being said, I have always perceived Crown Point was an important post that allows us to keep mastery of the Lake. If we abandon it, the enemy will be free to occupy it, placing us at a disadvantage at some point in the future. I will tender my advice only to General Schuyler. I trust officers that I place in these positions of authority to use their God-given wisdom to do what is best for this noble endeavor.

I do not shirk from giving guidance to my officers. This is imperative. General Schuyler who has health problems is dually mindful of the health concerns of his army. He informs me many are sick. What plagues his army more is the fever of discord and disorder. He says that the troops from different provinces are jealous of each other. They are making pernicious distinctions. The general must make these see that we are one army. There is neither Jew nor Greek, rich nor poor, Virginians nor Marylanders. We are engaged in a war of eminent importance. We cannot let disharmony among ourselves keep us from mutually contending for all that freemen hold dear. He must build order and at the same time unity. Schuyler must instill discipline with great exertion. He must remind the soldiers of the common vision that drew us into this fray from the very beginning.

Friday, July 19, 1776 — New York

The Committee of the City of New York has responded to my urging with a resolve that all persons deemed a danger to our efforts be forbidden to travel about. This is necessary as these may have the capability to relay intelligence to our powerful enemy, counteracting all operations for defense. The propriety of this action is founded upon the basic law of self-preservation. I am submitting the names of people that I consider inimical to our work. I am lending them twenty thousand dollars to carry out this work with their promise to speedily replace it.

I have heard little from General Gates. I am very frustrated by his lack of returns. I am going to write him to let him know that. Though I have not publicly sided with the field-officers, I do believe holding Crown Point is equivalent to holding the Lakes, maintaining communication, and retaining a supply chain. To lose this post would mean a closing off from three of the New England governments.

Lord Howe has arrived. He and his brother General Howe have been named commissioners both for military and civil matters. In the role of supposed peacemakers, they sent British Colonel Patterson, the adjunct to General Howe, to meet with me. I had Colonel Reed, Colonel Knox, and a few others join us. We were not surprised at their offer to dispense pardons for repenting sinners. That is quite gracious of them, but with Heaven's blessing, they will be the ones seeking America's forgiveness. I simply told him that those who have committed no fault want no pardon. We are only defending our indisputable rights.

Sunday, July 21, 1776 — New York

I received amazing news from Charleston. General Lee has relayed a victory by the men under his charge. In June, the masts of the British fleet broke the horizon to the fear of all those near that shore. On June 28th, the British sent nine ships to take over Charleston by way of overrunning our defenses there. Their hope was to hurl explosives into the fort from their bomb ketch called the Thunder while their other ships pounded the fortress walls. The men at the main fort stood their ground and continued pressing the deafening roar of our guns and cannons throughout the day. Ultimately, two of the English ships were disabled. Three more ran aground. One of those exploded from the cannon fire from our fort. Near midnight, the British ships slipped away humiliated. Sir Peter Parker and his fleet got a severe drubbing and I rejoice.

I have shared this with our men. The situation in Charleston is similar to ours. Excursions are being made. Some are being thwarted. We are outnumbered and outgunned. Their superiority on the water is staggering here too. Yet, in the hearts of our people pound the yearning to be free with the will to do what is necessary to attain it. We can defy all odds to achieve it. May this be the encouragement our men find in the quest for this city of New York. If it can be done in the south, it can be done here by God's Grace.

Monday, July 22, 1776 — New York

Colonel Knox is in great need for artillerists. I had him write down his ideas on how to supply this shortage. He has done so. Along with his ideas, I am transmitting this need to Congress for consideration. I am also requesting a light horse company. Several here have requested the opportunity to make up this troop.

We continue to look at the British fleet. I assume they are looking at us too. I have been told that they will not attempt an attack until the rest of their men (who are expected every hour) arrive. It bothers me greatly not to be able to disturb or trouble them. They sit out of our range. They have the superiority of the water as their best defense. I am not sure what we will do when they do come. I believe they have twenty-five thousand men available. We only have fifteen thousand men at best. We do have right on our side. We have men who truly have something for which to fight. This should help render our force equivalent to theirs. I am comforted that Mrs. Washington is a long way away from here. This allows me to fight without any concern but the task at-hand.

Wednesday, July 24, 1776 — New York

I am stretched beyond measure. I must reply to the adjacent States, answer returns from the field, react to the enemy's moves, settle disputes, coordinate the different departments, account for the inflow and outflow of monies, coordinate supply distributions, recruit troops, direct those troops to some battle formation, and more. Jethro suggested able men to help his son-in-law Moses when he saw him worked to the fringe of collapse. I likewise need more able men by my side. I am going to consider, with reluctance, asking Congress to enlarge my aides-de-camp. I pray they appreciate that it is only when I am in deep wanting that I ask for help. Other officers ask for surplus or adequacy so they may fight from a position of comfort. I, to not be a burden, try to make do with deficiency and only make requests when the water is over my head. Reed has been a great help to me, but he can only relieve so much.

Thursday, July 25, 1776 — New York

I am told that five more British ships arrived today.

Friday, July 26, 1776 — New York

According to reports, eight more British ships have arrived this day.

Saturday, July 27, 1776 — New York

Always, in the back of my mind are those two British ships sitting above us on the Hudson. I have received two of the three row-galleys from Governor Trumbull. The third is expected. Governor Cooke has not responded to my request for his contribution. Mr. Anderson has our fire-ships under construction though the progress is slower than I desire. When things are ready, I plan to make an attempt on the two ships up the Hudson. This can be done in isolation without the huge enemy fleet being alerted. Until then, I will continue to prepare obstructions for the channel opposite the works at the upper end of this island.

I am awaiting the whole of the Flying Company under General Mercer. Once they arrive, I have the mind to bring some annoyance to the enemy through them without putting too much hazard upon our posts.

Monday, July 29, 1776 — New York

General Mercer believes any attack upon the enemy on Staten Island is ill-advised as they have the command of the water around the island. I have instructed him to have nine or ten flat-bottomed boats built with the purpose of keeping communication open across the Hackensack and Passaic rivers.

I was informed this evening that twenty more British ships have arrived. Action is looming.

Tuesday, July 30, 1776 — New York

Congress has approved an exchange of prisoners with the enemy at a time mutually convenient between the two armies. We seek officers of equal rank be exchanged, soldier-for-soldier, sailor-for-sailor, and citizen-for-citizen with one exception. We would like to get Colonel Ethan Allen back so badly that we will exchange any officer his equal or inferior. I am hopeful that General Howe will agree.

Wednesday, July 31, 1776 — New York

With relief, I received a letter today from General Schuyler. He and General Gates have settled their disputes and are working in good agreement. General Schuyler was able to discover and apprehend some ringleaders of a dangerous plot, the details of which I have not been made aware. I am still not at peace with his decision to give up Crown Point in preferment of Ticonderoga.

Thursday, August 1, 1776 — New York

General Greene has seen forty more British ships come into the Hook.

I am greatly concerned at the divisions that have arisen among the troops. There is a fractioning between States, nationalities, rank, assignments, and the like. Our country is bleeding. Our men are doing their best to help the enemy by fighting each other. All distinctions must fade into one — American. To make this name honorable and preserve the liberty of our country should be our only emulation. In this cause as Americans, all distinctions of nations, countries, States, and provinces should be lost so that each may contribute as one hand and one heart to this glorious work which Providence has purposed.

Friday, August 2, 1776 — New York

The enemy is growing stronger by the day. Though we are behind, I am glad to say we are growing stronger too. Congress has released General Ward's regiment from Boston to assist us here at this quarter. Colonel Elmore is to repair hither with his regiments. Colonel Holman from Massachusetts has arrived with his regiment. Colonel Carey is also here. He is awaiting the arrival of his regiment any day. The third regiment of Massachusetts is soon to be set in motion hence. The enemy is going to make their grand push here soon. It is essential that every aid that can be obtained is brought here to meet them.

Sunday, August 4, 1776 — New York

Yesterday, Colonel Tupper carried out our plan to attack the two ships up the North river. I am flattered to hear that our men believe our galleys were able to hull the enemy ships several times by our shot. The damage on our galleys was significant and must be repaired before we make another attempt. Even so, I give thanks that we have been able to engage the enemy. Our men acted with great bravery and spirit.

Monday, August 5, 1776 — New York

Twenty-five more British sails arrived at the Hook today. It is reported that the Portuguese have seized some of our vessels. They have joined the British to our distress. They need Britain in their own war with Spain. Things are drawing fast to an issue.

Tuesday, August 6, 1776 — New York

As we await the fire to fall, I pour over our army and its organization. The glaring deficiency has not dissipated. We are in grave need of general officers, namely brigadier-generals. If Congress is delaying these appointments due to frugality, their reasoning will come at a higher cost. I cannot, as one man, effectively manage this entire army. A more reasonable excuse could be that they are unsure on how to reward this rank. Some would say that the oldest colonels should be considered first to the higher rank. This is the least objectionable, but does it bring the greatest talent to the position? If we choose the most abled in our ranks, this will greatly enhance our army and perhaps produce the greatest improvement of our exercise. However, such a move on merit at this juncture could insult the older colonels and cause their protests to be expressed through mass resignations. Congress could potentially choose some through political reward and give it to those who are not currently in this army. This would be the worst choice of all. I am going to submit these options to Congress and perhaps influence them to the most expedient — promote based on the oldest colonels in this army. Then promotions to fill their place can follow similar logic. The effects of each move often affects more than that which is obvious. Such machinations should not be an issue — if all are of one heart and mind. Sadly, our men are not perfect so we must account for such things.

Aside from the issues of war, there are side issues, such as prisoners-of-war, with which we must address. I am asking the war department to be more engaged to handle such things. I daily receive letters from British prisoners-of-war requesting parole, asking to be exchanged, complaining of conditions and treatment, to name a few. That the general of this army must consider such things when the enemy is sitting out on the water within my sight ready to strike is untenable.

Wednesday, August 7, 1776 — New York

Two deserters arrived this day from the British ranks. Their information seemed to match what we have been witnessing the last few days. Reports were that their army, which was so embarrassingly repelled in South Carolina by General Lee and his men, has arrived. The Hessians have arrived by ship as have the Scotch Highlanders. The British appear to have thirty-thousand men ready to fight, whereas we have barely ten thousand. Sickness reduces our strength here. Their plan, per these informants, is to attack New York and Long Island within the week.

So here we are. If we rely only on the justice of our cause, we will fail. We must not be slothful at a time as this. We must give our utmost exertions and trust Providence to do the rest. We will do the little things, but we are trusting in the Mover of Events to do the big things.

Thursday, August 8, 1776 — New York

I nominated General James Clinton to command the levies on both sides of the Hudson river. He is a native of New York and has experience in building fortifications around the Hudson. That familiarity will greatly aid him in this assignment. The New York Convention agreed to my nomination.

Friday, August 9, 1776 — New York

General Greene reported that last night near sunset, approximately one hundred boats brought troops from Staten Island to the ships. Three of those ships have fallen toward the Narrows after taking on board thirty tenders of soldiers. Their hope appears to be to hem us in by going above us where their other two ships sit and cut off communication and help, while the majority cut under us for a deciding blow.

Our troops continue to be enhanced. Colonel Smallwood is here with his battalion from Maryland. Colonel Miles is here with two additional battalions of riflemen from Pennsylvania.

Sunday, August 11, 1776 — New York

I have apprehended several citizens of Long Island whom I fear would do damage to our cause. Though I have not caught them in any treasonous activity directly, their code of conduct makes me suspicious. At this time where combat is nigh, I will not risk the safety of our men, nor the outcome of this enterprise. I am sending them to Connecticut to Governor Trumbull with the request that they be treated kindly in the chance that I have overreacted. I will let the New York Convention know of my decision. I delayed it as long as I thought possible. Now the threat is eminent. All potentialities must be reduced.

Monday, August 12, 1776 — New York

The Convention of this State has ordered their militia to station above Kingsbridge. Half of the militia in King's and Queen's counties are assigned to reinforce the troops on Long Island. General Morris and his brigade are taking post on the

Sound and Hudson's river to annoy the enemy in case they attempt to land. Militia from Connecticut are assembling and will march this week.

The British parade of naval strength is playing out great intimidation. It took them a full day to come up the harbor. They are flying their flags, saluting themselves with guns. The sailors and soldiers stand on the decks waving to crowds on the shore. We seem to have kicked a hornet's nest and everyone is against us. Some say they have near four-hundred ships, all with guns and cannons pointed in our direction. People are on their rooftops gazing at this armada come to fight our little army. I cannot help but feel the people viewing this are longing for the spectacle of a bully putting down a puny challenger. What some are thinking, including myself, is what an impact this contest would make if the puny kid whips the bully. Now that would make history. I revel to think of such things, but reality of the matter makes such whimsical musings useless.

General Ward's two regiments have recovered from smallpox. His men began marching to assist the northern army last week. The Massachusetts militia will take their place in Boston and throughout their colony.

Even as I am bolstering the army here, I was negligent in asking Congress to send one thousand cavalrymen to General Lee's aid in the south. With all that is on my mind, it is a wonder that I do not forget more things. I am writing Congress per his request. He believes if he receives these, he can ensure the safety of the southern States.

Tuesday, August 13, 1776 — New York

The enemy received thirty-six more ships to augment their fleet. At this time, all outcomes should be considered and we must plan for them. I have many papers in my station that could greatly jeopardize future successes should they fall into the hands of the enemy. I have taken precautions to have these boxed up and nailed. I am sending them to Congress for safe-keeping with Lieutenant-Colonel Reed. I will receive them back when our affairs here are circumstanced.

General Gates's letter was received today. He says that his army is still in a sickly condition. I am sending Dr. Morgan with medicines that I pray under the smiles of Providence will relieve their distress to some degree. Gates says the construction of vessels to command the Lakes there is going well. If these are assigned to General Arnold, I am confident that all exertions will be made for success. Sadly, Gates is still fuming over our disagreement on the abandonment of Crown Point. I do not want to deal with this discussion again. I am communicating as much to him. I will trust his judgment in abandoning that post and pray for the best.

Ninety-six more enemy ships have arrived. I am more concerned about that than rehashing old arguments.

Friday, August 16, 1776 — New York

Our men made another attempt on the Phoenix and the Rose, the two British ships up-river. We attacked them with two of our fire vessels. One grappled with the Phoenix before being driven back. The only damage the enemy received was the destruction of one of their tenders. Regardless, the enemy can know that we are resolute against the status quo.

I have divided our men now into five divisions. I have placed one in northern Manhattan Island, three on the southern end of the Island, and one across the East river on Long Island.

Saturday, August 17, 1776 — New York

I have great anxiety over the women, children, and the infirmed still here in this city. The enemy's approach is expected any hour and these poor creatures are in harm's way. In addition, when the British men-of-war passed the twelfth ultimo, the shrieks and cries of the women and children greatly disturbed our young and inexperienced soldiery. I am writing the New York Convention to do whatever necessary to move these to an area far away from this point of conflict. The army will be much more effective without the concerns for these.

Sunday, August 18, 1776 — New York

The harassing efforts we have made on the two ships up-river have paid dividends. This morning, both set sail with a favorable tide and rejoined the rest of the fleet south of us. This is a blessing as we had feared those two joined by others could help hem us in between two enemy forces. The disappointment is that these two moved past our batteries again with guns firing, yet neither received even one hit. It makes me fearful that our batteries will be ineffectual when the real action begins. If I can become discouraged seeing that, how much more does the enemy receive the opposite effect?

The good news is our reinforcements are arriving. I believe that with the smiles of Providence, our exertions will baffle the designs of our inveterate foes, putting us on a footing to defy the utmost malice of the British.

Tuesday, August 20, 1776 — New York

The good news of the Phoenix and Rose removal from the North river will be short-lived if the enemy's plans that have been told to me are accurate. The enemy still plans to attack us from above and to land troops on Long Island. For us to stop their landing here will be impossible. The area is so vast that we do not have the men nor the works to prevent it. Our greatest hope may be to harass them as much as possible. This seems to be all we can do. I dare not write this but would rather than say it aloud. The ability of this army to hold this city appears less likely by the day. Only the Mover of events can reverse our fortune.

Thursday, August 22, 1776 — New York

This day broke clear and bright. It is difficult to imagine such a morning when last night brought the most terrible storm this army has ever witnessed. It was like a hurricane. The sky was electric with lightning running three solid hours. Homes were struck and burst into flames. It seemed with every flash, a horrific pop was heard of something struck. The thunder soon followed. Reports have poured in all this morning of the casualties — from the storm, not a human battle. We lost ten soldiers who were struck with a single bolt. Three more were killed in another part of town. One soldier was struck leaving him blind, deaf, and mute. I wrote of the Mover of events having the ability to reverse our fortune. We cannot help but be silent and realize He is the greatest ally we can have, or our greatest enemy. May He be the former.

I suppose rumors are to be expected the closer a fear becomes reality. The New York Convention has let me know that many citizens here assert that I have ordered the burning of this city in the event our army is obliged to retreat. That maneuver has never entered my mind. These are the homes of families. We are fighting for families and for property. Far be it from me to initiate destruction that is an inherent practice of our enemy. I saw what the enemy did in Boston. They chased our families out of their homes. The enemy then burned them. I will not be surprised to see that repeated here. This very fear should cause the Loyalist to run to our side. Yet, they have not. I will refute such speculation to the Convention and put it in writing. I pray they rest in the fact that we are here to protect and set free our citizens.

Friday, August 23, 1776 — New York

The attack may have begun in earnest. Yesterday morning, the enemy landed on Gravesend Bay upon Long Island with several thousand men. Colonel Hand retreated before them and burned any wheat and provisions that he could not carry. At first, we thought they would march upon General Sullivan, so I sent six regiments, nearly five thousand men, to reinforce his post, but they halted last night at Flatbush, three miles from our lines. General Greene is extremely sick. General Sullivan is filling in admirably. He is a gifted officer. He will need his talent to embolden him for what lies ahead. Reinforcements to Long Island will be determined by the enemy's next steps. I have stationed several thousand more of our men on Brooklyn Heights.

Saturday, August 24, 1776 — New York

In taking stock of our available troops, I cannot spare more for General Sullivan at this time for fear the enemy will soon attack us here at the next flood tide. Our army is in high spirits.

General Schuyler has made the treaty with the Indians of the Six Nations and others at the German Flat. This will assist us in capturing enemy officers and soldiers. Anything to divert their attention or make the enemy feel the weight of the continent against them is welcomed.

Sunday, August 25, 1776 — New York

I received distasteful news today that some of our men on Long Island fired reck-lessly at the enemy with no effect. No good can come out of disorder and unsol-dierlike actions. Such behavior elicits so many handicaps. Deserters from the en-emy are afraid to leave the British for fear of being fired upon by the very army in which they seek refuge. Ammunition cannot be wasted as we know not how great an assault we shall soon be under. Every ounce of powder and every musket ball is needed. Additionally, every time fire arises from our ranks, an alarm goes up and down the line which may prove false. With enough of these, our men will not react when the real danger is upon them. Beyond this, constant alarms will fatigue our men when our purpose is to wear down the enemy.

I am ordering that the guards be in their place, that a brigadier-general be always on the lines to take command, and that men do not extend beyond the lines without orders and scouting purposes. No property of the inhabitants of this city shall be touched. All property shall be cared for and respected. We are here to protect, not to steal. We are here to defend not to invade. We are an army not a mob. We are not mere hirelings as the British employ, we are men who fight to defend and promote all things dear and valuable for ourselves and our posterity. This conduct should be pursued with all propriety. To remember that we are here because we made a choice between freedom and slavery is imperative. We have made the choice of freedom. We must obtain it by the blessing of Heaven through our conduct of righteousness and through our united and vigorous efforts.

Monday, August 26, 1776 — New York

Almost the whole of the enemy's fleet has fallen down to the Narrows. We are still led to think they will land the main body of their army on Long Island for their grand push. Skirmishing and irregular firing is occurring between their men and our advanced guards. Colonel Martin of the Jersey levies sustained a wound in his breast feared fatal. A private had a leg broken by a cannonball. Another received a shot in the groin from musket fire. What the enemy received in return is unknown.

The enemy's varied waves of movement make it difficult to form any strong positioning of our forces. We have received the addition of nine militia from Connecticut, which is helpful as some of our people are very sickly.

Tuesday, August 27, 1776 — New York

I have little time to diary, but there is one thing I want to record before this day begins. I am leading our men out this morning. The one thing I will warn this nervous group of men before me is that if I see any man turn his back today, I will shoot him through. I have two pistols loaded for that purpose. As strong as this is to convey to soldiers about to fight, I want them to find one reassurance in all this — I will not ask them to do anything that I will not do. As they are in the flurry, so will I also be. As they are fired upon, so will I be. As I call them to fight with every last breath, I too will fight as long as I have a breath, a leg, or an arm.

Wednesday, August 28, 1776 — New York

I have been in the saddle for almost forty-eight hours. I have had no time to write much less think. Things have not turned out as we had wished. We were indeed attacked viciously by the opponent from three sides.

Tuesday morning, they attacked us to our right where Lord Stirling was in command near the Narrows at Gowanus road. It had appeared their whole army was attacking from that side. I am told that our men held their ground and never flinched. It turned out, their attack there was to draw our attention to the right. Then the Hessian soldiers began to bombard us in the center where General Sullivan's lines were situated. We had thought this was their main thrust all along, but then Sullivan was attacked by the main of the British army from behind in an outflanking maneuver. Our men were greatly outnumbered, but they fought valiantly and inflicted a great toll on the enemy. The riflemen of this army made a major contribution to the carnage the British received. Our left side collapsed. Many of our men were killed, while others surrendered or were captured. Remnants were able to retreat. They arrived at the Brooklyn lines seeking safety and reinforcement ahead of the advancing British troops.

I looked through my telescope to see Lord Stirling and his men still holding the right side with all their might. They held the enemy for almost four hours trading blow-for-blow. I have never seen any group so determined to succeed or die. Sadly, they were attacked from the left side and closed in on from behind. Only one escape existed for Stirling's men, and that was through the marshes of Gowanus Bay. Lord Stirling sent the bulk of his men to retreat in that direction while he and about two-hundred or more men resumed the attack upon the British to cover the retreat of the rest. I grieve even as I write this. I cannot imagine the brave fellows that I lost this day, especially those of the Marylanders. Cut down time-after-time, they kept getting up, kept fighting. I had told my men I would fight with my last breath, last leg, and last arm. These men did that and more. They finally gave way. As I looked, the smoke cleared, their fighting was finished. Many escaped, others captured. The British ceased their engagement for whatever reason. We have time to make adjustments and decide what to do next. From what we can tell, we have lost seven hundred-to-a-thousand soldiers. Three generals are missing — Stirling, Sullivan, and Woodhull.

I am unsure what to do. Two Pennsylvania regiments just crossed the river to join us here in Brooklyn. They marched in with a show of great confidence. Perhaps not all is lost. The enemy is about a mile-and-a-half from us. Our riflemen are firing and holding them up. We are hemmed in on three sides with just the East river to our backs. How long until the British ships sail in behind us and this war will be over? I am praying that is not the case. I have sent Brigadier-General Mifflin out to reconnoiter the outmost defenses and to make recommendations. Our men are hungry and tired, but they cannot sleep, nor can I. We will brace for battle and pray for help from above.

Thursday, August 29, 1776 — Long Island, New York

I am unsure if last night was a Smile from Heaven or a frown. Rain just poured on us all night. Our men are soaked and tired. I dare not question the rain. Sometimes in the darkest of days, the Almighty is doing things that we do not recognize as blessing until days, months, or years later. Brigadier-General Mifflin says that fighting is not an option. He believes fleeing is the only way to save our fate and that of America. His reasonings are the men are exhausted, the rain is heavy, the ammunition is not dry enough to use, the enemy is ever-approaching, and Lord Howe's fleet may soon set in behind us. I have taken the prerogative to dispatch a letter immediately requesting that General Heath at King's Bridge send every flatbottomed boat or sloop to us without delay. In case this letter is discovered, I am writing to say that we need these vessels to relieve our men with the many battalions of fresh troops we have coming from New Jersey.

With this in motion, I called for the officers to meet with me to decide what we should do — fight or retreat. Upon unanimous advice of our council of officers, we have agreed to give up Long Island and retreat to safety on Manhattan. Our force is unable to resist the enemy. To divide our forces against the various directions of attack would certainly dilute our chances, not to mention risk a break in communication from the main part of the army. Extreme fatigue is present among our men attempting to guard such an extensive line without proper shelter from the weather. I suffer from the fatigue myself.

Though we are choosing retreat, it may be prudent to leave some militia here to prevent or retard the enemy's landing on the east of the Hudson river. General Mifflin has volunteered himself and the Pennsylvania regiment to serve as rear guard and hold the line until the army has departed.

The day is almost spent. I have given orders for the men to prepare to fight. I am fearful to tell them we are retreating as they may leave behind some of their guns and ammunition, which we will desperately need at some point soon. We have no idea how many in our midst are enemy spies. We must pull this off in total secrecy or we have failed before we disembark. We can trust no one. I have called for the least-experienced soldiers as well as the sick and wounded to start for the Brooklyn ferry landing, ready to load at nine tonight when whatever boats arrive.

I am waiting — and praying. The Lord's Favor has kept the Northeast wind blowing, which has kept the British fleet from moving. Sadly, that same wind that protects us hinders us too as the water is too rough for our men to cross. What are we going to do? Dear Lord, what are we going to do? General McDougall says we cannot retreat tonight, but the British are on the move. If we do not retreat tonight, we will be unable to retreat beyond tonight. Almighty God help us! I have told McDougall to stand pat, keep the men there, and be ready to load at first relenting of the wind.

The time is a little after eleven o'clock, the wind has shifted from the southwest. General McDougall sees boats crossing the river from New York. I cannot help but wipe the tears from my eyes and thank the Father in Heaven.

John Glover of Massachusetts was on the first set of boats. He has assigned his sailors and fishermen to navigate the swift currents in the dark and in silence. We have loaded our first set of men and munitions. I will get the next set of men to move from the lines and march to the ferry-landing.

I am keeping watch. All is going well. I am overseeing everything at the landing. I watch, wait, pray, and write. I have no idea when I will have a chance again. Despite defeat, this night is shaping into a life-rope. We are wrapping wagon wheels with rags. All orders are whispered with no other talking allowed but what is extremely necessary. Troops, supplies, horses, and cannons pass by me. All are being loaded onto heavy-laden but floating vessels. Mifflin and his men are doing a great job with our ruse. They are keeping the campfires going to make it appear our troops are in their places ready to make a defensive stand. This is the fear of the British as I understand it. They still cannot get over Bunker Hill and the losses they sustained from the valiant stand of our people. I have a full garrison on the Brooklyn Heights with cannon ready to address any enemy ships that might try to cut us off.

The work continues. It is four in the morning. We are exhausted but all is going well.

Just now, General Mifflin rode up with our rear guard! I admit that it was hard to keep my composure. I asked him why he had left his post. In the confusion, Major Scammell told him and his men that it was their turn to leave, that we were almost finished. We are not almost finished. I told him and his men to return to their post immediately or we have lost this. I have never seen such a look of disconcertion. Like good soldiers, they went back. I hope the British have not found us missing. I pray that we have not tripped so close to the goal.

Friday, August 30, 1776 — New York

Daylight is upon us. We are not nearly finished. A large portion of our army still needs to be evacuated. We are about to be exposed to the enemy's view. The curtain of darkness is being pulled back. What will we do? I am praying the Lord will do something. He moved the wind. He has guided our steps. He has navigated the currents. I have told my men to keep moving. Keep loading. Keep rowing. Hurry back, please more.

I cannot believe it. A light fog is forming. Please Providence Please. Keep moving. Keep loading. Keep rowing. Hurry back, please for more.

The fog has grown dense. We cannot see six feet in front of us. Glover says it is sunny in New York. It is just Brooklyn and Long Island that are covered with fog. I am writing this because no doubt exists why this is happening. We have prayed. God is answering.

Everyone has been loaded and moved. I have summoned Mifflin and his men to come. I am waiting on them now.

We are all on board the last boat. It is almost seven in the morning. Heaven has smiled on us. We have done what only Israel leaving Egypt was able to do. God is with us. I just looked back toward Brooklyn. The fog is gone.

Saturday, August 31, 1776 — New York

General Sullivan and Lord Stirling were taken prisoners during the engagement on the 27th. General Sullivan has written me to estimate our losses to be near one thousand men matching earlier estimates. I am in a hurry now to make new dispositions of our forces.

I cannot help but now take time to reconsider all the plans and actions that we took in New York. Why did we leave the Jamaica Pass open? Why did I assume the enemy would cut us off by water, but not hem us in by land? Our escape was a miracle, but how faulty was our fight. Courage was shown. Men stood their ground. We were outnumbered without doubt, but I fear we were also out-thought. I must do better, plan better, and anticipate better. What we did in Boston, they did in a much larger scale to us in New York. May we win the next contest. I realize we could have lost this in a single stroke. I dare not consider that we expediently can win this war. We must be prepared to persevere in a long-drawn out engagement.

Sunday, September 1, 1776 — New York

This is the Lord's Day. I am to make a joyful noise unto the Lord and enter His Courts with thanksgiving. At this moment, that is hard to do, but why would it be hard? He has blessed me with Mrs. Washington and the beautiful Mount Vernon. He has given me friends and family. He has allowed me positions of leadership and of substance. Providence has delivered me in every battle win-or-lose. Seemingly, most of my military experience has been defeat, but never final defeat. I live to fight another day. Muskets have fired at me on many occasions, yet I have never been scathed. My clothing shows the effect, but my skin has yet to suffer anything serious. This defies logic. I saw miracles on Dorchester Heights. I saw mighty miracles in retreating from Brooklyn — that the wind would change, that the fog would come and leave only after we were safely out-of-range, that the British did not push their advantage when they had us hemmed in, that the assassin's plot was found and foiled while in New York. All these things are noted miraculous blessings.

Monday, September 2, 1776 — New York

Though I have faced a setback, our Nation still trusts me. Our men are dispirited. They are apprehensive at best and in despair at worst. The militia continues to dwindle. Our army is not treated fairly when pay and commitment are measured against each other. The militia only adds to their dismay. We must do something to buoy our troops and to fill our ranks. Ten dollars to sign up is insubstantial. The militias are undependable. They come with requirements and exemptions that make organizing them for a thrust virtually impossible. Perhaps adding land as a reward for the regular army is the biggest incentive we can devise. A retirement pay after the war could also assist to encourage them. I am not sure what the answer is. I know our countrymen fear a standing army. Without one, I fear the independence of our Nation will be lost.

Tuesday, September 3, 1776 — New York

I am ordering Brigadier-General Mercer to set up a strong encampment on the Jersey side of the North river. He is to detach a force from Amboy, along with an officer and an engineer to lay out the works to make the ground defensible. He will need to gather a considerable quantity of provisions for the support of the camp.

Wednesday, September 4, 1776 — New York

A forty-gun ship passed up the Sound between Governor's Island and Long Island and anchored at Turtle Bay. We fired our cannons at her as she passed, but to no significant damage. Yesterday, I sent Major Crane of the artillery with a twelve-pounder and a howitzer to fire on her. The ship eventually moved behind an island for safety. Seemingly, no real damage was done to her.

Our communication up-river is cut off. I feel obliged to abandon this place. I made a promise that we had no intentions to burn New York though it grates me that the enemy could winter here in comfort and luxury. Though a strategic thought to burn it, Congress agrees with me that we should not. I say, "agrees with me." Congress is certain. I am not as I once was.

The enemy is moving closer and may be making a move up the Sound near Kingsbridge to hem in our army. General Sullivan has sent a letter saying that General Howe is agreeable to exchange him for our prisoner General Prescott. I would like to send them General McDonald for Lord Stirling as well.

Our money is nonexistent. The militia wants to be paid before they leave. Part of me would like them to leave and receive pay from the State governments from which they came. This would be easier, but it would bode better if they receive their pay from me here so that they will be more willing to return the next time. Our regular army would like to be paid too, as they are two months in arrears. Complaining ensues every day about pay. I wish Congress to supply us with compensation necessary to satisfy those who are sacrificing so much in this effort.

Friday, September 6, 1776 — New York

My officers have been sharing with me the wisdom and foolishness of seeking to defend New York. After conferring, General Greene gives a rational argument for abandoning this station. He agrees with me that our army is spread too thin over several posts. We are unsure at this point how many men are still with us. We also fear that the current scatter of the men makes it easier to cut us off and defeat us. Beyond that, the British have command of the waterways and our position here feeds to their strength. Drawing them farther into the country, away from their naval strength would seem to be the better option. Besides, two-thirds of this area is comprised of Tories. We are, in essence, sitting in enemy land. This area could easily be called New Britain given the enemies we are surrounded by here. Truly, great exposure exists for our cause if we remain to defend what may not be defendable. I am calling for a council of the officers on the morrow at the latest to decide the next step.

Saturday, September 7, 1776 — New York

I am now headquartered at the Mortier house north of the city. The council of officers met with me, but were greatly divided on what strategy we should take. I fear many of them are losing their confidence in me, based on some of their argumentative stances and multiple references to General Lee. As much as some view our defeat on Long Island a failure — more specifically, mine, I see some benefit from our activities there. We pulled the entire British force to one point of aggression. We have spared other parts and delayed whatever plans they had to move deeper into the continent. Our actions have also enabled us to know more how to plan. Where weeks ago, all that could be done was to guess what options were available to the enemy and prepare for all of them, now the enemy is stationed and a minimal of strategies at their disposal can be debated.

In the council meeting, a few called for complete withdrawal from all the island of New York with the sentiment again that the city be burned to the ground. However, with Congress's orders, this is out of the question. I expect my officers to respect the chain of command. They answer to me. I answer to Congress. Congress is to answer to the people. That is true in letter, but I am not sure the spirit of the thing is followed. It makes me look weak to some, but I will set the example and obey. With great reasonings to do otherwise, I have chosen to side with the majority for the time being and defend this plot of ground.

Sunday, September 8, 1776 — New York

The duty of the day is to write Congress the consensus from our council meeting on how and where to proceed in this war. The British have effectually sealed off our front. They are free then to hem our army from behind cutting off our communications, our supplies of stores and men, not to mention our means of escape if this is their preference. I have no confidence in the will of our troops to engage an enemy so large and well-armed after Long Island's retreat. I have a doubt as to the ability of our young and newly acquired men to fight a well-trained experienced foe. The situation would seem untenable by all accounts. Every other option at our disposal is fraught with manifold difficulties. As a result, taking a defensive stance at this instant and force the enemy to come to our position may be our best option to reduce their numbers. Bunker Hill continues to be a chapter in our minds for optimism, raising questions in the British minds. I will say a wise move by the British would be to surpass the bulk of our army, run roughshod in every corner of our Nation taking control of everything but this little ground where we are fortified. This makes sense, but with winter coming, I do not believe the British soldiers are willing to give up the comforts to which they are so accustomed. They would also not want to afford this army these luxuries in their place.

With these factors and the opinion of our officers, I am seeking a moderate approach. We will not completely abandon this city, but we will not put the whole of our force in it, nor exercise the full measure for its defense. The decision has been made to place five thousand of our men in this city. I am pulling out of the city all stores and ammunition except what is necessary to defend it. This robs the enemy of the chance to grab our supplies and use them against this army. Nine thousand troops are being placed at Kingsbridge. Our post at Kingsbridge is strong, high, and can be made even more an advantage. The enemy is moving eastward on Long Island to usward, so I am assigning the remainder of our troops between here and there to welcome the enemy and thwart their attack. I am thinking toward the winter. We have no winter clothes. Our tents are ragged. Our sick number one-fourth of our total at this instant. I am having them moved to Orangetown.

Congress is determined that the city of New York be kept at all costs. What they do not realize is that the cost may be our defeat and the reestablishment of Great Britain's flag. From an objective standpoint, the question is not will the British take the city, but rather when? The goal then for this army is to delay that habitation if possible. This is jeopardized by the number of our own troops retreating to their homes. In a lesser state of duty, I can understand. Our men are owed pay. They have little food. The enemy has money flowing daily across the Atlantic by ship, along with supplies and food. Even where they camp, the Long Island farms are giving them a buffet of choices and delicacies.

Monday, September 9, 1776 — New York

The good news in all of what I have written in ultima is that there are still patriots seeking to aid our cause. Governor Trumbull answers my every request as quickly and as ably as he can. He has dispatched the remaining regiments of his militia to New York with all expedition. Would that Governor Trumbull would take a seat in Congress, but then this army would lack a ready friend in Connecticut. I write that, but if men with the response of Trumbull were there, the Continental forces might not be so dependent upon one State.

I am requesting that the Governor not send his horses and men directly to this city, but rather keep them close to the Sound and in West Chester County. The enemy is expanding their encampments up the island. The presence of the Connecticut militia will give the enemy a second thought of attack if they are even remotely impressed with the deception that numbers of fighting men are pouring in from all over the Nation. Having the militia there too with their horses will enable them more rapidly to attack readily in any quadrant. The other reason for stationing them there is an issue that I am hesitant to express to my dear friend, the Governor. Militia, his included, tend to exempt themselves from the rigors of discipline required for a standing army. Such disorder and disobedience breed a virus that easily spreads throughout the army bringing complaints, divisions, disrespect, and rancor.

One other initiative from Governor Trumbull that I welcome but with modification. He is planning to put together a naval force to address and clear the enemy's ships on the Sound. If Commodore Hopkins joins in the efforts, I believe they will find great success. My modification is that the Governor wishes to man the naval effort with men from the Continental regiments. This is impossible. Our numbers are already low. These men are not trained for such service. He will do better to field this sea force by his militia or other men more familiar with the seas.

Wednesday, September 11, 1776 — New York

General Greene and six of our general officers have conveyed a letter to me which they have all signed. The British are on the move and have occupied Montresor's Island east of Long Island. They have occupied that island at the mouth of the Hudson river. My war council feels it is imperative that we abandon New York post haste if we are to salvage this war for independence. I am requesting a meeting with them early Thursday to investigate further their reasonings and suggested alternatives. In the council of many, is found wisdom.

Thursday, September 12, 1776 — New York

After a meeting of the utmost respect and open dialogue, we are of the same mind that we must abandon this city. The plans laid are for most of our men to travel north of Kingsbridge, while four thousand men under General Putnam stay behind to muster resistance against British efforts. A strategy to move munitions, arms, and supplies was put in place. Anticipating this a few days ago, I had sent a priority note to Congress to apprise them of the realities on the ground. I am hoping they see the need and approve of our officers' resolve reached today. Congress has neglected to act on first and secondhand knowledge of our situation, but I am hopeful they will trust the judgment of those who sit currently in the gun sights of the enemy.

Friday, September 13, 1776 — New York

We feel a noose tightening around our present position. This afternoon, four of the king's ships of war and two of his twenty-eight guns went up the East river and anchored above the city. This would reinforce my belief that the enemy desires to hem us in.

Saturday, September 14, 1776 — New York

I am gratified to find in their letter received today that Congress is trusting my judgment on the moves of this army. They have agreed to follow my lead in evacuating the city of New York. I have great anxiety as the enemy movements further solidify our belief that their plan is to cut off our means of escape. This I fear will occur in the next day or so, perhaps even tonight. Our stores are so great and numerous, no chance presents to move them all out of the enemy's reach unless they delay their attack. I cannot hope for this but can certainly pray. Moving our sick is a hefty task that endangers our every move and hinders our every plan. That be as it may, I will do all within my power to move them out of harm's way if only I can find some convenient place for their reception.

This evening, six more of the enemy's ships (including two men-of-war) have passed between Governor's Island and Red Hook, moving up the East river to take anchor near the six that arrived Friday. I have received one dispatch from Colonel Sargent informing me that the enemy has three or four thousand men by the river ready to sail to some location of assault. Another dispatch has been received from General Mifflin today relaying activity from his vantage point of uncommon and formidable movements poised for aggression. The water is boiling. I am at a loss as to where to set up for defense. I proceeded to Harlem to gain some insight, but nothing remarkable has happened yet. Our troops, stores, and sick are being moved in the interim.

Sunday, September 15, 1776 — Headquarters at Colonel Morris's House, New York

Three more ships of war came up the North river early this morning, suspending the movement of our troops, supplies, and infirmed. At eleven o'clock, they began to pound our grounds with heavy cannonade. Their troops began to land under their cover of fire between Turtle Bay and the city. We have thrown up breast-works to oppose them. I am riding out with all possible dispatch to the enemy's landing locale. We will attempt to push them back. I am hopeful that the main of our army and the total of our supplies and sick can be moved while we cover their retreat.

Monday, September 16, 1776 — Headquarters at Colonel Morris's House, New York

I write this entry early this morning as sleep has completely eluded me. I am found in great affliction. I rode with urgency in the hope of emboldening my men for-tified at Kip's Bay for our defense. I did not even get near our lines, but found the men fleeing with the utmost precipitation. Not only were they running, but the troops I sent to support them were retreating in great confusion as well. Our own guns and cartridges were discarded. Their knapsacks and hats were scattered on the ground. I found not one dead soldier of ours to rationalize a retreat, and only a small number of British in unified pursuit. I was reminded of the Lord's warning that when a nation is disobedient, one of an enemy will cause a thousand to flee. In a righteous contest, I find it unacceptable that the righteous would be the ones fleeing. I fell into a rage! Is this the soldiery with whom I must defend this Nation and secure our freedom? I found myself fighting — not the British, but my own men. My cocked gun pointed at my own troops, my whip flailing their backs. It did no good. They ran from me as from the British. I stopped just yards from the approaching enemy, all alone. I had told the men I would fight with every breath, that I would fight as long as I had just one arm or one leg remaining. The British marched slowly toward me as if savoring the moment. This was a stand I intended to make. I said I would die for my country and, at the heart of an army's coward-ice, perhaps I thought my death might help them rediscover their courage. As the enemy closed within seventy yards, I softly spurred my horse with my feet in the stirrups and began the gallop toward them — one hand on my pistol and another on my whip, reins hanging down. Just as I swallowed, one of my aides rode up, grabbed my reins, and pulled me away. Uncharacteristically, I cursed him. Sympathetically, he understood. I acquiesced to his leading.

We have lost many of our supplies unnecessarily because of the disgraceful conduct of our men, but their cowardice brought little loss of life. By Providence's Hand, General Putnam and the main of our army has arrived. We are now stationed on the Heights of Harlem this morning. Perhaps the enemy will seek to dislodge us here. With a semblance of courage, we can thwart them. Perhaps our men can show themselves worthy of the blessings of freedom. I am not putting my hopes in that at this moment.

Tuesday, September 17, 1776 — Headquarters at Colonel Morris's House, New York

From the depths of Kip's Bay to the heights of Harlem. I did not imagine in my mind that I could see such a turn of events, nor a sign of life in this Continental collection for defense. I am quartered in the Morris home atop Harlem Heights. My vantage point from here gives me a unique view of things and a reference point for our troops wherever they go. There is a knowledge of where I am. I am given a strategic view of where they are.

Yesterday morning, it was here at this desk that some came to tell me the British were advancing toward us with a small party led by a bugler hitting the notes of a fox hunt. How arrogant how they be! I want our troops to remember this consequence following the cowardice at Kip's Bay. We were no longer seen as an army to be feared, but as game, a common trophy from a side-recreation to be hunted. They were taunting us, thinking we will continue to run until we are treed.

I sent out some of Lieutenant-Colonel Knowlton's Connecticut rangers to investigate while I rode down to ensure our advanced posts were in a state of readiness. I then heard fire from the direction of Lieutenant-Colonel Knowlton's men. Our men at the front stood their ground. They returned fire even though outnumbered four to one. Eventually overpowered, our men fell back. I immediately sent three companies from Virginia's regiment under the command of Major

Leitch and Colonel Knowlton. I ordered some of them slowly to station themselves unseen behind the enemy, while a contingent met them head-on with the
hope that we could squeeze them in between. I added reinforcements. The British
began to retreat downhill in the exact direction of our men that I had sent to
entrap them. Sadly, our men fired too early before they could get successfully
behind them. The fighting grew with our side and theirs, adding men to assist. I
was delighted to see our men fighting back. Even those who had fled at Kip's Bay
engaged with a newfound courage. This was the spirit that started this war for
independence. Lexington and Concord cross my mind. These were brave men
knowing they were outnumbered, but refusing to back down. This is the resolve
we need. It is the resolve that I saw again yesterday. If only it would not show its
head and then disappear so frequently.

After a few hours, our men prevailed. The bugler and his hunting party began
to run from the hunted fox. Shouting and excitement ensued. Our men had found
their footing. It is hard to imagine that just two days ago, I could not keep these
men from fleeing. Yesterday, I found it hard to keep them from attacking.

I was greatly worried this was a ruse of the enemy to draw us into an ambush,
so I sternly called on our officers to rein in their men and return them to safety.
They did.

Our losses were small in quantity, but great in quality. We lost Lieutenant-
Colonel Knowlton with Major Leitch wounded. I am proud to note this here,
that a British deserter reports that our adversary yesterday was far greater than a
scouting company. He relays that our men engaged their second battalion of light
infantry, a battalion of their Royal Highlanders, and three Hessian companies of
riflemen. I estimate they lost around one hundred eighty men while we are looking at thirty. What a relief to see a fight and an encouraging blow to our enemy.
May we not forget it, nor the British.

Friday, September 20, 1776 — Headquarters at Colonel Morris's House, New York

I am again writing Congress to generate some solution to the fact that the enlistments of many of our men are about to end. This order of affairs renders our army
weak and our officers melancholy. They no sooner get a batch of raw materials

called men into a fighting orderly organization called an army, just to see them leave. Then the process must start all over again. All this goes on in the harrowing view of an enemy who outnumbers and outguns this one even at our greatest strength. Congress must act with expediency to remedy this. It is too much for the officers. It is (confided in my diary alone) too much for me.

It seems easier to complain and place blame after a victory. In the throes of defeat, I blame myself. In the splashes of success, I fault others. Both are excessive. Yet, I must judge myself, and others themselves. The public papers' reports are nearly true. Their inaccuracies of our outcomes, perhaps purposeful, temper our victories and exaggerate our losses, all the while deprecating my judgement.

Saturday, September 21, 1776 — Headquarters at Colonel Morris's House, New York

When the British fell back into New York after their routing of our forces from Kip's Bay, one deserter stated the citizens of New York welcomed them with open arms and cheers, that they carried the British soldiers on their shoulders, and pulled down the flag of our declared independent Nation. I dare to conjecture in my mind that our own citizenry has welcomed the poisonous viper into their midst and the rabid dog under their family table. News from last night lays credence to my claim. New York city caught fire last night. My understanding is that homes, churches, businesses, warehouses, wharves, and even Tory mansions were burned to the ground. Our own soldiery vowed not to burn it. Congress ordered we restrain such as well. So, why was so much of New York burned? Could it be the friends of Britain who have been our neighbors and betrayers have found not so appreciative a guest? Could it be our patriots left behind sacrificed their own city? Or did Providence have His Say? When I heard that the problematic area called "Holy Ground" had been burned to the ground too, it made me think perhaps the latter option was the Culprit.

Sunday, September 22, 1776 — Heights of Harlem

It has been a busy few days while the action has lulled. The enemy realizes the strength of our position on the Heights of Harlem. They are making strategic moves in their attempt to dislodge us while reducing the risk to their own numbers. They feel that they have the fox treed. They are moving cannons toward our location and bringing ships I believe up the Hudson behind us. We have placed obstructions in the river to thwart their navigation. They have upward of twenty-five thousand troops. As best as I can surmise, we have at most twelve or fourteen thousand fit for duty. I have taken time to write my dear brother. Next to this journal, he is one of a handful that I can share my deepest thoughts and woes. I put on paper to him what I have been thinking of late. I am overwhelmed and words cannot describe what I feel, nor what I face. If I had to do this all over again, knowing what I do, fifty thousand pounds could not induce me to undergo what I have. On this Lord's Day, I pray for things to change. I made a commitment. I will see it through. I would that others do the same. How this would lessen my grief and stress.

Monday, September 23, 1776 — Heights of Harlem

I do not believe I have a better opportunity to show the love of the Savior than in how I deal with the enemy in honesty and courtesy, keeping with every exercise of humanity. I give my promise to General Howe. I trust in his word given to me. I expect the British prisoners we hold to be treated well based on their behavior. I have equal expectations that they will treat our men which they hold with civility. To find ourselves fighting with the Nation to whom we once pledged allegiance and enter a conflict with men we once served beside is an unhappy contest. Freedom is what we desire. Great Britain has chosen a different path for us, one that we refuse to travel. The friend has become an enemy who seeks to force his will against ours. May this war end soon and to our favor. Providence determines what the end will be, so we seek His Favor above all.

Tuesday, September 24, 1776 — Heights of Harlem

I sometimes think I can pen eloquently what I feel and see. I read back over my old diaries and still am bewildered at just the raw information. No personality, no feelings, no insights. I then look at what I have penned since the onset of this conflict. Am I becoming too emotional? Provided I come out of this alive and we come out of this independent, I wonder if I will look back at this diary and feel ashamed of my complaints and unmanly whining. I may. But for now, this permits my fears, feelings, betrayals, discouragements, and hopes to be vented. By writing these things down, I am putting out a measurement — like a mark on a doorpost to see how tall a child is getting, or like a line drawn on a stick to see how high the water is rising. I like to think of this as a notation of my hopes, yearnings, and more than anything prayers. I pray to look back and see where I was and what God did to deliver me. There could be no higher praise for Him, the Disposer of all circumstances, than to see the record of all He has done. Looking back and perhaps even sharing this with others, may bring a certainty that there is a God in Heaven who reveals mysteries.

I am exerting my utmost to hold this army together. Enlistments are coming due. The men see no immediate gratification for their efforts — no real appreciation from their countrymen, no supplies and arms for their fight, no timely pay for their sacrifices, and no fair compensation for a long-term commitment. Others simply show up when they want, make some extra money, and return to the comfort of their domiciles when suffering ensues. If Congress does not remedy these deficiencies, this cause and this war is lost.

I have received a dispatch just now from General Howe concerning the exchange of prisoners. He writes as if he has done all things Christian concerning those of ours under his charge. Yet his very aide who bears his letter, not knowing what is in it, tells a different story. The fire of New York a few days ago has been blamed on several of our countrymen. They have been summarily punished, beaten, burned, and hung. None were given a trial. None were allowed to speak with a minister before their execution. All were refused a Bible. Everything good and true and right was denied. Do we serve the same God? Do we read the same Bible? Do we have the same ethic? It appears not.

I was greatly saddened at this news and the news that young Captain Hale was hung as a spy. He too was denied all charity and civility. Yet, it is my understanding that the final words of this young patriot were, "I only regret that I have but one life to lose for my country." I am informed that a board with a rebel soldier painted on it was brought to the execution. They supposedly wrote my name upon it and hung that semblance on a rope next to the captain. I am moved to tears by the depth of commitment and resolve that beat in the heart of one so young. May these words, and more this sentiment, be carried in the heart of every man and every woman in this country. I would hope that if my time arrives as his, that I will be as bold and resolute to utter the same words, even if I am not permitted to say goodbye to Mrs. Washington, John Augustine, Lund, and others so dear to me. I do not fear worthy to hang next to such a man as Captain Hale, but I know there is a cause worth fighting for and there is a purpose worth dying for. We are in it.

Wednesday, September 25, 1776 — Heights of Harlem

Men are deserting. Soldiers are disobeying. Troops are leaving in coveys. It is one thing to quit for one's own cowardice or rationalized reasons, but what they do not see is the effect they have on the remainder. For men to run off and leave in the cover of night is better than to announce broadly beforehand that they are leaving and state the reasons why. Disheartenment, defeat, and enjoining the deserters is followed by many others. The ship seems to be sinking. I may be the only one left on it. My needed aide, whom I spent so many months coercing to rejoin me, is feeling the same resignation. I had not written what happened on the 19th for hopes it was a rare occurrence of the most villainous of acts. Some things I dare not write — the sound of a man dying, the thud of a ball penetrating a man's side, the carnage a cannonball wreaks on a man's body. The other I seldom write is the offense of a man in full-scale desertion. Such was Reed's experience a few days back. In the heat of battle, Private Leffingwell began to run from the enemy. Reed pursued him and ordered his return to the fray. Instead of obeying his superior, he drew his gun to kill Reed. The hammer clicked but the gun did not fire. In a rage, Reed aimed his gun and pulled the trigger to the same effect. Providence must have been at the helm. Soon after, this army court-martialed Leffingwell with the sentence of death. As he knelt and confessed his cowardice, ready to accept the punishment, Reed showed the mercy I had not expected. He begged me for Leffingwell's pardon. I granted it but charged that the next offender would be killed without mercy. It is easy to say, hard to do, but necessary if order under enemy fire is to be maintained. I have carried it out on many occasions and will again.

I have hastily sent off a letter to Congress that may conclude my time as general of this army. In my mind, there is no way to hold this army together under the current system. As much as I respect Congress and faithfully carry out its orders, no substitute exists for being here on the ground and in the action. What Congress does not realize is that men will gladly engage at the moment of patriotism or in response to tyrannical actions. Joining this war is an impulse most cannot ignore. However, after the moment of initial encounter is over, there is a reframing of position, a measuring the cost that often reduces the sacrifice one is willing to expend. This makes my duty to hold, train, and meld a group of individuals into an army a Herculean task. This may sound as written in my defense, but it is a truth that any who seek to take my place will find. Our army of men have families back home who suffer in their absences. They have mouths to feed, bills to pay, relationships to grow, and loved ones to whom they long to return. To hold an army from all that, requires reward of the most basic expectations — clothing, shelter, weapons, powder, and pay. Congress must realize that these men are making investments in freedom that are unmatched by any other on this continent. Yes, they are doing it for the freedom of a nation, but what good is a free nation to many if they do not survive or at least have a fair opportunity to live and enjoy it? They are willing to die if they are equipped to fight. They are willing to stay if given the inducements to do so. I am asking Congress to give them payment in arrears with an advance, give bonuses for recruitment, give a suit of clothes, a blanket, and acreage at the war's end for every soldier who completes this noble task.

Still, without such provisions, enlistments are endurable if for a short time to those who come. Turn-over at the end of each period and the retraining puts this whole independence question at risk. Again, dependence on militia is unsatisfactory as there is no order, no accepting of orders, and constant claims of exemptions which lead to infighting and insubordination. Many go out into the communities which we have sworn to defend; they rob families and burn people's homes to cover up their unlawful acts. Like a dog who has the taste of a chicken, these men plunder the defenseless and gain the taste for more. I must constantly be on alert. I am the ever-present and, often, only punisher. There must be one army paid for and equipped. Moving Mount Atlas would be easier than to win this war with such men in the current circumstances.

Adequate and ample pay must also be provided for regimental surgeons. At the present, these are not being paid for their expertise. It has drawn out the scoundrel in many. Care is being given at a price. They are giving exemptions, furloughs, and health discharges for bribes. Many men are willing to pay a financial price to leave this foray rather than pay the physical and personal price for freedom. These surgeons are also using the stores and medicine liberally for their own proffer and, I fear, addictions. I must put up with such when our government is not willing to pay medical men with integrity. I must be up front with Congress on these matters and give them the bitter truth. Prayerfully, this will bring remedy or remove me from this torment.

Thursday, September 26, 1776 — Heights of Harlem

My focus has been inward the past few days, but an enemy is present below these Heights of Harlem. That enemy must receive my attention. We have no idea what blow the British seek to strike first. If they pursue us up here, they should leave with great loss of men. Knowing that they have this army treed, they could presume to make a move on Philadelphia, leaving just two thousand of their men in New York to keep us in check. I am sad to write, they could maintain that city against the whole of our army with few men. I need intelligence on any of their movements on land and sea.

Saturday, September 28, 1776 — Heights of Harlem

There are those who are soldiers and there are those who are willing to fight. Sadly, they are not one in the same. There is one though whose return from British hands I desire — Captain Daniel Morgan. He is intrepid in assault and inflexible in his attachment to our cause. If ever a man deserved promotion, it is Captain Morgan. I am asking Congress to promote him, but as he is in the hands of the British now, any prisoner exchange will be made easier if he is reported to be a captain at this moment. We have captains of theirs to exchange for him, but few above that rank.

Sunday, September 29, 1776 — Heights of Harlem

On this Lord's Day, I take rest and pray though I find that in my rest I worry still.

Monday, September 30, 1776 — Heights of Harlem

I am ordering General Lincoln and General Clinton to form a party to cross the Sound to destroy grain and arms that were left in our retreat of Long Island. They cannot fall into the British hands providing succor for them. Dispatch and secrecy along with sufficient men will be the key to Lincoln and Clinton's success. I look forward to a good report.

Wednesday, October 2, 1776 — Heights of Harlem

The British enemy is both smart and discerning. Rather than fight for their cause with their men, they recruit our own countrymen to advance their cause. Just now, it has come to my attention that some men from Westchester and Duchess counties are on the move to join the King's army. Such parricides! I have ordered our men to be on the lookout in hopes to intercept them at the North river and at the East river. If they make their pathway through the Sound, we have little hope of catching them.

Friday, October 4, 1776 — Heights of Harlem

It is with gratitude for some leniency that I received a letter from Congress allowing for a twenty-dollar bonus and one hundred acres of land for men who endure to the war's completion. What Congress does not understand, I perceive, is that they see this army as mine. They need to see this army as theirs under my command. They need to see that their affairs are unpromising if they do not act with vigorous exertions to fortify this body. They seek to conciliate me by saying they have voted to raise a larger army. What they do not see is a difference exists between voting battalions and raising men. Its execution falls to me and without proper provision, any efforts exerted will fail. In all this, they do not see that any setbacks in this campaign will energize the enemy in their recruitments, adding insult to injury, further reducing our chances of success. I will be writing them another letter. I would imagine that Congress will grow weary of my complaints and suggestions. In writing them, I feel the ability to explain better our needs covering options and consequences. In writing them, I feel too that I am carrying out the trust Congress and our country have reposed to me.

Saturday, October 5, 1776 — Heights of Harlem

It is with great gratification that I received a letter from the newly appointed governor of Virginia, my friend Patrick Henry. His letter and his bold character buoys my hopes. He has written to convey his best. He also has inquired how best to solidify the defense of our fair State. I have recommended to him not to rely on our army for his defense. We are spread too thin. We are poorly supplied to be of much assistance other than seeking to keep the British at bay in this quadrant. He may rely on his militia for immediate threats, as the ebb-and-flow of trouble are best met effectively by these. I have also given him guidance on how to buttress his defenses along the riverways and shores under his care. Batteries and obstructions have not proven to be effective against the enemy's movements along the river but can be a deterrent and delay tactics on their shores near their batteries. To his question of promoting and recruiting of officers, experience has shown that men will not subordinate to officers whose honor and position are undeserved. Those best to promote are those who have gained recognition and reputation in private life. This tends to transfer amiably into military life.

In negotiating the exchange of prisoners with the British, they are desirous to convey our men captured on Long Island in equal number for the men of theirs whom we have in our care. This is agreeable to me, but my concern is that our men captured in Quebec have been forgotten. They have been imprisoned longer than those in Long Island and have suffered no less injury. I am somewhat disconcerted as to why General Arnold sought to work this out, assuming an authority that does not belong to him. As the one who is in chief command of this army of the States, I would that General Arnold confer with this station, submitting to the authority who bears the burden of all outcomes.

Monday, October 7, 1776 — Heights of Harlem

It is encouraging to receive a letter today from Monsieur Penet. His attachment to our cause has aided this army in a multitude of ways. He is working here diligently to provide needed supplies and is confident he can provide them in great quantities. He believes he will have an easier time assisting us if he is allowed the title of my aide-de-camp, uniformed as an officer in this army. I am agreeable to his request. I am hoping that Congress will concur in sentiment.

We are blessed with many French gentlemen seeking to render service to our cause. The commissions which they hold upon entry into this army makes it difficult to place them. They seek to command men, yet lack the ability to communicate to their subordinates because of their inability to speak our language. This brings added frustration to my shoulders, placing them in an irksome situation as well. These genteel and sensible men have value I am sure, but until they learn the language, it is better no others are sent to my care. I must convey the same to Congress.

Tuesday, October 8, 1776 — Heights of Harlem

I am still overseeing negotiations for prisoner exchanges. What has been a pleasant surprise for me is that a few British prisoners wish to stay with us. Our enemy is aware of the names and ranks of the prisoners that we now hold. To hold some back or to not deliver the ones on their list may affect the return of some of our men. As a result, we are advising the prisoners who seek to stay with us and fight for our cause, to go along with the exchange. They can then escape back to us later. It would be a benefit to us. Perhaps they might be successful in bringing other like-minded friends with them. To see that the American thirst for freedom is being felt by those on the other side is uplifting. We were British once upon a time ourselves.

Wednesday, October 9, 1776 — Heights of Harlem

This morning, activity was engaged against two enemy ships and a frigate of twenty guns proceeding up the Hudson river. Their purpose is unsure, but it is surmised that their intent is to close off navigation and block our supplies. I had hoped that our chevaux-de-frise and batteries would have stopped their movement or at least injure their vessels. To our mortification, our work was ineffective. The enemy sailed by with the least difficulty. I am notifying all affected parties.

Sunday, October 12, 1776 — Heights of Harlem

Sunday worship was interrupted as dispatch reached me relaying that the enemy has landed at Frog's Point up the Sound, about nine miles from this locale. We have not ascertained the number of their men, but it may be a large proportion of their whole. In keeping with my belief that the British seek to get in our rear and put us in a vice, I have ordered works to be thrown up at the passes in that direction.

Witnesses have reported a great number of sloops, schooners, and nine ships went up the Sound this evening with many enemy soldiers. We do have the advantage. Frog's Point is strong and defensible. It has many stone fences, which provide cover for our response and bring obstacles for their movement.

I have sent two regiments of militia from Massachusetts to watch the ships which have not passed us and to oppose any landing of men. At this time, with my men few and scattered in this guessing game of conflict points, I am moving as many of my men as possible to East and West Chester to oppose the enemy. I hope they will be able to prevent the effecting of their plan.

Tuesday, October 14, 1776 — Heights of Harlem

Today has been a day of good returns. In all our haggling over prisoner exchanges, this army received a bump in confidence when Lord Stirling and General Sullivan were returned. Never had I been so glad to see two men. Never has there been a better time to see them.

To bolster this good news, General Charles Lee arrived, dogs in tow. My position does not seem so lonely when there is a true second-in-command. Though he is hot-tempered and ambitious, he does have a string of successes. The men also seem emboldened by his presence. To show Lee my appreciation, I have ordered that Fort Constitution be renamed Fort Lee. General Lee seems very appreciative.

Wednesday, October 16, 1776 — Heights of Harlem

With the British forces growing north of us and a realization that the Heights of Harlem are more vulnerable than I am comfortable, I called for a council of war with my officers — General Lee, Lord Stirling, General Health, General Sullivan, General Mifflin, General Clinton, and Colonel Knox. It was decided by all except General Clinton that we should evacuate all of York Island, leaving just a thousand men to hold Fort Washington as long as possible. This truly was an alteration to our plans, but one that proves necessary. Movement is to begin in earnest in one day, not more than two.

Thursday, October 17, 1776

Unity in this army is greatly appreciated. Our men began their move after lunch today. They seem more confident. If pride were my thorn, I would hesitate to write this, but I believe having Lord Stirling and General Lee in the fold brings a oneness. They also remove discouragement were I alone leading the move. The men seem to believe that if these two generals are involved, then a brilliant strategy to the move must exist. For this I celebrate.

Movement is slow with our sick being our chief burden, but they are a burden we willfully bear. We have crossed King's Bridge and are heading north along the Bronx river.

Saturday, October 19, 1776

The confidence that I sense from our men was confirmed in a message from General Glover who raced to oppose an incursion by the British at Pell's Point. He reports some two hundred ships on the move. General Howe seemingly landed four thousand or more troops at Throg's Neck. Thankfully, General Glover was on the alert. He sent seven hundred and fifty of his men to slow their assault. Our men were reported to have fought with fervor behind walls and trees hitting the enemy. They then would fall back behind more stone walls, firing again. This went on for a day before the enemy, having been inflicted with heavy casualties, retreated to regroup. I am now hastening to get our main army to White Plains. My prayer is that Howe moves with great trepidation, fearing our men are behind every wall.

To receive dispatch this evening informing of the destruction of General Arnold's fleet on Lake Champlain was disappointing. My consolation is that General Arnold was able to escape with the bulk of his men and slowed the British somewhat. General Arnold takes it to the enemy. This is what is needed so long as it is done wisely with losses minimized. For Arnold to take on such a fleet of British with a makeshift one, manned by novice seamen, is a testament to his tenacity. Congress has questioned his integrity and disbursements of public funds. I have seen no reason to question him myself. We are so poorly funded. I am not certain there is any to mismanage. I may have placed my officers in a tough situation as I keep Congress abreast of the army's expenditures under my command. They may expect that from every officer in the field. That is a fine expectation except when one is in the throes of war. Accounting must necessarily be delayed until the fury has passed.

Tuesday, October 22, 1776 — Valentine's Hill, New York

I received a return from General Schuyler requesting my peremptory orders regarding the next move of the army under him. My understanding from General Arnold is that General Schuyler has approximately nine thousand effective men at his disposal. I get the impression from Schuyler that this number is inflated. Nonetheless, I have no good foundation on which to render an order or an opinion as to what he should do next or where best to shelter for the winter. As a general who is a willing subordinate, yet prone to resign in the flurry of frustrations, I am suggesting he find haven at Ticonderoga. This garrison when supplied is almost impregnable to enemy attack. He will need to take steps to hasten the enemy's discomfort should the British lay siege. He should remove any carriages and draft-cattle from their access.

I have reason to believe General Arnold's recitation of the number of men at Schuyler's disposal may indeed be overstated. Every general thinks the other generals are faring better than they. Taking that into consideration, I am asking Schuyler to use the utmost discretion on the usage of militia to fortify his company. Militia in general waste stores. Their ability to submit to authority is in want. They breed dissension, division, and create more of a liability than an asset. This said, they are a necessary evil, good for the short-term and in the tyranny of necessity.

Thursday, October 24, 1776 — Valentine's Hill, New York

General Greene is stationed on Fort Lee. He is to hold it and Fort Washington as long as he is able. General Greene is an amazing man, never willing to let any hardship or obstacle stand in his way of success. He has shown grit his whole life. He joined this cause as a Quaker and was summarily read out of his congregation. He then was refused a commission because of a limp from an injury in his youth. This did not stop him. He chose to serve as a soldier. As such, he has risen in rank by his own merit. None has been charitably bestowed upon him. This is the reason I caution Congress not to choose officers by family or by favor, but rather by merit and hard work. Men like this take the hardships of battle without shrinking, willing to fight to a successful conclusion.

Monday, October 28, 1776

I am finding it more difficult to keep up with my daily log. We have been attempting to stay ahead of General Howe, his redcoats, and his added Hessian recruits. I am told their number far exceeds ten thousand. He is either trying to outflank us or he is seeking to move us into a confrontation in the open field. It is the same strategy they used in the previous war when we fought by their side against the French and the Indians. I am grateful to have fought alongside them. From that experience, I have gained an understanding of their strategy. The enemy has a trained well-equipped force. I fear we will be unable to withstand an all-out attack with our lesser-trained, poorly equipped army of men eyeing the fulfillment of their enlistment terms.

We are now dug in on high ground. If the enemy attacks, it may be to his detriment. We have the Bronx river to our left. Chatterton Hill is on our right. We have room for retreat to higher ground behind. I have militia stationed on Chatterton Hill, a small distance from our main army, which is necessary for good order. We wait.

Tuesday, October 29, 1776

The British dealt a blow to our position yesterday. Howe and his men attacked us in two columns. The redcoats' field guns exacted significant damage to our defenses. One column came directly at us, another column wheeled toward Chatterton Hill where our only defense was militia, which had no way of withstanding the thrust of a large enemy force. I ordered more men to the hill under Colonel Hasler and Colonel Smallwood. They did their best with the men they had, but ultimately, they were overpowered. We did not lose as many as the British by our count, but that may be because we retreated as quickly as we could to a half mile behind yesterday's initial line, across the Bronx river. Sometimes it seems the majority of our fighting is on the retreat. This may benefit our army in reducing the enemy's numbers and frustrating the British who are far from their homes and discouraged by the absence of the decisive blow they seek. My men tend to the same mindset as their general. A longing exists to engage, to move forward, to take the fight to the enemy, but circumstances prevent that. I pray that changes soon. Our men are digging in for the next affront.

Wednesday, October 30, 1776

The enemy has been on pause. I am not sure of their strategy or the reasoning behind their delay. I am certain they cannot attack this day. It is raining so heavily that movement is impossible.

Thursday, October 31, 1776

The heavy rain subsided late last night.

Saturday, November 2, 1776

I have ordered preparations. This may be the place of a decisive stand. We wait. The enemy is watching us. We are watching them. I imagine to their mind, we are treed. In our mind, we are positioned and ready, even anxious.

Sunday, November 3, 1776

Reports this evening state the enemy is on the move. I have given orders to prepare for a night attack.

Tuesday, November 5, 1776

One can only be on alert for so long. As morning gave way, we found instead of the relief of action, the relief of absence. The British have moved away from our position. Scouts say they are moving in a southwest direction toward Kingsbridge and the North river.

Wednesday, November 6, 1776 — White Plains, New York

At our officers' council, we tried to discern what the enemy's plan might be. Some said they were discouraged by our strong position, unwilling to pay the price of attack. Others believed they were moving for Winter quarters with the desire to resume conflict in the Spring. I believe they are positioning for one more stroke before ending the season's battles. It may be Howe's intention to move on New Jersey and then to Philadelphia, which is my greater concern. I could also see the enemy make another effort to outflank us. A chance exists that they could be moving toward the southern States for a Winter campaign where the climate is more agreeable.

In times like these, I believe I come across indecisive to my men. They come to me looking for answers and walk away in the same quandary by which they came. When General Lee is conferred, he has a firm opinion and can give confident direction. His insights are compelling, but in the back of my mind, I believe his aggressive strategies would mean immediate defeat. My strategies may mean defeat too, albeit prolonged. The freedom of every American being at-stake causes me a hesitation I was never burdened with before. As a soldier, I would swing into action with only my life and my family's personal loss at stake. As General, countless lives, families, freedom; yea, even a nation is jeopardized.

I am attempting to engage this army in this instant as it will soon dissolve with enlistments expiring. Officers are unable to recruit because of time, preparation, and lack of financial incentive. Of all the things I must face in war, seeking to maintain an adequate force or at least the shadow of one is daunting. I am writing letters to plead with Congress and the surrounding States to fulfill their promises made to me when I entered this fray.

Thursday, November 7, 1776 — White Plains, New York

I have asked the council of Massachusetts to do what is always the last resort — send militia to us to shore up our deficiencies. General Lincoln is best at bringing such independent souls into a semblance of an army. The request is for at least four thousand this instant with the hopes they will stay engaged until March by which time a new army will have been recruited and trained. This is my earnest hope.

At the least, it appears the redcoats will invest Fort Washington. From there, it is believed General Howe will make incursions into the Jerseys on his way to New York. Thus far, he has shown little success in his endeavors. He may be called to account as his progress so far falls short of his reputation. Once it is probable that this is his design, men will be sent to counter and harass his movement. I am making Governor Livingston of New Jersey aware of this speculation. He will need to alert and station his militia to stand the gap until this army arrives to bolster their efforts. I have requested that the governor have his citizens who live contiguous to the waterways, move their grain, animals, carriages, and personal effects post haste. The enemy will take these from them without regard to their allegiance to supply the enemy's needs and rob our Nation's families if action is not taken. I also have asked the governor to have the barracks at Elizabethtown, Amboy, and Brunswick inspected prior to our arrival. They need to make any repairs necessary to house our men.

Friday, November 8, 1776 — White Plains, New York

Reports have been received that three British vessels have moved up the North river freely with no effect given by our blockade or defenses. I am not sure that it is wise to risk men or stores on Mount Washington. I am writing General Greene to inform him of my concern. He is free to defend or to evacuate based on what he sees and knows on the spot. General Greene will face an unpalatable decision. He must ensure that all supplies, grain, stores, and stock be removed before the enemy's arrival. Should the inhabitants hesitate, he is to destroy them himself. This will raise the ire of our citizenry, but what they do not comprehend is that if we do not destroy them, the enemy will use them. Our destruction of them is a one-time loss of supply and profit to the owners. The British confiscation is a multiple loss — loss of supply and profit, but also loss of freedom, liberty, the Nation, and their land itself.

Saturday, November 9, 1776 — White Plains, New York

Being prepared for every possible attack is a difficult task, but it is one for which I must address. I must divide the army into four. I am putting seven thousand troops under General Lee east of the Hudson to protect New England. I am sending three thousand under General Heath to Peekskill to guard any incursions there. I am taking two thousand with me over the North river toward the Jerseys. Thought ensues that this area will be the enemy's main target. The remaining army will stay with General Greene at Fort Washington and Fort Lee.

Sunday, November 10, 1776 — White Plains, New York

I met with one of Governor Trumbull's commissioners yesterday. At first, what he told me was an encouragement. Then, as he left my company, I realized the move by the commissioners to recruit men will be detrimental to our cause. Connecticut is offering to pay their men an extra twenty shillings per month in addition to what Congress has agreed to pay. True, the increase in pay will meet and possibly exceed their State's quota. However, once their troops arrive to join the main body and talk around the campfire devolves to pay, jealousy, impatience, and mutiny will follow. When news spreads, other States will have an effectual bar thrown against their ability to meet their individual quotas. Dissatisfaction will drive troops with less pay to desert. This army will likely then face dissolution. All night long, I have wrestled with this predicament. How can I address this without offending my friend Trumbull? How can I not discourage Connecticut from showing initiative when it seems I counter that assistance? I fear that objection will cause this fine State to sit back and wait for my command, bringing delay in the provision of our needs. Nonetheless, I will write Governor Trumbull. I pray that he understands. On this Sunday, "pray" is the operative word.

Monday, November 11, 1776 — Peekskill, New York

I am writing Congress. Aside from Connecticut, no real movement occurs in levying an army as enlistments are expiring. Reliance on militia is dissatisfactory but necessary. Unfortunately, their commitment to serve is even less likely to extend past their agreement. General Lincoln is doing his utmost to keep those from Massachusetts in attendance, but as best I can judge, his persuasion will not suffice. I am in hopes that Congress will assist in enlisting an army and perhaps bring Continental inducement to supplant Connecticut's and now Massachusetts's design at a State stimulus. Troops cannot act in a common cause at different pay. This is not my singular opinion but the concurrence of all the generals.

Wednesday, November 13, 1776 — General Greene's Quarters, New Jersey

It has been an arduous route of about sixty-five miles, but our troops have crossed the Hudson with me. I left Peekskill to General Heath. I have ordered him to secure the pass through the Highlands next to the river. I am unsure what the enemy is planning, but his sights seem to be on Fort Washington. Their direction at this instant is Kingsbridge. Their probable next campaign may be a southern expedition. I am quartering men at Brunswick, Amboy, Elizabethtown, Newark, and in this neighborhood from where I now reside. Congress may wish that I move more around Philadelphia. This may become a necessity for which I will gladfully oblige.

Thursday, November 14, 1776 — General Greene's Quarters, New Jersey

One concern I have voiced to Congress is the need we have for field artillery and men to man it. Experienced officers and a few capable engineers are vital for its effective usage. Too often, men of experience are promoted to positions where they are less engaged with their talents, leaving a void by the removal of those talents. I am asking Congress to consider this. My preference would be to promote capable men with rank and pay but leave them in the position of best utility for this effort.

Saturday, November 16, 1776 — General Greene's Quarters, New Jersey

I am saddened to note in my diary that we lost Fort Washington today. I fear two thousand of our men were lost too. Yesterday, General Howe demanded surrender of the fort to which Colonel Magaw gave a spirited refusal. Receiving an account of the situation, I began to cross the North river to gain an assessment of the situation. I was met halfway by Generals Greene and Putnam who assured me that the men were in high spirits and would make a good defense. Contented in this response, I returned to our station.

This morning, the British attacked Fort Washington from the south. Magow rallied his men to thwart the assault, just to find that a body of troops attacked a second line by crossing the Harlem river. Colonel Cadwalader sent a detachment to oppose them but to no avail. Meanwhile, Hessian forces advanced on the north side. Our men were outnumbered. Colonel Magow was unable to fend them off. With no prospect of retreat across the North river, he has surrendered his post. With little consolation, I am told the enemy suffered great loss in this endeavor, as reports of numbers and actual numbers greatly vary.

I am in anguish over this and am mortified at the entire situation. I did not feel Fort Washington was in a good position, but the Colonel had assured me that his position was strong and could withstand two months of any enemy attempts. I regret that I did not go with my better judgment. I shared my beliefs with General Greene and gave him the option to evacuate the post, but he chose to hold on, believing it important to satisfy the resolve of Congress. I regret that I gave discretion instead of giving an absolute order to withdraw. In addition, this defeat has aided the British in giving General Howe a respite. I believe General Howe is under pressure and ordered this stroke to pacify England whose citizens are complaining of the huge investment of men and treasure. They have little to show the king for their efforts. They see no end to the hostilities in sight.

Sunday, November 17, 1776 — General Greene's Quarters, New Jersey

On this Sabbath, I find myself locked in self-evaluation, confession, and voicing my worries to the Lord. What have I gotten into? I love this country. I value freedom. I entered this conflict because I felt a mutuality amongst our friends. For me in the compass of a diary entry, it is impossible to describe the complexities of what I feel. I told Congress that short enlistments would be detrimental and costly. I conveyed to them in explicit terms of the evils of having to raise and train a new army every year. I have warned of the faulty promotion system that is based on favor and not outcomes. Yet, promotions and raises continue regardless of qualifications. Annual deficits continue in the levy of an adequate army. I am not a prophet, but what I shared with them over a year ago has occurred exactly as I foretold. This army was already deficient of men. In one fell swoop, two thousand trained and able-bodied men were lost to surrender or death. Being right does not placate me. Providence has given us a mind to anticipate. Being on the ground and on the front lines lend a certain sober assessment, which seems to be missing in the States and Congress. When we wish things to be one way and find things to be the opposite, we must respond to what we find and not what we wish. I am weary almost to death with the retrograde status of this fight for freedom. By most accounts, we have failed in Brooklyn, at Kips Bay, at White Plains, and now Fort Washington. I am sensing hostility and dissatisfaction throughout the camp. I fought to get Joseph Reed here to aid me. Even now, I feel a coldness from my closest ally. To make any comparison is inappropriate, but to say I have a better understanding of what Jesus felt at Gethsemane is somewhat certain. If I were to do this all over again, the wealth of Croesus could not induce me to engage in this burden if the truth had been told upon entry. My character demands that I continue. Expectations of my countrymen must be met. In time, I pray they will be.

May God grant us success in our endeavor. The angel that assisted Hezekiah would be a welcomed friend at this instant.

Monday, November 18, 1776 — General Greene's Quarters, New Jersey

Bold face forward, granite-steeled optimism on the outside though liquid on the inside. Our men must see hope and believe all is being protected against. Waging war rather than being the brunt of it must be the design of leadership.

Wednesday, November 20, 1776 — Hackensack, New Jersey

General Howe has landed men below Dobbs Ferry. He is advancing rapidly upon Fort Lee. Another loss of men cannot be afforded. I have ordered the Fort evacuated immediately, leaving all that cannot be readily carried to prevent unnecessary loss of men. I have ordered Beall, Heard, and the remainder of Ewing's brigade to move west of the Hackensack river. I am avoiding any attack that may come our way. We must get a new footing. We need a victory. God send a victory.

Thursday, November 21, 1776 — Hackensack, New Jersey

I have sent a dispatch requesting General Lee to join our army on this side of the Hudson and leave Fellows, Wadsworth, and their brigades there to take care of the stores. The enemy seems to have placed a priority on taking this area. The citizens of this side of the North river are counting on the Continental Army to protect them. If our troops fail to defend our citizens here, the citizenry will question this army's ability. I fear they will then end their supply and provision of men. This would be devastating to a young nation longing to be free. General Lee's move to join us will put forth the appearance of force. Perhaps this will deter any further enemy incursions.

The assessment of losses in the evacuation of Fort Lee are as follows — all but two cannons, up to three hundred tents, a great deal of baggage, and a thousand barrels of flour. Happily, the ammunition was carried away before the British arrival. I have informed Congress that we are retiring over the waters of the Passaic river as our army is insufficiently manned for the smallest probability of success.

I am requesting men be enlisted, including militia, from New Jersey and Pennsylvania. The Flying Camp troops have been a good aide to this cause. I have requested Congress supply them with money to meet their needs which can induce more to engage.

Sunday, November 24, 1776 — Newark, New Jersey

Great frustration ensues on my part to the infrequent correspondence from General Lee. I have made clear to him our need for his supplement to this army. I have made this a request rather than an order to show respect for his reputation and position. I am sending a letter to him today in hopes it will push him forward to this camp. I am told in the Scriptures that love hopes all things, believes all things. I wish to give him the benefit of the doubt that much of his correspondence has indeed been sent but lost to some unfortunate occurrence. Under this premise, I will write him today to inform him that his reply to me must have been intercepted by the enemy. Therefore, he must be careful in his journey to our aid. I have studied and will suggest the safest route for he and his army to follow to nudge him the more. As he leaves Haverstraw, he can follow the western road and stay between the enemy and the mountains on the way to our position. The more I affirm as a certainty that he is coming, I pray he will be inclined to accommodate. I am unable to convey the desperation from this head without the appearance of total dependency upon Lee and thus a relinquishment of my authority.

Wednesday, November 27, 1776 — Newark, New Jersey

Last night I received the favor of Lee's letter. I have been in anguish and robbed of sleep all night. The General has not left upon my request. I feel he would prefer that the army under me dissolve or be defeated. He then could point at me as the failure and rise up as the awaited savior of this Nation. It may be my own insecurities talking, but a power struggle from his side of the war is perceived. The enemy has been delayed by Providence and His timely heavy rains. The poor weather now subsiding has brought a march by the enemy across the Passaic not a safe distance from our position. Thankfully, they are still slowed by the muddy roads. Philadelphia may be their destination. Our troops feel abandoned in the cold and rain. They lack clothing and tents, not to mention a shortage of fellow soldiers for comradery and assistance. I have sent another letter emphasizing the need for General Lee to move now.

Thursday, November 28, 1776 — Newark, New Jersey

I am leaving Newark this morning with our army. The enemy is close to this town. We are unable to make a satisfactory stand. I am sending the men out in front. I will take the rear. With this little army poorly clothed and insufficient to make a stand, it is vital for them to see that I will stand between them and the enemy who pursues. If a soldier is to fall, I am willing for it to be me for the sake of liberty.

Saturday, November 30, 1776 — Brunswick, New Jersey

I have arrived in Brunswick. Hardly had we left Newark when the enemy arrived. My hope is that large and early succors might join this force. It is as if I am calling out into a canyon with only my echo returning my call. Our little army is diminishing in numbers. Enlistments run out in two days for many. Intelligence this morning reports one division of the enemy has advanced as far as Elizabethtown. An advancement of quartermasters from the British have crossed the river to this side, to acquire barns for their accommodations. Hessian troops are on the road through Springfield. The enemy must be aware of our plight. They have captured Fort Washington. Now they set their sights on General Washington. I am moving the rest of our stores toward Philadelphia in an attempt to stay one step ahead of a fast-approaching enemy. Where is General Lee? Where is the new levy of troops?

No sooner did I write those questions into my record of accounts, this evening I was met by a timely temptation. The Board of War suggested enlisting the enemy's prisoners-of-war to our service. The British do this to ours through intimidation and promises. This is not consistent with the rules-of-war. Such a practice is not befitting an army of integrity. We have joined willingly for our common benefit. Hiring mercenaries meet our immediate needs, but at what cost? True, some have joined our ranks because of the virtue of our cause. These are welcomed, but to lower oneself to entice others to chicanery is unacceptable. One must always keep a watchful eye on any such as these prisoners, for they can bring discouragement, betrayal, or even gunshot from behind. The Hessian soldiers care not which side is right, but which side pays best. They then only engage if victory is conceived certain. When a battle goes south, those who joined for such purposes desert with haste.

Sunday, December 1, 1776 — Brunswick, New Jersey

I was awakened early this morning with a letter from General Lee. I have told my men to keep me apprised of any troops moving to this head. I noticed the letter was addressed not to me but to Colonel Reed. As I have sent Colonel Reed on a mission, and not wanting to delay good news, I opened the letter and began to read. General Lee's malicious delay has now been explained. I am sickened by what I am writing in this entry. I now grasp what David wrote in Psalm 41:9, "Yea, mine own familiar friend, in whom I trusted, which did eat of my bread, hath lifted up his heel against me." What is worse than Lee's volitional delay is Colonel Reed's duplicity. It appears the man I have needed so desperately to conduct my duties efficiently, the man who hesitated to come to my aid, the friend came and now seems so distant, has emotions toward my person which anguish me. I know not what he wrote to General Lee in specific, but Lee's response in this letter that I have opened gives strong insight. It appears Colonel Reed has been carrying on correspondence with General Lee for quite some time. Lee thanks the Colonel for flattering him as a leader. Lee then commiserates with him that my "fatal indecision of mind" is a worse disqualifier for leadership than stupidity or cowardice. Now I understand the more fully why General Lee has hesitated and why Colonel Reed has been distant. Even now, he delays return from his mission and is absent in correspondence. If I had time and the Nation was not dependent upon selflessness in this contest, I could readily respond to such traitorous behavior. Do they not know that nothing could contribute more to my happiness than to be in the peaceable enjoyment of my own vine and fig tree, with Mrs. Washington by my side? Many enter this battle for monetary benefits or for national praise and position. I have entered it to see our Nation free from the tyranny of an oppressive government that demands voluntary enslavement of its distant citizens. I do analyze my decisions or the lack thereof. I do delay and move from one opinion to the other. I do consult the officers under my command when perhaps they would prefer that I make the bold stroke. I understand fully the frustration. We stay close to the enemy, but then we flee from the enemy when he draws near, just to move close to the enemy again when danger wanes. I struggle with decision because one faulty step means the end of our Nation and surrender to British chains. Mr. Paine, to whom we are blessed to have joined us for a stint, has said to me that this war is not for the sunshine soldier — that odds like this try men's souls, but such hardships will make triumph all the more sweet. This is what I believe. This is why I do not resign as General Ward or seek an end to my own enlistment as many of our men. Will they not see this?

I pray this diary does not fall into the enemy's hands or into my friends' hands as General Lee's letter has. I would be appalled and humiliated for any to read my true feelings. I realize that Colonel Reed and General Lee would feel the same. Are we not free to express our own opinions? Must we be censored from the feelings we hold deep down? I must respect their questions and doubts. It was not a gentlemanly thing to do to open another's mail. Truly this violates the Rules of Civility which I have sought to guide my conduct. I will forward this opened letter to Colonel Reed in the immediate and attach an apology on my part. It is enough for him to know that Sovereignty has revealed his sentiments. My only regret is that he did not address his opinion of my leadership to me personally. We have shared quarters as well as strategy and longings. I must be better at my occupation as a leader and friend to prevent any barrier for his honest assessments to be voiced.

The enemy is close by and it appears their designs are upon Philadelphia. Intelligence reports they are impressing wagons and horses. They are collecting cattle and sheep for a march to this station. I do not have the men to stand against them. If this army is not augmented quickly, I fear our cause is lost. I have in place four thousand men including militia. General Lee sits with a larger army of seven thousand. His assistance could bolster our forces and give us strength to stand. Not being able to count on General Lee, I am writing the Governor of New Jersey to send men. I have never expressed myself so strongly to the point of begging. Now is not the time to be cordial or proud. I have let him know there is either a lack of will in his officers or a lack of urgency in his actions to bring Jersey's militia in sufficient numbers to this head.

Not being able to count on reinforcements, I am instructing Governor Livingston to make ready for our retreat across the Delaware. All available boats and craft are to be in place on this side of the river and guarded. All parties are to be made available to assist our crossing. For the time being, I will use the Durham boats to send across all military stores, supplies, and baggage to safety on the other side. I am again writing General Lee to let him know that our valuable purpose may be lost if he does not move to our support.

Tuesday, December 3, 1776

The Savior told the story in the Gospel of Luke about a man who needed bread for a late-night guest. He had none so he rushed over in the night to ask a neighboring friend for food for his guest. The neighbor resisted, but because this man was persistent, the neighbor got up reluctantly and gave him what he needed. Persistence. Continued request. I am in need for sustenance as we are facing an unexpected and unwelcomed guest from British soil. In this vein, I am writing General Lee again beseeching him as my friend and neighbor to come to our aid with the army that I placed under his command. He gives excuses but those will not win this war. He may seek command and glory for himself, but there may be no command for him to assume. His delay may go into the annals of history as a curse to his name. So, I ask again by letter. I am informing Congress of my entreaties to General Lee. I am telling them that I am not surprised even a little at his reluctance to join this body. Philadelphia will be in jeopardy should Lee fail to answer my urgent requests. I am sending Colonel Stewart as my personal envoy to solicit a response from the good General. Having left Brunswick, I am now headquartering in Trenton. I am hoping my presence there will motivate the principal gentlemen of this State to perform their duty for the cause of freedom.

Thursday, December 5, 1776 — Trenton, New Jersey

I am going to recount to Congress several instances where lack of men has stymied any thrust against the enemy. They need to realize that militia, short enlistments, and an insufficient order of a standing army cost this Nation action, supplies, and hope. Lack of an army allowed the British to cross Hackensack. Lack of an army prevented a stand at Brunswick. Ten thousand more instances can show why success is a fleeting attainment. We cannot undo yesterday. Congress can help secure tomorrow if they will just heed the call of the one that they put at the head of this revolution.

Friday, December 6, 1776 — Trenton, New Jersey

I receive great support from the clergy of our Nation. It seems they are the confirming spirit of the Revolution. Colonel Muhlenberg is a great example. Though he refused my first call to serve due to pressure from within his family, he finally conceded and raised men from his own flock with a riveting sermon expounding on the fact that there is a time for peace and a time for war. He charged that now is the time for war. It is said that he had his military uniform on under his clerical robes. He then removed his vestments to reveal his intent to fight. He is doing very well in the south per reports I am given. I write this with profound gratitude that such men preach, pray, and fight. We could use a regiment of such men. They are not summer soldiers, but men committed to the cause. I believe we are engaged in the task for which Christ came — to set men free indeed.

Another clergyman by the name of Mr. Caldwell has fled Elizabethtown ahead of the British. He reports that General or Lord Howe has offered sixty days of grace and pardons, that no man is to be denied Howe's mercy for any who will lay down the sword. Overtures like this from the British could be because they believe we are on the cusp of despair and defeat. It could also be that pressure from across the sea beckons them to settle this dispute and return this Continent to their fold. I was invigorated by Reverend Caldwell's dismissive remark, "The Lord deliver us from Lord Howe's mercy." I cannot help but smile. Caldwell's stand gives me the strength to pick up the sword, face the hardships, call upon Heaven, and see this thing to its victorious end!

Sunday, December 8, 1776 — Mr. Berkeley's Summer-Seat, Pennsylvania

I received intelligence just now as I am traveling between Trenton and Princeton, that the enemy has attempted to get to the rear of our troops. Our men responded responsibly and have retreated to Trenton. The situation is dire. I am dispatching a letter to Congress to inform them that augmentation of this army is desperate, a moment cannot be lost. Again, I am not a prophet, but I have been clear at the onset that if men and supplies were not provided, this effort cannot succeed. May Congress, the States, and General Lee work to prevent the fulfillment of what was foretold. The British were reported Sunday last to have sailed one hundred and seventeen ships, leaving the Hook. It is believed that their heading is for the Delaware river to meet General Howe upon this route.

General Lee has still not responded. I have sent frequent expresses to him, lately Colonel Hampton, to ascertain his journey or lack thereof. I am now sending Major Hoops in the hope that he will hasten Lee's movement. Our troop numbers have been enhanced by the arrival of militia from Philadelphia and a German battalion totaling two thousand. Never have our men been so glad to receive aid. Our numbers are now between three thousand and three thousand, five hundred. Lee would bring us to over ten thousand, if only he will come.

We have crossed the Delaware into Pennsylvania. The day is sunny, but cold. I am hiding all boats on the Pennsylvania side of a little island in the river. The owners of the ferries are assisting our cause at great risk. We cannot make any transport across this river available for the British to pursue us. Their chase must end at the river. We need time. We need men. We need a break.

Monday, December 9, 1776 — Mr. Berkeley's Summer-Seat, Pennsylvania

Philadelphia must be secured. I am requesting that communication lines and redoubts be constructed between here and there on advantageous and commanding grounds to slow the enemy. Even the slightest rebuttal has been shown it can prove effective in allowing the people living in harm's way to regroup and resist by our side. Neighboring States and Pennsylvania must come to our defense. They must supply force against the enemy and prevent Philadelphia's fall. This country cannot afford the military stores held in Philadelphia to be lost to the enemy.

Tuesday, December 10, 1776 — Trenton Falls

Should I fall in battle or fail in war, I do pray that my diary and my letters (particularly those to General Lee and Congress for support), show that I did all I could to win this contest. They document how I was hindered by nonresponse, selfish motives, and a lack of motivation to stave off tragedy. General Lee has sent a return excusing his lack of response as a strategy to hold to the rear of the enemy for some feigned notion of defense. I am on the opposite end of the British force. They are pressing in with their whole army. He must make the utmost exertions to come to our aid. With any other excuse or delay, Philadelphia and even America may be lost. The enemy is seeking to move north and cut off passage for Lee at this moment. The enemy's numbers, per our intelligence, are two battalions of infantry, three battalions of grenadiers, several Hessian grenadiers, and more.

Thursday, December 12, 1776 — Trenton Falls

I have sent a dispatch to Congress this morning to let them know that our little handful is diminishing through sickness and other causes. They are concerned in Philadelphia. Many have abandoned that city. Congress has left for Baltimore. This band of few under my command, after many desertions, cannot hope to engage an experienced and out-numbering enemy. Congress must fulfill their commitments.

Friday, December 13, 1776 — Bucks County, Pennsylvania

When I need something to lift me up, it seems that God always hears my cry. As I received dispatches from soldiers in the field, I seek to respond with immediacy. I imagine that my prayers are received in Heaven the same way and that the Divine Author of my life is responding. General Mifflin has sent word that he has been successful in raising fifteen hundred men from Pennsylvania and that they are on the march to Trenton at the present time. Recruiting of a new army is said to be going well per reports received this day. The Delaware river divides the two sides of this war. Gladly, we have secured the boats for our men and withheld them from the enemy for crossing.

I await General Lee, which is my daily posture. I have sent General Putnam with men to secure Philadelphia as its defense successfully or unsuccessfully may render the verdict to our clash.

Saturday, December 14, 1776 — Headquarters at Keith's, Pennsylvania

With the enemy so close, I am instructing Lord Stirling to monitor the river and watch for the British crossing. He will need to be prepared to make an energetic defense the minute the redcoats' feet hit the water. To this end, Lord Stirling will need to keep his baggage, wagons, and supplies on some backroad heading to Philadelphia for retreat should his efforts fail. This will prevent the enemy from gaining stores from our shortages. This army under my command is too small to make an opposition so we have pushed through the Jerseys. General Howe's army is spread between Pennington and Burlington, with his main army in the neighborhood of Trenton. I am empowering Stirling to recruit a spy to get close enough to the British to discern their probable route. The spy is to gather intelligence from the enemy's gathering of supplies, horses, and boats with the hopes of narrowing the guesses to their intentions.

I am told that General Gates has seven regiments at his disposal. I am entreating him to make no delay but hasten his march to Pittstown. Even as I note this in my journal, do my orders have any authority with these officers, or do they roll their eyes and wait for direction from some commander they prefer? I have not time to question that. I sit in the capacity of Commander-in-Chief. I will continue to act as such. General Lee has other ideas. I have just received in-hand a letter from the General excusing his tardiness to his indecision as to what route he should take for the safety of his army. This sounds reasonable, until I remind him that I have already informed him of the best route and sent officers to validate said route. There seems to be a hedge between me and my small army, and the bulk of the segmented Continental army that I have assigned to other fronts beyond me. Do they plan my fall and then rally together in the rubble to bring victory from defeat? Such is a risky venture. Our defeat will only embolden the enemy and discourage our citizens from joining. This army must be maintained. My fortitude, defiance, and tenacity must win the day. I pray I can win over the men under every other officer's command. I am letting Lee know that boats await his arrival along the path that I have ascertained as best. His convergence upon Pittstown in concert with Gates and this army will provide a stroke against the British from which they may not recover. If only . . .

Governor Trumbull is requesting immediate aid. The superior naval force of the British has landed at many of the ports of Connecticut. They are threatening to make a move inward. Governor Trumbull has been my most ardent supporter. I am fraught with great melancholy that I am unable to send him the support he needs. I pray the spirit of his people can oppose and hold the enemy at bay. General Arnold is on his way from Ticonderoga. I am diverting he and his men to assist Trumbull.

Sunday, December 15, 1776 — Bucks County, Pennsylvania

I am vexed between two opinions. My hand has received notice that General Lee has been captured by the British in a tavern near Vealtown in the Jerseys. It is a great loss in that General Lee is a capable general with vast experience as a former British officer and, in recent years, a Continental officer joining for the cause of freedom. When engaged, I believe he has no equal on the battlefield. His loss dampens the hopes of our Nation.

The second opinion — cannot help but wonder if this is a smile from Heaven. Lee would not march to my aid. Lee has been a voice of discontent, doubt, and insubordination. The poison that he has brought to this army is hard to detail. Now, General Sullivan heads his army and is on his way to our aid. I fear many will not be with General Sullivan as their devotion lay more with General Lee than this Nation. Be that as it may, I welcome the movement of the army. No one person is irreplaceable. If one falls, another must pick up his flag. I do believe Lee's own hubris has led to his imprisonment. My only hope with him at this instant is that he does not betray the oath of loyalty he once professed for our cause. We shall see.

Cornwallis appears to be heading for winter quarters. This is a comfort if it is not a ruse. Philadelphia must prepare for their onslaught without hesitation either way. The British can attack for certain be it winter or spring. It is best to be ready while time allows and immediacy dictates.

Monday, December 16, 1776 — Bucks County, Pennsylvania

Many of the militia have left, taking their arms and powder. Once again, the unreliability of the militia must be remembered. I fear that the arms they take may be used against us. I am recommending to Congress quietly and unannounced to take up the arms from the militia. I can assist if they so choose. Congress must raise up a full-time army, one we can depend on, one where order is key, and where submission is instinct.

Tuesday, December 17, 1776 — Bucks County, Pennsylvania

Speaking of militia, when I see the movement of Massachusetts to protect their State by raising up six thousand militia, I am reminded of their best purpose. Men will rally to protect their families, homes, and properties. Just as Nehemiah had the Israelites build the walls directly behind their homes knowing that best effort is extended for one's own life and property, the militia are best utilized to this front, albeit they need direction to be effective. I am putting the militia under General Lincoln. He has a talent in preparing and organizing for a season the untrained soldier. Major General Heath is in that area following my order to guard the passes of the Highlands on into Jersey. If this militia under Lincoln is comfortable pushing out for a better cushion for their homes, I recommend he utilize the extra reinforcements to form an element of defense near Peekskill and Kingsbridge.

Wednesday, December 18, 1776 — Camp above Trenton Falls

I cannot recall when last I wrote my brother. I know he and the family follow the state of our afflictions not to mention the outcomes of our engagements. They surely worry and seek some seam of truth in the reports they hear. I can be honest with my family. To share my honest assessments is a consolation to me. What do I tell John Augustine? We are in an adverse condition. If things do not change, the game is nearly up. He will want to know why. I know what causes the ailments. What I long for is the cure. The cause of misfortune lies in too much dependence on militia, too little emphasis on raising an army, the defection of New York, Pennsylvania, and chiefly infamous the Jerseys from this effort. Short enlistments contribute and the insidious actions of the enemy bring a paralyzed fear to all who would engage. No one, in the cause of a nation, has ever encountered such difficulties as I now face. This is my educated guess going through the record of history. I am perplexed. I would like to extricate myself from this sorrow, but I cannot shrink from the justice of our fight nor consider anything other than hope lies just beyond the next hill.

Friday, December 20, 1776 — Camp Above Trenton Falls

The request was made to Congress in October for augmenting our corps of artillery and the corps of engineers. No action has been taken. I am taking the authority upon myself to provide for three battalions of artillery, which is necessary for the safety and defense of the States. Colonel Knox requests more, but I will rely on some States who have formed their own to fend for themselves. To assist in the recruitment, I am raising their pay by twenty-five percent to compete with the pay of that role within the French or English artillerists.

Some will accuse me that I have a thirst for power, that I am taking authority not vested in me. The exigency of the situation demands action. I submit to Congress's authority continually and communicate constantly my actions, needs, and requests. The existence of our army can possibly cease in ten days with enlistments expiring and soldiers defecting. The enemy is aware of our situation. It is a matter of Providence that they have yet to strike a fatal blow when we were well within the site of their gun barrels. Arduous preparations must be made. Full exertions must be extended. Desperation is the mother of invention. Desperate diseases demand radical remedies. I stand ready to be corrected and redirected. Until then, I will brace this army for a rousing defense.

I am asking Congress and the States around to raise one hundred and ten battalions. Outfitting these battalions with officers will enable the number to be increased. If our target is one hundred and ten, we may receive less, but we will have more than we have at the present. Money cannot be a chief concern at this moment when freedom and liberty hang in the balance. Tents must be obtained. A clothier officer must be appointed to supply the men. A commissary of prisoners must be appointed. The method by which prisoners of war are being handled is shameful. It all falls under my purview. I am short on supply of attention. Every officer who is at my charge has been sent out to carry on some other duty lacking a person of responsibility. We need a brigadier for every three regiments, a major-general to every three brigades. Over the corps of artillery, Colonel Knox should be put at the head and promoted to brigadier in rank and pay. Ammunition carts are needed, as well as carts for entrenching tools to make allocations easier.

Sunday, December 22, 1776 — Camp above Trenton Falls

On this Lord's Day, as we met for prayer and listened to a minister speak of the army of God, I was praying for guidance. A bold stroke is what we need, but how? Would the men be with me? Since General Lee's capture, I have found my orders go out without an echo back of dissent. Gates has arrived as has Sullivan. We are not strong, but perhaps seven thousand, five hundred now field our force. Just as the Church service ended, I was handed a letter from Colonel Reed pleading with me to act. His words were confirming what I have been feeling. Our army enlistments are up in nine days. Men are thinking of going home. Endless marches and setbacks play a negative role on our mindsets. Are we soldiers or are we marchers? What Reed wrote has really stuck in my head, "Our affairs are hastening fast to ruin if we do not retrieve them by some happy event." I agree. He suggests Trenton.

Monday, December 23, 1776 — Camp above Trenton Falls

With little sleep and much note- writing, I have decided that we will strike the British at Trenton in the night of Christmas. Intelligence informs me that Hessian soldiers primarily are quartered there. How long has Reed been wondering if I would act? His letter to General Lee still haunts my mind. I had lost his trust for lack of decision. I wonder if I am regaining it. His and the myriad of other opinions have no weight in this matter. I know that the best thing for this Nation is to strike the enemy. The clock is short of midnight. I am writing Reed with fear and a hope that he keeps it to himself. For Heaven's sake, Colonel Reed, let me trust you this time and onward.

I am having our men supplied with three days food. I have put every ferry and ford on alert and under guard. May Heaven grant us the stroke we need. The whole fight for freedom may be decided in just a few days. We cannot go on like this. Our Nation will not support it, nor will our men agree to drag this thing out. A dispatch intercepted from a Tory to a friend in Philadelphia informs that the British intend to attack Philadelphia once the ice forms for crossing.

Strategies and the potential for victory or defeat played in my head all night. I believe we need to attack Trenton as Reed suggested. Contemplating this, I believe we should attack it from three directions. I acknowledge that if all three are successful, the enemy will be surrounded and routed. The odds are, one of the three will face delay, perhaps more. Consideration of this outcome is warrantable. Even so, surprise will be the deciding advantage to this endeavor. I think we should send one thousand Pennsylvania militia and five hundred men from Rhode Island to cross down river at Bristol under Colonel Reed and General Cadwalader. They could then proceed to Burlington. I can send seven hundred men with General Ewing to hold the bridge over the Assunpink creek to prevent the British from escaping. I would then lead the third group and cross upstream at McKonkey's Ferry with Generals Greene, Sullivan, and Lord Stirling. We should plan then to converge on the camp of the enemy at Trenton. I am informed that they have stationed approximately three thousand battle-hardened men there.

Tuesday, December 24, 1776 — Camp above Trenton Falls

A chill is in the air this morning to go with a tension that I have not felt previous. I see it in our men. There is an expectation, almost a belief of total loss or a turning of victory in the immediate. I may be reading my own emotions into what I see. I believe we are at the breaking point — victory or death. Victory or death? This is the crossroad on which we now stand. It is sad to say that there would be relief in death, relief in defeat, or relief in both. Just to have this thing over, we could deal with the aftermath. Certainly, there is relief in victory. If the war is turned, that is relief. Even if it is not the final victory, the smallest of victory would change the outlook for all involved.

I called for an early council of officers but limited it to just the bare minimum to prevent any intelligence from being conveyed to the enemy. I posed to them several options — winter quarters, move to Philadelphia and prepare, or a surprise attack at Trenton (which I assumed would be considered a wild thought). The faces of our officers lit with the thought of an attack. Almost a revelry and excitement was present that I have not felt since the aftermath of Lexington and Concord. Ideas were just flying out of their mouths. It was then that I felt comfortable to share my notes from the thoughts last night.

We spent the rest of the day passing ideas back-and-forth. The officers, who to me are now the trustees of freedom, improved every idea I had. I call them trustees of the Nation's freedom because it is on the field of battle, not in some legislative hall, where the freedom will be won or lost. Decisions are made at a distance, but they are carried out by what these men in our camp do. The decision has been made that two divisions of our army will arrive at Trenton at approximately five in the morning as Christmas night turns to a new day. The attack will commence at six as daylight approaches. All movement must be done in silence. To differentiate the officers, each is to wear a white piece of paper or some other white material in their hats. Secrecy, silence, and surprise will be the key to our success.

Wednesday, December 25, 1776 — Camp above Trenton Falls

Action is too close at-hand. My mind is racing. Another night of no sleep. Our short time of planning has made me apprehensive. I am carrying my journal with me all day making notes and using paper from it to send out orders. Dr. Benjamin Rush has arrived from Congress to lend us his aid. Here is a man who does not just talk freedom, he invests in it from his own largesse. This is more than most, but he goes one step further and submits his own life into danger for the cause. How sweet it is to have one from that august body join us for this stroke. Colonel Reed is with him. I decided that our password would be "Victory or Death." As I jotted that down, it fell from my hand. I was a little embarrassed, but maybe a little glad that Dr. Rush saw my note. He must know the urgency of what we are about to attempt. Dr. Rush, trying to taper my disappointment at the end of this venture, told me not to expect much out of the militia under Cadwalader. If Dr. Rush has been privy to my letters to Congress, he would know that I have no vaunted expectations from any man in our militia. Their ability just to provide some noise or diversion is the limit of my expectations. Anything above that will be an extra benefit.

The boats I had secured are the ones we are utilizing for our launch. The Durham boats are my preference because of their ability to carry the heavy weight of men and some artillery. The largest Durham boat has the capability to carry forty men. There are ferry boats we are blessed to use as well due to the number of horses and cannons that must be carried across. Together, they should be able, with many trips, to deliver this fighting force. I have assigned Colonel Knox with the responsibility to organize and direct our crossing. He has proven relentless time and again in carrying out monumental tasks. We are taking eighteen cannons across along with fifty horses. We must exert ourselves to the fullest with the hope of some miraculous wave of the Almighty's Hand. I have knelt and prayed on several occasions. Our march is to begin at two o'clock this afternoon. Each man is carrying sixty rounds of ammunition. It is all we can spare. It is also what can be more easily carried.

Colonel Knox and I have reached McKonkey's Ferry. It is four o'clock. The weather is turning ugly, but at the present, we are on schedule. I pray our other two columns are at their points of crossing. I admire Knox's hand in pushing the men, artillery, and horses across. He is truly a brigadier even if not by title. I am going to cross with the first group and cover landing as Knox commands the launch.

As we crossed, I was captivated by the thought that these Durham boats brought to Philadelphia many of the items we enjoyed before the war. They carried valuable items such as iron ore, timber, and flour. Yet today, they are transporting the most valuable cargo they have ever carried — the fate of America embodied in these men.

The time is eleven o'clock at night. We are behind. The conditions have turned for the worse. Cold freezing rain is pounding us. The swift current is pushing the ice floes. The wind has picked up to almost a hurricane force. Even disembarking from the boats is treacherous. The ground is hard and slick. Most of the men are pulling down fences to make fires to keep warm while they wait.

Some of our men saw the struggle of men coming ashore and have formed a human chain to keep men from falling into the river as they get off the boats. The anchor of this chain of men clings to a huge tree up on the riverbank. The chain cascades down to the river. Men reaching to help. Men grasping in exhaustion to hold on. These men have such little clothing, few shoes, and hardly any cold wraps. Their bodies are ready to quit now, but their spirit presses them on. We have not even completed our crossing of the river. There is still a march ahead.

Every ounce of common sense says call this thing off. It is as if Heaven is seeking to turn us back. Victory or Death! We are at the point of no return. Like a baby dying in the womb, our mission seems to be gasping. May this baby fight to be delivered. The birth of a nation is at stake. I cannot let it be stillborn. The one solace I receive in this nor' easter is it covers the noise of our crossing. Surely the well-sheltered enemy looks out their windows, away from the fireplace with a smile of peace and a firm belief that if ever there was a night when attack is unlikely, it is this one. God, may they hold to that thought. Please give us the strength to push through this.

From my vantage point on the New Jersey side of this river, I see the boats are struggling. It is as if I am watching the disciples on the Sea of Galilee overwhelmed by the bitter storm as recorded in the Gospel of Matthew. Jesus had to descend from the mountain, walk out on the water, and rescue them. The ice is thickening. I could almost walk across the river as one would move across a stream from one rock to another. But those are not stones; they are ice floes. They are not grounded in the sediment; they are flowing rapidly. I pray the Lord comes down to help us too.

Colonel John Glover's Marblehead regiment of experienced watermen using the ferries and Durham boats are the only factors that keep our men, horses, and cannon from going overboard. My fear is how long can their skill overcome the elements? Have I made a mistake? Our number of men has declined from twenty thousand to three thousand, five hundred during the course of this campaign. Am I to watch the last three thousand or so drown? I am praying.

Thursday, December 26, 1776

It is three o'clock in the morning. It has taken almost ten hours. By the interposing Hand of Providence, our men have made it. We have not lost one man, one horse, or one cannon. There is no other explanation. Knox has just arrived with the last of the supplies and men. I hear his recognizable voice-of-command through the storm. He is one officer who does not need a white paper in his hat. All know he is the officer at the juncture of this exercise. We are three hours behind schedule. I am convinced the other two columns are facing this, but their crossing was to be easier. I pray they are patiently waiting at their designated neighborhoods, finding some warmth and dryness until we arrive.

An officer, not Knox, suggests that the element of surprise is lost and queried me concerning aborting the mission. We cannot. As much danger presents in retreating as there is in attacking. Let us face the defeat in attack if that is our fate. No sooner did I say that — the wind, sleet, snow, and hail are starting to fall harder. My paper is wet, my ink smears. Water runs off my hat. The brim is my only cover as I write. Almighty God, Elijah had the men pour water on the altar before the prophets of Baal. He wanted all to see that there is nothing You cannot do. You answered by sending fire from Heaven. The wood was consumed. All knew that it could not have been some random chance lighting, but Your Hand that worked the miracle. Are You pouring water on the wood in this forward thrust of ours to show Yourself even greater, able to give victory when none would be reasoned possible?

I have given the order for our two thousand, four hundred to march. It appears all are present and accounted for. On to Birmingham. I have never felt colder.

We have marched five miles. It is dark. I pray we have not lost a man. I have given orders for our column to divide. Sullivan will lead a force to the right on the River road. General Greene and I will lead the other half to the left following Pennington road. I estimate it is four miles either way to Trenton. I pray that Reed and Cadwalader's columns and General Ewing's column have had a better go of it and are awaiting our arrival. I have let General Sullivan remind his men to keep with their officers. I will do the same for ours. The men have no idea where we are going except to meet the enemy. We cannot risk them being lost. I fear we will be even later. The roads are muddy and iced over. The march will be slower than I anticipated. God give us feet for the path.

I just received a note from General Sullivan. He says his men fear their powder is too wet to fire. What shall we do? The only recourse we have, the bayonet. Weather is against us. The cover of dark is dissipating. Footing is poor. Men are cold and chattering. Is this a fool's errand? Have I wanted a win so badly that I have put the whole of our cause on the verge of defeat? Are we marching to our demise and to the chains, jeers, and mockery of the British? I cannot think that. But it is what will be recorded in the days ahead without some miracle. I dare not count on man, but I am counting on Ewing and Reed.

It is eight o'clock. We are just outside of Trenton. I see Colonel Knox's men at a distance. Smoke is rising from the chimneys. If I were at Mt. Vernon the day after Christmas, perhaps I would be enjoying the fire myself in this weather, not wanting to venture out until the ground dries a bit. It appears my intelligence was correct. I see markings of the Hessian soldiers in the old barracks down from King and Queen streets. The Assunpink creek bridge is just behind them. I am in hopes that General Ewing is stationed there to prevent their most available escape route. I have given the order for Greene and Sullivan to attack. May the Almighty who brought us through so much this night, carry us on to victory with this attempt.

The blizzard is at my back. The wind is blowing our troops into the Hessian first line of defense. I hear shots but can hardly make out what is happening. All I can tell is that even after a full night's march, our men are moving with purpose and renewed energy. How magnificent is this group of men!

The noise of shouts and gunfire grow louder. I just heard Colonel Knox fire cannon. Each column is to have their cannon firing ahead of them to clear the way. I feel like Moses on the mountain. Hur and Aaron are fighting for us below. No one holds my hands. I wish to hold theirs. This is the hardest thing to do as a commander — not be in the thick of it myself. I would feel so much better if I were down there and they were up here.

It is now 9:30 in the morning. The air is silent, but smoke filled. A shot is fired randomly here and there, two to my right, down below, one to my left. What is the outcome? Have we won? Have we lost? What are our losses? Do I still command an army? Is our Nation no longer free? I want to ride down, but I dare not. I will wait.

Colonel Knox just left. Heaven has smiled on us. The Hessians have surrendered. They are being rounded up and searched at this instant. Many of theirs have been killed. A large group escaped over the Assunpink bridge, just as I feared. I am in hopes that General Ewing has cut them off. By Knox's observance, he has not seen one American lying in the street, but many Hessians. What a blessing! I am riding down to survey the situation. I cannot wait any longer.

Friday, December 27, 1776 — Headquarters, Newtown

Even with the late advance, the Hessian soldiers were stormed upon so surprisingly that they were unable to respond due to indecision and fear as to how. We have captured twenty-three of their officers, and eight hundred and eighty-six of their men. I fancy not above twenty or thirty were killed. Our losses are none killed and just four wounded. Our victory would have been more thorough had General Ewing been able to cut off the retreat, but both he and Cadwalader, along with Reed, were hindered by the ice and the elements. They were forced to turn back. I must be understanding as the Commander-in-Chief of such things. What bothers me inwardly is the will of these men. I do not seek to elevate myself, but I want to see beating in these men the same heart that beats in Greene, Knox, and Sullivan. They had the will to overcome obstacles at least as difficult as what Ewing and company faced. Ours had the will to push forward, seeming to vie with each other in a race to the enemy despite exhaustion and a violent storm of snow and hail. Not one of these men under my command would abate their ardor. What a happy duty I have to convey this news to Congress. We had prayed for a stroke. Heaven has favored us with that and more.

Saturday, December 28, 1776 — Headquarters, Newtown

I am giving my men who entered Trenton time to rest. The enemy is on the move away from this army. I am sending General Ewing and Colonel Cadwalader with the troops under their command to pursue them. General Mifflin is to follow. As soon as our men are recovered from fatigue, we will join the whole of the Continental troops. I am writing General McDougall and General Maxwell to collect the large body of militia at Morristown and harass the enemy on the flank and rear. Though the Jerseys have disappointed me in their lack of investment, we will attempt to drive the enemy entirely from their province.

Sunday, December 29, 1776 — Headquarters, Bucks County

On this, the Lord's Day, we truly give thanks. This year of our Lord, 1776, has been a monumental year of resolve and a discouraging year of setbacks. The end of it though seems to justify the whole and make this coming year one of greater hope.

I am about to move out over the Delaware with the troops that are with me. General Cadwalader reports he and his eight hundred men have crossed from Bristol and are in Bordentown. General Mifflin has sent over five hundred from Philadelphia and three hundred from Burlington. He plans to send another eight hundred. With much difficulty but unity of purpose, we will move to join them and pursue the enemy and decrease his numbers. The British may have wanted to quarter for the winter and initiate the assault on our capitol in the Spring, but our goal is to change those plans and help them reconsider their objective.

I am writing General Howe, in the fullest respect as always, a letter. I am also enclosing a letter for General Lee. It is a draft on Major Small for a sum of money that General Lee may need as he is in British custody. Writing General Howe after a victory but not changing my tone is a great joy. I know we have had a victory. He knows it, but my attitude and temperament should show no signs of premature contemplations of the winds changing. At worst, we have been given a reprieve. At the best, the enemy is seeing that their efforts may not turn to their favor. Also a relief is to write regarding General Lee. I rejoice to show him favor in return for his vain treachery toward me. May my enemies remember these courtesies.

Monday, December 30, 1776 — Trenton, New Jersey

The stroke on the 26th has had the desired effect on our men. Congress has authorized me to use every effort to prevail upon the troops to stay with our army. I am seizing this and pleading with our men. No better time to do so then after a victory. Our regiments from the eastern States have signed on for another six weeks beyond their enlistments. In reward, I am giving a ten dollar per man bounty. I am asking our generals nearby to do the same. I need the armies at Morristown to try to make a strike on Elizabethtown. The enemy is confused and scattered. This is the time to get men from wherever we have a post. Let the enemy feel the sting of being surrounded in a strange land that is not their own.

Regarding the almost unlimited powers Congress has bestowed upon me, I want them to know that I have no inclination to use them beyond strengthening this army and giving it the best chance for success. The last thing we took up for liberty was the sword. It will be the first thing we lay down once our liberty is secured.

The Year 1777

Wednesday, January 1, 1777 — Trenton, New Jersey

It appears the British are strengthening their positions at Brunswick and Princeton. They have been said to have upward of six thousand in number. General Howe is said to be moving with another thousand from Amboy to their locations. Our armies are on the move to meet them. I am hopeful Jersey will raise up a militia. They should be motivated by the losses inflicted on them by the British oppression.

Just received word that General Howe is breaking camp and heading to this neighborhood. I have two choices. One, I can retreat with the whole of this army, but that will destroy every dawn of hope in the militiamen from Jersey. Two, I can call General Cadwalader and General Mifflin to join us in Trenton with their men. We can then boldly seek another lucky stroke. Our actions the 26th last has drawn activity. Cornwallis is seeking a stroke of his own.

Thursday, January 2, 1777 — Trenton, New Jersey

The time is later afternoon, the British have begun their attack in earnest. At four o'clock, their regiment hit Trenton. We are in an intense skirmish.

We have been pushed back across the Assunpink creek. The British have sought to pursue but thanks to Colonel Knox and his cannons, they have failed three times. Only the river and those cannons are keeping us free. The British have paused, but at first light with their numbers, a good chance presents they will surround us. I have ordered a handful of men to give a retort to any enemy bombardment and for our army to build fires as if to stay in camp for the night even though there is no way we can stay this night. It is cold and we are tired. We are more outnumbered. I called a council of our officers. Our choices are again retreat, which will steal the heart. The other option, we can move for an attack on another quarter, which may stoke our newborn confidence. We have decided to leave men to make the appearance of an encampment and to move toward the rear of Cornwallis's column near Princeton. Surely most of his men are moving to meet us here at Trenton, leaving their rear flank of Princeton with a skeletal army and many stores. We are moving our own stores to Burlington and leaving guards at the bridge and other potential crossing points. At twelve o'clock this evening we are moving out.

Friday, January 3, 1777 — Trenton, New Jersey

We have arrived at Quaker Bridge just northeast of Sandtown. Our men have made our escape into another planned confrontation. I am still in awe of these men, poorly clothed, hardly a shoe, yet resolute in our aspiration. Just to think that they are beyond their enlistments and more committed than ever. This over-whelms me. We are dividing our army of about five thousand, five hundred into two columns just as at Trenton. General Sullivan will lead his men to the right. General Greene will lead his to the left. I am sending General Mercer and a few men to destroy a bridge on the Kings highway to prevent the enemy's escape. Surprise is our advantage. The Lord Almighty must be our strength.

What a joy to report that we have won the day and in short order. Unlike my time at Trenton where I was on a hill overlooking the conflict, this time I deter-mined to ride into the fray with my men. You should have seen the smile on their faces. Nothing is better than to see an officer do what he has ordered of the men. I felt that as a soldier and more so now as their commander. The shock of the British was almost paralyzing. They acted as if the army upon them had dropped from the sky. They had all this time been moving toward Trenton to face our army supposedly surrounded. Then they find the army surrounded was not, and the army they thought hedged in at Trenton was upon them in Princeton. To them, it was as if we had passed through a wall. The enemy's fight was for survival. As a result, it was quite fierce at first. Our numbers and our zeal got the best of them, they went to flight. It was like a fox hunt. So, I pursued and vied my men to join me in this fine chase. Captain Hamilton and his artillerymen captured many British who had barricaded themselves in a college building. Their losses of almost five hundred British killed, wounded, and imprisoned in number are greater than our twenty-three. But our losses are painful due to the deaths of the valuable officers — Colonel Hazlet and General Mercer. All in all, the new year has had a great start.

Saturday, January 4, 1777 — Trenton, New Jersey

Our situation is much improved since two successive victories. The militia in Jersey are taking spirits and coming in fast to join this army. I do fear the militia from Pennsylvania will soon be leaving. In preparing for the worst, they have sent their blankets and supplies to Burlington out of the reach of the enemy. With winter upon us heavy, they will not suffer these hardships or discomforts for long. I fully understand. They are ill-clad and many lack shoes. General Howe seems to be on the move away from us to winter quarters. I am working to move our men to Morristown to gain the best cover I can for them.

Sunday, January 5, 1777 — Pluckemin, New Jersey

I am writing General Putnam to move this way. Our victories have been because of surprise movements. We must continue this advantage. The enemy will be more alert and more inclined to counter with surprises of their own. Putnam needs to keep as many spies in the field as possible watching the enemy and looking for opportunity. We need horsemen dressed as the people of the country, moving about as if for routine business reporting anything of consequence. He also needs to exaggerate his numbers in the hearing of those close by. The enemy must think we are stronger. Our victories of late should cause the enemy to give heed. Communication from that quarter to this quarter is vital.

I am writing General Heath to leave a guard at the Highlands and move toward New York. If the enemy is moving out of Jersey, perhaps because of our aggressions, they need to be challenged at every opportunity but always with great precaution. I need General Lincoln with his militia to move this way to Morristown. The constant need for crossings of the North river by our armies requires that all officers gather and secure boats for this purpose as circumstance dictates.

Tuesday, January 7, 1777 — Morristown, New Jersey

The enemy has retreated to Brunswick, completely evacuating Trenton and Princeton. I am not sure how long we can stay here in Morristown. Our men need cover. It is best provided here, albeit poorly. I cannot think of another place in which we can go at this instant. The benefit of this location is the shield that the Watchung Mountains provide from the British. I am having an upper redoubt built to keep watch. A signal beacon is to be constructed at the point of the mountain above this town. The Morristown area does have working iron forges, grist mills, sawmills, and most importantly, a gunpowder mill. All things considered, this place may be better than first thought.

Militia men are leaving daily due to the severe conditions. I am consoled to note that our active militia is harassing the enemy at various points. Sunday, our militia was able to kill or wound several Waldeckers. They imprisoned thirty-nine-to-forty with no loss of our own.

General Heath has written to inform that he is moving toward New York. General Lincoln is doing the same. I pray the enemy sees this and leaves this station to defend New York. Such a sudden change of events would find the enemy unprepared to make a stand in New York from what I can measure. If circumstance allows, it would be a key target to upstage them in New York. At this moment, it is a hope only. I am desirous that Heath and Lincoln also move some men to join me in this neighborhood.

Wednesday, January 8, 1777 — Morristown, New Jersey

As I have sent money to General Lee by the British General Howe, so now the British Cornwallis sends money for his Hessian and British soldiers along with medicine. His letter asks for my protection and assurance that the aid will reach their men. I am willing to oblige. What he does not know is that the Hessian and British actions of rape, pillage, and destroy have raised the ire of the militia of every State. I cannot be responsible for their response though I will try to dissuade. Perhaps Cornwallis should take a reconsideration of their actions if he does not like the consequences. He may feel as helpless with Hessians as I feel with militia.

Thursday, January 9, 1777 — Morristown, New Jersey

Colonel Baylor's letter written on the 1st has been received. He is requesting recruitment of a horse regiment and to appoint officers to lead. I am favorable to his desire. My only warning is that he must use great caution in choosing officers. They cannot be too young as they are unprepared. They cannot be too old else they lack energy. The officers must be gentlemen not ruthless, rash, or inconsiderate. They must be men of integrity. It may behoove him to appoint others for favor or relation, but Colonel Baylor must remember that this cause is not a private cause, but rather a public one. The instances of good and bad behavior in a corps of this service have been originated by officers every time. He is free to nominate officers, but I reserve the right to approve or reject them.

Congress has afforded me the authority to do what I venture necessary for the success of this effort. They have resolved to raise sixteen more battalions in addition to the eighty-eight voted on previously. In addition to Colonel Baylor's wishes, I am promoting Nathaniel Gist to Colonel and conferring on him the duty to raise up a battalion under his charge. Under the authority vested in me, I am seeking to remedy the problem of short enlistments. Any battalions raised from this point shall be for a three-year enlistment or until the war with Great Britain has ended. We are fighting for the States of America. Those States must be united in our cause. No disunity or divided purpose can exist. Every man must pledge their talents and their attachment to the United States of America if this contest shall reach a beneficial conclusion for all.

Friday, January 10, 1777 — Morristown, New Jersey

The people of this neighborhood have been overly kind to this army. New Jersey understands what is at stake for our nation and particularly for their State. I am touched by the men who serve in this army. Jacob Ford was one such man. He made his fortune in iron manufacturing. He was a man who could have served in

Congress or in the leadership of this State. Instead, he chose to put on the uniform of a soldier. He chose to fight for our freedom as a colonel in the New Jersey militia. Unlike many militiamen who come-and-go, take-and-leave, Colonel Ford was a dependable defender for our cause. He and his family have a stately mansion on a hill in this city. They opened their home to house some of our Light Infantry. I could write volumes of books about men like Ford.

I write all this because today I received a sad note from one of our Infantry. He has informed me that Colonel Ford has died of pneumonia. While Mrs. Ford should be taking time to grieve, she has, instead, been tending to the needs of our men. She says her husband would have wanted that. He died for freedom just like any man on a battlefield. I have ordered a military funeral for this fine patriot. I will be attending.

Sunday, January 12, 1777 — Morristown, New Jersey

It has come to my attention that the British are considering trying General Lee, now in their custody, for treason against Great Britain. They make this claim as if he had not surrendered his commission as a British officer. The truth is, he surrendered his commission after the previous war with the French and Indians. Only after having moved to this Continent as a private citizen did he join our ranks at the beginning of this war. The British know that full well. I agree with Congress that we should trade the Hessian officers whom we captured at Trenton in exchange for General Lee. If General Howe refuses, then we demand fair and kind treatment to General Lee. If they do not abide as gentlemen in this way, retaliation will occur on our part toward their officers under our care. As it now stands, the prisoners of the British under our possession are treated with the highest considerations. Abuse of such men is not tolerated. As Christians, we can do no less. We are to love our enemy though he be our enemy.

Monday, January 13, 1777 — Morristown, New Jersey

Congress has forwarded to me the account of one of our captains, a Captain Gamble, who has just been released from a British prison ship in New York. He reports horrible atrocities being conveyed upon our men who are unlucky to be held by the enemy. Such behavior is unwarranted and is against everything humanity holds dear. I am writing immediately to General Howe regarding this circumstance, which comes on the heels of my letter regarding General Lee. I know they call us rebels. They think such treatment is justifiable. With that same mindset, we could mistreat their prisoners. They have occupied our soil with the intent to steal our liberties, rights, and properties. I do not believe General Howe would want such treatment for his own men or his own brother. If that be the case, then he must remedy the situation at once. I am culpable if I do not speak out. I am boldly requesting a response from General Howe. If he chooses to continue in this abuse of our men, then his actions will regulate ours.

I will concede that some of intelligence informs us the British are hard-placed to find sustenance for their own men, much less ours. We face the same struggle. Common decency allows that if our men cannot be cared for in their prisons, then they should be released on parole so that they may fend for themselves. Others of our men who have returned home inform me that the British offer captives from war better treatment if they enlist in service against their own countrymen. This is untenable.

The complaints of our men imprisoned by the British are that they are cold, malnourished, and sick without treatment under the enemy guard. I cannot help but be melancholy as I look at my own camp. I realize that those miseries are the same for our own men in this camp at Morristown. I must do all I can to make my men who are sacrificing feel better in their station than the men on those enemy ships. But the question is how?

Friday, January 17, 1777 — Morristown, New Jersey

Would not call it necessarily hemmed in, but the enemy is at Brunswick and Amboy with its foraging parties extending far out to resupply their empty stores. I have ordered the militia and any in that area to harass and deter such foraging. The less opportunity they have to resupply and feed their men, the greater their distress in these wintry conditions.

Saturday, January 18, 1777 — Morristown, New Jersey

Colonel Dayton has written from Ticonderoga. He is concerned as his regiment's enlistments end in February. He believes if he could be allowed to move his men southward to the Jerseys where they and he are from, that they would be more apt to continue to fight for our cause. His men have suffered much being away from home. They have heard of the depredations the enemy has exacted on their families, kinsmen, and properties. Having them near their homes would give them more motivation to fight to the war's end. I am agreeable to this, but Colonel Dayton is under the command of General Schuyler. I will not undermine those whom I have placed in authority. If a commander does not rely on his officers, then he multiplies his workload and reduces his effectiveness.

Heading into the next campaign, it may be wise to have the levies of New Hampshire, Massachusetts, and other States serve in or near their States for comfort, ease, and a ready recognition as to why they need to stay enlisted.

Sunday, January 19, 1777 — Morristown, New Jersey

On this Sabbath day, I feel an inkling of a man with his finger in the dike trying to prevent the water from pouring out too quickly. Our men are ebbing out due to enlistments ending and harsh winter conditions. So, I am in a spirit of prayer this day. I am calling on the States to stay united in our cause if we choose to remain independent. The spring campaign should find the British on route to Philadelphia. I am writing the Council of Safety in Pennsylvania to send militia here at once and to encourage their militia here to remain. For them to fight and hold the enemy in this State is better than scurry to address them in their own. Their militia so far has been a ready contributor to the victories at Trenton and Princeton. They are trained, equipped, and seasoned. I know many of these deserve to go home, but for the sake of the cause, I am asking their State's leaders to encourage their continuation through the first of April.

I am writing Congress to assist in raising the army. I am urging States to send men, even militia. The Delaware is frozen. The enemy is moving men from Rhode Island. I have ordered every officer that I can spare to forage for men. Some I am sending to recruit. Some I am sending to gather those who are dispersed to previous stations and have not followed the main of the army after conflict. I am also sending officers to the hospitals. Many men went there sick and injured and have not returned since their recovery. One battalion of Philadelphia leaves today. Two more are planning to leave in a few days. The only men that have remained are those with whom I have bargained and pleaded, but such efforts of persuasion have an expiration date. The five Virginia regiments are now only a handful. Massachusetts have supplied about seven hundred militia, but their tenure is just to the 15th of March. I need Congress to turn out every man possible, especially from Pennsylvania, Maryland, and Virginia. Congress must do so quietly as we are putting up the ruse that our numbers are swelling. Supporting this deception is difficult if it is found we are begging for men. Some publications in New York are already reporting our deficiencies.

Monday, January 20, 1777 — Morristown, New Jersey

Report is that Governor Cooke is raising men to defend his State of Rhode Island, while not meeting his State's quota of men for the Continental army. I am exceedingly sorry to hear that. He believes, I suppose, that each State can raise their own defense and independently defend their State against the army of a whole nation called Britain. This is ludicrous to assume and a failed policy in practice. Should every State seek to defend itself only, then each State will fall one-by-one. The plan is for the States to pull together to produce a formidable army that can defend against the assaults of the British. Governor Cooke may think his men will fight harder for their State and that men from other States will not exert the same energy. He is mistaken, especially on the latter. Each State's independence is dependent upon the other States' assistance. Our success depends on a firm union.

Levies must be raised speedily. The war will be more favorably decided if I can deal a harsh blow to the enemy before he receives reinforcements from home. A draft must be used if volunteers do not readily come forth. People can hire others to take their place if need be, but the levy must be met. I am calling on every State in most pressing terms to do their part to raise the eighty-eight battalions that are needed without delay. I cannot conceive why Rhode Island has adopted this policy, but I am insisting on changing this injurious scheme. They must realize the benefits this Continental army has produced killing, wounding, and imprisoning two-to-three thousand British soldiers. The effect of this success has been to reduce the dangers in Rhode Island as the enemy is forced to move to where the threat lies. With their help, I hope to close this campaign gloriously for the United Independent States of America.

In a move that unites the States, the Council of Safety of Pennsylvania is requesting the opportunity to send a ship of meat and flour for our prisoners in New York. They are not sending them for the prisoners from Pennsylvania, but rather for the prisoners from across the United States of America. This is the attitude Rhode Island needs to see. I am writing General Howe to allow safe passage of this ship. We would do the same for them, of course.

Tuesday, January 21, 1777 — Morristown, New Jersey

The disagreeable account was conveyed to me that Lieutenant-Colonel Preston's militia from Cumberland County of Jersey has deserted him. This is the problem I face daily when relying on militia. They come into this army, get supplied with all resources, and then carry off to their homes everything put into their hands. I do not label them all, but a general lot of them plunder this army of the necessaries, retarding our efforts to oppose the enemy's designs. Every State must supply militia willing to stay until the 1st of April unless sooner discharged by the Commander-in-Chief. Otherwise, the most fatal of consequences may be apprehended. Those who serve in the militia dutifully and faithfully should be allowed indulgences, but those who leave prematurely or who remain at home when everything is at stake, should be given no privilege and no mercy.

Wednesday, January 22, 1777 — Morristown, New Jersey

I am pleased to report to Congress that General Dickinson and four hundred militia defeated a foraging party last night taking forty of their wagons, a hundred of their English draft horses, along with a number of sheep and cattle. The enemy was caught so off-guard and afraid that they fled with so much precipitation that our men could only catch up to about nine in flight. General Dickinson brings honor upon himself being able to take a group of raw militia and bring about such great results. Would that I had more Dickinsons to help with the militia complexity.

I am requesting again that Congress assist in providing officers to look over the payrolls of the several regiments. This is necessary to ensure that all have what they need, and none have more than they need. We have officers in the field risking life-and-limb for the cause who are unpaid, while other officers are by their firesides drawing pay as they give excuses for their absences from service. This cannot be sustained and bring about a favorable outcome. Such an officer over payroll could also ensure that pay to our men does not begin at their call, but upon their arrival to the army. Delay from Congress for parsimonious reasons is a mistake. It will cost more than the perceived savings.

In the next campaign, I do plan on dividing the army into three with need for three lieutenant-generals, nine major-generals, and twenty-seven brigadier-generals. We also need to equip three new regiments of light dragoons. One will be filled by Colonel Baylor per his request, along with two others. I will recommend Colonel Moylan for one of these. He is a volunteer who has stayed beyond his enlistment and since his departure from the quartermaster office.

Friday, January 24, 1777 — Morristown, New Jersey

The strategy to hold the British here while making noise in New York to draw some of their men there, gives us a divided enemy that is made vulnerable to our advance. I have ordered General Heath to begin an assault on Fort Independence just outside of New York to see if he can draw enemy numbers away from here. If so, we might be able to defeat them in both places. If only I had men myself to take advantage of this, should the British respond.

I am writing Governor Trumbull to exert himself to levy and supply the troops requested of his State by Congress, this September last. Militiamen bring a hardship beyond what they take home. Militiamen are farmers and tradesmen who are good at their agriculture and art. When they are removed from their work, the army and the Nation suffer for want of their supply. Having a standing army would allow men to work in the vocation as soldiers and others work in the vocation of provision. At some point, I pray Congress will realize this. In the meantime, our numbers ebb and flow. When they are large, we can move and defend.

When they are small, the enemy, with knowledge of the shortage, is free to engage. Their ignorance of our numbers is our only respite. I am asking the good governor also to send with their men supplies, extra shoes, stockings, and shirts to be deposited into the inventory of the quartermaster so all will have what they need.

I am sending a stern letter to the Governor of Jersey, Governor Livingston. He must get his militia under control. He sends the lowest of men with even lower men commanding them. They plunder the inhabitants of his State under the pretense that they are Tories and deserve it. Their lawless rapine causes the friends to our purpose to consider willful surrender to the British for protection. This should never be. If the militia are put under good officers, the militia will act better. They will then seek to protect the inhabitants instead of distressing them. The make-up of the militia will be a better lot of men too if all men come willingly to serve rather than pay some scoundrel a trifling fee to take their place.

Saturday, January 25, 1777 — Morristown, New Jersey

I am issuing a proclamation to stop the bleeding in our Nation. On the 30th of November last, Lord and General Howe issued pardons to any who will lay down their arms and pledge their fidelity to the king of Great Britain. They have also been encouraging others not to assist in the cause of the United States of America. As a result, it is incumbent upon me to discern who are our friends and who are our enemies. If our friends, then the citizenry must pledge that and stand with us. If they choose to be with the British, then they need to leave all they have and withdraw to the British lines. Should anyone not take this pledge and make it known, then they will be considered our enemies and treated as such. I feel a great sense of pain in issuing this as it sounds as though I am a dictator to take such a stand. The inimical effect of the British offer is serving its traitorous purpose. I have militia plundering us. Citizens are giving to the enemy. All say they want freedom, yet many want comforts and luxuries. Many sit on the fence hoping to fall under the favor of whomever the victor is. The signers of the Declaration of Independence put in writing where they stand. They are suffering for it. The time is for everyone in these States to sign their names accordingly and not be a Judas at the table.

Sunday, January 26, 1777 — Morristown, New Jersey

The State of New York is requesting assistance from the other States as they are being deprived of commerce while the British station there. They truly have a need, but I struggle to have compassion for them. Twenty-six bales of clothing shipped to this army were intercepted in New York and distributed among their people in their homes instead of to our men in the field of fire. It goes back to my proclamation on the last. This army will take only what it needs. It will gladly forward a portion to the residents of New York. Such kindness from us is not reciprocated. Whose side are they on?

We see the same in our hospitals. Doctors and workers are making money, stealing medicine, and walking off with comforts while our men who are sick and injured from fighting for their freedom perish for lack of care. Whose side are they on? A new appointment must be made to oversee our hospitals.

Recruitment officers say they are having great success, yet few of their supposed recruits are leaving their comfortable quarters to join us in the field of sacrifice and discomfort. Whose side are they on? We need all recruiting officers to require those signed up to move with expediency to the army's headquarters for training and assignment.

General Schuyler has requested ninety-four tons of powder. I do not have this amount myself, thus I do not have it to spare. Where can I find the powder we need? Congress must help. Powder needs guns. I am asking Congress for more. Guns need men. As things go, I may not have an army left in this army when promised reinforcements do arrive. Whose side are they on?

Monday, January 27, 1777 — Morristown, New Jersey

I have not heard a thing from General Heath regarding his success or failure at Fort Independence. I am sending him another letter with my thoughts on taking the city of New York if he believes it is doable with the British troops not well-supplied there. I am emphasizing that I need to hear from him more frequently. I cannot make the best decisions with partial information. General Lee was terrible in this. I do not wish to see that repeated. My own insecurity causes me to fear others' commitment when I remember General Lee and Colonel Reed's correspondence. Even in a season of breakthrough, it is sad I still feel this cloud.

Tuesday, January 28, 1777 — Morristown, New Jersey

I have received an express from General Sullivan. He is close to the enemy camp with a large part of our army. He feels this is the best place to be as his scouts do not have far to travel and they can make better certain of the British movements. He wishes to stay there with my blessing. I am very hesitant for him to stay that close. At some point, no doubt, the enemy will notice him there, see the numbers, and put forth an offense to save their cause and end ours. I prefer he move away under the cover of darkness. By doing so, he may leave the enemy confused should they find he was there and worry about his next destination. Of course, I do believe in the counsel of many there is wisdom, so I am asking him to consult with Generals Maxwell and Stephens.

Friday, January 31, 1777 — Morristown, New Jersey

To hold an army in the elements with poor supplies and great discomfort is difficult. When citizens are housing, hiding, and protecting deserters, it is even harder. I am writing every State to request they enact laws to discourage such activities. They can enforce the laws with officers of the militia and justices of the peace. Desertion will cease when the offenders find they have no place to go.

Monday, February 3, 1777 — Morristown, New Jersey

I was never more sanguine than to hope the enemy would surrender Fort Independence or evacuate it in retreat to York Island. General Heath has reported bad news that makes me wish he would not have written at all. He has retreated from the enemy due to the cold and the fear of being outnumbered. His retreat prevents at the least a menacing Continental presence around the enemy. The retreat also increases the likelihood of success for the enemy's foraging parties. Now, I need him to join me here. His letter brings light as to why the enemy is suddenly sending men and supplies to Brunswick. Their intention will be to attack us here in

Jersey. I will now need General Heath's men to counter any move against this neighborhood.

I am sending a private letter to General Heath. He excused his abandonment of his orders regarding Fort Independence as the belief that he was outnumbered and could be surrounded if he delayed. I will not call his act cowardice, but I will call it unbecoming an officer worthy of command. Strategy, patience, and a sober assessment of the situation was needed before retreat. Too much caution on his part has disgraced his army. His act has made our army appear farcical and scared in the eyes of the enemy. Based on what I know, if he would have stayed and surveyed the forces against him, he would have realized that the day could have been carried with a vigorous effort.

General Heath adds to his letter his request for a leave to return home to his beloved New England for a while. Maybe some time at home will do him some good. I will approve his leave provided it is short in duration. Other officers are making the same request before the spring campaign. Though this increases the risk of desertion, it lessens the bodies we must feed and clothe here. Beyond that, it enables our officers the opportunity to bring back much-needed supplies. Who better to communicate with our citizens our needs than someone who has suffered here with us? What I would not give to return to my own home and spend time with Mrs. Washington and our family. Mount Vernon is the place I love. It is partially the reason I fight, so that I might preserve my own vine and fig tree.

Wednesday, February 5, 1777 — Morristown, New Jersey

Congress has written to inquire as to the barbarity of the British and Hessian troops toward our soldiers, officers, and inhabitants of New Jersey and New York. I do know such acts have been perpetrated by the enemy. Strangely, the Hessians have treated our prisoners much kinder than the British have. I am sending out men to interview the inhabitants to get a sense of that to which they have been subjected. I will report back to Congress. I have already written General Howe on multiple occasions as to their behavior. I do believe that complaints we make are just castigated as those from their enemy, unpatriotic rebels to Great Britain. Only if they fear our reciprocal response, do I believe a change will be made.

I am hurriedly sending men out tomorrow in every quarter to remove from the enemy's reach all wagons, horses, cattle, sheep, and anything else that will give aid to the enemy. Having these withdrawn makes it harder for the enemy to artillery forward against us or Philadelphia.

Congress's letter mentioned that General Schuyler is requesting general officers for his assistance. I am glad Congress has received this from him. It helps substantiate the need that I conveyed to them on the 22nd.

Smallpox is spreading throughout our camp in every sector and cannot be stopped. I have ordered inoculations be administered to every man. I am also ordering that any recruits being sent this way be inoculated before they make the journey.

One last thing to note, many of the inhabitants, for fear of the British, have been forced to take an oath of allegiance to the King. This brings me great alarm. We have been negligent in gaining oaths from our own people. They say they support independence but then plead neutrality when the enemy appears. Once the enemy can get them into an oath, we have lost support from that quarter. I am recommending that every State require an oath to our cause in the immediate. Any who refuse must be forced to move to the British lines for the King's care. I am glad that we live in a country where a man's word, his oath, is his bond. By taking an oath to the United States, we will create a bond that the British will find hard if not impossible to break. I fear for the day when our honor and word carry no weight. If we no longer defend our oath with our lives, than there is nothing we hold that cannot be lost.

Thursday, February 6, 1777 — Morristown, New Jersey

General Arnold and General Spencer are stationed in Providence. Their desire is to attack the British and Hessians on Rhode Island. Arnold has sent me a map and a plan, but I cannot make it out. As a result, I am hesitant to give the approval. I will give him the tightest of terms before he engages — if it can be made with the strongest of probability and a certainty of success, then he may. If not, I would prefer he deter such. Its failure would bring melancholy to all involved. The advantage is not just to be gained over the enemy across the lines, but must also be maintained in the hearts and spirits of those who serve by our side.

Saturday, February 8, 1777 — Morristown, New Jersey

Per his request, I am giving Brigadier General Parsons permission to cross over into the east end of Long Island to remove all forage from the enemy. This strategy in the winter has been beneficial. Many Tories are in that area. I am ordering him to also write out an oath to our cause because one has not been formalized by New York or Congress. Any who will not sign it, may leave with only the clothes they wear, to join the British. We must not allow them to take anything else that might be useful to the enemy.

Monday, February 10, 1777 — Morristown, New Jersey

General Schuyler would like to send some of our army to defend the Lakes near Ticonderoga. I am recommending he use troops from New Hampshire and Massachusetts. What I am finding are jealousies and rivalries between each State. No man of one State wants to serve any man of another State. I am doing all I can to emphasize to these men that we are one people of one Nation with the same interest in this united struggle. That so far has proven insufficient. For the moment, we must let men serve with men of their locality so that harmony exists. Perhaps being divided by State will keep us united in effort.

Wednesday, February 12, 1777 — Morristown, New Jersey

When I required an oath, it was a line that had to be drawn to determine who was with us and who was against us. In the army under my command, it seems we are of one accord on this matter. Brigadier General Maxwell is facing a problem with some young men under his command at Elizabethtown. They refuse to take the oath of allegiance to the United States. They refuse to go to the British lines. This is untenable. If the men will not take the oath, they must be forced to leave. No choice is a choice. To allow such men to stay only provides intelligence to the enemy. It poisons the people on our side. Those whom he honestly believes are trying to decide what to do because their oath means so much, I recommend he show lenity.

Friday, February 14, 1777 — Morristown, New Jersey

General Lincoln has arrived with around two hundred and fifty men. He believes another fifteen hundred or so are on the march. I am not confident in his estimate based on the number that have arrived versus how many I was expecting.

Colonel Knox has written. He prefers to set up a laboratory and cannon foundry in Springtown, Connecticut on the Connecticut river. He says copper, tin, and other materials for the works are close at-hand. The enemy is at least twenty miles away in Hartford, so it should be a secure place. I have given my consent to proceed.

Saturday, February 15, 1777 — Morristown, New Jersey

Finally, our clothier-general has been appointed and has arrived. He is Mr. James Mease. He is working with great expedition to determine the clothing we need and to formalize that request to Congress. Congress must act with the same urgency. Complaints about clothing are chief at this head. The lack of this necessary item retards our enlistment of new recruits as well. No one wants to serve in an army where they are not cared for or supplied in proportion to the sacrifices these are willing to make. I am asking Congress to address this at once, along with sending money so that I may cover the pay and needs of these men.

Tuesday, February 18, 1777 — Morristown, New Jersey

Comforting winds do blow during this crisis. Brigadier-General Caesar Rodney is requesting continuance in this struggle. Here is a man who came ready to serve. He signed the Declaration of Independence, which cost him dearly at home. He has led troops bravely into battle. He has raised and held the militia together from Delaware. That was a task altogether ripe with complexities. He forwarded his troops from Trenton at my request with no concern for his own command. He not only has faced public affliction and wartime struggles, but he has had to battle his health as well. A disease has disfigured his face, so much so, that he wears a scarf to cover it. Troops are going home for lack of provision, pay, or praise. Yet in all this, General Rodney continues to serve until the culmination of liberty.

What a blessing that in the isolation of command, I know there are men suffering as I and even more.

Thursday, February 20, 1777 — Morristown, New Jersey

Good returns from Colonel Nelson of Brunswick. He successfully remedied the loyalist and traitorous efforts of Major Stockton on the morning of the 18th. His men killed four and captured fifty-nine of their corps. They brought with this victory much needed arms and blankets.

We have strong reason to believe the enemy is about to make a push. Their want of supplies is forcing them to do whatever it takes to make a large forage and collection of provender. Enemy troops are moving from Rhode Island to Amboy. Their numbers are near eight thousand, while ours is about four thousand, though our troops are leaving every day. I am ordering utmost vigilance to guard against surprise. We are in a feeble state. Readiness is our best defense.

In a time when men are going home, enlistments are ending, and recruiting is slow, I find myself vulnerable to any help that is offered, as is Congress. Monsieur Faneuil is a French officer who came to attach his name to our effort. He encouraged us with a plan to adjoin Canadians to this conflict with a promise of success. Our hopes were buoyed by such designs, but then he generated only thirty or forty men. Now he desires to raise a number of men from the French Islands, provided Congress supplies arms and clothing for them in advance. If his efforts prove successful, this would be a help. Sadly, many come from France in search of fame and adventure. They may mean well but expending resources in exchange for no results is costly. I have asked him to make his request directly to Congress. I am hesitant to decline his request as more is at stake than Monsieur Faneuil's discouragement. In this battle against the world's greatest army, help is needed from every quarter. Respect then must be paid to any who seek to help. I propose that Congress hear him out, but only expend resources in exchange for results. The ambition to lead is noteworthy, but to have men given without earning them is detrimental to our purpose whether they be Frenchmen or American. Many want to start out on top instead of beginning at the bottom, working their way up, and along the way gaining the experience that makes a better-seasoned officer.

The French who join our cause also face the disadvantage of language, which makes their effectiveness harder to attain.

Sunday, February 23, 1777 — Morristown, New Jersey

One of the finest Christian men I know is Governor Patrick Henry. He is willing to exert every possession, and even his person, for our liberty. He is working tirelessly to raise up troops for our cause. I remind him as I do every governor to not just send men, but also send supplies and arms with them. I am as short of the latter as I am the former. Governor Henry is also the first to congratulate me for successes that we lately have achieved. I thank the Lord this day for those successes. I pray that Heaven will rain down many more in short order. We rest in God's Hand. Rise up O Lord, let Your enemies scatter and those who hate You flee before You — and us.

Friday, February 28, 1777 — Morristown, New Jersey

As the Commander-in-Chief of the Continental Army of the United States, it is comforting to be the one that a British officer can write to when he is mistreated by our own people. The British have mistreated General Lee under their confinement. It was made clear to them that as they treat our prisoners, we will retaliate and treat theirs the same. My belief is that the British have responded and given General Lee more humane treatment. I then am alarmed to hear that in a Concord gaol, Lieutenant-Colonel Campbell is facing, per his writing, the most severe confinement — one which would not be meted out on the worst of criminals. I am requesting the Council at Massachusetts Bay to remedy this immediately. The British have many more of our officers in confinement. We, at present, have no hope for an exchange as their prisoners under our care are far less. In a war that is based on Christian values and morals, my desire is that when the enemy does wrong, I speak out. When our side does wrong, I do the same. It is God's Side that I desire to be on, the side of right. Only then can we hope for Heaven's Assistance.

A call for firearms comes to me daily from every quarter — a call I cannot answer. I am writing the States to supply these in the immediate. I am also calling for the States to hold their officers accountable for the arms they are given and to ensure that any who take leave of this war, leave their arms behind for the ones who we wish to take their place. It is the least we can ask of those who return to private life.

Saturday, March 1, 1777 — Morristown, New Jersey

The nation of Judah was to be judged by a nation more wicked than them — the Chaldeans. A higher expectation existed for the nation who had experienced God's Care and Revelation. I cannot help but think of this as I write Congress later concerning the inhumane treatment of Lieutenant-Colonel Campbell and Captain Walker. We demand humane treatment for our prisoners under British confines. Why should we expect more from them than we ourselves are willing to give? It is an emotional enmity that we carry rightly against the British aggressions. Retaliation is our only check at this moment. But how can our evils exceed the ones we seek to redress? Congress must write policy to deter such. Should the Hessians catch wind of our treatment of their men, mind cannot conceive the distances they will go in return.

Sunday, March 2, 1777 — Morristown, New Jersey

Robert Morris has written in a very honest and candid manner. He is a great supporter in Congress. He and many others believe General Howe is in an exceedingly difficult situation which should hinder any initiative. Basis presents for that belief, but what they do not see are the difficulties Howe faces are no greater than our own. His are surmountable. His troops are just shy of ten thousand in Brunswick and quartered onboard boats at Amboy. His men are well-disciplined, well-officered, and well- appointed. On the other hand, our men are four thousand at most. We are comprised of untrained militia — undisciplined, and often unmanageable. If ours are not bolstered soon, the game may be at an end. My duty is to be honest in my correspondence with Mr. Morris as with Congress. To do any less would be insubordination. Failures could also come if I am not forthright. I do not share most of what I see or feel with many others. The candidly honest surveys are reserved for this journal alone. Congress, I must share to Mr.

Morris, expects whatever difficulties we face in the field to be dealt easily with the mere utterance of "Presto begone." They have no concept of the struggles, challenges, and obstacles at this head. I wish for Mr. Morris to express this to them in as clear a language as he writes me. I do know our cause is good. I hope Providence will support us.

Monday, March 3, 1777 — Morristown, New Jersey

Brigadier-General Arnold is itching for a fight. If his men and arms are as deficient as mine, I urge him to refrain from aggression unless success is certain. He must content himself with posing a strong defense.

Many have been promoted of late by Congress without my consent or knowledge. I am afraid that Arnold has not been one promoted to major-general. This may lie at his ambition to deliver a striking blow, which will capture the admiration and promotion from Congress. To make a move like this out of personal hurt rather than national good is a separation every officer must make, favoring the latter. I am reminding him that if he has not received the promotion which I believe he has earned, he must trust that I will do what I can to rectify the slight.

Where I am not sure of Arnold's promotion or omission, Brigadier-General Andrew Lewis has informed me that he was omitted. He is greatly disappointed. He now renders his desire to leave this army. It is his opinion that if his valiance and diligence for this Nation has brought doubt to his merit for the major-general rank, then he should resign altogether and let another more worthy take his place. As if I do not have trial enough to hold an army together, keeping capable officers to command them is a worry I should not have to carry in addition. The French want men to command, yet they have not proven themselves in recruiting or battle. Congress gives them commission and pay with no experience to justify. Officers who have worked their way up through the ranks, fought, recruited, and led are then denied the merit that they have rightly expected. In a normal occupation of soldier, resigning would be understandable, but we are at war. Freedoms are on the line. No capable officer should quit or withhold themselves from service or entertain any small punctilios to persuade them to retire. As Governor Patrick Henry has said many times, "Now is the time for all good men to come to the aid of their country." Let those words resonate to General Arnold, to General Lewis, and to any other. If time would allow, it would do a good deed for these two generals and any of others subjoining to their complaint to spend time with General Rodney. Rodney is willing to serve as a General or as a Private. Freedom and Liberty alike will reward all men who exhaust themselves in this purpose. Here is the guarantee for all who are slighted — a steady perseverance in promoting the public good and carrying out their orders will secure for them the unfeigned thanks of a nation. They will then obtain the desired rank and more from a nation most appreciative. This is my constant consolation.

This is a hard day. Now a third complaint about promotions has been received. This one from Brigadier-General Woodford. Congress informed him of his new rank as Brigadier-General, but his name came after the promotions to Brigadier of General Muhlenberg and General Weeden. Woodford once commanded both. He assumed that he would be named ahead of them. What General Woodford conveniently forgets, he resigned his post after a conflict, against my advice and plea. Now, in his promotion, he finds the consequences of his hasty decision. He has appealed to me to remedy this situation. I will not. He must understand that this complaint carries as much weight as air when compared to this contest which jeopardizes all that we hold dear. His family and his happiness and the same for this Nation is dependent upon his steady and vigorous assertions.

Thursday, March 6, 1777 — Morristown, New Jersey

General Lee has written with the consent of General Howe to request a prisoner exchange of officers of ranks lower than the general and several troops more numerous than this one general. As much as General Lee desires leave of his confinement, Congress has stipulated that officers should be given for officers of equal rank, soldier-for-soldier, and citizen-for-citizen. I cannot have that precedent violated. Once compromised, it will prove a continuance of inequality in our transactions, always to our subservience.

I have written Richard Henry Lee in Congress regarding the passing over General Arnold for promotion. There is not a more spirited and sensible officer in the army of the United States. He is a man of action and a man of tenacity. No one's friend or neighbor should be given preference over one of our most seasoned generals. I desire a response. I hope specifically for General Arnold's promotion to major-general. If there is a reason that I am unaware of, I am requesting an explanation.

The letter that I have flattered myself to never write again, I now must write to Governor Trumbull. He has come to our rescue on many occasions. Sadly, militia from the south come when they want, stay only as long as they want, and then leave after a few days of arriving, content that they are on record for the fight. Those who stay refuse order. They carry a pride that their very sacrifice is in showing up, not realizing that duty requires their appearance and their remaining for life, liberty, and family. General Lincoln has done a grand job in the militia he commands, but their enlistment expires on the 15th. If the British knew our numbers and plight, we would not be left unmolested as of this entry. Smallpox remains a deterrent, but we are inoculating as many as come. We are requiring those who have not been vaccinated to remain in Peekskill until that service is rendered. I am requesting that the Governor dispatch two thousand men immediately.

Knowing the enemy's needs, I am writing William Deur of New York to secure the wheat and flour contiguous to the water and move them to the interior of the State out of the enemy's reach. These stores are needed by the United States army. I am asking that he also ensure that the owners of these supplies do not demand an unreasonable price for our usage. It is, after all, for their benefit that this army is engaged in the field.

Saturday, March 8, 1777 — Morristown, New Jersey

The inhabitants of Jersey are eyewitnesses to the distress and inconveniences exacted by the British. They see the need for raising their militia. Yet, the rich are trying to buy the poor to serve in their place. The result? The raising of troops is delayed in the haggling. The time is nigh for them to lay aside the distinction between rich and poor. Every man must take up arms for the public good. For Heaven's sake, our Nation's survival should be our sole concern. A letter is a poor carrier of inflection, but I am praying Governor Livingston will hear me well on this matter.

Monday, March 10, 1777 — Morristown, New Jersey

Add to the name General Caesar Rodney, Major-General Gates who agrees to serve as adjunct-general in this dire circumstance. Many consider remaining in the same office after great success an insult. But General Gates has informed me that he will cheerfully join me in Morristown to the second post upon this continent. He gives form and regularity to this new army. This is our greatest need at the moment.

As General Gates is leaving Philadelphia upon receipt of the letter that I am sending him, I beg that he ensures our prisoner, the British Major Stockton, will be treated with respect in that quarter. He was taken in arms as an officer of the enemy. He should be treated as the rules of war require and not as a felon.

Tuesday, March 11, 1777 — Morristown, New Jersey

Because of the requirements placed upon me at the back door of the enemy's forces, I am unable properly to discipline General Wooster. His retreat from the enemy at New Rochelle was injudicious and unwarranted. I pray his courage and the respect of the men under his command can be regained. With that in mind, I am ordering him to return to Kingsbridge. He is to do all he can to confine the enemy there. I believe he is salvageable.

Wednesday, March 12, 1777 — Morristown, New Jersey

As we anticipate the enemy's movement, I am burdened by the thought that our army is too scattered. I am convicted by a wise tenet of war, which says a superior army can be defeated by an inferior one if the superior one is divided. Every State feels in danger. Every officer desires more troops. In doing this, all are left vulnerable. I am requesting General Schuyler and the bulk of the rest move to meet us here in Jersey before the start of the next campaign. From this station, we can more readily send men to where the enemy threatens. With the bulk of the army here, we can deliver an early stroke, which may dictate the rest of the war and perhaps discourage further investment from the King.

The areas of greatest danger are Jersey and Pennsylvania. I believe Philadelphia to be the enemy's target, though Pennsylvania holds a disaffection to our efforts. Jersey which is now housing the enemy reluctantly may soon consider submission to the enemy in order to get the transgress behind them. As a result, we must bolster our army in the present and regain the resolve of our neighbors. It behooves the change in strategy to gather our forces together. I am writing the Council of Massachusetts Bay and others to inform them of this plan. To protect the Lakes in the north, we will garrison the forts and supply them with provisions. We will charge the men there to keep diligently the cattle and carriages out of the enemy's reach.

Friday, March 14, 1777 — Morristown, New Jersey

Let me consider the objects wished by Congress for me to achieve — confine the enemy in their present quarters, prevent them from being supplied, and subdue them before they are reinforced. Their wishes and mine are the same. The problem is, how can I effect this work when Congress has yet to supply the army to achieve their goals? Do they not know that I have but a handful of men poorly supplied? Do they not know the enemy is larger in number, trained, and singularly focused? Fighting is their occupation. Farming is ours. Fighting is their vocation. Business is ours. Finishing the job so they can go home is their aim. Ours is to stay home and leave only if necessity requires it. General Heath and his troops are leaving. Militia from this State are hard to find. Those who have responded faithfully have left their homes so many times that they have grown tired answering the call. I have not heard of any Continental troops on their way. I have requested the brigadier-generals to send recruits, even in tens and hundreds. Few arrive.

Congress has expectations, yet they meet none of mine, not even a response. I am in painful anxiety that if levies do not arrive, we will meet with a melancholy event. The enemy plans to move once the roads are passable. Our current, unprepared state-of-affairs will benefit their objective. We need men. We need officers for these men. Congress has provided officers, but not as many as I requested. Those provided are not certain to perform in battle. The number of our army in this quarter is now under three thousand. What solution can I recommend? I would suggest that each member of Congress take my place one week per month. I will take theirs. They, in this station, would fearfully see the need. I, in their place, would readily with expedition meet their needs because I would fully commiserate.

Saturday, March 15, 1777 — Morristown, New Jersey

General Sullivan imagines that he has been slighted in some way. I have looked back at my journal to see the documentation of how often Sullivan is concerned for his own vanity and popularity. He is always ready to resign if he feels he has been disrespected in some self-conceived way. I am writing him back honestly to let him know that I have no other officer in this army who has considered himself more neglected, slighted, and ill-treated than he. Any neglect of notice that he has observed has occurred by accident or circumstance, not by design. His suspicions of being slighted are poisoning his happiness. If he does his duty, I will commend him as I have to the present day. Rewards will follow. I am exhorting him no longer to suffer the imaginations of evils toward him. They do not exist. He needs to remind himself continually of the noble cause for which he fights. Such reminders will help chase away selfish concerns. Worries and complaints like this weigh me down. Sometimes I feel like I am the only one who realizes what is at stake.

Tuesday, March 18, 1777 — Morristown, New Jersey

A point when letters and dispatches fail to deliver a favorable response or at the very least any response. I am asking Major-General Greene to repair immediately to Philadelphia. He is to ascertain how we are to be supplied with arms and various other necessities in which we are exceedingly deficient. We must be provided with tents, articles of clothing, ammunition carts, carriages for entrenching tools, and tools such as tomahawks and hatchets. The quartermaster-general should be made aware of these shortages and pushed to answer how and when we should see these needs met. He must also meet with the commissary of stores to see how he is proceeding with the casting of cannon and the making of cartridges. However, General Greene's chief mission is to impress upon Congress the need for their ready response. They are in a safe distance from danger, but only for the time being. Their hesitancy to act endangers the Nation and themselves. Greene must acquaint them with my ideas for the upcoming campaign, where our strengths and weaknesses are, and everything regarding the army. I am also asking Greene to plead with Congress to supply us with cash from the paymaster with regularity. Without cash, avenues available to us are stymied by lack of pay. I trust General Greene. I have confided in him my deepest fears. I believe he can be the most persuasive of all our officers. No one has a better grasp of our situation and the dangers which lie just weeks away.

Wednesday, March 19, 1777 — Morristown, New Jersey

Outside my quarters I see our men shuffle about this camp hungry and cold. These are the men who have given us hope. These are the men who have buoyed our Nation's morale. Yet, they are of the most neglected sort. Smallpox is having its way among us. I am thankful for the ability to vaccinate them, though for many of our men, the inoculation proves more stressful than the disease itself. I have had to house the sickest in residents' homes here in Morristown. The home-owners are greatly dissatisfied with this arrangement, but what option do I have? And why are our citizens not willing to sacrifice a room, while these troops are sacrificing their comfort, their financial well-being, and their lives?

What stresses me more, is what my brother-in-law Bartholomew Dandridge writes. He says that God has chosen me as his favored instrument to bring about the salvation of America. Our victories at Princeton and Trenton have caused the papers like the Pennsylvania Journal to write of my steady hand and unassailable virtue. They say I retreat like a general and act like a hero. I do not feel like a general when militia ignore my orders. I do not feel like a hero when we have very few victories to my name. Beyond that, a hero would be vaunted in the minds of his countrymen, yet I am unable to move them to come to our aid. I am praying for General Greene's visit to Congress to effect a repentant change. So, I wait.

Saturday, March 29, 1777 — Morristown, New Jersey

It has been reported that our men and stores have been attacked by the enemy at Peekskill. General McDougal has not sent me a report yet. My understanding is that the majority of our stores were destroyed by our own men, some one hundred and fifty, who were protecting that head to keep these supplies from falling into the enemy's hands. The enemy came, I assume achieved their purpose and left.

Mr. Kirkland, the Oneida missionary, arrived this week with a chief and five of his warriors. The British have been doing all they can to recruit their aid against this army. They have told the Oneidas and the other Indian nations that we are weak, near collapse, and that our stores and land are theirs for the taking. I did all that I could to show them otherwise. I even invited them to go and meet with Congress. I am sending them with my letter of introduction. Thankfully, they said they saw enough to know the British are lying. They say they are comfortable remaining neutral and might even join the hostilities in our favor. They were also glad to hear that the French may soon be assisting this cause. I have shown them every civility the past few days. They left this morning to give a good report to their nation.

Sunday, March 30, 1777 — Morristown, New Jersey

Colonel Reed has resigned his post as adjutant-general. This leaves a void that must be filled with the new army coming. I pray a new army is coming or the old one stays. I am writing a letter to Colonel Pickering to offer him the position along with pay of one hundred and fifty dollars per month. My hope is that he will accept this offer. This vacancy can delay the activity, hindering our preparation.

Tuesday, April 1, 1777 — Morristown, New Jersey

With the ill-treatment of prisoners on this side, it is consoling that Congress has allowed the position of commissary of prisoners to be appointed. They recommend Elias Boudinut be offered this position. I am approving of this candidate. His pay will be sixty dollars per month. His duties will not be difficult once he puts the business into a proper train. He is to stay close to the army, to receive and distribute prisoners, to assure they have all they are allowed, and to ensure they are properly treated according to the rules of war. His most difficult job will be to obtain an account of expenses already incurred. Once this is underway, I wish to annex a new responsibility which will be of the utmost importance. Under the commissary of prisoners' care is a wealth of intelligence — enemy soldiers with various insights into the status and plans of the enemy. I wish for Boudinut to procure from these sources as much insight as possible.

General Lee, imprisoned by the British as he is, has requested for members of Congress to come to his guarded apartment for an interview. I personally feel it is to undercut the cause for liberty and to compromise the rights of the citizens of the United States. I have sought to dissuade members of Congress from going, as their own freedom would be endangered by acceding to a meeting. Gratefully, Congress concurs. I will write General Lee of their decision and let him know that Congress, not me, sees no advantage to such a meeting. I will encourage him that we are making every effort to assure his safety and the attainment of his liberty. Knowing General Lee's attitude toward me, I will attach the letters from Congress for his own review so that he will know it is not my decision, but theirs which I convey.

Wednesday, April 2, 1777 — Morristown, New Jersey

I have received intelligence that the British ships have taken on fourteen days of wood and water. They have sailed out of Amboy. I am not sure where they are headed, but I am alerting Philadelphia.

Thursday, April 3, 1777 — Morristown, New Jersey

To record that Governor Cooke in Rhode Island is hoarding supplies and men is distressing. Both are needed for our army in this State where the enemy has his sights. How I am to oppose them, God only knows. The Governor continues to build his army to guard his State. He fears a threat posed by the few Hessian and British soldiers there. What he does not realize is that the enemy's numbers there are decreasing daily. The majority of the enemy troops are making their way to

Jersey to confront the Continental army here. I would pray that I have earned his trust over these last few years. If I felt Rhode Island was in danger, I would not be requesting troops to be sent here. Rather, I would be sending them there. That is not the case, however. The safety of the whole confederacy is dependent upon every State furnishing its quota of men. I am pressing upon him the need to complete his allotment. If he is unable, then he should send militia. If he does neither to good effect, we may as well give up any resistance.

General Greene has reported back on one issue that has been discouraging to many of the officers — the issue of promotions. General Arnold is greatly distressed at being passed over for promotion. General Greene inquired as to how promotions were given by Congress. Their reply was that major-general positions were allotted in proportion to the men contributed by each State. Connecticut has two major generals already. They were not deemed eligible for another. Thus, General Arnold has been bypassed not because of his lack of merit but because of some ill-advised rationale of proportionality. I am writing General Arnold regarding this so that he may not think some nefarious coalition has kept him at bay. I rejoice that, even being overlooked, he remains in this army and in his command, doing all he can for the sake of liberty.

Sunday, April 6, 1777 — Morristown, New Jersey

On a day in which we remember the mercy of our God and the indulgence granted by our Savior, I am inclined to do the same. Bounties were offered for soldiers to enlist or reenlist. Many agreed to this call, received their individual bonuses, just to desert a few days later. I have authorized stern punishments for such men if caught. I am now being told that some would return to serve their time as integrity requires if only the punishment for such offenses be waived. I am issuing a decree of pardon for all who will return for whatever reason by the 15th of May next. Those who are caught who do not return under this indulgence will suffer.

Friday, April 11, 1777 — Morristown, New Jersey

The British are fitting their transports at Amboy to accommodate the movement of their troops. I am somewhat certain it is to make their first push at Philadelphia. Governor Johnson of Massachusetts visited our troops several weeks ago to determine our needs. I was comforted at his concern and his pledge to forward troops upon his return. I have waited in painful expectation of reinforcements, but they have not materialized. I am writing the Governor to remind him of his oath and that our army is worse off now than when he visited. Our chances in this war are dependent upon the governors of each State doing their part, meeting their quotas. Assuming they are doing their duty to persuade, a heavier hand may be required to move their men from comforts of home to the urgent call issued in the field.

Saturday, April 12, 1777 — Morristown, New Jersey

A feeling of home has livened my spirit. Mrs. Washington arrived a few days ago. This is the first day that I have had to sit with her. She has made my favorite breakfast of hoe cakes. I smelled them early this morning as I awoke. What a blessing the Lord has bestowed upon me in this dear lady. After we ate, I was glad to open a letter from my brother. He shares with me the efforts my sister is exerting to make stockings for me. How I love the institution of family. It is with my family that I can share openly all vulnerabilities. They have known me for my entire life. They have seen my victories and defeats. They pray for me. They write to me. They think of me. I can go to them when no one else will listen. They love me and would gladly bear my burdens if enabled.

How valuable is this resource when the army at my command lacks men? I have found it impossible to induce officers to bring men to the field. Short enlistments make this a perennial problem. If only the men at my disposal had signed three-year enlistments early-on. We very well might have driven the British from the Jerseys, perhaps even New York. But no. The ridiculous and inconsistent orders of most executives of the States impede the hopes of success. To be discouraged is easy, but across from me sits Mrs. Washington. In my hand, I hold a letter from my brother. Providence steels my resolve in this day of trouble — by His Grace.

Sunday, April 13, 1777 — Morristown, New Jersey

Home is my comfort, even today in Morristown. No sooner do I feel encouraged, then I get a letter from Governor Henry of my home State of Virginia. They know our need for troops, yet the plan they have set forth to supposedly bring me comfort, discourages me more. Their volunteer plan will never answer any valuable purpose. It cannot succeed in bringing the reinforcements we need. Instead, they put into question the continuance of our liberties. Virginia's "volunteer" plan is worse than short enlistments. Volunteers feel as though they are doing a favor to their country and are being infringed upon in the pursuit of their happiness. They come to camp with an air of superiority. They decide where they will stay, what order they will obey, and what hardship they will endure. They leave at any exigency of affairs even when a war is close to being won. They bring discouragement to the remainder who must stay. I cannot advise the volunteer plan of my home State. It is pernicious. I do offer Governor Henry some weight to his argument for this plan. He says great fear of smallpox exists and that this retards the collection of troops. I understand that full well. I fear smallpox more than the enemy; therefore, we do inoculations. Should not Virginia carry out this action throughout our State? We do need troops. I know the Governor is attempting to meet them in an expeditious manner, but it would be more advantageous to build this army through regular enlistments. This will take considerably more time, but it is worth the wait if only they begin the process.

Tuesday, April 15, 1777 — Morristown, New Jersey

With pleasure I received a letter of support from my planter friend in Virginia, Landon Carter. It feels good to recount to him that, though we have been outnumbered, we have harassed the enemy all winter, skirmishing with their foraging parties, attacking their picket guards, and distressing their movements. Lacking men, we must focus on a defensive war until men promised, arrive. The enemy's intent is still not discernable. I am praying the God of armies may incline the hearts of my American brethren to support this contest and provide for our needs. My longing, as I shared with Landon, is to see this thing brought to a speedy conclusion so that I might rejoin him in the happiness of domestic life. This is my fervent prayer.

Friday, April 18, 1777 — Morristown, New Jersey

Congress has written. I am delighted to note that. They are responding. I give credit to General Greene for this effect. However, they are concerned that factions exist within the army in this quarter. They have heard, as have I, that some are taking the appellation of "Congress's Own Regiment" and another group the appellation of "George Washington's Life Guards." This is very problematic. I have issued the orders to all officers that such distinctions will meet severe reprehensions. We are one army, the Continental Army with no distinctions and no divisions.

I am writing a return to Congress. They are comforted in the number of soldiers that Pennsylvania has retained in that part. They, like Rhode Island, are holding back soldiers for their own defense. For a body of leaders concerned with division, dividing this army's troops in the various States is inexpedient. The practice subjects this Nation to injury, not to mention a quick defeat. I need all recruits sent to this quarter. If all are collected here, I then can respond to the enemy's movements from this head quickly and effectively.

Sunday, April 20, 1777 — Morristown, New Jersey

Word has reached me that Boston is in great alarm. Rumor has it that the British are heading for Boston under General Burgoyne to decimate that city and punish its citizens. As a result, Massachusetts is withholding troops for their own defense. Again, like in Rhode Island and in Pennsylvania, if troops are withheld in every State, then our force is divided and easily defeatable. All intelligence tells me the British heading to Boston is wrong. I would venture to guess it is a feint of the enemy. All States must send their men to this head. From this point, we can then address any enemy stratagem.

Monday, April 21, 1777 — Morristown, New Jersey

Richard Henry Lee has written with the sanguine hope of assistance from France. As much as such help would be appreciated, it can provide no occasion for the smallest relaxation in our preparedness. I profess that I am one of the class who has never built any confidence in the French assistance. How can I hope for some outside nation to assist when our own people hesitate to fight? Delay has been experienced in appointing officers, many others are resigning, those who sign up are unfit, and recruiting officers carry out great abuses. This distresses me. I believe only when our people show resolve will any outside power be inclined to join in the fray. As it now stands, seemingly the call is for someone other than this Nation to fight our battles for us. This is an impractical footing from which to hope.

Tuesday, April 22, 1777 — Morristown, New Jersey

I responded yesterday, but Mr. Lee's suggestion of exempting all persons concerned in ironworks from military duty is still gnawing at me. Yes, we need ironworkers as we are in want of cannons and arms. But do they not see that in this area (and in a few others), the vast majority of the people are ironworkers? Shall parts of the country not have a militia or contribute to the army because they feel they contribute through their trade? Would this not leave those parts needed vulnerable to the very attack they are working to prevent? Why would we let the ironmaster be exempted from military service because of his contribution to the war, when the farmer's contribution helps feed the soldiers, the shoemaker contributes to the clothing of the soldier, and other manufacturers provide their contributions for the army? Every trade is vital. All must work in this effort, but what good is the cannon if there is no one to fire it? What good is the shoe if there is no soldier to wear it? What good is the food if there is no camp to eat it? Exemptions for service must be few, quantified, and named. Otherwise, there is great detriment to the cause of a free United States of America. I have a two-fold duty — secure manufacturing to meet our needs and prevent numbers under this pretext from withholding their aid in the military line.

Saturday, April 26, 1777 — Morristown, New Jersey

General McDougal's letter informs me that the enemy has anchored transports at Dobbs Ferry for possible incursions up the North river. Appearance is they are also moving toward the mountain passes to cut off communication between this army and the North river. I am ordering General Clinton to send as many men as he can spare to protect those passes, to awe the disaffected, and protect our friends.

General Glover was offered a brigade to command. I was approving of his name on this list of assignments from Congress. I am surprised and a little disheartened that he has declined the appointment. I am writing him this day. Diffidence is becoming in an officer, as humility is an admirable trait, one that makes it easy for men to follow. But modesty aside, I need General Glover to assume this command. The British take great heart in officers who resign as this brings question to our cause and doubts to our success. When an officer who at first stepped forward, recruited, and led men into battle resigns, the men scatter from the cause as well. Our blessed Savior referenced this truth when He quoted Zechariah, "Strike the shepherd and the sheep will scatter." Now is the time for listlessness to end. Officers must think no more of private inconveniences. They must step forward to serve. Else, the private inconveniences will become public enslavement.

With deference to our friendship, I am writing a letter to Dr. Craik today with a soft persuasion that he leaves his practice and family and fill one of two vacancies at our hospitals between the North river and the Potomac. He can choose to be Senior Physician and Surgeon of one of the hospitals or he can be Assistant Director-General of the other. The pay will be good with travel expense as well as forage for two horses. I am praying he will agree to one or the other. He has always helped me in my time of need as a lifelong friend. I am his friend and now am in need again.

Sunday, April 27, 1777 — Morristown, New Jersey

General Lincoln informs me there are many desertions of late. He states they are selling their arms to the British for just a few dollars. This case makes it clear. Our men are doing so because they are not being regularly paid. As I research the officers' requests for payroll, it seems the money has been distributed to adequately cover these needs. I suspect there are officers of these regiments who are taking the money under the pretense of paying their men but are using the money for their own extravagant use.

I am ordering General Lincoln to gather his men immediately to ascertain what is owed to them. He is then to order the paymaster to draw what is necessary to pay these men. He is to assure that each man gets what he is owed. General Lincoln must also alert the officers that once our regiments are drawn together, I will personally cause an exact scrutiny to be made into their accounts. I will surely hold them responsible for any indiscretions.

Monday, April 28, 1777 — Morristown, New Jersey

General McDougal has written to inform this command that the enemy has raided the stores in Danbury, Connecticut. I am ordering him to move quickly to block their retreat if they have not reached their boats at this time. As difficult as it is to get supplies, it is even more tragic when these are lost due to our inability to resist or our lack of alert to address. I must report this to Congress, but I know it will add supineness toward our support.

Wednesday, April 30, 1777 — Morristown, New Jersey

I have a fear of my papers, baggage, and other items of public import being captured or stolen. These items, including this diary, would give great aid to the enemy. As we are heading into the dangerous jeopardy of war, I cannot protect these items while seeking to carry out my command. I am asking colonels who I trust to nominate four men to be guards for these things. For such sensitive and important duty, I need men of integrity, men with family, men who are native to this country, men of stature, men who are clean and soldierlike, and men who have the highest allegiance to fidelity. From the point of stature, I desire men no taller than five feet, ten inches and no shorter than five feet, nine inches. Uniformity, courage, and commitment are essential to thwart any temptation or attack.

Monday, May 5, 1777 — Morristown, New Jersey

I was honored this morning to receive a letter from Congress approving the promotion of General Arnold to the rank of major-general. I am also gratified that when Congress heard of his bravery on the field in Danbury, having one horse shot from under him and another wounded, they sent him a fine new horse on which to fight, as a token of their esteem. The one issue Congress needs to address is that in the tardiness of their promotion, they promoted several who served under General Arnold ahead of him, making him serve the ones whom he has led. General Arnold shows bravery, enterprise, and industry in all he does and to the benefit of this Nation. I am prayerful that Congress will remedy this order of command.

Rumors persist that the British are making a move on Ticonderoga. In response, General Wayne has three thousand troops in that quarter discouraging the enemy's inclinations without great loss of blood. From what I can discern from the enemy's movements and intelligence gained, there is no plan to move on Ticonderoga. I am in hopes that some of those men stationed there will make their way to this head.

British General Howe has been giving sixteen dollars to any of our deserters who come to them with their arms. My understanding is that he is raising that bribe to twenty dollars. Congress needs to know this. Their inconsistency to pay our troops brings incentive for those not sold on our cause to default to the enemy.

Wednesday, May 7, 1777 — Morristown, New Jersey

It appears the enemy may be moving toward the North river. To slow their movement, I am writing General McDougal to fortify Fort Montgomery for resistance. Should the enemy make a move on them, we will be able to come to their aid. General Arnold is on his way toward Peekskill per my order. He can bring great assistance with intelligence that he has derived, as well as the skill he can employ for opposition.

I am angered the State of Massachusetts is making their men pay for their arms. I could understand the philosophy if it is to cover any arms lost or damaged by the soldier, but can they not see that these men are already sacrificing enough to join in this fray? I will do all I can to stop this practice.

Friday, May 9, 1777 — Morristown, New Jersey

Mr. Silas Deane and General Heath have sent me letters of recommendation for a Colonel Conway, an Irish gentleman who has been serving in the French army. They are requesting an appointment in our army for this man. I do not know who he is to recommend him. I will say that he must be more useful than others who have come from France since he speaks the English language and has a history of combat.

Sunday, May 11, 1777 — Morristown, New Jersey

The enemy with complete control of the water around us is making raids on our stores and fortifications. I gratefully record that though they harass us, they are unable at this point to make a decisive stroke. Their forays bring them losses even when they succeed in gaining stolen provisions. Attrition affects the enemy's stay. Seemingly, the sentiments of our people toward the cause of liberty are maintained and strengthening.

Governor Trumbull is aware of these raids. He has requested to keep two regiments of men in his State for response. Until Congress informs me of their disposition of reinforcements and enlistments, I cannot entertain any State keeping back men. We need them all at this quarter. From here, we will dispatch to wherever the enemy may threaten.

Monday, May 12, 1777 — Morristown, New Jersey

Being in this position, I depend upon the true situations as expressed by the officers on-site. I respond according to what they share, with the hope that what they transmit is accurate. With supplies and men in short supply and the spring campaign about to begin, I need to confirm our situation with an objective eye so that men and arms may be dispersed where needed. We cannot afford them to be wasted where unneeded. I am assigning Major-General Greene this task. He needs to determine if we need more posts of communication. He should check the forts to ensure they are ready for attack. He must check the waterways for weak points to the enemy. He can decide the greatest areas of passage for our army. I also need him to determine what posts are defensible and which need to be supplied. It will be helpful to know what areas have no possibility of successful defense. Then, we can move our stores and supplies from those places to reduce our losses. He needs also to determine where militia may best be placed for general defense and where the regular army may be deployed in eminence.

General Arnold has arrived today. I was going to send him to Peekskill, but he is haunted by what he calls insults to his character in Philadelphia, which caused him initially to be passed over for promotion. I am allowing him to go to Philadelphia to clear his name. This is what I would desire if it were me. I know he needs to get this weight off his mind so that nothing will impede his effective execution of duties in the command I have given to him.

Friday, May 16, 1777 — Morristown, New Jersey

I have received a very confrontational letter from Monsieur Malmedy. He complains that because Rhode Island issued to him a rank of brigadier-general, that the Continental Army should issue him the same. Instead, Congress appointed him to the rank of Colonel, which he feels is beneath his abilities. He believes such a change in rank brings question to his character as he has already reported to friends in Europe that he is a brigadier-general in the American army. His argument is that if one State recognizes him at the high rank, that all States must do the same. This is an error on his part. No State legislature's actions should be binding on any other State or on the continent as a whole. State legislatures only have local jurisdiction. Malmedy holds too high of an opinion of himself. If he wishes Congress to recognize him at the higher rank, he should ask for that favor, not demand it. His disposition is certain to cause him difficulties in the future. Like Cain, sin is crouching at his door, but he must master it. It is unfair to elevate one to a position unearned to the deflation of the American officer who has fought, worked, and earned his elevated rank.

I am writing Richard Henry Lee as my friend to find out what in the world does Congress expect me to do with these adventurers of foreign origin who have been given ranks as field officers? I am in hopes Congress will be more cautious in whom they promote. They must share what the rank means. When they award a rank to one of these foreign men, Congress needs to inform them that their rank does not mean a command is immediately in the offing. Their expectations must be set to reality and not to some dream of command or glory. This cause is too important for any one person to seek aggrandizement.

Three hundred Tory levies attempted an attack on General Heard's men at Paramus. Thankfully, he was made aware of it and moved away before they arrived. A heavy fog further complicated the Tory attack. It appears they lost ten men in the short fight as our men were relocating.

Monday, May 19, 1777 — Morristown, New Jersey

I have need of a new position. We have adjutant-general. We have commissary-general. We have quartermaster-general. Now we need a complaint-general. It seems any time a lacking occurs in some area of need, I must fill that need. In the lull of battle, or in the expectation thereof, men and officers find time to complain. That being the case, I received a letter from General Gates. He contends that there is an imputation of partiality in favor of this army to his in the north. He bases this complaint on the fact that he has not received the number of tents he requested. He knows full well that we lost a large bulk of our tents with the raid on Danbury. He also should be aware that this army is on the move and is in need of tents as well. His army is stationary. With the shortage of tents, they have the luxury of building barracks and huts where he now resides. Does he not know that if I had ample tents, he would get the amount that he has requested? I am asking him to recall if at any time I have ever omitted complying with a request of his when it was within my power to do so. I wish for one minute he would consider the load that I bear and the efforts I make without prejudice.

No sooner do I record the above entry, then I receive a letter from Major Colerus. He is upset that as a major, he has not received a place to serve. I will have to reiterate to him what I told him at the onset — when he gained a competent knowledge of our language, I would find a place for him to serve. This has not been out of neglect or disparagement of his merit. He has since improved his grasp of our language. I now have a vacancy in Colonel Hazen's regiment at

Princeton which needs one of his rank. Should he deem this not below him, I ask him to make his move in that direction immediately. If he believes this is beneath him, I have no other place for him. It is a laudable quality of an officer to esteem emulation, but I condemn those with lofty ambitions to expect this army to yield to gratify their views.

Friday, May 23, 1777 — Morristown, New Jersey

Brigadier-General McDougal writes of his concern of the impropriety of the diversity in the modes of training that our army now falls under. I am in full agreement. I am hopeful to soon have a regular system of discipline, maneuvers, and regulations throughout the army. All must learn how to march with a uniformity of training so that when they come together, they act as one. They must learn how to handle the noise of fire and how to respond when under fire. Training is greatly lacking at the present. May we, by Providence's Hand, find one who can help us achieve this purpose.

Officers have been leaving the army and our cause again. When a few are apprehended, they express the reason is for want of pay and necessities. I cannot object to this expression, but the cause for which we are assembled must take priority over comforts and disappointments. People leaving brings great discouragement and distrust for those who are staying. Only a bold courageous soldier will stay when he has every reason to leave. May all remember why we are here and the cost if we abandon our call.

Saturday, May 24, 1777 — Morristown, New Jersey

I can be grieved by the selfish ambition men display in preference to the nobleness of our purpose. Yet, just when I feel this is the plight of all mankind, my emotions are lifted by men such as Colonel William Lee. I had written Congress in request of an adjutant-general. Congress recommended Colonel Lee. I preferred Colonel Timothy Pickering because of my familiarity with his high character, military genius, industrious attention to the study of war, his education, and his zeal to take care of business. When he stated he was unable to take this position, Colonel Lee was brought in. He has served admirably, though he had a distrust for his abilities to fill this appointment. His humility and dedication to service have made him a fine addition. Then he brought a letter from Colonel Pickering stating that he had taken care of the business at-hand and would be willing to serve as adjutant-general if I still had that need. Colonel Lee immediately agreed to step down. He said he would serve gladly wherever needed. I am writing Congress that I had need of one adjutant-general and now have found the luxury of two. I am retaining Colonel Lee with Colonel Pickering. Both these men seek to serve in any capacity that America desires. What a blessing.

Sunday, May 25, 1777 — Morristown, New Jersey

The thought has occurred to me that some advantage might come if we were to surprise the British at Kingsbridge. I am writing Major-General Putnam of the idea, not to persuade but to gain his input, along with General McDougal's and General Clinton's. This attack would need to be done in the dark of night, and from the water. It would need to be cloaked under the pretense of moving men to Tappan, even having wagons loaded on that side of the river to give even our own men a belief that this is our intention. Or we could let the men believe we are embarking at Peekskill to reinforce our garrisons on the river. Either way, we could then swoop down upon the enemy at Fort Washington and perhaps even take Fort Independence. Sadly, deception even of our own men is necessary as any time something is shared with too many, it quickly becomes known by our enemy.

Monday, May 26, 1777 — Morristown, New Jersey

In my prayer time yesterday, I was convicted of the spiritual and immoral state of our men. As I went to worship, very few of our men were in attendance, nor have many attended in Sundays past. Do they not think we need God at this time? Do they really think God will favor those whose fidelity and love toward Him are superficial? I cannot imagine the Divine Hand to favor our cause if we are drunk with wine, promiscuous with women, and engaged in gaming which takes from one to benefit another followed by laughter of all but the loser. Such activities are ruinous to an army, to families, and to even the ablest officer. I have assigned chaplains to every regiment. I am asking every officer to require the men to attend Sunday worship regularly. May God change us. May He incline our hearts toward Him. We cannot win without Him, nor do we want to. This Nation can only long endure if it is grounded and built upon the Bible and the God who authored it.

Tuesday, May 27, 1777 — Morristown, New Jersey

With all my being, I labored to get a commissary-general to this place to meet the needs of this army. No sooner did Congress approve one and appoint one, they ordered him to Philadelphia. He has been absent ever since while our men starve. I have sent request after request but to no avail. I am ordering the assistant commissary-general to repair to this camp immediately.

I was riding later this day and I met a man who informed me that Brunswick can be had. He also led me to believe that there are spies among our officers. I am unsure of this man and have him under surveillance.

Wednesday, May 28, 1777 — Morristown, New Jersey

General Howe has written to me demanding that we return to them the number of their men we have in our possession equal to the number of our men he has released back to us. His letter hints a threat against the remainder of our prisoners under his confinement if we do not oblige his request. I am not certain what Congress is doing on this matter or if they have for some reason released less than received. When our men imprisoned are at stake, I am going to urge Congress to act in a manner that best protects them. Our Nation must be fair and do right in our exchanges and in our treatment of the enemy under our care.

The enemy advanced on our post at Boundbrook. They retreated when our men went out to meet them. Long-range firing occurred but to no evident harm. I have just returned from checking the conditions there.

I have decided to move my headquarters to Middlebrook, which is closer to the enemy so that I might respond more expediently when they begin to make their move. Our soldiers are tired as am I. Our bedding is nonexistent with the men continuing to make their bed on the ground. I am just grateful that it is warm now. Our rations are poor. Our men grow fatigued with long watches in the night with nothing to see. Though we are not ready for action, action may be the best remedy to our situation as it will reinvigorate the men in camp and bring more men to our fellowship. Each time activity occurs, there is the hope that this war will soon be over. I pray with a favorable outcome.

Thursday, May 29, 1777 — Middlebrook, New Jersey

I am thrilled with the news of Lieutenant-Colonel Miegs's success against the British at the Harbor in New York. His men sailed on their whaleboats to one side of Long Island. He then had his men carry the boats to the other side. There they embarked upon the enemy, killing six, capturing ninety, and destroying twelve brigs and sloops. Our men also destroyed one hundred and twenty tons of hay, corn, oats, and much merchandise of the enemy. Miegs then sailed back to New Haven within a twenty-four-hour period. Amazing industry these men have. Their work has greatly distressed the enemy. We are seeking the offensive, though we are few. Often, the brave few are the ones who can make all the difference in this war.

Saturday, May 31, 1777 — Middlebrook, New Jersey

It is reported, and I have no cause to doubt, that the British set sail out of New York. It is believed their intentions are still Philadelphia. With troops on board, it is figured they are bound into Delaware Bay. I am writing Governor Patrick Henry to put his militia on alert and have them well-supplied with ammunition. If the fleet lands on his coast, he needs to have his militia engage in the immediate even if the whole of his militia has not arrived. This may discourage the enemy or at least cause him to rethink his strategy. The British need to receive the impression that there is an unfavorable disposition of the people toward them. Militia's quick activity is the thing for which they are best-suited. Organizing and assembling them is counter to their nature. Such order reduces the thrust of their zeal.

Eighteen transports appear to have arrived in York perceived to be foreign soldiers, if their uniforms are any indication. It is supposed that they have arrived to reinforce General Howe.

While Mr. Deane is working hard overseas to gain support, he is making promises that can bring trouble to this army. Case in point, he has sent Monsieur Ducoudray on his way to Philadelphia to assume command of our artillery and the rank of major-general. This is extremely untenable. General Knox has served admirably and has our artillery on the best footing. He is one of the greatest men in this army. He is also one on whom I rely above almost all others. He would take such a move as an insult. General Knox is a native. He is committed to our cause. He has sacrificed incessantly to see this thing to its favorable conclusion. I am strongly writing Congress to find some other purpose for the Monsieur. I will not countenance General Knox's replacement or reduction in authority, nor will I subject him to another.

I realize the complexity of this situation as we do need foreign help, foreign input, and foreign supplies. With prudence, policy, and the most respecting of feelings, I pray Congress will redirect Monsieur Ducoudray to some other position of usefulness for our cause — one that is equally fulfilling to this man who has come to render aid.

Sunday, June 1, 1777 — Middlebrook, New Jersey

Desertions outnumber enlistments. I have made this known to Congress who expects me to put forth a valiant defense for our liberties. It is very unlikely that any effectual opposition will be given to the British with the numbers and state of our army at the present. I have informed Congress that General Howe's offer to our men of immunity and a bounty to join him is enticing many of our men. As a result, I see men who are here one night and with the enemy the next. I am grieved that men whom I have fought with and fought for have turned their arms against us. Such treachery, I cannot comprehend. Do they not know what we are fighting for? Do they not understand that the oppression of the British is what drove us to this separation? I will grant that this avenue we have chosen is hard, but it seems to me that right is always hard. It is this struggle that will lead to a satisfaction when the fight is done. I cannot imagine being content having surrendered or taken the easy way. I could not live with myself even under my own fig tree and vine. I have asked Congress to counter Howe's overtures, but no response has come. A simple yea or nay would relieve me, but none is forthcoming.

Tuesday, June 3, 1777 — Middlebrook, New Jersey

I am gratified to report that I have received requests today from men having been seduced by the enemy to join them. They now wish to return. The treatment promised did not pan out as they wished. These deserters have realized afresh why this engagement was launched at the first. I look back at my entry just two days before and realize that Providence works in the favor of right sometimes sooner than later. Now I have the dilemma. If we let these return, it will bolster our numbers and encourage these here who have considered switching sides to stay the course. At the same time, these who have deserted may have an injurious effect. They may prove to be sunshine soldiers as Mr. Paine so aptly described. They may also be spies sent back to gain more intelligence. The reverse could also be true. They may bring useful intelligence to this head. I am of the mind to write Congress to encourage a sound policy of reentry. I also desire them to make offers to counteract the enemy's temptations. Pardon and indulgence, I believe, can be offered with caution, but their position in this army cannot be fully restored. To reestablish these men in the same stations as when they left will discourage those who have chosen to suffer with a steady devotion. We know the enemy is dubious. The British call out like the prostitute in the streets declaring that surrender brings relief and is easier than resisting temptation. May we see resolve in our men — those who have left and those who have never strayed. I will await Congress's guidance.

Friday, June 6, 1777 — Middlebrook, New Jersey

The French gentlemen who have come to aid our cause are bringing great uneasiness in the artillery corps especially with regard to Monsieur Ducoudray. The very thought that he should supersede General Knox is untenable. The artillery of this army has served well for two campaigns thus far. They are attached to our cause and to each other. They have shown thus in the field. They have earned their rank and command. To allow a French officer or any foreign officer to join this conflict and assume the same rank in this army that they had in their home country is illogical. We have no idea how the rank they claim was given, nor do we truly know if the rank they claim is legitimate. To place these over the men who have served valiantly here is reprehensible. It is also poor policy for someone loosely connected to our cause (for the sake of personal glory) to take over a command of men who are warmly attached to the rights of this country.

It is easier to prevent evils than to remedy them once they occur. So, I am proposing one of two solutions to the issue of foreign officers. The first, we could create a second artillery division for these French officers to command. This is unlikely to succeed as they have not learned our language. Also, men native to our Nation will be hesitant to serve officers they do not know, nor are certain of their fidelity. Besides, our own men have had difficulties raising men for their own command. How can creating another division not increase the realities of our shortage of enlistments? The second option is likely the best. I would suggest the French officers be spread over our existing units and that rank of our own commanders be dated prior to those of the French officer. In this vein, we can promote our own above them to give the French officers a place to serve while not superseding our current commands.

Saturday, June 7, 1777 — Middlebrook, New Jersey

I was gratified to see more men and officers at our Sunday services today. With the campaign at-hand, our standing with our greatest Ally is of the greatest necessity.

General Schuyler has left Philadelphia and now General Arnold is in command there. I am having him make ready for British movement to his quarter. This army is ready to join him at the first alarm. I just need to ensure that it is not a false alarm as any movement from this head prematurely could prove fatal. I am suggesting that he and General Sullivan give each other notice by signal lights upon the heights. The signal beacons are to be pyramid in shape, made of logs and filled with brush. They are to be sixteen feet on every side of the square base and project up between eighteen to twenty feet high. They are to be built on the peak of prominent mountains, each within view of the other. Upon a movement of the enemy or an emergency, they are to be lit. This will notify our men to go to their meeting places and prepare to respond.

Tuesday, June 10, 1777 — Middlebrook, New Jersey

I am in great concern for our men held in British hands. Every prisoner returned to us is found in the poorest of condition. They attest to being held in large spaces, no fire for warmth, little food, and no clothing. When one is sick, they are ignored and surrendered to the path of their ailment. No effort is rendered to treat their maladies. This is inhumane. We treat their prisoners with the greatest of care. Our men do with less so that their men may have equal provisions. It is almost pitiful that we cannot afford prisoners. The other options are more hated — to release them or kill them. So, we must care for them. Duty demands it. The Rules of War by Christian gentlemen require it. Yet, General Howe continues to mistreat our men while depending on our commitment to civility regardless of their actions. He complains at the mistreatment of his men, yet I have offered the British to invest an agent among us to make sure that their prisoners are well-treated. Such a gesture has not been afforded to us.

A prisoner exchange could be a cure, but the terms which General Howe proposes cannot be agreed to. I am proposing an equal exchange of men in number and rank. I will concede that General Lee, who has been mistreated in their custody, must be held by them longer until we can capture a man of equal rank for which to make an equitable exchange.

Thursday, June 12, 1777 — Middlebrook, New Jersey

A new strategy is unfolding to help buffet the enemy. A corps of rangers under the command of Colonel Daniel Morgan has almost been completely formed. They will be a light-infantry group. As such, they will be exempted from the common duties of the line. They are to cover the left flank of the enemy, particularly covering the roads from Brunswick toward Millstone and Princeton. Upon movement of the enemy, they are to fall upon their flank and gall them as much as possible while always alert to not be surrounded or caught. I am asking him to consider an idea that I have been entertaining — that he dresses a company or two as Indians. Let them attack with screams and yells attributed to the manner of the Indians. This may have a good consequence of unnerving the enemy. It will also make the impression that many more are hiding who are against them than for them.

Saturday, June 14, 1777 — Middlebrook, New Jersey

General Howe began his march out of Brunswick last night. The first of his troops have reached Somerset Courthouse and halted there. His rear is still in Brunswick. I am uncertain if he intends to march on toward Philadelphia or if he is wishing to draw us down from our heights. I do believe he desires to bring a stroke upon this army before moving to Philadelphia.

Monday, June 16, 1777 — Middlebrook, New Jersey

It is probable that if General Howe does not receive the reinforcements he has ordered from Europe, he will move many of his troops from Canada and then make their march on Philadelphia by way of the Delaware. I am asking General Schuyler to keep me apprised of any activity he sees in the north to confirm my opinion.

Upon any enemy movement in this neighborhood thus far, the militia has responded in a spirited manner. It has harassed the enemy throughout this country. We will hang at his rear. If General Howe seeks to cross the Delaware, he will do so with great difficulty. Generals Arnold and Mifflin will be waiting at their front to the west with Continental troops and militia. We will close in on them from the rear if they choose to cross. To strengthen this army, I have ordered General Putnam to send troops down from Peekskill, along with Generals Parson, McDougal, and Glover. I am leaving one thousand at Peekskill to deal with the few enemy troops in the area of New York. Once these troops arrive, my army will be respectable and can oppose the enemy and perhaps inflict some damage.

Tuesday, June 17, 1777 — Middlebrook, New Jersey

The enemy is well-fortified where they are currently stationed. I do believe General Howe's strategy is to attack this army before moving to Philadelphia. That thought is confirmed by the fact that he has moved most of his army with light packs and arms while leaving the bulk of their baggage, provisions, and wagons in Brunswick. I am requesting General Sullivan to draw part of his troops from Sourland Hills to reinforce our right as this is our weakest extremity. It will likely be the target of Howe. The remainder of Sullivan's troops can gall the rear flank of the enemy.

The seeming certainty of attack is felt by the people all around us. A spirit resides in them and this army that I have not seen in a while. All are greatly animated to this cause at present. Should the enemy delay or cease to attack, I will release most of the militia back to their homes. I will request that they hold themselves in readiness for any sudden call. I would like to retain two thousand militia with our Continental troops to lessen fatigue and duty.

Friday, June 20, 1777 — Middlebrook, New Jersey

General Schuyler is alarmed by a report from an enemy spy captured named Amsbury. I do not feel Amsbury's information is correct, but he stated that a British force consisting of British regulars, some Canadians, and Indians were on the move to this head under General Burgoyne. I do not believe this is their design, but I will have General Putnam hold four Massachusetts regiments in reserve at Peekskill to be ready for dispatch on a moment's notice.

With favorable notice, General Sullivan has intercepted an enemy's letter informing that they are in despair to carry out their schemes for lack of force. They are having to resort to bolstering their troops through flattery, bribery, and intimidation. As encouraging as this is, I must always act with caution. Deception can lull our men into complacency.

From this post, I am at a loss as to why there is a delay of the Massachusetts and New Hampshire troops. I have written on several occasions of the pressing need for these, but in vain. I pray that General Schuyler will have a greater influence upon them.

The main body of the enemy marched back to Brunswick again burning homes as they returned. I am not sure what precipitated the sudden change. I can only assume their original design to cross the Delaware was discouraged by the spirited way our militia assembled against them along with their shock at our Nation's people flying to arms in every quarter to oppose them. I have been riding horseback often these last few days in an attempt to discern the enemy's intentions and how to counter them. I am thankful that it has been my practice to take great care of my horses. Each morning I check on them and give them my attention. This is for their well-being and my distraction. My routine has been to rotate between two so that I will always have a fresh one ready to ride. This has served me well.

Sunday, June 22, 1777 — Middlebrook, New Jersey

The enemy is on the move again. This morning they have evacuated Brunswick and taken residence in Amboy burning more homes as they march. I detached three brigades under Major-General Greene to fall upon their rear. I am keeping our main army upon the heights for support should an occasion present. Colonel Morgan's regiment of light-infantry attacked and pressed the Hessians. General Wayne's brigade joined in pursuit and drove the enemy to the east side of the river where they sought shelter in redoubts built there. Inhabitants in that quarter inform us that General Howe, Lord Cornwallis, and General Grant are with their men now on that side.

General Greene confirms my impressions of Colonel Morgan and General Wayne. These two and their men pressed the enemy, superior in number, with courage and ferocity. This valiant group of men now formed bring great aid to this cause.

Wednesday, June 25, 1777 — Camp at Quibbletown, New Jersey

I have moved this army nearer to Amboy upon the advice of my officers so that we might find greater ease in annoying the enemy. I have advanced Lord Stirling's division with some other troops to the neighborhood of Matuchin meeting house. After reconnoitering the area, I decided not to move more men there because it is low ground with a scarcity of water. To defend is disadvantageous. I have light parties staying near to the enemy to alert us if we need to move upon them or move from them — whichever proves necessary. From what we can tell, the enemy is poised to move across the Sound to Staten Island.

A dispatch from Congress by the hand of Mr. Hancock congratulated this army in view of the retreat of the enemy out of New Jersey. They believe this is a declaration to the whole world that America cannot be easily conquered, that our defeat may be an unattainable object. They interpret the recent events as a confirmation that my conduct and decisions have been correct. I am glad they carry this opinion. Perhaps this will make them equally favorable to come to my assistance for enlistments, terms of enlistments, cash, and supplies. This is my hope.

Thursday, June 26, 1777 — Middlebrook, New Jersey

General Howe has advanced his whole army from Amboy to Westfield. From there, troops have been sent across to Staten Island. I imagine they intend to use this as a base from which to advance in the direction of Philadelphia.

Saturday, June 28, 1777 — Middlebrook, New Jersey

General Howe's troops have returned from Staten Island. All that I can consider is their initial movement was a feint to draw a general engagement on disadvantageous terms. It may also be their object to cut off our light parties and perhaps possess the heights and passes in the mountains on our left. All this is speculation. Perhaps, other than our harassing with light-infantry, no general response from us has caused them to question their strategy. Nevertheless, I have immediately moved our force to further occupy the heights. I am dispatching Brigadier-General Scott to hang on their flank and have ordered Colonel Morgan to assist with his corps of riflemen.

Sunday, June 29, 1777 — Middlebrook, New Jersey

Probably no more a strategic place exists to camp than this area. We are lurched on a high hill overlooking everything around us. The terrain is rugged. We are safe here, but we must discern the plans of the enemy and respond accordingly.

Once again, General Howe has moved his troops. This time he moved his whole army back to Staten Island, totally evacuating the State of New Jersey.

Tuesday, July 1, 1777 — Middlebrook, New Jersey

It appears from reports and the movement of Howe, that their designs are to move up the North river to unite with General Burgoyne coming from the Lakes. Burgoyne and armies of Canada have their sites on Ticonderoga. General St. Clair confirms the enemy's activity in that quarter. General Putnam has ordered Nixon's brigade to a state of readiness. I am ordering that Nixon and his men embark immediately with their baggage to Albany and then beyond to assist the northern army. He can move as soon as General Varnum's brigade and General Parson's brigade can get near enough to Peekskill to take their place. My officers believe, as do I, that Howe will seek to take control of the Highland passes and at some point, join with Burgoyne's forces. Their intentions will be for Philadelphia. I am asking General Putnam to take the most effectual manner to obtain militia for reinforcements to counter Howe. There is not one moment to lose.

Wednesday, July 2, 1777 — Middlebrook, New Jersey

Governor Turnbull is requesting arms for his militia. I am sorry I am unable to comply. More men are showing up at this head. We lack arms to supply these. Our commissary-general records receipts of more arms than we have men, yet every State is deficient. I cannot conceive where the arms have gone. A small amount has gone over to the enemy with deserters. Militia have carried off theirs I am sure. There is no accounting for these. Perhaps some of our troops have more than one's own use would require. Though it hinders this army, there is just no way to tell. My hope is that the Governor will be able to supply his men from his own State while doing all in his power to forward the troops lacking to fill his quota.

I am urging General Clinton to call out a respectable body of militia from New York to join General Putnam without loss of time.

I have just received a letter from Major-General Schuyler letting me know he has received a strong supply of provisions from Congress. I am relieved to hear of this provision. I do believe General Burgoyne was not sent from Europe on a feint, but rather he has come with an eye toward glory on the battlefield. He is here to deliver a master stroke with strenuous effort against this army beginning at Ti-conderoga. With this army, I am at a loss of what I should do. I am holding here until the British intentions are clear. I am apprehensive. If I move to Peekskill, then I may provide an opening for Howe in Philadelphia. Staying here and wait-ing may put this army at risk should he take possession of the Highlands. At this point, all I can do is consult and do the best we can.

Friday, July 4, 1777 — Morristown, New Jersey

On this first anniversary of our Declaration of Independence, it is difficult to find a footing of celebration while the matter is to be determined. With a bold spirit, we chose to separate from the King and Great Britain. This need had been well-recognized for many years, but few had the courage to acknowledge it publicly and take a stand. My friend John Adams was one of the few who was unashamed to declare the need. Even now, not all our countrymen are happy about this di-vorce. Yet, I know that once it is won (and I pray it will be), all our neighbors will rejoice and benefit from it. I am just sad that so few are paying the price for a majority who will benefit at so little sacrifice. That said, it is the troops and even the militia who have come out with a realization of what their service will mean to their families and the generations to come. My own decision to join this fray was a personal one. It was one that I undertook with a reliance upon the Unseen Hand. I joined for the benefits that freedom and independence offer. I have dreams for this Nation, for my family, and for our friends that I cannot express in words.

I am gladdened as I look back to have seen Providence work every step of the way. There is no other way to explain the fact that our army still exists and that our Nation and its Congress still operate independently. This very day, I give thanks to God that the Pennsylvania militia poured out of their homes to meet the enemy with such vigor to the chagrin of General Howe. They exceeded my most sanguine expectations. I am grateful Jersey has been evacuated just in time for its inhabitants to spare many farmhouses, as well as secure their hay and grain harvests. Those who have lost their homes, I have been able to send wagonloads of meat and flour to supply their wants. I am also blessed to be able to release many from the Pennsylvania militia, not only to lessen the burden to meet their needs, but also to allow them to go home just in time for the season of reaping. I could count my blessings for the rest of this day, but work is to be done at this instant. I choose to walk this day in worship. Today is not the Lord's Day on the calendar, but it is a day I will be mindful of Him just the same.

Monday, July 7, 1777 — Morristown, New Jersey

I am writing Governor Cooke to let him know that General Howe has withdrawn. He seems to have designs in two or three locales that are not in this State. Cooke still should be on alert just in case the enemy returns.

We are still uncertain where the enemy is headed, but the deserters have informed us that the enemy has fitted berths on their transports for the light horse. They have taken in provender, enough for three or four weeks. Officers' baggage is being forwarded. Their ships are watering. I believe they are preparing for a heading upriver.

Thursday, July 10, 1777 — Morristown, New Jersey

From the returns I have received, it appears General Schuyler has abandoned Ticonderoga with the excuse that he had not more than seven hundred men and fourteen hundred militia under his command, not near enough he says to counter General Burgoyne. This is the worst of my expectations. It appears he has evacuated our posts on the Lake. I await more explanation from Schuyler. As it now stands, there must be a check on General Burgoyne's progress. Our levies are currently deficient. Militia must be called up immediately. I am asking Congress to send an active and spirited leader to lead this militia. I will not leave it to their calculations. I must recommend ever so strongly, General Arnold. He deserves more than militia, but if that is what he is given, he will make great utility of them. He is active, judicious, and brave. His presence will embolden the men. They will rally to his command with great animation. Besides, he is more familiar with that area. He knows the routes and important passes.

As for me, I believe General Howe is going to take the Highland passes and meet with General Burgoyne in that area. I will move my army up the North river immediately to see if we can counter them or land a major offense.

Saturday, July 12, 1777 — Pompton Plains, New Jersey

General Schuyler has sent requests to this quarter as well as to Congress for tents. We have none to spare. He requests horses and drivers. He will have an easier time procuring them there. He asks for cannons. We have none to spare. He desires a large reinforcement of men. I cannot part with what I have. What I can send to him, I have in the last few days — kettles, musket-cartridges, sixty barrels of powder, lead and cartridge paper, and a number of recruits on-march from Massachusetts. Colonel Putnam is on his way to him with his regiment. General St. Clair should be there by now with his force. A number of militia have turned out. With all this, General Schuyler should have a force at least as big as Burgoyne's, if not superior.

Our march to the North river has been delayed by the rain. We have stopped at Pompton Plains. The very moment the weather allows, we will be on the move with great expedience.

Sunday, July 13, 1777 — Pompton Plains, New Jersey

General Schuyler's letter was received in my hand a few moments ago. I am at a loss as to why General St. Clair has not reached Schuyler by now. There is no word as to his whereabouts. If he and his troops were delayed or had taken another route, we would have heard something. If he and his men were captured, there would have been news of that as well. I wait impatiently for news of their fate.

Tuesday, July 15, 1777 — Camp at the Clove, New Jersey

General Schuyler writes that General St. Clair has not been captured by the enemy, but has camped at Bedford. I am incredibly happy to hear that. I really feared that they had been taken prisoners. I have written back to General Schuyler. It is hard for me to comprehend his reasoning to evacuate Ticonderoga based on what I have been told regarding its fortifications and men. Report is that Schuyler actually had five thousand men in the fort with high spirits and well-supplied with numerous militia marching to their succor. The Council of Safety in New York has sent me a letter from General Schuyler himself attesting to those numbers just a few weeks before. If that is the case, then I cannot rationally countenance that retreat.

This notwithstanding, Schuyler has been a good general. He is loyal and faithful to keep me apprised of the enemy's movements and his. It can be expected failures will occur under fire. As a result, I will remind him that all is not lost. We should never despair. We have faced tough circumstances before that were unpromising. To our surprise, things got better. Providence has moved on our behalf. I have no doubt, He will again.

I am asking General Schuyler to send down any vessels he can spare for this army as we desire to sail upriver to meet General Howe and General Burgoyne if circumstances will admit. We are currently waiting on some movement and are camping at the Cove.

Wednesday, July 16, 1777 — Camp at the Clove, New Jersey

Great news has come to this quarter. The daring endeavor by Lieutenant-Colonel Barton and forty men was successful. They were able to move in and out of the enemy lines to capture Major-General Prescott and one of his aides. Finally, we have a man of equal rank to exchange for General Lee. This also enables us to exchange Lieutenant-Colonel Campbell and the Hessian field-officers for an equal number of ours in Howe's hands. This will remove at least one ground of controversy between us. I am sending the letter to him immediately with a willingness to release General Prescott to him with the promise that he will then release General Lee upon his arrival. Or if he prefers, he can release General Lee. We will send General Prescott. I will do neither until General Howe accedes to the exchange. Until that time, General Prescott is to be removed farther from the Sound and guarded with great diligence. I do not doubt he will try to escape. If word gets out, the British could endeavor to free him in the same vein that he was captured.

I have asked Colonel Prescott and his regiment to join us without loss of time. General Knox advises that they halt at Trenton along with General Nash's men until we know what move General Howe will make.

Friday, July 18, 1777 — Camp at the Clove, New Jersey

I have not heard from General Schuyler since July 10th. I am hopeful that all is well, and that General Burgoyne has not pursued success with rapidity. I am hoping that General St. Clair has formed a junction with Schuyler before Burgoyne comes upon them. I am writing General Schuyler to be apprised of their situation. I am also informing him that General Arnold is on his way from here to help check Burgoyne. I must again brag on General Arnold. He was withheld the honor of rank as a major-general which was his due. He had every reason to refuse to come to our aid. He could have remained in Philadelphia until the question of his promotion was settled. I would have understood that, but instead, General Arnold laid aside his claim for the time being for the good of this Nation. He is even willing to work in concert with General St. Clair, a man whom he should be ranked superior to but is not currently. General Arnold is a man of action, bravery, and engagement. General St. Clair, I must note in my journal, has not proven to be of equal ingenuity as Arnold. The evacuation of Ticonderoga seemingly was his decision. He has yet to give an account as to why.

I am writing the brigadier-generals of the militia in Connecticut and Massachusetts to send at least one-third of their men to meet General Arnold at Saratoga or any other place General Schuyler or General Arnold should direct. The liberties and interests of the United States depend upon it. I am advising these generals to enlist the men for a period of time. They can then let them rotate off to be replaced by another third of their militia. This will encourage the men by allowing them to work their harvest and take turns bravely defending their country. The enemy has grown brutal with the aid of mercenaries. Now with savages, they seek to add murder to desolation.

Sunday, July 20, 1777 — Camp at the Clove, New Jersey

Not knowing what General Howe and General Burgoyne intend, I have sent Lord Stirling with his division to Peekskill guessing that Howe will make his move up the North river. I am sending General Glover from Peekskill to join General Schuyler as he still believes his force is inadequate to oppose Burgoyne.

Monday, July 21, 1777 — Camp at the Clove, New Jersey

I am writing General Putnam to see if he or General Sullivan have seen any activity of the enemy on the water. I need to know, are any of the enemy's ships going up the Sound, are there any anchored, how many ships do they see, and do they have troops on board? I am anxious to know.

Tuesday, July 22, 1777 — Eleven Miles in the Clove, New Jersey

I am informing Congress of my embarrassing situation of having no intelligence as to what the enemy is doing. At last count, one hundred and twenty of their ships were in the New York area. Many have sailed out, but their destination is unknown. I am asking Congress to place the militia in a state of readiness. They need to appoint lookouts at the Cape of Delaware who will be diligent to report and specifically describe the number and types of ships they see. They should give an idea as to where the enemy ships may be headed. Congress is to pass this information on by the speediest conveyance.

General Schuyler's latest return has arrived. I am elated at the change in his demeanor and outlook on this war. It may be that General St. Clair taking the blame for the evacuation of Ticonderoga has renewed his resolve. I may flatter myself that taking a positive tone in the last letter has encouraged him of my faith in him and in our circumstances. He reports that he has found two advantageous spots to post his men. The General also has taken strides to remove all cattle from the enemy's reach. He is attempting a blockade of all the roads to retard their progress.

General Schuyler has taken a greater measure. He is impressing upon the people in that sector that if they do not join in this effort, the consequences will be fatal for them, their families, and their country. Toryism must not be tolerated. Taking the wrong side will hurt them worse than the sufferings of this war. Schuyler needs to remind the people that General Burgoyne will use every art of deception to move the people away from our cause. He desires their pledge of allegiance to their nation. The enemies of America have one chief aim — to sow division and jealousy among our people. A nation cannot be divided and stand, just as an army cannot be divided into many parts and have any hope of victory. May Congress remember this in all their deliberations. We must be one.

Thursday, July 24, 1777 — Ramapo, New Jersey

General Schuyler is making up for his previous lack of correspondence. He sends a letter today intimating his great need for more men. Many of the militia expected, have not arrived. I am sending General Lincoln to take command of the eastern militia and to join the northern army. He is to work in concert with General Schuyler. Lincoln has gained the respect of the eastern militia. I promise myself that his entry into the northern front will turn the men out and cause them to serve cheerfully bringing about the desirable end. I believe the best assistance that Lincoln can bring is to dog Burgoyne from the rear. The enemy will be very hesitant to proceed if he believes his rear flank is vulnerable.

I am moving now with my men to oppose General Howe. We have arrived at Ramapo this day. He and his fleet have left the Hook. I believe they are heading toward the Delaware. I am asking General Putnam to order General Sullivan and Lord Stirling to move their divisions toward Philadelphia. Other than two field pieces of artillery for each brigade that remain behind, the rest of the field artillery needs to go with the beforementioned divisions. I need General Putnam and his officers to decide how many of their troops they can spare to respond either this way or to the eastward as the occasion shall require.

Friday, July 25, 1777 — Ramapo, New Jersey

Mr. Benjamin Franklin's son William, the loyalist and once colonial governor of New Jersey, has written me from prison in hopes that I could get his release as his wife is in ill-health. I have written him to let him know that it is not within my power to supersede a resolution of Congress, but that I will forward his letter to them. I understand why he is imprisoned and support it. With that said, the delicate situation of his wife's health would give exception for Congress to allow him to see her. He would need to give assurances to return and follow whatever restrictions Congress may lay upon him. I would hate for a man not to have the privilege to see his wife one last time if death should soon befall her. That is my opinion from this vantage point.

Wednesday, July 30, 1777 — Coryell's Ferry, New Jersey

We have been on the move, but now are halting at Howell's Ferry and Trenton. Here, we are on proper grounds to oppose the enemy should they make ready for an attack. I am hoping General Gates has made the water ready to oppose the British ships. I have ordered General Sullivan to halt at Morristown and be ready to move northward or southward as the occasion dictates. General Howe appears to have abandoned General Burgoyne, but I cannot help but look behind me for fear Howe has circled to my rear. I am ordering General Gates to alert me if he sees any appearance of a fleet.

Thursday, July 31, 1777 — Coryell's Ferry, New Jersey

I have just received information that the British fleet has been spotted at the Capes of Delaware. I am instructing General Putnam to send his two brigades immediately toward Philadelphia. He is to engage the militia from Connecticut and New York as soon as possible. No doubt exists now. General Howe will make a vigorous push to possess Philadelphia. I also need Putnam to alert General Schuyler of Howe's movement. Now, Schuyler can oppose Burgoyne full force without fear of Howe coming up against him.

Friday, August 1, 1777 — Chester County, Pennsylvania

A surprising event has just been reported. Yesterday around eight o'clock in the morning, the British fleet sailed out of the Capes of Delaware. I am filled with anxiety. We have no idea what the British are up to. I am sending General Sullivan's division and the two brigades back across the river. I am calling on General Clinton to reinforce General Putnam with the New York militia. I am calling on Governor Trumbull to have the Connecticut militia ready. If General Howe is attempting to take the Highland passes, this will be greatly injurious to Connecticut. I am sorry to move all these men back-and-forth. These troops are weary.

The constant alarm may dull their response, cause them to question my leadership or the fight altogether. We are playing cat-and-mouse. I fear we are the mouse.

Sunday, August 3, 1777 — Philadelphia, Pennsylvania

I have been hesitant to let French officers of questionable ranks come into this army to command our American troops even when their motives are sincere. Congress desirous of foreign assistance gave commissions to these men, but thankfully did not put them over our field officers per my request. Now, I find a complication that I had feared. Brigadier-General DeBorre arrested a Tory, tried him, and ordered his execution. It was carried out. I know the Tory deserved this fate, but this was not within the jurisdiction of martial law and is therefore illegal. The authority to try and execute an American citizen or an American soldier is not General DeBorre's to carry out. He has brought discontent, jealousy, and murmurs among the people. Now, he has brought charges against Major Mullens. He has had him arrested and awaiting trial! This is the last worry with which I should have to contend. I am writing to correct him in the firmest manner possible without causing enmity between this army and the French who have joined us. I am also allowing the trial of Major Mullens, but have ordered that no punishment will be exercised other than what I decide upon completion of his trial.

Monday, August 4, 1777 — Philadelphia, Pennsylvania

This army, having moved to defend the city of Philadelphia, must decide what the enemy's strategy is, now that they have moved. At least I have had time to visit with Congress face-to-face. Congress has passed a resolve this morning that General Schuyler should leave his command of the northern army and join us here along with General St. Clair, to answer for the failure at Ticonderoga. They asked that I choose another to replace him there. I have asked Congress to make this decision. They have conferred and decided upon General Gates. I am writing Gates to proceed to that post with all expedition. I am in hopes he can restore the face of affairs in that quarter.

The Council of New York has written me with great concern. The misfortune at Ticonderoga has left many in the northern and eastern states fearful and discouraged. I understand that fully. What these States do not understand is that regardless of the successes Burgoyne now celebrates, if the States would just come together and put forth even a moderate exertion, Burgoyne would leave this continent a defeated and ruined man. New York is requesting that I send more men and arms to their sector from this main army. What they do not understand is that this move would jeopardize the whole war. They are worried about Burgoyne, just a fraction of the British army. I am dealing with the main army of the enemy under General Howe. If I can keep General Howe at bay, whatever successes Burgoyne now experiences will be temporary. The eastern States have not responded to my calls for militia. Few come and those who do are inconsistent in service once they arrive. I still have a confidence that the eastern States will awaken to the danger and raise themselves to the task of dealing with this enemy. If they do, no army can take this land.

Tuesday, August 5, 1777 — Germantown, Pennsylvania

I have written my brother John Augustine today. Just writing him makes me feel at home. With him, I can be honest for I know he prays for me and supports me along with my family. My sister and the rest of his family have pulled through the smallpox. I cannot believe Virginia has made inoculation illegal and punishable with a one-thousand-pound fine. Surely, people can see the amazing benefits of inoculation. This army still stands and has lost very few because we took the advantageous step to inoculate our troops and our recruits. I have enough to occupy my mind without having to fret over the smallpox.

Our men are exhausted. They march and then they countermarch, all in this oppressive heat. Fatigue and injury retard their movement. I am grateful that while we are trying to decide where the enemy will strike with the bulk of their army and ships, our men can take time to rest and recover. Taking time to rest is like stopping to sharpen an ax. It may appear to be a waste of time, but it makes that ax and this army more effective.

A call has gone out for a public inquiry into the fall of Ticonderoga. Officers who were responsible have been called to defend their actions to either regain public trust or be made a public example. This whole event has brought about a shade on a bright prospect, but I am hoping the cloud will be dispelled with the entrance in that head of General Lincoln and General Arnold.

Thursday, August 7, 1777 — Germantown, Pennsylvania

There has been no sign of the British fleet. They have not been seen or heard from since they left the Capes of Delaware. My best guess is the fleet is moving around Long Island into the Sound with a plan to cooperate with General Burgoyne. General Schuyler believes the northern army still needs reinforcements. I am asking General Putnam to confer with his officers to see if they could spare Court-land's and Livingston's regiments. It appears Burgoyne is on the move toward Albany. I have my men back on the move to station themselves where we feel the enemy may engage.

Monday, August 11, 1777 — Bucks County, Pennsylvania

We have crossed the Delaware to meet the enemy somewhere in the eastern States. I just now received a dispatch that believes the British ships were seen about sixteen leagues south of the Capes of Delaware. Is their intention Philadelphia again? Can I trust anything that comes to me? It is as if this army is marching in the dark with no fire to guide us and no enemy fire to draw us.

General Putnam reports that the British General Clinton has left York Island. I would think that he may seek to attack Putnam from the south and Burgoyne to come down upon him from the north. We need to know how many men they may have and how many regiments of theirs are left on the island. I am ordering Putnam to send spies to make an estimation. The numbers reported will help us discern their intentions. Report is also that wagons and horses are moving toward Kingsbridge. Part of the British transports may plan to land there with troops to attack Putnam from that quarter.

Wednesday, August 13, 1777 — Bucks County, Pennsylvania

I am afforded great satisfaction this day after receipt of a letter from Governor Clinton of New York. With great alacrity, he has assembled his militia to meet the threat General Burgoyne poses on the eastern States. I am not surprised that a general turned governor would appreciate the need for men and grasp what is at stake for all of us. Now if his neighboring States will follow his example, if our people will unite and rise up, the British will find themselves surrounded with no succor to stay. They would gladly get on their ships and sail back to their homes if our people decide to let them. Tories and loyalists discourage such action from our countrymen. Governor Clinton has a great hatred for such traitors. It excites him to move. Now that General Gates has taken over the northern army, Congress has given him the discretionary power to make requisitions of the States of New Hampshire, Massachusetts, Connecticut, New York, New Jersey, and Pennsylvania. I pray all heads of the States will cooperate with him as he seeks to set that sector in order.

Saturday, August 16, 1777 — Bucks County, Pennsylvania

I have received a follow-up letter from Governor Clinton. He has informed me that some Indians are making a stir at the behest of the British on our northern army. I am sending Colonel Morgan's corps of riflemen, about five hundred men, to fight the Indians in the same manner they fight. I will have General Putnam prepare sloops for their transport along with any provisions they will need. Unlike most military maneuvers where surprise is an advantage, Colonel Morgan and his corps have proved so effectual that the mere mention of their arrival brings fear to the enemy and Indian alike. With this in mind, I am instructing General Clinton that it would be beneficial to spread the word that Colonel Morgan and his riflemen are moving to that quarter. This may cause the quick evacuation of the savages, emboldening our northern army.

I am advised that the militia are gathering under General Lincoln. New Hampshire's arrived under General Stark and more of the Massachusetts militia has arrived as well. I am calling on Lincoln to begin attack on Burgoyne to his rear. No army can effectively move forward if there is fear of attack from behind.

Such a situation will require Burgoyne to peel off some of his men at each move to man posts to cover their rear flank. The more he peels off, the less force he will have to face our attacks on his front. In the interim, his progress will be slowed as he will be required to advance circumspectly.

Sunday, August 17, 1777 — Camp at Crossroads

Foreign officers, especially from France, are coming over in droves. I am grateful for their interest and their desire to serve by our side. Sadly, most come requiring troops to command. Enlistments are short. Those who are enlisted have generally been recruited by the officers for whom they serve. The French officers do not have a base nor the language from which to recruit. I cannot, on the other hand, take men from the American officers to whom they are pledged, nor can I replace an American officer with a French officer. The situation is like a minister wanting to lead a Church. He wants a Church full of congregants given to him, instead of doing the work of the evangelist to bring them to his flock.

All this supposes that the French help is pure and sincere. I feel at times that France seeks to use us to weaken their natural enemy. This will also bring them trade and financial benefit from these shores. They do provide us with arms which we need. At times, I will find a serviceable officer from their numbers. Why bring this issue up? I just received a letter from Mr. Benjamin Franklin who is in France diligently working on our behalf to gain true assistance. Mr. Franklin desires a commission for Monsieur Turgot. These who come from foreign soil wish to be taken into the highest confidences and stations of this army. These men have not been tried in our battles. They have not earned the respect that a General Lincoln or General Arnold has. I am writing Mr. Franklin to illuminate these complexities in the hope that I will not insult him, but rather have him figuratively pull up a chair at my station and understand my hesitancy.

I know Mr. Franklin wishes me to do the same in his station. He is seeking favor of that government. To do so, he must conciliate their desires. To refuse applications for a commission in this war puts his purpose of gaining French investment on shaky ground. I would that he realizes that though a decline of position here may hinder his efforts, it would be better that then for them to arrive here and be mortified at not being granted the position for which they came. I believe that would bring far worse damage. Honesty upfront is needed. It is true that Mr. Franklin may not be making promises at all, but his recommendations are perceived as a promise of position in this army. To this, he must be aware and extra cautious.

Tuesday, August 19, 1777 — Neshaminy Bridge, Pennsylvania

The Marquis de Lafayette arrived in camp today. He is a young man, perhaps nineteen years of age. He admits that he is inexperienced and young, but wishes to take command of a division. He informs me that Congress has bestowed upon him the rank of major-general. He has also stated that I can trust him with a smaller command if I feel he needs a little seasoning. He informs me that his two aide-de-camps are to be given commissions as well. I could not hide my displeasure at the predicament in which Congress has placed me. I simply told him that he needs to confer with Congress. I abruptly returned to my quarters to note my complaints and frustration. I thought Congress said they would give such men from foreign soil honorary ranks henceforth and not actual command posts. I have written Congress at-large concerning such men, but it seems certain that my insight has afforded little attention. I am going to write a member of Congress instead of the body of Congress. I will apply for aid from Mr. Benjamin Harrison to decipher what Congress wishes for me to do. The Marquis is back in Philadelphia. If they meant for his commission to be honorary, they need to clarify that to him and not leave it to me. If they do indeed intend for him to assume a position of command, I need them to tell me where I should place him and what area of our Nation must we put in jeopardy to pacify a foreign country. I will follow their lead as I am required to do, but they must consider the hardships and jealousies that they are placing upon my shoulders to bear.

Wednesday, August 20, 1777 — Bucks County, Pennsylvania

The enemy's fleet has not been seen since the 8th instant. I am now of the opinion that General Howe is setting his attention on Charleston, which is the only place of significance to the south. My great fear, which I regret to consider, is that General Howe could be making appearances in this quarter and then another quarter to drag this army all over the country. This would then open the door for General Clinton to raise havoc in the east and to join force with General Burgoyne to inflict some great damage to our Nation. All the while, our army is being led by one feint after another simply to remove the obstacle our force presents.

Friday, August 22, 1777 — Bucks County, Pennsylvania

To support my conjecture that Howe would move to Charleston, I take inventory that Charleston is a large port with extensive commerce, large military stores, and the ability to increase his arms. I cannot consider moving this army southward to that location. The disadvantage the Continental army has is our inability to maneuver by the seas. Wherever he sails, he does so with expedition and ease. This army must march in all kinds of inclement weather to reach wherever he has landed. By the time we arrive to where the enemy was, he has moved on to another sector. I am proposing to Congress that it may be best for this army to wait upon the enemy in the east as there is still the likelihood that at some point, Howe will make a junction with Burgoyne. The other alternative would be to converge on Burgoyne to the north. I have called a council of general officers. They share my sentiment. I will move my army toward the Delaware and await Congress's decision after deliberation.

I just received notice that all my considerations were in error. The enemy's fleet has entered the Chesapeake Bay. Now no doubt exists that they will make their approach upon Philadelphia very soon. I am alerting Governor Trumbull to make ready. I have summoned General Sullivan and his division down to me.

By a masterful stroke, General Stark has struck General Burgoyne near Bennington. A letter intercepted from Burgoyne shows his situation is desperate. He needs everything. What great news as we head into perhaps the greatest conflict of this war. The northern army needed a lift. That is what we received. As I told General Schuyler a while back, when things look darkest, it seems Providence always steps in.

I am ordering for all troops here to march toward Philadelphia. To witness Congress working in concert with the needs of this contest is good. They ordered the removal of stores from Lancaster and York to places of greater safety out of the enemy's reach. I am gratified they took this step. It is one step less that I must take.

Saturday, August 23, 1777

We will be within five-or-six miles outside of Philadelphia by this evening. I am letting Congress know that I intend to march our men right down the streets of that city to bring confidence to our countrymen. My design is that we march down Front street and up Chestnut street. The city, in the meantime, must construct several works to defend the city with all industry. Lookouts must be placed at the Capes in case the enemy brings a small number of ships to hit the city by surprise.

Sunday, August 24, 1777 — Wilmington, Delaware

The city gave our men a great welcome as we marched through their streets. I had hoped it would influence those in the city who are disaffected. The returns from our march were quite the opposite. I am told that the people were very disheartened to see the condition of the men they had hopes to defend. I flatter myself to think that if Congress and the people of this city see how our men suffer, sacrifice, and do without, they will rouse themselves to our aid and the aid of their country especially in this moment of danger.

Monday, August 25, 1777 — Wilmington, Delaware

General Greene's and General Stephen's divisions are just outside the city. I have instructed them to march in. Two other divisions are not far away. Pennsylvania militia are gathered. More are on the way. Sadly, some of them are unarmed. I am taking strides to get weapons to them immediately. They have turned out with great alacrity. I will be riding out tomorrow to examine the grounds toward the enemy. I am unfamiliar with this area as a matter of defense.

I just received information that the enemy has landed almost two thousand men near the Head of Elk. This troubles me as a good many of our stores are there. We have not had time to remove them from the enemy's access. I am ordering Major-General Armstrong to send the militia there as quickly as possible. The enemy's first step will be to obtain horses, carriages, and cattle. They must be met and hindered.

Tuesday, August 26, 1777 — Wilmington, Delaware

I just returned from the Head of Elk after an early ride this morning. The enemy has not moved from where they debarked. I saw but a few tents in their camp. I cannot determine the number of men who are present. By an act of grace, our quartermaster was able to remove all the stores from the enemy's reach except for about seven thousand bushels of corn. He and some men will try to recover some of that too, but the enemy may prohibit their success. A part of the Delaware militia is there. About nine hundred of the Pennsylvania militia are marching that way. I am about to move part of this army in that direction today once they are armed and supplied with ammunition. The heavy rains the last few days have delayed our activity.

Wednesday, August 27, 1777 — Wilmington, Delaware

General Sullivan's expedition into Staten Island was not as successful as he had hoped per his letter. We believed he would have accomplished more, but I am not able to judge the reasons. I need him to join me here, but only after his men's injuries have been tended to and they have had time to rest. It is possible to push men so hard that when they arrive, they effect little good.

Thursday, August 28, 1777 — Wilmington, Delaware

There is one commission for a foreign officer that I do not object to; it is the one Congress has requested for Count Pulaski. He is a Polish officer who has fought and sacrificed greatly for the independence of his own country. He now comes here to do the same for us. Not having seen him lead, I am hesitant to put him over a brigade of infantry, but his experience in the cavalry of Poland makes him a good candidate to lead our horse service. We have had a vacancy in this area for a while. This will give him time to acclimate himself with our army. It will also give me the opportunity to measure his usefulness.

Friday, August 29, 1777 — Wilmington, Delaware

The enemy advanced a part of their army to Gray's Hill. I am unsure if they are going to camp there or are just posting a guard while they gather stores left in that town. Our light parties were able to capture thirty-to-forty of their men. In addition, twelve deserters from their navy and eight from their army have come into our camp. They have brought little intelligence. They do report that the enemy had several horses debilitated by the voyage.

Saturday, August 30, 1777 — Wilmington, Delaware

I have been riding, reconnoitering the country and the different roads. I will be doing the same today.

I came up with a plan that is effectively harassing those who have landed. I formed a light horse corps by drafting one hundred men from each brigade and placing them under a brigadier. Just now, twenty-four British soldiers have been brought in by Captain Lee of the light horse.

Sunday, August 31, 1777 — Wilmington, Delaware

A small skirmish ensued between one of our advanced parties and an advanced party of the enemy this afternoon. After a short while, the enemy retreated. They had one officer and three men killed. We had a private wounded.

Monday, September 1, 1777 — Wilmington, Delaware

General Howe has issued a declaration to the inhabitants at the Head of Elk pledging they will be safe if they stay in their abodes. He offered pardons to any of our men who have taken part in our "rebellion" if they will return their allegiance to the King and turn themselves in to a detachment of the King's forces. I translate this to mean, they will destroy and burn homes unless people come out and swear loyalty to the enemy. He is still up to his usual seduction.

Many have turned out for the Maryland Eastern Shore militia. The one problem, they lack arms. I am trying to address this. I am requesting that Congress allows me to send General Cadwalader to lead them, get them arms, and bring order to their corps.

Wednesday, September 3, 1777 — Wilmington, Delaware

Congress is requesting an inquiry with General Sullivan relative to the affair at Staten Island. The thing did not come out satisfactory. There is question as to General Sullivan's conduct in that battle. He has agreed to the inquiry with the stipulation that Colonel Smallwood give his testimony. He was a firsthand witness and can vouch for General Sullivan's command in that fray. This is fair.

The enemy came out this morning against our light advanced corps. They brought three pieces of artillery and gave heavy fire but fell prey to our expert marksman. Our men drew the enemy out and then fell back in a ploy. The enemy pursued right into the sites of our riflemen. The belief is that the enemy was trying to secure Iron Hill, but failed. They did leave a picket at Couch's Mill. It is now reported that we had about forty men killed or wounded in that skirmish. As best we can tell, the enemy lost many more.

Friday, September 5, 1777 — Wilmington, Delaware

I am directing Brigadier-General Maxwell to send a man under flag with a letter to the Howe brothers requesting a prisoner exchange — their General Prescott for our General Lee. They have not responded to my first notice. I have heard that they came to us under the flag and we fired on them. If that is the case, we need to deal with the one who broke the rules of propriety. We should never be guilty of such an offense. While Maxwell's officer delivers the letters, I am wishful that he can get an idea of the layout of the enemy camp. I am asking General Maxwell to send out reconnoitering parties to survey the enemy's situation to see if they can determine what the British are up to.

Sunday, September 7, 1777 — Wilmington, Delaware

The enemy's main body now has a post at Iron Hill. Ours is about eight-to-ten miles away at a village called Newport. The thought is he will spread his troops out to cut us off from help in the east and secure horses, cattle, and forage from the countryside. This seems a poor plan as he will be easier to overcome if he is so spread out.

Tuesday, September 9, 1777 — Wilmington, Delaware

The enemy advanced within two miles of us yesterday. Their goal seemingly is to get around us to our right, passing Brandywine, and taking the high point on the north side of the river, coming between us and Philadelphia. We cannot allow that, so at two o'clock this morning, our army marched to take the high ground near Chad's Ford.

Thursday, September 11, 1777 — Chester County, Pennsylvania

I am headquartered in a rock house situated near Brandywine creek. It is an area where people are clearing fields to build homes, raise families, and start lives for themselves. The air is crisp. The Brandywine creek runs amongst the tallest of trees, glistening at every turn as the morning sun rises. The grass is lush for grazing. The trees and grass combine for an invigorating aroma. I can almost drink it in. I raise my head to inhale deeply that scent. I wonder if I lived here, would I take this for granted? A hill descends from this home down to a branch of the creek. That same hill rises behind me to an overlook. This is America. In the stillness of the morning, I wish this were all behind us. What a life we can live in this land. The British should go back to their country and enjoy theirs. Let us enjoy ours. In the quiet beauty of this moment, I realize why this fight must be carried. The men and tents that dot this landscape bring me back to the reality of war. It is not the battle itself, but what follows that drives us. With that said, the peace and serenity can only come through the cannon and musket fire of confrontation. When the smoke finally settles days or years from now, I pray we are standing free. When that time comes and I hope it will, I must bring Mrs. Washington back to this spot. She would love this place. But for now, I must meet with our officers. A battle is lurking at this pristine spot.

The time is midmorning, I have just been alerted that approximately five thousand Hessians have positioned themselves across from our men at Chad's Ford. No sooner have I been told that, I am now hearing cannon fire. Where is Howe?

The time is eleven o'clock, the fire fight continues at Chad's Ford. Now I am told another dispatch of British troops are marching to Trimble's Ford. How can it be that ford? This is the one ford that I did not secure! If Howe has divided his troops then they are in a vulnerable position, I am ordering ours be divided. I am sending one division to meet those crossing Trimble's Ford. I am sending another to join the men in repelling the Hessians.

General Sullivan just sent a dispatch, the intelligence was wrong. No British troops are crossing Trimble's Ford. I am ordering our men to halt until we know what is going on. All I know is the Hessians are on the attack.

The time is now two o'clock, General Sullivan just sent a frantic message, the British are crossing at Birmingham Meeting House. I am sending Sullivan now with his division to hold the enemy at bay until reinforcements arrive.

The Hessians are now crossing into Chad's Ford against General Wayne. I am trusting Wayne can hold his own. I am taking General Greene's division to support General Sullivan at Birmingham.

Sullivan and his men are outnumbered and struggling to hold their own. General Greene is rushing down with his men to support Sullivan.

The time is midnight now; we are back at camp. What a disaster. General Wayne and General Maxwell and their men were pushed back and overpowered.

General Greene, in support of General Sullivan, was unsuccessful in reversing the British at Birmingham. He had to retreat as well. I was able to retreat along with our men — thanks to General Pulaski.

Friday, September 12, 1777

Second guessing, checking on our men, setting defenses, and regret took the place of sleep tonight. I never dreamed we would be so overwhelmed. All things have been going well. Our ranks were increasing. Our spirits were high. I am faced again with the harsh reality — the British outnumber us, outgun us, and have the mobility that we lack on the water. They are experienced soldiers. We are a volunteer, sometimes soldier, sometimes farmer collection called the Continental Army. General Howe was able to outflank us. We were totally ignorant of his movements. Intelligence gave nothing to prepare us. What intelligence we received was false as seen with the first report that the enemy was crossing at Trimble's Ford. We have lost a good number of men with first counts of wounded, killed, and captured. The Marquis de Lafayette was shot in the leg but braved well. General Woodford was shot in the hand.

The one thing I can be heartened by is that I watched General Sullivan and his men at Birmingham Meeting House. The British would overwhelm them and push them back. Each time, Sullivan and his men had reason to retreat, but they would not. Each time, five times as I have heard, they pushed back against the enemy, reclaimed ground, and made them pay for every moment of their two-hour clash. This may be why our men seem to be in good spirits today. The enemy gave them all they could. Yet, this army still stands. America still is.

There is a tree on a companion hill from where I sit. It is tall and bending over the field below. Next to it sits a home that has been abandoned for how long, I do not know. A thought that crosses my mind — I can imagine that tree giving a testimony of what it witnessed here, for generations that follow. If it could speak, I believe it would say an army was on this site that was willing to fight for all things good and true, no matter the cost. May it stand for decades to come as a monument to these men. Whatever our losses are when the final totals come in, we are resolved to gain compensation in redcoat losses the next time.

Sunday, September 14, 1777 — Germantown, Pennsylvania

We are now headquartered in Germantown. It is the Lord's Day. Many would be angry at God for their plight, especially two days after Brandywine. I am not angry. I knew when we entered this struggle, as with any struggle to redress a wrong, difficulties would present. I think that not standing for what is right would be much easier. Sadly, retreat from such virtue steals away all that one is to be in this life. It just leaves an empty shell of cowardice and what could have been.

Congress reports that Monsieur Ducoudray is busy putting up works on the Delaware. I do not believe they will be done in time. Even if they are, at this rate, the enemy will have better use of them than this army. I have ordered the meadows on Province Island to be overflowed. I am posting General Armstrong and his militia along the Schuylkill to throw up redoubts at various fords.

Congress has recalled General Deborre from the army until an investigation of charges against him are investigated. Report by those of General Sullivan's command is that Deborre acted very poorly in command of his brigade at Brandywine. From their viewpoint, Deborre should never be sent into combat again. I believe Congress will concur.

Monday, September 15, 1777 — Buck Tavern

Congress has requested the presence of General Sullivan to commence the inquiry into the Staten Island event. I understand the need, but I object to their call currently for two reasons. One, we are near another action. I cannot spare another general at this moment of battle. We are already short of brigadiers. Beyond that, Deborre has been withdrawn. Smallwood is head of the militia from his State. General Gist is absent by order. Lincoln had to leave to cover for St. Clair. For this reason, I am not asking that the inquiry be dropped but just postponed. The second reason that I object is General Sullivan's performance at Brandywine. Had Congress seen him in action, I believe his performance and courage against overwhelming odds would give them the light to see that whatever occurred at Staten Island was not due to some failure of duty on General Sullivan's part.

Congress reports that General Gates is having success in bringing order to the northern army. He now has it on a respectable footing.

The enemy in these parts is stationed at Dilworthtown. We are moving to get between them and Swedes' Ford. Work is underway to protect our right flank, which tends to be the enemy's violent inclination when aggressions commence.

We need Congress to provide us with blankets and clothing for our men. The cold weather is upon us.

Wednesday, September 17, 1777 — Yellow Springs, Pennsylvania

The enemy moved yesterday from Concord toward Lancaster road with a design on our right flank. We have adjusted our position. We are on the move to Warwick.

Congress has heard that the British have four thousand men situated in the Jerseys. If they have that many, their purpose is not a feint. I am in hopes General McDougal with the militia can join General Dickinson and make a strong show against them.

Friday, September 19, 1777 — Camp

I have crossed over at Parker's Ford. I am waiting on our main body of men to complete their crossing, which should be in an hour or two. The river is deep and moving rapidly. It is hampering our move. I am marching my men and stationing them at various places along the river where the enemy might cross. General Wayne and his division are following at the rear of the enemy. General Smallwood and Colonel Gist with their troops should be joining him soon.

I had hoped to attack the enemy a few days ago, but our lack of provisions and the heavy downpour of rain made such an endeavor impossible. Without an attack, the enemy is moving rapidly toward Philadelphia with little-to-no resistance. I am in hopes I can meet them soon and prayerfully before they take Philadelphia. If they do take that fair city, I hope it will be at great cost to them. I am informing Congress of my movements. That last part, I know they will not want to hear. It grieves me to think that we may lose Philadelphia, but after what happened at Brandywine creek, the enemy seems to be a boulder rolling quickly down a mountain gaining speed and bringing damage without any means to stop or redirect them. I pray for Heaven to intervene.

Monday, September 22, 1777 — Camp

I have never heard of an army losing a war because of lack of blankets. I have heard of losing a battle for lack of strategy, or lack of leadership, or lack of weapons, or even lack of numbers, but blankets? If we do not have cover for our men, they will certainly get sick, some will die, most will be too weak to fight, and many will leave their posts. I am asking Lieutenant-Colonel Alexander Hamilton to go into the city of Philadelphia and ask the citizens for contributions of blankets, clothes, shoes, and any other necessities they can supply our soldiers. By our count, a thousand of our soldiers are marching barefoot. Our countrymen in Philadelphia still sleep in their homes (though uneasily), while our men lay in the field virtually naked. It is a sad state-of-affairs. For me to press this after Brandywine creek is hard, but how can we fare any better down the line if we have few men and those who stay are ill-cared for?

Tuesday, September 23, 1777 — Camp

I am sending Baron D'Arendt to move immediately and guide the troops at Fort Island below Philadelphia to deter the British from gaining navigation on the Delaware. We have sunk chevaux-de-frise near the fort to hinder their movement. The enemy will attempt to take Fort Island, remove our obstacles, and sail upriver to join their land forces. We must do all we can to prevent this junction.

I am gratified that Congress has adjourned to Lancaster. This takes some pressure off this army. Our Congress must stay out of harm's way. If the enemy gets them, I fear the enemy gets the Nation. If the enemy gets this army, the game may be over anyway. We can countenance losing the city of Philadelphia as long as all who are valued there are removed. I did not think this in the past, but thankfully our government is one that can be carried out regardless of location. Besides, our government really is not in some capital but in the houses and hearts of everyday Americans. This is a government that answers to the people and not the other way around.

The enemy's advanced parties may be in Philadelphia this evening. I thought of taking their rear, but our men are greatly fatigued after trying to keep pace with the enemy and force a confrontation. Tomorrow, we will march toward Philadelphia ourselves. We hope to form a junction with General McDougal and the Jersey militia under General Dickinson. I am also waiting on General Wayne and General Smallwood. I am asking that all Virginia militia who have arms to move to this head immediately. Those who have no arms need to wait in Fredericktown in Maryland until they can be provided. I am in hopes Congress can procure the needed guns.

I am calling on General Putnam to detach as many rank-and-file under proper officers to proceed expeditiously to reinforce me. There is no time to lose, no excuse acceptable. I am desirous to bring a defeat to this enemy's army opposed to us here. It is of the utmost necessity.

General Howe is advancing on Philadelphia.

Wednesday, September 24, 1777 — Camp near Pottsgrove, Pennsylvania

One of the greatest helps I can imagine at this moment is Colonel Morgan and his corps. I sent them to General Gates to assist him. I have heard of no real activity in that quarter. General Burgoyne may have been dealt with or he may be on the move. I have been so occupied here with Howe and the main of the British army, that Burgoyne's little contingent has not captured my notice. What Colonel Morgan brings to this fight is the unseen and the unknown to the enemy. They fear he and his men. This would be a great help and a great concern to Howe and the British. I am writing General Gates, not with a command, but a request that he send Morgan immediately as things have not fared well for us here.

The enemy believes Colonel Morgan and his corps are brutal and fight savagely. That they accuse us of what they do so well is interesting. Last Saturday, General Wayne and his division camped outside Paoli's Tavern. Deep into the night, the British rushed our men in the darkness and savagely drove their bayonets into our men. Enemy snipers then fired from the darkness at any of our men who were discernible in the dark. Wayne was able to escape with most of his men, but two hundred were killed. Some one hundred were captured. It was a massacre. May all of America be enraged and take arms against this enemy. The British offend and dare offer pardon for our offenses?

Saturday, September 27, 1777 — Camp near Pennibecker's Mill

No favorable change has occurred in our affairs. We have suffered another loss in this quarter. At the advice of the council of officers, Commodore Hazelwood sent two frigates, the Delaware and the Montgomery, along with a few other vessels to disrupt the British from building batteries near the city to prevent our shipping. The Delaware was captured. Some say there was a mutiny on board. Others say it was disabled by enemy fire. Either way, it is another loss that weighs heavily upon my command.

Sunday, September 28, 1777 — Camp near Pennibecker's Mill

Congress informs me the northern army has had a breakthrough against Burgoyne and that his defeat is just a matter of time. That is good for our cause. It supports my case to get Colonel Morgan here.

Monday, September 29, 1777 — Camp near Pennibecker's Mill

General Smallwood has joined me with his Maryland militia, but their numbers are down to around one thousand due to desertions. General Forman will join me today with nine hundred Continental troops and militia from Jersey. We are going to move about four or five miles today. We will see if we can make an attack on the enemy after we reconnoiter the enemy's situation.

Wednesday, October 1, 1777 — Camp, twenty miles from Philadelphia, Pennsylvania

The British now have control of Philadelphia. Many reasons exist as to why we have failed in our objective to stop this from occurring. The men, however, are in good spirits despite their lack of blankets, shoes, and clothing. Saying they are in good spirits when they lack basic necessities is hard to imagine. I believe this is a testament to the type of men under my command.

News about the northern army is a pleasing and an important circumstance. I am hearing of their success from many avenues. I cannot help but feel somewhat envious. I hope Congress will remember the situation in that quarter was in a state of defeat, but with time and perseverance, it was turned around. The same will be the case for our situation at this head. Our army has received the rest that it needed. We are regaining our footing.

Friday, October 3, 1777 — Camp, twenty miles from Philadelphia, Pennsylvania

We have intercepted two letters from General Howe dictating their plan to reduce Billingsport and the Delaware forts. I shared this with my general officers who were unanimous in the opinion that we should make a strike on the enemy troops at Germantown. We spent the day planning our attack. We have received reinforcements. Our number is happily up to eight thousand regulars and three thousand militia. We now have a force that can more readily contend with the enemy.

In our deliberations, it was decided that Generals Sullivan and Wayne will lead their divisions into the town flanked by Conway's brigade. They are to enter by way of Chestnut Hill. General Armstrong with the Pennsylvania militia is to fall upon the left and rear of the enemy by way of Vandeering's Mill. Generals Greene and Stephen will take a circuit with their division flanked by McDougal's brigade by way of Lime-kiln road and attack the right wing. The militias of Maryland and Jersey led by Generals Smallwood and Forman will march by the old York road upon the rear to their right. Lord Stirling with General Nash's brigade and General Maxwell's brigade will form a corps de reserve. This seems to me to be an agreeable strategy. With surprise as our advantage, we may now be able to surround the enemy and change our fortunes. This is my prayer.

Before we set out, I need to share what is on my heart and, more so, the fire that is in my belly. I do not choose to motivate, but rather to state clearly to our men why we fight and what is at stake. I will gather our officers and as many men as can join us. I must let them know that in this foray we are about to embark on, we are to no longer allow the enemy triumph over us. We have had enough losses. The turn of the tide in this war needs to begin now. We are mocked. We suffer wounds with no recourse. This has gone on almost since the inception of this Nation at Britain's hands. We cannot resign our wives and children, our parents, and friends to be vassals to an insulting foe. We cannot neglect to contend nobly for all things dear to us. Our rights, our lives, our honor, our glory, and even our shame should urge every man to fight and not turn from the enemy. We must be brave. We must be firm. If we show ourselves as men, we will truly end this thing victorious. I know we can win this.

We are setting out for our march at seven o'clock this evening. We have fifteen miles to cover before we make contact with the enemy. May the Lord give us favor. I have given our men my charge.

Saturday, October 4, 1777 — Camp, twenty miles from Philadelphia, Pennsylvania

Morning is breaking. The enemy is silent. An unexpected heavy fog occurred. I am unsure if this is a good thing for us or a bad thing. We can begin our attack covered by fog. The retarding factor may be that we cannot see what each other is doing, nor are we able to signal to each other. My prayer is that once we encounter the enemy, the fog will lift on this action as well as on our cause.

I have given the signal for Sullivan and Wayne to move. A picket is just ahead with enemy troops.

The firing has begun. The enemy is retreating. Our men are pushing forward. Now, may our men pour in from their various quarters. I cannot see what is going on. It seems repetitious — the sound of heavy fire, then it recedes, our men push forward, the sound of heavy fire, it recedes, our line moves forward. Sullivan and Wayne seem to be having their way.

As best I can tell, it is almost eight o'clock. I am hearing fire from our left column. Greene is engaged. The fog is still heavy. I am in hopes that our men can make out who is with us and who is against us.

I am following our men. I can see heavy enemy fire coming from a stone house. I am ordering a few of our men to surround it and keep up the fire. I am ordering the rest of our men to keep moving behind Sullivan and Wayne. We are moving forward. The enemy is in retreat. I cannot see, but I believe the front of our assault must be getting close to Howe's quarters. This thing is working!

I am hearing fire all around us. Are we surrounded? Wait a minute, sober thought reminds us, our men are coming in from all quarters. We should be hearing that fire around us. If only the fog would lift.

Up ahead, from what I can make out, our men are running toward me, why?

Sunday, October 5, 1777 — Camp near Pennibecker's Mill

The day was almost won. Perhaps even the battle. For a moment, the rolling boulder of the British army was stalled. But the fog. The men were retreating. I could not understand why. Had the enemy reinforcements arrived? I tried to get the men back in order, to regroup, and to resume our push but it was to no avail.

From what we can gather, it seems the fog kept our men from knowing that the fire they were hearing was from our own men, not the enemy. A real problem was that the men leading ran out of ammunition and fell back. The troops behind were to carry on the fight, but seeing the men ahead of them retreat, they assumed that General Greene's guns were enemy fire, that they were surrounded. They fled in confusion, following the lead men who were moving back to get more ammunition. I do not know how many of our men fought our own men in the malaise of fire and fog.

I must write Congress. Reaching back to a tired but true excuse — unforeseen accidents and unavoidable difficulties robbed us of a significant victory. Several good things have come from it. I do not believe we have lost as many men as the enemy. Our new troops have been tested by fire and proved valiant. Had there not been fog and confusion, I believe the day would have been a complete victory. The enemy has been shown to be vulnerable. For the first time in this conflict, we have seen the main of the British army retreat. This gives us succor. General Sullivan once again proved to be a strong general and a good leader who does not pullback from the fires of battle. I know Congress wishes an inquiry of the misfortunes at Staten Island, but General Sullivan has proven twice in just a few weeks, under my watchful eye, that he is gallant and beyond reproach. He may have made some errors, but I believe his loss at Staten Island was for the same reasons we faced the unsatisfactory results yesterday. I could just as easily be questioned concerning my performance of late.

Monday, October 6, 1777 — Camp near Pennibecker's Mill

General Howe's letter came to me this morning. I was interested to open it for hopes that the battles two days ago would bring some conciliatory sentiment. I am always hoping for good news and trust that over time, good news and glad tidings will befall this Nation and this army. Sadly, as I read his letter, he complains that the inhabitants of Philadelphia were victims of our actions, including destroying some of their mills. I am unaware of any civilian harm. This army has never sought to burn and destroy any of our countrymen's belongings. I am glad to see finally General Howe has some concern for the inhabitants of this Nation. This would be the first. It is he and his army that have burned houses and barns, raped women, and killed the innocent. I will write as such back to him, but of course in a gentlemanly manner.

On a comical note, if there is any room for such, a dog of General Howe's has fallen into our custody. The man who found it brought it to me for sport. How did he know it was General Howe's dog? The owner's name was found on the dog's collar. I am returning the dog to him with a note. He must know that I am civil and will do right even down to the least of God's Creation.

Tuesday, October 7, 1777 — Camp near Pennibecker's Mill

Our loss at Germantown appears to be greater than I first thought. We seem to have lost one thousand soldiers either killed, wounded, or captured. This is a regrettable figure when I consider how close we were to victory, and that the laziness of the weather would turn certain victory into something short of that. I am told the British were making plans to retreat to Chester when the confusion and loss of ammunition brought about our premature retreat. The enemy's losses are reported more than what we experienced per a few deserters who have come over from their side.

I am taking time to rest our soldiers and to bring some sober reflection of the previous action. My prayer is they will be emboldened in hindsight and learn how to prevent such things in the next. Our numbers are being replenished. General Varnum with a detachment of about twelve hundred men are on their way to our camp. Five hundred militia from Virginia and two hundred from Maryland have joined this army, along with General Gibson's State regiment of over two hundred and fifty. When the whole of our reinforcements arrives, we will have thirteen brigades, which will require as many brigadiers and six major-generals. We are lacking in officers. I am asking Congress to supplement them. I am recommending General McDougal for the post and after inquiry to reinstate General St. Clair.

General Forman's brigade of militia from Jersey has left us. It is believed that news of the enemy in their State has prompted their move. I have approved it. The British have taken Billingsport with little opposition. I believe it is of no significant value. To record that two whole crews of seamen and their officers have deserted to the enemy is shameful. The good news on the waters comes from Captain Brewer who arrived here with his fleet. He says his men are inspired with greater confidence since four enemy ships tried to weigh the chevaux-de-frise near Fort Island. Our galleys and garrison on the fort were able to launch such a volley to render their effort fruitless.

General Hawkes Hay of Haverstraw reports that a considerable number of armed vessels and eight transports have arrived at the bay opposite his position, landing troops at Verplanck's Point.

I am sending Colonel Christopher Greene, along with Colonel Angel, to the garrison Red Bank. They are to coordinate with Colonel Smith (who commands the garrison at Fort Mifflin) and Commodore Hazelwood (who commands the fleet on that river) to strengthen our blockades along the river. I am having cannon and supplies sent to supply Red Bank. A race by the enemy will ensue to take this garrison to maintain their hold on Philadelphia. I am sending men and artillery there. I am instructing the Colonels that they must rush to the fort and be willing to fight the enemy if they find them contesting its acquisition. The defense of the Delaware depends on their exertions.

Wednesday, October 8, 1777 — Camp near Pennibecker's Mill

I am writing Governor Livingston in New Jersey to make ready his militia. They need to swing to the aid of General Putnam at Peekskill. The enemy is making a move in that direction to perhaps take the Highland passes including our forts. They then may come in behind General Gates and the northern army, placing him potentially between two fires. This could force his retreat and reverse our successes in that quarter. I have had to reduce General Putnam's force because of our dire need here. As a result, the militias in that sector must join together to repulse the enemy.

Saturday, October 11, 1777 — Skippack Camp

Lieutenant-Colonel Smith informs me that the enemy is firing on the Mud Fort along the Delaware river. His plan is to move his men away from the fort to protect them, but the only place they can go is to an open field. He only has two hundred men to defend against perhaps one thousand of the enemy. With the weather poor and already having many sick, he is unsure what to do. I am advising him to build up a bank against the picket to his rear, to help defend it from the shot. He can then throw up some blinds within the fort which will provide additional protection. If he needs to move his men, I suggest between the Stone Fort and the lower battery where his men can find shelter until Commodore Hazelwood can attack from the water.

Monday, October 13, 1777 — Headquarters

Commodore Hazelwood has brought great success in defense of Mud Fort. His three galleys and a floating battery caused the enemy to surrender. He has taken fifty-eight prisoners of war. This brings me some solace when I must note General Putnam has lost the Highlands, including Forts Montgomery and Clinton. I am awaiting more information.

Wednesday, October 15, 1777 — Headquarters

Governor Clinton has given me a more complete account of the loss of Forts Montgomery and Clinton. Our men put up a brave resistance, but were faced with a far superior number. General Putnam was put at a disadvantage after Brandywine when I had to reduce his troops to the preservation of these under my watch. I had hoped the neighboring militia would have come to his aid. I know Putnam did all in his power to solicit their help. I do believe the British general Clinton will seek to destroy any of our vessels he finds on the Hudson river. I am asking the Governor to see to it that more flat-bottom boats are constructed a few miles from the river, out of sight, so that they can be hauled to the river should our army need them.

The good news of the day is that Providence has given favor to the northern army and General Gates. General Burgoyne has been defeated. This is a huge blow to the enemy. The British may have Philadelphia. They may have been able to drive us, but they have been unable to defeat us. They cannot say the same for their army in the northern front.

Insecurities and self-pity prevail upon me this day. It will be shared nowhere else but here and to no one else ever. I cannot help but ask why is General Gates seeing the victories and the accolades while I seem to be stuck here in the mud, unable to move as prey to the enemy? I fear that I am losing the confidence of Congress. I did not feel this pressure when Gates and I were struggling at our different corners of the war. But now that a decisive stroke has been made in his sector, the failures and futility in this neighborhood does not bode well for me. Even my potential victories are turned to nothing in the fog. Will Congress remember the efforts that I took to reinforce Gates and bring greater assurance of his success? Even now, Colonel Morgan and his corps are there and have contributed significantly to Gates's success. Yet, when I am in need, and it has been over a week, little assistance comes from that quarter. If I were in Congress and did not know what I know here on the front, I would question the selection of Mr. Washington to lead this army. Perhaps, I would consider a change in leadership. This weight and darkness hang over me. I am praying for Providence to do what He does, and swing to my aid. I need a victory and a decisive one. I would love to say that if we win, I will accept rejection and even demotion. I do believe this is my heart. But on the surface and a little below, I wish that my efforts and sacrifices would be rewarded. This is enough for me to write. May this writing never see the light of day. I will hold to a Scripture that an old preacher shared about the Lord's Judgement Day. He will say to those who have served Him, "Well done, good and faithful servant." He will not say, "Well done, good and successful servant." I will do my best to be faithful and leave the rest to Him. Setback after setback, what else is there for me to do, but have faith and be faithful?

Friday, October 17, 1777 — Matuchen Hill

I am writing Mr. Wharton, President of Pennsylvania. The enemy has invaded this State and taken over its capital. Yet can they only bring together twelve hundred militia in the field? Maryland is sending militia to this State as is New York and New Jersey. Both these States have had to deal with the enemy in their respective quarters. They raised enough militia to thwart the British designs even without Continental troops present. Pennsylvania has also done poorly in meeting their four-thousand-man quota. They have never been over one-third of the requirement. Now it is less than that. You would think a State occupied as this one, would rouse the people to come and fight for their State and their own homes. Such apathy is difficult to comprehend. I am going to ask Mr. Wharton to institute a draft if he must, to fill his quota. He needs to do it with all alacrity. New England and Virginia have initiated a draft. They are finding it quite effective. The British are governing the Delaware river at the present. They do so from the capital of Philadelphia. I hope to at least shame this President into caring enough to fight his own battles. We are here to help.

Today is proving a trying day. Late this afternoon, I received two letters from Congress intimating that they are about to promote Brigadier-General Conway to major-general over many of his superiors. I am generally not so animated in things like this, but I will write Richard Henry Lee, in particular, to air my anger over this pick. General Conway is unfit to be a major-general. All the brigadiers and their subordinates know it. Not a day passes where I do not receive resignations tendered from this army and its officers. I must plead and beg them to stay. I do all I can to appease those who are disgruntled. Within the last six days, twenty commissions at least have been tendered to me. I know for a fact that if General

Conway is promoted, a stampede of more resignations will occur. This army will suffer or dissolve over it. I, myself, would be tempted to if I did not love and owe this Nation so much. General Conway's merit and importance to this army is only in his imagination. His maxim is to leave no service of his untold. I have never spoken out so harshly of a man than this. I pray Congress realizes that for me to come out so strongly means something must be amiss in General Conway.

Saturday, October 18, 1777 — Philadelphia County

I am assigning the Baron D'Arendt to take command of Fort Mifflin on Mud Island. He is to coordinate with Commodore Hazelwood and Colonel Greene who commands Red Bluff. I have full confidence in D'Arendt. I have placed him at this fort because I believe the success of this campaign depends on holding it. If he is successful, the British may be in position to be defeated or at the very least leave Philadelphia shamefully. That is how much weight I put behind this command. He is to let me know what he needs, pass on intelligence the minute he hears it, watch over his ammunition, and keep me apprised of the state of the garrison. May the smiles of Heaven be upon this army.

I am writing my dear brother John Augustine. He is greatly worried about this army and me specifically. I have been too busy to keep him abreast of our condition and activities. He had written previously to let me know that his son Corbin has married his sweetheart. I am writing for my brother to give them my best wishes for a long-lasting and joyful marriage. Out here in the field, we miss so much the day-to-day life of home and family, of events and celebrations. I know Providence has designed things otherwise for me, so I will trust in Him.

Sunday, October 19, 1777 — Philadelphia County

General Putnam sends congratulations to me concerning the surrender of General Burgoyne to General Gates and the northern army. That victory should afford the highest satisfaction to every American. I am consoled that General Putnam gives me some credit for my part as Commander-in-Chief. Things are looking good in the northern sector and in New York despite some losses of forts. General Putnam informs me also that his wife has died. Again, the cost of being in this battle pulls us from our dear ones. Often men die on the battlefield, but some-times men on the battlefield lose people at home and cannot be there to care for them. I do know and will remind General Putnam in my condolences that all of us must die, but we take consolation as Christians. It is appointed once for all of us to die. We would prefer to choose the circumstances surrounding that event, but that is not for us to decide.

Wednesday, October 22, 1777 — Philadelphia County

President Hancock informs me that he is retiring from Congress. He has been of ill-health, and personal matters at home require his attention. He has been good to me. I pray for his health to return and, as Providence permits, that he returns to public service if he desires. I am offering him an escort to General Putnam's station. I am then asking General Putnam to provide him an escort from there to Mr. Hancock's home.

No sooner do I restore Baron D'Arendt to his post as commander at Fort Mifflin, I now receive a letter from Lieutenant-Colonel Smith wishing to resign from Fort Mifflin to rejoin his corps. I suppose he thinks he has done something wrong. He may just be miffed he has been replaced after doing an adequate job in command. He forgets that he was placed in that command because the Baron was ill. I cannot remove the Baron from his position permanently simply because he took ill. I wish for Lieutenant-Colonel Smith to stay there. He should continue to do his duty and assist the Baron where he is in need. It is a shame that pride and feelings get involved. I have both, but I refuse to let them interfere or cause me to resign from my duty.

Friday, October 24, 1777 — Philadelphia County

Colonel Greene sends good news. Four battalions of Germans, about twelve hun-dred men, arrived at the fort at Red Bank. They demanded the fort's surrender. Colonel Greene declined saying they would never surrender it. The enemy's can-nonade began to fire. The German soldiers pushed forward against the fort, some passing the pickets. Colonel Greene's men fired so ferociously that the enemy had to turn and run. By Greene's count, seventy of the enemy were killed. Another seventy were wounded and taken prisoner. He has asked to send them to Burlington. I believe that place is insecure. The British could easily make off with them. I am directing him to send them to Morristown.

We are recording small victories in this part. We celebrate one large victory by the northern army along with a few smaller ones in the north. All totaled, it seems things are going better for us all things considered.

Saturday, October 25, 1777 — Philadelphia County

General Putnam has forwarded to me a copy of General Burgoyne's capitulation. I am glad to see it confirmed. I have not received one line from General Gates and have no idea what he has planned. General Putnam is seeking guidance on his next move. As I have not heard from Gates, I cannot comment for sure regarding strategy. I would assume that he should form a junction with Gates and go after General Clinton, driving him out or boxing him in at New York.

General Lincoln was wounded in the leg during the activity that brought the end to General Burgoyne's hostilities, but it appears he will be able to keep his leg. I was glad to report to him the news which I just received from Commodore Hazelwood. During the attack on Red Bank, the British sent ships to support their troops. Our fleet responded. The British lost a sixty-four-gun ship called the Augusta and a frigate called the Merlin. The rest of the enemy's ships retreated down river. Commodore Hazelwood believes he can retrieve the guns from the sunken vessels if they are able to keep the enemy ships away while they do it.

Monday, October 27, 1777 — Skippack Road

We have two unfinished frigates up the Delaware which we are unable to use. We lack men to man them in any case. I am recommending to the Board of Navy that these two frigates be sunk immediately to keep them from falling into the enemy's hands.

I received a letter from my friend Mr. Landon Carter greatly concerned that, in all the events that have taken place, I am putting myself in harm's way. He believes America cannot risk losing me. What a blessing to hear that. I have told him that I am willing to put myself in harm's way if that is what it takes for victory, but that I am not reckless. He has also shown great concern for the losses we have experienced. I am reminding this dear friend what I remind myself daily — Providence is ordering everything for the best and in due time, all will end well. This is my earnest prayer. I pray that it be so and soon.

Tuesday, October 28, 1777 — Philadelphia County

Lieutenant-Colonel Smith is at odds with Colonel Greene and Commodore Hazelwood. He is taking offense in many directions. I am reminding him that I trust him and that I expect him to do his duty. I am also letting him know that the safety of those forts and that river are dependent on the three of them working in concert. Will there ever be an end to pettiness? So much more is at stake than who commands whom. What is more important is who defeats whom. I must remind myself of this in my dealings with Congress and, I fear, with General Gates.

Thursday, October 30, 1777 — Headquarters near Whitemarsh, Pennsylvania

I am sending one of my own family up to General Gates to solicit reinforcements. No one of this family is better-acquainted to our situation than Lieutenant-Colonel Alexander Hamilton. He knows the state of this army and the situation with the enemy. Gates needs to be apprised of both. Gates should be concerned about both. This war will not be won in one sector while it carries on in another. Gates has already dispatched men to Putnam. This tells me that he realizes the men he has is more than what he needs. He may have some other plan to help in this war which may be why he is keeping the remaining men with him. If he has no plan of action, I need him to send men without a moment to lose. With extra troops, General Howe can be hedged in Philadelphia. We can then cut off his supplies, placing him in the same shape as General Burgoyne found himself previous. By Heaven's Hand, he can then meet the same end.

General Clinton of the British is believed to be on his way to this neighborhood to reinforce Howe. That would be disastrous for us if we have not the same assistance from our allies. I need General Gates to send Colonel Morgan and his corps specifically. Their usefulness can turn a situation.

I am sending a personal letter to General Gates congratulating him on the victory over General Burgoyne and the full surrender of the British army in that sector. I want Gates to know that I should have been notified of this by his own hand. I cannot understand his reticence in communicating with me as his Commander-in-Chief. I am still accountable to Congress for all the armies. I have a better understanding of what the army needs as a whole. I fear General Gates is communicating only to Congress because he believes they alone are his superiors.

Saturday, November 1, 1777 — Headquarters near Whitemarsh, Pennsylvania

I am writing Congress of my disappointment that we have not been able to wage an attack on the enemy. The heavy rains, the lack of clothes, the want of ammunition, and the absence of men would make any endeavor an unfavorable one I believe.

I am letting them know that I have sent Lieutenant-Colonel Hamilton to meet with General Gates to gain reinforcements for this sector. We need these extra men to handle any attacks by the enemy and, more optimistically, to enable us to bring the battle to them. Gates may have other plans, but I am letting Congress know that I can see no greater priority than to defeat General Howe and his army. That alone would remove any fears we have for the future.

In our attack on Germantown, many bits and pieces of the enemy's papers have provided us with needed intelligence. The suddenness of our attack kept them from forwarding these to a safer area. We are separating and arranging these bits and pieces to gain better insight into the enemy's strengths, objectives, and strategies.

I am letting Congress know how each State is doing in meeting their quotas. Such a poor showing I pray will convince Congress to be more persuasive. We need to gain clothes and blankets for our men. Our numbers are already decreasing by the day. The cold will take more through the sickbed and desertion.

The last thing I need to communicate to Congress is the issue of the Marquis de Lafayette. He greatly desires a command equal to his rank. I believe he has misconstrued the sentiment of his commission from Congress. Since he has been here, I have grown to appreciate his zeal for our cause and the great expense he has taken to support it. He has quickly learned our language. He is attentive to every order. I have now seen him in battle at Brandywine. He has proven to possess bravery and military ardor. I feel at this point, we might consider giving him a command. I would dare consider what damage his return to France would do with his expectations disappointed. He has encouraged other Frenchmen to accept the situation and rank where they find themselves and not to complain back home. This alone bodes well. I leave it to Congress to make the decision, but I am willing to take a chance now that I know him. Every objection that I have had for him has been satisfied.

An agent for the British prisoners in our possession has brought six thousand Continental dollars to provide for our Hessian prisoners. I am very suspect of how he accumulated this money. I feel it may be counterfeit. I am going to convey to Congress that my preference is that hard currency be all that is accepted to care for prisoners in our care. By the way, we take care of them with or without their army's support. It is the right thing to do.

Sunday, November 2, 1777 — Headquarters near Whitemarsh, Pennsylvania

I am issuing a proclamation in every State that all deserters who return to their corps by January next or to the nearest recruiting officer shall be given full pardon for their crime. Those obstinate offenders who do not avail themselves of this indulgence will be arrested and punished to the full extent their treacherous behavior deserves.

Tuesday, November 4, 1777 — Headquarters near Whitemarsh, Pennsylvania

Major-General Dickinson proposes a good plan to help me here by utilizing the militia there. He proposes that General Gates and General Putnam with their men join him in an attack on Long Island and New York to drive out the enemy stationed there. He believes this can be affected especially if the New Jersey militia attack at Staten Island. The benefit to me here would be that the reinforcements General Howe is expecting would be tied up in New York, unable to render aid to the enemy in this quarter. I look forward to seeing what they decide. Our situation depends on it. Either send reinforcements to help us or keep reinforcements from helping the enemy.

I have ordered the engineer Major Fleury to Fort Mifflin to give guidance on how best to fortify that post and increase the effectiveness of its defense. He has proven useful everywhere he has been sent. Though his rank is inferior to that of Lieutenant-Colonel Smith, his department is of a different nature in this army. It should be given discretion, and he should have freedom to execute his judgments. Working in concert is what every part of this army must do if we want to realize a successful end to these hostilities.

Sunday, November 9, 1777 — Headquarters near Whitemarsh, Pennsylvania

It is hard for me to conceive that any would ever doubt that the Creator exists, and that He is not content to create and then just stand by and watch the thing destroy itself. Such is true today. I see God's Hand everywhere I turn. In my darkest hour, He sends a ray of hope and a blessing of relief. When my enemies conspire against me, God seems to always bring it to light. As Jesus said in the Gospel of Luke, "For there is nothing covered, that shall not be revealed; neither hid, that shall not be known." I received a letter that contained the following paragraph, "In a letter from General Conway to General Gates, 'Heaven has been determined to save your country or a weak General and bad counselors would have ruined it'." I am writing General Conway to let him know. I want him to never miss the truth that what is done in secret will be brought into the light. Such was the case of Colonel Reed and General Lee. So, it is again. I give thanks on this Lord's Day that there is One on whom I can always count.

I come back to the contemplation, why has Gates been so successful in that line of battle? Two names come to my mind at Saratoga — General Benedict Arnold and Colonel Daniel Morgan. I know the effect Colonel Morgan and his riflemen have to weaken the front of an enemy. They are able to target and take out enemy leaders. I know also of the activity of General Benedict Arnold. He will not sit still. He does not pull back from battle but rides in full force. Accounts have been arriving of how Gates was hesitant to engage the enemy, wishing the enemy to come to him on his terms. All the while, it sounds as if General Arnold pushed the issue at every opportunity. He was turning battle-after-battle into victory or, at the least, bringing harsh casualties on the enemy. I am hoping that whatever praise Gates gets is true praise, not fabricated praise. If Conway never let an action of his not be told, how much more could Gates take credit for the work Arnold and Morgan are doing. Besides all this, I am the one who sent Arnold and Morgan up to that quarter to regain what was lost by General Schuyler.

As long-serving men like John Hancock are slowly leaving government service, a whole new Congress sits in their place. I personally barely know the new men who fill these positions. They may easily take all the news they hear from the war at face value. That troubles me as Gates may be dispatching directly to them his successes, leaving out credit or concern for me and this army now stationed in Pennsylvania.

A comfort today is that the minister who spoke at our service referred to the book of Psalms, I believe it was in chapter nine, "When mine enemies are turned back, they shall fall and perish at Thy presence. For thou hast maintained my right and my cause; You sit upon the throne judging right." May this be the case for me as I trust in the Lord.

Monday, November 10, 1777 — Headquarters near Whitemarsh, Pennsylvania

I have received two letters from the new President of Congress, Mr. Henry Laurens. I am satisfied at his election to replace Mr. Hancock. I do not know him well, but thankfully his son John is one of my aides-de-camp. This should help me immensely. Whatever I report, Mr. Laurens can gain a confirmation from his son. I do not wish to use his son in this manner. I will deal honestly with our army and our Congress. I just know that if a question arises of my conduct, Mr. Laurens can find verification from one he knows in the camp — his son.

I am reemphasizing to Mr. Laurens that we should move the bulk of our resources to this front if possible. Defeating General Howe should be our chief goal. To achieve this, we need supplies, ammunition, and reinforcements. We also need cash. The militia has the advantage. They can come and go as they please to take care of their businesses, farms, and affairs. Thus, they have money and provisions for their needs. Our Continental troops have signed on as soldiers. That is their business. As a result, they and their families must be provided for by the government they serve. When they are not paid, it is a dereliction of the duties of our government, specifically Congress. I am pressing Mr. Laurens on this. Surely his son can vouch for the inconsistency and shortage in his own pay.

One other issue has occurred that I need Congress to remedy. Commissions of rank and promotions are all necessary. They may not realize that when they date those commissions an earlier date as a favor to a junior officer, it places that junior officer over men who were their superiors just a few days before. It breeds disorder. It brings disunity. Merits should be noted. Promotions should be dated accurately.

Wednesday, November 12, 1777 — Headquarters near Whitemarsh, Pennsylvania

Lieutenant-Colonel Smith reports that the enemy batteries are bringing great damage to the works of Fort Mifflin. I am encouraging him not to evacuate. They must defend that ground to the last extremity. I am sending reinforcements to relieve his tired troops. I am also ordering General Varnum to supply the fascines and palisadoes so that his men can repair at night what the enemy damages during the day.

Thursday, November 13, 1777 — Headquarters near Whitemarsh, Pennsylvania

Major-General Heath is seeking advice on what to do with the prisoners taken in the surrender of General Burgoyne and his men. There is thought that they should be sent directly to Britain and remove them from the field. The problem with that is, once they arrive in Britain, they will be placed in garrisons. Then they or others will be sent to replace them here. I am directing him to stick with the orders of exchange that we and the enemy had agreed upon previous. This will slow the process. It will also keep the enemy in the dark as to how many he has in the field and how many we have in our custody.

I am writing my friend Patrick Henry to address again my displeasure at the response of Pennsylvania and the neighboring States to the invasion of the enemy. These inhabitants seem to be lukewarm and disaffected. When New York was invaded by Burgoyne, that whole State and its neighbors poured out to defeat the enemy. I am told that at one point, fourteen thousand militia from different States joined General Gates in his efforts. Here, only around one thousand four hundred militiamen have joined. I have fought the enemy always with a great shortage of men in comparison to what Howe has. The only succor we have received is that the enemy believes we are double in size and that we are strong. This has kept them from carrying out our defeat in earnest.

Friday, November 14, 1777 — Headquarters near Whitemarsh, Pennsylvania

I have received complaints again from General Howe regarding our treatment of his men who are now our prisoners of war. I must again reiterate to him that his men are being treated humanely as far as I am aware. I am offering for him to send a person into our camp to confirm the condition of his men. I would like for him to allow the same. He would rather accuse than confirm. In the same way, I get horrible reports. He will not allow a man of ours to confirm or contest what is being told. I am sick of the whole ordeal of trying to get him to come to some agreement to exchange prisoners. I am going to offer to accede to his terms and do just a general exchange. The friends and family members of our soldiers in the enemy custody call upon me daily for their relief or retaliation for their mistreatment. I recoil at the thought of treating our prisoners in like manner, but it may be necessary for the relief of ours with them. I place it in Howe's hands.

Sunday, November 16, 1777 — Headquarters near Whitemarsh, Pennsylvania

Brigadier-General Conway has tendered his resignation to me. I suppose the fact that his undercutting with General Gates was made known to me, has prompted this act. I would be more than happy for him to leave and return to France to serve there. But it is not my duty to accept it. I must forward it to Congress. I am sure he expects it to be received with great grief. He deems his importance to serve here to be requisite to the freedom of America. I will treat him kindly and gentlemanly. If Congress desires that he continue to serve, I will be cautious but give him the benefit of the doubt. I will extend forgiveness to him as I have to Colonel Reed and even toward General Lee in the British confines.

Monday, November 17, 1777 – Headquarters near Whitemarsh, Pennsylvania

I am sad to report that Fort Mifflin has been evacuated. Our men acted valiantly, but the volleys from a specially constructed enemy ship were more than they could withstand. This ship drew so close that her men were able to toss grenades into our fort, killing our men on the platforms. Some say the captains of our galleys did not actively address this enemy ship, but that will have to be determined by inquiry.

I do believe Fort Mifflin could have been saved, but I would have had to send troops from guarding our stores and hospitals. Our stores would have been exposed. The British could have gained them to starve us out. They also would have been able to take our ammunition stock. This was untenable to me. The better option which I had hoped for was reinforcement from the northern army, but they ignored my request and never came. I sent an aid up the North river to spur them on. Excuses and no movement were all my man received.

We now need to hold Red Bank to keep the enemy from weighing the chevaux-de-frise. I am sending General St. Clair, General Knox, and Baron de Kalb to decide how best to secure it.

I am being told that Congress feels this army should have been more enterprising in confronting Howe and his army. This frustrates me to no end. Have they not seen our numbers and those of the enemy? Do they just want a quick end to this war, regardless of who wins? How can we confront the enemy naked?

Tuesday, November 18, 1777 — Headquarters near Whitemarsh, Pennsylvania

I am letting General Varnum know that a body of the enemy marched from Philadelphia across the Middle Ferry. They have boarded ships at Chester. I am hearing numbers between fifteen hundred to three thousand. Some believe they are leaving. I believe it is a feint. I am advising General Varnum to be alert and expect an attack at his quarter.

I have written Richard Henry Lee in Congress. Because of our relationship, he often is my most ready contact for effective response in means and not just words. Colonel Pickering has accepted another office, so I am in need of an adjutant-general to take his place. The candidates are as follows: Colonel Lee was recommended by Congress. He is of a good hand, but I do not know how correctly and to what ease. Colonel Wilkinson is one that General Gates speaks well of, but I am unfamiliar with him. It is said that he is a good grammatical scholar, but I am not sure of his diligence. Major Scull is highly spoken of for his knowledge of service, strict discipline, correctness, and diligence. Colonel Innes is recommended by General Woodford. I hear he is a man of good sense and educated. I leave it to Congress to choose.

We are also in desperate need of a quartermaster general. He needs to be proficient at this duty as our army has suffered greatly for lack of clothing and supplies. We scarcely ever have more than a two-day supply and often run short of meat and bread. We are also greatly lacking salt. I see no chance of it being resupplied from the east as winter is fast approaching. Congress may not realize it, but such wantings clog this army's progress.

I am praying for news of help from Russia, or that France will engage in war with Britain. Either European activity would greatly enhance our prospects as things sit now. I hate the thought of depending on foreign aid when domestic spirit should meet the demand.

Wednesday, November 19, 1777 — Headquarters near Whitemarsh, Pennsylvania

Colonel Hamilton reports that General Putnam has yet to send troops to reinforce this quarter. He may have other ideas concerning New York, but the greatest need of this Nation is here against General Howe. I am letting Putnam know that I am greatly disappointed in his reluctance to obey an order and that I hope in the future they will be followed. If he is worried that obedience will put his army in jeopardy, he needs to know that blame will lie with me. He needs to forward troops immediately. He needs to let me know how many are coming, what route they are taking, and when I can expect them.

Saturday, November 22, 1777 — Headquarters near Whitemarsh, Pennsylvania

Lord Cornwallis has not returned to Philadelphia. I believe he is about to make a move at Red Bank. I am ordering General Greene and his men to make a junction with Glover's brigade. They must meet the enemy before they reach Red Bank.

Sunday, November 23, 1777 — Headquarters near Whitemarsh, Pennsylvania

Red Bank has fallen to the enemy. Fort Mifflin and Red Bank mutually depended on one another. When one fell, it was almost certain the other would be unsustainable. Had we had the men to attack Cornwallis in the rear flank, we might have been successful, but Cornwallis and his men moved too rapidly. Our men evacuated. It was a good decision. The cost of men and supplies would have made the loss a lot worse. The superior force of the enemy could have easily closed off supplies and retreat. Had that been the case, all that camp would be removed from our disposal. As it now stands, General Varnum was able to save most of the stores, arms, and ammunition. We did lose a couple of heavy cannon. Our people burned the majority of our vessels posted there rather than have the enemy take them. General Greene is in Jersey awaiting Glover's brigade. Colonel Morgan's corps are on their way to assist. Once they are gathered, if an attack can be made on Cornwallis with a prospect of success, I will order it done.

Tuesday, November 25, 1777 — Headquarters near Whitemarsh, Pennsylvania

I called a council of war yesterday to consider the question of an attack on Philadelphia. Our officers were at odds on many points. I sent them away to have time for themselves to weigh all the options. Each is then to write to me as to their personal leaning.

The vote has come back in the negative. Eleven officers opposed the attack — Greene, Sullivan, Knox, Baron de Kalb, Smallwood, Maxwell, Poor, Paterson, Irvine, Duportail, and Armstrong. Only four were for the attack — Stirling, Wayne, Scott, and Woodford. Based on the opinion of the council of many, we have chosen not to attack at this moment.

Wednesday, November 26, 1777 — Headquarters near Whitemarsh, Pennsylvania

I am still dealing with the Marquis de Lafayette. He is pressing for a command. We have done all we can to get him the experience he needs. He engages every opportunity with both feet. General Greene has reported from Jersey that he sent the Marquis out with four hundred militia and the rifle corps to attack a picket of the enemy. It amounted to about three hundred men. The Marquis and his men were successful — killing twenty, wounding many, and taking another twenty prisoners. Greene says the Marquis is determined to be in the middle of danger. He reminds me of General Benedict Arnold. We have vacancies in some of our divisions. I think it would be fitting to try him out in leading one. I will request the approval of Congress.

Friday, November 28, 1777 — Headquarters near Whitemarsh, Pennsylvania

The enemy has brought several ships into the city. It appears they have found a passageway through the chevaux-de-frise. I believe they may be planning to send them up the Delaware to destroy what watercraft we have left in this area. Some think they may attack this army as well. That would be my optimistic hope. I am ordering General Greene to push forward expediently with the rear brigades.

Tuesday, December 2, 1777 — Headquarters near Whitemarsh, Pennsylvania

I am ordering General Putnam to waste no time securing the North river. It is the only river that allows the enemy to connect with Canada. It runs through the whole State. Losing it would break our communication between eastern, middle, and southern States. It is also how we get our chief supply of flour for this army. Obstructions must be put in place to discourage or slow the enemy. I am asking him to meet with the French engineer Colonel Radiere for the best method of doing so. I believe this all needs to be done by the spring as I expect the enemy to try to take Albany in the next campaign. It is the only city of any importance in that State for which that they do not have control.

I am informing General Gates that by resolution of Congress, he is to gather his men and try to regain the posts the enemy has taken, drive them out, and refortify those forts for a strong defense. It is sad that I must reference Congress to get him to consider my orders. I am reminding him that I have not heard a word from him. I have no idea how he is doing with the previous resolution of Congress requiring him to repair the old works. I also want him to know that we have lost Fort Mifflin and Red Oak. I am inferring the true reason is because he did not send reinforcements in a timely manner. Those who did come were nowhere near what I requested.

The enemy's line extends from the Upper Ferry to Kensington upon the Delaware. It is defended by a strong chain of redoubts connected by abatis. Keeping this in mind, I have not decided on a winter camp. We need a location that can be safe, out of the enemy's reach, have natural barriers of defense, and allows us the opportunity to cut off at least one avenue of supplies to the enemy.

Thursday, December 4, 1777 — Headquarters near Whitemarsh, Pennsylvania

General Howe moved out of Philadelphia with the bulk of his force. He left a few men behind to guard his redoubts and lines. We are expecting an attack.

Friday, December 5, 1777 — Headquarters near Whitemarsh, Pennsylvania

The enemy moved to Chestnut Hill in front of, and about three miles off, our right wing. I sent the Pennsylvania militia out to confront their light advance parties. Brigadier-General Irvine was wounded.

Tonight, the enemy has moved quietly to our left. We think they have settled for the night, but we are watchful and ready.

Saturday, December 6, 1777 — Headquarters near Whitemarsh, Pennsylvania

No movement of our enemy. We are not sure what they are planning, but we are alert and ready.

Sunday, December 7, 1777 — Headquarters near Whitemarsh, Pennsylvania

The enemy has moved farther to our left. We are certain they are about to attack. I am sending Colonel Morgan and his corps along with the Massachusetts militia to cover our flank.

It is reported late this afternoon that Colonel Morgan, his men, and the militia gave a warm response to the enemy closing in. The enemy sustained considerable losses.

This evening, the British have been marching and countermarching. We are watching their maneuvers and expect an attack at any moment.

Monday, December 8, 1777 — Headquarters near Whitemarsh, Pennsylvania

This afternoon, the enemy marched in total, back toward Philadelphia. I have sent light parties to try to pick off their rear.

Tuesday, December 9, 1777 — Headquarters near Whitemarsh, Pennsylvania

Our light parties were unable to catch up to the enemy. No more losses were received by the enemy. From what is reported from the city, the enemy lost around five hundred from their excursion. I fear that number is exaggerated. We lost twenty-seven from Morgan's corps, killed or wounded. The Massachusetts militia lost between sixteen and seventeen wounded. I wish they had made an attack. I feel it would have had a favorable outcome.

Wednesday, December 10, 1777 — Headquarters near Whitemarsh, Pennsylvania

I am writing Congress concerning our adventure. I was unable to write to them during all the movement of the enemy. They do have their committee here in camp with us. They can attest to what occurred as well.

Friday, December 12, 1777

We left camp yesterday. We were crossing the Schuylkill at Madison Ford, when the first division and part of the second spotted a body of the enemy consisting of about four thousand men. They were led by Cornwallis. They were possessing the heights on both sides of the road. Our men repassed. We watched to see how we might attack. It turns out the enemy was guarding the pass while they were foraging the neighboring country. General Potter and part of the Pennsylvania militia came upon their advanced party and gave them quite a fight before they retreated to their superior numbers.

Sunday, December 14, 1777 — Headquarters near Gulf Mill, Pennsylvania

Congress intimates (in their letter just received) that our men are poorly stocked because I am not exercising the authority granted to me upon the citizens where we now reside. I am not a dictator. Our inhabitants take a suspicious eye to any military unit that seeks to force its will upon the people. Our Nation respects legislation and civil authority. They have been taught to obey willingly. Congress must encourage its citizens. The State authorities need to issue resolves urging the people to support the army defending them. If they do this, I do not doubt that we will have a great increase in supplies.

Wednesday, December 17, 1777 — Headquarters near Gulf Mill, Pennsylvania

General Burgoyne is requesting that Congress and I let him depart on parole before his men. I do not think this is wise as he would have access to our towns. He could report back detrimental evidence concerning our situation. He has offered an alternative. He asks for permission to travel back to Britain. He says if we let him, he will report to the British government that we are stronger than they thought, that the British army cannot defeat us. He says that he wishes to advise the King and Parliament to recognize our independence. If he is sincere, this would be useful, but I do not believe he is sincere. I also believe General Howe would beg to differ.

Friday, December 19, 1777 — Headquarters near Gulf Mill, Pennsylvania

I am writing the President of Delaware to let him know General Howe may be seeking to establish a post at Wilmington to countenance the disaffected of that State and use that location as a source to supply his troops in the winter. That city would give them a post on the Delaware river in that quarter. I am sending General Smallwood and a good group of Continental troops from Maryland to get there before the enemy. I do believe the enemy will try to take it. I do not have enough men to counter them. As a result, I need Mr. Reed to call out as many militia as he can and place them under General Smallwood's command.

I will be sending an engineer with Smallwood to help build the defenses. The quartermaster general is to coordinate with the needs of this division, but I am urging him to try to gather the supplies he needs between Pennsylvania and that post. This will deprive the enemy of accessible resources. The British are sure to come behind him. He needs to keep his men and officers on duty. He should be very sparing to grant furloughs. They must keep their hand to the plow for we know not when trouble will come. I hope that he can gather up stragglers from other brigades to enhance his numbers. I pray he can get the men clothed properly. He is to alert me of anything passing up and down the river from that quarter.

Monday, December 22, 1777 — Valley Forge, Pennsylvania

I am sending to Congress the list of our deficiencies in the commissary department. Unless vigorous exertions are extended, I fear this army must dissolve. General Huntington has told me that his soldiers would rather fight than starve. They are ready to march if that will get them food. The commissary says no meat or provision is available to give. Huntington says he does not know how long he can hold his men together. General Varnum quoted Solomon in saying that hunger will break through a stone wall. That is good for he has not had bread in three days or meat in two. He says his men cannot be commanded if they are not supplied. Varnum also states that I cannot expect virtuous principles from our men if their necessities go unmet. Filling the quartermaster general position and the adjutant general position will help if Congress allows. Regardless, all complaints are laid at my feet as if I am the unfeeling cause.

I have a conundrum. No easy answer exists. I can keep the men in camp, but they will be naked, cold, and hungry. Humanity declines that choice. I could release them to the towns in the area which would be preferable, but then the army would be divided, easy to cut off, and unable to provide protection for anyone. Thus, the Nation would fall into peril. Continued existence declines that choice.

As a result, I have chosen to keep our men in camp at this place called Valley Forge. Here, our men can protect the area, secure what stores we have, and maintain an army. The men are beginning to hut. I pray it will be done quickly. They are beginning with brush huts and staying in their tents. Once the temporary shelters are in place, the men will proceed from this place, cutting trees to make more suitable huts out of wood. This will provide better shelter from the harsh winter that is already pressing upon us. I am thinking of putting a bridge over the Schuylkill so that our parties can keep an eye on the enemy and converge on them if necessary, in an easier manner.

Congress wants me to send troops to defend Jersey. At the present, we do not have men to do that. I will, once our camp is set, send some to at least work with militia for better protection.

Tuesday, December 23, 1777 — Valley Forge, Pennsylvania

I could not sleep last night for I could not let the matter go. I am writing Congress on the heels of my last letter to let them know with great emphasis that, without supplies, our army only has three options — starve, dissolve, or disperse to find the means to survive (which may come through desertions as well).

The enemy set out yesterday after I sent my letter to Congress, to forage and gain sustenance in the countryside. I felt it was a good opportunity to attack. I was then told the men would not rouse. They had a form of mutiny last night over their lack of provision. It got ugly. The exertions of a few spirited officers put it down. The commissary was brought before them. He told them he had not one hoof to slaughter and only twenty-five barrels of flour left. The men seem pacified for the moment.

I then sent a few of them to harass the enemy foragers. I also sent out many of my own to forage for our men. If we hit a few days of bad weather, we may be facing this army's destruction. I have made call-after-call to Congress. They send promises but not one provision has appeared. I am going to unleash upon them all that we are suffering.

At this moment, we have over two thousand, eight hundred, and ninety-eight men unfit for duty because of no shoes and no clothes. This is a shame. Our men feel like outcasts from our own countrymen. It is as if they are suffering for some wrong they have done. How discouraging! It is for the defense of these neighbors that our men have left everything. It is a horrible reflection of this Nation and its supposed commitment to liberty and freedom. Everyone wants it, but no one wants to give to it. It seems Congress rules it be, but they make no provision for it to come to pass. Here I am in the middle. I am seen as a complainer and a do-nothing general to Congress. The men see me as a man making requirements but seeming to make no effort to provide for their most basic necessities. General Howe's dog has been treated better, fed better, and housed better than these men. We returned that dog. If he were here, he would be on a roasting stick. We had eight thousand, two hundred men in camp fit for service. The men spent all night sitting by the fire instead of resting because of no blankets in their huts. Our numbers continue to decline as a result.

This Nation sees these soldiers as unfeeling as sticks and stones that can layout in sleet and snow and be unaffected. They then expect this inferior army with all these disadvantages to defend against, yea even defeat, a superior army which has all its provisions, warmth, shelter, food, and clothes. The enemy sits by the fire-sides comfortably in the city of Philadelphia, while our men occupy a cold bleak hill sleeping under frost and snow with no blankets or clothes. Congress then meets with their Board of War to judge our ineffectiveness. To recruit men into this army when they are told what it costs to be in this army is difficult.

Speaking of men in this army, I cannot grasp how great these men of our army are — at least the ones who are still here. They have no reason to fear reprisal if they desert. Few have suffered for leaving. They are not bound by pay. They hardly ever get paid. These men suffer in the cold, disrespected and criticized, facing death and defeat for one reason — they love this country and long for it to be free. I have every reason to quit. Congress is looking for reasons to release me, but I will say this — to serve with these men is an honor. Congress should act if they value these men in the slightest. I have walked this evening amongst General Muhlenberg's men. They have set up their camp on the outer lines facing toward Philadelphia. His men have been together since January of 1776. They all come from the area of Woodstock, Virginia. What I love about the way our camp is set up, men from the same neighborhoods and upbringings cling together. They provide distractions and comfort for each other. They laugh. They reminisce about the old days and good times together. A bond exists in the different areas of our encampment that brings a warmth that no hut or fire could ever provide. Once again, I am drawn to the reason why I love this country — it is because I love its people.

Thursday, December 25, 1777 — Valley Forge, Pennsylvania

Today is Christmas. The temperatures are cold. We are not sixty miles from Bethlehem, Pennsylvania. We have been told in these hills of Valley Forge there is no room for us. I see the stars out this evening. I remember that night when Mary and Joseph reached another Bethlehem. Shepherds were out in the fields keeping watch over their flocks by night. They looked up at the stars too. What they heard was good news of great joy that would be for all people. I am alone on this hill near the Schuylkill with my thoughts and a small fire that I have built. I told my military family that I needed solitary time to think. At the present, I cannot leave this hill this evening. I am wanting, longing, praying that angels might appear to me this evening with some good news of great joy. No sooner do I write this by this quaint fireside, I feel a conviction creep in, a whisper addressing me, "Has God not already given me what I needed most?" That is right. A Savior. Again, "Has God not brought you through so many tough times already?" Well yes, He has. The last question, "Do you think He will not do the same in this and the things to come?" Well, yes, I know God does not change. So, what should I do? I know the answer. Trust Him and push forward. Wait on Him and in due time, He will deliver. He always has.

A peace has consumed me. This Christmas has special meaning. I can now relate to that evening almost two thousand years ago, that blessed event. In our depredations and struggles, tonight I feel myself truly finding a calm. The night is silent as the fire crackles. The night is a holy night for me.

Tuesday, December 30, 1777 — Valley Forge, Pennsylvania

The peace I found a few nights ago is eluding me now. Evil seems to be attending my way. I gave my concerns to Congress about General Conway's promotion from brigadier to major-general. I was completely candid. What does Congress do? They promote him to major-general. Not just that, they make him the in-spector-general in the Board of War which is to oversee me. I believe Congress finds it easier to push the dirty work that they intend on an outside board. This way, they can claim no responsibility for any egregious acts. General Conway writes that he is only in that position to serve me. He referenced the bad blood between he and Baron de Kalb, which was because of his own actions. I am letting him know that great reluctance presents from the other brigadiers and that some remonstrance may come from them. But as for me, I will respect Congress's de-cision. I will work with him the best I can. Only here I write, I will watch him ever closer.

Wednesday, December 31, 1777 — Valley Forge, Pennsylvania

I am writing Governor Livingston to move any Jersey shore food supplies away from the enemy's access in Philadelphia. The British army is foraging and would find great succor in those provisions. Congress has said I can order the inhabitants to do that, but I prefer to work through the civil authorities if they will act.

In a few days, I am sending all our light horse to Trenton to recruit and camp for the winter. They will also be able to provide protection from enemy incur-sions. I will let Governor Livingston know this too. He is concerned that the en-emy may try to invade his State again.

Governor Livingston brings one thing to my attention that allows me to share what our army is facing in this quarter. He says the wounded and sick in the hospitals in Jersey are poorly cared for. They are virtually naked and uncovered, he writes. I have let him know that our army is naked as well in this neighborhood. Our prisoners of war held by the enemy are in the exact same shape. Seemingly whether a soldier is sick, imprisoned, or in camp, the suffering is the same. This is the state of our affairs. Perhaps Livingston will be obliged to bring some sem-blance of care and provision from the people in his State. They rose to drive out the enemy. Maybe they can do the same to clothe their friends.

The Year 1778

Friday, January 2, 1778 — Valley Forge, Pennsylvania

To revisit a complaint, I had some time ago requested Congress set up a board to help meet the needs of this army. I suggested it be called the Board of War. In response to my request, Congress has done that, but I am greatly chagrined at the men they chose for this board. General Mifflin, General Gates, General Conway are on that board of five. My three greatest critics and enemies are on this board. Now they have been given authority over me. Congress may as well add General Howe and Sir Howe to complete the set.

With his new power, General Conway visited this camp. I was respectful and cordial, but I refused to hide my disdain or to pretend that we did not have strong differences, particularly in character. Now, I receive a letter from Congress stating that General Conway has complained of my behavior toward him. He states I gave him a cool reception. I am sending copies of all letters that have passed between Conway and me for their review. I will not profess friendship with a man who is my enemy, but I will honor his position though I am against the fact that he is in that position. I know my command is now jeopardized by this board of war, but I will do all in my power to carry out my duty regardless of what hostilities rise against me. My allegiance is to the Author of all things first. I will be held accountable to Him for my actions. I wish to honor Him in all I do just as Job sought the same. May those who rise up against me, remember that one day they too must give an account.

Monday, January 5, 1778 — Valley Forge, Pennsylvania

I received a letter today from Congress covering many issues for which I have requested their attention. The one glaring omission in their letter was dealing with what was most important — the clothing and provisions for our men. I am going to call them out on this as long as I man this post. To my great displeasure, it was necessary that coercive measures were used by this army upon the inhabitants of this countryside to gain clothing for our men. I detest what we have done and even more that we are forced to do it. The inhabitants were alarmed and greatly displeased. They should not live in fear of their own army. In the same way, we are their army. The citizens should want to provide for these men. Fire cakes can only sustain an army so long.

My greatest fear in all of this, once we seize provisions to meet our needs, how long before we seize luxuries for our wants? Such activity only breeds licentiousness, plunder, and robbery. Once these activities are initiated, they prove difficult to suppress. Our men could easily fall into the mindset they are "owed" such things. They would reason then that their actions are not robbery. Every sin has an excuse, a justification, or an explanation. I will countenance none of the above. I pray that we will never do this again. I hate it.

Thursday, January 8, 1778 — Valley Forge, Pennsylvania

I received a letter today from Colonel Samuel Webb who was captured in the conduct of a battle. He is now a prisoner of war as of December 10, 1777. He is requesting special favor to be released due to the hardships of imprisonment. While I empathize with the sad and troubling hardships he must be facing, he must realize other men have been prisoners of war to the British since early 1776 when General Thompson was defeated at Three rivers. Others come to mind who have been in British hands since August of that same year. They all would clamor loudly if they were to hear that I effected the release of one who has been in British confines a mere twenty-eight days. Since he is desperate to be exchanged and released, I will put it to him another way. If he, as miserable as he is now, had been a prisoner of war since March of 1776, would he not be greatly offended if I worked to get an officer out who had just recently been arrested? It would be as if, as time passes, those imprisoned the longest are just forgotten casualties of war. May that never be. They certainly will not be forgotten by me. Not a week goes by that I am not negotiating and pleading with General Howe and Lord Howe for frequent prisoner exchanges and better treatment for those who are there.

Friday, January 9, 1778 — Valley Forge, Pennsylvania

Congress has decided no prisoner exchanges will be made for those captured during the surrender of Saratoga. They demand Great Britain ratify the convention of Saratoga first. This will bring great frustration to General Burgoyne. I am alerting Major-General Heath in Boston to protect themselves against an escape attempt by Burgoyne and his men. After securing their holding place tightly, they need to remove all arms in the Boston area, so that if an escape presents, the enemy cannot get weapons to use against us.

I received a letter from a Baron Steuben with letters of recommendation from Messengers Franklin and Deane. It seems he has strong credentials and may be of help to this army. I am grateful at the polite manner he expresses his willingness to serve me and join this cause for liberty.

Tuesday, January 13, 1778 — Valley Forge, Pennsylvania

While I have had misgivings concerning foreign officers who come to join this contest, I am making note of one to Congress for promotion this day. The Chevalier de Mauduit Duplessis was one of the first to join our army from France. He has shown courage and gallantry at Brandywine, Germantown, and Fort Mercer where he united the offices of engineer and commandant of artillery. He made great improvements on the works at Red Bank. He saved artillery and stores upon its evacuation. In addition, he imperiled his life in blowing up the magazines to keep them out of the enemy's hands. Based on all these acts of courage in the defense of this country, I am asking Congress to extend to him the brevet of lieutenant-colonel. Because recent activities have delayed my request, I am asking them to antedate it effective November 26th, 1777. I am aware of the contribution that Monsieur Fleury has made. His and Duplessis's service starts were almost the same in France. To prevent jealousy, I am asking them to give the same date to the promotion of the Monsieur.

Wednesday, January 14, 1778 — Valley Forge, Pennsylvania

General Duportail took over the design and planning for our post here. He has shown a mind for great defensive positioning. Despite our scarcities, our men have followed his plan. We have over two thousand huts, each housing up to twelve men. In almost a month's time, the open field of Valley Forge has become a rudimentary city of wood huts, guarded by five redoubts in strategic places tied by miles of entrenchments. We are well-positioned for an attack from the British. Now if we can get our men as prepared for battle as their camp is for defense. To do this, they must first get healthy. Our great enemies right now are the cold, the hunger, the discouragement, and the sickness.

Friday, January 15, 1778 — Valley Forge, Pennsylvania

Now that our men have shelter, the officers and I have taken quarters in a rock house that faces Valley creek with the Schuylkill river running to our North. It is simply beautiful here. I took a walk alone this afternoon to the Valley creek in front of us and followed it the short distance to its confluence with the Schuylkill. Tall trees are everywhere. The temperature is cold, but that cold almost cuts an awakening within me. The sound of the creek rolling is deafening. What draws me on these lone walks is how each step seems to remove a burden from my shoulders. Every few feet, a different worry dissolves. The deeper I go into the woods following this creek, I feel as though I am in a different time. God overwhelms my being with His majesty and a peace. I am confronted with guilt that I fret instead of trust. He is on His Throne. He is not troubled or worried how this war, or any other conflict, will end. In the end, His Kingdom will come. His Will shall be done.

Regrettably, I had to return to Headquarters to resume the responsibilities from which I temporarily walked away. Our men are suffering still. Needs are not being met. The enemy is foraging just across the Schuylkill from us. What are their plans? For those who care, the freedom of the nation must be purchased through hardship. My officers caught me a few times this evening looking out the window, oblivious to the strategies discussed. I understand why our men are drawn to desertion. The beauty of life beyond this bottom floor window calls for us to lay down our arms for the joy of living. As I refocused, I remembered we have taken up arms to maintain that joy of living.

Tuesday, January 20, 1778 — Valley Forge, Pennsylvania

I have written Major-General Benedict Arnold with the hope that his leg injury heals up quickly and he can join me at this quarter. I need his assistance for the next campaign. He was perhaps the primary reason for our victory at Saratoga. I know he can do the same here in Philadelphia when he is healthy to join us.

I am writing General Lincoln who is recuperating from his injury as well. I am anxious to have General Lincoln back in the field too. He is effective in battle and highly competent in commanding militia.

Sir William Howe complains of ill-treatment of one of his men in our custody, a Mr. Elyre. I am convinced the degree of harshness extended to him as compared to other prisoners was of his own making. If I am wrong, then I can imagine that our men, hearing of the mistreatment of our brothers held by the British, compelled them to exact the same. I must investigate this, but I will not let Sir Howe off the hook as he bears much of the responsibility. His willful mistreatment of our men is well-attested.

I am asking Howe for the release or exchange of a young college student whom the British arrested and put in the prison camp. This young man is not affiliated with this army. He was just an innocent passerby. I will gladly make an exchange for this victim of circumstance. His parents are yearning for it.

I am writing the governors to let them know of our needs in general. Prayerfully they will feel a compulsion of passion to bridge the needs of our men.

While I am writing governors, I do want to make note that Governor Livingston has in his State's custody John Hendricks, Baker Hendricks, and John Meeker. They have been arrested for traveling to New York and carrying on illegal correspondence with the enemy. They are set to be tried as traitors with the punishment of death on their horizon. This is the gravest fear that I have when we employ spies. They are to be so convincing that the enemy trusts them, takes them into their confidence, or at the least, lets them mill around, gathering intelligence undetected. If they are good at what they do, our own people will believe they are loyalists carrying on subversion to our cause. This is the case with these three. I am writing with a yearning that my dispatch will go undetected. I need Governor Livingston not to pardon these allies of ours outright as this would bring suspicion to their charade. These three cannot profess innocence either. I am in hopes that somehow the Governor can throw the case out for lack of evidence or put them under a faux parole. We need men like these and the intelligence they harvest.

Wednesday, January 21, 1778 — Valley Forge, Pennsylvania

I am sending a thank-you note to Captain Henry Lee and his men. They were trapped in a house and told to surrender. They refused and caused such a fuss in firing, that the enemy backed away after great loss.

I rode out through the camp today and have been delighted to smell bread being baked in each brigade. We still lack food, but thousands of loaves of bread are being made as supplies are received. I sense morale being lifted. Belief spreads, like the waif of baking, that our period of suffering may have an end in sight — or in smell. I long for the day when our men will hunger no more.

Thursday, January 22, 1778 — Valley Forge, Pennsylvania

I am grieved to hear from Colonel Walter Stewart that while our men are starving and naked, the people of Pennsylvania are providing daily provisions to the enemy in Philadelphia at a nice profit of hard currency. I am asking Stewart to see if he can find how this is occurring. I am getting hints that we have some officers taking bribes to look the other way. If so, these traitors will be dealt with severely. I am sending General Potter who is well-acquainted with the roads in this area to find what route these provisions are being delivered and block that access. Additionally, I want anyone caught in the act to lose their wagons, livestock, and supplies on board. They are to be summarily punished for all to see as an example. They have had fair warning. No excuse will be accepted.

Sunday, January 25, 1778 — Valley Forge, Pennsylvania

At this writing, General Putnam has not responded to my orders to rebuild the forts and build defenses on the Hudson. He has also not given me the count of his troops as I have requested. I am hesitant to think it, but perhaps his proximity to General Gates has made him less responsive to the Commander-in-Chief.

Monday, January 26, 1778 — Valley Forge, Pennsylvania

Under the orders of the Board of War, British officers were arrested delivering supplies and clothing to their prisoners of war. This was a mistake. I had given permission to the British along with passports so they might care for the men in our custody. In exchange, we are passing their lines to care for ours. We have limited how many on each side can assist, but for the Board of War to order this without checking my correspondence with General Howe subjects our men in prison to further hardships.

Tuesday, January 27, 1778 — Valley Forge, Pennsylvania

General Gates requests the use of Hazen's regiment in Albany. I am in dire need of this regiment here at this front. I am already short of men. But what can I do? He is on the Board. He may have a need that he is unable to reveal in a letter. I will acquiesce to his request, but he needs to know this army is not a supply base for needs around the continent. We have a real enemy, the bulk of their army less than twenty miles away in our capital city of Philadelphia. The only advantage to sending them that way is it will reduce the numbers we must provide for during the winter in this quarter.

General Charles Lee has sent a letter. He is now on parole and is being treated well. I have let him know that I have done all in my power daily to arrange for his exchange. Now that we have the enemy's Major-General Prescott, we can achieve that exchange. He is requesting passage of Mrs. Battier to him, in the meantime. Her husband has been very gracious to General Lee. I note in this journal alone, I have a great moral question in Lee's request for the passage of another man's wife.

Friday, January 30, 1778 — Valley Forge, Pennsylvania

In the constant flow of letters concerning care for prisoners of war with Sir Howe, he has been very condescending toward our Nation, our government, and our Congress. I have made a point to be gentlemanly in all my correspondence. Now, I am making a point to require the same of him. I have not indulged myself with invectives toward the rulers of Great Britain. I wish the same courtesy.

Monday, February 2, 1778 — Valley Forge, Pennsylvania

Governor Livingston sends me a letter detailing how a wicked design against him was detected. He is shocked that someone he considered a friend could be behind such a thing. He thought he could always identify the enemy as one who wears a red coat. What he has found is that enemies can come from any quarter — even our own friends and countrymen. He has just a taste of what I feel daily. I am encouraging him, as I embolden myself, that all who stand for what is right will pay a severe tax in a station of trust such as his — and mine.

Tuesday, February 3, 1778 — Valley Forge, Pennsylvania

Intelligence informs me that the enemy will make another run at foraging the countryside. I am sending Brigadier-General Wayne west about fifteen miles from the Delaware river between the Schuylkill and the Brandywine to gather all horses, cattle, sheep, and provender from the enemy's reach. He is to bring all that he can acquire to this American army. He must give each person a certificate of promise to pay, detailing the articles taken. The quartermaster general or the paymaster will then inform them when and where to collect their pay. We will not steal from our own people. My preference is that we pay competitively what the British sometimes offer, but that is not always possible. If there are areas too far to carry the provisions back, I am asking General Wayne to destroy those supplies and animals where they are. He is to give a certificate to the owners so that they can receive pay for what we must destroy. I pray they know this is in the duty of protecting them from a stronger enemy who would use these supplies against them.

Sunday, February 15, 1778 — Valley Forge, Pennsylvania

Richard Henry Lee has sent me a good piece of guidance for managing the grenadiers and light-infantry developed by Lieutenant-Colonel Frazer. We are currently raising our own, so the timing is perfect. His guidance will be implemented at this head as well.

What is most interesting from Mr. Lee is notification of letters circulating in New York and Philadelphia supposedly from me to Mrs. Washington and other friends. These are forgeries seeking to remove the trust our citizens have placed in me. I pray they will be ineffective even for a single soul. I have lived my life in a transparent manner always seeking to follow proper decorum and a life that mirrors what the Judge of all men desires in every man.

Speaking of Mrs. Washington, I have been negligent in noting that she has arrived here at Valley Forge on the 10th. I may forget to note it as I hardly see her. Once she arrived and saw the condition of these men, she organized the officers' wives to knitting clothing, patching others, and providing items of warmth for those in serious need. She goes hut-to-hut caring for these and enters the tents of those still building their more permanent structure. Hardly do we get to spend a night together, but there is a great comfort for me when she is here. I am so thankful to have a great wife. In my daily prayer, I tell that to the One who provided her for me.

Mr. Richard Henry Lee lets me know that the Assembly of Virginia is busy recruiting volunteers for this army. This sounds good, but volunteers will not be as effective. I have stated the case clearly that volunteers serve at their will, not ours. I have asked these States on numerous occasions to enlist a draft instead to meet their quotas. But beyond this, they must provide for the ones they send, and then send provisions for the others who are here. We are in a sad shape. Mrs. Washington and the officers' wives can only do so much. I lay the majority of the blame on one of the Board of War members, General Mifflin. How he could get promoted to this board when he was completely derelict in his duty with these men is beyond me. Our men are naked, cold, and hungry. Their plight lies at Mifflin's feet. I have practically begged on my hands and knees for help. Yet, he has hardly ever set foot in one of our camps.

I am writing Governor Clinton, who has been a faithful ally, to send supplies to our men in this camp. I desperately am soliciting him to procure cattle to be driven here. I am encouraging governors of other States around him to do the same. The continuance of this army is dependent upon it. I am issuing a personal address to the inhabitants of New Jersey, Pennsylvania, Delaware, Maryland, and Virginia for the same.

Friday, February 27, 1778 — Valley Forge, Pennsylvania

Baron Steuben has been in camp for a few days. He appears to be a man with a knowledge of military conduct, strategy, and execution. He also has a penchant for training.

General Putnam is in distress for want of money in that quarter. I am requesting Congress to provide.

Congress has asked me to send a major-general to Rhode Island. We are short as it is, but I will comply.

Colonel Proctor's corps deserted, which adds to our need of men. It does, however, reduce our number of men to feed by a small fraction.

Our loss of matrosses in the last campaign was immense. To fill this vacuum, I am asking Congress to send Colonel Harrison's regiment of artillery to march here from Virginia as soon as the roads permit.

Sunday, March 1, 1778 — Valley Forge, Pennsylvania

I received a kind letter from my lifelong friend Bryan Fairfax. Though he agreed Great Britain has committed many abuses, he differed with me and our friends over taking arms against the King. He believes he can restore peace and remedy the grievances if given the chance. He is mistaken. The chances for peace are as likely as the mist remaining at the noonday sun. He laments the bloodshed and offenses in this country, but I have let him know we have acted as we should. Bryan does not see that Great Britain drove us to rebellion so that they might strip us of all rights and privileges. In the process, they have distressed millions, brought ruin to thousands, and brought woe to numberless families. Victory is the only solution for our cause. I still contend to him, and to any who ask, that the determinations of Providence are wise and inscrutable. He will always work things out for His gracious purposes.

Monday, March 2, 1778 — Valley Forge, Pennsylvania

Brigadier-General Wayne has acted valiantly and with good intelligence. When confronted by the enemy, he brought damage upon them. He then knew when to retreat as the numbers were not in his favor. I am calling upon him with all exertions to destroy all forage within the enemy's reach, put as many obstacles as possible in their way, and to drive off all horses and cattle. I am writing General Pulaski to assist.

Thursday March 5, 1778 — Valley Forge, Pennsylvania

Baron Steuben has met with me this morning to discuss the unsanitary conditions of the camp. The way he spoke, you would think he was describing the unHoly Ground in New York minus the drinking establishments and prostitutes of course. What offends him (and I agree fully) is the stench and the filth that pervades our camp. Men just relieve themselves anywhere. Every person must be alert as to where they step. We have women and children who have followed us here. I cannot imagine what they think. I say that, I can imagine because Steuben has described it through a translator in candid terms. He is reforming our military hygiene and setting the camps accordingly. General Duportail was a master of setting up our defensive positioning. Baron Steuben is setting the camps on a sustainable health position. When sickness is rampant, this is exactly what we need. I am embarrassed that I did not put this in place at the onset. No matter our experience, we can always learn — especially me.

Saturday, March 7, 1778 — Valley Forge, Pennsylvania

I received a complaint today from Mr. Wharton, President of Pennsylvania. He and his citizens are distressed over the procurement of supplies for this army through compulsion of the residents of this State. He must know that I am sensibly concerned for what has been done. Anything abusive will be punished. In the same sense though, this State should meet the needs of the army to whom they plead for protection. Because they have neglected their responsibilities and because this army is struggling to stay alive, what their residents should have given willingly, has now been taken by impressment. We will not steal. We will pay with a promise anything taken. To prevent such acts from occurring again, the President should use his position and that of government to provide for this army. This would bring a harmony between the people and their military arm. This army and the people have a mutual dependence. As a result, both should be faithful to their duty.

General Howe also extends a complaint. He says one of our soldiers violated the flag of truce. An inquiry is being made to ascertain the guilty party. Punishment will be exacted. I feel like Mr. John Adams the day he took the defense of the British at the Boston Massacre. Our own people make mistakes at times. When they do, right knows no national banner or allegiance. Our Nation has been wronged. We are fighting for independence. But when we do wrong in that effect, the Overriding Judge compels us to repent and make right that wrong.

Sunday, March 8, 1778 — Valley Forge, Pennsylvania

I have written a long letter to Congress due to the addition they made to the resolve for prisoner exchange. They initially set forth that exchanges should be done speedily for the sake of those imprisoned. This has given our recruits and enlistments comfort. Their worst fear going in is to be imprisoned. Our soldiers have known going in, that if they are captured, their countrymen will make every effort to gain their freedom with the utmost priority. While General Howe has been difficult to deal with and slow to act, I finally got him to the point of a general exchange. Now Congress dares to muddy it up and delay it for some unforeseen day in the future. What this says to our men is that if they get captured, they will be abandoned. This causes them to not reenlist. It causes recruits and volunteers to turn away. I am laying this out to Congress on no uncertain terms for our Nation's cause and for my honor as their representative to the enemy. The army demands this exchange as do the families of those imprisoned. More than this, the sufferers in the enemy's confines demand release and relief.

Congress has made two errors in their resolve which brings harm to our Nation. The first, they say that an officer should be exchanged for officer, soldier-for-solider, and citizen-for-citizen. They should not have included citizen-for-citizen as this gives the idea that imprisoning citizens is acceptable when it is not. But now because of Congress's over-step, citizens are being taken. Their other error is in referencing the enlistment of enemy prisoners and deserters to our army. I have complained excessively that the enemy should not be doing this. Now Congress includes the verbiage which sounds as if this is our practice while we plead the enemy restrain from this luxury.

Brigadier-General Parsons requests an attempt to capture the enemy's General Clinton. Clinton is currently in Captain Kennedy's house in New York. He is lightly guarded. Access to him is available from the back of the home by way of the waters that flow behind the property. With secrecy and surprise, General Parsons believes it can be carried forward with success. I am for the effort if all things are right and he can gain a good idea of the guards posted. I am suggesting that the men he enlists for the effort be dressed in red as the British soldiery to allow them greater access. I stand by for further developments.

Tuesday, March 10, 1778 — Valley Forge, Pennsylvania

The Marquis is worried that his aborted effort in Canada may bring him dishonor abroad. He desires a bold stroke to rectify it. I am asking him to delay this enterprise. He only imagines a stain on his reputation. The effort was thwarted by weather. He has no control of that. He has acted bravely and has gained my trust and that of Congress. This is proven by the command in which a man so young as he has been entrusted. With the state of this army, premeditated strikes would be detrimental. Opportunity is the key decision factor for the next move on the enemy.

I am sending Major-General Sullivan to take over command of the forces of Rhode Island upon their government's request. I do not see this as necessary or helpful to our cause, but I must accede to the will of Congress.

Wednesday, March 11, 1778 — Valley Forge, Pennsylvania

General Burgoyne has sent me a flattering letter of well-wishes for my person and my character, but not our cause. He has been approved for release. I have returned courtesies, but our Nation's freedom and liberty override any personal approval that I might receive. May our hostilities end in our favor. Only then, can we think of reestablishing friendlies.

Baron Steuben is formulating a plan for turning our men into a formidable army. He has requested that I raise to one hundred my Life Guards for his initial class of trainees. He has one caveat; he wants them to be composed of more than just Virginians. It is interesting that today of all days, he would make that request. It was two years ago to the day that I gave out orders for a group of men, native-born Americans from Virginia to join my company with the duties of guarding my person, our staff, my papers, and our provisions. I needed men then of sobriety, honesty, and good behavior. I wanted them to be clean in appearance, model soldiers, neat, and spruce. These men have served me well except for Thomas Hickey, the one who betrayed me, plotting my assassination. I will relent to his request. I know of no finer soldiers than those in my Life Guard which currently totals forty-seven. Perhaps, Von Steuben can reproduce this type of man throughout this army.

Thursday, March 12, 1778 — Valley Forge, Pennsylvania

Congress has removed the impediment to our prisoner exchanges. Sadly, I believe their initial delay has harmed the potential to see these done in an expedient manner.

Friday, March 13, 1778 — Valley Forge, Pennsylvania

Captain John Barry has made our Nation proud. He and a few men in four rowboats moved down from Burlington. They were able to move through the water with muffled paddles and arrive at Port Penn, where they were able to take two of the enemy's transports from Rhode Island with forage and supplies. They had to burn one at the enemy's rebuttal. They may have to burn the other. They also captured a schooner with eight double-fortified four-pounders and twelve four-pound howitzers. They intend to hold this no matter the cost. Barry's men captured thirty-three of the enemy troops in the process. Just a little ingenuity and initiative in small pockets make a difference. They show benefit exists in volunteers who are driven by the rights that freedom affords them.

I have envisioned a plan to use four hundred Indians disposed to our freedom to divest themselves from the savage fighting among themselves and join us as scouts. I believe their contribution will be a benefit. We can raise half their number from the north and another half from the south. The southern force can come from the Cherokee primarily. I am asking Colonel Gist to help with this in the south. I am asking a missionary to the Indians by the name of Kirkland to help us recruit the Oneida. He has a great influence upon them. If we can get them here before the campaign begins, I believe we can have some advantages. I am writing General Schuyler, James Duane, and Volkert Duou to make this their area of enterprise.

Speaking of missionaries, I received a kind letter, but late received, from Reverend Israel Evans. He is calling on our Nation for a time of Thanksgiving effective December 18th. My first responsibility is to join the reverend and all clergy to point this Nation to a complete dependence upon that All-Wise and All-Powerful Being. Only in Him our success stands or falls.

Saturday, March 14, 1778 — Valley Forge, Pennsylvania

General Pulaski has tendered his resignation from his present command due to language barriers and the manners of this country. He does not wish to resign from our cause nor lose his rank. I celebrate that. He is a gallant and brave man who has accomplished much already in the preservation of our liberties. His wish now is to form a new and independent corps of sixty-eight horse and two hundred infantry. I propose he raise this from our Continental bounty as well as through the draft.

Governor Livingston wishes to raise up a light horse division in his State. My wish is that any who desire to join this group bring their own horses, arms, and accoutrements. These would be under the Continental service for a short period to meet our need. They can then return to the post of their home States. My preference is that General Benedict Arnold command these when he returns to service from his injuries.

I am advising Governor Livingston to cease from the search and imprisonment of the enemy's deserters. That they have left the enemy is enough. By allowing them to remain free, we may encourage more to leave the King's command. This will reduce the enemy's ability to fight.

Monday, March 16, 1778 — Valley Forge, Pennsylvania

Congress resolves to commence the inquiry of the failed efforts at Fort Montgomery and Fort Clinton in the State of New York. I am ordering General McDougal to lead this with the assistance of Brigadier-General Huntington and Colonel Wigglesworth.

My greater mission for General McDougal is to take command of the different posts in the Highlands. I need him to make the works ready for defense. Governor Clinton has said that when he finds the time, he will offer his aid. I know that General McDougal would prefer a post in the principal theater of action, but his work making this area defensible is for the public good. Once this is done, another can be positioned to take his place. I will return him to this main army forthwith. The Governor believes men are needed in that quarter as he fears the enemy is being positioned for another run at New York. I disagree vehemently. I have made that known. Hopefully soon, Congress will see the reality of my viewpoint and reposition troops down here.

I am letting General Putnam know of my assignment of General McDougal to his post. He is positioned to this place, because he is the one for whom New York initiated the inquiry. They believe Fort Montgomery and Fort Clinton were lost because of General Putnam's lack of urgency due to his age, because of his good nature, because of his easy temperament which brought on a lack of preparedness, and because of his frequent intercourse with the enemy. All these will prove out in the inquiry one way or the other. I want him to know that upon a successful clearing of the charges, I will return him to his command in Connecticut. I will then forward new levies to him with the greatest expedition.

Governor Clinton has suggested that one officer command Forts Montgomery and Clinton, and that a separate officer command the remainder of the forts in and around Highland Pass. I believe this is an ineffective strategy as one commander can respond and move troops as needed to whatever various posts are under attack. I do not, however, believe any danger is imminent for these posts. I believe the enemy's northern army is simply present as a matter of defense for Canada.

Tuesday, March 17, 1778 — Valley Forge, Pennsylvania

A very troubling issue has arisen. We have given every State a quota to raise troops to join the Continental Army. In Massachusetts, several towns and districts are recruiting deserters from General Burgoyne's British army to join this army. The inhabitants prefer this. They would rather an enemy deserter do their fighting than they themselves. Do they not see the danger in this? Who will fight harder — the one who is unattached to this State and Nation, or the one who is intimately concerned owning land, a home, and having a family? It is like Nehemiah in the Holy Scriptures who assigned the citizens to rebuild the part of the wall of Jerusalem that was directly behind their personal homes. Naturally, the citizens gave their best efforts when the wall was to protect their own homes and families. Besides this lack of connection, enemy troops are more apt to return to the enemy and take our arms and intelligence with them.

I do not doubt for one minute if General Burgoyne were still here in this fight, he would prefer his deserters join our numbers to fill part of our quota. That way, once the war ensues, his men can return to him. His numbers are bolstered. Our numbers fall far short of what we need and what we think we have at the onset. I am demanding that the President of the Council of Massachusetts, Mr. Bowdoin, desist from this immediately and issue extreme punishments for any continuance.

Wednesday, March 18, 1778 — Valley Forge, Pennsylvania

In the course of worry and correction of what is going on in this army and around it, I am flattered by a Reverend Timothy Dwight who has written a poem about Joshua's Conquest of Canaan. He has dedicated the work to me. I am so thankful that people see how desperately I am attempting to drive the enemy out as Joshua did. With the Lord's Help, I know we too can be successful.

Thursday, March 19, 1778 — Valley Forge, Pennsylvania

I have had the pleasure of watching Baron Steuben direct our men. From dawn-to-dusk, he has the men drilling and working. His first phase is impressive. He is training my expanded Life Guard in the military disciplines and battle techniques. He reports he is not far from releasing them to train other men in the basics, under his watchful eye. I am intrigued by the way this man who knows little English can train men who know primarily only English. He does have some translators, but his gestures and personal demonstrations effectively get his points across. His translators do put his instructions on paper in English for a ready reference. If I had time and it would not affect my standing among the men, I would be pleased to fall in with them to learn all that he has to teach. The men are pushed by Steuben, but they seem delighted to be instructed. I think our men are gaining traction despite the human suffering. Slowly, I believe he can produce an army that is able to stand toe-to-toe with the enemy.

Friday, March 20, 1778 — Valley Forge, Pennsylvania

Brigadier-General Cadwalader has written to rejoin me in this army. There is nothing that I would desire more. I will always have a square on my floor reserved for him. But what I desire and what I need are opposites. I need him to remain where he is and assist with the recruiting of this army. We are so far behind. The campaign is due to begin at any moment. General Howe is receiving reinforcements daily. I believe he plans an attack soon. I cannot hope to face him unless this army is replenished. General Cadwalader is immensely helpful to this regard.

Regarding men, we need them, but I also need to feed the ones I have. This is not happening. Our men have gone six days without food. We have had many horses starve to death. They were being drug outside the camp, but the smell emanating from them was horrific. As hungry as our men are, I am surprised few have used the horsemeat to reduce hunger pangs. As exhausted as they have been, burial of the horse corpses did not register as a priority. The Baron has addressed this unsanitary existence. Before drills, regardless of hunger or unrest, he has every camp inspected for cleanliness, and requires all the dead buried — man or beast.

He is teaching the men that even in suffering, order must be present to prevent more of the same.

I am requesting that the Marquis and General de Kalb join me in this quarter. I have a division ready for the Marquis de Lafayette to lead. I have another one for de Kalb.

Saturday, March 21, 1778 — Valley Forge, Pennsylvania

Speaking of drilling, this army is taking shape. I was able to watch Baron Steuben work our men on the Grand Parade field. Close attention was paid to everything he ordered. The training officers under him ride out to the different divisions throughout the day to pass on his instructions. The troops are now simulating battles with each regiment carrying out their orders. He makes them repeat the exercise until it becomes second nature. A few days later, he brings them a different scenario. They then work to master the strategy for that possibility. Before his arrival, our whole existence as an army was to rely on instinct and reaction. Without the ability to hold an army for a length of time, this has been our only recourse. With the training the Baron is bringing, I believe a whole new type of army is being birthed. The British have no idea what is being formed just miles from their comforts in Philadelphia. I am encouraged that such regimen will cause the men to want to stay beyond enlistments. They have a reason and a hope now. The Baron's demands and the visible results are causing the men to almost forget they are hungry.

Sunday, March 22, 1778 — Valley Forge, Pennsylvania

We have had another roadblock to our prisoner exchange. General Howe is listing Ethan Allen as a Colonel because of some correspondence that I had sent where I abbreviated his title to Colonel, instead of his true position Lieutenant-Colonel. I am in hopes Howe will reclassify Lieutenant-Colonel Ethan Allen so that we can include him in our exchange.

Wednesday, March 25, 1778 — Valley Forge, Pennsylvania

I am writing General Heath to remove any of General Burgoyne's men from the Boston area. The enemy forces in Newport may move to free them and bring them into their fold for the next activity. I need him also to forward all recruits to this quarter whether they have been vaccinated or not. We cannot waste another moment. We can inoculate them here once they arrive.

It has come to my attention that Colonel Armand at Yorktown is striving to raise a new and separate corps. His was reduced to so low a number that I reassigned his men to another regiment. If he seeks to raise a new corps, he must begin by gaining Congress's blessing. He has acted as if I gave him permission. I am writing him to let him know that he must have misunderstood me. Again, he must go to Congress.

Friday, March 27, 1778 — Valley Forge, Pennsylvania

Major-General Armstrong is equally alarmed at our deficiency of troops. Some States have shown no will to meet their quota. Others are half-hearted in their recruiting. A few have drafted to meet their quota but have done nothing to ensure their draftees leave their homes. Then we have Massachusetts trying to get enemy deserters to meet their requirement. We must fill our numbers as Howe is filling his. The only thing that keeps Howe from attacking and putting an end to this thing is his ignorance of our numbers. I do not believe that ignorance can endure long.

The enemy finds greater strength by reducing our numbers through the arts of deception. In the towns, they are speaking of their might and our dim chance of victory. I am convinced that most of this damage is perpetrated by the British prisoners in our midst, especially the enemy officers who are being confined. They confirm the disaffected, frighten the lukewarm and timid, and convert others to their opinion. We are in desperate need of a prison exchange to rid these nemeses from our midst.

Some of our people do not need the enemy's spur, they are selling horses, cattle, and every necessity to the enemy in the name of profit. We have made examples of those we have caught, even executing a lieutenant found guilty of this, but the deterrent has done little to stop the intercourse.

Tuesday, March 31, 1778 — Valley Forge, Pennsylvania

I am writing General McDougal a very confidential consideration. General Howe has gained two thousand, five hundred men by some counts. Reports are that more are coming to them. We must gather our whole army in this quarter to fight theirs, or perhaps divert a portion of their forces by an activity to the east. I am asking General McDougal to confer only with Governor Clinton and General Parsons to contemplate an attack on New York. If one were successful, this could draw a portion of Howe's reinforcements away. By dividing their army, our prospects improve. I look forward to their views.

Wednesday, April 1, 1778 — Valley Forge, Pennsylvania

Baron Steuben is not the only one getting our men in fighting shape. General Henry Knox has taken this time at Valley Forge to drill the Continental Artillery under his command. He has assigned fourteen-to-sixteen men to train on each field piece. He has each man take turns in the operation of each component. Knox ensures that each artilleryman has a working knowledge of every facet. After instilling this comprehensive knowledge, he assigns the men to a particular function and gives them time to perfect it. Once this is done, he has the men work on timing and accuracy. Each day, they improve. The battalion of artillerymen has never performed better. They are itching for a fight in earnest.

Friday, April 3, 1778 — Valley Forge, Pennsylvania

When it comes to commissions and ranks awarded, I know of no better qualifier than what men do on the field of battle. Captain Henry Lee is one that I am recommending to Congress to the new rank of major. His bravery, zeal, and prudence are exemplary. He and his light dragoons have rendered great service to this war effort. I am asking for Captain Lee to become part of my family here in Valley Forge. I can give him a command of two troops of horse with the assistance of Mr. Lindsey and Mr. Peyton. They operate as independent partisan corps.

Colonel Josias Hall has been court-martialed for failure to obey orders of a superior. I am writing to let him know that I concur with the findings of the board. An army cannot stand if men will not follow the orders of their superiors. Subordination on the grand scale is soon to follow. With this said, Colonel Hall has humbly accepted his punishment. He has offered to resign though he says he has a constant fidelity to our cause for freedom and independence. He says that even out of the service, he will do all he can to bring this war to a successful end. These are the types of men we need in this army — men who make mistakes, repent, and accept punishment but refuse to give up our purpose. I am writing him to request he stay in the service and stay in his rank of colonel. With officers leaving right and left, how encouraging it is to find a man who understands what patriotism is.

Saturday, April 4, 1778 — Valley Forge, Pennsylvania

My sensibilities are a little wounded by Congress's refusal to bend on their resolves regarding prisoner exchanges. I am writing them to protest. I am here on the ground. I have dealt with the enemy all these months to enact an exchange. I know what is fair. I know what will work. Extra obstacles break good faith dealing. They also prolong the time our men must suffer in the enemy's hands. I am in hopes they will reconsider.

Wednesday, April 8, 1778 — Valley Forge, Pennsylvania

General McDougal believed the transports coming from New York were filled with troops. The ones that have arrived thus far have had very few of the enemy's troops. The question then follows where did they go? General Lee on parole in Boston believes they went to Rhode Island to replace those sent to Philadelphia. We shall see.

I have asked McDougal to determine the prudence of an attack upon New York. If he believes success will incur, then move the men. If he does not, then I am requesting he send Van Schaick's regiment to this head.

Friday, April 10, 1778 — Valley Forge, Pennsylvania

Congress has given me permission to raise five thousand militia. I am gratified at their approval, but they do not see that they extended a similar power to me last campaign. We were unable to get even one thousand with this authority. Militia can be very costly. They seldom stay past a few weeks. Congress needs to reinforce our army. They need to do something to stop the daily flow of capable officers leaving this army in huge numbers. Today, General Muhlenberg wishes to resign. I never dreamed he would ever think of leaving early. General Weedon has informed me of his intention to resign. The Virginia line has been greatly harmed by the rash of officer resignations.

I am willing to try anything to hold this army together. I am suggesting half-pay be offered to officers who agree to remain until war's end. This will cost the Nation nothing at the present time but will greatly motivate officers to stay. It is good to count on some provision after one's service ends. It is an emolument that can help an officer bear under the depredations they now face. The heart of patriotism holds an officer and a soldier for a while, but over a time of hardship, that inducement loses its hold. Rank is a motivation, but even rank and additional pay lose their luster as suffering ensues. This is especially true when the officer considers how his family is suffering back home. A half-pay to me is the answer. It will be gratified through the success of this war, by achievement of rank, and by a constant monthly financial reminder that their service has been appreciated by their Nation.

I am also asking Congress of one location change. I need the clothier-general to be posted with me. Only then can the needs of the men can be supplied in an expedient manner.

Saturday, April 11, 1778 — Valley Forge, Pennsylvania

The lack of return of officers from Colonel Moylan's cavalry is vexatious. I am asking him to find out who is on leave with properly acquired furloughs, who is negligent, and who is absent without permission. For those of the latter two, I will make examples of them forthwith.

Monday, April 13, 1778 — Valley Forge, Pennsylvania

Just as I once rode over my properties to see that our men were fulfilling their duties, I have ridden out to the Grand Parade ground to observe Steuben at work with our soldiers. Today they were working on the speed in which they fire, re-load, and fire again. With amazing speed, our men are mastering this essential process. I had fancied myself as being rather efficient at this. After watching our men, I feel I need to slip off from their earshot to sharpen that skill myself.

The Baron took me to the side. Through his translator, he beamed with praise for our men. He said that it can take up to two years to properly train soldiers in the field. With this army, in less than two months, he says our men are responding with alacrity. He also conveyed the fact that in Europe, he gave commands. The men obeyed. That was it. But with our American men, he says he must give a command, demonstrate the command, and then follow with an explanation as to why it was given. I suppose this is the characteristic of any man who has the mind-set of freedom. The people of this nation cannot be ordered. They can be in-structed when they willfully desire to learn. Most Americans demand to think for themselves and respond according to their own free will. What a people this land has bred!

Tuesday, April 14, 1778 — Valley Forge, Pennsylvania

I am filled with vexation when I look at the condition of the horses in the light dragoons. These were exempted from the fatigues of winter camp. They were al-lowed to stay in comfortable quarters with the duty to recruit other men, acquire horses, and keep their current stock in a healthy condition. Now that the cam-paign is upon us, what do I find when they ride up? They have spent so much time galloping about the country, neglecting their animals, reducing them to a worse condition than the horses who have survived the winter here in Valley Forge. How do they dare answer this Nation on this matter? I am furious!

Wednesday, April 15, 1779 — Valley Forge, Pennsylvania

I rode out today to the Grand Parade to catch a glimpse of the good going on in our army. I sat on the hill watching as the Baron had the whole army executing drills to better grasp the intricacies of charging with bayonet. The men have accomplishment beaming on their faces. They are moving with precision from disciplined formations. I do not believe the British have such an expert teacher on this side of the ocean. I rejoice that Steuben is ours.

Friday, April 17, 1778 — Valley Forge, Pennsylvania

In our council of officers, we are considering three general plans of operation. One — attack Philadelphia and destroy the enemy's army there. Two — attack in New York, split the enemy's force, and hopefully conquer both with more bearable numbers. Three — wait at some well-fortified camp and make ready for the enemy attack. I am showing no preference as I want the officers to give their honest thought-out assessments. For my own vote, I note in this journal. I am moving men here as fast as possible. I am hoping to have the strength to deliver a devastating blow to the British. Currently, ten thousand of their troops reside within a few miles of us. They must be as tired of fighting us as we are of fighting them. They need to experience loss. They need to feel that we are not going anywhere.

Monday, April 20, 1778 — Valley Forge, Pennsylvania

Lord North has issued two bills to Parliament. He is calling for pardons for all who will lay down arms and pledge allegiance back to Great Britain. He expresses the King's longing to have his nation back in harmony. They say they will do their best to accede to some of our requests. Their offer of specious allurements of peace poses a snare to our people. They are offering a peace on the principles of dependence. It will produce supineness and disunion. Should our citizens give in to these temptations, Great Britain will return to their abuses. It is their nature. Any resistance afterward, they will be put down. France helps keep this boat afloat with provisions. Their constant threat to join us has held Britain at bay. But if we give in to the seductive overtures of the enemy, foreign allies of ours will be unwilling in the future to join, knowing that this Nation folds after a period of self-denial.

Conversely, building this army of ours will force Britain to consider recognizing our independence. Our strength and spotted victories will embolden others to join us, knowing that we do not expect anyone to fight for us. We will fight. We will welcome others to come alongside. It will benefit them to take the fight to a common enemy to prevent further offenses worldwide.

To this end, we need to invite other nations to join us. We need to build up our intelligence of British affairs — size, strength, intentions, operations, and preparations. Every one of our States must join us in this cause. Congress must make decisions instead of delaying. Even if they reject some of our proposals, we welcome that over silence. With acceptance or rejection of ideas, we can then move forward in a more certain direction. As long as they delay, we sit inactive, nothing is attempted, and the men lose heart.

Congress worries about a standing army. I understand that fear, especially in peace time. But we are not at peace. We are at war. Our army is not one standing. We are an army fighting. There should be no fear of the army. Our army is made up of our citizens who long to return to private life on their own land, with their own families, thriving in their chosen vocations. At this moment, these men are in rags, hungry, shoeless, leaving blood marks in the snow as they walk. They have sacrificed more than most, especially more than those in Congress. Humanity and common decency demand their care. I have never seen a breed of men suffer as these men have suffered. Yet, most remain at their post with hardly a murmur.

Congress must be decisive so that the enemy has no time to deceive our people. The offenses exacted on this Nation by the British are inexcusable. Britain has abused our citizens unprovoked. We cannot coexist as a nation with them, but once the war is decided in our favor, we can then commence commerce beneficial to all.

Wednesday, April 22, 1778 — Valley Forge, Pennsylvania

General McDougal has sent his return stating that he and his officers believe a strike on New York has little chance to succeed. I accept their advice. This gives us greater clarity on what we must do. General Gates is about to resume command of the northern army. I need General McDougal to move this way and take command of his division.

General Lee is one step closer to freedom. He is on parole and should soon be part of an exchange. I am writing him today to celebrate its certainty. I invite him here to join this army and help me. With General Gates, we can solidify our strategy for the next campaign.

Friday, April 24, 1778 — Valley Forge, Pennsylvania

I went to the other side of the Grand Parade to pay my respects to David and Elizabeth Stephens. They have been allies to our cause here at Valley Forge. That three-hundred-acre parade ground below their home is their land. What we use to train on, they use to grow crops to support their family. Sadly, this year, our occupation has cost them a year of production. They even opened their home to General Varnum to use as his brigade headquarters until his hut was completed. Where many in Pennsylvania are reluctant to lose income and productivity for the sake of this army, the Stephens are the opposite. At their invitation today, I shared a meal at their table. I am thankful for patriots like this family.

After our meal, the hill on which the Stephens's home sits provides a broad view of the Grand Parade. The Baron often monitors the troops' exercises from this vantage point. Today, he was down in the field barking out orders. I had the privilege to watch him without any interference or conversation. Below me, on that massive field, were thousands of our men working as one through their drills. It is from this place that I really gain an appreciation for the size of this army. A geographic spot noted in the Bible came to my mind today — the plains of Megiddo. Many battles have been fought on those plains in the land of Israel. We are told the final battle to end all battles will be waged there in the last days of mankind. It will be called the Battle of Armageddon. The Lord Jesus will conquer evil once and for all. His Kingdom will then come. There will be peace. I do not know if the Grand Parade field will ever amount to more than a training ground, but it is ideal for a true battle. I am looking for our own Armageddon on this continent. We want King George's kingdom to leave, for God's Kingdom to be tasted — in a free United States of America.

Saturday, April 25, 1778 — Valley Forge, Pennsylvania

Congress has made a call for a council to be formed of major-generals and the chief engineer. They leave out the commanding officer of our artillery which is General Knox. I am taking offense to this. I am asking them to include General Knox in this meeting. No officer nor unit has performed as valiantly, orderly, and effectively as this department. They should be included. I am not sure as to why the prejudice against General Knox, but it is counterproductive in our aim for victory over the British.

Sunday, April 26, 1778 — Valley Forge, Pennsylvania

A court-martial has concluded against Hetfield. The guilty verdict seems well-founded, but the evidence of the trial showed that he was enlisted through coercion. I am writing Governor Livingston to inform him that I agree with the verdict but believe that confinement is punishment enough. I think capital punishment is excessive. I write this on the Lord's Day. May everyone understand on this day of all, that we, as members of humanity, have been offered a reprieve from what we deserve by our dear Savior's sacrifice.

Monday, April 27, 1778 — Valley Forge, Pennsylvania

I am appreciative of Congress's reply to Britain's offer of pardon if we lay down our arms and silence our complaints. Congress wrote, "The United States cannot, with propriety, hold a conference or treaty with Great Britain until they lay down their arms, remove their armies, withdraw their fleets, and acknowledge our independence." Amen, so let it be!

Wednesday, April 29, 1778 — Valley Forge, Pennsylvania

I am ordering General Putnam to forward all recruits and drafts to regiments in this quarter as fast as possible. I need him then to return to Connecticut to arrange and forward militia.

I am still astonished that our recruiting officers in the various States are still counting deserters from General Burgoyne's army toward their quota. The British army relishes their troops serving as our reinforcements. They will not be vilified upon their return to the British side, but will be rewarded for the arms, clothes, and intelligence they bring with them. They will also be commended for the dissention they brought to our camp while they were with us. We are counting on men in whom we cannot even confide. Experience publicly seen has shown that recruiting deserters does not work. Lieutenant-Colonel Smith left with two detachments of these men. All of them are gone. Colonel Henley left Boston with sixty of these. He is now in this camp with a handful. They will soon be gone too.

Thursday, April 30, 1778 — Valley Forge, Pennsylvania

Our army has lacked uniformity in discipline and maneuvers. Since the commencement of this war (other than when I drilled our men at the onset), no one has been available to fill this great need. But now, we have been blessed with Baron Steuben. I am presenting him to Congress to be our inspector-general. He has a zeal and intelligence for which we have longed. He desires to hold the rank of major-general. I must attest that he is worthy of that rank. In his time at Valley Forge, our collection of men is being formed into a competent army. Not only has he trained in maneuvers, but he has brought order to the camp, cleanliness to the post, and showed us what is healthy in the conduct of our daily activity. The Baron is flexible to his duties, knowing they will fall beyond what is generally expected. He is willing to take this extra burden as he has a burning desire to see our Nation victorious and free.

I will set him up with two ranks of inspectors beneath him — one will be lower officers to inspect the brigades. These will be called brigade-inspectors. The other branch will superintend these. Lieutenant-Colonel Fleury is joining the Baron as an inspector at his request. He will hold the rank of lieutenant-colonel. I have struggled with how to employ foreign officers who desire a role in this army. I believe we have now found a place where they can render profitable service. I would like to give this inspector corps their regular pay according to their rank, plus an additional pay of twenty dollars for brigadier-inspectors, and thirty for their superintendents.

Friday, May 1, 1778 — Valley Forge, Pennsylvania

I should have gotten to this sooner, but the many calls for my attention have delayed my duty to call every officer to either pledge an oath of allegiance or of abjuration according to the resolve of Congress.

Congress has compromised in answer to my request for half-pay for officers. My urging was that all officers should receive half-pay of their salary for the rest of their lives. This is to be passed on to their widows. Congress has acceded partially to half-pay for seven years once the war ends. This does not go far enough, but it is more than we had. It should give our officers a reason to stay until war's end. A provision to Congress's liberality is that each officer must pledge allegiance to this Nation. Those who refuse will be ineligible for this stipend.

I must make a note and hold this day with great rejoicing. General McDougal and Mr. Deane bring me tidings of great joy and a most appreciated answer to my silent prayers. The French frigate Sensible arrived on our shores bearing news that the French have joined America in this Nation's fight for independence. The Sensible with its twenty-six guns is just a token of the support we can now expect from across the waters. Our fight has been vindicated.

Sunday, May 3, 1778 — Valley Forge, Pennsylvania

General Schuyler sees little prospect of engaging the Indians in that quarter to assist this army. The enemy has made a strong impression on their minds that assisting us would bring calamity to their people. If we can keep them neutral, I shall consider that a win. With France joining this contest, the Indians may be more inclined to help. At worst, they may refrain from hostilities. This frees up our army and militia to deal with the one enemy rather than a myriad of attacks from other opponents.

Our officers, along with some dignitaries who are visiting our camp, have requested a formal celebration to commemorate France's entrance into this contest. Baron Steuben and Colonel Knox are to arrange for a Continental display on the Grand Parade. We will schedule it for Wednesday, May 6th.

Tuesday, May 5, 1778 — Valley Forge, Pennsylvania

I am writing Major-General Heath to continue to prepare for war as if France were not allied with our purpose. We have no idea what the enemy will do as a consequence of our recent favor. We also do not know how or when France will join this contest in full. Even if Britain can no longer get reinforcements following the change of circumstances in Europe, the enemy can still combine their forces and effect an unfavorable result on this continent. We must be zealous, dedicated, and prepared. The States cannot be lax in meeting their quotas. On the contrary, my prayer is that they are energized even more by recent events.

The enemy is packing and loading. They appear to be planning on leaving Philadelphia. Intelligence is sparce as to their next move. Some believe the West Indies to confront the French navy. Some believe they plan to move toward New York. Others believe it is a ruse to lull this army into complacency and then deal a final blow. We have seen some two hundred of their light transports leave Philadelphia, but we are unsure if any troops were on board. If New York is their debarkation, new recruits and militia (especially from Connecticut and Massachusetts), should be moved to the North river. This includes those on furlough, those drafted, and those just released from the hospitals. If the movement is a ruse and the efforts are to be focused on Pennsylvania, then all these should be moved to this quarter with all expedition.

I need General Heath also to be mindful of prisoner exchanges. They hold more of our officers than we do of theirs. The only card we hold is if we can get General Burgoyne's officers to request an exchange. This would even the score somewhat, though we want those who have been imprisoned the longest to be released first. This will not work on the British side as Burgoyne's men have only been held for a short duration. This may not matter to the British.

I do believe New York is their likely destination. New York is too valuable for them to evacuate. With this in mind, we must be ready to move upon any confirmed enemy transports to New York. Posts must be fortified along the North river.

Wednesday, May 6, 1778 — Valley Forge, Pennsylvania

What a glorious day. Ten thousand of our men welcomed the sunny warm weather with drills on the Grand Parade. I was honored to inspect our men. They then formed battalions and carried out maneuvers as if in battle. The culmination of the day, a significant show of national unity was presented as thirteen cannons fired at once. The power of all thirteen states pulling together resolve to dislodge the British from our soil. The French are coming to aid us. Sickness is passing. A new day is dawning. General Greene has been kind enough to distribute an extra quantity of rations for the men. On this day, they deserve to feel fed and satisfied.

Thursday, May 7, 1778 — Valley Forge, Pennsylvania

A gentleman from France has given me three sets of epaulettes and sword-knots. They are beautiful to behold. Because I do not have much to give officers for whom this army's success has been afforded, I am sending one set to General Benedict Arnold and another to General Lincoln. This will be a testimony of my sincere approbation of their activities. Though we have many fine officers, these two I believe stand head-and-shoulders above the rest.

Tuesday, May 12, 1778 — Valley Forge, Pennsylvania

Congress has requested a commanding officer for Fort Pitt and in the western company. They desire to have General McIntosh at that post. He has been a gentleman of the highest regard in this army. I prefer not to part with him, but at Congress's request, I will send this man with a firm disposition. I constantly end my letters with, "your servant." I write this to Congress. I am to be their servant. I write this to officers in this army. I am to be their servant. I write this to my friends. I am to be their servant. There can be no pride or loftiness. As Jesus led and washed feet, so I must do the same. This means often denying myself of what I feel I need. I still believe that it will work out in the end.

As a servant, I seek to bring about the best outcomes for every person and every asset entrusted to my care. I had recommended the Continental frigates on the Delaware be sunk to keep them from the hands of the enemy. The Navy

Board rejected this advice believing that if the enemy approached, they would have ample time to sink the ships. I let them know that the enemy's approach would be so quick, that no time would be allowed to respond. I am not a prophet, nor do I take pleasure when my predictions of evil come true. The enemy has taken possession of these frigates. Now they have our vessels to use against us. This is a regretful occurrence.

My notations in this journal ebb-and-flow like my emotions in any given day. I turn now to record one Lieutenant-Colonel Allen. An original something in him commends admiration. He has suffered long as a prisoner of war. Even so, his enthusiasm for our calling has increased. Since his release, he seeks to serve this cause for freedom and desires no special favor or even an ambition of a higher rank. This is patriotism. This is sacrifice. This is a man who understands the thing for which we are striving.

The French have sent their intentions to Parliament on our behalf. The response from Parliament has been shameful. It should motivate the French and our Nation all the more.

Governor Livingston writes that his efforts to raise a militia have been successful above what he had dreamt. I am encouraged by this influx of militia, but he has misunderstood my request. I just asked that they be readied. If I had the means to supply them, that would be an advantage. As it is, I have no provisions for them, nor any action in which to engage them. What I desire from him and those in his region is to form their militia into what can be referred to as "minute companies" like those at the initiation of this war. They need to continue to conduct their normal business as citizens but have the arms and readiness to respond immediately as the moment dictates.

Wednesday, May 13, 1778 — Valley Forge, Pennsylvania

Brigadier-General Nelson of the Virginia militia has raised a cavalry to join us at this head, which will reinforce this army and provide them some rest.

The British have sent messengers to Madrid to inquire of their intentions now that France has entered the war. They are demanding to know if Spain will join the French in our cause or sit neutral. Clearly, the enemy is disturbed by the recent occurrence. To see their energies divided is a delight. I believe the only way we will not be successful is if we lack virtue, prudence, and management of ourselves. Righteousness exalts a nation. The opposite will bring it down. How can we expect the Creator of all that is good, to come to our aid if we do not seek His Face and pattern our lives accordingly?

Sunday, May 17, 1778 — Valley Forge, Pennsylvania

With cautious delicacy, the Marquis de Lafayette has made me aware of a singular brigade refusing to sign the oath of abjuration or allegiance. I find it odd that the officers of only one brigade would carry this opinion. As short as we are at this moment, I am advising the Marquis to let it go if they will continue to join us in this fight. To me, their reasons are excuses which cannot be well-defended. That being as it is, I believe the oath should not be coerced at this time. They will swear or not swear. May their own conscience guide them. If they look at the infringements made upon this Nation and the jeopardy to which our freedoms and properties are now placed, perhaps they will see the wisdom of this oath. What Congress has asked is nothing new under the sun. The oath should not have raised a concern. I am unclear as to their true objection.

I am assigning command to the Marquis, the area between the Schuylkill and Delaware. He is to stay near the enemy lines, monitor communication, gather intelligence as to the enemy's movements, and to harass the enemy should he evacuate Philadelphia. With this said, he will be over a valuable resource in these men. He is always to be alert. He is always to be on the move so that the enemy is unable to get an idea of their situation. This would enable the British to plan some form of attack. He is to attack only if assured of success. He must be willing to retreat in an efficacious manner. One other thing I ask of him, he must make sure that the inhabitants are not abused or stolen from by this party under his command. Others have been sent out and brought harm to our own citizens. The Marquis will do well to find from the residents any offenses and then make efforts to remedy and console the offended.

Monday, May 18, 1778 — Valley Forge, Pennsylvania

As noted earlier, Congress has agreed to the half-pay for our officers though at a lesser period than I felt most influential. With that said, they have not made it known to our men in a formal manner. I am begging Gouverneur Morris, for God's Sake, this measure needs to be communicated formally. It is one thing to hear from me, but another to see it as an official documented resolve of Congress.

General Mifflin is seeking to be reemployed in this army. I will not oppose his reinstatement. But Congress should be aware that any man who steps in and out so readily, depending on the circumstance, is not to be preferred to the one who stays connected through the bitter and the sweet. General Conway who had resigned is now making overtures through his friends to regain his commission. I need to know if Congress is going to allow this. They already know where I stand with General Conway.

The above notation brings a joy to me. Its writing reminds me that the three men who sought to undermine or replace me have been disbanded. Some friends called their actions toward me a cabal. I suppose that is what it was. The very enemies of my position were gathered by Congress, an unknowing Congress, to form the Board of War. Everything they did was to harm me publicly and in this army. I thank God their efforts were not crowned with success. The Author of life, of my life, has always stepped in when I needed Him. He says do not take revenge. Vengeance is His. I have found the promises of Scripture proven true time-and-time again. Many doubt His Existence. They doubt because they refuse to recognize what He does all around them continually.

Congress has given me permission to share the half-pay measures with our officers. I believe this will make a big difference in retaining good men.

The Marquis and his detachment have already incurred the ire of the enemy. He struck with fervor and retreated when wisdom demanded it. He lost nine men, but the enemy lost many more.

The enemy seems to be gathering stores for their journey out of Philadelphia. I am alerting General Gates to make ready. The quartermaster-general and the commissary of provisions are exerting themselves to be prepared for movement. I feel for the prisoners in the enemy's hand. They will be drug along with the enemy's army to a place perhaps more miserable than the current. How I long to complete an exchange.

Tuesday, May 19, 1778 — Valley Forge, Pennsylvania

The President of the Council of Massachusetts has written to let me know recruiting of deserters from the British army has been censored and should no longer occur. If they find it in practice, they will punish the offenders. They have initiated the draft, but it seems they are using this to increase their militia. I would prefer it was to enlarge this army. I will trust all things will be well in the end.

Sunday, May 24, 1778 — Valley Forge, Pennsylvania

General Howe has written with a favorable view of making the prisoner exchange. I have let the commissary-general of prisoners, Mr. Boudinot, aware. I am having him report to me at this camp forthwith.

Monday, May 25, 1778 — Valley Forge, Pennsylvania

The enemy is circulating letters that are said to have been written by me. They are forgeries, but the writer of this art has some acquaintance with my family and its make-up. I have to wonder if a loyalist exists in our family's midst who is concerting with the enemy. I have not the time to consider further. What I pray for is that our citizens give them no weight. I pray that my actions thus far have removed any doubts as to my character or commitment.

France's involvement is as welcomed as a vaccination from the pox, but I am fearful that it will bring a hesitation in our work. We must make ready for war. We must prepare for a long and drawn-out one. I would rather our men be pleasantly surprised at an early end, then for me to have to plead with them when an expected short end is unrealized. Our great work is not finished just because the French choose to align by our side. This is still our war to win or lose.

We have nearly three thousand sick in this camp. Thus, we are unable to respond to the enemy's movements in quick fashion, much less follow them in a timely manner. I believe the enemy is aware of our State. The British may gain the spirit to act against us before they leave.

To assume the role of Commander-in-Chief to all the Continental armies rather than just this one under my watch is a great relief. The recent fall of the "Cabal" has brought General Gates a more submissive posture toward the authority of the command with which I have been entrusted. I am ordering him to make ready his troops for the British arrival. Prior to the disbanding of the Board of War, I felt I had no choice but to plead. I now have the ability to stand and require. Not only are my men faithful, but his men have decried any effort to undermine my authority or replace me. I have never been one to take advantage of trust given me. My letters concluding with "your servant" I pray furthers the confidence that I seek nothing but the success of this army and the freedom of this Nation. I digress. I am ordering General Gates to hold all recruits in his quarter. He is to make the militia ready. I will keep him abreast of events here. I trust he will do the same for me.

Thursday, May 28, 1778 — Valley Forge, Pennsylvania

President Laurens of Congress objected to the half-pay measures for our officers on the grounds that these do not suffer more or risk more than the soldiers in the line. I agree with him, but half-pay is a necessary evil for competent leaders. Without them, the men on the line do not execute as they should. In disorder, they will lose a lot more. Laurens also worries about the budget going forward, which is why he only acceded to a seven-year commitment post-war. I understand this as well. We must look beyond the war at being fiscally responsible. I pray our Nation never gets to the point where we have a large portion of our residents depending on the public dole. Half-pay, not exceeding a colonel's pay, is not enough to provide for any person in their yearly needs. This amount is a reward, a bonus, but not enough to keep them from work afterward. I hold to Scripture, if a man will not work, he shall not eat. The half-pay is more of a payback for what the Nation has taken from such men of enterprise in the duration of this war.

Friday, May 29, 1778 — Valley Forge, Pennsylvania

General Gates believes, I gather from his previous return, that I am withholding men from his command. Of interest to note is that it is he who withheld men from me. General Lee did the same in the past. It is funny how those who commit the offense, assume the offense is committed against them. I suppose they think all deal as duplicitous as they. I am assuring him that if the quotas of the States are unmet, this is not my fault. I plead with them daily. If quotas are not met, then our command is in want of men. This is the case for the army under my watch. I assume it is the case for the men under Gates. He requests reinforcements from this quarter when I still have the bulk of the enemy posted at my door. I am ordering all Jersey troops to his post. I will join them if the enemy moves from here.

A box of hard money was captured from the enemy at the battle of Princeton. It then disappeared. Many thought it had been misplaced perhaps with the ammunition, though was not found there. Guilt began to point at a subordinate officer in this army. Governor Clinton writes that the box has been found. The guilty has been dealt with. As goes our virtue, so goes our war. I pray all understand this premise.

Saturday, May 30, 1778 — Valley Forge, Pennsylvania

To read the letter of my friend Landon Carter has been a pleasure. He always brings kind words to my side. I know he does not do it to flatter as his integrity would prevent it. Nonetheless, he does not realize that every success this army or me has experienced has been due to Providence. He protects. He directs. His frequent interposition has saved the day in the darkest of situations. No other explanation can be had. Our prospects have brightened recently because the Author of all that is good has extended relief to usward. My dear friend was aware at the designs against me from the three schemers. Our men and Heaven itself intervened.

I am sending Major Lee with his three companies of dragoons (as opposed to the two originally assigned) to move toward the North river. The quartermaster-general is to give him the route, encampment, and halting days. He is to move rapidly but not press his horses as to weaken them prior to battle. They are not to burn fences. They are to protect every person and property on their journey.

Friday, June 5, 1778 — Valley Forge, Pennsylvania

A change in British leadership has come to my attention. General Howe seems to have been recalled from his command. He ships out shortly. Intelligence informs that General Clinton is now in command of the British troops in this quarter.

The evidence convinces me that the British are moving toward New York. I am having General Dickinson to break the militia in his command into small parties to obstruct the roads as best they can. They are to harass the enemy as they move. I want these men to hide in the trees, bushes, and hillsides and to fire upon this enemy night and day.

Tuesday, June 9, 1778 — Valley Forge, Pennsylvania

I have received my first dispatch from the enemy's new commander General Clinton. He is requesting a rite of passage for a Doctor Ferguson. I must seek Congress's approval. My fear is that he will serve only to spread disaffection.

Wednesday, June 10, 1778 — Valley Forge, Pennsylvania

I was honored to receive my brother John Augustine's letter. It is a taste of home. I must confess to him and myself, we have been waiting fourteen days for the enemy to evacuate. Many of their stores and baggage have been moved. Most of their troops remain here. It has been relayed to me that their commissioners Lord Carlisle, Governor Johnstone, and Mr. William Eden have arrived. I am curious if these were the cause for their delay. Some say they are willing to allow us to make our own terms if we will remain in our dependence upon Britain. Here we are at war, and they arrogantly speak of what they will "allow." I cannot even consider retreating to their abusive arms.

Virginia is lax in providing the troops according to their quota. I am letting my brother know that twelve hundred and forty-two will not suffice when we have requested a minimum of thirty-five hundred. Maryland and New Jersey are close to their numbers. My home State should do the same.

My brother tells me that Billy Washington is sick. I pray for his soon recovery. Perhaps Mrs. Washington, who left yesterday, can bring our family comfort comparable to what she has brought me at this head. I miss her being with me here, but the campaign is about to heat up. I prefer her to be far from danger.

Friday, June 12, 1778 — Valley Forge, Pennsylvania

I am writing General Gates to give him a general direction of the enemy. I do not believe they will venture into the heart of the eastern States. The majority of the populace there will certainly not give them a favorable welcome. I expect, for that area, they will seek to burn the coastal towns and lay waste their coasts. If they are going to the North river, I will send part of my army to meet them in concert with General Gates. They should expect no success by a coup de main. The enemy is truly evacuating Philadelphia while their commissioners seek an audience with Congress to pursue a negotiation.

Saturday, June 13, 1778 — Valley Forge, Pennsylvania

I received a letter from Major-General Lee with some very honest questions along with his assessments of this army, the enemy, and our strategies. I welcome such inquiries as no one man has all the answers. Any plan must be considered in the positive and negative to bring about a more successful outcome. He is concerned about the instances when I move a major-general from one division to another. He feels this puts that major-general and the division he goes to on an unfamiliar ground. I try to avoid such moves, but sometimes in the heat of action, those moves are necessary as I seek the best effect. Besides, my daily orders speak of every major-general and their activities. I do this so the army is familiar with every major-general, their record, and their achievements.

It seems Mr. Boudinot and General Lee believe the enemy may move upon Maryland. I do not believe that is where they are headed, but I have prepared should that be the case. We are moving stores and provisions from the Head of Elk. We are placing boats upon the Susquehanna for the transportation of our troops if that is necessary. More than anything, I am glad that General Lee has turned his thoughts and attention to this war again. It would be nice if we see his talents fully engaged in the service of this country. I hope his time spent under enemy confines has made him more friendly to our quest over his personal advancement.

Thursday, June 18, 1778 — Valley Forge, Pennsylvania

Baron Steuben has requested a meeting with Congress at York which I assume is to define his powers as inspector-general.

The enemy has officially evacuated and is on the move. Estimate is they have about three thousand men who have boarded the transports. I have put six brigades in motion. The rest shall follow with all possible dispatch. We will head to Jersey and adjust as the enemy's destination is ascertained.

I am sending Brigadier-General Wayne with the first and second Pennsylvania regiments (once under Conway) to Coryell's Ferry leaving an interval between he and General Lee. They are to march to the North river unless they receive intelligence that the enemy is headed toward South Amboy. They will make changes if that news arrives.

With Dr. Ferguson on my mind from the British requests, I am now closely monitoring all intercourse between the enemy and our army, and between the enemy and our inhabitants. Their letters will be inspected. Anything insidious will be suppressed. Too much is at stake to let our guard down or to assume those we trust are truly with us.

As we move from this cantonment, I am grieved by our losses. To ascertain the exact number is difficult, but it is estimated that we have lost two thousand of our soldiers here at Valley Forge. Never in my wildest nightmares did I imagine losing so many men to something not combat-related. I am saddened by the loss of so many. The one bright spot is that we are leaving this place stronger, better-trained, and more resolved. If a furnace shapes the metal and makes it harder, then I believe we have been forged in the fires of suffering in this valley. How sovereign is our God to do such a work at a location called Valley Forge. I do not believe this was an accident. This area is known for forging metal. Our metal is marching out to be tested. May God go with us. I pray we never have to return to such hardships again.

I am waiting on the men to finish preparation for our march. We have gathered all my papers. We have closed the door on my Headquarters here at the confluence of Valley creek and the Schuylkill river. If the Lord grants us victory. I wish to return to this place and stay a night or two. I want to enjoy the beauty of this place. I want to remember all that was lost and found at this special place.

The Baron Steuben has challenged the men. They stand in tight formations. All are ready. We are moving out, anxious for a test on the battlefield.

Friday, June 19, 1778

I am assigning General Arnold command of Philadelphia. His wounds, not healing, prevent him from active service which is to my regret. While in Philadelphia, per the resolves of Congress, he is to assure tranquility in the city, give security to the residents, restore city government, and ensure that any private property taken by the enemy is returned to the rightful owner. Any stores or provisions left by the enemy should be forwarded for this army's use. The quartermaster-general is being made available to General Arnold as he has need.

Saturday, June 20, 1778 — Ten miles from Coryell's Ferry

I am with the army on the move. We are about ten miles from Coryell's Ferry. We should make Jersey by tomorrow. I am instructing General Gates to make forage and provisions his chief concern.

Sunday, June 21, 1778 — Ten miles from Coryell's Ferry

Major Wemp is escorting warriors from the Seneca nation. They are on their way to Philadelphia to inquire of the whereabouts of Astyarix. They have heard he is held in captivity somewhere. I am asking General Arnold to use all civility toward them and do what he can to help. However, I have warned them in the past, and General Arnold is to repeat to them, that if they do not cease from all hostilities, once the British are gone, I will turn this whole army against them and any other

Indian nation who have taken a bloody part against us. They need to know that we will cut them to pieces.

General Arnold is to let them know that Congress will order Astyarix's release as soon as he is found. He is then to give the Seneca warriors trinkets and the like. He is to give an abundance more, in their presence, to our friends in the Oneida and Tuscarora tribes who have traveled with them. I want them to see how we treat our friends who seek to live in peace with their neighbors. After this, General Arnold is to order the Senecas to their homes immediately.

We have not been able to leave our post near Coryell's Ferry. The rain has impeded our travel.

Monday, June 22, 1778 — Headquarters near Coryell's Ferry

General Dickinson has caught up with the enemy, but at a safe distance. He reports that their destination is still unclear. They currently reside at Morestown and Mount Holly. Rain is still slowing us. As soon as we have dried out and cleaned our arms, we will be heading to Princeton.

Wednesday, June 24, 1778 — Headquarters, Hopewell

I am instructing General Dickinson to employ some men from the Jersey militia who know the roads and lines of communication to assist in our safe passage. They are to effect our offensive operations with greater precision. As it now stands, I am instructing the following of the enemy and the direction of attack as follows: Colonel Morgan's corps of six hundred are to gain the enemy's right flank, Maxwell's brigade is to hang to their left, General Lee's men with General Scott's detachment should gall the enemy's left rear flank, and General Cadwalader is to take his two or three hundred Continentals and militia and march on the enemy's rear.

Thursday, June 25, 1778 — Headquarters, Kingston

General Lee has objected strongly to our attack on the enemy, so I am sending the Marquis de Lafayette with General Poor's detachment to join General Scott.

They are to use the most effectual means for gaining the enemy's left flank and rear and render as much annoyance as possible. My hope is this will impede the enemy and disrupt their march. If he sees an opportunity where success is sure, I would like for him to try to strike the enemy with his full force. I am cautioning again that he is to do this only if a high chance of succeeding is present and little chance of being defeated or captured. Preservation of our deficient force is essential.

Friday, June 26, 1778 — Headquarters — Cranberry

General Lee has voiced his displeasure at the responsibilities laid upon the Marquis. He now wishes to reenter the contest. To keep from humiliating the Marquis and from alienating General Lee so soon after rejoining this army, I am asking him to take charge of the whole left and rear flank enterprise. I reserve one point of restriction. If the Marquis has some plan that is approved by the general officers, General Lee is to acquiesce to his initiative and aid in the activity as best as possible. General Lee has agreed to my request.

I have spoken with the Marquis, and he has responded very politely and understandingly. I am grateful for this young man. I hope that he attains the glory and honor that he so desires.

Saturday, June 27, 1778

The enemy is now at Monmouth Court House. They have positioned themselves wisely with almost their entire front secured by a morass and thick woods. Their left and right flanks have tree cover. They are more exposed to the rear. It is a beautiful day for a battle. The grass is lush. The trees are in full bud. Fields are plowed. Corn is growing in the fields. Everything is right to put into practice what our men have learned. I have held them back like a horse that senses he is near the barn. The time is upon us to release the reins and let them fight. The only obstacles to slow our men will be the marshes and the thick wooded areas.

I am sending a strong detachment under General Lee to move on their rear if possible. The enemy is aware of our proximity. I just received a report that the enemy has moved their best troops — grenadiers, light-infantry, and chasseurs of the line to their rear.

I am detaching the Marquis and his men to move to his left toward English town. I am having Maxwell's brigade, General Wayne with a thousand men, and Morgan's light-infantry readied. I am moving Morgan's corps to the left to hover around the enemy's right flank. I am sending General Dickinson with seven or eight hundred men to their left.

I have decided that if the enemy is able to get about ten-or-twelve miles from where they are situated now, an attack will lose all prospects of success. I have decided that the moment they begin to move from their present position, we will attack from the rear. I am letting General Lee know to have his men sleep with their arms and be ready to advance on the shortest notice.

Sunday, June 28, 1778

The time is now five in the morning, General Dickenson has informed me that the front of the enemy has begun their march. I am sending orders at the present for General Lee to move and attack. May the Lord bless and protect us, please.

I am hearing firing. Hallelujah, the battle has begun! We have trained all winter thanks to the Baron. We are ready. More than that, we are in the necessity for action. I am moving the main army now to support Lee.

We have marched five miles. Our own men are retreating toward us! I am riding to rally them.

Monday, June 29, 1778 — Fields near Monmouth Court House

The fire has ended. General Lee, I am ashamed to say, ran in retreat with the fire of one shot and the appearance of the enemy's light horse. How could he! He gave me nothing but excuses days ago. He did not want to attack so he quit. Then he joined again when he saw the Marquis was taking his command. I acquiesced to his request to resume command. He was sent back to lead. He was given the opportunity he requested. And he retreated?! It was as if this was his plan all along. He is currently under arrest. A court-martial is scheduled.

Enough on that. What a glorious day yesterday was! I rode into the retreat of our men. By God's Grace, I got them turned around. We quickly regained the formation taught by the Baron. We moved forward. It was as if the men were wanting to fight, not retreat, but they were following the command of General Lee reluctantly. Our officers joined me in rallying the men. Other officers repositioned our artillery. They opened fire to push the enemy back. The enemy regrouped and made a second charge. We were able to push them back again. The British were pounding us with cannon, but our men would not move. We matched them cannon for cannon. It was like this army was in one accord, an orchestra with each playing its part.

Our left wing attacked. Our second line moved forward. Lord Stirling on my left opened fire on the enemy. Our infantry stopped their advance in that direction. I put General Greene in command of Lee's brigades and sent him to our right down by the new church to sweep around to the rear of the Court-House. I had the rest of our column move directly to the Court-House.

The enemy pushed to their front. Heavy fighting ensued. Our men for the first time engaged in successful hand-to-hand fighting with bayonets. I could tell in the mass collision, that the British troops appeared surprised and disheartened to find an army as capable as themselves. Being repulsed at their front, the enemy made a move to our left but were bravely rejected by detached parties of our infantry. They made a move to our right and were making headway. General Greene then turned some artillery on them. He was able to stop them. General Wayne charged up with a body of troops and kept a severe fire upon them. The enemy's flanks were covered by woods. Their front still had the obstacle of the morass. I sent General Poor and his North Carolina brigade toward their front through a narrow pass. They attempted it but found too many obstacles in their way.

The enemy retreated to a secure position. Nightfall hit. Our men were exhausted as was the enemy. Our men slept in the field on their guns. The enemy slipped away during the night. It is believed they are embarking for Sandy Hook. From what we see of the graves the enemy dug for their dead during the night and those we buried this morning, their losses are near one thousand men. We may have lost three to four hundred brave soldiers. Both sides lost some to the intense heat. I fear we may lose more in the next day or so.

Our men performed better than I have ever witnessed. The officers seemed to vie with each other for zeal and bravery. So many of our men distinguished themselves. I cannot even account for all the brave individual acts being reported.

I am overwhelmed with thanksgiving. This is one of my happiest days since the beginning of the war. We did not finish the enemy off. I believe we could have if Lee had not retreated. We have shown the enemy and ourselves that this thing can be done. I give thanks to the One who always works all things for our good.

I have broken away from our men for a moment. I have dismounted off my horse in the middle of this once active battlefield. I am sitting under a tree. I have pulled out my diary to write. A thought has struck me. This moment cannot pass me by without reflection. Gazing across this field, I see a few bodies left, being gathered. Lives have ended here. Years ago, they started off with such joy to parents who loved them — American and British alike. There were hopes and dreams for each. But on this day, July 2, 1778, many men exited this life. All that remains is a body with a stilled heart.

In the brisk time of moving, guessing, strategizing, fighting, then moving forward or retreating with the men remaining, we leave some behind. The futures for many were stopped on a piece of ground in this field — some by cannon fire, some by bayonet, and some by musket shot. No one foresaw it. Each considered it before conflict. It is before that soldiers come to terms with their own mortality. When the battle is done, only the surviving move forward. Again, under the shade of this tall tree, silence and reflection are all I can muster. Journeys terminated on this field. The truth is many men have fallen. There was a final thought, a last word, a gasping plea to Heaven. May this nation understand the sacrifice that each man lying on this field has paid for freedom.

I am cognizant of the fact that I must move on to Brunswick. I just cannot at this moment. If I had my way, I would stay under this tree, look out across this field, and ponder for days. This field will produce again. Bodies will lay under it, returning to dust. I wonder if the farmer of this field will think of the patches of ground under his feet where life moved from this life to the eternal? Surely, the farmer in a day or two will. What is grievous to me is how few of the future generations of farmers and families will contemplate the ultimate price that Joe paid, John paid, Paul paid, Amos paid, Benjamin paid, or Henry paid. Each has a name. Each came knowing what was required. How I love these men. One day, George may lay in a field just like this one. I will not regret that. This cause is worth it.

Friday, July 3, 1778 — Brunswick, New Jersey

The count of enemy casualties continues to mount. We have over one hundred in our confinement who were wounded and left at Monmouth, including forty privates and four British officers. If it were in my power, I would have no losses of our brave men. Sadly, we lost several. I have been notified that Lieutenant-Colonel Banner of Pennsylvania and Major Dickinson of Virginia were killed. These, as all who died on our side, were patriots. We will make sure their death was not in vain. I cannot help but consider how much less our losses would be and how much greater our victory had General Lee not retreated at the first. He will answer for this if the court-martial trial finds any dereliction on his part.

The enemy appears to be moving to Sandy Hook, so I am moving to the North river. I do not believe there can be any success in hampering their embarkation. That area is well-situated for their protection. I am leaving at their rear Colonel Morgan, his corps, and the Jersey brigade to hover near, gather deserters, and prevent depredations.

Our march today has been tough. It is extremely hot with little water. We have lost several men and horses to the elements. The march is also on sandy ground making it more difficult and slower. I am informing General Gates that we intend to cross the North river at King's Ferry. If he sees the enemy entrench that for defense, I am asking that he communicate that to us. If they are not there, I need him to secure that area by throwing up some works and stationing some cannon there for our cover.

Saturday, July 4, 1778 — Brunswick, New Jersey

On this second anniversary of our Declaration of Independence from the King and Great Britain, I have the pleasure to write my brother John Augustine of the events which have occurred recently. I am happy to let him know what Providence has given us in the activity at Monmouth. It is from Him we are given our liberties. Mr. Jefferson so rightly put the chief of those liberties is to worship Him freely. The second right, not clearly stated, is the one I have pleasure to exercise in this letter to my brother. It is the right to enjoy our families and find strength in this God-given institution. I suppose this right could be considered under the phrase "pursuit of happiness." The bond to the Author of life and the family bond are what makes this Nation great. It is what has sustained us thus far. I believe these bonds will bring us ultimate success.

I am asking my brother to encourage our friends and family in Virginia to make vigorous measures to fill this army. If they do this, our inconveniences can be suspended in an expedient manner. The enemy appears to be traveling through the Jerseys and moving by water around to New York. I still do not believe they will see many recruitments with France now involved. Their numbers are static. Ours increase from abroad. We are in a better position than we have ever been.

Sunday, July 5, 1778 — Brunswick, New Jersey

The left wing of our army has crossed the North river today. We are moving only as health and heat allow.

Monday, July 6, 1778 — Brunswick, New Jersey

The right wing has crossed the North river today.

General Franks sends me word concerning General Arnold. He has a violent oppression in the stomach. I am wishing him a full recovery from this and his leg injury.

By some counts, Sir Henry Clinton has experienced a diminution of two thousand troops and his numbers continue to decline. I pray that is true.

Tuesday, July 7, 1778 — Brunswick, New Jersey

The second line which forms the rear division is moving across the North river now. Every movement of this army reminds me of the orderly way the Lord had Moses move the children of Israel. Each tribe went in certain order. Each went carrying their assigned baggage.

I am asking Lord Stirling to move General Lee's court-martial from Morristown to Paramus Church as many officers will be called to testify. I cannot have them pulled off the line for any length of time. It is interesting, General Lee has left one prison, that of the enemy, to go to another prison, that of his friends. In both instances, his status can be attributed to only one fault — his own.

I need Congress to settle the issue of rank for our officers. Their disorganized manner of increasing rank mistakenly promotes younger officers over superior ones. They do not stop to consider who has served, where they have served, and for how long they have served. It gives reason for resignation. I need them also to consider their commissions to foreign men who come to join our ranks. Their choices can be discouraging to those who have fought and earned their ranks versus those who have simply come to jump ahead of them in the line of promotion.

Saturday, July 11, 1778 — Headquarters, Paramus, New Jersey

The left wing of the army has advanced four miles from here and nineteen miles shy of King's Ferry. The other two divisions are moving in that direction in proper intervals. The enemy is stationed in three camps — one on Staten Island, one on Long Island, and one on New York Island. They appear to be in no mood for an offense. This has enabled me to move our army in a leisurely manner. Great peace and purpose exists among our men as we march.

The French fleet is said to have arrived off Chesapeake Bay. It is said to be under the command of Count D'Estaing. The enemy is rushing to ready their large ships for an encounter.

Sunday, July 12, 1778 — Headquarters, Paramus, New Jersey

I received a vote of approbation and appreciation from Congress today for the victory at Monmouth over the British army. That is their word, "victory." I believe it is truly what we experienced. Their vote shows that even on the darkest moments when it seems everyone is against me, Providence steps in to turn things around. This has been true my whole life. I give thanks on this Lord's Day.

Tuesday, July 14, 1778 — Headquarters, Paramus, New Jersey

In expectation that the British fleet may move around the Sound to avoid the French fleet or to draw them to some favorable quarter, I am asking Governor Trumbull and the States nearby to gather every armed vessel and frigate possible. They are to make ready to join together to provide a hindrance and a harassment to the British. We can do this to at least help our naval ally France.

I am writing a letter of introduction and gratitude to the French Count D'Estaing for his assistance in this war. I will ascribe to him the state of the enemy, their numbers, and their strengths as well as weaknesses from our vantage point and experience. Our army is fifty miles above New York. We are working our way down to them. We need to establish some sort of signal system between their navy and our army. I am sending my aide Mr. Laurens. A letter cannot answer questions that arise or explain what is needed in a timely manner.

Friday, July 17, 1778 — Camp at Haverstraw Bay, New York

I am sending Lieutenant-Colonel Hamilton to join Mr. Laurens before the Count. He has a good grasp of our strategies as well as our supply condition. To join Laurens and Hamilton, I have decided to also send Lieutenant-Colonel Fleury. He is a Frenchman who has been in our ranks. He has acted with zeal and courage in the line of battle. Where may be a language barrier or some suspect of trust may exist, Fleury can fill the gap and give Count D'Estaing confidence to act on our communication. The French fleet has twelve ships of the line and four frigates now sitting off Sandy Hook.

We are considering attacking the enemy in New York or possibly in Rhode Island. We are equipped and ready for the former. I am writing General Sullivan to make ready for the latter by raising up five thousand men from Rhode Island, Massachusetts, and Connecticut. He is to establish suitable magazines of provisions. He needs to have pilots who are familiar with navigation of the ports of Rhode Island and the adjacent coasts, ready to go on board to assist the French Admiral. The one thing I must warn General Sullivan, as well as our army and Congress, is that we must not rest upon the aid of the French. We must make all preparations and movements as if we are in this all by ourselves. If he does not think five thousand men are enough with that mindset, he needs to gather as many as he believes are necessary.

Wednesday, July 22, 1778 — Camp near White Plains, New York

I am sending the Marquis in command of the regiments of Varnum and Glover along with the detachments under Colonel Jackson. They are to move to Providence, Rhode Island, by the best route available. He is to then subject himself and that body of men to Major-General Sullivan. If for some reason, he finds the British are marching to this head, I desire that he countermarch to join us.

11 o'clock p.m. — Count D'Estaing has just reported through Colonel Laurens that the waters are too shallow for his ships to enter the bay of New York. He is thus setting his sights on moving on the enemy at Rhode Island. The Count plans to move as soon as the Chimere Frigate rejoins him from the Delaware river.

We are currently camped at White Plains. I am sending Mr. Laurens to General Sullivan in Providence so that he might be aware of this movement and be ready to cooperate.

Friday, July 24, 1778 — Camp near White Plains, New York

I am writing Gouverneur Morris regarding the commissions Congress is assigning to foreign men. This practice drives out our own officers. It places the hands of this army under the care of foreigners who do not have a stake in this Nation — no family, no property. To promote these over men of our own country who have served, fought, and suffered is unnatural.

Men who come from foreign shores come under the guise that they merely want to join us in our cause as volunteers. Then they ask for rank without pay. Then they ask for pay according to their rank. Then they ask for a higher rank. And then they complain because they did not get the rank or the pay they desired. Then they resign after our own men have. We are then left with no army with which to fight.

I will convey to Mr. Morris very frankly, these men are foreign fortune-hunters who fit into one of three categories — adventurers, spies, or ambitious men. Many of these write letters of recommendation for themselves. They forge an American officer's signature below it. Several foreign gentlemen appear to be making their way to Philadelphia at the present to obtain rank above our native and active officers.

Even the Baron Steuben who has served well as inspector-general and has vastly improved this army, now wants to surrender his position, and take up a command in the line. Our existing officers appreciate his contribution but will take a dim view if he is allowed a command beside or over them. Our brigadiers especially will resent this as he has been given a title major-general for his role as inspector-general. If placed on the line, he will succeed them in rank and command. Our brigadiers are the ones who have valiantly fought the fight for which the Baron has only invested a training regimen. I found very quickly the officers' attitude recently when we marched for Brunswick. I was lacking major-generals. I assigned the Baron to conduct a wing to the North river as a pro tempore. This excited great uneasiness among the brigadiers. The move has been a point of complaint ever since.

I will close my entry with a reminder to this issue. I am a citizen of the world who is not warped or led away by attachments merely American. Yet I confess, I am not entirely without them.

Sunday, July 26, 1778 — Camp near White Plains, New York

The Baron has shared his intentions to travel to Philadelphia to tender his resignation to Congress because he has not been given a command in the line. The prospect of losing his service to this cause saddens me. He is a vital piece. I am prayerful he will reconsider or agree to some other position by which to pacify his ambition, while carrying out the best service for this Nation.

Monday, July 27, 1778 — Camp near White Plains, New York

Having sent the Marquis to command the troops to assist General Sullivan at Rhode Island, I am now of the mind to send Major-General Greene to join him. Greene is now ably serving as our quartermaster-general. I have never seen such vigilance to meet our needs. I would that he could have been in this place of service before Valley Forge. It would have made the winter more bearable and our losses less significant. That being the case, I am now sending him as a major-general to join Sullivan and the Marquis. Greene is from the Rhode Island area. He is familiar with the land and the people. Our best prospect of success is to have him take lead there over half of the troops now under the Marquis. I am writing the Marquis about the change. I am hopeful that he does not feel I am showing any disrespect to his leadership or abilities.

Monday, August 3, 1778 — Camp near White Plains, New York

General Arnold is doing better. He is considering a move to some command in the navy. I am in hopes that he recovers and joins us. We could use his experience and zeal.

I am letting the Count D'Estaing know the British seem to be moving their fleet. We are unsure if they are going to meet the French fleet or if they are going to provide reinforcements on the coast. They could also be attempting to draw part of the French fleet to divide it for a better engagement or to distract the French from our plan upon Rhode Island. They could even be loading up to leave this continent but that seems unlikely.

The French fleet needs water onboard for their men. I am contacting Governor Trumbull to gather water and send it by as many vessels as are appropriate for the task.

Monday, August 10, 1778 — Camp near White Plains, New York

It was a relief to receive a letter from the Marquis today. I have worried several days now that he would be offended by my direction of General Greene to take the lead. With the Baron's dissatisfaction in not being given a command and with many of our own officers upset at foreign usurpers taking their commands, I feared the same would be true for the Marquis. And then I get his letter today where he states that he is happy to submit to General Greene and will do all in his power for the success of this engagement. He states that he is happy to serve as an officer or to serve simply as a man on the line. This young man came with an ambition to lead. He pushed me to get him a command. He has acted bravely in battle, displayed great leadership in command, and now he shows the humility to serve in any capacity. Seeing this progression is a testament to his maturity, to his growing humility, and to his true desire for the freedom of America above all else.

Sunday, August 16, 1778 — Camp near White Plains, New York

Misfortunes, misconnections, and bad weather have prevented the French fleet from entering upon the enterprise against Rhode Island. This has deranged our views for its prospect. General Sullivan and our men are ready to engage at first sight of the French fleet's return.

Monday, August 17, 1778 — Camp near White Plains, New York

Report has it that Count D'Estaing met the British fleet at sea and were close to engagement when a terrible storm hit which prevented the attack. It would have meant sure destruction of much of the British fleet, but instead both fleets were damaged by the storm. We hope for quick repair. The French fleet brings great hope to our Nation.

Thursday, August 20, 1778 — Camp near White Plains, New York

To receive a letter from my good friend Brigadier-General Nelson from my home State of Virginia was such a pleasure. Congress made a call for men to join this army as light cavalry as long as they brought their own horses and provisions. Nelson writes that many responded, but when they arrived in Philadelphia, our army had already moved to New York. As a result, they were returned home to Virginia. I would have loved to have had their assistance here, not to mention the comfort old and new friends bring. Nonetheless, I am encouraged by their desire to serve.

I am not sure what to think of the French fleet. They have still not returned. There is thought that they were disgruntled when our men arrived in Providence and set up for attack without the orders of the Count. I am not sure if this is true, but as of this moment, the hope we had garnered is waning. I shared with our men not long ago that we must be glad for the French but move and plan as if we are in this alone. This increases our preparedness and decreases our disappointment. But, like our men, I am still disappointed if all that we have had was a "potential" ally.

When I think of the Hand of Providence, it is interesting. This battle was engaged against the enemy early on in New York. Now, two years later, here we are again in New York. What will be the effect? I await to see.

Friday, August 21, 1778 — Camp near White Plains, New York

General Greene informs me differences are brewing between our Continental troops and those few French troops who have joined us. I am imploring General Greene to do all he can to pacify this. We need to foster a harmony with this potential ally.

Rumors of the French fleet's activity reach this head frequently. Major Howell of Black Point reports that he saw the British fleet sail out of the Hook to sea. Soon after, severe cannonades were heard on the ocean. My hope is that the French have exacted some damage to the British fleet. At this moment, there is no news.

Tuesday, August 25, 1778 — Camp near White Plains, New York

While at Valley Forge, I sent a request for gold specie as this was more acceptable than paper money. Congress has not responded. I am sending a private letter to the President of Congress to find if they have delayed an answer or chosen to refuse without notifying me. I will accept either answer but hope they will answer positively and soon. We are in want of intelligence that can only be gained by specie. I need to know what the enemy is doing. At this moment, I have no means without some reward.

In the meantime, I am sending different persons into the city of New York who do not know each other. I have asked them to gather intelligence and report back to me. What this group finds should provide some general ideas as to the enemy's position, provision, number, and intentions. I am also requesting Major Clough to send someone, without paper, into the city on some design of personal business to ascertain intelligence for us. He is to provide this person with money to make some purchases of personal wares, thereby removing any detection of his true aim.

The activity in New York makes me even more desirous of information. The British are embarking cannon and other matters. One hundred and forty transports have come down to the Hook. They may be preparing to engage this army or to move the war to another location. Perhaps their desire is to change the seat of war to the eastward to deal with us and the French fleet together. At this point, I have no firm idea.

Wednesday, August 26, 1778 — Camp near White Plains, New York

General Sullivan reports a reverse of prospects regarding the French fleet. Lord Howe does seem to be moving toward the relief of Newport. We are in hopes the French fleet is apprised of this and will respond accordingly. Should that not be the case, I am instructing General Sullivan to determine the propriety of remaining in Rhode Island. If he does move out, he needs to keep his troops together as we may soon need them eastward. If the enemy is moving in that direction, General Sullivan will be able to discourage their plans. Part of this army will join him at first word of any action in that quarter.

Not knowing what the French fleet is doing, it is best we put the best face on the situation. We should offer the opinion that they have sailed for Boston for repairs from the storm. This will reduce the discontent of our men or any prejudice that may ensue. I am asking Major Heath to do the same. If we let the French fleet be criticized, the public will lose confidence in this alliance, the disaffected will be contented in their opinion, and any volunteers will be discouraged. It will also cause States to hesitate in rendering supplies. We must make the most of our misfortunes.

Tuesday, September 1, 1778 — Camp near White Plains, New York

I am greatly troubled at the divisiveness that has arisen between the officers under General Sullivan and the men of the French fleet under Count D'Estaing. The last thing we need is trouble amongst our allies. Nothing would embolden our enemy more and make us a laughingstock in their quarters. I know our men are upset that the French fleet left them in Rhode Island without explanation. I know nearly six thousand of our men were placed in jeopardy with the approaching British fleet and transports. And I know they are exasperated at the perceived hesitancy of the French to engage the enemy and disembark their troops. But the French fleet has brought hope to the United States. It has brought fear to the British empire.

To make matters worse, our own officers signed a protest and had it delivered to the Count blasting him for removing his fleet from harm's way. A prejudice already exists between this country and theirs. Not that long ago, our people fought on the British side against them. All that has changed. Count D'Estaing assures me that the damage from the storm prevented his naval force from taking on the enemy. The Marquis, who was the lone officer not to sign the protest letter, assures me of the Count's sincerity. The Marquis states a prejudice exists in our army toward the French volunteers who have joined our cause. The Marquis says he has experienced that same lack of trust toward himself. I must remedy this at once.

I am writing General Sullivan of the detriment he and his men are doing our alliance. First impressions last. That protest letter was a terrible first impression. He must know that the French are a people old in war, that they are strict in military etiquette, and that they are willing to take fire when others shrink from it. This misunderstanding of the Count's actions and the letter that followed must be squelched. We cannot have the public or the whole of our army aware of the rift. I am writing General Greene also to assist in this matter. The Count sailing from Newport to Boston for repairs brings question as to what is really damaged. I fear the greater harm is to our alliance because of dissensions, feuds, and jealousies. I need Greene to bring reconciliation. I have confidence he will.

I am writing the Marquis with my personal apologies. I hope he will overlook the letter of those who do not think or consider the consequences of their uneducated ramblings. I will let him know that what was written was highly impolite. Yes, hopes were disappointed. That is understandable. He must understand that the response of our officers toward the French fleet would have been even greater expressed had our own fleet disappointed. What the French and the Marquis must understand is that we are a free people in a republican form of government. Each person is free to speak their mind regardless of who it may hurt. These freedoms often bring positive results, but sometimes they bring negative ones too. He must understand it is the nature of man to be displeased when hopes are disappointed. This is true of the Americans, of the French, of the British, of the Canadians, and of people from every corner of the world. I need the Marquis to help heal this injury. He is looked up to by this Nation, by this army, by this Commander-in-Chief. He is admired by his own people as an officer who has bravely fought in our conflict. The Count sees him as a friend. He is the one who can bridge this gap and move our alliance forward against a mutual enemy. This is my request to him. Sometimes I flatter myself to think that I am the only one who holds this cause together with all its pieces, that if I cease from this position, the freedom of our Nation and our friends will collapse. At times, it is evident this is the case. For such a time as this I have been called. I realize too, in the words of Mordecai to Esther, if I fail, God will raise someone else to carry out His Will.

Wednesday, September 2, 1778 — Camp near White Plains, New York

I need to reach out to the Count, but how? If I address the letter, I may be giving him (one I do not personally know) some hint that I am upset with him too. If I ignore the letter, it will seem that I do not know what my own men are doing — right or wrong. I am going to just offer my condolence for the damage the storm made to his fleet. This will give credibility to his reasonings. I will acknowledge with regret the insults that my men have inflicted upon him. And I will offer him help in repairs. I will take special care to get him the supplies his men need, even at the expense of my own. I also need to keep him apprised of the hardships I face as Commander-in-Chief so that he can know we are metaphorically in the same boat.

Friday, September 4, 1778 — Camp near White Plains, New York

General Greene brings me good news. A few of our men encountered a British expedition group by surprise. With great courage, they rallied against this contingent of the enemy. They fought valiantly. Colonel Laurens, with little men or notice, was especially effective. One Frenchman, Monsieur Tousard, lost his arm in the struggle and his horse, but fought back and escaped the enemy's grasp.

Six o'clock p.m., I am encouraged by a letter from General Sullivan — a reconciliation has taken place between he and the Count. This is an answer to prayer.

Saturday, September 5, 1778 — Camp near White Plains, New York

Sometimes help offered becomes a hindrance instead. Gouverneur Morris has offered a half-bounty in silver to induce recruits to join this army. This is a sacrifice for sure, but it will bring an obstacle that may never be overcome. To offer silver or gold to recruits causes those who are serving for devalued paper currency to demand the same. If they are not given hard currency, then many will desert. This Nation has no means to generate or supply that amount of gold or silver. Rather than help, this move can hurt our efforts or even dissolve our army. Paper currency must be the only object of reward offered to anyone at any time. It will serve to build up confidence in our currency rather than take away all value.

Friday, September 11, 1778 — Camp near White Plains, New York

There is interest in invading Canada. Some believe it will reduce the enemy's hold on this continent. Others believe it will distract the enemy and divide their force. More conservatively, it could reduce the enemy's supplies and reinforcements. I do not believe this is tenable, but I will inquire through Brigadier-General Bayley to see what their feelings are toward our cause, what armies have they available, how active have they been in opposing the United States in our quest for freedom, and would Canada care to unite with the Independent States of America? I would like to discern their opinion of American politics and more so American clergy. As this Nation seeks to stand under God with the freedom to worship Him and create a nation in His image, that spirit and His Aid are the overriding factors which will determine our success or failure. If the Canadians have a heart for Him, then we have more of a basis on which to unite.

Count D'Estaing has written to reaffirm his support for our cause. Additionally, he expresses his deep disappointment in not being of more assistance. I am writing him back to reassure him that our luster as leaders is more determined by our hardships that are overcome than our victories that are won. I sure hope that to be the case for me. I am assuring him that while his fleet is in Boston, the enemy will set their sights on destroying that fleet which will greatly reduce our chances of success in this war.

The Count must also know that as his fleet is in repair, I am torn on what to do. The enemy can navigate up and down our waters with purpose or in feint. Because we do not know their intentions, if we march to where we believe they will attack, they can turn back and take an important and undefended point. If we march to where they are going, we may be lured into a trap as their ground and naval forces pinch us in a place where retreat is unavailable. As a result, I must do all I can to secure the North river and have this army spread along the road that leads to Boston in case we must move in that direction to protect the French fleet.

Saturday, September 12, 1778 — Camp near White Plains, New York

General Grey of the enemy has again burned many houses in Bedford. Now he has embarked to hover around the coast. Lord Howe seems to be heading to Newport. I am apprehensive all of this is a distraction, and the true focus of the British is on that French fleet in Boston. I am alerting General Sullivan of this. He is to inform me if he sees movement of the British from his quarter in Rhode Island toward this head. With his word, we move.

Still more inquiries are coming in of invading Canada. I am more convinced today than ever that such an expedition would be foolish. We would need to equip the soldiery for the cold and have provisions laid up before. We would need familiarity with that area which we do not have. Another objection would be for our men. They understand fighting on this soil for it is our land and our cause. Canada would seem more of a conquest or a fight for another nation perhaps cool or warm to independence. All the while, such an endeavor would bring additional neglect to our own families and property. I will continue to dissuade Congress with my opinion. I will list the complexities to consider. We are barely supporting our army locally. How can we expect this Nation to support us at a distance?

Wednesday, September 23, 1778 — Fredericksburg

My brother John Augustine writes that he is a granddad again. I am so happy for him. I wish he would have conveyed if the child were a boy or a girl. I suppose he is too excited to notice. Through the newspapers, he is remotely aware of what we are facing. He wants to know what has come of the court-martial of General Lee. I too wish to know whether it has met Congress's approbation or disapprobation. As to his question of the British's next move, he and I are both left to guess. All I can do is prepare. Intelligence to this head would be appreciated. To see that life goes on for my family — weddings, births, business, and pleasures — is pleasing to me. I wish I were part of that. I remind myself that this is why I am fighting.

Friday, September 25, 1778 — Fredericksburg

Speaking of family, the Marquis de Lafayette is more of a son to me than any I have ever called dear. His letter today speaks of his efforts to reconcile the division between the American line and the French. I am thankful that God has given us an intermediary between us and them. He has requested a picture of me. I am flattered, but to give him one seems to be for my vanity and not for his gratification. I do not understand why he or any man would hold me in such regard.

He still voices an entreaty for a move into Canada. I am going to lay out my reasons against it but will encourage him to let Congress know his thoughts. I dare not censor him on this issue. May the right decision be made.

Saturday, October 3, 1778 — Fishkill, New York

Congress desires to secure Charleston should the enemy proceed in that direction. I am sending General Lincoln to take command in that neighborhood.

I have moved my men to Fishkill until the enemy's intentions in the Jerseys are decided. I have detached another brigade toward New York along with Pulaski's corps and militia. Lord Stirling will take command of the whole. I have sent General Putnam to secure West Point.

Colonel Baylor was taken by surprise by the enemy who were out foraging near the Hackensack river. He escaped but lost about fifty men and seven horses. The brutality of the enemy executed upon our men is in keeping with their evil bent. Colonel Butler was able to gain some revenge by catching up with some Yagers near Tarrytown. He killed ten and took eighteen prisoners.

Rumors flow as to the direction and intent of the enemy. They brag of having taken over several towns, but they have yet to take this army or our arms. Until they do that, they really have not succeeded.

Sunday, October 4, 1778 — Fishkill, New York

Lord Carlisle of the British has brought numerous insults against France and her men serving on this side. The Marquis has taken exception. He has challenged Carlisle to a duel. He has written for my permission to take a leave to follow through. I cannot let him give in to his passions nor to his offense at insults. In the same way, I must do all I can as his general (and an adopted father as he calls me) to discourage such actions. He may bring chivalry in the attempt but cost this Nation at his loss. He must see there are bigger things for which to die than some mere insult. If a duel could pacify things, I could have easily challenged Lord North to one. That would not have comforted this Nation for the offenses of the British, nor ended British hostilities. I do not want the Marquis exposed. I will not refuse his request nor approve it.

Gouverneur Morris poses three questions to me in his latest letter — Can the British prosecute the war? Do they mean to stay on this continent? Should we raise barriers to their departure? He posed the questions, but then gave his answers. He believes the British cannot continue in this war. He believes the enemy will stay on this continent. And he thinks no impediments should be placed to prevent their departure. I love a well-thought-out discussion, but this is not one well thought-out. The real question should be, can our Nation continue to prosecute this war. The answer is no. We cannot while we lack supplies and men to fight it. The enemy I believe knows this and for this reason they stay. This Nation cannot stay in this war also because our currency has no value. Our citizens extort our men for arms, horses, and food we desperately need. Congress continues to forestall decisions regarding rank-and-pay. If we cannot continue in this war, then we will fall slave to the British. Then, by no means, are they going to leave this continent.

We need God to intervene. With the state of the French fleet, we need the Spaniards to intervene too. The British navy, I believe, is too strong for this French fleet. Gouverneur Morris needs to consider the questions laid bare by our army's needs. By no means should he hide his answers under a bushel. All that we do in the days to follow depend upon Congress and our citizens to resolve and act.

Monday, October 5, 1778 — Fishkill, New York

I had written Edward Rutledge several months back to find how things were in his quarter. He has never answered. Now that Charleston seems to be a potential target, I have sent General Lincoln in that direction to take command. I need Rutledge to answer. I need him to assist Lincoln. Congress is making all exertions for the defense of South Carolina.

Tuesday, October 6, 1778 — Fishkill, New York

The Marquis is on his way to Congress to gain a furlough for the duel that he demands for his nation's honor. I am asking Congress to help discourage him. I am also writing Count D'Estaing to do the same. This young man is precious to our contest, an intermediary between our two nations, and he has caught my tender regard as well.

Wednesday, October 7, 1778 — Fishkill, New York

I still believe the enemy is moving toward Boston with the object of the French fleet. I am, however, taking measures to defend the Highland passes and to interrupt the British navigation of the North river. We cannot extend our entire army to Boston and leave strategic points vulnerable. This would tempt the enemy to reverse their direction to our chagrin. I am having the roads to Boston cleared and repaired so that this army can move quickly should the need arise.

Saturday, October 10, 1778 — Headquarters near Fredericksburg

The Count informs me the enemy may think little of moving toward Boston this late in the year, especially attempting to go round Cape Cod. With this stated, it does appear the British are leaving New York at this moment. We are unsure of their destination if it is not Boston. It could be south. It could be east. I ordered two brigades to leave Danbury and head for Hartford. I am, on this intelligence, sending a third. I am alerting General Heath.

Wednesday, October 14, 1778 — Headquarters near Fredericksburg

I have had the misfortune to hear that the Raleigh frigate has become a prize for two British ships after a long resilient fight. Seeing no way out, Captain Barry ran the Raleigh aground, got his crew ashore, and set the frigate afire. His attempt was defeated by the perfidy of one of his crew who stayed on board and extinguished the fire.

Thursday, October 15, 1778 — Headquarters near Fredericksburg

Brigadier-General Lewis has been placed by the Board to be commissioner of Fort Pit. The desire is to make peace with the Indians in that quarter who have sided with the Tories. General McIntosh requested this assistance. He is greatly frustrated by the attacks he deals with daily from that side. No one appreciates more fully the frustration General McIntosh feels then me. I am convinced Providence tries the patience, fortitude, and virtue of men by difficulties of many sorts. We must hold firm. To use an odd phrase, we must shape our coat by the cloth we have. Or in other words, if we cannot do as we wish, we must do what we can.

The enemy seeks a vigorous campaign if I correctly interpret their actions. I believe their greatest hope is that we will defeat ourselves or, in frustration, resign our freedoms for the want of peace. We must not give in. I would love to send men to assist General McIntosh, but feeling the enemy may act upon Boston, or Rhode Island, or turn on this army where we now sit, I am unable to relinquish one man. I would hope the frontiers of Virginia, Maryland, and Pennsylvania can raise up men for their own defense. If a militia is needed, it should be formed, but only when an attack is imminent. I have found they will not stay long if danger is not immediate.

I am writing General Lewis to also inquire of my lands in that quadrant. I know they are unprotected. I hope they have been patented. I would hate to lose all my investments when I have not time to give them attention.

Monday, October 19, 1778 — Headquarters near Fredericksburg

I am asking General Heath to move our men toward Charlottesville, Virginia, as they are unable to be supplied where they now reside.

Thursday, October 22, 1778 — Headquarters near Fredericksburg

The enemy has left Sandy Hook with one hundred and fifty sailing. I still believe they are moving toward Boston. If I knew how many men they left in New York, I could more easily ascertain their intentions.

Seditious papers are being circulated by the enemy to excite dissentions and mislead our people. I do all I can to suppress these, but they go through so many avenues that it is virtually impossible to stop them. At this present, these seditious papers threaten our people with more predatory behavior and flagrant destruction. This should be nothing new to our ears. They have burned homes. They have taken clothes right off people's backs. I do not see this as a furtherance of measures but rather an admission of what they have already done.

Sunday, October 25, 1778 — Headquarters near Fredericksburg

Count D'Estaing has sent a comforting letter that he has given his disapprobation to the Marquis's wish for a duel. I am heartened by his influential persuasion as one of the Marquis's own countrymen. I have looked for some common ground of concern with the Count. Perhaps Providence has worked that out in our mutual care for the Marquis, our intermediary. I cannot help but think how in a higher sense, God has sought an alliance with man. Because we were at odds, He sent His Intermediary in His Son, our precious Savior, to bridge our gap. And, in that concern for Jesus, we would respond in a way favorable to His honor. This pleases the Father God in that He sees our care for His Son. Thus, we are brought together. We are seeking to care for the son of France, the Marquis. The Count, I believe, finds this favorable.

Monday, October 26, 1778 — Headquarters near Fredericksburg

Now it is reported that the ships that sailed from New York did not have many of their troops but rather invalids and officers recalled to Britain. With that stated, what can we anticipate from the enemy at-hand?

I was honored to receive a letter from Lieutenant-Colonel Aaron Burr who is seeking to rehabilitate from an injury he sustained in battle. He requests that his pay be suspended until he is back in service. This is a grand gesture but would be unjust. The service to his nation brought injury in the first place. He should be compensated as he recovers his health and reenters the fray.

Tuesday, October 27, 1778 — Headquarters near Fredericksburg

Major-General Scott reports some officers wish to resign because they were not assigned to the corps for which they belong. Any who leaves or resigns for this reason will be punished to the full extent a court-martial will allow. Officers who believe they should serve when and where they please should not be in this army. At the present need, we must bear with those unworthy to command. I believe they make this complaint for they think other corps are wintering in more favorable locations. They need to know that no corps and no man is wintering anywhere while danger is present.

Count D'Estaing reports that his repairs are near completion. He will soon be upon the water to fight for our common cause. How I pray this will be the case. I am sharing with him the hope that Spain will soon join this battle to reduce the burden and exposure of the French fleet.

Saturday, October 31, 1778 — Headquarters near Fredericksburg

The enemy has not made a move. I am writing the Count to let him know I still believe Lord Byron may make a move into Boston. We are doing all we can to fortify that town for his defense. We need to secure the other seaport towns as well.

Friday, November 6, 1778 — Headquarters near Fredericksburg

In our march, Major-General Phillips has written, with the utmost politeness, his concern for the health of the troops. I am glad to see a general care for his men and to carry that care to the point of being an advocate for them. I believe generals like this can count on their troops performing well in battle because the men know their commanders have their best in mind. I am assuring him I will endeavor to confine the march's inconveniences to such as are unavoidable. I am also asking the commissary and quartermaster-general to move throughout the army to assure that needs are being met.

Saturday, November 14, 1778 — Headquarters near Fredericksburg

Congress is pressing me to make an effort into Canada to move the British out. They want me to form a junction with them either as allies or to combine with them as one Nation on this continent. The Marquis has championed this opinion and brought Congress to favor this expedition. (I almost fear he clothed this proposition to conceal its real intent. I am ashamed to even note this, but times like this cause me to question not just a friend, but sometimes all friends). I have voiced with the Marquis and Congress the obstacles regarding such a move — the state of our provisions, the condition of our troops, the difficulty of the cold, the straining of our communication, the lack of our naval power, and more. The number one objection, however, rolling in my mind is the fact that the French are for it. As much as I honor the Marquis, he is French. I wonder if this was an idea placed in his head by his native country and innocently accepted under the pretense that it is for the good of the United States. We are grateful for our allies. We wish for more, but we must always keep an eye open for those who wish to help us too eagerly.

France would benefit greatly from having control of Canada. They are the best fishermen. They have a natural quantity of resources. They have ports that would be beneficial. Ample commerce is to be gained from the Canadians and the Indian nations in that area. Beyond that, even though they are our allies, they are jaded with the flaws of humanity. Any government who sees the benefits will be tempted to extend from our good to their own profit and power. Canada could also increase security for the islands now in French control. It would not be long before the French would try to subject us to their rule. They would be in a prime position geographically, militarily, and with naval supremacy to make our obedience sure. We would be trading in one master, the British, for another master, the French.

At the present, no one wants to consider our ally in such light. But we cannot let the urgency of the present jeopardize the freedoms of the future. No nation can be trusted beyond its bound of personal interest. I hope I am mistaken. My experience makes me more vigilant.

Monday, November 16, 1778 — Headquarters near Fredericksburg

I am working on a plan to winter our troops. Last winter, the whole of our army was kept at Valley Forge, aside from those under General Gates and a few protected posts. Provisions for such a large group were inadequate. We almost lost an army to starvation and exposure to the weather without clothing or blankets. Though we are stronger together, the complexity of outfitting such a group is too difficult. I must be able to devise a way to put troops closer to provisions in various areas. Having them separated extends the circle for each to forage. Because we have had little engagement this year, I am afforded the luxury of time to plan better.

No sooner do I say lack of activity, I have received notice that an attack occurred at Cherry Valley on Colonel Allen's regiment. Our frontier is continually harassed by banditti. I am sending General Clinton with his two remaining regiments to that quarter near Albany. I am asking him to confer with General Schuyler to see if some offensive operation is practical. If not, I am desirous that he stations troops in areas more apt to be attacked. Count Pulaski is at Cole's Fort near Minisink with his legion of two hundred and fifty horse and foot. I want that augmented by another two hundred and fifty or so. Colonel Courtland and his men are strategically posted at the present between Minisink and Rochester.

Friday, November 20, 1778 — Headquarters near Fredericksburg

I am against an expedition into Canada, but I must prepare for it if Congress so orders. I am writing General Schuyler to gather advice on the best route to enter Canada. The most recommended route is through Lake Champlain. I do not believe this is feasible as the British have control of that lake with their naval strength. Schuyler envisions building two ships there on the Lake in which to confront the enemy. To build two ships without the enemy's knowledge is impossible. I dare not think they would let the project get far along before they would act to destroy them. Another option is to move men by way of Coos. It would not take much for the enemy to dispatch men to block that route. I feel the best way to invade Canada and confront the enemy there would be by Lake Ontario. We could make motions on Lake Champlain. We could even do some post work along the Coos to distract them while making preparations and moving vessels upon Lake Ontario. Come Spring, the ruse would be discovered, but by then, we may have enough strength to move forward. All this said, I believe none of the options are worth pursuing because success of such is improbable. I have voiced my objections and concerns. I am now praying that Congress will receive wisdom. I am asking General Schuyler on his way to Philadelphia to meet with Congress, to stop by New York. I would like him to confer with Governor Clinton who should be in Albany in a few days. I believe the Governor has better insights.

Monday, November 23, 1778 — Headquarters near Fredericksburg

Major Whiting and Mr. Clyde have written to say that, though we did experience losses at Cherry Valley, they were less than we had reason to apprehend. Now it is also confirmed that the fort manned by Colonel Allen was not attacked as first thought. With attacks in many quadrants, Congress requests that I dispatch troops to each place of concern. To do so would greatly weaken this army. Should a concerted enemy attack be discovered, it would make it more difficult to discipline and harder to rally our men. We can only do as much as we can. Militia should be the first line of defense in the frontier areas.

Tuesday, November 24, 1778 — Headquarters near Fredericksburg

Count Pulaski has sent me a return to consider where he and his men would be best-situated to protect the frontier. He is now located at Rosencrantz, which is a good location as is Cole's Fort. Subsistence may be hard to find. I am authorizing him to stay in that vicinity but to take the liberty of moving where he believes things would be best adapted for accommodating his corps.

Count Pulaski has requested to return to his country. It is a frequent refrain for which I struggle. Good officers in our army have shown themselves zealous, active, and effective. How I long for these men to stay. I know they have personal matters to attend. I too have reasons to leave. I cannot bear the thought of surrendering my post for personal care when so much is at stake. With this written, I have told him that once things are in order, he may go to Philadelphia to gain the approval of Congress. I will send Brigadier-General Hand to take over that command.

Friday, November 27, 1778 — Headquarters near Fredericksburg

To the issue of winter cantonment for this army. I have settled on a plan I believe will have our men scattered enough to provide but gathered enough to respond. I am sending my plan to Congress. Nine brigades will be situated along the North river. Of that group, the North Carolina brigade will be stationed near Smith's Cove to protect the pass and secure West Point. The Jersey brigade will be at

Elizabethtown to cover the lower part of Jersey. The other seven which are comprised by Virginia, Maryland, Delaware, and Pennsylvania troops will be encamped at Middlebrook. Three Massachusetts brigades will be stationed for the defense of the Highlands. One will be stationed at West Point. Two will be garrisoned at Fishkill and the Continental Village. The remaining three brigades (those of New Hampshire, Connecticut, and Hazen's regiment) will be posted in the vicinity of Danbury. This will allow for protection of the country lying along the Sound. I am parking the artillery at Pluckemin. I am placing the cavalry as follows: Bland's regiment at Winchester in Virginia, Baylor's at Frederic in Maryland, Moylan's at Lancaster, and Sheldon's at Durham in Connecticut. Lee's corps will be in Jersey. They will act as an advance post. I am leaving Albany Clinton's brigade, Pulaski's corps, and some detached regiments and corps. Command will be as follows: General Putnam at Danbury, General McDougal at the Highlands, and I am headed to Middlebrook.

This varies from what was done last winter. Much has been learned from Valley Forge. Such suffering I wish never to see repeated. Providence worked it for our good last winter according to His Purpose. He has also instilled wisdom to do a different thing this winter. The troops are hurriedly hutting as snow is falling. I am writing Mr. Reed personally, in addition to my letter to Congress. I need his help in initiating actions, which will raise the value of our currency and to help reduce the exorbitant prices that profiteers are placing on this army. I am also soliciting his prayers.

Saturday, December 5, 1778

I was on the way to Middlebrook when I received word that the British with a large fleet had secretly sailed near King's Ferry and disembarked. I have turned the men around. We are heading in that direction to address the enemy's intentions. Intelligence from a source who has never let me down reports they are planning a move on Monmouth to forage in that area.

Monday, December 7, 1778 — Paramus, New Jersey

I am asking Governor Livingston to have the militia remove all stores and live-stock from their access. I am also taking the extra step to ask him to send men to the homes of those disaffected. They have insight to the enemy's designs and often store up supplies for the enemy's usage. They do it under the guise of saving things for their families for the approaching winter, just to turn around and stock the British.

Wednesday, December 9, 1778

The enemy has sailed back to New York. I am not sure what their purpose was, but I am now headed back with our men to Middlebrook.

Saturday, December 12, 1778 — Middlebrook, New Jersey

Joseph Reed has now been chosen as the President of the Pennsylvania govern-ment. I am glad this has transpired. I am writing him to keep him apprised of developments on this end. I have let him know of the enemy's move toward King's Ferry. I am at a loss as to why, at this late in the season, the enemy would make such a move. The only logical answer is they thought it possible to gain the High-land pass. When they found it well-fortified, they resigned that aspiration. The negative effects of this activity were limited to a few burned log houses. The greater damage was that it slowed our Maryland, Virginia, and Pennsylvania troops four days from hutting.

With Mr. Reed in charge, I pray he will bring punishment to the murderers of our cause — the monopolizers, forestallers, and engrossers. I would to God that some of the worst would be hung on gallows five times the height of Haman's. Along with this irritant, General Lee continues to be a burr of his own. He has published an article in the newspaper telling of how he has been mistreated and that the facts of his case have been misreported by some evil design of this command. I would cherish the opportunity to refute him in the same papers. I have too much to do with this army for me to waste time defending my character. With this said, thousands will not believe him. Tens of thousands may who are unfamiliar with the facts. The esteem of our people is the one thing that keeps this army together. That respect encourages more to join. I cannot bear the thought of having our citizens misled. If only they could see the presence of a red-coated enemies on our soil. I hasten to think that the greater enemy wears our Continental vestiture. I have always honored General Lee even when he entered a party against me. I have respected his rank. I have consulted with him as an equal. No jealousy has ever been seen in my behavior, yet he continues to accuse otherwise.

I desire nothing more than tranquility on my own land in my own home with my own family. Many temptations come to draw me in that direction. But I know that what lies between me and that condition are hostilities that must be addressed. To lay in leisure and let others fight is easy, but what satisfaction can that be? Beyond this, no guarantee exists that allowing others to fight for us will bring a favorable result. We must all fight. We must all sacrifice. We must be one. The enemy is aware that we are not. This may be what precludes them from leaving.

Sunday, December 13, 1778 — Middlebrook, New Jersey

Congress has requested I write our ministers in France of the desire to bring the emancipation of Canada from the clutches of the British. They wish that I describe it in a way that will cause France to join us in this endeavor. My desire is to comply strictly with the wishes of Congress, but when I believe such a measure is wholly wrong and doomed for defeat, I must at least let them know with all frankness. They have allowed me this in the past. This gives me the freedom again respectfully to object. If they require it still, I request the freedom to enunciate the difficulties that such an activity portends. My requirement, should they demand my influence, is that they give explicit instructions on how to write such a letter. Even as I hold reservations in proceeding, I am preparing for an expedition against Niagara upon their order. We are having stores placed in Albany. I am alerting General Schuyler to give us the best insights on how to succeed.

General Benedict Arnold writes that some differences exist between he and the Board of War. I am unaware of those, but the Board has requested troops in Philadelphia and Trenton further to secure those locations. I am sending Colonel Hogan's North Carlina regiment to assist. This is all I can spare.

Wednesday, December 16, 1778 — Middlebrook, New Jersey

Sir Henry Clinton has denied the request for the exchange of prisoners upon our terms which are fair and equitable. As a result, no exchange will be made at this time.

Mr. Henry Laurens is stepping down as President of Congress. He is being replaced by John Jay. I have enjoyed my relationship with Mr. Laurens. He has been a great help. I am also delighted that Mr. Jay is now holding that seat. I respect him and rejoice in his leadership which I have seen displayed in many facets throughout the years.

Friday, December 18, 1778 — Middlebrook, New Jersey

I am writing in response to Mr. Benjamin Harrison's letter regarding the state of our Nation and its government. He is currently speaker of the house of delegates in Virginia. America has never stood more in need of patriotic, wise, and spirited sons to take the helm of leadership. States should desire and even compel the ablest of men to serve in Congress. This army and this country suffer from the lack of good men in leadership. Many abuses have been produced as a result. How can constitutions be written, laws be enacted, or offices be filled when we lack the men virtuous enough to carry out what is best for this Nation at the yielding to one's own personal benefit? I am grieved that the ablest of men sit in ease and luxury unable to exert the energy and sacrifice to create and sustain a better government. Only honest men must be employed. The enemy rejoices in such inadequate governance. It encourages them to fight on.

Virginia to her credit has raised the number of troops per their quota. The negative is that they have not forwarded those troops to this army. I am asking Mr. Harrison to help rectify that.

I am writing General Schuyler to consider the foray into Canada. He must consider that we will need at least an additional ten thousand men just for this venture with a proportion of artillery men, attendants, and retainers. I want him to draw up the plan and the route so that the impossibility of such an adventure may be clearly seen. Though I will not word it in that way in my letter, I do want the truth to be seen. If I am wrong, let his plan show it. If I am correct, may Congress cease this discussion.

Saturday, December 19, 1778 — Middlebrook, New Jersey

Baron Steuben writes to update me on his plans regarding areas of needed attention. I am glad to see him involved after desiring to leave recently. I am pledging to him my support. I am also emphasizing my high regard and appreciation for him. Not a year ago he came and set this army on a sound military footing. I will be forever grateful.

Tuesday, December 22, 1778

The Marquis is determined to return to his home country because of the prospects of a European war. I am sending a letter to Mr. Benjamin Franklin to be of any assistance that the Marquis may need. He is very dear to me. I wish him success in his home country. He has experienced it in this one.

Wednesday, December 30, 1778 — Philadelphia, Pennsylvania

My dialogue by letter continues with Mr. Benjamin Harrison regarding the deficiencies of our government. We need men in Congress who will not slumber nor sleep, but who will attend to the needs of this Nation and this army. Many now suppose the war is over and we have won. They assume that now all they need is to get their local state-of-affairs in order. Men who think this way have no idea of the reality on this front. Their States may be in a safe position at the present, but America is sinking into irretrievable ruin. Idleness, dissipation, and extravagance are present. The violins are playing. People are dancing while their own infant Rome is burning. Men have come, served, and then retired to their homes. But the trouble is not over, yea it may be worse than ever before. Is this not the time for all good men to come to the aid of their country? I ask the question, where is Mason? Where is Jefferson? Where is Wythe? Where is Nelson? This is not the time to retire. I have not, though I easily could have and turned this thing over to General Gates or General Greene. Our Nation needs all of us. Mr. Harrison needs to know this. He needs to convey this from his position. Our money is losing value. Yet, our needs have not waned. Our currency is buying less and less of what we need. This problem is one of a myriad that must be solved. I cannot do that from this post. I cannot do this alone.

Thursday, December 31, 1778 — Philadelphia, Pennsylvania

General Schuyler has been acquitted of the charge of negligence for not being at Ticonderoga when General St. Clair evacuated it. I would like now for him to retake command in that quarter. I await his decision.

The Year 1779

Monday, January 11, 1779 — Philadelphia, Pennsylvania

I am conferring with a committee of Congress in dealing with our need for a commissary-of-prisoners officer. They are in favor of such a position. For it to be effective, I am writing them to prescribe what I deem as necessary expectations for this post: (1) He should reside at the headquarters of this army. (2) He is to only make exchanges with the approval of Congress, the Board of War, or the Commander-in-Chief. The first two can only be accepted if given in writing. (3) If he plans to enter enemy lines to bring provisions to our men in British custody, he must have the Commander-in-Chief's approval as to what he is taking, when he is going, and the locations in which he seeks to go.

On another matter of protocol, no instructions or orders should be given this army from Congress or the Board of War without going through the Commander-in-Chief. Now that we have dealt with the attempt and failure of Conway and others, I must be more direct of communications. A successful enterprise of our army can only be carried out if there is only one giving orders. I serve Congress. The Board of War gives guidance. Ultimately, I am the one who must give commands. I must be the only one the army looks to for guidance. A free intercourse has occurred between Congress and New York recently. That must be restrained.

I must deal with the hostile acts of the Indians on our citizens in the frontiers. We seek peace with the Indians. We desire their peace to make a way of life for themselves, unencumbered by this Nation. It is the whole reason we recognize each Indian people group as a nation in and of itself, independent of the United States. Recognizing their sovereignty does not give them the right to kill families and destroy homes. I have sent out an expedition under General McIntosh to bring safety back to the frontiers. The expense has been made, but now some in

Congress wish to renounce this work when the results sought have yet to be realized. Our citizens demand something be done. They make calls on this army daily. We must be a protection for them. If we renounce an initiative toward an enemy when it gets difficult, this will encourage our enemies to strike and keep striking, knowing at some point we will give up and surrender to their wishes.

My new strategy against the incessant attacks by the Indians is to move from a defensive posture to an aggressive one. I am ordering General McIntosh and militia to attack the Indians in their home country. So far, they have not seen a personal cost to their heinous acts. The British pay them handsomely. The spoils they gain from their victims push them for more. Taking it to their homes where they live may be the only thing that will make them reconsider.

Saturday, January 16, 1779 — Philadelphia, Pennsylvania

I must communicate to Congress the options for this army and this Nation in the next campaign. A decision needs to be made as to which of the three likely options should be pursued in this year's campaign. Regardless which decision is made, more men will be necessary. Two options are offensive. These will need more men than the last option, which prioritizes a defensive posture. States are offering great bounties to recruit a larger army. I am heartened by the push by the States to meet their quotas. Sadly, their bounties can be excessive and vary by State. This brings jealousies when the men come to this army and, in a lull of activity, discuss what they have received in compensation. It breeds jealousy. On top of this, Congress wants to offer a greater bounty. My preference is for States to cease their bounties altogether. Let the Nation offer one bounty that holds for every State and every soldier so there is no feeling of competition. I would suggest there be one Continental bounty of one hundred and fifty dollars offered for the army. Adequate provisions should be given to the recruiting officers.

The three options that should be considered are as follows. One option is to expel the enemy from their current posts of New York and Rhode Island. This option can be broken into two approaches — attack the enemy at each at the same time or attack the enemy in New York forcing the British to evacuate Rhode Island to reinforce their men in New York. The second option is to attack Canada by way of Niagara while holding our current position in the States with a defensive strategy. This may bring a liberation of Canada. It could garner their assistance, but this has potential to backfire. The third option is fully a defensive posture. We can secure our frontiers with small parties dealing with the Indians and hold up in our current quarters daring the enemy to risk exposure in attacking our strongholds.

The Canada option would require this army to raise an army of twenty-six thousand men. A number that we have never had. From experience, I see little chance of raising one this size. At best, we have stood at about sixteen thousand active troops. That is with recruiting, drafting, and militia. As the value of our dollar decreases and the more men see a way of making a good living away from the army, I fear that gathering men will be more difficult this year. Even if we could raise an army of twenty-six thousand, how would we provide for them? We have not been able to supply the small army we have now. Valley Forge is a good reminder of how inept we are to care for our own. So, the option of attacking Canada is the least likely as I have pointed out over the last few months.

Expelling the enemy from their current posts would be desirable and decisive. This strategy gives a chance to end this war altogether. But, to do this, we would need the extra men. We would need to extend our entire force probably upon New York with the hope that the enemy would move down from Rhode Island. Placing our whole force anywhere exposes all other important points in this Nation. It leaves an open door for the enemy to go from two strongholds to many more.

Of regret, the third option seems to be our safest route. In this posture, we risk no great loss that would discourage support from abroad. We will be able to retrench our expenses and adopt a general sense of economy. Congress can then make move to the relief of public credit. Hopefully, they can restore the value of this Nation's currency. Doing so will also give this Nation time to care for our soldiers. This Nation needs to take steps to make them comfortable while building up their supplies and arms for a stronger engagement beyond this campaign season. In the defensive strategy, this army must be in places where it can easily be subsisted but also at places where the enemy can be restrained.

The defensive plan will have some disadvantages. It will show idleness, which will cause our allies and enemies to think we are weak. The truth is, we are weak. We can never let either know that. Our allies need to know we are in the fight and the fight is winnable. My prayer is that they will then continue in negotiations with our ministers for further aid. Another disadvantage in sitting still is that it will give our men idle time. This always leads to dissension, arguing, and immorality. The last disadvantage to be enumerated is that if this army sits still, the spirit of our neighbors will wane. The disaffected will find more reason to criticize the whole question of liberty.

I have been in Philadelphia since December 24th. I have used this time to acquaint myself with Congress and to answer their questions. I have also enjoyed my time with Mrs. Washington. Duty calls though. I am uncomfortable staying away from our army. The Commander-in-Chief should be with the army, unlike the British command that enjoys the luxuries of the cities while their men settle for lesser things. None suffer like our men. I need to suffer with them.

Monday, January 18, 1779 — Philadelphia, Pennsylvania

General Schuyler, after being exonerated from his charges, informs me he would like to return to private life. He is declining my offer to resume his command. I sometimes feel I will be the last one to blow out the candle and lock the doors. I pray he reconsiders.

Wednesday, January 20, 1779 — Philadelphia, Pennsylvania

The defensive strategy has not even been settled upon and I am already seeing the negative effects of an idle army. The officers are complaining. They are offering their resignations if rank, pay, and pensions go unsettled. When we were at Valley Forge and the enemy was near, survival was all they thought about. When the French sent their fleet and when we gave a strong showing at Monmouth, the officers were contented knowing that the war could be near its end. Now that we are held up in our places and the enemy is settled into their comfortable quarters for the unforeseeable future, discontentment turns to realization. Many see their once-fellow officers in private life making a profit and doing very well financially. These are with their families, enjoying the benefits of freedom when freedom has not yet been secured. This just causes those who have remained to want the same for themselves and their families. The yearning is natural, but one that cannot be sustained with this war's outcome in question. The longer we wait to engage in battle, the officers will use leisure to dwell on their hardships and voice their discontent.

I must revive the question of half-pay and pensionary benefits for our officers with Congress. Our representatives may not see it, but the public good will only be promoted if we settle this issue. This will induce our officers to remain to war's end. I am of the mind that a seven-year half-pay is good, but a lifetime half-pay would be infinitely better. Congress worries about the expense. The likelihood of these soldiers living past seven years after the war is minimum. They know this. But, seven years is not near as tasteful to the mind as lifetime. Besides, every husband and father worries about the care of their wives and children when they are gone. They do not want them to lose what they gained in the war — their homes and land. More than that, a man does not want to think he is leaving his widow and children in want. Carrying this pension to their survivors brings a special motivation. It brings gratification. Not only will they have secured the freedom of America, but their sacrifice will benefit their descendants.

Friday, January 22, 1779 — Philadelphia, Pennsylvania

This morning, I have requested permission to leave Philadelphia and return to the army.

Congress has approved my request. I am leaving Monday for Middlebrook. My time here has been constructive, but next to being at Mount Vernon, being with the men is my most satisfying abode.

Monday, February 8, 1779 — Middlebrook, New Jersey

So glad to be back in the mix of things. I am dispatching Count Pulaski and his legion to move from Minisink to Lancaster. He and Colonel Armand are to complete their corps of infantry. Because they are unaffiliated with any State, they need Congress to give them written authority to recruit in any State. Once their corps is filled, I am sending he and his men to South Carolina under the command of Major-General Lincoln. We are hurriedly sending other men to South Carolina as this may be the object of the enemy's next action. The one thing I need our officers to guard against is the destruction of property of the citizens as they march. They are to move with expedition, but to be mindful of the health of their men and horses, halting when necessary.

Friday, February 12, 1779 — Middlebrook, New Jersey

There are women who are gaining passes to go to New York under the pretense of seeing friends. What they are actually doing is buying goods in New York so they can return to their neighborhoods and sell them at a tidy profit. The State of Jersey has caught some of these. Jersey confiscated their property which by law, they are right to do. I would rather these passes be given out with more caution. Seizing property of individuals by any of our State governments is disagreeable at best. I am asking Mr. Reed to inquire thoroughly any request for passes. He is then to give such only when little chance exists of ulterior motives. These should then be cautioned as to any unlawful conduct. This will help on the front end. Should a person be found in violation, not only should their property be taken, but they should face punishment themselves to deter others.

Wednesday, February 17, 1779 — Middlebrook, New Jersey

I have neglected sending a letter of thanks to Mr. Laurens for letting me and Mrs. Washington stay with him in Philadelphia. I must extend my gratitude. I also need to inquire of reports that we may soon see Spain enter this contest with us and extend a loan of thirteen million dollars.

The enemy is busy on Staten Island. I am ignorant as to their designs. I am also impatient that I have heard nothing from Georgia regarding enemy activity in the south.

Friday, February 19, 1779 — Middlebrook, New Jersey

The enemy made an attack from Staten Island at Elizabethtown earlier today. I immediately put in motion General Smallwood with the Maryland division and General St. Clair with the Pennsylvania division to form a junction at Scotch

Plains. They are to reinforce General Maxwell. I was anxious to see what the enemy had planned next. However, as soon as our men were near, the enemy retreated and sailed back to Staten Island. I do not know what to make of their action except either to forage or to see what our strength and reaction would be.

General Conway's poor leadership as quartermaster-general has come under the review of Congress. They wish a military decision upon his punishment. This is not amenable to a military tribunal as he has resigned from the military. I do take consolation that God will deal with our enemies, that everything done in the dark will be brought into the light. I have seen this now on several occasions. I am a Commander-in-Chief who seeks to do all to honor the Author of our liberties and to win the trust of my fellowmen. I have received great criticism and attacks in this journey, but every time, I have found Providence stands as my guard.

Friday, February 26, 1779 — Middlebrook, New Jersey

Baron Steuben has submitted his treatise on military tactics for my review. He has written it predominantly in his language. It is beyond understanding to the Continental comprehension. He must get someone who is familiar with our language to write it with proper diction in the English language. This must be done without deviating from the military science he so aptly knows.

Sunday, February 28, 1779 — Middlebrook, New Jersey

The Board of War has received strong complaints as to an uneasy and disordinate spirit among the prisoners at Charlottesville. I am sending Colonel Bland to take command. He is to restore order and bring sensibility to the officers there.

Monday, March 1, 1779 — Middlebrook, New Jersey

The rumors of war in Europe, along with the prospect of the entrance of Spain, would attend valuable consequences if only we could know they are authentic. Our currency would gain value. Our recruiting would be enhanced. We would gain a certain spring to our affairs in general. For now, we do our part. Naturally, we hope for more assistance.

Wednesday, March 3, 1779 — Middlebrook, New Jersey

Several inhabitants and a few civil officers of the Jerseys are lodging complaints of ill-treatment against a number of our officers. Their list includes Major Call and Mr. Heath who are in Virginia wintering, and Captain Van Heer and Mr. Skinner who are with me here in Middlebrook. Governor Livingston has brought this to my attention. He suggests some sort of compromise would prevent further trouble. I would rather the charges be fully investigated. If our officers are found guilty, they should be dealt with according to civil or military law. If they are innocent, I propose they should be acquitted. The question as to their character should be removed.

I do believe, and I will honestly share this with Governor Livingston, most disputes between inhabitants of the States and our officers revolve around the former entering our camps selling liquor and taking clothes, provisions, and accoutrements as pay. Our officers are instructed to prohibit such and punish any violators. This brings contention. I am advising this governor and all others to pass some laws making such transactions illegal. This would relieve our officers and army of many destructive consequences. Just as Nehemiah had to ban the sellers on the Sabbath to Jerusalem with a stern warning and harsh punishments, our States must do the same to protect the integrity of this army and prevent disputes.

Thursday, March 4, 1779 — Middlebrook, New Jersey

Because of Indian attacks on our frontiers, an offensive operation has been in design. Sixteen brigades will be dispatched. Two regiments will be incorporated into this plan under Malcom and Spencer. Two more will join under Webb and Sherburne.

Our move must be carried in secret as long as possible. Otherwise, the Indians may attack us before we are ready, or gather reinforcements from the Tories, Canada, and the British. They may evacuate into the forests to avoid detection until the heat has dissipated. This army is facing a formidable enemy in the British. I am asking the governors to raise up their inhabitants and militia to join this effort since this action is for the safety and benefit of the States. In raising fighters, the governors need men who are familiar with the woods and familiar with the style of fighting known to be exercised by the Indians. Active rangers and expert marksmen are vital for the desired effect. Militia must be engaged at the last moment to save ammunition and to have them fully engaged for the period when danger is apparent. If they are held longer, they tend to lose interest.

Saturday, March 6, 1779 — Middlebrook, New Jersey

I am writing General Gates regarding our plan against the Indians. I would like for him to lead this expedition if his health allows. If it does not, I will pass on the command to General Sullivan. In thinking through the strategy more, I desire that we send four thousand Continental troops to join the troops raised by the corresponding States. Our wish is to punish and intimidate the hostile nations. I pray it will countenance and encourage the friendly ones. The brunt of our action will be against the Six Nations. We seek to cut off their settlements, destroy their crops, and bring them mischief of every kind. If they start to be concerned for the protection of their own homes, they will not attack and jeopardize ours. To prevent succors from Canada, I suggest presenting a false appearance that this army is planning an invasion of Canada through the Coos and along the St. Lawrence river with the French fleet. This will cause those north of us to worry more about their own fortifications and less about the Six Nations' defense.

Monday, March 8, 1779 — Middlebrook, New Jersey

We have suffered a temporary setback in Georgia as the enemy has taken possession of the capital there. They gained a few supplies, but other than that, nothing of consequence is lost. Their victory is an insignificant one too, in that the militia of Georgia only amounted to twelve hundred men. When they saw the British coming, they retreated rather than engage. General Lincoln is gathering an army to dispossess them.

Spain and the two Sicilies may be greeted as our allies. Russia has rejected the British overtures. All in all, things are working in our favor abroad. This dispute with Britain may be decided soon. That is our hope. Mrs. Washington is with me. She brings me joy each day. She helps with our men. She gives me comfort, which allows me to focus on the troubles at-hand.

The Marquis has written of things in France. The King has a new child there. As things go well in France, I could readily see the soldier Marquis become the statesman Marquis. This transition into a new walk of life will be welcomed I am sure.

Thursday, March 11, 1779 — Middlebrook, New Jersey

Baron forwarded his work on The Regulations for the Infantry of the United States a few days ago. I have reviewed it and am returning it to him along with my notes. His question of what title to give it was submitted to me with various options. The aforementioned title is the best I believe as it is the simplest. I have sent a copy to Congress with my approbation. I look forward to seeing this work put into practice. It will benefit this army and gratify its author.

Sunday, March 14, 1779 — Middlebrook, New Jersey

I returned from worship today and found a letter from Sir Henry Clinton. In the Lord, His answers tend to be yea and amen. Sir Clinton's answers tend to be nay and refusal to consider. He has rejected our plans for a prisoner exchange. Congress has authorized me again to send commissioners to meet with the same from Britain. They are directed to work through the objections so that some exchange can be made to reduce the suffering of prisoners on both sides. I am sending this potential solution to Clinton. I will await his answer which will probably end with a nay or refusal to consider.

Monday, March 15, 1779 — Middlebrook, New Jersey

Answers from Congress often fare no better. Their answers are usually "let us consider" or no answer at all (as if they never received the question or are too busy to be troubled with the issue). We need to complete our battalions. I have been waiting on Congress to procure some method to do so. I have asked them numerous times. Though I do not want to be a bother, I cannot wage a war without men. I will send them another letter with the request.

Enlistments are coming to an end. They must be refilled. Desertions are still occurring though not as many as last winter. The States continue to complicate recruiting for the Continental force. Inequitable bounties are still being offered by different States. For instance, Virginians are given a premium for joining while Pennsylvania offers very little. Men in Pennsylvania will not join unless their State matches Virginia's offer. Their argument has merit. Why should they suffer the same for less money? This is why I am for a Continental bounty only, with the elimination of State bounties.

I further believe if the States are exerting themselves less to raise men, it is because they are hopeful in the rumors of foreign investment into this war. They may be under the false pretense that foreign involvement increases the likelihood of success, lessens the time before peace is obtained, and thereby reduces the need for their efforts. Such aid may not come. If it does, I fear it will be as the French fleet's assistance thus far — a floating hope like a fanciful dream that never materializes anything significant. On the other hand, the one foreign nation fully engaged is the enemy. The British's verbiage shows no thought of evacuating. They speak of further engagement and committing what is necessary to win. Their whole empire could fray if they let just one possession attain independence. The enemy has made a serious goal of southern conquests in this Nation of late, while burrowing down to hold their existing possessions on our soil. Again, I write this to myself for it seems no one else will listen. This war hinges on our willingness to raise men and fight. We must move as if we are the only one in this war and that no one else will enter. From this position, success is achievable, disappointments reduced, and a surprise blessing if some nation does truly render aid and not intents.

In addition, clothes, arms, ammunition, and supplies are needed. The States must provide these. They can help also by sending men already supplied. We hear of clothes being paid for, packaged, and sent to this army, yet few if any ever arrive. The States must find where these supposed purchases are being distributed. I fear it is among profiteers who provide for the highest bidder — American,

British, or Canadian. Some have been found rotting in some warehouse unattended. That is the problem with bureaucracies.

Lieutenant-Colonel Laurens has asked permission to move to the southern front. He believes his talents are needed in that area. He is brave in battle, a patriot to this Nation, and a fervent believer in our freedom. I am writing a letter of introduction for Mr. Laurens to John Rutledge, Governor of South Carolina. I will also add a last line stating my desire to have him back in my family here if a change of affairs occurs there.

Tuesday, March 16, 1779 — Middlebrook, New Jersey

Last December, in writing Mr. Harrison, we spoke of the void in our Nation's government for capable and intelligent men. In my journal, I asked the questions, "Where is Jefferson? Where is Nelson?" among others. I am delighted that at least one has answered the call of their Nation. This one has agreed to leave the leisure of private life to join when the need for good men is so great. Mr. Thomas Nelson has written that he is returning to a seat in Congress. Never has there been a time when cool, dispassionate, reasonable, and attentive men of integrity were more needed. Our affairs at the present require no small degree of political skill. Mr. Nelson fits the bill. He has answered his Nation's call. I pray more will return.

I cannot help but consider the posterity of this nation. If we are successful in this noble quest for independence, will the tendency to care for one's own affairs prevent good men from rising up when this nation faces some crisis in the future. Clearly, many of this generation do not care what form of government and oppression exists as long as they are at ease. I fear this will be the case in the future as well. Freedom requires sacrifice. So does righteousness. The Savior said if we are unwilling to take up our cross and follow Him, we are unworthy of Him. For this nation to stand for years to come, that cross must be borne by those who follow us. We must always strive to be worthy of Him. This is our only sustaining hope.

Saturday, March 20, 1779 — Middlebrook, New Jersey

Mr. Henry Laurens writes that the enemy has retreated at Fort Augusta. I am writing to get more information as to the facts of that good news.

There is talk of arming slaves for our cause. Slavery is a great atrocity. I believe that the virtue and national affection to freedom will be a great inducement for many slaves to serve. Such service will thereby render the institution of slavery irksome. I believe working and fighting side-by-side with men who were once slaves will produce a discontent in those who hold and those who are held in servitude. It may lead to a mass eradication of this inhumane practice. That is my prayer. God who works everything for good can even use the oppression of the British to cause those who oppress others here to repent of their sins. This should provide weight to the clause that all men are created equal, that all should be seen and treated as such.

Monday, March 22, 1779 — Middlebrook, New Jersey

I have directed General Rawlings and his corps consisting of three companies to march from Fort Fredric in Maryland where he is guarding British prisoners, to move to Fort Pitt once militia can replace him. He is then to move to Kittanning and throw up a stockade fort. Once that is completed, he and his men are to do the same at Venango. Colonel Brodhead at Fort Pitt needs to supply whatever tools Rawlings will need. Colonel Gibson is to march to join Colonel Brodhead at Fort Pitt and await word to attack the Indians. All these movements must be made in secret to provide the advantage of surprise. Watercraft must be procured for the movement along the Allegheny. They need to cultivate friendships with the western Indians. They are to engage warriors to assist and guide them from the Allegheny to the Indian towns and to Niagara. I will require prompt and accurate information for every step of this activity. I place that upon Colonel Brodhead as his chief responsibility.

Friday, March 26, 1779 — Middlebrook, New Jersey

Good intelligence informs that the British are moving troops to New London. They are utilizing sixteen transports (with a flatboat each), a sloop of war of sixteen guns, with five or six privateers. All are moving up the Sound as of a few days ago to join the Thames and the Scorpion. The Admiral in a sixty-four sailed from the Hook with the design to move the frigates for an expedition of New London. General Clinton is reported to have gone there himself. We have no means to prevent their descent.

Sunday, March 28, 1779 — Middlebrook, New Jersey

In thinking through the supposed movement of the enemy toward New London, I must think it is too late in the year with the elements too formidable for such an endeavor. I cannot help but believe these are going from New York to Rhode Island for the purpose of withdrawing troops from the latter. Still not knowing the true intent, we must be on guard at all points.

Wednesday, March 31, 1779 — Middlebrook, New Jersey

I am writing our Continental paymaster Mr. James Warren who is from Massachusetts. I am convinced that the depreciation of our currency lies at the root of why the enemy is still on this continent — aided by stockjobbing. The guilty parties are in our own camp. The British could be right, we will conquer ourselves. Can we not gather enough virtue to prove them wrong? I fear we are letting a little pelf cloud our eyes to the rights of our citizens now and those millions yet to be born. We are squandering the blood and treasure masses have sacrificed thus far for the avarice and aggrandizement of a few designing men. Heaven forbid that we become victims of our own lust for personal gain. Every State should present laws to prevent such monstrous evils. Our cause is noble. It is the cause of all mankind.

We must not sleep or slumber when so much depends on what we do right now. Extortioners, forestallers, and speculators must be forbidden to operate. They must be punished when they do. Supplies must be affordable. Troops' pay must have value. Heavy taxes must not impose on one's ability to serve. At times like these, even with the vital importance of the struggle, the fallen nature of humanity inside this Nation may require conquering before the British, Indians, or Tories.

Saturday, April 3, 1779 — Middlebrook, New Jersey

Citing health reasons, Lieutenant-Colonel Aaron Burr is requesting my permission to retire from the army. I am never agreeable to losing a good officer, but I understand the many reasons men give. The most acceptable is when their health no longer allows them to serve. As soon as he takes care of his public accounts, I will grant him permission.

Sunday, April 4, 1779 — Middlebrook, New Jersey

A rare "yea" has been received from Sir Clinton regarding a meeting of commissioners to negotiate the exchange of prisoners. The date he has requested does not permit time for our commissioners to assemble. I am requesting a deferment to the 12th instant. If it were at all possible, I would rally to the day he chose, because any delay could quickly bring his rejection. I have no ability to meet his date. I am in prayer that he will accept the latter option.

Wednesday, April 14, 1779 — Middlebrook, New Jersey

I have been stewing over the latest packet from Congress and Mr. Jay. I am not so disgusted with Congress, but rather with the source that has made their inquiry necessary. General Gates is up to his old tricks and his constant push to discredit me in the eyes of Congress, the public, and this army. He has brought false charges and groundless accusations against me regarding expenditures and plans for a Canada invasion. The demanding duty taken by me and my family at this head to accumulate, record, and retain copies of all correspondence often seems like a waste of time. Then I receive an accusation from this familiar source. I realize again why I take these measures — evidence, means of defense, and discrediting lies. General Gates has sought to impugn me at every turn. Now he accuses me of seeking a task into Canada that will be fruitless. I will play the attorney in my response to Congress, stating the truth and supplying my own packet of irrefutable evidence. I will send them returns between me and the General. I will also include my letters to Congress which I have sent every step of the way. They need to see that both they and Gates have been apprised and consulted with every decision.

On Canada, Gates is wrong. I said we would only invade Canada if the enemy evacuated this Nation. I did prepare for the invasion on the chance Congress would order such an act. But every step I took were steps that would not be wasted. Preparations were made that could be rerouted from Canada to other fronts as the need arose. He accuses me of exorbitant expenses for an invasion that would probably not occur. The only expenses spent uniquely for Canada were for snowshoes and leather for moccasins. Both of which could be used in other locations. Most supplies purchased were along the Connecticut river so they could be distributed to Canada or to Boston just as easily. I have written on many occasions to Congress citing the many reasons why an expedition to Canada would be fruitless. I have documented such a move would be harmful with the situations of the army and enemy as they exist today.

Gates says that I have not exchanged letters with him but once in December. I have pulled copies of our correspondence over the last few months. I have written him over fifty times. He has written back around forty times. Every letter I write has a purpose. I have not the time to just write letters to write letters. Exchanging pleasantries is done with the letters that need to be written and as a preface to what must be discussed. True, the last month or so, our returns have been few. We are wintering in quarters. Little need presents to correspond. I did write him and offer him a chance to lead the expedition against the Indians who are harassing our frontiers. Such a command would afford him a somewhat easy victory with great appreciation from our citizens. I offered this to him knowing his ill-will toward me. I never make decisions based on personal feelings but for what is good for the public account. I am sending Congress a few extracts of these letters. Even when the cabal between Gates and Conway was discovered, I continued to do what was best for our Nation. I wrote to him in a manner that was respectful of his position. Even with his underhand intrigues, I wrote for his insights to military questions. To have to defend myself troubles me, but in this case, I must. I am willing to share all evidence and allow Congress to make their decision. Gates has nothing to counter except accusations rooted in ambition, bitterness, and jealousy.

Wednesday, April 21, 1779 — Middlebrook, New Jersey

I am writing Colonel Brodhead to inform him I cannot countenance moving troops from their present positions on the frontier as it will expose us to hostilities in those regions.

Once the Six Nations have been successfully dealt with, I would like Brodhead to consider an attack on Detroit while it is winter. Only when the rivers and waterways are frozen, is the enemy hampered in their response. In the winter, the British find themselves more like this army — confined to the march, denied naval means.

Thursday, April 22, 1779 — Middlebrook, New Jersey

I am pulling Maxwell's brigade from the Jerseys and asking Governor Livingston to cover their posts with militia. I would rather the States enlist militia for defense purposes, as marching militia out of their State is expensive and they are prone to defection in a short time. To not exert themselves to raise men is to the States' disadvantage. They clamor for protection but do nothing for their own. I fear that the bigger a government grows, the more its inhabitants will depend upon it instead of their own industry. This leaves them weak. The Nation and its government will become weak soon thereafter.

I am also withdrawing troops from the Monmouth area. The enemy has had a negative influence in that region. They are not using arms there but arts. The result has been mutinies, desertions, and corruption. Having them engaged in action rather than idle in defense, at least for that group of men, is the only saving choice.

Friday, April 23, 1779 — Middlebrook, New Jersey

As Congress sends a packet to me regarding accusations from Gates to hold all accountable, this must work in the opposite direction. I need to hold Congress to their word. I seem to do this often. I am writing them to ascertain why our Continental frigates are in port. They are useless sitting. They require troops to protect them while sitting. They challenge the virtue of good men when idle. Would it not be better to send them south to meet the British in Georgia? Enlist brave and capable men to officer them. They can make a dent in the enemy, gain booty for themselves along with personal accolades. They will also provide exclusive benefits to their respective States, not to mention the gratitude of this Nation.

Rumor has it that Monsieur Gerard plans on leaving these waters and returning to France with his fleet. Will not the enemy see this as a triumph and an open invitation for further depredations? Why is Congress allowing the Bermudan ships to exchange their salt for our flour and then return to annihilate our trade? Why would we allow such? Why would we trade what we need to a posing friend who returns to be an aggressive foe? Why has Congress not done something to restore the value of our currency? As it now stands, a wagonload of money will not purchase a wagonload of supplies. I may be out on a limb so soon after General Gates's accusations, but I must not back down from my own censor. The freedom of millions in the future is at question.

Saturday, April 24, 1779 — Middlebrook, New Jersey

General Greene has done all that is humanly possible to help as quartermaster-general. He feels he is on an island where no assistance comes from our citizens or our government. He believes his reputation is depreciating by the day. He wishes to resign this post. I believe he has done a good job. If given time, he will meet the needs of this army and transform his department. If he will not stay in that position, I will gladly let him succeed General Lincoln in the south.

Friday, April 30, 1779 — Middlebrook, New Jersey

Pennsylvania seeks a trial against General Benedict Arnold with several charges hinting of corruption. I have not known this to ever be an issue with General Arnold. I do believe he is grieved for being passed over for promotion on numerous occasions. He has not been given credit due him for the role he has played in key victories. I lay part of that at the feet of General Gates. He is a man of action.

Yet, because of injury, he has found himself inactive in military matters serving more as a public official. I believe he is an officer who needs action. I pray for his recovery. I desire he return to a command where this Nation will be eternally grateful for his patriotism, gifts, and conduct. I will do all I can to expedite his trial so that he can be vindicated. If he is guilty (I will not say he is not as I have no access to evidence), he will be punished according to military or civil law. I can scarce afford the officers needed to be the witnesses and jury, but I must submit to the wishes of the government of that State.

I will remind Pennsylvania when she is so outraged about some acts of Arnold, that there are accusations to be made toward this State. Pennsylvania has failed to raise their allotted battalion. They have not supplied militia for their own defense. They suppose that the Continental army will meet their need. We face attacks from the Indians in our frontiers. Pennsylvania has a few of those frontiers in need of order and defense. This State has not even supplied the six hundred that I requested for the current action against the Indians to secure safety for their own people. I must tell my friend Mr. Reed, who is President of Pennsylvania, that we will not be able to offer the protection for which they had hoped. Mr. Reed complains that his State is unguarded and exposed where other States are better protected. He is right. Virginia is well-protected because Virginia raised the men to carry out the work. New York is doing the same. I have no preference for one State over the other, just as I will show no favor to my friend Mr. Reed over the governor of a neighboring State whom I hardly know. I will supplement for each State's defense as I am able. My main concern is the enemy who has crossed the sea to enter our towns and homes. It troubles me to be so firm with a friend, but I must let Mr. Reed know the facts and the faults. He then must act accordingly. He knows my situation better than most. He may get pressure from his constituents, but the duty begins with his neighbors.

Saturday, May 1, 1779 — Middlebrook, New Jersey

Count d'Estaing has shared his intention for his squadron to leave for France. Other than some hope, the French fleet has done little for our cause. Even unloading their soldiers onboard to help us would have been a succor. They have never left their ships as best as I can tell. Monsieur Gerard has been so kind to meet me at my camp over the last few days to gain my approval for their departure. I believe he can tell that I am disappointed. I do not believe they have kept their promise to help. He asked what I request be done by this fleet on our behalf before they leave. I have given several options, all of them in keeping with the purpose for which they came. As a first option, I asked Monsieur Gerard to have Count d'Estaing's squadron to move from Martinique to New York. I will invest the whole of this army in that quarter, including militia of the neighboring States to meet them there for the reduction of the enemy's fleet and army there. They can then move to the Delaware and do the same. I believe we stand a good chance for success. However, I am requiring their assurance of cooperation before I make such a commitment with this army.

If this option is not agreed upon, I then have suggested that Count d'Estaing proceed with his squadron to Georgia with this army. We should be able to capture and destroy the enemy's fleet and army there. With that handled, he can proceed to New York and capture or destroy the enemy's fleet in that port. I believe either scenario can be done before Lord Byron's fleet arrives from Britain. This will put them at a disadvantage at best. It will discourage them at the worst and cause them to reconsider this war as their losses accumulate.

This might also open the field for them to move to Rhode Island and capture and destroy their vessels at that head. If this is done and the American States are made secure, this army would then be willing to join them in a move on Canada or in other areas where the enemy has a stronghold. Basically, my request is no different than what it was when they arrived. I suppose my main request, knowing that they wish to depart, is to act. For them to go with my blessing, I am simply asking them to do now what they promised. I am praying they will agree so we can get this thing over. My honest expectation is that they will do nothing. As I have stated many times, America must fight to win her own freedom. We can count on no one else.

Sunday, May 2, 1779 — Middlebrook, New Jersey

I have taken this day of worship to pour out my heart to the Almighty God. They say rats leave a sinking ship, sometimes the rats leave with the ship. This is dishonorable to record. I regret writing it. The Author of life is dear to me and near to me. He has told us in His Word that we can come boldly before His Throne, that we are to come to Him in spirit and in truth. I must come before Him in truth, not in a faux positive manner. For my needs to be met, for the needs as a nation to be met, I must come before Him and honestly present those needs. I am also to come before Him as the publican who beat his chest and pleaded for God to have mercy on him a sinner. Jesus said this man left with his prayers answered. I come the same way, not in some pretense to get what I want, but in humble adoration making my petitions known. I ask that the French will help us. I ask that our army does not dissolve. I ask that those who have become disaffected will have a change of heart. I pray that those in leisure will become active. I pray that those who are extorting us in this war will see the error of their ways, that they become allies not obstacles. I pray the Tories will see this war is a benefit to them, more than their current sentiments or past alliances can achieve. I pray General Gates will repent and fight by my side. I pray Congress will act and not table issues for another day. I pray for a quick victory so that I might return to my home and enjoy the freedoms gained — to worship, work my land, and pursue my ambitions for life, liberty, and the pursuit of a happy state. More than anything, I desire my trespasses to be forgiven and that Heaven will be mine when my last breath is taken. All these I pray. As our dear Savior prayed, I close this Sabbath with the earnest prayer, Thy Will be done on earth, in this Nation, as it is in Heaven. Providence knows better and gives better than we can ever ask or think.

Monday, May 3, 1779 — Middlebrook, New Jersey

I arose from my prayer time this morning to a bit of good news. General Schuyler writes that some of the hostile tribes of Indians on the western frontier desire peace with us. We can make a partial peace with these who desire it, but not with the whole. I believe the mind of many of these Indians is they desire peace when danger is near. Once the danger has left, they return to hostilities. Rigors should be made to punish those of their company who have brought the hostilities, even as we move for peace. This will deter others from carrying out future aggressions. Peace is great but there is a price for past sins. In this process, rewarding peace to those willing to attain it will reduce the confederacy aligned against us. It will make our success easier to accomplish. Perhaps, it reduces the investment of men who would otherwise be made if we must fight the whole. We must still consider any detachments coming from Canada against us. To thwart this, every artifice must be employed to cause those in Canada to fear invasion on their soil. This will induce them to keep their forces at home.

The call for peace from a portion of the hostile enemy could not be more welcomed considering the news I just received from Colonel Malcom. He says many of his regiment, including officers, refuse to combine with Colonel Spencer's regiment and serve under Colonel Spencer. Malcom reports his men are threatening to resign and return to serve in their respective States rather than serve anyone but him. This is blatant mutiny. I have told him I will not bend to their threats. Spencer is to use whatever means necessary to force compliance from Malcom's men. If I must, I told them, I will dispatch this army to bring the instigators to submission. I face this from time- to-time. It grieves me. Allegiance is not to an officer or to a personality or to a State but to the United States, for the freedom of all. If one truly values liberty, we must serve regardless of the name at the head of the regiment. Colonel Malcom must use that influence to compel his men to serve for the greater cause. Families are losing their homes to these hostile sorts. Are these men willing to let homes be destroyed and family members be killed until their wishes of who they will follow are granted? God forbid it.

Governor Clinton brings favor with his report that his one thousand men requested have been raised. I am thankful this governor never disappoints. He complies with every request I make for public service. Can Pennsylvania and Mr. Reed not take note of this and do likewise? Governor Clinton is seeking guidance for prisoners he has taken on the frontiers. I am gladdened that he has such a problem. However, my authority only extends to military prisoners. His State must make the decision as to the disposition of all others.

Tuesday, May 4, 1779 — Middlebrook, New Jersey

Governor Livingston has written that his pay of his State's militia has really enhanced his recruiting for that branch. Sadly, that pay is higher than what our Continental troops are making. This brings dissatisfaction. Militia come and go for a higher pay when Continental soldiers stay at their post full-time for less pay and greater suffering while missing the comforts of home and family. This cannot be sustainable. The option would be to pay Continental troops on par with the militia which the United States cannot afford. Equal pay is not fair either. One does not pay full pay for part-time work, nor does one pay part-time pay for full-time labor. I question the philosophy of paying militia in general. Militia is called out for a specific danger to their friends and family. Must an inducement be made to draw them out? I rather think that love of their friends and family would draw them out regardless of reward or pay. Large bounties for State enlistments and for the militia continue to be a fertile source of evil. I pray they will stop this. I bring this same issue up time-and-time again, yet no one seems to be listening. If my concerns were only proven by words, I could understand the hesitancy. But, the state of the army, the number of desertions, the lack of readiness all give evidence to these words. They have ears to hear, but do not understand. They have eyes to see, but do not perceive.

Wednesday, May 5, 1779 — Middlebrook, New Jersey

Three New York papers record Lord North's speech declaring Britain's intentions to vigorously prosecute this war. The British papers report reinforcements are being sent to this continent. Our hoped-for European war driven by the French seems to be nonexistent. This allows the enemy to bring more resources to put down our "rebellion." The States are not exerting themselves to raise men for the Continental army. They still hold out hope for a ready peace. If only they knew the French fleet desires to leave. If only they read the papers. I am asking Congress to address the subject with the respected legislatures. With our action in the frontiers about to be underway and the Virginia levies going southward, this army is in a reduced state, unable to pose a significant defense should the enemy decide to attack. Congress needs to use their influence to buttress our force.

Saturday, May 8, 1779 — Middlebrook, New Jersey

I fancy Mr. Reed does not see the irony in his last letter. He believes I am showing preference to other States at the risk of his. He states he is losing trust in my care for himself and Pennsylvania. He does not realize it is easier to cry for someone to help you than for you to step out and take measures to help yourself. This is what Pennsylvania has failed to do thus far. Back to the irony of preference and trust. Not long ago, I discovered by accident (Providence's Hand I should say), that Mr. Reed preferred General Lee to my command. Having made secret returns with General Lee, does he not realize that he is the last who should complain about lack of trust? I write this only here. I have forgiven him. I have seen repentance and loyalty on his part after the matter was discovered. May that incident come to his mind too. I believe if he will recall that event and my response, his trust will be restored. His perceptions corrected.

Gouverneur Morris writes to discuss his meeting with Monsieur Gerard and the news of the French fleet's soon exit. He is curious as to which of the options I posed to Gerard is my preference. I believe that the enemy is focusing on the south, so the French strength should be exercised there first. A striking blow would benefit that region. Success would be certain. Who knows, a victory in that region might bring a great change to this whole Nation. At present, there is weakness, want of energy, disaffection, and a languor among our people. I believe if the enemy is unchecked, they will attack Charleston next, forcing us to make all efforts to protect South Carolina. This will give them a complete hold of Georgia as our troops evacuate to defend Charleston.

I am letting Gouverneur Morris know our army is now but a skeleton. If the enemy seeks to press us, no likely defense is to be made unless Providence intercedes. Why would He, if our own people lack the public spirit to make any effort at all? Our currency is in rapid decay. The times are dark. No harmony exists. A general apathy seems to have infected our populace. I will hate to go back and read this is the future. My complaints and hopelessness seem to pervade each day's entry. At times I think I would not be surprised to see the British flag waving above our homes and courthouses. I could see me hung as an instigator of all discomforts, as the lone thorn in the side of peace.

Sunday May 9, 1779 — Middlebrook, New Jersey

Yesterday, I sent my complaints to Mr. Morris. Today after service, I have had time to count blessings. I look out of my quarters to see officers drilling their men because their men requested an extra session to improve. I see other men cleaning their guns. I see a hope in the eyes of men like General Greene devoted to the path, hand to the plow, unwilling to look back. I walk the grounds and see huts being cared for, men helping each other, even a song being sung around a camp-fire. The men salute me. They give me their full attention. They are respectful and seek my comfort, answering my every command. They are cordial. At times they just visit with me as if I were their closest friend. These have left their homes. They have trusted their families to the Lord's Care. They love this country. They hate all kinds of evil. They have denied themselves luxury even knowing that men outside this army bathe in it. Gouverneur Morris needs to join our work in Congress. He needs to give vigor to this cause. If an epidemic is to be spread, do not let it be the pox; rather, let it be the patriotism and love that lay in the hearts of these men whom I am privileged to command. I may make mistakes in the next campaign. This army may be overrated. I will face many other moments of gloom, but I pray I do not forget what I see in this camp. Heaven and these men are my hope.

Monday, May 10, 1779 — Middlebrook, New Jersey

General Maxwell informs me that the 1st regiment of New Jersey are discontent with their pay. I knew this defensive strategy would bring this. When the soldiers have nothing threatening their lives, some will focus on perceived injustices. I am directing Maxwell to remind his soldiers that this army is cared for deeply. At times, this army was not fed and suffered insufficient clothing. That is not the case at the present. May it not ever be the case again. General Greene is doing a good job getting things in order for the comfort and provision of our men.

Tuesday, May 11, 1779 — Middlebrook, New Jersey

Complaints of the 1st regiment of New Jersey have been weighing on me. I am writing Congress. I do believe under further consideration, that the officers of that regiment are not given the provisions they need. Many officers are wearing the same clothes as the soldiery with no distinguishing marks to warrant attention. The officers have been patient regarding pensions and other benefits. I believe if informed, Congress will see the danger this poses to our Nation and do all they can to obviate my worries.

There is want of reliable intelligence for this army. This deficiency is often filled by ambiguous characters that concern me as to the information they bring. I am asking Congress to provide the article of specie for a secret service, which will then enable us to dispatch reliable parties into the enemy's abode, give them cover of a business, and allow them supplies to support their pretense so they are not arrested and tried in the courts.

Monday, May 17, 1779 — Middlebrook, New Jersey

Several ships have sailed from New York. Their destination is uncertain. We have made a concerted effort to move men to Virginia and southward to meet the enemy there. This sudden movement of the British may be to delay our detachments to allow the enemy a good footing before we contend with them. I am of the mind to continue with our plan and hasten the levies forward. We must be on alert for deception of any kind.

What remains in New York, by most accounts, are two frigates of twenty guns, two sloops of war, and a few privateers to protect a large number of transports. I am suggesting to Congress that our frigates to the east be moved to this port to deliver an important blow to their stronghold there. I believe this experiment may be worth the try. I will await word from Congress.

Thursday, May 20, 1779 — Middlebrook, New Jersey

Another day, another return from Mr. Joseph Reed. He writes that it is not just the State of Pennsylvania that feels exposed by this army's lack of attention, but that other States feel the same. He does not name the other States. I will answer his letter as I have before. We will carry out our duty. We will do all we can to cover all the States, but those States must do their part to provide succor for this army and men for their own protection in addition.

Tuesday, May 25, 1779 — Middlebrook, New Jersey

Congress is alarmed at the enemy's recent movement into the Chesapeake Bay where they burned houses, sacked the town of Portsmouth, and destroyed several small vessels. They must know that this army can do little to stop this at present. We are dealing with the frontiers. We are moving men southward. The solution to the problem is a larger army, which comes with more men being added to the Continental army and more men added to each State's militia.

That the enemy in New York does seem to be stirring to some important enterprise is true. They have collected vessels at Kingsbridge and are drawing their forces together at this head. With several locations threatened, perhaps Congress and the States will deliver an army to us. It may also be that the enemy is seeking to reduce our force from the western frontier. We must be on guard.

Sunday, May 30, 1779 — Middlebrook, New Jersey

Major James Monroe has requested transfer southward to assist where action is likely to soon occur. He is a man of great zeal, character, and activity. He served valiantly at Trenton. He was even wounded as he pressed the fight. I have seen him serve bravely as an officer in two other campaigns under Lord Stirling. I have granted his wish. I am informing Archibald Cary of Virginia of Major Monroe's value with the hope he will appoint him to the place of his desire.

Monday, May 31, 1779 — Middlebrook, New Jersey

Since my nemesis General Gates has declined the opportunity to lead in the western front, I am dispatching General Sullivan to that command. He will have at his disposal the brigades of Clinton, Maxwell, Poor, and Hand, as well as the individual companies raised in Pennsylvania. Clinton's brigade will rendezvous at Canajoharie and either form a junction with the main body at the Susquehanna or at the Mohawk river. Clinton is to travel light with only provisions needed in the journey to meet Sullivan. This way they can travel undetected by the enemy. Sullivan will then assemble his group at the Wyoming Valley of Pennsylvania and proceed to Tioga. He needs to establish intermediate posts as necessary for the security of communication. He must leave just enough troops for this purpose without diminishing his operating force. I am instructing him to make attacks rather than receive them. He is to attack with great impetuosity, accompanied with as much shouting and noise as can be generated. Nothing will terrify the Indians more. If after taking it to the Indians, they wish a peace, they must give evidence of their sincerity. This can be accomplished by handing over the prime instigators from their fold, including Butler, Brand, and other mischievous Tories.

These Indians who desire peace must join our men in attacks on Niagara and upon the shipping on the Lakes. This must be demanded as a token of their friendship. If they comply, then we can assist them with the supplies they need. Caution is required even then. Their savagery must be watched. Trust will be a long time coming from these hostile groups. Their history of treachery must not be discounted.

Wednesday, June 2, 1779 — Middlebrook, New Jersey

Good news on our men. As we seek to quarter and supply them, the aim of this army is to do little harm to the inhabitants of this land. Inconveniences are sometimes necessary, but the desire is to minimize those. Often, even the least inconvenience is met with complaints from the people we defend. With this said, the Dutch Reform Church of Raritan sends a letter of appreciation. They say our army is doing their work while behaving in a gentlemanly manner. I appreciate this. I feel a great pride in this army. I trust the goodness of our cause and the exertions of our people under Divine protection will bring peace which flow from piety and religion.

Thursday, June 3, 1779 — Middlebrook, New Jersey

The enemy has some important enterprise in contemplation. I sent the Virginia division under Lord Stirling yesterday to meet them. Baron DeKalb follows this morning with his Maryland troops. I will set out this day with the main army toward the Highlands. I have doubled my efforts to put this army in ready. The quartermaster-general has seconded our motion with supplies, though horses, wagons, and provisions are few. He has done a good job overcoming the obstacles of scarcity. I am glad to have one so diligent in that position who is also present to see and meet our needs.

Friday, June 4, 1779

Stony Point has been evacuated by the forty men we had stationed there. They were outnumbered. They refused to risk falling into the enemy's hands. The enemy is attempting to take hold of our garrisons at strategic locations. I am hoping that we can get there in time to blunt their efforts.

Sunday, June 6, 1779 — Ringwood Iron-Works

The enemy fired on Verplanck's Point from Stony Point and from their ships on the river beside. Being invested on the land side by force, our seventy men there capitulated and surrendered. The enemy then advanced with five thousand men below Continental Village with the hope to gain Nelson's Point. Thankfully, they made no action and removed to the two points gained. The enemy has since remained with two divisions on opposite sides of the river. Part of their fleet has moved down river. The remainder of their fleet stands in that position with seventy sail and one hundred and fifty flat boats. They are fortifying Stony Point and intend to hold this very strategic fort. Their movements are perplexing, but the grand scheme seems to be to take the Highlands' posts. If nothing else, they have succeeded in cutting off communication for us along King's Ferry.

Friday, June 11, 1779 — Headquarters, Smith's Cove

The enemy has posted one thousand troops at Stony Point where we had forty. They have posted five thousand troops on Verplanck's Point where we had seventy. Clearly, our want of men makes any place we hold vulnerable. The States' only means of defense seems to be the hope that the enemy will not be too aggressive. These two posts now in enemy hands provide comfort to the disaffected. They also allow the enemy another place to gain supplies.

General Gates writes of his optimism that he can take New York. He wishes my agreement. He overrates the army under his care or undervalues the enemy's. The enemy in New York has now nearly eleven thousand men. I am not sure what General Gates is thinking. In the back of my mind, I wonder if he is trying to get me to issue an order for sure defeat propelling him to head this army. He has already shown that he baits me and then makes accusations that cannot be supported. The enemy I face has but six thousand men. I have no way to address them with the main army. My only strategy with which I can proceed is to hinder their progress.

Monday, June 21, 1779 — Headquarters, Smith's Cove

On the western frontier, General Sullivan writes he is disappointed in the Independent Companies coming for Pennsylvania. I am not surprised. He has also experienced difficulties which he had not anticipated. I am confident he can overcome them. A body of troops are coming from New York under Lieutenant-Colonel Pawling. Once they achieve their first objective, two hundred of these will go to join Sullivan's group. Governor Clinton is personally assuring this. He has even offered to lead them himself. I am asking him not to do that. Pawling is more than capable. We cannot risk Governor Clinton. He is doing more for our cause from his current position in Albany.

I am asking General Sullivan, if he can spare them, to send Colonel Armond's corps and Captain McLane's company to rejoin me here.

Friday, June 25, 1779 — Headquarters, New Windsor, New York

The British have lodged a complaint that our officers under their confinement were given parole, but have not returned at the end of that parole. This is a violation of military etiquette. Their break with protocol will make it harder for others of our men to gain parole. I am asking Mr. Beatty, our commissary of prisoners, to cooperate with Major-General Greene to determine who these men are, if they are truly military prisoners, and to remedy the problem through punishments and other measures necessary.

Sunday, June 27, 1779 — New Windsor, New York

Major Benjamin Talmadge is a man who has my utmost trust. He, above all others, can camp nearest the enemy without being apprehended. He protects our inhabitants from the forays of the enemy parties and gathers intelligence all the while. He is also astute at gaining agents for our cause. One of his came lately, requiring ten guineas for his information. The money was given just to find that the information was days old and already in the papers. Besides that, the numbers he reports to me on the enemy are rarely accurate. I am requesting a replacement for this one. I have found a man near the enemy by the North river who has reached out to help us with intelligence. He is well- regarded by the enemy. If I find he is sincere, he will be a great aid to our preparations.

Monday, June 28, 1779 — New Windsor, New York

I am requesting Major Henry Lee find someone who can get into Stony Point undetected. I need him to report what he sees, how the garrison is laid out, where the troops are posted, and, if possible, draw a rough sketch of the works. I also need him to give me an accurate account of the armed vessels employed below.

Thursday, July 1, 1779 — New Windsor, New York

General Sullivan continues to face obstacles in the expedition on the western frontiers. I had instructed General Clinton to travel secretly. The best way to do that was to travel light with just enough provisions to get him to General Sullivan. Regrettably, either General Sullivan did not communicate that to General Clinton, or General Clinton did not heed this advice. Clinton instead is moving slowly with a long train of men and three-months supplies for his brigade. The enemy has taken notice of him. They will probably fall upon his men with their full force. If only wisdom could capture his attention.

I am apprising General Wayne of a potential move on Stony Point. I have thought long of dispossessing the enemy here and at Verplanck's Point if the opportunity presents itself. The enemy has since moved some troops from Stony Point. A man in the area has brought intelligence that a hidden approach may encroach upon that garrison. I am asking General Wayne to gain some insights into the likelihood of success of such an endeavor, to study the area — the garrisons nearby, the state of the creeks, the strength of the fortifications, and the number of vessels in the river. His reconnoitering will give the information we need to decide yea or nay.

Sunday, July 4, 1779 — New Windsor, New York

Thus far, the 4th of July has come and gone with little activity on the actual day of our Declaration of Independence. In a way, I appreciate the silence to reflect on why we are fighting. To observe this day on the Lord's Day is even more gratifying, to worship and reflect on His Hand. We are outnumbered and our number diminishes by the day. Many times, it has appeared that all is hopeless. Every time we reach that point, Providence steps in to aid us. He governs the affairs of men as Mr. Franklin has said on numerous occasions. May we be faithful. May He see us through to the end. He will be praised. Thanksgiving is offered now and will be then.

Monday, July 5, 1779 — New Windsor, New York

I am writing Mr. Reed to concur with General Sullivan's disappointment. Pennsylvania is not assisting the Continental army in protecting their own frontier. Their lack of response is injurious. It may exceed injury. I have invested a large part of this army to assist the State, which contends they receive less than equal treatment from me. If they do not assist in the immediate, more may be lost than just the frontier. I have stretched the string on my end to the point of breaking. I have nothing left to do but compel that State to do its part. Now is the time to come forth.

Major Talmadge informs me of a terrible loss — his papers. In those papers are our correspondence and strategies, not to mention the state of this arm (though I have shared little with him, knowing how close he is to enemy lines). More to be lost are the agents who have worked on our behalf in enemy lines. The enemy may discern from these letters particularly the identity of our spy "H." This man, who has risked so much, will lose his life because of carelessness. I am instructing Talmadge to communicate the loss of these papers immediately to "H" so that he can get out of New York before he is discovered.

Tuesday, July 6, 1779 — New Windsor, New York

I have just returned from a visit to our posts below New Windsor where I now reside. I have been studying the enemy's fortifications as I consider an attack on Stony Point and Verplanck's Point. I believe I have developed a strategy. I will be working with our officers to refine it.

Wednesday, July 7, 1779 — New Windsor, New York

The enemy embarked a body of troops at Frog's Neck on the Sound. From what we can ascertain, this body of eighteen hundred consists of grenadiers, light infantry, and a few Hessians. They proceeded eastward. It appears they may be headed to Connecticut. I am letting Governor Trumbull know. I am also having Glover's brigade to proceed the same route not far from the Sound. He can form a juncture with militia to meet the enemy if they choose to descend. They will probably continue their destructive habit of burning homes and meeting houses. I wish I were able to obstruct this enemy wherever he lands, but this army is too small. I must direct it to the areas of greatest impact. Terms of service are expiring. Sickness, death, and desertions reduce our force even more. The remainder are in the western front or are moving to the south to stop the enemy there.

Friday, July 9, 1779 — New Windsor, New York

Stony Point looks to provide an opportunity for success. The deserters report of a sandy beach to the south of that fortress. This route is obstructed only by a slight abatis. I am working with our officers, engineers, and our quartermaster-general to invent an effective plan.

Saturday, July 10, 1779 — New Windsor, New York

We have settled on a plan. I will send Brigadier-General Wayne to attack Stony Point. If he succeeds in that endeavor, then he is to turn that garrison's guns on

Verplainck's Point. All must be done in secret. Approach is to be along the water on the southside, crossing the beach. Wayne is to send advance men to remove obstructions, secure sentries, and drive the guards. Then the main group is to advance with fixed bayonets and muskets. Each officer must know what parts of the line they are to possess to remove confusion. Other parties will advance by river to the north. This may serve the dual advantage of distracting the enemy while cutting off their potential retreat. The invasion will be at night so each man should wear a white feather or cockade, or some visible badge for discernment at night. Those without will be considered a foe. Secrecy must be the ultimate concern. It only takes a few minutes for a plan to be divulged, just one deserter can sink the whole endeavor. Only men that Wayne can fully rely on should be recruited for this plan. A small detachment of artillery should be ready should the Stony Point advance succeed. This will allow a rapid turn on Verplainck's Point. I have ordered a couple of light field pieces for the enterprise. The enemy's cannons can also be drafted once the garrison is ours.

Brigadier-General Parsons reports the enemy has brought havoc at New Haven burning houses as is their custom. I am having General Heath to move with two Connecticut brigades on the enemy. I hope the militia will be animated enough to join.

Sunday, July 11, 1779 — New Windsor, New York

The depredations of the enemy must be publicized. Such villainy should never remain in secret. The victims are convinced, but those still in their homes may feel the same will never happen to them. If we let all know, perhaps more will join to answer such atrocities.

Monday, July 12, 1779 — New Windsor, New York

I am asking Governor Trumbull to do all in his power to assist General Heath in making a vigorous rebuttal to the enemy. The enemy's numbers are inflated by rumors. They number no more than two thousand — a number which Connecticut can push back.

Wednesday, July 14, 1779 — New Windsor, New York

General Wayne believes all is set for an attack on Stony Point. I am giving him the approval to carry it into execution tomorrow night unless some unforeseen change requires its deferment.

Thursday, July 15, 1779 — Fort Montgomery

I am asking Brigadier-General Muhlenberg to march toward Stony Point. He is to go with one day's provision so as to march light and undetected. He is to stay there until I inform otherwise.

Friday, July 16, 1779 — New Windsor, New York

The first returns from General Wayne's attack have shown success. I am awaiting further reports. I give thanks to the Lord.

Monday, July 19, 1779 — New Windsor, New York

A slew of activity has occurred since my last entry. Things have been fluid, but they have taken a successful turn in total. General Wayne's action caught the enemy by surprise. In the critical climb, General Wayne received a head injury from a musket-ball. He would not let it deter him from his duties of leading the men with unshaken firmness. Lieutenant-Colonel Fleury and his men were the first to enter the enemy's works. He struck the British flag with his own hands. Having taken this garrison at a loss of many of the enemy soldiers, our men then turned to fire upon Verplanck's Point. Miscommunication in getting the light artillery in place, delays in moving the cannon, and the inability to juncture below caused this part of the enterprise to be halted. It was a good thing that we did not prosecute further. General Howe's full force had time to gather. Seeing our position on Stony Point, he returned to his place of security. We did gain a strategic post as well as artillery, supplies, and provisions for our men. Now what to do with this gain?

Tuesday, July 20, 1779 — New Windsor, New York

After surveying the grounds of Stony Point myself, I have concluded we cannot hold it. This garrison will require fifteen hundred men to secure it. We do not have that many men to spare for one post. Great work and expense would be required, in addition, to prevent it from falling to the enemy as it has fallen to us. I have decided we will evacuate it. This means the enemy most likely will take it back without a shot. The good thing is, they will find a need to invest more of their men at that one spot and spend the money themselves to secure it. This will mean less depredations in other areas. Our losses in this endeavor are inconsequential. The enemy cannot say the same. Their spirit is dampened. Our men's confidence is heightened. The mind of the people around see that we are still an army that can produce significant successes.

Sunday, July 25, 1779 — Headquarters, West Point, New York

Lieutenant-Colonel Fleury has requested a furlough for a few months to tend to personal business in France. I cannot help but approve. Here is a man who entered this army in 1777 with a captain's commission from Congress. He joined the service as a rifleman. I have had my doubts about many foreign men coming to our cause. Most came only for glory and rank motivated by selfish ambition, primarily. Fleury has come with the right intentions — wanting only to serve and be commended only as his service warranted. He moved from captain to brigade-major because of his zeal and activity. As a major, he served in the infantry then the cavalry. He has gained approbation each time from his commanding officers. He then became a field engineer. Serving with intelligence, Congress promoted him to Lieutenant-Colonel. In that post, he was a sub-inspector and commanded a corps of light infantry. Of late, he stormed Stony Point. He was the first to enter their works. Here is a man from France who has done things the right way. He is brave, well-informed, judicious, and indefatigable. I set him before every foreign ally as an example of what they should be. I also present him to our own native troops to show the benefit foreign men can bring to our cause.

Wednesday, July 28, 1779 — West Point, New York

I am sending Major-General Howe to repair to Ridgefield with his command. He is to assist General Glover's brigade in protecting that area from enemy incursions. The enemy is numerous in horse. With a good deal of celerity, they can bring a force superior to his. I am cautioning him to not risk his men but be on guard. He is to stay in places where it would be dangerous for the enemy's cavalry to explore.

Thursday, July 29, 1779 — West Point, New York

The Maryland Journal has published an interesting article entitled "Queries: Political and Military," which have been written by the hand of General Lee. Mr. Reed has forwarded the article for my knowledge. On one hand, it is flattering that Lee contends the fate of this Nation rests with one man — me. But the flattery ends there. He questions if that should be. He also questions my strategies, my fitness to command, and what credit I should gain when it appears General Gates and General Arnold are really the two who have kept us in the game. Mr. Reed sends it to me for General Lee references him on occasion as an ally and insider. Reed does not want to be drug back into that. He has refuted Lee's contentions and has renounced them at every turn. I am grateful for Reed's quick response. I had prayed he would remember, in questioning my preferences and trust, that he is the one guilty of infringing on both a while back. Now that prayer has come to the positive answer. I thank the Lord that each thing Lee does only brings dishonor to himself. His actions serve to remind Congress and Mr. Reed of the sacrifices that I make. I have never boasted of my abilities, even at the onset of this contest. I stated clearly this task was above my abilities but that I would sacrifice and suffer for the desired outcome. I said I would not pull back regardless of difficulties. I said that I would see this through. So far, by God's Grace, I have kept my word. It still disappoints my most sanguine expectations to see my name brought into question in Maryland and in any other State. I desire the approbation of my countrymen, not their disapprobation or doubts.

Friday, July 30, 1779 — West Point, New York

Intelligence that can be depended upon, reports General Cornwallis has arrived, and that Admiral Arbuthnot is not far behind with seven thousand troops. A number of transports have also arrived at Sandy Hook.

Sunday, August 1, 1779 — West Point, New York

I am an alien when it comes to European affairs. Knowing what alliances are being formed or not formed would have a great bearing on how I plan for this army at my command. It is one thing to be ignorant of things foreign, but I regret to say I am in the dark with what our own Congress is doing or not doing.

The two greatest evils that can befall a state of war are a reduction of men and a want of money. This army faces both. We lack men. Though we have some currency, it has no value because of the redundancy of printing it. I lament the former. I feel the ill-effects of the latter.

Friday, August 6, 1779 — West Point, New York

Governor Thomas Jefferson who has just taken the place of Governor Patrick Henry has written regarding how to proceed with the prisoner Lieutenant-Governor Henry Hamilton. Hamilton has been over Fort Detroit for the British. He has led the enemy's Indian affairs. He was surrounded and capitulated to our forces. In confinement, the citizens are demanding a severity of punishment upon him. The reason is that it is told he offered the Indians money for the scalps of our people brought to him. His cruelties are well-known. I have suggested those offenses be published for the world to read. He should not receive one act of kindness that other prisoners do receive. This is even more supported when the British make requests for indulgences for this one man.

Tuesday, August 10, 1779 — West Point, New York

Major Henry Lee has submitted plans for an attack on the enemy at Paulus Hook. I am gratified by Major Lee's aggressive nature to prosecute this war upon the enemy to the fullest measure. I do believe he needs to rethink his plan somewhat.

If what I know of the enemy's number in that neighborhood and the amount of men Lee is considering investing, I feel the gain will not measure up to the potential losses. Secrecy would be the key ingredient to success, but one deserter, one slip of the tongue could bring disaster. I would suggest an alternative to his attack. He should consider going at it from the water by way of Newark Bay. If these boats were discovered by the enemy, they would assume the attack is on Staten Island. This would prevent an alarm at Paulus Hook.

Monday, August 16, 1779 — West Point, New York

It has come to my attention that Spain has offered to mediate some sort of peace settlement between Britain and our Nation. Britain has declined. I am not surprised. Britain believes they can take us through attrition. I am assured they are aware of our problems. They must have problems of their own not to attempt a decisive stroke.

Tuesday, August 17, 1779 — West Point, New York

Offers are received weekly from some who seek to be informants on our behalf. Major-General Howe has suggested one. I have had some dealings with this one, but I believe he is reckless. He has the potential to raise suspicions upon himself (if he truly is on our side). I hazard to guess he may be a friend to the highest bidder. Though some information he has given has been accurate, I must be guarded against any acting in double character. I will honor General Howe in giving some financial reward for his services when they are actionable. I will also keep him at a remote distance from this army.

Baron Steuben in his office of inspector-general has incurred expenses that go beyond what his salary can compensate. I am requesting Congress give him an allowance beyond his pay and cover any expenses he incurs in carrying out his necessary service.

Sunday, August 21, 1779 — West Point, New York

Blessed are the feet of those who bring good news. This was such an appropriate message this day from the chaplain at this quarter here at West Point. Yesterday late, I had the honor to receive a return from Lord Stirling reporting that Major Lee has succeeded at Paulus Hook. I await more details. I am extremely thankful that we have now put together two victories — Stony Point and Paulus Hook.

Monday, August 23, 1779 — West Point, New York

More information is arriving of the victory at Paulus Hook. Major Lee was able to gather intelligence to show that the garrison was in a state of negligent security. He attacked with Lord Stirling covering his flank. Beforehand, they secured a way of retreat if the attack failed. It did not. Lieutenant McAllister was able to capture the Standard. I am sending him with it to report to Congress the good news. These men did everything right. They covered every scenario. They pushed the issue with hardly a flaw.

Thursday, August 26, 1779 — West Point, New York

I am writing Jeremiah Powell, President of the Council in Massachusetts. I am forwarding the names of the men from their State who were issued paroles from the enemy and have not returned by their deadlines. Such behavior is ignominious to their character, dishonorable to this country, and damaging to their fellow soldiers in the enemy's hands. We cannot hope to be successful if we act in any way contrary to the word of honor we give. Even the enemy corrected such behavior. Can we allow the villain of our freedoms, the oppressors on our shores appear more virtuous than this Nation of people? God forbid. I am directing the President to do all in his power to force these men to return or suffer worse punishment at our hands.

Wednesday, September 1, 1779 — West Point, New York

Major Lee has exercised prudence, bravery, and enterprise in the reduction of Paulus Hook. He has a complaint at my allowing Lieutenant McAllister to carry the enemy's Standard to Congress instead of Captain Rudolph. I am unsure as to his objection. I believe he is dismayed to have been ordered to retreat from Paulus Hook so soon after taking it. As with Stony Point, the statement has been made to the enemy. They have paid a price for their aggressions. The state of our army at the present does not allow us the luxury of leaving men at posts that are either unsustainable or provide little benefit to the overall war effort. I ascertain this because he requests I write my orders to him on paper so he can defend himself against any criticism that might befall him. My directions were given to him verbally because we were unsure of the situation of that garrison and by what means it might be obtained. I will concur to write these to the best of my recollection.

Friday, September 3, 1779 — West Point, New York

Two good officers now have voiced dissatisfaction over one thing or another. First it was Major Lee. Now, it is my close confidant Major-General Greene. Both have no animosities toward me as their commander, but both disagree with some things that are required by circumstances. General Greene never wished to be quartermaster-general, but his industry was what we needed in that position. He is an amazing tactician in the field. It was at a cost to remove him from that post to handle supplying the army. He has been ideal for the position of quartermaster-general because he knows the needs of the army in the field. He understands the tools an army needs to achieve success.

General Greene seeks to hold both positions concomitantly. Congress has issued the resolve that no officer shall hold more than one commission at a time. Looking over the rules of armies over the years, this has been a good rule. To Greene's point, I have allowed him to take command in the line as the situation necessitated. He did so at Monmouth. He did the same under General Sullivan another time. He is more than capable to serve both, but common sense is the best reasoning for him to not hold the two at once. As quartermaster-general and in the lineal command of a division, it could be argued that he supplies his division with preference to the others. This would bring contempt not to mention excuses for failures in the field. As adept as General Greene is for the field command (and I will continue to use him as the issues warrant), he serves a greater purpose for the army as quartermaster-general. I pray he will understand this and continue doing the superb job at that station.

Tuesday, September 7, 1779 — West Point, New York

The enemy continues some grand scheme, if the large detachments from New York are any indication. Their work on New York Island and at Brooklyn give credence to the belief they are making these posts strong against attack to sustain them with the fewest men possible. This will allow them to move out as they have been doing, perhaps to counter France's successes on the Virgin Islands and Jamaica. I could see the enemy moving on Georgia and South Carolina even more to make up for their losses on the Islands. This will give their government in Britain some compensation for these defeats.

Mindful of this, it bothers me that General Lincoln has not been able to amass a sizeable force. The one he has assembled is in a feeble state. Congress must not withhold any exertions to make them better. Though I do not have much, I will gladly dispatch what I can to that end. I believe I can spare the two North Carolina regiments upon Congress's word.

General Sullivan is having success on the western frontier. Everything that was hoped for is now coming to pass. I am optimistic that in a short time, the Indians will be pushed back and made hesitant to engage again.

Congress is giving me more insight on the European turn of events, which is greatly appreciated. Russia does not seek to aid Britain. The Porte are unable. Spain and France pose an obstacle in the English Channel, but no significant activity has been reported. I could see Denmark, Holland, and Portugal join England as all three have a dependence upon her. This would be a formidable force. I flatter myself to believe this will all be over before any have opportunity to join. That includes the hope that France and Spain come to our aid. If nothing else, the French fleet is wreaking havoc for Britain on her Islands. That distracts them from a full run on this Continent.

Congress is suggesting a certain person to aid with intelligence. I feel this person may be able to assist a time or two. Not residing within the enemy's confines, I do not believe he can do more without raising suspicion, bringing danger to himself. The others they have employed have not produced any useful information. I am letting Congress know that the people who will be best to offer intelligence are those who reside on the enemy's side, whose local associations raise them above suspicion and gives them opportunity to make the most useful of observations. It is with these that I seek to employ and endeavor to establish correspondence.

Sunday, September 12, 1779 — West Point, New York

General Sullivan is now in the heart of the Six Nations with four thousand men near Newtown. The Six Nations with their warriors have been assisted by British regulars and Tories, commanded by the two Butlers, Brand, and a Captain McDonald. These enemies were able to hold out for eight days. They then found their predicament in such a state that they fled from General Sullivan's divisions. They have left behind trinkets, packs, camp-kettles, and many arms. We may have lost at most one hundred men, but Sullivan and his men were able to destroy fourteen of their towns and all their crops. The goal of this enterprise is two-fold — one, make sure the Indians understand that their cruelties will no longer go unpunished; and two, the British are unable to protect them when they do.

The enemy continues their conflagration of New Haven, Fairfield, and Norwalk. Women and children were all that were in these towns for their defense. The British took great pride in their victory over them with two thousand of their "brave" regulars. How anyone can side with these beasts is beyond me. Tories deserve what they get.

Thursday, September 23, 1779 — West Point, New York

John Beatty, our commissary-general of prisoners, has met with Mr. Loring about prisoner exchanges. Again, the British pose another obstacle for the exchange. They continue to press for privates to be exchanged for their officers. We hold to the same stance as before — officer-for-officer of same rank, regular-for- regular, and citizen-for-citizen. The more we do to remove obstacles, the more the enemy presents new ones and revives old ones. They believe that over time, we will wear down and concede to their unfair offer. We will never do that. It appears they have as little concern for their own men in our hands as they do for our homes that they burn. As it now stands, we may never be able to bring about an exchange.

Friday, September 24, 1779 — West Point, New York

One of our most effective men of intelligence, "Culper Junior," is requesting permission to leave his present employment. He wants to dedicate himself to giving information wholly. I would not recommend this. He will bring greater suspicion to himself. He will open himself to easier detection. In the cover of his usual business, he affords himself greater opportunity for observation while maintaining his personal security. In his current occupation, he commends himself the ability to move in and out of the enemy's sight as a citizen seeking to provide for his family. If he is not seen in that realm, then questions will be asked as to his income. Questions he may ask and places he is found will make him suspect.

That aside, I am advising him to use a variety of methods to convey information. Writing notes in books and pamphlets will be effective. Also, writing letters to friends while placing guiding notes (discernible only to the recipients) on the back of several pages in the letters is another mode. To further the pretense, writing many letters will reduce any attempt for discovery. Letters of import can be folded differently to let the recipient know when they contain intelligence.

Tuesday September 28, 1779 — West Point, New York

The enemy has sailed four regiments from New York. A more considerable embarkation is on foot along with a body of cavalry. Any explanation for their movement would be no better than conjecture. Events in Europe and in the West Indies may have caused their commander to consider a scattered aggression.

General Sullivan may be nearing completion of the enterprise on the western frontier. Report is that whole settlements of the Six Nations have been destroyed except for those of the friendly Oneidas. He should now be advancing on their exterior villages.

General Lincoln has made a successful attack at Stone Ferry on the rear guard of the British expedition as they attempt their move on Charleston. Lincoln continues his brilliance of what he can do with untrained and disorderly militia. As

General Greene has a talent in the quartermaster office, as Baron Steuben has a talent to train, General Lincoln has a talent with militia. I know the results were not as fully successful as he wished, even though he did deliver a good blow to the enemy accelerating their retreat from Charleston. I regret that the Virginia succors have been delayed in reaching him. I believe the enemy will make another attempt in South Carolina. If they can take that State and Georgia, it would provide them two States to counterpoise their losses in the Islands. They appear to be evacuating Rhode Island. They may invest three-to-four thousand men to the southern States, which, in their weakened condition, poses a big temptation.

Thursday, September 30, 1779 — West Point, New York

The whereabouts of Count d'Estaing is a mystery. Guesses and rumors come from all corners. This may be intended to keep the British as confused as we are. I rejoice that the French fleet seems not to have abandoned us after all. May this be proven soon.

Monday, October 4, 1779 — West Point, New York

With great relief, I received a letter this morning from Congress that Count d'Estaing is still in the fight to rid this continent of the enemy. I propose he move to New York. I believe it will deal a striking blow. Perhaps this action can change the enemy's opinion if we hit them at the place they cherish most as seen by their extensive fortifications at that head. I am ordering up twelve thousand militia to be ready to move on New York — two thousand from Massachusetts, four thousand from Connecticut, two thousand, five hundred from New York, two thousand from New Jersey, and one thousand and five hundred from Pennsylvania. I am trusting every State to provide for transportation, ammunition, and supplies of their respective men.

I assume General Sullivan has completed his task on the western frontier. I am directing him to move to this quarter with his men, leaving only a few to hold the frontier garrisons. I am also writing General Gates to move his men to this head, unless he has plans to join the effort in Rhode Island. I am directing Major Lee to meet the Count at Monmouth with a letter detailing the options for our coordinated attacks. I have taken the liberty to countermand the two regiments of North Carolina, provided things are to our advantage southward. Congress has sent three Continental frigates to South Carolina. If they have no assigned action in which to engage, I prefer they join the Count's fleet. I am sending two pilots to help guide the Count up the North river and to wherever else the war may lead. Having pilots familiar with the waters here will prevent mishap and delay.

I am writing Count d'Estaing to detail the different options and to apprise him of every complexity. Some of the enemy's ships had sailed for South Carolina to join the attack there but hearing that the French fleet was potentially on route for New York, they returned to defend that stronghold. The British have an estimated fourteen thousand men in New York. Their fleet there is comprised of the Russell seventy-four, the Europe sixty-four, the Renown fifty, and the Roebuck forty-four with a number of small frigates. In my opinion to take New York, it would take over thirty-thousand men. We cannot collect that many men in three weeks' time, so the French fleet would need to wait for a while, inactive. They could take this time to attack the enemy at Rhode Island. This is well-fortified. To overtake it would probably require four weeks. Unfortunately, an attack on Rhode Island would still require blocking any naval exit from New York. This would divide the French fleet. I am sure the Count has his own ideas. I rejoice in a generous succor their help affords. My heart pounds in my chest at the thought that the long journey of suffering may soon come to an end thanks to our foreign friend.

Thursday, October 7, 1779 — West Point, New York

Major Henry Lee has requested specie for payment of spies. We have little to spare. If we start using hard currency more, than our own paper currency will continue to depreciate. Because he has promised it this time, I will oblige, but I must dissuade him from offering that again.

Mr. John Jay has written to inform me he has been appointed as a minister plenipotentiary to Spain with the object of negotiating a treaty of alliance with them. I congratulate him on this appointment. I pray he finds success in gaining more assistance for this noble cause. I also hope his replacement will be as helpful to this army as he has been.

Monsieur Gerard just left my headquarters. He has sought to dampen my enthusiasm. He says Count d'Estaing may be unable to stay for the duration of time this undertaking may require. I am sending General Duportail and Colonel Hamilton to the Count to disclose every circumstance. My prayer is that he will understand what can be done and join without reservation. I will assert my utmost efforts to rally at least twenty-five thousand men. We will expend every resource of this Nation in a vigorous fight to shorten his time commitment. This is the sad state-of-affairs. This Nation is promised help, but we must beg, plead, and accommodate every whim just to get a promise translated into action. The borrower is slave to the lender. I feel myself slave to the lender of aid.

Saturday, October 9, 1779 — West Point, New York

Samuel Huntington has been appointed President of Congress to replace Mr. Jay.

General Sullivan has completed his expedition on the western front. He has achieved every expectation. I rejoice.

General Cornwallis and his men have returned to New York in anticipation of Count d'Estaing. He has also ordered transports of troops to Rhode Island to secure it for attack. May they find a ready and swift attack from our side so that they will not be disappointed for action. May that engagement though bring the British great disappointment in defeat. I await Count d'Estaing just like the British.

Saturday, October 16, 1779 — West Point, New York

General Sullivan has achieved complete destruction of the country of the Six Nations. His men have driven them out of an area where they could attack our inhabitants under the inducement of British reward. General Sullivan was able to accomplish this without losing but forty men to the enemy or to sickness. The Mingo and Muncey tribes living on the Allegany met similar chastisement from Colonel Brodhead and his six hundred men. All this, we pray, will convince these that Great Britain can provoke them to hostilities but will not stand up for them when the consequences are rendered. Perhaps they will comprehend our desire for peace with them. We want all families, Indian or American, to live in peace on their own land in their own settlements.

A bit of more good returns, we were able to capture two transports with four hundred Hessians who are now under our confinement in Philadelphia.

Mr. Jay has left for Spain. Mr. John Adams is on his way to France.

Wednesday, October 20, 1779 — West Point, New York

For fifteen days, we have waited for Count d'Estaing's arrival off the Hook. Each day we peer out of our door like the father looking for the prodigal son in the Lord Jesus' parable. The father was delighted when he saw his son a long distance away. I hope to match that if I can only see the French fleet. Even the top of their mast would bring me the utmost joy. But still none. I am filled with anxiety and impatience. What are we to think of this cat-and-mouse game with our own allies? I am writing the Marquis. He may be able to excite some action. The time in which he would receive my letter, read it, and respond is a long time by ship. I hope that the letter I write will be considered void and will meet his on the seas with good news of freedom.

The enemy is as expectant as we are. They are throwing up works on Staten Island and on the Narrows on Long Island. They are also fortifying the point at Sandy Hook. Obviously, they are worried. Cornwallis ordered eight ships to be sunk. He is about to sink another ten to limit the French entry in the channel. His plan seems to be to make the passageway so narrow that only one ship at a time can pass. Their hope is that they then can summarily defeat each one as it attempts to pass. All this bids me think the enemy is either horribly frightened or greatly confused.

Thursday, October 21, 1779 — West Point, New York

The enemy appears to be making plans to evacuate Stony Point and Verplanck's Point in case the Count appears in New York. They continue their preparation for New York's defense as they await the French prospect. The British also are reported to be abandoning New Port with the plan to deal with kingdom issues that have transpired on the West Indies.

Friday, October 22, 1779

President Reed of Pennsylvania has succeeded in raising the one thousand, five hundred militia that I requested. I congratulate him and his State for finally meeting a quota. He now has requested to lead this group himself. I am content with that, but he desires a commission from this army to do so. I would find it politic to oblige, but the truth is our officers never are comfortable with people given rank who have not earned them in the line. Regardless of who makes the request, for the harmony of the army, I must do what is best for them even if it draws ire to myself.

Monday, November 1, 1779 — West Point, New York

We continue to watch for the French fleet while making preparations for their arrival. The British have evacuated Stony Point and all of Rhode Island. They have assembled the whole of their troops here in New York aside from what they are investing in southward. They are not sparing labor or resources to fortify key points in this city. If the French fleet does not show, I expect the British to descend upon us like an enraged monster. I feel that with this campaign almost spent, they will need some bold stroke to appease their arms, the Tories, and the ministry of Britain.

I am more concerned at this moment for the depreciation of our currency, which grows worse by the day. If only Congress would act to support our currency, I believe our men can draw upon our public virtue to drive the enemy into the sea.

Tuesday, November 2, 1779 — West Point, New York

I received a dispatch from General Gates. His courier brings many excuses to explain his delay — want of horses, bad roads, Congressional requests to name a few. I regret this as the lack of his men and information may have deprived me of some bold act or some needed defense. I am calling on him to come to me without a moment's delay. I grow weary of General Gates.

Friday, November 5, 1779 — West Point, New York

I am asking Mr. Henry Laurens to use his influence to try to stop the decline of the dollar. The lack of Congressional activity, coupled with our own country-men's acts of stockjobbing and speculating reflect a complete disregard for patri-otism and virtue. A few days ago, I wrote that by summoning our virtue, we can drive the enemy to the sea. I am prayerful virtue is still to be had. When I look outside my quarters, I just see a virtuous few who struggle in silence, fighting while others live with complete apathy.

Not a single syllable has been heard from Count d'Estaing. No report of any engagement that he or his fleet have made, not one assistance in any quarter that I am aware. Yet, here are my men making expensive preparations day-after-day for a groom who may never show.

Thursday, November 11, 1779 — West Point, New York

I am writing General Duportail and Colonel Hamilton to give them my thoughts and some direction. They have been waiting to inform the Count of our prepara-tions and plans, but he has not shown. Now I wonder if Congress knows some-thing. I am holding them there for just a little while longer. I will have to recall them soon. I am instructing them that at this late in the season, I do not expect the Count to arrive. If he does, no enterprise can be prosecuted with the weather our obstacle. I do not want them to share my plans with the Count until direction from Congress gives us instruction. I am telling Major Lee the same. We will withhold our pilots from the French fleet except for one to secure their safety on the chance they arrive.

Tuesday, November 16, 1779 — West Point, New York

The enemy is laying siege to Savannah. They seem to be laying strong fortifica-tions. They have appeared there with more men than we anticipated. I see no way to reduce that number any time soon. Our men attempted to dislodge them a few days ago but were unsuccessful. I am telling General Gates with the activity there and the lack of activity here, to halt his troops in Danbury.

Thursday, November 18, 1779

In this lull while the winter season is upon us, it is important that I do not waste time. The number of our troops by muster-rolls total almost twenty-seven thousand, including regular army, militia, and officers. That number is near-sufficient if that number were true. An army is always greater on paper than it is in actuality. To judge an army by those present and fit for duty is better. That is really the only number you can count on. The sick of course reduce the number on paper, but enlistments expiring shrink both.

I am going to take liberty again to revisit the draft and terms of enlistment to Congress. Each State should be given the ability to raise the men they need on their own, without individual State bounties. Whatever number they are short should be enhanced through a draft in each State. In my proposed plan, the drafts and the recruitments must be for a one-year term. They must report to this army by January 1st. This will give them the winter months to get seasoned, accustomed to camp life, trained, disciplined, and equipped for the coming campaign. With such a plan, this army can then make plans on what business must be conducted. Their expiration would be the following January. My longing is that they would love the cause and stay in it. Regardless, by October of the year of their enlistment, our officers can determine what the need will be for the next campaign. That will be reported to the respective States per their quotas.

As the various recruitment methods are going currently, men show up throughout the year. They often arrive in the middle of a campaign. These men have no time to acclimate to the camp life nor can they gain the training to be of any significant help to the effort. It is a hodge-podge method where patches are placed on the quilt. They are being sewn in without giving them time to be shrunk and cut for proper and enduring placement. My prayer is that Congress will adopt my plan instead. Or I pray they will forgive my intervening in matters that they may determine out of my realm of input.

Wednesday, November 24, 1779 — West Point, New York

Things are not going well in Savannah per General Lincoln's letter. I fear a disaster is near. I see no way to get our men to that quarter in a timely or safe manner.

Friday, November 26, 1779 — Peekskill, New York

The enemy is preparing for a considerable debarkation of troops from New York. Their destination is unknown. It may be to secure South Carolina and Georgia. Congress is requesting that I send the whole of the Virginia troops. I do not believe I can spare them. I will let them know that their departure will put this army in a weaker state. But, at their order, I will send them. I fear that sending these men is an act of futility. Traveling by land, their numbers will be greatly reduced through fatigue, sickness, desertion, and the expiration of enlistments along the way. I do not believe they could get there in time to offer succor. I would suggest Congress arranges a way to move them by sea. That poses a danger though, in this late season. They could easily be washed out to sea by a boisterous storm or placed in the throes of the enemy's ships. If they do decide to send them by sea, they will need six weeks-worth of provisions in case they are carried off-course.

Wednesday, December 1, 1779 — Morristown, New Jersey

We have returned for winter encampment in Morristown. If the current conditions are any indication, this is going to be a hard winter. Mrs. Ford sent her son to meet me on my way into town. He had a message that Mrs. Ford wished to speak with me. Her husband, Colonel Jacob Ford, died a couple of years ago when we were camped here the first time. When I arrived at their home, Mrs. Ford came out to greet me. She has offered her home to me and my officer family as headquarters. She had already moved her family into two small rooms before I arrived. She has opened the remainder of her home to my discretion. We are so blessed by this family and many others who have done the same throughout this journey. We have moved in. About thirty of us are hutting in this beautiful home. My papers have been unpacked. We now ready for the work.

Saturday, December 5, 1779 — Morristown, New Jersey

The main part of our army is up on a hill about three miles from the Ford home. It is one of the highest places in the area. Henry Wick and his family have been gracious to let almost ten thousand of our men hut on their land. Mr. Wick has been a successful farmer on his fourteen-hundred-acre farm. His family produces wheat, corn, hay, and rye. They have an apple orchard from which they make cider. He has a bountiful vegetable garden to provide for his family's needs. Thankfully, he has many trees, which he has obliged our men to cut down for their quarters. Our men have wasted no time. We are racing to beat winter.

Tuesday, December 7, 1779 — Morristown, New Jersey

Rumor has it that many British ships will be sailing from New York to England once they determine that the French squadron has left the coast. What is not a rumor is that it appears the enemy seeks to increase the depreciation of our currency. They are engaging in counterfeits to expedite this. I am writing Congress in hopes they can take action to stop this monetary attack.

A considerable part of our army will be moving to Georgia once we know that the French fleet is near the coast.

Governor Livingston has received some harsh criticism of late. I am encouraging him with the wisdom I have found in the many attacks upon my character. The best answer to calumny is to persevere in one's duty. Stay silent. All will work out if we do.

Friday, December 10, 1779 — Morristown, New Jersey

The Wick family has opened their home to serve as a headquarters for General St. Clair for the time being. He is grateful. So am I.

Sunday, December 12, 1779 — Morristown, New Jersey

I am mortified at the ill success of our allied arms against the enemy at Savannah. The one golden strand in this misfortune is that our French volunteers and the

American armies worked together. Despite the failure of enterprises, they have grown in esteem and confidence for each other. Upon Congress's request, the Virginia line is being directed southward. The troops began to march yesterday with the rest leaving in a few days. I have desired vessels be used to transport the convoy, but it appears that has been declined.

Monday, December 13, 1779 — Morristown, New Jersey

Governor Clinton has received accusations from the inhabitants of the area toward a few of our officers. I regret to say that sometimes, in the course of events, things in the military line cannot be supported by civil law. If he finds that this is the case, and no egregious offense has occurred, I am asking him to prevent the intended prosecution. If crimes have been committed by our officers toward the public, I wish them to suffer the full penalty of the law.

Tuesday, December 14, 1779 — Morristown, New Jersey

Brigadier-General Woodford has done an excellent job getting the artillery ready. The rest of the Virginia troops will move tomorrow. I am sending them from Head of Elk to Williamsburg, and from there to South Carolina. I am asking General Woodford to be on guard. As these men march through their home State, desertions will take place. He must be vigilant to take every precaution to prevent this as far as possible. They need to move rapidly as the interests of America may essentially require it. As an officer, his duty is what I require of every officer, namely train and prepare the men for the field, supply their necessary wants, restrain licentiousness (which may be the most important requirement for our success), support and honor the dignity of the corps, be attentive to their clothing needs and their uniform application, have arms and accoutrements always in order, and abide strictly by military rules, regulations, and orders. The regularity of well-organized troops must move like clockwork.

Wednesday, December 15, 1779 — Morristown, New Jersey

I am saddened by the news this army will be deprived the services of Major-General Sullivan. He has written to inform me that he is resigning. I am always disappointed when I receive these notices. I personally wish every man would stay with me to the end. Every day men leave, officers resign, and I am left to pick up the pieces. I must continually fill holes with untried men. I often must settle for less than qualified men. By God's Grace, more often than not, someone comes along and fills the spot admirably. This can only be by Providence's Hand. If it were not for Him, I would worry infinitely more. I would be devasted even further.

To add to the sadness, General Sullivan informs me that the intrigues of Mr. Conway continue in conjunction with General Gates and others. He shares that these and others seek to slander me. They use every method in their power to convince Congress and our citizens that I am inept. They report that this Nation is in danger as long as I lead it. I come back to the advice that I shared with Governor Livingston. The best answer to calumny is to persevere in one's duty and be silent. All will work out if we do. By the Disposer of events, I trust this will be true every time.

Thursday, December 16, 1779 — Morristown, New Jersey

I rode up to Wick's Farm to check the progress of the camp construction. This is a strategic location. Roads are going in every direction from this spot. On a moment's notice, we can respond to the enemy's movements. We also possess a vantage point that completely prevents a British surprise upon this army. Supplies are plentiful. More can be had. The British have New York. I regret that. However, I am grateful for this place.

Friday, December 17, 1779 — Morristown, New Jersey

Reverend Mr. D came to me this day to say that Congress has employed him to be a missionary to the Indians in Canada. He asserts he will take liberty while amongst the enemy to report back any intelligence that may assist this effort. He is a Frenchman on top of that. His help could be a blessing. I am not sure at this time if his offer is sincere or if he means mischief. Even among the clergy, a lot of wolves in sheep's clothing are present. If Congress finds that he is worthy of confidence, I will be glad to oblige. I am asking Congress to send me their instructions for him once he is approved and allow me to add some additional instructions.

Saturday, December 18, 1779 — Morristown, New Jersey

People are going into New York selling their produce. They are buying goods on their return and offer intelligence to us regarding the enemy. I fear they are in this more for their own emoluments than to the business that they profess. The information that they have produced so far is vague and unactionable. General Parsons says other men have offered to gather intelligence for us but will have to charge a fee. I am suspicious of many for fear the enemy has sent them. Intelligence is worth money if it saves lives and gives us an advantage, but every care must be made. Besides, I am not sure how we can pay for any of it when I consider the scant supply we have of hard money. The depreciating value of our currency is no help either.

My nephew George Augustine Washington has shared his warm desire for service in this army. I think it is late for him to start upon a military career, but I want to satisfy his wishes if possible. I will see if General Woodford can find a place within his line if the State recommends him for commission and the Board of War approves. I hesitate to mention this to anyone for fear that he will be given a commission upon my request alone. Then other men will feel their reasonable expectations have been skipped over on behalf of my nephew. I am very honestly seeking General Woodford's quiet inquiry into this matter. If there is the slightest concern, I want his request to be rejected. Once the war is over and I am not in this position, then he can come in on his own merit if he still desires a place.

Tuesday, December 21, 1779 — Morristown, New Jersey

The enemy is still held up in New York. The assumption is they will soon depart for the West Indies or more likely the southern States. The army here is to be kept on guard as all the transports and rumors could be a feint to allow the enemy to make a move at this head. I am writing Major-General Heath at West Point to be ready to come to our aid should the enemy move on us. The militia needs to be kept on standby in New York as well.

I believe Sir Henry Clinton is feeling pressure from home to make a move. It is said that he is receiving criticism for his inactivity when his force is far superior to ours. He is aware of our lack of men and supplies. As we depend on intelligence, he does too. He is aware that we had to send our horses at some distance from us so they could be supplied forage. If he were to turn on us here, we would have little to respond. He could easily destroy our huts and supplies and make the winter months impossible for this army to remain in existence.

Wednesday, December 22, 1779 — Morristown, New Jersey

Major-General Greene is having trouble finding shelter for our officers. The local magistrates are refusing to assist. This brings a perplexing dilemma. We do not seek to bring distress or incommode upon the inhabitants when avoidable. But our officers are serving this Nation and those inhabitants. If the magistrates will not help bring covering to our officers, they must be told with one more application that their rejection will require a more aggressive action to house our men. I want General Greene to make this last request in writing. He is to require a response from them in writing so that they are on record. Then we can show that we have exhausted every civility. I can never understand the unwillingness of our own people to care for the men who are contending for their liberties. The nature of man is to want things, but to expect them to come without effort, sacrifice, or inconvenience? Nothing worth having can be had in that manner. It comes back to Mr. Patrick Henry's contention that many would prefer life, peace, and financial security even if involved enslavement or removal of all rights.

Saturday, December 25, 1779 — Morristown, New Jersey

I rode up earlier today to give our men my Christmas greeting. I will not take for granted where they are this day — in the cold, as opposed to many of their countrymen who celebrate in the warmth of their homes with their families. At least my men are warmly in their huts this Christmas day. That is some consolation.

What delighted me was to see Lieutenant Hovenburgh of the 4th New York Regiment working on his hut. He has followed my desire to the letter. I have a standing order that no officer shall be hutted until their men's lodgings are complete. Officers command, but they command best with a servant's heart. Jesus washed the feet of His disciples. He says the greatest are to be the least. I have followed this practice as Commander-in-Chief. I desire that same attitude in every officer. To see our officers have taken this to heart is gratifying.

December 31, 1779 — Morristown, New Jersey

It is the eve of a new year. If today's arrival is any indication, this will be a great year. Mrs. Washington has come to my side. I am always relieved to have her company. She was led to the Ford mansion by one of my guards. We all ran out to meet her. Mrs. Ford heard she was coming and made a special meal to welcome her. What a great evening we had.

Before turning in for the night, Mrs. Washington shared with me all that she had been tending to at Mount Vernon. She also shared about the rigors of her travel here. The one comfort she said she found in this town, next to my presence, was how this home reminds her of Mount Vernon. I must agree. Though not the same, it has a feel of home, especially now that my helpmate has arrived.

The Year 1780

Sunday, January 2, 1780 — Morristown, New Jersey

I have often complained about foreign men coming to join us in this contest requesting commissions, the majority of those being from France. They have brought a burden to me and many complaints from our men. I am delighted to write again in my diary today that this is not true for some. The Marquis de Lafayette is a delightful exception. Though he left these shores to serve in his home country, he has been a blessing to this Nation and especially to me. When adversaries rise at every corner, it is a relief to find one who seconds my opinions and holds me in such high regard. Often, I dwell on this one who has taken charge when it was needed, who has taken a lower position when that was needed. He simply wants to serve for our purpose in any capacity where he can be of assistance.

Add to his name, Brigadier-General Duportail, Colonel Laumoy, and Lieutenant-Colonel Gouvion. Congress has requested that they be retained for the coming campaign. I am asking that they stay until the conclusion of the war unless their Nation needs them for some war that may arise in Europe. Congress also asked for Colonel Radiere to remain. They must not have heard the news that Colonel Radiere is no longer among our number. He died in battle. We owe him a debt of gratitude. I will join my letter with Congress's requesting the French Court allow them to remain.

Tuesday, January 4, 1780 — Morristown, New Jersey

Brigadier-General Irvine informs me he is in an embarrassing and distressful circumstance regarding provisions. I am writing him back that we are of the same scanty pittance. He is borrowing from the inhabitants in his quarter but says it will not last long. I am directing him to do all in his power to estimate the cattle (no milch cows) and provision in the vicinity of his command to assess how much the local inhabitants can spare to the army. He is to ask for their assistance. He is to provide them a certificate for anything given so that in due time they can be paid what their stock is worth at the time of giving it or at the time payment is available. My preference would be to value it at the time of receipt. Weights and measures should be attended by one or more inhabitants to insure fairness. Tender care should be given to each with respect to obviate those clamors of feelings that may arise. The local magistrates should be able to help gain the public's aid. We are only looking to gather what the neighbors can spare, never wanting to leave them in want. If the inhabitants or magistrates will not comply, then provision must be taken through compulsion which is the least favored of all options. Even then, this must be done with the utmost respect for the integrity of this Nation.

Colonel Brodhead has written for permission to invade Detroit. He and I agree that a winter campaign would be of great advantage versus a summer one. Regrettably, this army is not in a condition to take such a step. We lack men and supplies. Even with the addition of militia, the enemy's numbers show our army and militia there unequal to the attempt. It is a sad state-of-affairs when opportunity presents itself to bring a stroke upon the enemy, but we are too anemic for an attempt. This army is unable to send reinforcements as we have sent part of our army to South Carolina. Many others are about to leave due to terms of service expiring. Brodhead suggests another option — an attack at the Natchez. This would be easier for him. Even then, Fort Pitt might be exposed. I am too unfamiliar with the Natchez completely to deny his request. I am asking that he gather his numbers and decide his path of attack. Then he can apprise me of his plan. Whatever he does, I must emphasize that it must be done in complete secrecy. Surprise is the only thing that can substitute for lack of men.

Wednesday, January 5, 1780 — Morristown, New Jersey

Britain has come closer to our terms on prisoner exchanges. One hang-up I face from the Continental side of prisoners, we have the enemy's men in confinement, but some States have also taken enemy prisoners. This is a poor practice. The enemy has more of our officers than we have of theirs. Any exchange of officer-for-officer puts them at an advantage. If we can gain the enemy prisoners from the States, then we will have a better opportunity to get our own officers back.

Saturday, January 8, 1780 — Morristown, New Jersey

Our men have been almost perishing from want. They alternate between being without bread or being without meat. Often, they are without either. I join them in this suffering for I cannot dare eat while they starve. I will not set my needs above theirs. Too many in leadership feel they are so important that they are entitled to better care while those under them do without. There is no Commander-in-Chief, no general, no Congressman, no magistrate, and no king so important that they cannot be risked for the greater cause. Every one of us is replaceable. I have found that to be true in the turnover of my officers. Some officers I do not want to lose, but we have been able to persevere without them. Where one falls, another man from the line steps up to assume that role.

Our men have borne suffering with patience and without approbation of their countrymen. They are fighting for these who do not appreciate them. They are undeterred because they are fighting for higher purposes — God and freedom. These are men of virtue, but how long can they remain virtuous? At some point, starvation pushes them to recourses that they would normally not grasp. Depredations due to hunger have occurred in some instances. If our fellow citizens do not lend a hand, the evil will increase. Before long, it would not just be our soldiers who suffer but virtuous inhabitants too. I am calling on the States to make extraordinary exertions to satisfy the needs of their army — emphasis is on "their" army. They are in the field for them. They are fighting on behalf of their friends and neighbors.

As a result, as I have instructed General Irvine to gather the provisions his brigade needs, I am instructing Colonel Ogden to do the same for the army at this head. He is to call upon the respective counties of the State for a portion of the grain and cattle (no milch cows). I am addressing the magistrates of every county to induce them to assist in this business. If the requisition is not complied with, then we will raise our own supplies the best manner we can. This will be to the chagrin of the inhabitants and ourselves. I want Colonel Ogden to focus on

Essex county with dispatch to call upon the justices. He is to deliver my written address, which will detail the true sufferings of our troops.

He is to let them know delicately that if they do not assist immediately, we will begin to impress the articles called for throughout the county. With everything we gather, market price will be given at the time of receipt or at the time of payment. Again, my preference for economy sake is for the price at the time of receipt. We also need to press for wagons to transport any grain we receive.

Sunday, January 9, 1780 — Morristown, New Jersey

Sometimes men who are starving and taking action to meet their necessities, need a distraction. I believe this is the reason General Irvine is requesting an attack on Staten Island. It will engage the men. Perhaps with even a small victory, it will supply them too. I am not unwilling for him to make this attempt provided he weighs the cost. He must ascertain the state of the ice in the Sound, especially at Halstead's Point and Blazing-Star Ferry. Irvine must also gain insight into the state of Paulus Hook, the condition of the North river, and the practicality of relief coming from New York. He needs to obtain intelligence as to the enemy's strength, situation, and works. Everything he does must be done in disguise and under false pretenses, even with his spies that he is utilizing. The chance always exists that a spy may as easily work for the enemy as for us, hurting both while profiting both ways.

Wednesday, January 12, 1780 — Morristown, New Jersey

I am instructing Lord Stirling to join General Irvine in his attempt on Staten Island. They must cooperate upon the best place of passage. Colonel Hazen is marching this morning with a detachment from his command. He should reach Connecticut Farms tomorrow and form a junction with Irvine by Friday. I will send them one hundred and fifty pairs of shoes for those who are without. I will also spare forty thousand musket cartridges. Colonel Ogden should be able to assist with supplies and intelligence. I want him to have Colonel Ford to daily (and sometimes more often) check the state of the ice for crossing.

Thursday, January 13, 1780 — Morristown, New Jersey

Colonel Hazen made the journey to junction with General Irvine a day early. We cannot have so many men seen at one time. It will draw the enemy's suspicion. I am suggesting General Irvine give the appearance he is returning to his camp. I am asking Lord Stirling to have the men in sleds, who are to assist them, meet in Springfield (again to avoid sending an alarm). I sent General Stewart's detachment to join the enterprise. I have ordered them to halt in Quibbletown under the pretense to forage there.

All things look ready for attack. I am leaving it to Lord Stirling to decide if an attempt upon the enemy openly will succeed. If he deems it will, then he needs to act promptly before the weather changes. He will need to keep an eye on the North river in case the enemy sends down reinforcements upon news of an attack. The British surely do not want to lose so valuable a stronghold as Staten Island.

Friday, January 14, 1780 — Morristown, New Jersey

I have directed Lieutenant-Colonel Dehart with his detachment of two hundred and fifty men to move from Paramus to Newark then to Bergen to watch the enemy along the North river and Paulus Hook. He is to communicate to Lord Stirling any information that applies to his activity. Some inhabitants are aware that something is in agitation. They are preparing to plunder the Island afterward. This is to be prevented as far as possible. If Lord Stirling is able to come upon the Island, he must inform the inhabitants that if they are found with arms, they will be treated as the enemy. Their effects will be taken as plunder. This is a strong statement that may be misinterpreted. I want Stirling to issue this as a warning. I am instructing him not to see it through. To tell the wheat from the tares is difficult. I do not want those who are for us to be mistaken as enemies and suffer undeservedly.

Colonel Stewart's men have passed by me at two o'clock today. Artillery passed by this place at four o'clock. I had ordered five hundred axes with shovels and picks for Stirling's use, but found there were only one hundred and eighty in store. These will be sent, nonetheless. I wish I knew the weather and its rending passage from the Island to Bergen Point. I do not. I am trusting the execution of the enterprise to Lord Stirling. To do this is hard, knowing that the outcome falls on me — success or fail. I am encouraged though that I have found Lord Stirling to be an officer in whose judgment our Nation can rely. It comes back to the question, what if something happens to General Washington, would the war be over? I am replaceable. Lord Stirling would be a fine man to carry on as would General Greene or General Arnold.

Thursday, January 20, 1780 — Morristown, New Jersey

I am appreciative that my request for supplies has been attended to with a cheerful zeal by the counties of this State. It should satisfy us from any recurrence of want.

Saturday, January 22, 1780 — Morristown, New Jersey

General Greene informs me that some believe I am benefiting from the public expense above the state of our army. He is not in their company nor does he share in their accusations. Whoever has voiced such should come to my quarters. Appearance and facts must speak for themselves. Currently, I am quartering with eighteen of my family in Mrs. Ford's kitchen with little wood to burn. Most of our group are sick with colds. My fundamental principle is to share the common lot and inconveniences of this army. I can accept attacks for my shortcomings and bad decisions, but fabricated abuses are another matter.

Monday, January 24, 1780 — Morristown, New Jersey

Captain Rochefontaine, a foreign officer, writes that while he was tending to army business, Lieutenant-Colonel Stevens took over his quarters. This is an unlucky thing that is bound to occur in this army. We are a collection of moving pieces, never knowing when or where one goes and for what purpose, not to mention if they will return. I am asking General Greene to accommodate Captain Rochefontaine as he is a foreign ally helping from a distant shore. Unlike our men, he cannot request a short leave to visit family or gain some relief and encouragement from home.

Tuesday, January 25, 1780 — Morristown, New Jersey

Not only do our inhabitants appear to feel an agitation is soon coming, but the enemy has also doubled the garrisons at Staten Island and at Paulus Hook. It may be a coincidence as the enemy may be planning some attack of their own. If the weather holds and the ice passage is maintained between New York and Paulus Hook, the enemy will easily be able to augment their force with great facility. I have information that the enemy is moving sleds of wood between New York and Hoboken. This may afford us the opportunity to strike some of their covering parties.

Thursday, January 27, 1780 — Morristown, New Jersey

I am ordering General St. Clair to cover the country near the enemy lines where traffic is entering and leaving the city of New York. He can harass the enemy. Perhaps, he can slow the traffic of goods supplying the enemy. I desire that he also gain a more accurate perspective of the enemy's condition on Staten Island, Paulus Hook, the ice on the North river, and any other information that might be beneficial. St. Clair can also provide help by determining the number of ships and flat boats at the enemy's disposal. He may be able to discern what stratagem is under the enemy's consideration. General St. Clair is to mind the security of his troops, but if he sees an opportunity that has a good chance for success, I will give him discretion to launch an attack.

I have just received information that the enemy made an attack on some of our towns in Jersey on the 25th. Homes and meeting houses were burned along with a church. They plundered some inhabitants. They have taken a few privates as prisoners. I am dispatching Colonel Hazen to that area with two thousand rank-and-file to prevent such an occurrence again.

Friday, January 28, 1780 — Morristown, New Jersey

Colonel Willett has a plan to burn the enemy's transports iced in at Turtle Bay. I have consented to this experiment. I am suggesting the men of Webb's regiment wear red coats as disguise when they join in the enterprise. I am prayerful for success in each of these plans now underway. It is early in the season, but with such inactivity of late, any blow would be a potential harbinger for the coming campaign.

Saturday, January 29, 1780 — Morristown, New Jersey

I am sorry to find that Congress has made no requisition for reinforcements for the coming campaign. We need those reinforcements to fill the places of those whose terms are expiring and further to supplement our ranks. I have expressed our needs. I have shared that a difference exists between an army on paper and those fit for duty. I believe a complacency comes from the belief that peace is soon to be had. What our people do not realize is that a well-manned army with ample provisions is the greatest guarantor of peace. If we are strong, the enemy will want peace. If we are strong, the enemies of America will think twice to break peace. And, if we are strong, foreign allies like France and Spain are more likely to join us. I am writing Eldridge Gerry in Congress to plead that he use his influence to meet our ignored needs.

Tuesday, February 1, 1780 — Morristown, New Jersey

We have had fifteen snowstorms so far at this head. The cold cuts right through us. I am grateful that our men hutted before the worst hit. Many trees were felled to construct their quarters, but thankfully we still have wood to burn.

As Mrs. Washington is here, so are many other wives. God knew what He was doing when He provided someone to walk through life with us. Private Martin's wife has been near his side for the last few weeks. Today, we received joyful news on this cold morning. She has given birth to a son. They have named him Joseph, Jr. Joy is present in the camp. I rode out from the Ford place to personally greet this little one into this world. I pray that before he is able to walk, he will find himself in a free nation. His father and mother are doing their part to bring that about.

Friday, February 4, 1780 — Morristown, New Jersey

Chevalier de la Lucerne has written some great news. The Germans have declined the British request for troops. This is a delightful turn of events. If the British cannot receive succors across the ocean, they may be more apt to carry out prisoner exchanges to bolster their numbers. They will likely attempt to recruit locally as well, but knowing that the British seek dominance of the Thirteen States, their entreaties should meet with little positive response.

Saturday, February 5, 1780 — Morristown, New Jersey

I am sending stain to Major Talmadge to be used by our agents in conveying intelligence. I am suggesting that letters be written to friends and family concerning domestic matters. In between the lines and at the bottom of each page, they can communicate with the stain the intelligence intended. In this manner, these letters will pass through the hands of any enemy who comes upon them in an unsuspecting manner.

I do wish Culper Junior would find a more direct method to relay his information to me. I value what he sends, but the circuitous route by which he sends the intelligence sometimes reaches me at a point where it is too late to act. I am suggesting to him some men whom I trust to be the direct recipients of his messages. I am also willing for any ideas he may have. I am asking Major Talmadge to bring a better expedience so that Culper Junior's work can be of fullest utility.

Monday, February 6, 1780 — Morristown, New Jersey

I am seeking to combine Colonel Armand's corps with the late Pulaski's. This will leave Colonel Armond without a command. I am gladdened by his willingness to accept this. He sees the wisdom in such a move. What is notable, like the Marquis, he is not preoccupied by rank or pride. He just wants to serve in any capacity for the freedom of our Nation. I would like to think that I could step down from Commander-in-Chief of this army and become a brigadier-general or a major in this army for the sole purpose to see our people free. I believe that lies within me. That determination has not been placed upon me, but in many ways, I believe I would not only adhere to the demotion but rejoice in the lessening of burden. To me, it would be easier just to fight the enemy in front of me when action is begun, then to haggle and plead for the existence of the army, form the strategies to defeat the enemy, and protect against actions that would bring defeat. Britain's defeat means a loss of a property. Our defeat means the loss of freedom and liberty, perhaps even life for us who are fully invested. Yes, fighting on the line would be preferable, but I am not sure my sense of the whole would allow it.

As Commander-in-Chief, I have engaged an interesting company called the Marechaussee. Their activity has reduced our losses and maintained our numbers beyond what they normally would. They maintain order, put down squabbles, deal with instigators in the camp, go after deserters, spur stragglers, and man the rear for those who linger near the picket without a pass.

Wednesday, February 8, 1780 — Morristown, New Jersey

This army seems to have run into a good train of favor. The shortages of this army are being filled. Men are sacrificially serving. Intelligence is arriving. The enemy is having to face obstacles not seen before. Baron Steuben is now using his expertise in helping Congress know what this army needs. He is helping me focus our options of an offensive or defensive strategy. At the present, a defensive strategy is all that our number of men can consider. Our financial condition as a nation makes economy a priority. Congress is looking to combine or reduce battalions as we are short of good officers to lead them. This will also reduce our expenditures for officers.

Sunday, February 19, 1780 — Morristown, New Jersey

Several of our soldiers are complaining of the New Jersey Judge Mr. Symmes who had forced our men to stay beyond their enlistments. I believe his motives are right, but if we force men who join to stay beyond their commitments, then no one will want to join for fear they will have to remain. This is an injury on the backend of our recruitment. The injury on the frontend continues where States are offering bounties higher than what other States or the Continental Army can offer. Once a few men are signed for one thousand pounds for shorter enlistments, the rest who signed for less pay and longer enlistments become disenchanted. They demand equal pay or resign. This will cause our military system to become completely unhinged. It is another concern that often makes serving in the lines a better occupation for this commander.

Wednesday, February 22, 1780 — Morristown, New Jersey

Traffic is being implemented with avidity to bring supplies to the enemy in New York. All this is done by our own people living outside of New York. They are trading freedom for a large profit. I am assigning the task to Colonel Willett to retard this practice. In addition, he needs to establish intelligence lines between Secaucus, the city, the North river, Bergen, and this headquarters.

I have taken a walk down from headquarters. It is hard to think with so many coming and going. I passed the Life Guards who are stationed around the Ford house for my protection. A couple asked to go with me for safety's sake. I declined. They know me well enough by now. I needed time to think and pray. Another snowstorm hit two days ago. Everything is covered in white. I have tried to separate myself from the suffering and cold for a moment. The snow has always held a magical mystery with me. Though our sins be as scarlet, He shall make them whiter than snow. Our sins are weighing on me. My sins, but also the sins of my countrymen who betray our cause. I think of the famous evangelist, another George, George Whitefield. He made a mighty impression on this nation, even in men who were not as prone to religion like Mr. Franklin. We need another Awakening, not just for freedom but for righteousness. I sit on a stump of a downed tree out here in the snow. I am praying for God to continue to aid our cause for victory for certain. More so, I pray for the hearts of our people to have a regard and a return to Him.

Monday, February 27, 1780 — Morristown, New Jersey

General Lincoln reports better news southward. He is building up defenses. The Spaniards' activity in Florida is hoped to draw the enemy to that quarter to protect their possessions there. It may at least distract them and divide their forces further. From my perspective, their resistance to recognize our independence is costing them in many sectors — their islands, Florida, in Europe, and alliances in America. If pride would allow them, common sense would win the day. They could realize the betterment for their nation to settle for peace. This will save face and save possessions. The lives saved will be the most significant benefit of all.

Wednesday, March 1, 1780 — Morristown, New Jersey

Spring is not far away. Winter seems as though it will not leave without a fight. We are longing for the warmth. I am reminded of getting up early to hunt when I was young. The morning would be cold and dark. The whole time, I would long to see the sun break the horizon. Then, I would be able to see clearly, but more, the sunshine breaking forth brought warmth with the promise of more warmth as the day progressed. This army has been in the coldest darkest winter that I can remember. March is here. Now, we wait for spring to break forth in the same way. We long for the sun's warmth to chase this frigid weather away.

Sunday, March 5, 1780 — Morristown, New Jersey

Chaplain Hays, in this morning's service, spoke about the woman who took the lamp and went throughout her house looking for the silver coin she had lost. He spoke about how valuable that Divine Kingdom is, how we are to value it and search for it like that dear lady. He also turned the message toward judging ourselves so that we will not be judged. His application was insightful as he said we must take the lamp of God's Word. We are to search our own lives just as diligently for the presence of any transgressions that we should put away. I am doing that today in my own life.

I found another application today as I read the orders General Stirling has given his men. His orders are an effective promulgation of the established "Regulations for the Order and Discipline of the Troops." What is lacking with General Stirling (I have touched on this very slightly at our last interview), those regulations addressed must be followed by close attention to their performance. Some hear them, others read them, some inaccurately attend to them, while a few completely disregard them. This will continue to be the case until the principal officers of this army begin the work of reformation by close inspection. Officers of every denomination must inspect narrowly into the conduct of the army placed under their care. If they do not, we will see the creep of neglect in discipline, want of order, irregularity, waste, abuse, and embezzlement of property. Each officer must expend a portion of their time each day inspecting the affairs of their command to ensure that the regulations are being dutifully followed. Deficiencies can then be addressed and corrected. This will generate a uniform army with working arms — clean, supplied, and ready at a moment's notice.

If I were not overwhelmed with the multiplicity of letters and papers received daily, I would expend a greater portion of my time on the military parts of my duty. Every time that I have had the opportunity to inspect our men with the few rides that I can make into the camp, I have found many instances of inattention and relaxation of discipline. Such things lead ultimately to agitation, theft, and even murder in the camp. I pray this is soon rectified. The officers need to take that same lamp of regulations and search out the army under their command to clean things up, so that all can succeed as we desire.

Monday, March 6, 1780 — Morristown, New Jersey

The message of Chaplain Hays resonated with me all day. The power of his message and the call for introspection brought an awareness to my walk that I have not had in a while. The delivery of the message also made an impact on our men. Before us yesterday morning was this old chaplain. He had some disorder of the shakes. He has for some time. As he held the Bible, it shook in his hand to the point that he could not read it. He laid it on a nearby stump, slid his glasses on, and began with a low and quiet voice. As we strained to hear him, no one moved. It was as if everyone in the camp exerted themselves to catch what was said. As he got into the sermon, his voice would rise and then fall. The execution was exceptional and shocking from a man of such unsteady posture.

I had the chaplain to my quarters to join my military family for a meal. He shared his story with us. It made us all appreciate even more what it means to be an American living free in the land we love. In his younger years as a merchant, he had gained great wealth. He even was once a partner with our patriot Robert Morris. But then Chaplain Hays lost it all. He said he was on the cusp of taking his life when he had a visit from the Lord. He did not see Him, nor did he audibly hear Him, but he said His Voice was unmistakable. He was pointed to several passages in the Bible. The chief one stated that he was to seek first the Kingdom of Heaven and God would add all things to him. With that, he left the enterprise to recapture lost wealth. He began to preach God's Word. He has never regained his earthly riches, but he has a comfortable home in New York. He told us that the greatest riches of which he had ever dreamed were given to him. He paused. He had just said no earthly wealth had been restored. The old chaplain could tell we were at a loss. He then broke the silence to tell us that his wife, his son, and his daughter all gave their hearts to the Lord as he had, not long before. With tears streaming down his eyes, he said these were the greatest riches that he had ever dreamed. Chaplain Hays says he knows now that they will spend eternity in Heaven together.

What a night! If anyone questions my stationing chaplains throughout this army, they just need to have a meal with Chaplain Hays, or Reverend Schibler, or General Muhlenberg. This virtue, if it can just infest our ranks, will give us victory over any enemy. We might not even have to draw a weapon.

Tuesday, March 7, 1780 — Morristown, New Jersey

Since leaving New York, the enemy's ships are believed to have been injured by the violent and constant storms in their journey southward. We are told the Spaniards' fleet has embarked from Havana. The hope is they will be able to deliver a stroke upon the deranged enemy.

With information from the quartermaster-general and commissary-general, I am informing the States of where provisions are needed for the army in their respective jurisdictions.

Wednesday, March 8, 1780 — Morristown, New Jersey

I am authorizing Major General St. Clair and Lieutenant-Colonels Carrington and Hamilton to proceed to Amboy. They are to try to negotiate a prisoner exchange and establish a general cartel. If the enemy will not agree to negotiate on an equal footing, I am instructing them to end the official talks. Then hopefully, they can have private talks with the British commissioners on proposals for future agreements. If they do enter a general cartel, I would like for them to include southern prisoners if possible. The enemy holds more of our officers than we do of theirs in the northern sector. They also need to endeavor to advance sufficient sums of money to pay for supplies and board for our men in captivity.

Wednesday, March 15, 1780 — Morristown, New Jersey

The Board of War requests that I detach some men for an expedition with several of our frigates. They also ask for permission to let General Arnold lead it. I do not at the present have men to share. I am not opposed to the endeavor and will be pleased for General Arnold to lead it. I just cannot authorize sending men when this army is in the current state.

Friday, March 17, 1780 — Morristown, New Jersey

Today is St. Patrick's Day. It is a celebration of the day St. Patrick came to Ireland and Christianity entered their shores. I am allowing a celebration at the encampment this day. The Continental army has a strong composition of Irishmen. Currently, seven of our eleven brigades here in Morristown are commanded by Irish gentlemen who were either born in Ireland or have parents who were. Some estimate that our army is almost one-fourth Irish descent. I am not sure of that, but I do know that the Irish serving these ranks are men of activity and bravery. At Monmouth, it was the Irish from the Pennsylvania line that gave me time to regroup at the first retreat. Their numbers in that group are so prevalent that General Henry Lee calls them "the line of Ireland." That the Irish would be fighters makes sense. They have been mistreated. They have been rejected. They have been jeered at. Yet, in their belly is the fire of freedom.

One last thought before I turn in. Sitting in one of the huts of the Second Pennsylvania brigade, I looked out the door watching the men celebrate. I was hit with a familiar longing. How I would often prefer building one of these huts, living with these men, sitting around the campfire telling stories, and waiting on the next orders to fight. It seems to be a less complicated life. With that written, I am where I am. I volunteered for this weight. I truly do not believe I would be content without it.

Saturday, March 18, 1780 — Morristown, New Jersey

I have received a letter from the Marquis which is sweet and bitter. It is sweet to receive his letter, but bitter that he has not received any that I have written. This grieves me as I consider that he may think I am not writing, but simply professing to write. I know how he values my returns. I will hope in the trust he should have by now that I am always honest. Having been told of dispatches sent from others like General Gates or Mr. Reed yet never receiving them, I am insecure as to other men's measure of my honor.

I am letting the Marquis know (and I hope he receives this one), that our eyes are turned to Europe. Great Britain is finding no takers on her overtures for alliances. Europe can help us best by not helping our enemy. Europe can bring conclusion to this war with just a little assistance in this Continent, which would benefit us and them at the same time.

Tuesday, March 21, 1780 — Morristown, New Jersey

Baron de Kalb is requesting General Greene have some boats built. At the present, the means of building them are lacking. I suggest he search several rivers in his area and make use of the best he can find. I am directing him to position what he finds in Newark Bay. I believe this is the most likely place where the enemy may attack our army. We are trying to convince the inhabitants to move their livestock away from the path that the enemy may take. The inhabitants in this quarter are reluctant to move their stock until the moment of danger because in this season, they have no other place to gain forage for their animals.

Wednesday, March 22, 1780 — Morristown, New Jersey

Congress has developed a new system for recruiting men. I am disappointed they are making this arrangement so late in the season. If their plan is successful, the recruits will still need to get to this army, be trained, seasoned, and organized to be an effective force. By the time that occurs, the campaign may be near decided. Governor Livingston is doing his best to assist. He has requested field officers from the Jersey line to go throughout his State to recruit. He feels if they are sent to their respective counties of origin, they will have better results. I agree. I just wish he would have initiated this sooner. He is requesting that these recruits be able-bodied and effective men. I would add that they should be inspected by the inspector-general or one of his sub-inspectors. These men should not be unsound, or too old, or too young. If they are, I will not allow the recruiter to gain a bonus for these.

General Livingston is offering a one-thousand-dollar bounty for each man who joins. He is offering a two-hundred-dollar bounty to the recruiting officer for each they bring into service. The Continental bounty added to this is for the soldier's clothing, land, and other benefits. I am still against individual State bounties. But at this time of need, I cannot afford to raise exceptions.

Sunday, March 26, 1780 — Morristown, New Jersey

The southern army under General Lincoln is my chief concern. If we let the enemy grab a foothold there, it will strengthen them and give them another base from which to foster attacks. Their success at Charleston would weigh heavy on the minds of the people in this quarter. Congress needs to extend their efforts to that head.

Tuesday, March 28, 1780 — Morristown, New Jersey

General Arnold has written me regarding the enterprise of frigates suggested by the Board of War. I am reiterating to him that we do not have the men to spare with the things going on in the south. In addition, enlistments are expiring here. If he wishes to lead the enterprise, I have given him my blessing. But he also hints that he may wish to go overseas for his health. He is requesting a furlough. I am beginning to think that General Arnold does not wish to reenter the field. He has seemed hesitant to engage in any activity. He is constantly citing his health with sundry other excuses. I believe the longer he languishes in idleness, evil lurks at his side. Arnold is attacked for many reasons where he is now stationed. I am not sure that any of the attacks are valid. He tends to complain. I assume he is lashing back. My wish and expectation is to see him in the field. His real strengths are evident in the fight and the flurry of activity. It will silence accusations. It will render him the glory and approbation for which he thirsts. Mrs. Arnold has given him a newborn son. I pray this addition will refocus his talents.

I am sending General Duportail, our chief engineer, to assist General Lincoln in preparing the works for the enemy's affronts.

The Indians have made two incursions on our frontiers. They have taken five inhabitants of Tryon County, killed one, and captured another thirteen militia at Skenesborough. I may need to send Colonel Brodhead back to address their hostilities. I had hoped the last time would be the remedy.

Thursday, March 30, 1780 — Morristown, New Jersey

John Mathews from Congress has written. He has heard that the Roebuck and transports have arrived in New York from southward. I have seen no evidence of that. The Russell from Savannah did arrive with some provision vessels from the Cork. The enemy seems to be looking to make a considerable move at this head. Even as I keep my eye on them here, intelligence indicates they are moving another two thousand five hundred men southward. A lot of activity is occurring, yet there has been no contact between the two sides.

I am putting Major Henry Lee with his whole corps of horse and foot in readiness to march to South Carolina. The horse will go on land. The foot will go by water and meet the horse at Petersburg. I need Lee to go to Philadelphia to gather the articles needed for such a long march.

Friday, March 31, 1780 — Morristown, New Jersey

Nothing of substance came from our commissioners meeting at Amboy regarding a prisoner exchange.

I do not know what we will do in this quarter or what General Lincoln will do in the southern quarter without men. The enemy is hurting for men too, but their numbers far exceed ours. Their men have little choice but to stay and fight. They are, for the most part, so far from home. The few men we have can easily just leave and go when it suits them. They have a choice. That choice is working against our cause.

Sunday, April 2, 1780 — Morristown, New Jersey

The enemy is about to make their embarkation from New York to reinforce Sir Henry Clinton it is assumed. The estimates of how many are leaving are too varied to report with any assurance. Belief is that Lord Rawdon's brigade, Brown's brigade, Fanning's brigade, and two Hessian regiments, along with the forty-second are all part of this group. Perhaps their number is close to two thousand, five hundred as cited before.

The choice of how to assist southward or defend here are equally embarrassing to me. We have not the men to make an offensive move. Our whole rank-and-file in this quarter are no more than about ten thousand, four hundred men. Two thousand, eight hundred of those are about to leave with expiring enlistments. The enemy in New York alone has about eleven thousand rank-and- file. Additionally, they have control of the waterways. We have no naval force to speak of at all. Our magazines of flour and salt are lacking. West Point is at risk. We could venture something against the enemy in this quarter. This might reduce the pressure southward. The advantage we have here, as opposed to General Lincoln in the south, is the internal strength of the country.

My great fear is southward. I am asking Congress for permission to send the Maryland line and the Delaware regiment to assist Mr. Lincoln. They may not get there before Charleston is taken, but at least they can be there to prevent the enemy from taking the whole Carolinas. I am going to send them to Philadelphia to gather supplies for their march in anticipation of Congress's approval. The quartermaster-general and commissary-general are already there. Baron de Kalb can command that detachment. Once supplied, I will have him move down the James river to prevent desertions. Going through a home State is always a temptation to break away.

Baron Steuben carries the same concerns I have for this army and for the threat south. His experience gives credibility to my concerns before Congress. The Baron believes the measures by Congress to raise men is far too late to be of much succor. He would like to augment the cavalry, but I doubt the practicability at this time considering the Nation's treasury is exhausted. The Baron wants to raise up additional regiments. Money aside, officers would need to be recruited, but provision for officers already on duty is sparce. Every day I receive threats from officers to quit because they are not being paid. Their basic needs are not being met. I have let Congress know that if they cannot meet the needs of the officers, they should let them retire with whatever promises they have coming after the war. We then can take the remnant of their regiments and combine them with others that are officered.

Some say we should invest this whole force to the south. The frailty of this argument is that if we leave this quarter unprotected except by scattered garrisons, the enemy here will hit us at our weak points. By a dozen inflictions, they will render the thing over.

I can go on about the problems. I have been inured to difficulties for so long in the course of this contest, that I have learned to look upon them with more tranquility than before. Vigorous exertions will be required to overcome the present difficulties, but I am far from despairing it can be done.

Monday, April 3, 1780 — Morristown, New Jersey

I am writing Congress to deal with the needs of our officers. I repeat these things over and over. I fear the repetition will only breed resentment. However disagreeable, the situation of our officers must be tended to or we will have none left in service. I do wish they would serve for patriotic reasons knowing they will be taken care of at the culmination of this conflict. That is faith. Sadly, they have received many promises that have not come to fruition. As a result, the promised care after the war has little merit for reliance. If freedom and liberty are of the value that I place on them, no greater payment could be received then the prize for which we are fighting — freedom and liberty. Once those are attained, security and financial blessing will follow. I know this, but I cannot run the army on my own sense of purpose. To obviate the reduction of officers, an army must be raised, paid, subsisted, and regulated upon equal and uniform principles.

We have chosen the defensive strategy of late out of necessity. It again has bred what I feared it would — comparison of circumstances among the men and complaints over inequality. When the men are in the fight, all these shrink in level of importance. As it now stands, they have time to compare and contrast. This is natural. Their complaints are well-grounded. I believe the army would be better-situated if all military affairs could be conducted under the direction of Congress.

This alone would give harmony and consistency that the various State approaches now prohibit.

Thursday, April 13, 1780 — Morristown, New Jersey

The enemy's fleet, which fell down to the Hook, has put to sea. The assumption is they are heading southward, but this could be a feint. We cannot be too guarded here if it is. Major-General Howe has already considered this. He has brought the fascines and gabions within the works of the Point. General Heath is superintending the recruiting in Massachusetts. Officers who assist in recruiting need to know that any expenses they incur will not be reimbursed by this army. What they get per recruit is what they must use for their expenses. I do not want any murmurs when they return.

Saturday, April 15, 1780 — Morristown, New Jersey

General Lincoln has written for approval to make an expedition against St. Augustine. The plan is well-founded, but I cannot approve it. We barely have enough men to defend ourselves. Another embarkation from New York is headed southward. The total number of men is undetermined. The appearance is they have no cavalry or draft horses with them and no more than fifteen dragoons. When the British General Clinton made his voyage, it is said many of his horses were thrown overboard in the violent storm. They may not want to risk more. I do believe if the enemy can take Charleston, this will become the principal theater of the war. Different States are raising supplies to be sent to General Lincoln's men. Congress has asked me to dictate where those supplies should be allocated. I do not have enough familiarity with that area. I am asking General Lincoln to direct. I have written the governors of those States to refer to him.

Monday, April 17, 1780 — Morristown, New Jersey

The Maryland division finally marched this morning with the first regiment of artillery, eight field pieces, along with what are attached to the brigades. Our want of wagons delayed their departure.

Massachusetts has applied for an expedition against the enemy at Penobscot. It is of great importance, but our circumstance does not give us any prospect of success. We have no fleet. The enemy has a respectable one on the coast. We would need our allies to join us with any chance of victory. Beyond this, we do not have the number of men to spare to send. A siege would be necessary, but the enemy has plenty of reinforcements to break the siege. They could then deal a significant blow to our efforts. Deficiency of money and magazines also seem insurmountable. Opportunities are presented to me daily, but we do not have the men nor the supplies to take advantage of those initiatives. If only we had men. If only we had supplies. If we did, it would not be long before the enemy would be driven from this Continent. If only. Providence please.

Wednesday, April 26, 1780 — Morristown, New Jersey

Colonel Laurens has written that the enemy has been able to pass the bar with a sixty-four-gun ship and a number of other vessels. Decision was made if the enemy could not be stopped at the bar, no need existed to defend the town. This puts the affairs in the South in a dangerous situation. The enemy should have the latest detachment from New York near Charleston any time. Now another embarkation is looking to depart New York soon. The garrisons at New York cannot surpass eight thousand at the present. Perhaps, the enemy may attempt something on us here to secure their conquest southward. To make, retard, or prevent their next embarkation may be in our power.

Total confusion presents in every department of this army. Congress has appointed a committee to rectify this. With this being the case, I am paralyzed in what I can do. I am sharing this with Mr. Laurens as he is both my friend and confidante.

Friday, April 28, 1780 — Morristown, New Jersey

Upon Mr. Adams's request, James Bowdoin, President of the Council of Massachusetts, has sent me a copy of that State's proposed constitution. I am honored they would consider me a person worthy to review their planned government. I have not the time to give it a thorough review. My cursory review makes me think it will be a judicious form of government assuring the liberty and happiness of the individuals. It corresponds with my expectations for every State. I just pray we can get this war over and commence with the work of governing a free people.

We are informed that forty-seven transports from South Carolina have arrived in New York. I do not know what this means. I am having General Howe collect as many boats as possible on the river and repair those that need it. This army may need to move quickly. All things must be ready.

Cattle have been distributed by the commissary-general with a large portion coming toward this camp. Report is that our own General Howe halted their drive and distributed many that were destined for our camp to his various garrisons. I am giving orders that this be prevented and repaired immediately. We need those supplies. They must not be diverted. The commissary-general has distributed them in proportion to the need. His plan must be followed. We may not get all we want, but at the least we all get some sustenance.

I am also directing General Howe along with all generals that our arms are in short supply. Any man whose enlistment has expired is to leave the guns provided by the public in the camp. Any who traded their own gun for a better one at the public expense, must leave the better one and return home with the one they brought. This is common sense. Carelessness makes the order necessary.

Sunday, April 30, 1780 — Morristown, New Jersey

I am sorry to note that our Spanish friend, Don Juan de Miralles, has died in our camp. He came to express his friendship and provide needed arms. While here, he was hit with a violent bilious. After nine days, a period was placed to his life. Our physicians did all they could. He was given every care within our power. I am writing Don Diego Joseph Navarro, governor of Cuba, concerning this unfortunate bit of news. I pray that his family and nation will find comfort.

Friday, May 5, 1780 — Morristown, New Jersey

I am flattered by a copy of a letter that the French gentleman Chevalier de la Luzerne sent to Congress and his government concerning me. He stated his time with me convinced him more than ever of the very great advantages the republic derives from my service. He says my virtues have gained for me the affection of this army which I command, as well as the confidence and respect of the officers. What a blessing and encouragement to receive such a nice letter. People may think I am stoic and unmoved, but this writing has shown the opposite. At this point of frustration, words like these reignite my fire. They cause me to press on. I believe I am more tranquil in adversity as stated previously, but just as my officers have a limit to their patience, my peace can be tested as well.

Monday, May 8, 1780 — Morristown, New Jersey

I have just received more good news. The Marquis has landed on this continent. He is making a fast approach to this camp. I cannot express the joy that I feel. Every man should have a friend. Every leader needs an encourager. Every soldier needs the example of one who fights for the cause and nothing more. They need to see one who will not quit until the thing is concluded. All these are wrapped in my friend the Marquis. He is a friend to my personal benefit. He is a dedicated soldier for our public utility. He is a double blessing.

Sunday, May 14, 1780 — Morristown, New Jersey

The Marquis has arrived! He comes bearing good news. He has informed us the French court is sending a fleet and an army to cooperate effectually with us.

Our finances are as they are. Our magazines are empty. To construct a plan to fill both so we can be of assistance to our abled ally is necessary. I am writing James Duane in Congress personally to gain his assistance. I cannot suggest this to Congress, but because he is my friend, he can suggest it as his own idea. We need a committee from Congress vested with plenipotentiary authority to draw out men and supplies as they are needed. This committee needs to be attached to this very spot of command so that all needs can be judged and met with urgency. Having a committee from Congress on-site will also enable me to discuss our condition and opportunities more honestly. This will enable them to make decisions in a timely manner without the deliberation of the whole body of Congress. I do believe if the whole of Congress could be here, they would meet our every need. There is just a time and distance element that breeds doubt and delay. If the French fleet does come (I am convinced by the Marquis that it will), the independence of America is within reach. That is, if we do our part to have men and supplies ready. I am going to suggest further to Mr. Duane that he man this committee with General Schuyler who has the military experience and knowledge to best guide the committee. He will gain great help if Mr. Mathews is added along with the Chancellor.

Monday, May 15, 1780 — Morristown, New Jersey

The Most Christian Majesty of France seems to be leaning toward the destruction of Halifax and the naval arsenals and garrisons there. He does so because these seem the most effectual in support of the enemy's operations on those seas and in the West Indies. I am directing Major Heath to gain information about the fortifications in Halifax, the number of men, vessels, and the like. I wish for him to employ a few men to help in this. A draftsman or two would be beneficial. Their drawings of the fortifications can aid in the design of our combined strategy. These can be compensated handsomely based on the intelligence they bring. The pay can be increased in proportion to the useful information they continue to gather. A few skillful pilots should also fall within his responsibility. These can give the French a better grasp of the coast and harbor.

Tuesday, May 16, 1780 — Morristown, New Jersey

As I think on what options are best for the French fleet to target, I believe New York should be the first object to reduce that post. I would that the Marquis advise Count de Rochambeau and Monsieur de Ternay of this. He needs to urge them with the strongest terms to proceed with fleet and army expediently to Sandy Hook for this purpose. I realize they may want to begin at Rhode Island or Cape Henry. But with the enemy's naval strength divided, this is the time to hit them in the New York Harbor. To hit anywhere else will give them the ability to move ships and men, or to put up obstacles in anticipation of the French's next move. I am resigned to the fact we are at their service. Their decision will be the one we will support. I just pray they come. We will work with them and support them with the utmost zeal.

Thursday, May 18, 1780 — Morristown, New Jersey

General Wayne has written to gain help in the Charleston area. It is a sad position that there are thousands of things that we might do, but currently all are impracticable. We hold out hope from our allies. I will write our States to join the plea of Congress.

I am calling Governor Clinton to have his Assembly act on providing the supplies and men needed for the soon advance upon the enemy. He needs to do it now. His Assembly is gathering. Though this may not be on their agenda, having them reassemble to consider our needs will waste time and opportunity.

Congress has approved my request for a committee from their membership to assist in our war efforts. I am thankful as this will remove many obstacles.

Friday, May 19, 1780 — Morristown, New Jersey

I am asking the Marquis to write the Canadians a proclamation as an officer of the French and American army to let them know that the French fleet will soon be in our midst. The time is good to rally the Canadians to their ancient friendship with France. The Marquis can assist us perhaps in making Canada part of the American confederation with all its privileges. This proclamation needs to also warn them not to aid the enemy. Else, they will face the backlash.

Sunday, May 21, 1780 — Morristown, New Jersey

I am asking General Schuyler to work with the committee to consider every variable, potential landings, and effective actions to be considered by the French fleet and their army. All advantages and disadvantages must be considered. They must also anticipate what provisions are needed to accompany any strategy. We must have all these things thought out so that when the French land, we can confer with them and act before the British have time to respond.

Thursday, May 25, 1780 — Morristown, New Jersey

The committee has prepared a circular letter to be sent to every State detailing the deplorable state of this army and the vast needs we have. They also detailed very well what is at stake if the States do not respond. They have highlighted what can be gained if we will join together for this one consequential push. Their letter is compelling. I just need them to consider one other thing — the supply of men. They seem to want to go with the old system which has added to our misery. A draft is the best method to meet our needs and hold the men for the duration of the war. This will enable us to focus on the enemy and not recruitment. Depending on militia is not economical. It is akin to leaning on a broken staff. We must use militia, but we must never depend on them.

Saturday, May 27,1780 — Morristown, New Jersey

We are reduced again at the extremity for want of meat. Our men are at half, a quarter, even down to an eighth of their daily provisions for this necessary article. They have borne these shortages with patience and forbearance due to the officers' exhortations and example in suffering with the men. There does come a breaking point. Thursday evening a mutiny occurred among the men in the Connecticut line. After a good deal of expostulation from their officers and a few from the Pennsylvania line, the men went back to their huts. They thought the trouble was over, but a few hours later, the instigators returned with packs of men resorting to violence. Colonel Miegs sought to quell the riot with great propriety, but he was struck in the head. Two colonels from the Pennsylvania line came to his aid. They were able to suppress the mutiny. After some deliberation, these officers report to me that the men were not just upset over lack of meat. They have not been paid in five months. They have been firm to the commitment to our purpose, even willing to go without pay, trusting that I would make it right. But when they had to deal with hunger on top of no pay, things just reached a boiling point. Their other complaint, which joins mine is the reduction in the value of the currency by which they are paid. The currency does not buy what it once did. They want compensation to match the value of what was promised. I have no solution for this. I have written repeatedly for Congress to address this burden. If only our men could be given their daily provisions, I believe the other complaints can be dealt with in due time. I am grateful that officers acting in my stead were able to bring a calm to this uprising. Sadly, they are occurring throughout the army camps. West Point is facing similar issues. The garrison at Fort Schuyler is confronted with them as well.

I have received three New York Gazettes and found one paper in the camp held by a soldier. These four items contain the offer from the enemy for our men to desert. These copies are being distributed by some treasonous source throughout our camps. When the men's needs are unmet and they are not paid, how much more impactful are the enemy's inducements? The States and Congress must step up to meet these needs or there will be no army, just a Commander-in-Chief.

Sunday, May 28, 1780 — Morristown, New Jersey

I am writing Joseph Reed. He has been my aide. He has been by my side. He has suffered in the past what our men suffer. Now in his position as President of Pennsylvania, I am imploring him to come to our aid. If only Reed were on the spot here, he would see the need. He would realize we cannot recruit people to abject poverty and starvation. Men would rather be in the militia. They can stay at home, come when needed, receive a stipend, and then leave at will. By far, this is a better situation than being in the regular army, but a disorganized militia cannot hope to defeat an organized, larger, and well-funded opponent.

Too much reliance is placed on the French and Spanish fleet. They are larger in number but are no match for the British on their own. Our Nation must come to the battle and exert itself fully. France and Spain will not remain by our side if we do not carry the bulk of the load. Fighting men must come primarily from the United States. Provisions for those men must also come primarily from the United States. Reed's State has the resources, particularly for flour. Four States produce the bulk of that needed substance — Maryland, New York, New Jersey, and Pennsylvania. New York has already given all it can spare. New Jersey has been exhausted by this army spending the majority of its time in their State. Maryland can give more. Delaware may be able to contribute. Pennsylvania can give a lot more. If she does not, then we can undertake nothing. This crisis at every point is extraordinary. Extraordinary expedients must be summoned.

Monday, May 29, 1780 — Morristown, New Jersey

Canada is demonstrating which side she is on. A detachment consisting of about five hundred men under Sir Jay Johnson has penetrated New York by way of the Mohawk river. A larger force has been accumulated in Montreal to invade the area of Fort Schuyler. I am writing Brigadier-General James Clinton to move supplies and arms into the garrison of Fort Schuyler for support of the troops. That Fort is cut off at the present. Clinton and his brigade are to move toward King's Ferry, then to New Windsor, and then halt in Albany for further instructions. His purpose will be to open communications with that garrison and deliver to them flour and salted meat. I would advise one hundred barrels of flour and the same quantity of salted meat — more if they can provide it. I am praying that his State can provide for these men. Any time I send a brigade like this, I must warn them to watch for the enemy, avoid being trapped or surprised, and by all means do not risk these troops. Men are in as short supply as flour and salted meat.

Wednesday, May 31, 1780 — Morristown, New Jersey

General Greene is facing frustrations as the quartermaster-general. He is short on currency. The currency is short on value. As a result, gathering new provisions is difficult. He is distressed by what he is unable to do. I am encouraging him to do what he can. He has at his disposal carriages, old camp-equipages, and boats. He can use the boats, tied together, to form bridges. All boats found need to be supplied with cables, anchors, plank, and scantling. As we are moving to prepare for the French fleet, Greene needs to distract the enemy by spreading rumors that we are considering invasions of Penobscot, Halifax, or Newfoundland. Whatever materials he cannot find, he must make an appeal to the councils of the States of New York, New Jersey, and Connecticut.

I am personally writing my friend Joseph Jones in Congress for his assistance with a perilous attitude that has permeated each State. Each State is concerned only for their State. As things stand, each State sees that there is one army, the one from their State. They have no concern for the men coming from other States. The resulting consequence is this United States army is changing into thirteen.

These armies no longer look to Congress for their direction, but each native accepts direction only from his State. As a result, the power of Congress is on the wane. I fear the aftermath. Congress must speak in a decisive tone. Congress must be vested with powers from the respective States to enable it to prosecute this war on a united footing. As it now stands, one State will comply with Congress. One ignores Congress. Another meets Congress's requisition by halves. The old way cannot continue with unwarranted jealousies. Delays responding, because of the need to have deliberation at each State Assembly, hurt the cause. The word "United' in United States must mean something. Otherwise, we are just States. I am hoping Mr. Jones can voice this with some persuasion and unite all parties.

Thursday, June 1, 1780 — Morristown, New Jersey

We have received word through the newspapers in New York of the surrender of Charleston. Report is that one hundred sail of vessels entered Sandy Hook. I cannot help but believe this is the fleet with Sir Henry Clinton returning from southward. Now buoyed by his success in the south, he is now encouraged by the distresses in our garrisons to attack in this area — principally West Point. I am therefore having General Howe take measures to prepare for the British incursion at his post. I am forwarding supplies to that garrison. I am asking Connecticut for salted meat to be sent. I am having General Howe gather any cattle the inhabitants have to spare.

Friday, June 2, 1780 — Morristown, New Jersey

The French fleet is presumed to be landing in Rhode Island. My understanding is they will do this to land their sick, gain additional stores, and gather intelligence before they set out again on our behalf. I am sending General Heath to meet them along with Dr. Craik to make sure homes are set aside to serve as hospitals. I also need General Heath to set up a market between the inhabitants and the French. This will enable them to purchase what they need, but not at excessive prices.

Sunday, June 4, 1780 — Morristown, New Jersey

I am writing General Gates to form a general disposition of his army. I also would like to know if he has taken care of his personal business so that he can, if he wishes, join us in the field. If he so does, I am requesting that he meet me here at my headquarters. It is like walking on eggshells with this general.

Monday, June 5, 1780 — Morristown, New Jersey

The Chevalier de la Lucerne has written to offer any aid he can render. I am delighted to have his help. I am assuring him (and myself) that I will make use of his offer as infrequently as possible.

Tuesday, June 6, 1780 — Morristown, New Jersey

As West Point seems more and more the destination of the British, I must remind General Howe to keep his troops together and not divide them for any dispatch purpose whatsoever. If the enemy comes, he will need the whole body to overcome their designs.

Wednesday, June 7, 1780 — Morristown, New Jersey

Enemy troops under General Knyphausen left New York and made an intrusion into the Jerseys on the 6th. They moved the next morning to Connecticut Farms. They then proceeded just above Elizabethtown where he resides at the present. Baggage and cavalry are being moved to him at this moment.

Some of our men have just rode up this evening to inform me that Knyphausen moved from his station a few hours ago to within a half mile from Springfield. A detachment of our advanced Continental corps, along with some Jersey militia, galled them with great spirit and zeal. The enemy was forced back after about forty minutes. They suffered significant losses. It is a question whether they wish to forage or if they are attempting to draw this army out into the open.

I have set this army in motion toward Springfield.

Thursday, June 8, 1780 — Springfield, New Jersey

The enemy has been content to stay at a distance. Report has it that their General Sterling was wounded in the leg. Major Lee and his men exhibited great spirit in the encounter. I am writing him to thank him and to request his men join us at this quarter with his cavalry. They can catch up to our rear and look for forage. I would like to see the Major at my quarters Saturday.

Thursday, June 15, 1780 — Springfield, New Jersey

The enemy remains nearby. I believe their purpose is in the vicinity of the North river and terminating at West Point. I have yet to hear returns from General Howe as to the number of his troops and their readiness for attack. I am suggesting he quarter two thousand, five hundred men. If he does not have that number available, he can bring in some militia to reach that number. I do not want him to have more than that as there will be too many men for whom to supply provisions. Governor Clinton can be applied to for men if he is short. I need to ensure we have three days of provisions available for the men.

Sunday, June 18, 1780 — Springfield, New Jersey

The Jersey legislature has made the mistake that I have stood against for a while. They are drafting men from their militia and holding them under their own officers instead of letting them be incorporated into the Continental battalions. This is dangerous to our cause. We cannot have thirteen armies. We must have one. I am begging that Governor Clinton rectify this with their legislature post haste.

Monday, June 19, 1780 — Springfield, New Jersey

I am writing the Committee of War concerning the lack of information from the individual States regarding the requisition for men and supplies. With no information, there is no way I can plan; nor, can I effectively cooperate when the French fleet arrives. I have no data on which to proceed. The interests of the States, the reputation of our country, the justice and gratitude to our allies, and my own character demand that the States' government assemblies act and inform of their progress without delay. I am at a loss of what to do. I am urging the Committee to send another letter to the States imploring them to respond. The fate of our Nation is at stake.

Tuesday, June 20, 1780 — Springfield, New Jersey

Stony Point and Verplank's Point were established more for a viewing place to monitor the enemy, not for a garrison to defend. The men who are there need to be prepared for an attack from the enemy. They are to put up some degree of opposition. Then they are to prepare for retreat. Boats are to be readied for this sole purpose. Plans are to be made to evacuate with stores and cannon. The officers there are not to burn these posts as they may reuse them once the danger has passed. They are to maintain a ten-to-twelve-day supply of provisions at each.

It is Fort Schuyler that we must defend with all our might. The fort is a strategic garrison that could hurt the whole effort if it is lost. In fact, the whole security of the western part of New York depends on our hold of that post. I am directing General Howe to throw in a hundred barrels of flour there at least. He is to apply to Governor Clinton for a hundred barrels of beef. These resources are to be inspected by the commissary before being stored.

Our cavalry is nonexistent at this post. I am pulling the Marechaussee corps of horse from their duty. They are to join the line in the field. I am ordering General Glover to join me here. I am directing General Heath to order all officers recruiting in Massachusetts to join us at this instant. They are to march here with their drafts from that State.

Wednesday, June 21, 1780 — Springfield, New Jersey

I know General Greene will be happy to receive his next order. He tires of just being the quartermaster-general. He prefers to take the field. My request will fall within that scope. I am placing him in command of the brigades of Maxwell and Stark with orders to cover the country and guard our stores. He is to protect those under his command and keep them from surprise.

Sir Henry Clinton is said to be on Staten Island with four-to-six thousand men. I cannot penetrate his designs. I am calling on the whole of Moylan's regiment to join me. I am sending out Sheldon's as reconnoitering parties and parties of advance.

Thursday, June 22, 1780 — Springfield, New Jersey

One has to love officers like General Greene. No sooner do I send him out to cover the country, he runs straight into the enemy not far from here. We immediately moved this army out of Springfield for a better posture of defense. Generals Greene and Dickinson kept the enemy occupied until the numbers forced them back. The British have taken over Springfield. Of course, they burned the village, meeting house, and private homes. They then returned to their previous position. I am gratified that Greene took over when he did. He bought us time. As I always say, in the guise of coincidence, Providence delivers.

Friday, June 23, 1780 — Whippany, New Jersey

The enemy has crossed back over to Staten Island. There seems to be no reason for their action other than their designs on West Point.

Sunday, June 25, 1780 — Whippany, New Jersey

The enemy has made incursions with little loss. We have not suffered much more. What pleases me is that I have never seen the militia more invigorated universally. They deserve the praise for posing a vigorous resistance the British will not soon forget. I know that I will not. Their spirited display is greater than anything that I have seen from them through the entirety of this war.

The ladies of Pennsylvania have pulled their resources together and sent a gift of almost three hundred thousand dollars. Mrs. Joseph Reed has headed this effort. She is now writing other women in the various States to do the same. Seeing our Nation pull together and our States reach out to each other gives me some comfort that my pleas are being heard. The money they have provided and what they will raise, I am inclined to use for shirts for our men. They have been lacking these for a while now. The Continental provisions do not include this article. We have been too busy just trying to gain food and arms. If other moneys are sent, I will dispatch it to the hospitals for the care of our wounded. I have written Mrs. Reed to convey my thanks. I am also writing Mr. Reed to remind him that we need an augmentation of our troops which only he and the State can provide.

Tuesday, June 27, 1780 — Ramapo, New Jersey

With West Point being threatened and the enemy active again, I cannot help but believe they are trying to retard our support for that post. The result of their activity is not what they expected. They have animated our militia and given stimulus to the States to assist our efforts.

I am writing Governor Trumbull to continue to push to meet the quota we have requisitioned for men. Voluntary service is lacking. Politicians use indolent excuses of "All is well" to avoid expense and inconvenience. Such attitudes will protract the war. They risk the perdition of our liberties.

Thursday, June 29, 1780 — Ramapo, New Jersey

I received an interesting letter from Mr. Robert Livingston in Congress. He is suggesting relieving General Howe of his command at West Point. He says the State of New York has lost confidence in him. He suggests replacing him with General Arnold for whom the State and the militia hold in high regard. General Arnold has voiced through other channels the same desire. He has stated that his request for a leave of absence was merely because he thought there would be no activity this campaign.

I value General Arnold but am suspicious of murmurings that he has political or selfish motivations. I have the utmost regard for General Arnold as I have expressed on numerous occasions. However, I cannot relieve a general from his command for no apparent reason. This would deliver a severe wound to Howe's feelings. If I find a need for General Howe in battle, this will give me the opportunity to move him to the line. I believe he would appreciate such a transfer. I can then move General Arnold to his place at West Point. The problem that I have with this strategy is that if war does demand officers, I prefer to have both generals in the field. Arnold is too valuable to guard a post when he can inflict great losses on the enemy.

Friday, June 30, 1780 — Ramapo, New Jersey

New Hampshire has shown great zeal in forwarding drafts. I am sending General Stark to meet them and march them to this head, along with the one thousand militia that State has engaged. The drafts need to be inspected before the march. They are to be able-bodied and fit. If they are not, they must be left as they will be an incumbrance and great expense.

This is the time for America, with one great exertion, to put an end to this war. I will warn every State that if this is not done, we will be unable to prosecute the war. We will have to fall back to a defensive position once again which could lead to our soon defeat.

Tuesday, July 4, 1780 — Bergen County, New Jersey

Since we have declared our independence has now been four years. The good thing is that we have been acting independently these four years. The bad thing is we have done little as a nation to retain it. Freedom cannot be purchased by bits-and-pieces. Liberty also cannot be retained by installments. It is quite the opposite. Slavery comes little-by-little. The more we resign our rights, the more we compromise our individual freedoms, the more we will return to the condition of servitude.

Now the French fleet and its army are ready to help. For all of us (including the Spaniards if possible) to achieve our goal of defeating a common enemy will take a concerted effort. We must exert every effort. I am beginning this day in prayer. I am asking the Author and Finisher of our Faith to wield His Hand to our cause. We need Him to move in the hearts of our people. We need Him to defeat our enemy for His Glory. Following this, under His inspiration, I am writing my friend Mr. Reed again. I am pleading with Reed to use every tool at his disposal, even martial law if that be what is needed, to contribute men and provisions to this war. The maxim of good government is the one I will remind him of — the best way to preserve the confidence of the people is to promote their true interest. He may fear acting. His legislature may encourage the status-quo. He needs to know one thing is for sure, should this thing go south, his legislature will gladly lay our defeat upon him, never on their own complicity.

Wednesday, July 5, 1780 — Bergen County, New Jersey

It is times like this that I miss our active generals. General Putnam has stepped aside due to his health. He writes to say his health has improved. He should be visiting his men in the next week or so. I rejoice in that but wish for one more step. I need him to join his men and help me lead.

Monday, July 10, 1780 — Headquarters near Passaic, New Jersey

With Charleston having fallen to the enemy, there is a call in Congress for an investigation into the matter, especially concerning General Lincoln's conduct. I am fully confident in General Lincoln's leadership. I know in my heart he did all that anyone could. With this said, I will never oppose inquiry by Congress. Inquiry causes every leader to evaluate his actions as well as the costs that may follow. General Lincoln would feel the same, but he is now in the confines of the enemy. Nothing good can come from bringing men out of the line for an inquiry while the chief defendant is suffering as a prisoner of war. The men on the line must stay there to prosecute this war. There will be plenty of time afterward to see what was done right or wrong. I am sure those inquiries will include my actions, decisions, and command. My chief concern regarding General Lincoln is to get him back to our side through whatever prisoner exchange we can negotiate so long as he is not given priority when others have suffered longer in the enemy's hands.

Tuesday, July 11, 1780 — Headquarters near Passaic, New Jersey

I am dispatching Major Lee to Monmouth to meet with General Forman who awaits the French fleet expected at the Hook. He is to impress pilots for their ships. He is to also impress cattle, vegetables, and anything else that the French fleet may need refreshed. Lee is to give certificates for any supplies taken from inhabitants. I do realize that such certificates are a promise to pay. If I were an inhabitant, I would think those certificates are only good if the Continental Army is successful. The Continental currency paid will be worthless if the British win this war. This must weigh on their minds. This situation supports the preference for specie over paper. Gold and silver have value no matter who wins. May the Lord help us win.

If Lee finds State troops or militia without a superior, he is to take command. If they have a superior officer, that officer is to cooperate with Lee's assignments. He is also to look for the fleet and give me notice when they arrive.

Friday, July 14, 1780 — Headquarters near Passaic, New Jersey

I have settled on a plan for the reduction of the city and garrisons of New York in the enemy's hands. This must occur with the French fleet's assistance, along with at least forty-thousand men. I am directing General Greene to make every necessary arrangement and provision for this operation. He is to appeal to the States to provide everything Congress has requisitioned. If our batteaux are in deficient numbers, Greene is to proceed to Albany where the plank and timber needed to build is more readily available.

I just received a letter from General Heath. The French fleet arrived at Newport on the afternoon of the 10th. I entreat Congress to press every measure in their power to put us in the condition to wage this intended cooperation with vigor and efficiency.

Saturday, July 15, 1780 — Headquarters near Passaic, New Jersey

I have delayed contacting General Knox to move cannon and stores to this quarter until the last minute. Now that I know the contest is about to resume, I am directing him to bring all he can for the siege and attack on New York.

Sunday, July 16, 1780 — Headquarters near Passaic, New Jersey

The Marquis has written with concern. He had misunderstood my letter when I was detailing the obstacles that our gathered forces would face in the attack on New York. It was not to dispel the attack, but rather to give full disclosure of the difficulties. My intention was not to discourage the move or to make it seem that taking New York was an impossibility. Quite the contrary, it is my chief option. I must write him to clarify. This is always the problem with writing. Things come across unclear. Then the time delay clarifying proves an obstacle on its own.

I will also write Count de Rochambeau to let him know that we are ready to do whatever they ask. I do wish we could repay them for their sacrifice, time, and expense. May the glory on the battlefield give them what we cannot. I have directed the Maquis (with my clarification letter as referenced above) to answer any questions face-to-face with the French officers. I ask the Count to take the Marquis's words as if they are my own. The Marquis knows our situation. He has fought by our side. He knows our limitations and strengths.

Wednesday, July 19, 1780 — Bergen County, New Jersey

The French have eight ships in port, two frigates, and two bombs, and upwards to five thousand men. As grateful as I am for this force, it is inferior to the British fleet under Arbuthnot and Graves. The French tell us another fleet of theirs is expected soon. Rochambeau does not believe his army will be ready for action until four weeks have passed.

Thursday, July 20, 1780 — Headquarters near Passaic, New Jersey

General Putnam came to see us a few days back. He appeared greatly aged since our last encounter. On his way back home, he had a seizure and now has a paralysis. I do not believe our Nation will be able to benefit from his gifts. As if this has not saddened me enough, I just received a resignation letter from Brigadier-General Maxwell. He has served well in this army from the commencement of the controversy. If any deserve to retire, it is General Maxwell. How I wish though that he would not.

At times, it is as if I have entered one of Mr. Shakespeare's tragedies. The Marquis writes that Count de Rochambeau and Chevalier de Ternay have given him letters listing the reasons why M. de Ternay is hesitant to enter the Hook based on d'Estaing's arguments a while back. He feels his ships are too big to enter the harbor and must stay off Long Island to deal with the enemy at sea. I am unfamiliar with maritime affairs, but I do believe control of the port is essential. Otherwise, our operations must become more precarious.

Another problem with them staying out at sea is that we have been promised arms and powder. If they cannot come in themselves, we are in need that they send the arms and powder so that we will have what we need to carry this campaign to a favorable outcome. Otherwise, we fall back to a defensive posture while our succor, the French allies, float off our shores. As it now stands, we are four or five thousand arms short. We are two tons of powder in wanting.

Count de Rochambeau wishes a personal audience with me per the Marquis's letter. I would like nothing more, but I have an army to attend to as we may be the only one willing to fight. The British may solve this problem for us. I have just taken possession of letter from Colonel Hamilton, which states the enemy is intending to embark New York for Rhode Island to confront the French squadron.

Monday, July 24, 1780 — Bergen County, New Jersey

I am alerting Major-General Howe of the enemy's intention on the French fleet off Newport. I am directing him to order forward the militia from New Hampshire and Massachusetts. They are to rendezvous at Claverack. I need him to also let me know if our arms have arrived in Albany.

Thursday, July 27, 1780 — Preakness, New Jersey

The levies are pouring in slowly. Pennsylvania has not even generated four hundred, and she thinks she has done well. I am moving our men at the present toward New York for one purpose, to take the pressure off the French fleet in Rhode Island. If the enemy sees that New York is in danger, perhaps they will move back to this sector or divide their forces. Either would be favorable to what our allies face at this moment. The Marquis needs to push Massachusetts to gather their full complement of men. If he can succeed in that, then he needs to press them for arms and ammunition if for no one else, but their own men would suffice.

Monday, July 31, 1780 — Robinson's in the Highlands, State of New York

I am writing Rochambeau to inform him that Sir Henry Clinton has sailed the main part of his force with about eight thousand men to attack the French fleet. I am glad the French have had time to get their men settled and prayerfully ready. I need to let him know that if I had time to get there, I would gladly assist. Unfortunately, there is no way we can achieve that. The best I can do is provide a diversion.

Our army with me has crossed King's Ferry. The transports with the remainder of our troops should cross King's Ferry and join us today. I propose we then move rapidly down toward Kingsbridge. If Sir Henry has taken the men (I think he has), we have a good chance to strike a blow upon them. This would gain an advantage for us in this quarter. General Heath and his men may be able to assist the French in Newport. They can give the enemy a welcome they did not expect.

The enemy has cut off communications with Fort Schuyler. The men there have few provisions. To prevent this valuable post from falling into the enemy's hands, I am sending General Fellows to detach five hundred of his militia to join the brigade under General Van Rensselaer. I am writing General Van Schaik at Albany to supply provisions and wagons and whatever else may be needed to expedite the march. The enemy must be removed to save this strategic post and to guard the harvest upon the Mohawk river, which is necessary for the sustenance of this army.

Tuesday, August 1, 1780 — Peekskill, New York

I am requesting that Governor Livingston order his militia to be in a state of readiness with the intent to march to Dobbs Ferry to meet me there upon my notification. Some of the men the Jerseys have raised for this army have been kept in hold for their State army. I am asking him to forward those to this army with all possible expedition. I am requesting that Major-General Dickinson command the Jersey militia. I am calling on General St. Clair to form the light horse. He is to be ready to move under the command of the Marquis de Lafayette. I am writing the Marquis to make sure that Count de Rochambeau and Chevalier de Ternay know that my plan is an attack on New York based on the enemy's movements.

Wednesday, August 2, 1780 — Peekskill, New York

The quartermaster-general was able to secure enough arms in coordination with the States to provide for the men in this enterprise. Fifty tons of powder should be supplied by France. We need another fifty from the French fleet. I am asking the Marquis to secure this. I do not want him to ask the admiral or the general to do anything in which they would be disinclined. I cannot risk them taking a step that will risk their fleet. If some accident were to occur to the harm of their squadron, I know it would damage our relationship. Perhaps it would cause them to leave our aid altogether. I feel as though I am walking gingerly in the dark, hoping not to snap some twig to give the thing away. They need to know we will do everything within our power from this head. I hope circumstances will ultimately favor us.

Thursday, August 3, 1780 — Peekskill, New York

News just arrived that the British fleet is returning to New York in response to our movement on New York. I am letting the Marquis know we will move back across the river to Dobbs Ferry. I am writing General Heath to consider returning the militia to their homes to lessen our financial burden for provisions. I will leave this order to General Heath as our allies may desire the militia to stay a little longer for their defense.

I am ordering General Arnold to take command of West Point and its dependencies, including Fishkill to King's Ferry. The infantry and cavalry that advanced to the enemy lines east of the river are also under his authority. Once the New Hampshire and Massachusetts militia each reach twelve hundred, the New York militia is to be released to the main army on the west side of the river. When the Massachusetts Bay line reaches fifteen hundred, the New Hampshire militia is to join the main army too. Colonel James Livingston's regiment will garrison Stony Point and Verplanck's Point. Arnold is to make sure the works are completed at West Point. He is to have ample provisions always in store in case of sudden attack. This is true for the garrisons as well.

Saturday, August 5, 1780 — Peekskill, New York

The Marquis has written that Chevalier de Ternay is averse to entering the harbor of New York. I do not think a blockade is possible without their entrance. I will submit to their concerns and hope a siege can occur. I find myself at their whim. We are desperate for succor from France and the West Indies. We cannot keep the militia out so long with such little chance of activity. We need to decide if we are going to make an offensive move. If not, we need to let the militia go home at once. The minds of our citizens cannot help but be discouraged if we stand at the point of readiness and then do nothing.

The Count de Rochambeau has written with appreciation for the hearty response the States have exerted. Their ardor is attributable to their interest, their duty, and their gratitude for the sacrifices the French have made to aid our cause.

Sunday, August 6, 1780 — Peekskill, New York

General Greene has written to resign his post as quartermaster-general. He wishes to return to the line of battle and lead from that head. I regret his resignation of this post. He has been extremely helpful in bringing that department back into order. I do know it is a burden. His heart is to command men. I am asking he stay until his replacement is named.

Congress has directed a junction of the Continental frigates to rendezvous in Delaware and join Ternay's fleet.

I am working at the present to establish communication across Dobbs Ferry to aid our land transportation and facilitate our bread supplies. I am directing General Arnold to ensure this is completed.

Friday, August 11, 1780 — Orangetown, New York

Rumor has it the enemy is about to embark again. I do not believe it is possible they would make another move on Rhode Island, nor do I think it possible they would experiment with West Point. But, just in case, I am having all on alert. General Arnold needs to keep the Massachusetts and New Hampshire militia at his post until we receive more intelligence. I am requesting he send sixty artificers from Colonel Baldwin to me.

Colonel Pickering is the man to replace Greene. He should be appointed quartermaster-general formally soon. In the meantime, I am having Colonel Hay to deposit some stock of hay at Fishkill. The men are not to use it if pasture is available for their animals.

Saturday, August 12, 1780 — Orangetown, New York

I impatiently await the second fleet of the French. Little hope of success exists without it. We need this to enhance our force to an amount that can run against and overpower the enemy. The French will not move without this addition regardless of our wishes.

General Gates has yet to comply with my request as to the size and condition of his force. I am making another request. It is impossible that we detach some of the enemy southward until we know what we have there and what we need. I am in hopes he will respond.

Sunday, August 13, 1780 — Orangetown, New York

I am requesting General Arnold provide Colonel Hay the number of men needed to cut wood for the winter. An unsatisfying event is transpiring at this post. Many enemy prisoners are escaping from West Point to this location because they say they are being denied water or they are given water at an exorbitant price. I am ordering General Arnold to remedy this. I know he has had to deal with many existent problems since his arrival. I also am keenly aware that there is no way he can solve them all in a few days. In the same way, he cannot possibly have been made informed of many problems as perpetrators cover their offenses.

Joseph Jones in Congress writes that Congress is of the mind to suspend General Greene from the line because of some grievances made while he was quartermaster-general. Some inhabitants were unhappy with the impressments made when provisions requisitioned by Congress went unmet. This is the problem with every deficiency of this army. The needs are not met. For the good of the country, the army must be held together. It must be manned. It must be supplied. This will anger people just as forcing medicine to one's child draws complaint. The leadership of this army does not know better than the inhabitants, nor does this command believe it is the parent. All I know is that for this army to contend for the freedom of our Nation, needs must be met, or all must be surrendered. Like medicine to the child, forced compliance sometimes is for our Nation's own good. General Green was doing the distasteful work, which is the chief reason he is resigning. No man can hold that station for long. General Greene is a patriot. Where others would simply retire because they have had enough, General Greene seeks to see this contest to its end. To remove Greene from his line of command with his talents to fight and win would harm the public good more than all grievances put together. I am requesting that if inquiry is necessary, then one must be carried out, but let it be while he remains in the service of his country. I will be the first witness on his behalf. He should not in any circumstance be suspended without a trial. No officer would ever serve if this precedence were established. The one thing that has held the officers here the longest has not been their pay or rank, but rather their love of country, of honor, and of seeing their labors crowned with success at the liberation of their neighbors.

Wednesday, August 16, 1780 — Orangetown, New York

Turnay is requesting the second French fleet meet him in the Boston Harbor along with our frigates and sloop, the Saratoga.

Thursday, August 17, 1780 — Orangetown, New York

General Heath has requested permission for the militia to be released from the Count's service. He would like the same as he desires to rejoin the army here. I understand his desire, but the Count still requests the militia there. The Count has also specifically requested General Heath stay at his side as he is pleased with the service Heath provides. I am asking the General to please stay there.

Sunday, August 20, 1780 — Orangetown, New York

Congress must reconsider the status quo as to raising provisions and men. It is the same chorus. This army does not have the ability to meet any opportunity that may present itself. Supplies are not being provided. Horses are now being sub-sisted by force, which gives rise to civil disputes. We have tried influence and persuasion. Neither have produced results. We have no other remedy but to force compliance. Pennsylvania has been of little help in sending men. The men they have sent have been well-supplied. Every State should do the same with regard to supplies and more in regard to enlistments.

The southern States are doing all in their power to gather magazines of bread, forage, and salted meat. They will need around eight thousand men to hold against the enemy and perhaps drive the British out.

Some could argue that it is good the army is daily decreasing as shortages will cease to be a problem. With no supplies, there will be no army. With a small army, there will be no strike against the enemy. The more we stand in a defensive mode, the more the remaining army will grow dissatisfied and leave. The more leave, the less we have to make a defense. In this case, it will not be long before the British can raise their flag again over every town and possession. Men like me will hang on gallows as monuments to deter future objections. I will not hang alone. Every person who has sought the mantle of government for this United States will either pledge an allegiance, suffer punishment, or join me at the rope. None want this.

A need presents for a solution. Congress has been calling for troops. The coun-cil, that has been by my side representing them, has done their part. But calling for troops is not working. I do not know how many more times I must write this. If I had the time and inclination to look back over this journal, I am sure that there is a repetition that begs me skip this one. I have made the same repetitious folly to Congress. We do have allies now, but should this army dissolve, how dishonorable will it be to let a friend carry on our work? I fear that if we allow the French to carry the war for us, then the French will become our new masters. This goes against the very reason shots were fired at Lexington and Concord. A preemptory draft is our only effectual option. The draft should be for the entire war or at least three years.

Had we formed an army by this means at the onset, we would not have had to retreat across the Delaware in 1776. We would not have had to fight at Bran-dywine. We would not have lost Philadelphia. The Enemy would not be fortified in New York. We would not have suffered at Valley Forge. Our towns would not have been ravaged. Our homes would not have been burned. Our dollar would not be of so little value.

This army's insignificant numbers, dissatisfaction in service, and its crumbling to pieces have given the enemy hope that if they just stay around, we will soon collapse from the weight of hardship and apathy. The old maxim is the counter to this — the strongest way to secure peace is to be well-prepared for war. If Congress will only initiate the draft across the States, our army will be robust. With a formidable army, American lives will be spared. The enemy will determine to pacific measures. Half-pay to the officers who serve will be the most politic and effectual means of recruiting and keeping them to the end of the war.

Monday, August 21, 1780 — Orangetown, New York

I am writing Count de Rochambeau of the options we face in a combined operation upon New York. The first, we attack with full force on York Island. The second is we attack with a principal part of our force upon Brooklyn, leaving the remainder to secure our communications on York Island. The third option (which is my preference), we divide our forces and attack both islands at once. To do this, we can move to establish ourselves at York Island and Long Island. Upon attack, the enemy would face a dilemma as he would be unable to move enough men to any quarter without surrendering the quarter they reduce. The key to any offensive will be naval superiority. As such, we eagerly await the second fleet. These are just a sketching of what I believe we can do. I am asking Rochambeau what he thinks is best and what he desires. It may be any one of these three, and perhaps a mode completely different. We long to act.

Thursday, August 24, 1780 — Orangetown, New York

Though we are freeing General Greene from his quartermaster-general duties, I am asking him to forage down to Bergen and then to the English neighborhood with the Light Infantry and four brigades from his own wing. The necessities of the army must be gathered — forage, hay, grain, horses, as well as cattle, hogs, and sheep fit for slaughter. All these are to be forwarded to this army. Receipts must be given to the inhabitants. Once he has completed this object, he is to draw off his troops and join this army.

Saturday, August 26, 1780 — Orangetown, New York

General Arnold writes of the licentiousness of the soldiery under his new command. I face the same here on occasion. He requests permission to execute the plunderers and the deserters. I am giving him permission to execute the chief of the plunderers and all deserters as examples. I hate for this to be done. But if it saves this Nation and prevents further offenses, it will be sadly done.

Monday, August 28, 1780 — Orangetown, New York

European Intelligence just received makes a campaign in this part doubtful. I am writing General Heath to release the militia unless Rochambeau has some objection. Our allies are requesting the works on Butt's Hill to be reinforced. I do not believe this is necessary, nor will it provide any benefit. But if our allies desire it, we will oblige to do it with the delicacy of our relationship being as it is. This is an expense with little utility. We are short on resources but knowing the cost that the French have expended to come here, it is the least we can do.

More news has come that the second fleet was delayed at the Port of Brest in France by a British fleet. This puts it out of our power to act upon New York. The good news is the French frigate Alliance arrived with arms, powder, cannon, and clothing for our army. I am writing Congress to work to get these forwarded to this army without delay.

Wednesday, August 30, 1780 — Orangetown, New York

Several of our officers and men are held as prisoners of war in Quebec. They are suffering under inhumane conditions. To get them the supplies they need there is not easy. I am asking Lieutenant-General Haldimand to transfer those prisoners to the British in New York. This will grant us the ability to provide for their needs more easily. Colonel Ethan Allen is requesting we bring about an immediate exchange of enemy officers for these in Quebec. I understand his zeal, but it is not right to get these men freed while others have been in confinement for a longer period of time.

Saturday, September 2, 1780 — Bergen County, New Jersey

I have moved to this place to cover a forage that the enemy has been taking advantage of in our absence. Our proximity to New York and their posts there gave the enemy this opportunity which we seek to remove.

Having received intelligence that the enemy is in preparation for some important movement, it is believed their target is this main army or the posts in the Highlands. I am making my army ready. I have sent a note to General Arnold to take every precaution to put the posts of the latter in a good defensive standing. I have let him know that the two State regiments of Connecticut are to form a junction with Colonel Sheldon to protect the fortifications on the North river. General Arnold needs to collect his detachments and move the stores and garrisons from the post at King's Ferry. He is to order sixty boats to that place with five men each to expedite the evacuation if needed.

Sunday, September 3, 1780 — Bergen County, New Jersey

Information has been shared with me that a few days ago, Sir Henry Clinton approached a person to act as a spy with the instruction to go to Rhode Island to ascertain the French fleet's situation. Thankfully, the person declined and was kind enough to inform us of their intrigues. I am notifying Count de Rochambeau that the enemy may be planning movement his way. I cannot imagine the enemy would divide their forces again from New York and risk their hold there. We must prepare for every eventuality.

I am pleased General Schuyler took the initiative to take some Indian leaders to the French fleet at Newport. Several Indians had formed alliances with the French in the last war. This reunion served the purpose of giving the Indian nations further proof that the French are aiding us. It is hoped this will counter any attempts the British make to discredit our alliance. We need the Indians to join us in our efforts or at the least not assist the enemy. My understanding is that Rochambeau and his men were very courteous to the Indian visitors. They gave the Indians great tokens of honor and respect. I am grateful to the Count for this. I will write him to commend his actions.

Wednesday, September 6, 1780 — Bergen County, New Jersey

I am writing Congress that many of our officers are being paid the set fee that was agreed upon when they entered the war. This amount has not kept up with the cost of living as our currency depreciates. They seem to be adjusting this for some officers, but not others. I am asking that they remedy this at once. I am also alerting them at the scarcity of our meat supply.

With great dissatisfaction on many fronts, I record General Gates has lost a significant battle in South Carolina at Camden. I am mortified at the loss. I am mortified that he has not communicated this to me. I have written him on several occasions to ascertain the state of his army there and for information on the enemy's designs. I note only to myself, that I had recommended General Greene for this post, but Congress chose Gates instead. I cannot conceive this would have been the outcome had General Greene been in command. As of this notation, I still have no details. I am awaiting further news. This changes our plans.

I must countermand the Maryland troops who were marching to this army to redirect southward along with any recruits they have raised. This is a disaster. Only a vigorous measure can relieve our affairs there and check the enemy. Major-General Gates has been a thorn in my side and a secret adversary. This event, as the news is slowly coming in, brings him great dishonor. I can honestly write, that though he has contended with me instead of cooperating, and though he has sought to undermine me at every turn, I have wished him the greatest of success for our Nation's sake. The events and his actions are frustrating. I take some solace that his defeat brings sadness to me. If I were in this for myself, I would have celebrated anything that brings him shame. That is enough internal investigation. We must put the pieces together and save this thing.

An uprising occurred in the Pennsylvania line over the promotion of an officer whom the rank- and-file were very much against. Many had determined to quit the contest entirely. Thankfully, General Wayne and General Irving were able to calm the storm. General Wayne has written me himself because he fears I might hear a rumor that he started the fiasco. I have not been told such. Even if I had, I would not believe it. General Wayne is strong on fidelity. We are a band of brothers. We will rise above every injury — real or imaginary. We must persevere in this arduous struggle for the glory that awaits, should peace and independence be ours.

Thursday, September 7, 1780 — Bergen County, New Jersey

General Arnold writes to inform me of his plan for engagement if the enemy comes up the river. I am in agreement with him. I cannot think how things southward could have gone differently were General Greene in command at that front or General Arnold (had his health allowed). I am glad to have General Arnold back engaged. When he is idle, he seems to get into trouble. That was the case this past April when he was accused of misusing public funds. Thankfully, he was acquitted, but doubts always arise when he is inactive.

Friday, September 8, 1780 — Bergen County, New Jersey

The paper money of these States is not accepted in some countries who wish to render us aid. I am asking Congress if they can raise up specie or foreign currency for the maintenance of four or five thousand men who wish to ally themselves with us.

I need Congress to encourage support from the States in the south. We have some sort of an army left there. I intend to raise and send more. They will need articles of bread, meat, forage, horses, and wagons. Speaking of men, we are short of them still. With enlistments running out, we may have no more than six thousand left in this quarter. I will not be able to enter any engagement unless this is changed.

The recent movements of the enemy in New York appears to be nothing more than loading ninety vessels to be sailed back to Britain with a few invalids. However, rumors still prevail that the enemy plans a descent upon Virginia to make use of the victories they have experienced recently in the south. I am informing Count de Rochambeau of our predicament. I do not take joy in delivering the bad news. As a good ally, I must disclose everything. He has requested to meet me for some time now. I believe that this is the time to get together so we might consider different plans and settle on one. Then, when the second fleet arrives, we will be ready to act. I am suggesting that we meet on the 20th instant in Hartford.

Sunday, September 10, 1780 — Bergen County, New Jersey

General Lincoln has written of a plan to meet with the British General Phillips to arrange an exchange. I am sending the commissary of prisoners to join them. To receive General Lincoln back into this army would be great. All the while, we must not forget those who have been long-held by the enemy. Anything I can do to gain their release, I will do as long as it does not benefit the enemy unequally.

Tuesday, September 12, 1780 — Bergen County, New Jersey

I am writing the French admiral, Count de Guichen, to join the appeals of the Marquis and Chevalier de Turnay. We must have naval superiority if we are to win this war. Congress has given me the lead in our cooperation with the French. I am taking it upon myself to reach out and clarify our distresses. I must tell him, as I have Rochambeau, that our situation is critical. We are exhausted financially. Our army is diminishing. To have to admit our true condition shames me, but again I must be honest with those who seek to assist. General Clinton has around ten thousand regular troops in addition to militia in this quarter. Lord Cornwallis has seven or eight thousand men and complete possession of two of our States — Georgia and South Carolina. Of report, North Carolina is now at his mercy. I believe the enemy is sending a detachment to Virginia. We have thirteen States in this Union. We have lost almost all of four including New York. Turnay is blockaded at Rhode Island. The savages are desolating our frontiers in the other States.

I assume the primary object of the French is our independence. Even if that be the case, they can benefit from a humiliation of the British. I am sending my letter through Chevalier de la Luzerne as I know of no other channel that I trust. I will be putting so much insight into the state of our affairs that the enemy might move with alacrity upon us should they discover that I give credence to their belief that this army is at the point of unraveling.

I am also writing John Rutledge, the Governor of South Carolina. I know he must be wondering where this army is. He is probably curious as to what we intend to do to expel the enemy from his State. At this point, he must know we desire to do just that, but we are unable at the present. He must call upon his people and the surrounding States. They must raise up five thousand men for this army for the duration of the war or for as long as possible. He cannot depend on militia. They have shown at Camden how ineffectual they can be. He needs to gather resources for the five thousand, along with the men I will be sending. They will need meat, corn, wheat or rice, and transportation. Salted meat is needed, perhaps as much as four thousand barrels. I need him to convey to me the force of the enemy, the posts they occupy, the condition of these posts, and what reinforcements they may derive from the people of the country. I also need him to tell me the best place for our men to disembark should we be able to move in his direction.

More returns are coming from the collapse at Camden. It appears the militia turned and ran in the face of the enemy as Lord Cornwallis heard of their attack and fell back to repulse it. When General Gates was unable to regather the militia, he fled with them. He is said to have even passed them up per Colonel Hamilton's information. In fact, reports are that he rode almost two hundred and forty miles over three days in a northern retreat all alone.

Where General Gates proved unworthy of his rank, General de Kalb and the Continentals from Maryland and Delaware fought valiantly. Even taking a saber wound to his head, de Kalb continued to fight. He called for his men to charge the British. Seeing his example, they pushed forward. The enemy realizing his influence upon his men, chose to take him out. They hoped that his fall would cause his men to retreat. He took eleven shots to his body. His final act was to stab and kill a British soldier before he fell dead himself. Baron de Kalb is a man I will always respect. He was a true soldier and faithful to our cause to the very end. Men like de Kalb keep me confident that this contest will end in our favor. Providence has seen to it.

Wednesday, September 13, 1780 — Bergen County, New Jersey

Speaking of men who inspire me, Captain Hendricks Solomon and his tribe from Stockbridge have been in this war with us off-and-on from its onset. He is requesting to return home since no further action is expected in this quarter. He and his men do not wish for pay, but rather clothing articles instead. I do not have any to give them but am asking Congress to provide for these great allies of ours. They have lost their chief and many warriors for our cause. This Nation is forever grateful.

Thursday, September 14, 1780 — Bergen County, New Jersey

General Arnold is requesting permission to send down two of his cannons to Colonel Gouvion. I have no objections to this move provided General Arnold has what he needs to defend West Point. I am asking him to detain Colonel Putnam's men. He is to ensure that Colonel Hay is obtaining the flour that we need for the posts in the Highlands and at West Point. I am letting him know that I will be going to Hartford to meet with the French admiral and general. I am asking him to keep these things to himself so the enemy might not make a move in my absence.

Friday, September 15, 1780 — Bergen County, New Jersey

Again, I am writing Congress to build up our army with a draft. Militia will not do it. That was proven again in Camden. Militia are good at the point of attack. They can be assigned for ambush and for shooting from the forests, but they will never be able to compete with a regular line from the enemy. Congress believes if we have a lot of men, that will compensate for lack of a regular army. Their object should be to have a good army not a large one. Every exertion should be made to impress upon the States of North Carolina, Virginia, Maryland, and Delaware to raise a permanent force of six thousand men each. With this, we can expel the enemy from our country. Without them, we will continue to slide backward.

If we choose to move southward, we will need ample provisions, especially for a voyage from this point to there. If these needs remain unmet, we will face an insuperable obstacle.

I believe I have all things in order in this camp. I am placing General Greene in charge upon my absence. I plan on leaving tomorrow to meet with Count de Rochambeau and Chevalier de Turnay. Greene is to use all prudence and discretion. He is not to seek action or accept one if it is not on advantageous terms. If he hears the second French fleet has arrived, he is to put the army under marching orders to move toward New York. He will need to have boats collected at the North river and form a bridge over the Harlem river. He will need to call upon the States of Maryland, Delaware, Pennsylvania, Jersey, and New York to redouble their exertions for collecting provisions and forage, as well as put their nearest militia under marching orders. He must keep me apprised with every bit of information he receives. I am having Colonel Tilghman at his disposal to relay all information.

Monday, September 18, 1780 — King's Ferry, New York

I had written our generals for their opinions concerning the wisdom of attacking New York or making our next move to the south. I requested they reply before my meeting with the French leadership. Major-General Arnold was kind enough to meet me today at King's Ferry to give me his input. He looks to be recovering well and was animated in his opinions. He is always a man of action. He reports that things are shaping up at West Point. He seemed regretful that I would not be able to see his progress. I do not want to disappoint him. As a point of encouragement, I told him that I intend to stop by his post on my return from Hartford. He seemed delighted.

Wednesday, September 20, 1780 — Hartford, Connecticut

Though being absent from my army gives me anxious thoughts, the need for ally support made this trip necessary. I have arrived in Hartford to a warm welcome from Count de Rochambeau and Chevalier de Ternay at the Jeremiah Wadsworth home. We had a good meal this evening. We plan to strategize tomorrow. After much concern and doubts, these men give me hope that they intend to fight with us to the end. A verse I continue to quote in my lament is Proverbs 13:12, "Hope deferred makes the heart sick, but a longing fulfilled is a tree of life." I have often been sick hoping for the French to assist, receiving their promise, but then seeing no action. Accounts have been received that they have made inroads for our cause on the seas. On this Continent, I have seen no real succor other than from the men who are fighting in the lines wearing various French uniforms. May the next day bring some concrete action.

Thursday, September 21, 1780 — Hartford, Connecticut

Our meetings seem to have been a success. General Rochambeau and Admiral Ternay have responded zealously to our plight. They are not deterred by our state-of-affairs. Rather, they are more encouraged that their assistance is not wanted to lessen our casualties, but sincerely needed to secure our freedom. I have assured them our Nation will do all in its power to make their investment fruitful. We have decided if the French fleet from the West Indies arrives by the beginning of October, we will move to attack the enemy in New York. If the fleet does not arrive in that span of time or soon after, then we will plan our coordinated attack southward.

Friday September 22, 1780 — Hartford, Connecticut

With a joyous exchange, I am leaving with renewed hope. I cannot wait to get back to our army and make our plans more exact. Rochambeau and Ternay expressed the same desire to get back to their men and get ready to move. In fact, one of their aides stated their ships were already preparing for New York because they were encouraged by my visit. I am stopping off at West Point, and then back to Bergen County.

Monday, September 25, 1780 — Robinson's House, West Point, New York

I have arrived at West Point. They cannot find General Arnold. Some from his officer family have agreed to accompany me on my inspection in Arnold's absence.

I am appalled at the state-of-affairs here at West Point. It makes me wonder if this is the reason Arnold has disappeared. None of the preparations that he assured me had occurred have been performed. I find this post to be in the most indefensible of states. I have never seen such poor readiness. It is as if he wants this post to fall. They are trying to find Arnold now.

I have just been given some papers. A man by the name of John Anderson was stopped on the road to New York by chance. Upon suspicion, our militia men guarding the road searched him and found papers detailing the plans to capture West Point. They were written in General Arnold's hand. Upon further questioning, the man captured was found to be British Major, adjutant-general John Andre'. For a fee, Arnold had chosen to betray his country. I am horrified at this revelation. This is the man I defended. This is the man I fought to get promoted to major-general. This is the man I counted on when effort, action, and industry were needed. This is the man clearly overlooked by Congress time and again. This is the man who I prayed would soon rejoin this army. This is the man who I prayed our other generals would emulate. This is the man I shared my meals with, disclosed my great concerns, and shared secretive army plans. Who better to bring value to the British? I could grovel on this now. What I have written is enough. Now I must put the pieces back together. I must defend against the danger that may come because of this betrayal. Judas was in my midst and I had no idea. The Savior knew at that Last Meal. I did not at our last meeting at King's Ferry. I am sending Colonel Hamilton to see if he can catch up with Arnold before he escapes to the enemy.

I am handing command over West Point to Colonel Wade. He must get this post back in shape immediately. He must be vigilant. The enemy contemplates some enterprise upon this garrison. It has been made vulnerable for this purpose. I cannot doubt the enemy will not act even knowing their plotting has been discovered.

I am putting Lieutenant-Colonel Gray in motion with the regiment in his command. He is to place half of his men to occupy the middle and north redoubts on the heights above this place. He is to put the other half above Mandeville's.

I am ordering Lieutenant-Colonel Jameson to take every precaution to prevent Andre's escape. He is to be sent to me with such a party and as many officers as necessary. Mr. Andre' is to be treated with civility though he is not a common prisoner of war.

I am sending Colonel Gouvion to find and arrest Joshua H. Smith who was part of the plot between Arnold and Andre'. The plan was concerted in his home. I would not have known that had Arnold not referenced him at the end of one of his letters to the enemy. Smith is to be delivered to me as well.

Arnold has escaped. He was seen boarding the enemy's Vulture sloop of war. We should do whatever is in our power to capture this traitor and bring him to justice. His offense is a crime against this whole Nation.

I am directing General Greene to put the division on his left in motion for King's Ferry as soon as possible due to the alarming transactions now discovered.

Tuesday, September 26, 1780 — Robinson's House, West Point, New York

My suspicions were never roused when there were inroads for General Arnold to oversee West Point. I wanted him in battle. I thought that is where he wanted to be. That he wanted this post was a surprise. When I had an officer already in command, I offered him a position near it. That was not to his desire. When the opportunity presented itself, I gave Arnold what he requested. I never dreamed that he had planned to sacrifice it. I suppose thoughts to this treason will be with me for the remainder of my life. I suppose hindsight will help guard my future decisions.

Going over the papers Arnold gave to Andre', the traitor told the enemy the number of men we had, the state of the post, the best plan of attack, and the disposition of our artillery in case of alarm. He even ensured the areas suggested for attack were left unfortified. He did this not for thirty pieces of silver, but I am told twenty-thousand pounds. These papers were not delivered to the enemy. Providential interposition has brought this plot to light. I am resigned to the question, what if? What if he would have gotten away with it? What if the weather had not cloaked our escapes? What if more traitors had been in our midst? What if France was not allied with us? What if? Providence, God, is the only One who has spared this Nation. He always comes at just the right time. I believe it is even because of Him that the enemy has not pressed their strengths against us. I believe He has kept them afraid when, from a military standpoint, they have nothing to fear.

I am calling for Major-General Heath to leave his post in Rhode Island with the French fleet and join this army here. I will write Count de Rochambeau to explain.

I am writing Congress to inform them of the recent traitorous occurrences. I am also asking them to reward the militia who captured Mr. Andre'. They were said to have been offered a large sum of money and as many goods as they would like to release him. They refused. They deserve the thanks of their Nation.

Wednesday, September 27, 1780 — Robinson's House, West Point, New York

I am still concerned about West Point's security. I am having troops distributed all around this post. I am ordering ten days provision to be supplied at each point. Because of Arnold's intelligence to the enemy, they have perfect knowledge of our defenses. They can attack with utmost precision. We need information on the enemy's designs. I am having some militia cut wood and some to guard the stores at Fishkill.

I am directing Mr. Andre' and Mr. Smith to be delivered separately to the army under General Greene. They are always to be kept apart. They are to be secured with around-the-clock guards.

I was thinking back this evening to our time a few years back in Morristown. Benedict Arnold had met with me in the Ford mansion to discuss his next assignment. Back then, he was the fighter that I wished all men would emulate. A memory has struck me. It was the earnest expression that he made concerning his undying love for our nation. He went on to flatter me detailing his loyalty to my command. Was that truly who he was? Did he once possess that felicity, but then somewhere along the line lose it? Or was he pretending then, saying what he thought I wanted to hear so that he might gain stature and financial reward? I am perplexed if that large a change was made. I am mortified if it was all an act. I am not sure which.

Friday, September 29, 1780 — Tappan, New York

I have received a letter today from the villain Arnold. He has written that what he did was because of his love for this Country. He states that his rationale may appear inconsistent to the world. He is right. It is inconsistent, better said a fabrication. He is asking me to give mercy to his wife and to hold her innocent of his actions. I must do that, though I have doubts. Her responses to me proved untrue upon my arrival. Regardless, I will give her the benefit of the doubt. Arnold asks that we forward his clothes and baggage to him. He even offers to pay money for their value. I assume the money comes from the money given him for betrayal. I will not. He can throw that money into the Potter's Field. Last, he closes his letter as my most obedient and humble servant. This is from the man who put my life in jeopardy, who tried to coordinate the British attack with my arrival at West Point. Of all the ways to end a letter, I have to question Arnold's mental competence to close this letter this way. May God be the judge of Mr. Arnold. I pray that we can exact His Verdict.

Sunday, October 1, 1780 — Tappan, New York

I am directing General St. Clair to repair forthwith to West Point and take command of that post until further orders. He is the nearest man I trust. He will have at his command the Pennsylvania division, Colonel Meigs's regiment, Colonel Livingston's regiments, and the militias from New Hampshire and Connecticut. He must move quicky to provide the security of that post. I had given orders to evacuate Stony Point and Verplanck's. I have reconsidered this. These two posts will prevent the enemy from coming upon West Point by surprise. They can both retard the enemy's progress, giving Heath and his men time to prepare a defense. I will have these two posts evacuated only when it appears the enemy is about to take them. Dobbs Ferry can serve as an outpost. The biggest threat is if a single enemy vessel moves up the river, our men may overreact. They are to hold their ground until they see several enemy vessels. Then they must move to act. The east side of the river must be patrolled. This is the easiest place for the enemy to land a body of men by surprise. The men at King's Ferry should be moved up the North river except those that are needed for communication.

Monday, October 2, 1780 — Tappan, New York

At twelve o'clock today, Major Andre', Adjutant-General to the British army, was executed by hanging. He requested to be shot, but the practice and usage of war demand he be hung.

Wednesday, October 4, 1780 — Tappan, New York

John Mathews of Congress writes that Congress has agreed to one-year enlistments for the new recruits. They feel this meets my request. It does not. I have written that they should be no less than one year. I wrote that they must be for at least three years or for the duration of the war if we wish to secure success. Until an army is on foot for the war, the Independence of the United States will scarce be established. Congress believes men cannot be drafted. They are wrong. They believe a bounty is inducement enough. It is not. Each year the bounties must be increased but those who come for the bounty often leave once they have received the bounty and then when times get hard. One-year enlistments mean that just as men are coming into this army, recently trained ones are leaving. A healthy army is comprised of old soldiers. A sickly one is composed of new ones. Lives are lost as each new group of levies are being seasoned for battle. With a seasoned army who have been in service for longer than a year, we can take advantage of opportunities to defeat the enemy. With a new army, we are unable to seize the opportunities. The war drags on. We need a permanent force. I will write this again to Congress and to Mr. Mathews. Why in Heaven's Name can they not understand?

I am also writing James Duane in Congress the same. To make Congress feel like they are doing a good thing by fielding a temporary army takes little. Their expectations jump with every bit of good news. When we give a check to the enemy, Congress and our inhabitants feel we have won a victory. When we gain any little advantage, they feel the war will immediately end. The history of this war is a history of false hopes and temporary expedients. I am even now afraid of a little success because such favor lulls us into security. Supineness soon follows. This seems to be our National character. Some take a false hope from my interview with the French allies at Hartford. What they do not see is that nothing with certainty was determined. What we agreed to were possible plans on the supposition of possible events.

Thursday, October 5, 1780 — Tappan, New York

Brigadier-General Cadwalader has written of his regret to not have taken a commission when Congress offered it to him. He felt at the time of the offer that the war was near a conclusion. He assures me of his attachment to me and this cause. I wish that he would join now. We have had one general flee in the face of danger at Camden and another general turn apostate and attempt to sell his country.

This campaign began with such hope, but ends with little to show for it except two lost States to the enemy. The French fleet and army sit in a harbor inactive. Spain's activity has been minimal. We spend half our time without provision. In a little time, we will have no men. False hopes and temporary devices are our daily bread. Our case is still not desperate if virtue exists in our people and wisdom can be found in our rulers.

Friday, October 6, 1780 — Tappan, New York

As to whether West Point will become the headquarters of our army when we go into cantonments for the winter is a matter of great question. With the diminution of our present force and little prospect of new recruits, the importance of West Point compels us to center our force on the North river.

I am having General Greene take command of the Jersey and York brigades, and of Stark's and Poor's brigades. I am directing him to march to West Point. The first Pennsylvania brigade marches that way tomorrow. I will send General St. Clair from West Point with the second Pennsylvania brigade and Meigs's regiment to replace them.

When Greene arrives, he can dismiss the New Hampshire and Massachusetts militia with my thanks. This will reduce our costs. He is also to send off all spare wagons and riding horses to reduce the weight upon our forage. He must see that the works at West Point are completed. The more he does to improve that situation, the less useful will be the intelligence that Arnold has shared. He must be certain of the availability of ample magazines of wood. The artillery, corps of sappers and miners will be under his command, along with Livingston's regiment and Sheldon's dragoons. I have the utmost confidence in committing this important post to General Greene.

Saturday, October 7, 1780 — Tappan, New York

I am communicating the names of the three persons who captured Major Andre' and refused to release him even after great offers were made to them. They are John Paulding, David Williams, and Isaac Van Wart. I am asking Congress to reward them with a handsome gratuity.

I have detached the Jersey, New York, and New Hampshire brigades with Starks to the Highland posts. They will relieve the Pennsylvania line.

At the present, the weather is cold and wet. We are making a tedious march with my army. My intention is to proceed to the neighborhood of Passaic Falls.

Sunday, October 8, 1780 — Passaic Falls, New Jersey

Now I am getting letters from General Gates. If it were not so tragic, it would be humorous that now after a great defeat, he writes faithfully. He is still in charge of the army southward, but I expect an inquiry soon to be demanded from Congress. He would like to take a position near the enemy, I suppose to regain his stature. This would be foolish with such an inferior force. They just need to keep the enemy in check with light irregular troops under Colonel Sumpter and other active officers. A new army with provisions must be collected and arranged before any action can take place.

The enemy has the advantage with naval superiority. They can move men at-will by the water. By the time we hear of their actions and march, they have embarked and moved to their next stop of depredations. We are best to hold where the posts are most valuable until circumstances change. The fatal policy of temporary enlistments makes this necessary. The enemy appears to be preparing to embark from New York. They may be heading southward still. Assumption is their object is to make a further extension of their conquests in that quarter.

The French fleet is still blocked at the harbor of Newport. Count de Guichen and his fleet are nowhere to be seen. The old proverb continues to ring in my head, "Hope delayed makes a heart sick, but a longing fulfilled is a tree of life."

Tuesday, October 10, 1780 — Preakness, New Jersey

I am writing Count de Rochambeau a line to keep communication open. I have let him know of Arnold's treachery. I now am informing him of Andre's execution. He needs to know also that we are strengthening our post at West Point. I want the French to know we are not discouraged, nor have we lost heart. This campaign has not been as productive as we had hoped, but the next should bring better success. The operations of the Spanish in Florida should provide a useful diversion to the southern States.

Wednesday, October 11, 1780 — Bergen County, New Jersey

My friend Mr. Benjamin Franklin writes me from France. The Marquis has brought his letter to me. He is doing a great service in France. He has been instrumental in the help we have received. He wishes that after the war that I tour France with him. This is a kind offer. I will have to see what condition my domestic duties are in before I make that commitment. I am writing him back cordially, but also to see if he can assist in our greatest need for the article of money.

Colonel James Wood has command at Charlottesville. He has kept that post in tough times. He has made sure that it is well-supplied. He now wishes to be relieved this winter. He is deserving of this, but now his services are essential at his present station. I am requesting his continuance at least a while longer. To have a qualified officer there familiar with the situation is better than to bring in a stranger unacquainted with the business at-hand.

Congress writes with a desire to reform this army, reduce its regiments, and send some officers home. They think rearranging things will assist. Again, they are wrong. I am praying for wisdom in our rulers. I dare to write for my own eyes — wisdom seems to be in short supply. I must answer them as their subordinate who will comply. I must also answer them in rebuttal as one with whom they have invested the authority to conduct this war. I do not believe we need fewer officers. We do need more capable ones. I do not believe we should reduce this army; rather, it must be increased. If they let officers go, they must give them half-pay for life. This will ease any ill feelings, but if they relieve one officer for assumed lack of productivity, how many capable ones will feel their name will appear with the next assumption? Officers take pride in their positions. They often suffer more than their men for less pay than they could get outside the army. They do this because of patriotism, love of country, and a belief in the cause. They also know that when the war is completed, that rank will be a lifelong badge of honor respected among their neighbors. This has been the case, historically, in every other country where men have served. Daily, good officers are leaving for various reasons. I believe Congress should let attrition take care of their concern.

The number of regiments may be reduced if Congress chooses, but the men in each regiment must then increase. Congress flatters itself that this army just needs eighteen thousand men in aggregate. They are wrong. Let me put solid numbers to my argument. We need two thousand, five hundred men at West Point. We need fifteen hundred scattered between Fort Pitt, Fort Schuyler, and other frontier posts. We need fifteen thousand at least in this quarter. That already totals nineteen thousand men — one thousand over Congress's total. We need an army of men southward. We need a quartermaster-general and staff. We need an inspector-general and staff. We need a paymaster and staff. We need a cavalry. We need a corps of engineers. We need doctors. We need hospital workers. We need recruiting officers in each State. I could go on. I believe we need a standing army of thirty thousand men in total. In addition, we need militia to augment that. We need terms of service to extend to the end of the war. We need half-pay for life. We need better bounties for officers to recruit. We need one United States army and not thirteen armies of the respective States. I am pleading with Congress. Please meet our needs. Now is not the time for politics and self-interest, The public demands safety from its representatives. This is the best way to meet

498   Johnny Teague

the public's needs and secure our quest for freedom. They should keep that in mind if they wish to remain in Congress.

Friday, October 13, 1780 — Passaic Falls, New Jersey

My friend, Lieutenant-Colonel John Laurens, writes to share his relief that the Arnold villainous perfidy was discovered. I have thought a lot about this, even as recent as last night on my pillow. The thought of Arnold's plan succeeding causes me to tremble. What adds to this hurt is when I revisit the thought that Arnold planned it in such a way for the enemy to catch me at West Point. It breaks my heart that he would seek my own demise and combine two events with one stroke — the fall of West Point and the capture and death of my person. Providence interposed at the most remarkable and conspicuous time to rescue West Point and me. This has not been a rare occurrence. God has come to my aid throughout my life. He has been especially evident in this war. As I knelt to pray this morning (as is my custom), I gave Him thanks again. As I write this, I give Him thanks. As I will soon return a letter to Mr. Laurens, I will give Him thanks again.

Saturday, October 14, 1780 — Passaic Falls, New Jersey

Congress has done as expected in ordering an inquiry into General Gates's conduct at Camden. They have directed me to appoint an officer to command the southern army in his room until the inquiry shall be made. To save time (and in a covert admission that they placed Gates there against my suggestion), they are pleased to leave the choice up to me with their preapproval. For the second time, I am presenting General Greene for this post. I am sending General Heath to relieve him at West Point. General McDougall will command it until he arrives.

Sunday, October 15, 1780 — Passaic Falls, New Jersey

I am forwarding a New York paper to Congress, which contains nothing material except an address from the traitor Benedict Arnold to the inhabitants of America. I do not know which is more to be lambasted — the confidence that Arnold has in publishing it or the folly the enemy believes it will produce among a people who have been duped by so infamous a character. Hubris never ceases to amaze me.

The enemy has disembarked from their ships in New York supposedly with some new object of agitation. My informant there is hesitant to give me intelligence as he fears Arnold knows who he is and has the British watching his every move. I have assured him Arnold had no idea of who he is, nor does any other. Prayerfully, he will gain some assurance as things settle down. I need him to continue his good work.

I am writing Governor Jefferson to make ready for an enemy attack. I believe Virginia is the next incursion. He is to move all public stores from the navigable waters.

Monday, October 16, 1780 — Passaic Falls, New Jersey

General Greene writes that attacks have occurred on the frontiers. He has detached Gansevoort's regiment to address them. I am informing him the enemy set sail with around two thousand-and-upwards toward his quarter. He needs to pull five hundred militia up the river and put Stony Point and Verplanck's Point in readiness.

Speaking of savages on the frontier, Colonel William Malcom has had success against a party of savages in his quarter. He has suggested evacuating Fort Schuyler and set a post below it. I do not believe this is wise at the present. As his men's enlistments expire in December, so will his command. I will be sending a Continental regiment to garrison the post. I still expect him to take measures to lay up winter supply of provision, wood, and other necessities for the regiment that will replace his.

Wednesday, October 18, 1780 — Passaic Falls, New Jersey

The command General Greene is entering will be attended with peculiar difficulties. I know he is leery of these, so I am writing to give him confidence. He has the ability to handle each problem. He has done so his whole military career under my watchful eye. This is why he is the one I have chosen to send. I regret I have no idea the true circumstances southward as General Gates never shared them with me. Greene has requested a little time at home before taking this post, but I cannot allow it. The issues in that head are in such a state that no time can be lost. I would love to go home to Mount Vernon myself, but cannot leave my post either. Duty demands we stay at the helm.

President Reed writes of his gratitude that Arnold was caught. I remind him like I do any who mention this event that Providence alone overruled the enemy's designs. The timely discovery of this betrayal can only be attributed to the Overseer of all things.

Saturday, October 21, 1780 — Preakness, New Jersey

Colonel Varick and Colonel Franks, both aides-de-camp to General Arnold have requested inquiries to show they were not complicit nor knowledgeable of the traitor's plan. I am assuring them that they have been investigated. All are assured of their unimpeachable character. I do not blame them for being concerned. I, too, have come under some scrutiny for trusting General Arnold. I have questioned myself ever since.

The British are advancing toward the borders of North Carolina which is alarming. It is thought the ships which have lately sailed from New York may intend to cooperate with them. The enemy may have even received reinforcements from Europe with the last fleet. They are also moving from the northward toward Lake George. Another is moving from westward toward Schoharie. Governor Clinton is making a disposition of force to counter. I am sending two Continental regiments to his assistance.

Fort Pitt is in need of provisions. I am asking Congress to obtain the necessaries from the State of Pennsylvania.

Sunday, October 22, 1780 — Preakness, New Jersey

I am sending Baron Steuben southward to join General Greene. His expertise with raw troops will help form, train, and regulate them. His work there is essential.

In compliance with Congress's request, I am asking General Greene to nominate a court of inquiry into the conduct of General Gates. It is proper that it be done in that quarter as the witnesses and the requisite information are there. I wish for Baron Steuben to preside over this court. The jury will be officers of the Continental troops who were not present at the battle of Camden. They are to conduct themselves with the greatest impartiality.

I am requesting Governor Thomas Lee of Maryland to assist General Greene in every way possible to furnish men and supplies for the army to be newly formed southward.

Monday, October 23, 1780 — Preakness, New Jersey

Mr. John Mathews of Congress is requesting safe passage for his wife back to South Carolina. He says that he is suffering for lack of money in Philadelphia. He has nowhere else to get it as he serves our Nation. He does not mind doing without, but would prefer his wife not suffer too. I have assured him that I will do the best I can to help.

In return, I am asking him to consider the state of this army. The enemy is making progress. The one good result in all of this is that the British army has spread itself too thin. They are vulnerable everywhere. I see no chance to change the situation unless we have an army with arms, clothing, and supplies.

Tuesday, October 24, 1780 — Preakness, New Jersey

See how Providence works! I am praying for wisdom among our rulers. I just received a letter that New York has appointed General McDougall to Congress. I hate to lose a good general, but it blesses me to have a man of wisdom there who understands our situation. He has been in battle. He has seen the ineptness of a temporary army. I welcome this change. I give Him thanks.

Thursday, October 26, 1780 — Preakness, New Jersey

I am sending Brigadier-General James Clinton to take command of the affairs at Albany and the frontier. He is to proceed there at once. He is to pay particular attention to the post at Fort Schuyler.

Monday, October 30, 1780 — Preakness, New Jersey

The Marquis is a man of activity. He desires even more ardently than I to end this campaign on a happy stroke. He wishes to invade New York. What this young general does not see is that we must consult our means rather than our wishes. He may endeavor to better our affairs by attempting things that may make them worse. I regret to deny him, but the enemy's force is too great for us at the present. It is a melancholy fact, but all we can do is to gain a more certain knowledge of the enemy and act accordingly.

Sunday, November 5, 1780 — Preakness, New Jersey

Governor Clinton has written of his success over the savage invaders of his frontier. He personally led his militia and drove them out. I am grateful for a head of State who knows what it is to fight, sacrifice, and lead. He does not wait for someone else to do his work. He takes it on himself.

The enemy has laid waste our magazines of bread. I fear that I will need to bring flour from the southward for our troops at and near West Point. I need the Governor to tell me what his State can procure so that I will know what I need to gather from Jersey, Pennsylvania, and Maryland.

Complaints are coming in from the Troops in New York that they must do garrison duty at Fort Schuyler. This troubles me. I would assume they would be agreeable to guard their own frontier. Pennsylvania and Virginia guard their own State. I will make sure Governor Clinton is aware of these complaints. I cannot imagine him countenancing such.

Our affairs southward have taken on a more pleasing aspect. The people in the Carolinas and Virginia have been pushed and pushed by Lord Cornwallis. British Major Ferguson covering Cornwallis's flank pillaged and burned many homes in his path, laughing as he lit the fires. The people had enough. They gathered some one thousand men and caught up with the enemy at King's Mountain in South Carolina. Ferguson boasted of his position and his Tory strength. He even declared that God Himself could not overcome him. Our brave patriots climbed that mountain and attacked. Sharpshooters covered them from the tall trees. The enemy was being cut down. They raised a white flag, but Major Ferguson cut it down. They raised another. He cut that one down too. Finally, Ferguson was shot and drug away by a leg hung in the stirrup of his horse. He was soon found dead. The Tories of his party surrendered, but the rage of our men and the brutality exacted by General Tarleton excited our people to kill the enemy where they stood. Thankfully, it is reported that Colonel Campbell rode into their midst to stop them from committing the crimes that are emblematic of the enemy.

Monday, November 6, 1780 — Preakness, New Jersey

Governor Abner Nash of North Carolina has shared some intelligence regarding the enemy's movements in his State. I am grateful for his information. Every governor should be as engaged. He is concerned about the condition of things to the south. He is also worried about the enemy's plans. I do not have the men to send to him, but I am confident that the southern States will call forth the resources of the country to meet their present need. I am assuring him General Greene is very capable and is taking command there. Baron Steuben is on his way as well to bring training to the troops in quick fashion. Major Lee, a seasoned officer, is also on his way with his legion.

Tuesday, November 7, 1780 — Preakness, New Jersey

The enemy is active in New York State. They are destroying country as low down as Schoharie. Another group has repassed Lake George and proceeding to St. John's. They have a considerable force at Ticonderoga. I am sending the remainder of the New York brigade from West Point to Albany. The enemy has destroyed grain in the western frontier. I am not sure if we can compensate for that loss from the States of Pennsylvania, Delaware, and Maryland. Our army is in daily want while the enemy is deriving all their needs from New York, New Jersey, and Connecticut. They hardly need their shipments from abroad. In some wars, giving aid to the enemy is thought to be a crime. Whereas in the United States, the penalty is so light that hardly a concern is given. I am suggesting it be made a capital offense like in other countries. With a few select executions of profiting citizens and merchants, I believe this traitorous activity will stop. Everyone is up in arms over Benedict Arnold. They should be. I say that selling and giving aid to the enemy is of the same evil.

The good news of the day is that a prisoner exchange has been exacted with the British. In this transaction, Major-General Lincoln has been returned to us, as has Brigadier-Generals Thompson, Waterbury, Duportail, and Lieutenant-Colonel Laurens. All totaled, we have returned one hundred and forty of our officers and all our privates in New York amounting to four hundred and seventy-six. This is extremely gratifying. After all our efforts to effect an exchange, one has finally occurred. Now it is hoped that more will be conducted.

Wednesday, November 8, 1780 — Passaic Falls, New Jersey

I am instructing General Greene to have flat boats constructed to furnish a means for our men to cross the rivers and check the enemy's actions. He is currently forming a flying army of which I fully approve.

I am writing General Lincoln to congratulate him on his exchange. I want him to know that as much as I value him in this army, I understand if he desires to take some time at home. He can still assist us from home for a period of time to secure funds and subsistence for our troops this winter. I would rather he do this than be a participant in the camp of their hunger, cold, and lack of clothes. He may prefer to suffer with our men. I leave that to his discretion. Nonetheless, we need someone to help us gather the necessary supplies and clothing to care for our men.

Governor Jefferson needs to know the enemy may soon be landing on his banks. It would be good policy if he removes the troops of the convention to a greater distance from them. He should also help secure flat boats so that our men can cross the rivers and molest the enemy at every turn.

Saturday, November 11, 1780 — Passaic Falls, New Jersey

The enemy has gathered a large amount of hay at Coram. Major Benjamin Talmadge has submitted a plan to destroy the enemy's stored forage. He wishes permission to implement it. I am granting his request and sending Colonel Sheldon to furnish a detachment of dismounted dragoons to assist. The one thing I ask is that he secretly carry this out. He must always secure a means of retreat.

Thursday, November 16, 1780 — Passaic Falls, New Jersey

A plan has been in my head to make a strike upon the enemy on the northern part of New York Island. I am getting our men set but doing it all under the guise of foraging for winter. I am directing General Heath to send a detachment to White Plains or as low down as he can go on Thursday the 23rd instant. His men are to remain there upon their arms. The enemy may see them and attempt to surprise them, so a vigilant lookout is to be kept. Patrols must scour up and down several roads. He is to form this detachment merely as a foraging party with wagons in-tow. Guard boats are to be on alert to communicate any enemy movements. Five boats of the largest size are to be moved by carriage above Dobbs Ferry. Five good watermen from the Jersey line are to be in each. I am detaching the Massachusetts and Connecticut line to West Point to give him fourteen hundred men at his disposal. I will transmit no more to him by letter. I will send an officer soon to detail the rest.

Monday, November 20, 1780 — Passaic Falls, New Jersey

General Sullivan is now a member of Congress thanks to the State of New Hampshire. Another answer to prayer. General McDougall is there. Now General Sullivan holds a spot. Mr. Sullivan informs me that Congress is seeking to abide by my wishes for the army. I am so grateful to hear this if it is truly carried out. To have done this three-or-four years ago would perhaps have allowed us to be home by now. Looking back does no good. If this is brought into effect, we may be sooner where we want to be than if no change was made.

I need Mr. Sullivan to now work on getting the provisions for our men — primarily clothing. By the time the winter clothing is sent, we are in summer. What is sent and what is received is also at a huge disparity. Clothing sits often on docks or in warehouses falling prey to moths and cankerworms. I wish they would hire some eminent merchant who has a mind and foresight for business to order what we need and plan its delivery. A good businessman can ensure that we receive what we need when we need it. Shipping clothing material is preferred to clothing as our regiment tailors have a better means to make use of it. They can fashion what is needed for each regiment.

Congress needs to not fool themselves into thinking we can rub by this campaign as we did the last. That makes as much sense as the assumption that if a man can roll a snowball the size of a horse, he can continue to roll it to the size of a house. Matters can be pushed only so far. Our men have not been paid for ten months. Every department is in debt. Our money has no value. A loan from a foreign aid is what we need. I am unloading all this on Mr. Sullivan because he has a military mind. He has lived in the army's camp.

Tuesday, November 21, 1780 — Passaic Falls, New Jersey

The plan to make a strike on the northern part of New York continues to unfold in my mind. I make notes in the middle of the night as thoughts come to me. I awake in the morning trying to make sense of the notes I made. Some get lost between the hours of slumber. Some things get clearer. Some get murkier. From last night's thoughts, I am asking Colonel Gouvion to proceed to Fort Lee. Then with great secrecy, he can move along the margin of the North river opposite Spiten Devil creek. I am asking him to make observations regarding the enemy's works on Fort Washington, their huts, encampments, and barracks. He should note landing places on the Island where it would be easiest to debark troops, and where they could make their approach least-noticed. He needs to observe the enemy troops on parade in the mornings to ascertain a more exact number. He needs to decide what the probability is of moving down boats on carriages below Fort Lee. I will send a patrol toward Three Pigeons for their security but will not let that patrol know what Gouvion's men are up to.

I am instructing Colonel Moylan at nine o'clock Friday morning on the 24th to parade his regiment at Totawa Bridge with two-days provision. He is to detach forward parties toward New Bridge, then upwards to the bridge near Demarest's. This will be done to secure the crossings on the Hackensack. He is to prevent any person from going with intelligence to the enemy. He is also to patrol from the

Marquis's old quarters below the Liberty Pole toward Bergen Town, Bull's Ferry, Weehawk, and Hoboken. I rely on his punctual execution.

I am directing General Wayne to march Friday morning with his division toward Newark. They are to remain in this position until retreat-beating. When he arrives at Acquaquenoc, they are to begin a forage with a few wagons that will be sent down to him. He must have two -days provision cooked. Three would be better. All of this must be done in secrecy.

I am directing Colonel Pickering, our quartermaster-general, to provide the boats we need with padding for the oars. They are to be in good shape with repair material on-hand. On Thursday at twelve o'clock, these are to be placed on carriages pulled by fine horses to the North river below the mountain. They should remain there until Friday morning. Hay and grain must be ready to feed the horses. On Friday, they are to carry the boats to Acquaquenoc Bridge and arrive there early that afternoon.

Wednesday, November 22, 1780 — Passaic Falls, New Jersey

Orders are given to Lieutenant-Colonel Humphreys to proceed to West Point immediately. He is to communicate only with General Heath. On Friday, he is to repair to the detachment at White Plains. I am letting him know our contemplation is upon the enemy's post on York Island. The troops are constantly to be upon their arms. They will be put in motion precisely at four o'clock. The main body will be kept compact with patrols of horse and light parties. Upon signal, Sheldon's regiment and the Connecticut State troops should push forward to intercept the enemy.

The Marquis will lead the attack on Fort Washington with Light Infantry. General Knox is to provide cover with his artillery.

Thursday, November 23, 1780 — Passaic Falls, New Jersey

Our plan was perfect. The enemy was unaware. Regrettably, the enemy sent vessels down the river which intervened, all by accident I am sure. Our efforts were never carried out. I was proud that our men did all that was asked, and in the time in which they were asked. This gives me confidence that we can make a strike on the enemy even with the few men we have. I have seen Providence's Hand work for our good many times by accident. Though great time and effort went into this planning, I will not conclude anything but that this was His Protection.

Saturday, November 25, 1780 — Passaic Falls, New Jersey

Congress has made promotions again based on State proportions. These tend to always bring complaint. General Knox was passed over. I am writing Mr. Sullivan to make sure no younger officer passes General Knox or, undoubtedly, he will quit the service. He is too valuable to lose.

Monday, November 27, 1780 — Passaic Falls, New Jersey

I am directing General Wayne to march to the neighborhood of Morristown for winter cantonment. I am asking that we minimize the number of horses in each camp as forage will be scarce. I have directed the quartermaster-general to procure ox-teams for the service of winter. They are subsisted easier. The soldiers and waggoners have less chance to abuse them as they would horses. Magazines of provision will require frugality. Great effort must be taken to prohibit any abuse of the inhabitants or their property. These have borne the burdens of war enduringly. They have never failed to relieve the distresses of this army. If new recruits come in, he is to see that they are trained and fit to join the line in the Spring for maneuvers. Discipline must be required as we will be marching in cooperation with the first corps of France this campaign — by God's Grace.

Tuesday, November 28, 1780 — Morristown, New Jersey

I will be wintering with the troops at New Windsor. The Pennsylvania line will be four miles from hence in huts constructed last winter. The Jersey line will be at Pompton. The Connecticut, New Hampshire, and Rhode Island lines will be in the Highlands. The Massachusetts line will be at West Point. Moylan's regiment of horses will be at Lancaster in Pennsylvania. Sheldon's will be at Colchester in Connecticut. One regiment of New York will garrison at Fort Schuyler and another at Saratoga. The remainder of their line will be in Albany and Schenectady.

I rejoice that Major Talmadge and the second regiment of dragoons were able to destroy the valuable magazines of forage the enemy had stored at Coram upon Long Island. He not only burned three hundred tons of their hay, but burned their barracks and a vessel containing their stores. In addition to this success, he took fifty-four of the enemy as prisoners.

Friday, December 8, 1780 — New Windsor, New York

The Light Infantry corps under the Marquis has been broken up. I have had them rejoin the lines and regiments from which they first belonged. This leaves the Maquis without a command. I am giving him the opportunity to move southward. He can take a command there or he may remain with this army, though it may be in a period of inactivity. I will let him decide based on his European advices. If he chooses to go southward, I will write dispatches to facilitate his move under General Greene.

Sunday, December 10, 1780 — New Windsor, New York

Report from New York is that the enemy is about to move another detachment. I conjecture it will be southward. The detachment is said to be comprised of one battalion of grenadiers, one battalion of light infantry, one battalion of Hessian grenadiers, Knyphausen's regiments, and the forty-second of the British army.

Count de Rochambeau is quartering his second division in Connecticut rather than in Massachusetts. This is preferable to me as it will be closer to the probable scene of our next operation.

Wednesday, December 13, 1780 — New Windsor, New York

General Greene has been on my mind a lot lately. I know that he faces an arduous task. I dare say it is more of a task than he imagined. It is shocking how poorly the state-of-affairs can be under neglectful leadership. The one who sought to supplant me, General Gates, could not even take care of the duties that had been assigned to him. Yet, he felt he was ready for a bigger challenge? I have found as the Lord has said, if we are faithful in little, He will give us greater responsibilities.

General Greene has intimated in a recent letter that his reputation could greatly suffer if he fails at this post. He needs to know that if he succeeds, he will be praised and add to his reputation. If he is unsuccessful, all will know that it was an impossible task. His military reputation will still be intact. I face the impossible daily.

Thursday, December 14, 1780 — New Windsor, New York

The Spaniards are on the move from Cuba to the Floridas. If his Most Christian Majesty's fleet under Chevalier de Ternay could move to meet the Spaniards and inflict a blow on the British in that quarter, it would aid our cause. Portugal has given a friendly disposition toward our cause for which I am grateful. If we can get all these foreign allies to work together, we may have a superior maritime force that will put an end to this question once-and-for-all.

I am writing Chevalier de la Luzerne to see if he can deliver clothing for this army. Our want of those articles makes an uncomfortable cantonment, but alas, we are accustomed to want. We never flatter ourselves that relief will come.

Our letters are delayed at this season. The dragoon horses have been exhausted. We have sent them to winter cantonment with the men. The quartermaster-general has not the funds to furnish an express even on the most urgent of occasions.

Friday, December 15, 1780 — New Windsor, New York

Confirmation has been made that the British are making another debarkation with a detachment of two thousand, five hundred to reinforce Lord Cornwallis. The enemy intends to push their operations southward this winter.

For the Independence of the United States, it is essential the common enemy should relinquish their conquests in South Carolina and Georgia. No means ought to be left assayed in efforts to dislodge them. We will need the French assistance in this quest. The defeat at Camden and the loss of men and supplies at Charleston has greatly hampered our efforts in that region. I believe General Greene and Baron Steuben can take the raw recruits in that quarter and resurrect our prospects in time.

I am suggesting a plan to Rochambeau. If the Spaniards target Pensacola and St. Augustine according to their plan, with the enemy spread out, they should find success there with rapidity. They then can move up to meet the French and subdue the enemy in the States of South Carolina and Georgia. I am writing the governor of Havana to see if they will cooperate with us conjunctly. This will be in their best interest. For if the enemy is allowed to station themselves in Georgia and South Carolina, they can easily make a move on the Floridas. This will allow them to regain that area or at least harass the Spaniards there. I can raise up another one thousand troops. Hopefully, Rochambeau can add double that. These corps and troops can be collected under General Greene in conjunction with the Spaniards to form an army that the British cannot resist. If the French can bring their fleet from the West Indies as well, this will enhance a force far superior to what the enemy can assemble in this continent. Though I wish the United States would provide the force for our own defense, it is encouraging to see that, in our infancy, we have gained such potential support from abroad.

Sunday, December 17, 1780 — New Windsor, New York

To correct a strong friend like Governor Trumbull of Connecticut is always difficult. Last winter, he asked that our cantonment of horse be moved to some other State. I let that go without remark. Again, this winter, he is requesting that Sheldon's regiment take their quarters to Massachusetts. This repeated interference by the Governor must be addressed. I must remonstrate very pointedly to him against such repetition of this practice. We have a purpose as to how we quarter this army. We do it considering how best we can secure our capital posts, how we can cover our country, what is most convenient, and what keeps our army close enough together to respond to any threat. If Connecticut can move that regiment to Massachusetts, then Massachusetts may want to move it to New Hampshire. Then, New Hampshire may seek to move it to another State. I know that Connecticut is providing quarters at Colchester for the French cavalry. Trumbull fears they will have insufficient forage. The Governor needs to know I have taken this into account, making apportionment accordingly.

Mr. John Sullivan in Congress has raised the question of promotions within this army. That is a complicated issue. If we were one army, this would be easy to handle as all promotions should be lineal. If this army were comprised of thirteen separate armies, this would be easy too. But this army's composition is of both, making promotions complicated and ripened with complaints. I have tried to eliminate all State distinctions early-on in this war, but the States continue their practice of promoting within. They then require this confederate army to recognize their ranks. We must take things as they are and make the best of them. Maybe the next war, we can have just one army. I pray there is not another war to remedy this.

Wednesday, December 20, 1780 — New Windsor, New York

No succor appears to be coming from a second French fleet. I am disappointed at this news from the Chevalier de Chastellux. My hope is that the Spaniards can make up the difference. The movements of Lord Cornwallis during the last few months have been retrograde. If we had the army and the naval force we expected, we could take advantage of this. We could also reduce New York as the enemy has made many detachments of late. Regrettably, we have not the force to do anything but be spectators at this quarter. We have moved as many men as possible southward under General Greene. We hope it continues Cornwallis's backward motion.

In our favor (I cannot write or say it enough), Congress has moved from depending on temporary expedients. They are now making vigorous efforts to establish a permanent army. If Mr. Franklin can gain a loan from the French, we may have all we need to conclude this contest.

Thursday, December 28, 1780 — New Windsor, New York

I have believed the reduction of the post of Detroit would give security to the western frontier. As I have not had the Continental force to carry it out, Governor Jefferson has written of his intention to try with his Virginia militia. I welcome this wholeheartedly. If every Governor would take it upon themselves to make inroads where the enemy is near, this army would have less burden to carry. I am giving direction to Colonel Brodhead at Fort Pitt to send what men he can spare, along with the Continental company of artillery. Colonel Clark of Virginia will command this operation upon Detroit. Clark is asking for the six-pound cannon. I am deterring him from its usage. Experience has taught us that it cannot batter a common blockhouse at the shortest range. I am directing Colonel Brodhead to provide four fieldpieces with sixteen-hundred balls, one eight-inch howitzer with three hundred shells for it, two royals, grape shot, five hundred spades, two hundred pickaxes, some boats, and one traveling-forge. Even if Virginia is not successful in this attempt, it will provide a diversion and give the enemy employ in their own country.

The Year 1781

Tuesday, January 2, 1781 — New Windsor, New York

Confirmation has arrived that the enemy embarked from New York on the 20th ultimo with sixteen hundred men composed of British, German, and Provincial corps.

Wednesday, January 3, 1781 — New Windsor, New York

I am saddened to hear an alarming defection of the Pennsylvania line has occurred in the Morristown cantonment after a New Year's Day of too much drinking. Reportedly, almost twenty-four hundred men rose in mutiny against their officers. Their complaints — no pay for twelve months, no food, no clothing, great suffering, and the grouse that they have been kept beyond their terms of enlistment. General Wayne, Colonel Butler, and Colonel Stewart did all they could to quell the revolt but were unsuccessful. They are said to be marching toward Philadelphia with six pieces of artillery to bring their grievances in person to Congress. I am fearful that if they get to Philadelphia, many more malcontents will join them. Congress will be in danger. I fear also for the inhabitants of Philadelphia. On the other hand, if we can raise troops to counter them, this may drive the mutineers into the enemy's hands. The enemy will surely seek to induce them to join their side. Even if these do not join the enemy, they may scatter, never to be found again. Two thousand, four hundred men? This will weaken our force and greatly augment the British. Who is to say that this mutiny will not spread to other encampments? I am asking General Wayne to cross the Delaware with them and seek to draw from them a list of their grievances with a promise that we will do all we can to gain remedy from Congress. I will venture to set out toward Philadelphia myself to see if I can help.

Thursday, January 4, 1781 — New Windsor, New York

Upon second thought, I am fearful to leave these troops lest they revolt in my absence. They lack pay, flour, clothing, meat, and everything the Pennsylvania line lacks.

Friday, January 5, 1781 — New Windsor, New York

Everything I feared on behalf of this army is starting to be realized. I have long apprehended the consequences from the complicated distresses of this army. Now I am told that some officers were killed by their own men, others wounded, and the lives of several soldiers have been lost. This was not inflicted upon us by the enemy across the line, but by our own men. They have not been cared for, but I had hoped that dignity and virtue would have prevented this. I say that, but dignity and virtue are the only things that have sustained us this long in such want. Per General Wayne's aide-de-camp, this body is on-march to Philadelphia.

This camp is quiet. How long can I hope for that to remain? As it now stands, these men do not know what has happened in Morristown, but I cannot keep the news from them for long. These in my camp suffer under the same pressing hardships. I cannot just wait for Congress to act. I am writing some of the governors of the States around us for their immediate succor. We need flour and meat. We need an immediate supply of clothing. We need three months' pay at least to be given to each of our soldiers.

Sunday, January 7, 1781 — New Windsor, New York

I am sending General Knox who is familiar with our distresses to carry my letter to the governors of Connecticut, Rhode Island, Massachusetts, and the president of New Hampshire. Our men are tired of seeing merchants get richer and more comfortable, while these men with little provisions fight to protect those merchants. The northern army is in need. So is the southern army under General Greene.

We may obtain supplies from France, but I do not count on it. We have been disappointed so often before. I can see France's argument. They must grow weary of our requests. They must feel that if we cannot fight for ourselves, how can we maintain a government in the aftermath?

The Pennsylvania line is now in Princeton. Intelligence says the enemy is moving into Jersey in response to the revolt. We need guard-boats to keep a lookout. I am sending Colonel Hull and the militia to guard our stores at Ringwood.

I am unsure how bad things can get. I know we have been here before. I fear we will be here again. My only hope is in Divine Providence who has delivered us from this place in the past. I trust He will again.

Monday, January 8, 1781 — New Windsor, New York

I have been deliberating on making a move for Princeton myself, but the governor of this State and the general officers advise that I stay here and trust my officers. To remain still is difficult for me.

Troops at several other posts still seem quiet with no indication of outrage or defection.

Tuesday, January 9, 1781 — New Windsor, New York

General Greene writes that a dispute has risen between General Smallwood and Baron Steuben. Smallwood believes he has seniority. He is hesitant to give it up to the former. I am hoping Greene can convince Smallwood that the Baron is extremely necessary there at this moment.

The defection of the Pennsylvania line continues to fester. Their demands are exorbitant. It appears we will need to dissolve the line altogether. I am happy the remainder of the troops give no signs of defection. God only knows how long that can last or what the consequences will be if they continue to be neglected.

Wednesday, January 10, 1781 — New Windsor, New York

I have sent directions to General Heath to assemble all the general officers at his quarters tomorrow. I need to meet with them. I need to have their advice on whether to use force against our own men as they continue their march.

Thursday, January 11, 1781 — New Windsor, New York

The enemy sent two men to the Pennsylvanians with incentives to leave us and join their side. I am grateful that our mutineers have arrested them both and will be having a trial to decide their fate. At least these men have shown an attachment to our cause even in their discontent.

Friday, January 12, 1781 — New Windsor, New York

One day is different from the one that follows. General St. Clair writes that mutineers have made it known that if their terms are not met, they can obtain what they need elsewhere, intimating their second thoughts on the British offer. I am directing one thousand men to be prepared and held in readiness. If no hope of a reasonable compromise follows, I will seek advice from the governors as to our next move. I will have them ready to call up militia as well.

Major-General Howe has written to lead this detachment. I think in a point of policy, General Parsons or General Glover would be better apt to lead. I will leave it to these three gentlemen to decide. I am asking General Heath to pay attention that each work is manned and provided for, and that the guard-boats are watchful. If any force on the water is seen, they are to fire alarms at Stony or Verplanck's Point. A field piece should be stationed at Fort Montgomery. We must watch the enemy. Mutiny may have been their signal for a decisive stroke against us.

General Wayne writes that as things now stand, it may be better simply to dissolve the Pennsylvania line and start anew. This may be the best remedy to be sure the thing does not spread. If we bend to their demands now, what will cause others to exit in like manner?

Sunday, January 14, 1781 — New Windsor, New York

General Heath sent a woman into one of our remaining regiments. She gathered information that our men will take no hand in putting down the Pennsylvanians. This is a fear. I cannot relax discipline to appease the men, nor can I refuse to act for fear they will not obey. I choose to count upon our soldiers' fidelity. I trust they will follow my directions.

Mr. Reed, president of Pennsylvania, met with the mutineers. He has hammered out an agreement. With it, the Pennsylvania line has been handled. Half of the men were discharged from duty. Another half were given a three-month furlough. Very few have been retained. I am not sure how many of the furloughed will return. It does not matter.

The two agents from the enemy who sought to induce the discontents to join their side were summarily executed. Even our dissenters vowed to not be "Arnolds" to our cause. May this name serve this usage in infamy.

Monday, January 15, 1781 — New Windsor, New York

I am writing Congress in full concerning the unhappy mutiny, the perplexing state of our affairs, and the distressed condition of troops at West Point. All of this is on account of the lack of provisions, clothing, and food. I cannot hope to visit men in rebellion and change their minds without some relief in my hand. This is something upon which Congress must act.

Congress wishes to detach the French troops from Rhode Island. They want them to march by land to Virginia. I do not believe it would be safe to separate the land and naval force of the French while the enemy is blockading the harbor at Rhode Island.

Speaking of our needs, my heart is lifted a bit when I see what Mrs. Bache and the ladies of Philadelphia are doing to bring some clothing relief to our men. The sense of patriotic exertions by these ladies have furnished a useful gratuity for the army in this severe season.

Monday, January 22, 1781 — New Windsor, New York

Another mutiny has erupted. This time in the New Jersey line. I am sending General Howe to take a detachment from West Point to deal with the mutiny. I am having him rendezvous the whole of his command at Ringwood or Pompton. He is to compel the mutineers (about two hundred) to unconditional surrender. He will grant no terms while they are in arms-in-resistance. I am unsure how many of General Howe's men will act, but I flatter myself that they will do their duty.

Where I now sit, our army is fed day-to-day by flour. We have received few if any cattle. The salted meat that we had on-hand is now exhausted. I am writing the States to assist. Otherwise, this plague of mutiny will spread quickly to wipe us out. It is more dangerous than the smallpox. To inoculate our men, we just need our Nation to meet our needs. That is all we ask.

Thursday, January 25, 1781 — New Windsor, New York

Reports are coming of inhumane treatment of our men in the prison ships off the harbor of New York. I am writing the officer in charge of their fleet to allow a representative of ours whom they trust to ascertain if the complaints have merit. If they do, I ask they be remedied. If they are not, the British will be vindicated of this one evil.

Saturday, January 27, 1781 — New Windsor, New York

This morning, General Howe has let me know that the mutiny of the Jersey line has been put down. Some six hundred men detached with General Howe in swift pursuit. The Jersey line threw down their arms and surrendered. Two of their leaders were shot by my orders. Several of their own followers were forced into the firing squad to shoot their leaders.

The complaints of the men of Pennsylvania and the Jerseys of being kept beyond their term of enlistment were mostly incorrect. The majority had signed for the duration of the war. The remainder of their complaints were true, but all of us have faced such suffering. The price of freedom is that which I willingly accept.

Monday, January 29, 1781 — New Windsor, New York

For fear of revival of the discontents in the Jersey line, I am asking General Howe to place other troops, in whom we can rely, near them to cover their responsibilities. The New Hampshire detachment and artillery can be detained for this purpose.

Wednesday, January 31, 1781 — New Windsor, New York

The recent mutinies reinforce my belief that we cannot have thirteen armies or one army with thirteen masters. Congress must be vested by the States with power to enact laws to keep our army manned and supplied. In the meantime, I have no doubt that the same bountiful Providence who has relieved us before, will enable us to emerge from each future difficulty and crown our struggles with success.

Good news on this day, Brigadier-General Parsons and Lieutenant-Colonel Hull attacked the enemy Delancey's corps at Westchester burning their barracks and a large quantity of their forage. They also were able to take several of Delancey's men as prisoners. These officers succeeded with three companies of our Continental troops and a party of volunteer horsemen. This is the battle we are to fight. Fighting among ourselves or fighting against Congress will never win our freedom. I believe with Providence's help, the only way we can lose this war is if we defeat ourselves. I strongly believe this is the reason our enemy seems so inactive. They are just waiting for our hoped-for demise.

Thursday, February 1, 1781 — New Windsor, New York

Lieutenant-Colonel Dubuysson finds himself imprisoned at the hands of the enemy. He has written me on several occasions to do a partial prisoner exchange to get him free. I cannot set the precedent of engaging in individual prisoner exchanges. One, it would not be fair to show preference to one over many who have been held for a longer period. Two, if I were to devote my time to individual exchanges, I would not have time to prosecute a war.

Saturday, February 3, 1781 — New Windsor, New York

I am writing Congress for a proper gradation of punishments in our military code. As it now stands, officers often apply arbitrary punishments for various offenses. Congress needs to set some standard to which all can reference.

Also, a standard should be given to the officers, particularly colonels, who furlough their soldiers without any approval from the Commander-in-Chief. These furloughs are used excessively. They come at a point where our manpower is already deficient. Congress should issue a certificate that cannot be easily forged to be given to every soldier on furlough or discharge. They then can present it to the nearest magistrate when they arrive at their destination. If a soldier is found without this document or who has not presented it to the magistrate, they should be treated as deserters and punished accordingly. Virginia has put such a plan in place. All the States should make it a requirement.

I am writing Major General St. Clair to give the greatest attention to recruiting. The Pennsylvania line must be reestablished.

Sunday, February 4, 1781 — New Windsor, New York

Congress is looking at appointing ministers of war, finance, and for foreign affairs. I believe this is wise. Having all of these dealt with as one means that things that need attention in one area are negated by an over-concern for the whole. Each department needs a separate and unique eye.

Trade between our inhabitants and the enemy is on the increase. Two or three years ago, men would shudder at the thought of supplying the enemy. But now, it is pursued with avidity. Such activities drain this army of provisions, tear down the barrier between us and the enemy, corrupts the morals of our people by a lucrative traffic, weakens our collective opposition to the enemy, and gives the enemy opportunity to gain intelligence to everything among us. This is perpetuated by the smallest of penalties. People who enter such traitorous activities know that the only punishment will be the forfeiture of goods found. I am contending again that Congress should make this a capital offense. One or two main players should be executed to discourage the rest.

Tuesday, February 6, 1781 — New Windsor, New York

Governor Jefferson writes of the enemy's incursion into the State of Virginia. Their depredations with impunity are mortifying. More will come in the future. I believe before the next campaign they will establish a post in Virginia. As concerned as I am about this, I pray the Governor will not allow this threat to keep him from supplying the needs for the southern army. The enemy's strength in the Carolinas makes it necessary to build up the southern army to stop their progress.

Arnold, the traitor, has brought off a raid on Richmond. We must employ every exertion to stop him. He must suffer for his betrayal. I believe Cornwallis is using Arnold in that head to divert our attention from his own army's activities.

The enemy's fleet is said to have suffered severely in the recent storm. One seventy-four is said to have been stranded, perhaps lost. Another is said to have been dismasted. It has been towed to Gardiner's Bay. One of their ninety guns has been driven to the sea. This is a good time to act upon them with the French fleet.

Wednesday, February 7, 1781 — New Windsor, New York

Baron Steuben is doing a good job assembling recruits for the southern army. He is also excelling in gathering those who had been furloughed.

I am directing the officer commanding the New Jersey troops to move their men to Morristown. He needs to garrison them in the huts left by the Pennsylvanians.

Saturday, February 10, 1781 — New Windsor, New York

In conference with Count de Rochambeau, our next operation should be upon the enemy in New York, provided we have naval superiority by then. I am instructing General Knox to make preparations for the siege of New York. He will need to gather the arms, powder, heavy cannon, and other essential articles for this activity. The French may be able to supply some of what we need, but we cannot count on that. He needs to plan for an army of twenty thousand men. The general idea of this operation will be two attacks — one upon York Island, the other upon Brooklyn on Long Island.

If for some reason we are unable to execute a strike on New York, Knox needs to consider the option of a strike on Charleston. If successful there, the army will then move to reduce Savannah, Penobscot, and other places.

Thursday, February 15, 1781 — New Windsor, New York

I am directing General Heath to have all the light companies under his command completed to fifty rank-and-file each. He is to assemble the whole at Peekskill. They must have shoes and other necessaries. He is to consult the quartermaster-general to prepare wagons.

It appears M. Destouches will go toward the enemy at Rhode Island while the British fleet has been weakened after the recent storm. Mr. Abuthnot of the British is intent on escorting his disabled ships to New York. The hope is that Chevalier Destouches can take advantage of this situation. He may also decide to detach a portion of his fleet to Chesapeake Bay in quest of Arnold. I do believe Arnold will keep his fleet under protection of land batteries to defy naval attack. He will also be able to collect provisions from the country in that part.

To assist Destouches southward, I am sending twelve-hundred men to advance to the Head of Elk to embark in cooperation. I will not delay this march to the Bay even though I have heard nothing from Rochambeau or Destouches. Our men will march so that if the French agree, we will be ready to act. If they disagree, we have lost little in the exercise. If they do agree, Rochambeau should embark about one thousand of their own troops with many pieces of siege artillery. Arnold's forces consist of about fifteen-hundred men. With our combined forces in this attack, it should not take long to terminate Arnold's activity. This will be of immense importance to the welfare of the southern States.

Saturday, February 17, 1781 — New Windsor, New York

With great elation I record this late in the evening that General Morgan and his men have scored a signal victory over Colonel Tarleton and the flower of the British army. Having General Greene and General Morgan engaged in that quarter is quickly turning the situation around. The only fear is that the area States will take this victory (and the one over Ferguson) as a sign that the war is near-done. The States will then become slothful in their duties. With this recorded, General Greene's strategy to force Cornwallis to be torn between two fronts was brilliant. Cornwallis could move on Greene and leave Camden open to Morgan. Or he could move on Morgan and leave Charleston open to Greene. Cornwallis sent Tarleton and eleven-hundred horsemen and troops to address Morgan's thousand. Morgan's strategy was equally admirable. He backed his untrained men against the river. As a result, his men had to fight or die. They chose to fight. Lining his sharpshooters in the front, he was able to knock down several of the British. These sharpshooters then retreated. Three hundred militia waited. They fired their shots. More British fell. The militia retreated to be replaced by four hundred Continentals. Waiting on the other side of the hill, Morgan had his cavalry ready to attack. In all, ninety percent of Tarleton's men were killed or captured. We only had twelve killed and sixty wounded. This is one of the many blessings that I will give thanks for tomorrow on the Lord's Day.

Monday, February 19, 1781 — New Windsor, New York

Governor Clinton is requesting that I detach two regiments to guard their western frontier. I understand the melancholy picture they give of their distresses. I sincerely wish I could help. To have an offensive strategy against the enemy in the coming campaign, I cannot spare one man. I hope the State will know that if danger increases, I will do all in my power to assist.

Tuesday, February 20, 1781 — New Windsor, New York

I am writing the Marquis to be ready to take command of the men I have sent to Peekskill from General Heath as well as another detachment of Jersey troops. Those troops amount to a total of about twelve hundred in rank-and-file. The Marquis is to march these men to Virginia in conjunction with the militia and some ships from Chevalier Destouches's fleet. He is then to march them to Pompton and then to the Head of Elk. The Marquis will need to coordinate with the quartermaster-general for transportation, route, tents, entrenching tools, and the like. He is to work with the commissary-general for provisions. He is to engage the clothier general for shoes and clothing. Additionally, he will need to consult with General Knox for artillery and stores. Whatever supplies are unavailable, he will have the recourse of impressment.

If boats are ready at the Delaware, the Marquis is to move the men by water. If the boats are unready or the river not open, he is to march them by land. When he arrives in Virginia, he needs to work with Baron Steuben who now commands in Virginia. Together, they must familiarize themselves with the rivers in that area, particularly the James river, seeking what harbors best afford security and shelter. The Marquis is to do nothing that would screen Arnold from due punishment that is afforded for treason.

I am writing the Baron to work with the Marquis. That the Barron obviates any chance for Arnold to escape through North Carolina is imperative.

Thursday, February 22, 1781 — New Windsor, New York

I am concerned that the Marquis will need more men. I am asking General St. Clair if he can form a battalion of eight companies of fifty rank-and-file each in time to leave with the Marquis. St. Clair needs to know this detachment will be temporary. The men will return to him after the exercise. If the companies cannot be completed to fifty each, whatever he can assemble should be sent.

The Chevalier Destouches has taken on the goal to rid the coasts of Virginia the troublesome neighbors. I am hopeful they will be successful. I am apprehensive the enemy will be able to use the land batteries to secure their vessels. If nothing else, the hope is that Destouches can block Arnold in the Bay.

Today is my forty-ninth birthday. Many in my family of officers have blessed me with some food items and a few gifts. Every year, I wonder will this be my last year? Over the last few years, my birthdays have come and gone without notice. Let it be said, I spend my birthdays in the field with our men. The day is no special day for them, so it should not be observed as a special day for me. But this birthday seems different. In many ways, it seems we are seeing things move in a positive way. The enemy is spread too thin. The southern army is finding success. This northern army has a possibility of dislodging New York. Rebellions have been put down. Patriots have risen to the occasion. Traitors have been discovered. Heroes have been uncovered. Usurpers have been humiliated. This is the day I give thanks that God gave me birth. He has a purpose for me. My prayer is that it will be a noble one, that I will not fail Him. Each birthday is a new start for me (when I have time to reflect on them). May this be a new start where the coming campaign terminates this war. That is my prayer. May our people return to virtue and faithfulness. May our army be cared for with ample provisions and respect.

May the enemy leave our shores. May the United States of America find our long-sought-for freedom. May this be the best year I have ever lived!

Friday, February 23, 1781 — New Windsor, New York

With detachments moving southward, the enemy may take advantage of the weakened state of this army. I am pressing for the recruits of Massachusetts Bay and Rhode Island to be hastened to this army. I am also directing militia be made ready near West Point and Westchester. Governor Livingston needs to have the Jersey militia properly arranged if the enemy invades by way of Elizabethtown. I am writing General Heath to have every post ready and supplied. Stony Point and Verplanck's Point must be defended to the last extremity. The beacons on Butter Hill and on mountains opposite of Fishkill also should be examined. They must be put in good order to fire on moment's notice.

Saturday, February 24, 1781 — New Windsor, New York

Count de Rochambeau has sent a letter today expressly wishing me a happy birthday. What a flattering distinction to be paid on the anniversary of my birth from this much-needed ally.

Governor Clinton has written another letter requesting two regiments be sent to guard New York's western frontier. If we can make a blow on the enemy in New York, ample time will present to deal with the frontier. At the present, no such aid can be given elsewhere.

Sunday, February 25, 1781 — New Windsor, New York

The Marquis has arrived in Pompton. He is troubled by enemy ships of the line at New York. He has received some intelligence from a man whom I do not trust who says a large reinforcement is leaving New York to support Arnold. This is not true. About six hundred men may be on board two frigates at the present, but they cannot hope to sail for another week. He has received the clothing he needs for his men. He still lacks shoes. I am asking him to endeavor to get them from Philadelphia.

The British fleet has been repaired. The British have naval superiority again. I am informing the Marquis of the importance of keeping a fast-sailing vessel at the Head of Elk to correspond with the French commodore. As he marches, he needs good officers to stay at the rear to bring up the part of his army that is tired, lazy, and drunk.

A body of men have supposedly landed at Cape Fear under General Provost from Europe. I am ordering the entire Pennsylvania line southward as a result. The Marquis should endeavor to get the Ariel, the Trumbull, and any other public vessel to go around the Chesapeake to harass the enemy.

Monday, February 26, 1781 — New Windsor, New York

Now that Congress has agreed to augment our force with a permanent army, it is imperative that the States comply with the requisition.

I am calling on General Wayne from his leave to take command of the Pennsylvania line. He is to lead it to Virginia.

Tuesday, February 27, 1781 — New Windsor, New York

Lord Cornwallis and twenty-five hundred men have entirely divested themselves of baggage. They made a push to catch General Morgan. Thankfully, Morgan escaped and returned to General Greene. Cornwallis now has turned his sites on General Greene and his army. I am grateful Greene is doing what I have always encouraged our officers — do nothing to risk the army you have, only strike when it is in your advantage. In keeping with those wishes, he has moved to avoid confrontation with Cornwallis until he can gather sufficient militia to augment his force. Lieutenant-Colonel Lee with his legion was able to keep the enemy at a distance with frequent strikes. With the time that Lee gained, Greene and his men were able to reach the Dan river and take boats across to safety, out of reach of the enemy.

Colonel Lee has since surprised a British detachment in Georgetown, South Carolina. They took several of the enemy as prisoners, including some officers. We only lost one man, with two wounded.

General Lincoln is busy recruiting. He has asked me to consider pardons for deserters with the belief they might return to this army. I have found such pardons ineffectual. Deserters believe they can leave their post, return to private life, receive a pardon in time, and resume life as they choose. The more pardons I give, the more desertions increase.

The Marquis is on the march to the Head of Elk.

Thursday, March 1, 1781 — New Windsor, New York

Good news came today in a letter from Count de Rochambeau and Chevalier Destouches. They intend to move their whole fleet to the Chesapeake Bay with a detachment of eleven-hundred French troops. Their plan is to leave on the 5th of this month. The Count is requesting an aide-de-camp to assemble the militia in Virginia in coordination with the commanding officer there. I am asking the Marquis to send Colonel Gouvion to Baron Steuben to relay this intelligence. They are to press preparations for the arrival of the French troops. I am fearful Arnold will escape before the fleet arrives in the Bay.

I am setting out for Rhode Island to meet with the French before they sail. I hope to deal with any difficulties this operation may incur. Cornwallis appears to have twenty-five hundred men who are penetrating the country with great rapidity. I am giving the Marquis latitude to concert a plan with the French general and the naval commander for a descent into North Carolina. The goal will be to cut off the detachment of the enemy and intercept Cornwallis if possible.

Thursday, March 8, 1781 — Newport, Rhode Island

The whole fleet went out this evening with a fair wind. I am hopeful the Marquis has everything prepared for falling down to the Bay on a moment's notice. I have no information regarding the British fleet in Gardiner's Bay.

Friday, March 9, 1781 — Newport, Rhode Island

My business is almost finished here. The leaders and citizens of Newport have shown effusions of esteem, which give me peculiar satisfaction. I will soon be returning to my dreary quarters at New Windsor with a fresh zeal and abundant reasons to give thanks to Providence for His favorable interpositions on our behalf.

Sunday, March 11, 1781 — Newport, Rhode Island

The British have publicized that their fleet left yesterday for the Chesapeake. I am glad the French fleet had a head start. I am praying they reach the Bay before the enemy.

Tuesday, March 13, 1781

The journey from Newport toward New Windsor has been a pleasant one so far. I may be able to make a few stops to visit our friends along the way. We are seeing small traces of Spring. The air is fresh. We have hope under the protection of Heaven to secure the blessings for which we are contending.

Saturday, March 17, 1781 — Hartford, Connecticut

I am entreating Governor Hancock of Massachusetts, as well as governors in the neighboring States to procure the levies to complete their deficiencies. They are to forward them to their places of rendezvous expeditiously. We are at an important moment. Our allies are doing their part. This bold attempt upon the enemy depends on naval superiority. This is something we hope for but can never be certain.

Wednesday, March 21, 1781 — New Windsor, New York

Many letters await my attention since my departure for Newport. A manifesto and declaration have been delivered to my hand. Great Britain is at war with the Dutch. To see this is pleasing. Because of the evils exacted upon this Nation and others by Great Britain, many have turned upon them — France, Spain, the Irish, the Dutch. One would think Great Britain could see what their abuses have wrought, and change. I see no change at the present.

Report has it that the Admiral Destouches has arrived at Hampton road. Baron Steuben and a number of militia are bearing down on Arnold. These are ready to cooperate with the Marquis and General Viomenil who leads the French troops. The Marquis has advanced his detachment to Annapolis. His hope is to move under the protection of the French fleet. General Greene is gathering strength. Lord Cornwallis is said to be retreating. Things seem to be going well. I just know that we have fought this war with unrealized hopes. I cannot relax. I would move from this quarter if I had better intelligence of the enemy's designs in New York.

I received a letter from General Heath with complaints that the Marquis and foreign officers are leading the detachment southward. Jealousies are the last thing we need at this moment. Circumstance alone made me decide to choose Colonel Gimat and Major Galvan over native-born Americans. I meant no slight toward my confidence in General Heath or his men. These three were available and un-occupied with other duties. Beyond that, since we are coordinating with the French, to have men who speak our ally's language is important. I would hope by this time, our officers would know I have the sincere disposition to make every one of them happy as circumstance will permit.

Congress has written to inform me the Articles of Confederation have been ratified. This was an event for which I have long wished. I am hopeful this will give Congress the power it needs to prosecute this war with one army rather than thirteen. I pray it also gives Congress the authority to draw men and supplies as needed without hesitation from the States who now agree to work as one under a recognized authority.

General Greene's letter is in the stack. He gives me relief that in all his move-ments, he has saved all his baggage, artillery, and stores. Greene's strategy seems to be hit-and-move. When outnumbered, he retreats and regathers. Such strate-gies often put provisions at risk. Greene has used his quartermaster-general expe-rience for his advantage.

At one point, Greene had grown his force with militia to four thousand, four hundred men. Cornwallis's men were outnumbered. Greene knew it. He was stationed at Guilford Courthouse in North Carolina just twelve miles from the enemy. Cornwallis attacked Greene confident to win the day against our raw recruits. For more than three hours, they fought. Greene informs me that his men fared well, but were outmaneuvered. He got as much out of his fresh troops as one could have hoped. He retreated with his men, leaving around seven hundred and fifty of the enemy dead. Greene lost about four hundred (I grieve over every man we lose. They have paid the ultimate price). I do applaud General Greene for his military abilities. I told him that little was expected. If he failed, his military reputation would be sustained. If he succeeded, he would add luster to his military stature. He has done that full well. He has released a large portion of his militia. He is now carrying out his strategy of hit-and-run.

The enemy has sailed reinforcements from New York on the 13th to aid Arnold and Cornwallis.

Friday, March 23, 1781 — New Windsor, New York

Congress has postponed their appointment of a man to lead the new department of war. I had hoped by now they would have settled on my suggestion of Mr. Schuyler.

I am in a critical and disagreeable state of suspense. We have heard no word from either fleet. If the French would have left Newport on my request, the destruction of Arnold's corps would have been complete. The British fleet would be debilitated by now. The undertaking now is more at risk as the enemy has the opportunity to meet or beat the French to the Bay.

Monday, March 26, 1781 — New Windsor, New York

Major-General Armstrong writes that he has recovered from his health issues. He is also regretful for decisions he has made. I am reminding him that we ought not look back except to learn from our errors. What we have done in the past is irremediable. Using the past to help us steer clear of the shelves and rocks and gain wisdom is the only way we navigate the intricate path of life.

I am writing to him what I am noting here, our affairs are in a perilous crisis. The Hand of Providence I trust can bring about the deliverance for which we long. His deliverance in the past, in our deepest distress and darkness, has been too luminous for me to doubt the happy outcome of this contest. Though I do fear our victory may be so distant that I will not be here to enjoy it. Every morning and every hour, I pant for this work to be done. I long to rest in retirement with domestic and rural enjoyments.

I still think this war could be over quickly if the States will do their job in recruiting for this army. They would rather wish well than act well. They expect me to build with the brick they furnish, but it is absent of straw. I am the one they call upon to furnish the men and the means for the desired outcome. Often, it is too much for me. Congress must act. The States must comply. Retirement seems a dream.

Saturday, March 31, 1781 — New Windsor, New York

From what I can discern, all is bad news. I write this because of a letter just received from Chevalier Destouches. The French fleet met the British fleet on the 16th. The fleets were somewhat equal, but the British had more guns. After a lengthy battle, the British prevailed. They now have possession of Chesapeake Bay. The French have returned to Newport. What will we do next? I suppose that when things are darkest, this is when Providence brings Glory to Himself in our rescue. This is my daily plea.

Wednesday, April 4, 1781 — New Windsor, New York

Everything seems to be in a critical standing. I am writing General Lincoln to gain his assistance in sending forward men from Massachusetts. Every State must use every exertion to gather their men so that this army can check the enemy in this urgent hour. General Greene's present force will not allow him to give any effectual opposition currently. We are at the point of depending on the militia, which is a place I would rather not be.

Congress requests my papers be compiled into books for future reference. They are allotting extra money so I can employ what we need to get this done. I will comply with their wish. I see the necessity of this endeavor. I believe my papers will be important in success or defeat. They may be my only defense in the latter. My letters reveal I have pleaded without end for men and provisions. I have been hindered to act for lack of both.

Thursday, April 5, 1781 — New Windsor, New York

The Marquis grieves over our loss of opportunity. I join him in the melancholy of the moment. He must not get discouraged, nor should I. The only consolation is that we did everything practicable to accomplish the task. I believe the French did the same. I do wish the Marquis would not have headed to the Head of Elk thinking the French fleet was nearby. I also wish he would not have moved to Annapolis when he did. Nevertheless, we move forward. He needs to leave his heavy artillery in Baltimore. The light pieces with the two smallest mortars are to go southward with any ammunition for the Pennsylvania line. I am requesting him then to proceed to Philadelphia.

The complaints from General Heath regarding foreign officers leading our men to the Chesapeake Bay is wearing on me. I wish to appease them so that they see I trust their abilities. I believe in sending the Marquis along with Colonel Gimat and Major Galvan to Philadelphia. I can then give General Heath and his men an opportunity to march southward and take an active role in our offensive or defensive campaign.

Friday, April 6, 1781 — New Windsor, New York

I have considered the vast importance to reinforce General Greene. To send the Marquis to Philadelphia and then await more troops from General Wayne will take too long. The British have reinforced Cornwallis with fifteen hundred more troops. I am asking the Marquis to reverse course. He should put his detachment under General Greene and the southern army. Once this is in motion, the Marquis can go to meet with Governor Jefferson in Richmond to inform him of what is being done and what is needed.

With this change of mind, I am going to inform the Marquis that I may need to relieve Colonel Gimat and Major Galvan and replace them with native officers from their regiments to maintain peace. The Marquis needs to prepare these two officers for that likelihood.

Rumor from a gentleman near the enemy lines has it that four parties have been sent out with orders to kill Governor Livingston, Governor Clinton, and myself. It may not be true, though that is always a possibility. I am informing these so that they can take precautions.

Sunday, April 8, 1781 — New Windsor, New York

General Wayne writes that he has faced many obstacles in raising the levies from Pennsylvania, but he has had some success. I am directing him to have the corps ready without a moment's loss of time. The southern army is in dire need.

I am writing Congress to let them know the levies that each State has raised, marking the deficiencies. Some States desperate to fill their quotas have resorted to temporary enlistments against Congress's direction. Want of men and want of money makes it impracticable to fix a time for any definitive plan in this campaign. All future operations depend on contingencies.

The New York line is greatly dissatisfied. Since they have received pay has been near sixteen months. The Jersey troops are in the same predicament. I am asking Congress to send them some portion of pay to stop desertions or worse evils.

Major Talmadge is a man of activity. He has submitted a plan to cut off overtures from the enemy in Long Island to the disaffected in Connecticut. Currently, some eight hundred refugees and deserters from our cause are said to be at Lloyd's Neck. It is a community of potential Arnolds. I am for the plan if the British fleet is not nearby and if Talmadge can obtain two French frigates to provide cover.

Monday, April 9, 1781 — New Windsor, New York

False hopes and "if onlys" seem to rule my morning. If the French fleet had arrived at the Bay first, we may have seen a decisive turn to our affairs in the southern States. I could then have seen Arnold in gibbets. The world would see we are worth supporting. But as I shared with General Armstrong, it does no good to reflect on the past except to learn from it and reduce the repetition of mistakes.

I am writing John Laurens in Paris to let him know where we stand. He must get us loans so that our present force can be augmented with men and provision. At the present, even if provisions were raised in other States, we do not have the money to pay the teamsters to deliver them. They no longer will accept our certificates. Our troops are near-naked. Our hospitals are without medicines. Our sick men are without nutriment. Our artificers are disbanding. We are at the end of our tether. Deliverance must come now or never.

Tuesday, April 10, 1781 — New Windsor, New York

The Chevalier Destouches is seeking to undertake an expedition to Penobscot. If the States can effect it, the effort will be worthy of our attention. M. Destouches must judge for himself the situation of the enemy's fleet. He knows better than I what may be attempted with prudence. If the attempt is made, it will need to be done by a coup de main to prevent the enemy from moving a part of their fleet to interrupt before its conclusion. I suggest they use frigates, including the forty-fours without any ships of the line. To send more would cause the enemy to send more. They need to gather the number of troops necessary to succeed without depending on the militia. That area is too spread-out to be a resource for any significant militia.

Wednesday, April 11, 1781 — New Windsor, New York

I give the Marquis credit. By a maneuver of his men, he was able to remove the British ships from before Annapolis. Sadly, this has put him at a point farther from being an aid to General Greene. Militia will not be substantial enough to help Greene if General Phillips remains in Virginia or goes farther southward. I need the Marquis to communicate immediately with Greene who can tell him whether he should move forward to join him or remain where he is. Greene may feel the Marquis needs to keep watch over Phillips should he form a junction with Arnold. Lafayette must get shoes for his men before any march can be undertaken. His officers need to be given time to write their friends and family. Their mission was to be a temporary one. Now that it has been extended, provisions need to be sent to them. I depend on the Marquis's assiduity and activity.

Saturday, April 14, 1781 — New Windsor, New York

The Marquis writes often as a son. For this I am grateful. He is a young officer who has far exceeded what any of his age perhaps could. He still needs seasoning as a leader. Humbly, I take time to guide him. He wishes to make another effort against New York. I commend him for this, but I have him where I need him.

Monday, April 16, 1781 — New Windsor, New York

Colonel Harrison has accepted a civil appointment in the State of Maryland, which leaves me in need of a secretary. I am writing Jonathan Turnbull to see if he can fill this place. He will live as sparce as I do and will be paid one hundred and fifty dollars a month.

General Burgoyne is in ill health. His death would deprive us a beneficial prisoner exchange — one that could amount to the equivalent of one thousand and forty private men or officers. I am writing the commissary of prisoners to renew a proposal for an exchange before it is too late.

Wednesday, April 18, 1781 — New Windsor, New York

General Greene has yet to gain the honors he seeks in the field. I know he deserves them. The chances of war are various. Even the best-concerted measures that promise the most flattering of outcomes can and often do deceive us. He is still striking the enemy. He has said so aptly, "We fight, we get beat, we rise, and we fight again." This is one capable general. I am doing all I can to supply his needs. He has let me know Virginia is exerting every effort to his satisfaction. I thank Governor Jefferson for that. I am urging Congress to use every means to get the Pennsylvania line there as well as recruit and equip Moylan's dragoons. For now, General Greene must continue to peck at the British until succors can arrive.

When it comes to jealousies and hurt feelings, General Greene writes that Baron Steuben was discouraged that the Marquis was given command in the recent effort. He needs to know this is not for lack of confidence in his ability but rather a language and relationship decision. Lafayette was to deal with a French land and sea force. He is better equipped to do this than the Baron.

Saturday, April 21, 1781 — New Windsor, New York

The Baron's dissatisfaction continues to hold my mind in thought. How can I appease the Baron and not offend the Marquis? I believe the best answer is found in the fact that the Marquis wants to be by my side if he is not in command. If I can get him here, I can appease the Baron. I need to convince Lafayette that it can benefit him for us to work and strategize together at headquarters. I am writing to let him know I am desirous of him being near me. He will be conciliated if he believes occasions will present for significant activity at this head near New York. I will leave it to his choice.

Sunday, April 22, 1781 — New Windsor, New York

I am writing the Marquis again to let him know great advantages will come to him being where the French army and the American headquarters are. I am going to be clear that I wish for him to return to my side.

I have received another note from the Marquis this afternoon. The British have published a letter supposedly coming from me to my brother Lund. In that letter, it sounds as if I was critical of the Marquis. I do not know what I wrote in that letter, as personal letters are not generally copied when written in haste. I must be honest and let him know that the point referenced in this supposed letter was an event where he acted to my chagrin. I will always be honest in my letters to all addressed. My letter to the Marquis in response to his concern is no different.

Just when I am trying to move the Marquis to these quarters, an unforeseen attack is made against it. I believe firmly there are two sides of spiritual forces. Providence and the good is on one. Evil is on the other. It far surpasses British capabilities and manipulates them with its contemptible weight.

Another letter has been received from the Marquis disclosing sadness. He has faced a rebellion in his ranks. I am concerned for the temper in his detachment as well as the continual desertions. Any time a State raises levies and sends them to this army, they soon forget their men. When their men are killed, desert, or are in need, the States act as if it is no longer their concern. They seek neither to replace the fallen, return the deserter, or meet a need. No wonder their men feel discontented.

We must endeavor to compensate for the loss of State supplies. I am sending from this post twelve hundred shirts, twelve hundred linen overalls, twelve hundred pairs of shoes, twelve hundred pairs of socks, and one hundred hunting shirts. I know the Marquis sought to get these from Philadelphia, but nothing was provided. I am urging the Board of War to assist in holding the States accountable. In addition, the Board needs to notice these deficiencies and move to address them before an emergency arises.

The Marquis is still desirous of an act upon New York. The French ministry has rejected a siege of New York at the present. The enemy has seven thousand men in New York. That far outnumbers what we can muster. The danger of the southern States is more immediate. Phillips must be held in check. This is the task the Marquis's detachment must meet if he remains there.

Monday, April 23, 1781 — New Windsor, New York

Governor Jefferson is requesting I give orders for Fort Pitt to afford every assistance for the reduction of Detroit. This request may have to be delayed. Report is that Colonel Connolly is rounding up the refugees around New York to join Sir John Johnson in Canada. Their object is Fort Pitt. Several hundred persons around his garrison are ready to join the enemy. I am writing Colonel Brodhead to take measures to remove every suspected person in that neighborhood.

Monday, April 30, 1781 — New Windsor, New York

The Count de Rochambeau has received copies of a newspaper that published a supposed intercepted letter of mine that condemns the French allies. This letter was another supposedly written to my brother Lund. The enemy is changing my letters and publishing them to break alliances. I could discount their publication as just that. Honesty prevents me from doing this. The general import of the publication is true. I was upset that the French delayed their move to the Bay. I had not said that to them. Though when I met with them, I pleaded they leave earlier to beat the British to that head. I have shared my disappointment with others too. I must admit to the Count that this part is true. I was disappointed, but now understand their delay was for want of supplies. I pray he will consider the issue addressed and that the bulk of the letter untrue. We are grateful for the French. We need them. As I fight to maintain this alliance, a force is pushing against it.

I am writing Major Talmadge to help me gain the help of our unnamed informant in New York. I have offered a liberal reward for his service. I am directing Talmadge to urge our friend to let us know whether another embarkation is planned, what amount, the destination, and what force will remain on Long Island. This and any other information would be greatly advantageous.

My brother Lund writes of a terrible personal loss for him, and me, at the hands of the enemy. Lund was forced to go on the enemy's vessels to furnish them with supplies. If he refused, they threatened to burn down my home and barns. I would rather have lost my home than for Lund, as my representative, to be seen going on the enemy's ships and providing refreshments. He should have refused outright their demand for all to hear. And if they used force, then yield to their request, being unprovided for defense. This would be preferred to his feeble opposition. I am not sure what the consequences will be. I am requesting Lund move all valuables of mine from my home that are not bulky and that can easily be hidden. I am willing to lose it all for this Nation. My brother needs to remember that. No cost is too great!

Tuesday, May 1, 1781 — New Windsor, New York

I am still troubled by Lund's response to the British. Beyond that, in the past when I thought of the enemy marching into Virginia, I wondered how long it would take for them to get to my home. I am surprised they showed any restraint at all. As this war continues, I could easily see my home being torched, along with others like Jefferson's and Adams's. What I am most thankful for is that Mrs. Washington was not home. I am so grateful she is with me. She tries to always spend our cantonment with me between campaigns. This helps sustain and refresh me and our men. The fear I have now is, as long as the enemy is in Virginia, where is a safe place for her to stay? I do believe she is safe with this army when we are unengaged in battle. When a contest ensues, seldom is there enough notice to remove innocents out of harm's way. New York is unsafe. Philadelphia is not either. Virginia? No. Boston? No. I suppose this is one of those times where I am to trust her chiefly to His Hands. I need His Wisdom at the present to know what location is safest for her.

The State of Massachusetts sent nine thousand dollars to go toward the pay of their troops in this army. I have given it to the quartermaster-general to distribute per their wish. I want every State to supply their men. Military impresses destroy the good will of our countrymen.

I fixed with Ezekiel Cornell of the Board of War on some articles of clothing, arms, and military stores to be sent from this army to supply the wants of the southern army.

Friday, May 4, 1781 — New Windsor, New York

Baron Steuben reports that twelve of the enemy's vessels have advanced up the James river as high as Jamestown. He is unsure how many troops. The Baron has sent a few militia to move our stores from Richmond into the interior of the country.

Saturday, May 5, 1781 — New Windsor, New York

The Marquis writes that the spirit of discontent has subsided within his detachment. Desertions have ceased. For a twenty-four-year-old man, he shows such wisdom and initiative. He is inherently a leader. He took the measures into his own hands. He gathered what the men needed on his own credit. Truly, his men must see his sacrifice and be drawn to him. Any leader who will put his men first and forsake his own comfort for those under his command will generally always be exalted. He continues to add to the everlasting monument of his attachment to our fight for independence.

Sunday, May 6, 1781 — New Windsor, New York

Count de Rochambeau has informed me Dr. Franklin had made a promise that we would provide his troops certain provisions. I complied with the request taking from our own men to do so. This is an embarrassing situation. The States know our wants. I have repeatedly written to them detailing what is needed for them to provide. I have directed General Heath to go to each State with the hope that he can convince them to act.

Thursday, May 10, 1781 — New Windsor, New York

I am sending letters of introduction of General Heath and a restatement of this army's needs to the various governors of the States. If we gathered all the beef from Saratoga to Dobbs Ferry, we would not gather enough beef to feed this northern army for even one day. The eastern States have ample supply of this article. I wish for them to exert every patriotic impulse and forward provisions to this army immediately and regularly. If they do not, I doubt that I can hold this army together. In meeting the needs, the Marquis squelched the discontentment. Meeting the needs of this army is the only thing that will prevent dissolution.

Friday, May 11, 1781 — New Windsor, New York

Congress has not moved on the issue of promotions. I am apprehensive the committee who had this matter under consideration is now sleeping in Congress. That they adopt some mode is necessary. Thus, disputes and discontentment can be abated. Some promotions that have not been acted upon are also in the hands of Congress. Mr. Tilghman has been my faithful assistant for nearly five years. He joined this war in 1776 in the flying camp. He has been a captain of the light infantry. He has been in every action which the main army has been concerned. He has often served without pay. More often, he refused it. He has even declined rank when he felt he was unworthy. If ever a man was deserving of the commission proposed, it is he.

Congress has also deferred, to our disadvantage, ministers of war, foreign affairs, and finance. It seems they have postponed the first, delayed the second, and disagreed on the third. Of these three, I see the minister of finance position being the greatest need.

General Lincoln reports flattering accounts of obtaining men and supplies. I knew he would deliver.

Colonel Dayton reports that ten ships of the line with upward to four thousand enemy troops have left New York. They appear to be going southward. The enemy continues to reduce their force in New York.

Monday, May 14, 1781 — New Windsor, New York

Count de Barras has taken over command of his Most Christian Majesty's fleet along our coast. He has requested an interview. I am suggesting he and Rochambeau meet me at Weathersfield on Monday, the 21st of this month.

Mr. Schuyler has found a faithful and trustworthy man from whom to gain intelligence. To be apprised of the enemy's designs and guard against them will be essential to disconcert their plans and protect our frontiers. He further informs me there is talk of the inhabitants of Vermont leaning quite favorably toward the British. They are said to have formed some sort of agreement with the enemy. I do not know if I can believe the bulk of these citizens would fall on the side of such villainy. I am persuaded that most are well-attached to our cause. For those who are not, may they receive the punishment they deserve.

The troops on the frontier are suffering terrible consequences. They must be speedily supplied. Though I do not have the ability to meet their needs, I am sending them partial of what we have on-hand to give them some relief. General Clinton has agreed with neighboring States to supply our needs. I will forward a portion to those in the frontier. We all are suffering. I just cannot let one group suffer more than another. We are in this together.

General Patterson of West Point reports that the enemy is on the north side of Croton in force. Colonel Greene and Major Flagg, with forty or fifty men, have been cut off at the bridge. He has sent Colonel Scammell with the New Hampshire troops to march for their assistance.

Another rider has appeared. The enemy retreated when they saw the New Hampshire troops marching, but not before inhumanely murdering several of our soldiers.

Information has come to me that the enemy has sailed fifteen vessels and several flatboats near Fort Lee.

Tuesday, May 15, 1781 — New Windsor, New York

It has been a while since I have been able to boast of any naval successes from our side. Commodore John Manley had given us great success early in the war. After his capture in 1777 and release in 1778, he has not seen any significant success. Thankfully, we have Captain and now Chevalier John Paul Jones. He has arrived with articles of military stores and clothing but was late in coming.

I know that was not his fault. The Board of Admiralty gave him forty-seven distinct queries. He answered each one in detail to the satisfaction of Congress. What is amazing about Captain John Paul Jones is what he did in Europe opposing the British there. He captured two of the enemy's ships under our flag. He made a number of prisoners. Though he did not gain a total victory, he did enough to make Britain and the world know that this Nation can stand on any continent and put up a valiant fight against the greatest of odds. When the enemy demanded his surrender after losing nearly every capability, it is said Mr. Jones retorted, "I have not begun to fight." I believe he represents the spirit of this Nation when we are pushed to the brink. I could say the same with all our hardships and deficiencies, we have not begun to fight.

Wednesday, May 16, 1781 — New Windsor, New York

I have now received the full report of the enemy's attack at Croton on Monday. Colonel Delancey of the British, along with sixty horse and two hundred foot, surprised a part of our advanced troops that morning near the Croton river. Colonel Greene was mortally wounded. Major Flagg was killed. Thankfully before his death, Flagg made a good disposition of his small force. They lost only two men besides himself. Both of these men will be sorely missed. Colonel Greene had

distinguished himself in defense of the post of Red Bank, in 1777, when he defeated Count Donop. Echoing John Paul Jones, the enemy needs to know that
regardless of our losses, we have still not begun to fight. Three officers and a surgeon were taken prisoner.

Thursday, May 17, 1781 — New Windsor, New York

I have received intelligence the enemy troops who had sailed near Fort Lee Monday are now building a blockhouse and some other works near that post. If they
complete their work, it will be difficult to dislodge them. I am asking Colonel
Alexander Scammell to take his battalion (which I formed for purposes like this)
and endeavor a strike by surprise. Captain Lawrence who commands the New
York levies near Dobbs Ferry can assist. Any available Jersey militia may be employed as well. The directions I am giving Scammell is to do nothing out of rash-
ness, act if he is certain of success, be sure to guard against ambush, and have a
means of retreat.

General Foreman of Monmouth has written to inform me twelve large
transport vessels and ten topsail schooners and sloops made sail from Sandy Hook
on the 12th. They were steering southward.

Friday, May 18, 1781 — New Windsor, New York

I am setting out for Weathersfield for the interview with Count de Rochambeau
and Admiral Barras.

Sunday, May 20, 1781 — Weathersfield, Connecticut

I met with Governor Trumbull who has given me his opinion that if an important
offensive operation should be undertaken, he has little doubt we will be able to
gain the men and provisions adequate to our wants. This is a comfort to hear.

Monday, May 21, 1781 — Weathersfield, Connecticut

Count de Rochambeau and Chevalier de Chastellux have met with me this day. The British fleet appeared off Block Island, which prevented Count de Barras from joining us.

Wednesday, May 23, 1781 — Weathersfield, Connecticut

It has been a productive meeting with Count de Rochambeau and Chevalier de Chastellux. The French are ready to act. They intend to march toward the North river. Our object will be New York. This seems to be our best option. We do not have the men nor the supplies to march southward, nor do we have the naval force. To stop the progress of the enemy in this quarter will be essential. General Rochambeau agrees. The enemy has reduced its force considerably in New York on land and sea. The French fleet in the West Indies can move to Sandy Hook where they can shut in or cut off Admiral Arbuthnot. Count de Barras and his squadron can meet Count de Grasse's there in cooperation.

Thursday, May 24, 1781 — Weathersfield, Connecticut

In our strategy for our next object, the French army will march soon and form junction with the American army on the North river. The Continental battalions from New Hampshire and New Jersey will complete our numbers. Numbers are key. The attainment of New York is probable unless we fail to provide the necessary number of men. Once the enemy hears of our advance, they may move some of their force from southward, which will give relief to the southern States.

New Hampshire is far short of her quota. One sixth of what New Hampshire has sent has been lost by various casualties of war. This State must make up their deficiency. They must cover those who have been lost. I am calling for them to enlist men for three years or for the duration of the war. However, at this crucial time when cooperation with the allies is vital, I will accept even short enlistments as long as they go to the last day of December of this year.

I strongly feel the enemy has reduced their force in New York, because they have seen that we lack the energy to raise and supply recruits. They have come to believe a defensive strategy is all of which we are capable. Their reduction in New York invites us to take advantage of this moment. If we do not, the enemy will likely defeat the southern army. They will then move this way to render New York secure against any force. Then we will never be able to move them. Rochambeau is depending on us to have the men. He expects us to be a competent partner. I am calling for some militia to be on standby so that we will not disappoint.

Saturday, May 26, 1781 — New Windsor, New York

I was elated to receive a letter from the Honorable John Laurens written from the Court of Versailles. He informs me the French are granting the sum of six million livres to be applied for the purchase of arms, clothes, and other needs for our troops. He writes the French fleet of twenty sails are departing the West Indies on the 12th. They are proceeding to this coast. What a blessing. Tomorrow is the Lord's Day, but I will not wait until then to give Him thanks. I sense a change in the air. Providence is working His great work. All because He is able.

Sunday, May 27, 1781 — New Windsor, New York

Rochambeau is only leaving two hundred French troops to guard their heavy stores and baggage in Providence. I am stationing five hundred militia there to help preserve the works and secure the harbor.

The time to hit New York is ripe. The enemy's detachments southward forces them to make a difficult decision. They must either sacrifice the valuable post of New York or recall part of their force. Perhaps this will turn the tide southward in our favor. I am writing the States around us of the good fortune that can be ours in this campaign if they will simply raise the troops necessary. I am also calling on all governors again to have their militia on standby. I will require no more than necessary. I am calling on Pennsylvania to hold sixteen hundred militia in readiness too. Each State must make vigorous exertions to supply not just men, but also provisions, means of transportation, and clothing.

I am apprehensive of a formidable invasion of the northern frontier. The enemy is moving from Canada collecting a considerable force at Crown Point. This would be an inconvenient diversion from our plan on New York. I cannot spare men for that defense. I am calling on the invalid corps from Boston and Philadelphia that are fit for garrison duty to march to West Point to provide some succor. I am having Fort Schuyler abandoned as well as the German Flats. Every man we can pull, must be drawn into this camp.

Monday, May 28, 1781 — New Windsor, New York

If the enemy evacuates New York upon our success, another detachment may be necessary. I am calling on Colonel Elias Dayton to have his officers prepared to join this main army.

Thursday, May 31, 1781 — New Windsor, New York

General Phillips of the enemy has died. The command of the British army in Virginia now falls to Arnold. Mr. Arnold, our Judas, sent a letter to the Marquis. As soon as the Marquis saw who had signed it, he refused to read it. He sent it back. The Marquis has informed the British he will deal with any officer but Arnold. His rebuttal to Arnold meets my approbation.

Major Talmadge's confidante informs the enemy in New York has no more than four thousand, five hundred men, with perhaps some ability to call up six thousand militia and refugees.

Friday, June 1, 1781 — New Windsor, New York

In my planning for the object of New York, I have been remiss to mention in my diary the progress General Greene has produced southward. He is outnumbered for certain, but he continues to engage the enemy. He gets the most of every contest. Thus far, Greene has been able to push the British forces out of Fort Watson, Fort Motte, and Fort Grandy. General Marion and Colonel Lee deserve credit as well. In all of this, he should feel satisfied, as should I. Regrettably, to raise any sense of accomplishment when want of supplies and support prevents closing any deal is difficult. The General writes that he may have to withdraw from South Carolina and even from North Carolina. It will not be attributed to his abilities or exertion. He had Camden in his possession but lost it in the end. The enemy suffered the greater losses. I am letting him know that our strike on New York may reinvigorate his strength and restore his string of successes.

The Marquis writes that eight hundred recruits are ready to march from Virginia. He says perhaps another four hundred may come from Maryland. If General Wayne has no more discontents in his detachment, he should be on his way southward. All of these would greatly bolster General Greene. I could use these men, but I am willing to part with them and do with less. The French troops marching to North river will help supply my lacking.

Monday, June 4, 1781 — New Windsor, New York

The Marquis writes that Lord Cornwallis formed a junction with Arnold at Petersburg, Virginia. They marched to the James river to be joined by troops who sailed from New York on May 13th. They are now set up in Richmond.

Robert Morris writes he has accepted the appointment of Congress to be our Superintendent of Finance. I have the most sensible pleasure at this news. The value of the dollar and our financial strength stand in equal importance to troop levels for this war effort.

Tuesday, June 5, 1781 — New Windsor, New York

Governor Rutledge of South Carolina visited my camp today to discuss Southern affairs. He is soliciting aid from me as I so often do when I visit or write governors of other States. I have convinced him through a candid discussion of our circumstances that the best help we can give is to divert the enemy to New York. We will be glad to move southward if we are able to acquire naval superiority and can transport our troops.

Wednesday, June 6, 1781 — New Windsor, New York

I went against my custom. I rejected the enemy's agreement to exchange prisoners northward. The reason is that such an exchange would give them more troops. The men we get would be unable to assist in this campaign due to the close of their enlistments. I cannot allow the enemy extra men while we are unable to add to our own.

Congress has approved new rules for promotion. I am hopeful this new plan will satisfy those who have been denied or discontented because of inequities.

Thursday, June 7, 1781 — New Windsor, New York

Governor Jefferson is requesting my presence in Virginia. Lord Cornwallis is reported to be advancing to Hanover Court House. The Marquis is retreating before him toward Fredericksburg. The enemy General Leslie has embarked on the James river with about twelve hundred men perhaps the object of Alexandria.

John Mathews has written from Congress. He has a good grasp of our condition. He flatters me in his measurement of my determination not to sink under the weight of perplexities. He is right. My mind is fortified against and prepared for the most distressing accounts. The game is not yet in our hands, but we can play it well in all we do. I trust our errors will enable us to act better in the future. I am certain that even with setbacks and some ruin, it is in our power to bring the war to a happy conclusion.

I am encouraged by Mr. Morris taking over the financing of this war. I do not suppose that by some magic art he can do more than recover us by degrees from the labyrinth of our financial hole.

Friday, June 8, 1781 — New Windsor, New York

I am just now getting around to responding to Governor Jefferson. He and I are both alarmed at the enemy making incursions into our home State. I want Jefferson to know that I would like to be present to defend our homes and properties. If I were to have the freedom to share our true condition (which I cannot for fear the enemy will intercept this return), he would agree to the path I am taking. Until the enemy is defeated here or evacuates, we must remain at this post. If and when such does occur, we will follow the enemy without hesitation southward even as we must scramble to raise the funds for transporting the artillery, baggage, and stores of this army. Regardless of difficulties, we will move in his direction at that point.

Wednesday, June 13, 1781 — New Windsor, New York

The French have decided to leave their fleet harbored at Rhode Island. I understand their argument as opposed to moving the fleet to Boston. I am desirous that Rochambeau begins his march to the North river as soon as circumstances admit. The British ships are cruising off the Hook. A considerable British army is between Richmond and Fredericksburg. We are uncertain of their destination. With their superiority, they are at liberty to march where they please. On the water is the same. With their superiority, they can sail where they please. I am informed that Count de Grasse is soon to leave the West Indies to join us on this coast. Rochambeau has requisitioned de Grasse's fleet, along with six to seven thousand men to accompany him. Upon their arrival, the advantage should fall to our side. My only regret is that Count de Grasse's stay upon our coast is limited.

One change to our original plan, Rochambeau has suggested Count de Grasse move toward the Chesapeake Bay instead of New York. He believes if victory can be gained there, they can then move toward New York. I am open to the strategy, but I believe it would be better to give no specific guidance until we get closer to his arrival. Things can change between now and then. If he were able to go to Sandy Hook first, he might be able to block up any fleet there, enter, and reduce New York. He then could move to the Chesapeake. I am just hopeful he will come. The liberties of America could be soon realized with promises kept.

I am writing Chevalier de la Luzerne to emphasize the need for de Grasse to bring troops with him. Having extra French influence weigh in could make the matter more certain.

Thursday, June 14, 1781 — New Windsor, New York

General Greene has written of his successes in South Carolina. Lord Rawdon has abandoned Camden with precipitation. He has left all our wounded taken on the 25th of April last along with fifty-eight of his own. He burned his own stores and many buildings which is their custom. General Greene and his men have taken Fort Augusta and the town of Ninety-Six.

Saturday, June 16, 1781 — New Windsor, New York

I ordered the invalids to continue their garrison of West Point but will add no more.

Sunday, June 17, 1781 — New Windsor, New York

I am preparing to move this army from this headquarters to Peekskill in three divisions.

Mrs. Washington was going to set out soon, but she is extremely unwell. I am praying for her health to return.

Thursday, June 21, 1781 — New Windsor, New York

Brigadier-General Clinton examined two prisoners taken lately by his scouts. The enemy appears in Canada to have not moved toward the frontiers, nor have they made preparations to do so. I regret that I sent reinforcements northward considering this new information. I am recalling those for the campaign upon New York. I am writing to request Governor Clinton cover the vacuum with militia and volunteers from that area. I do not want to leave them vulnerable. I will send an officer to assist in assembling a force in that country. I believe Brigadier-General Stark will be ideal. He is brave, heroic, and has a good reputation in those parts.

General Irvine is disappointed in his unsuccessful attempt to fill the Continental brigades. The States have not helped. I do not want him to relax this effort. He needs to rouse the spirit of the country and put himself at the head of the cavalry. Any troops who join without an officer are to fall under his command. They need to all make their march southward.

I am happy to report that Mrs. Washington has perfectly recovered. She will set out for Virginia in a day or two. Of all the allies that I hope for, two are indispensable — Providence and Mrs. Washington. With these two, I can bear all things.

Sunday, June 24, 1781 — New Windsor, New York

Count de Rochambeau writes he has arrived at Windham. He is expected to halt his troops two days in Hartford. He plans to visit my camp once his troops have arrived. I will be happy to meet him in Peekskill, which will be our camp by then.

Monday, June 25, 1781 — New Windsor, New York

I am sending six hundred militia from Berkshire and Hampshire to the New York frontier to assist General Stark. I am directing Stark to establish his headquarters in Saratoga. He is to detain four hundred Massachusetts troops. He is to send two hundred to Colonel Willett on the Mohawk river. He can draw support from the men of the Green Mountains.

The hour is late. We have moved this army to Peekskill. Mrs. Washington set out toward Virginia. I am having her halt in Philadelphia until she receives assurance that all is safe at Mount Vernon. She is still somewhat weak after having been sick for almost a month. It may be a kind of jaundice. I am prayerful for her safe and healthy travels.

Mr. Reed writes that three-to-four thousand troops from France have arrived at Charlestown. He says the enemy is weak in that town, not exceeding four hundred and fifty men. This must be a mistake from Reed as intelligence reports that Lord Rawdon's troops alone in that area amount to many more. The French intend to send two thousand of their number to St. Augustine and New York.

Thursday, June 28, 1781 — Peekskill, New York

Mr. Morris is seeking to repeal the tender laws, before a new species of paper. This is a good move to gain credit with the public. In the short time that he has been in his new position, he has benefited this army greatly. I am obliged also that he was able to acquire the article of flour for our men. This is especially welcomed as I do not believe any was soon coming from Pennsylvania. General Schuyler informs us of the considerable quantities of flour upon the North river. The ease and cheapness of its transport should induce Morris to secure even more.

Our strategy upon New York is becoming firm. We will surprise the enemy posts on the north end of York Island. We have fixed the enterprise for the 2nd of July. This enterprise will be combined with an attempt to cut off Delancey and other light corps outside of Kingsbridge. General Lincoln will command the first detachment. Duke de Lauzun will command the second detachment. Rochambeau has requested to march to Bedford.

Friday, June 29, 1781 — Peekskill, New York

Rochambeau will be in Newtown this night.

The Marquis informs me Lord Cornwallis, after attempting a surprise on the Virginia Assembly at Charlottesville, returned to Richmond without succeeding in any valuable purpose other than destroying some stores at the forks of the James river.

I am saddened the Marquis reports many in Virginia are very dissatisfied with Baron Steuben's conduct during the Cornwallis raids. A discomforting coexistence seems to be growing between the Baron and the Marquis. Both men, we need. Both men, I respect. My hope is they will cooperate for this cause. I long for them to see the value that each brings.

Saturday, June 30, 1781 — Peekskill, New York

I am directing General Waterbury to collect as many men as he can and march them to junction with Colonel Sheldon at Clapp's on the 2nd of July by sunset. He must not exceed that time on any count. He is to bring four days provision ready cooked. He is to carry no baggage. The movement must be as light as possible. He must keep his movement in profound secrecy. I will give him further orders at Clapp's.

I am writing Governor Clinton of our plans for the attack on New York. I continue to review it in my mind for weaknesses or potential dangers. We will begin with an attack on the enemy's post on the north end of York Island on Monday night. This will be led by General Lincoln with two regiments formed into four battalions under the command of Colonel Scammell and Lieutenant-

Colonel Sprout. He needs to bring a detachment of artillery under Captain Bur-beck. A water-guard should accompany them under Captain Pray. General Lincoln is to make Fort George upon Laurel Hill his primary object. This will open communication with the main, afford asylum for the troops, and secure a retreat in case of necessity. From there, he is to damage Fort Knyphausen and Fort Tryon, then relinquish them. The artillery men are to be proportionally divided for three attacks. If they find success there, they are to draw boats across the Island from the North river into Harlem creek. They can cover them under the guns of Fort George. With each success, he is to signal by cannon so that all may know of his progress.

If they are disappointed, he is to retreat by water and push over to the Jersey shore. He can then assist the attempt that will be made on the 3rd by the Duke de Lauzun upon Delancey's corps lying at Morrisania. Lincoln will land his men above the mouth of Spiten Devil creek and march to the high ground in front of Kingsbridge. He can be concealed there until the Duke's attack is announced by firing. He may then dispose of his force as he sees fit. He needs to make the enemy think there are more to his party than really exist. This can keep the enemy from coming over the bridge to the Duke's right or from escaping that way. I think of Gideon when I write this. May we see the same success.

Upon conquest, I shall march the remainder of this army with the hopes the French force will be near at-hand. I will be at Kingsbridge in the morning of the 3rd. Upon a signal of success, I need the Governor Clinton to march his militia toward Kingsbridge, bringing three or four-days provision. I have General Clinton ready to send down regular troops upon the hope we shall succeed.

Sunday, July 1, 1781 — Peekskill, New York

I am directing General Waterbury to march his troops to form a junction at Clapp's on King street with Captain Sheldon and the French troops under the command of Duke de Lauzun. He is then to place himself and his troops under the Duke who will need his insight for that part of the country. I know he will do so with cheerfulness and alacrity.

Monday, July 2, 1781 — Peekskill, New York

General Lincoln's detachment embarked last night near Tellers Point below Ver-planck's Point. He is to repair to Fort Lee and reconnoiter the enemy's position. If the prospects are favorable, he is to make a surprise attack. If they are not, he is to land above the Mouth of Spiten Devil creek and cover the Duke in his opera-tion upon Delancey's corps.

I am asking Rochambeau to proceed tomorrow to North Castle where he will continue to assemble his entire force. This will put him in direct route to receive his provisions. It will give him a direct way for his troops to advance to White Plains or some other destination as the situation demands.

General Knox has arranged to transport the heavy stores from Philadelphia. Once they are in motion, I can communicate to him where to advance them. My plan seems disconnected because so many contingencies present with so many parts in motion. Ultimately, our enterprise will be against the posts upon the north end of York Island. The main objective is to defeat the corps of refugees under the command of Colonel Delancey of Morrisania. If we succeed in the attempt on these posts, we will then do what we can to secure them. I will then call upon General McDougall at West Point to move the militia to join us. We will then move forward against the enemy.

At three o'clock this morning, I commenced my march with the Continental Army to cover the detached troops. We will be ready to act upon their success.

We arrived at Valentine's Hill about sunrise.

Tuesday, July 3, 1781 — Valentine's Hill, New York

The operation of this day has ended — not to our wishes. Duke de Lauzun was unable to reach the point of action at the appointed hour due to the fatigue of his troops.

General Lincoln did all he could. His detachment of eight hundred fell down the North river in boats. They landed at Phillips's House before daybreak on this side of the Harlem river near where Fort Independence once stood. He was attacked by the Yagers, which ended the opportunity of surprise. General Parsons had possessed the heights near Kingsbridge and could have prevented their escape had Lincoln's attack been engaged before notice was sent. General Lincoln lost five or six men. He had about thirty wounded in his skirmish.

I spent a good part of the day with General Duportail reconnoitering the enemy works on the north end of York Island. I have retired our men at Valentine's Hill. Duke de Lauzun and Waterbury are on the east side of the Bronx river on Chester road. Tomorrow, the American army and the French under the Duke will march to White Plains.

Wednesday, July 4, 1781 — White Plains, New York

Though I desired this army to meet with Rochambeau's at White Plains today, he informs me his men are weary. I am asking him to let them rest another day though my anxiety wishes they would push through.

I have marched our men to Dobbs Ferry this afternoon. I have marked a camp for the French army to our left. Duke Lauzun and his men are camped at White Plains. Waterbury's are at Horseneck.

Thursday, July 5, 1781 — Dobbs Ferry, New York

I went to visit the French army, which has arrived at North Castle.

Friday, July 6, 1781 — Dobbs Ferry, New York

The French army has formed junction with our army on the grounds that I marked out for them.

Sunday, July 8, 1781 — Dobbs Ferry, New York

I had the privilege to review the French and American armies. Rochambeau's aide remarked to me of his amazement that this United States army seems to be of a voluntary kind. It holds together though destitute, without uniforms or shoes. He talked about the variety of men in this army — fourteen-year-olds and older, negroes, mulattoes, men of every race and color, though so different, yet well-schooled in their professions. He truly felt our men are the elite of our Nation. I agree.

Friday, July 13, 1781 — Dobbs Ferry, New York

The Marquis reports a favorable turn in his affairs. It appears our southern army is gaining the superiority over Lord Cornwallis. General Greene continues his train of successes. He has clarified previous reports. Augusta has indeed fallen, but Ninety-Six is under siege.

We are awaiting more Continental troops and militia to join this army and Rochambeau's. I am formulating a new plan I will not write in dispatch. I believe (the French fleet have hinted the same) that we may need to make a move southward while our attacks on the north have kept the enemy focused on these parts. If we can scatter and divide them further, we may be able to take them in the south. We can then restrict them to the area of New York. This will allow us to squeeze them completely off the continent. Everything must be kept secret. I am not sharing this with any of our officers. I am only hinting that some plan is in the works.

For a movement southward, I need the Marquis to draw together a respectable body of Continental troops. He is to take every measure to augment his cavalry. He needs to note the magazines available and their location. I am not giving him reason, but it will supply this army in transit. We need a chain of communication between this post and Virginia. I need the Marquis to also establish communication with the coast. We need to be apprised of any troops detached by sea from Lord Cornwallis's army.

Mr. Morris is doing his best to set up magazines of supplies at various stops within each State. Thus far, the States have not set up magazines of flour at any place. No salt meat has been put up in Pennsylvania, Jersey, or New York. Connecticut is sending seven-or-eight thousand barrels of meat and fish. Two thousand have arrived at this post so far. Massachusetts has put up little salt meat. What has been raised was consumed by recruits at Albany. Rhode Island has raised one thousand barrels. Only six hundred remain in Providence. The requisitions of Congress have received little attention. I am just thankful to have an ally in Mr. Morris. He begs and pleads for these articles. This allows me to deal more with the contest at-hand.

One last thing to note southward, I am trying to deal with the conflict between Baron Steuben and the people of Virginia. I may have to remove him from that quarter. He has become very unpopular. His strength is in training troops. He does not realize civilians are not as inclined to snap to attention at his command.

Greene's victories have opened a door for us that I had not thought possible before. His work is giving the French an even better estimation of our abilities.

Some French frigates attempted to break communication between the British and the Loyalists at Lloyd's Neck. The French were unable to get the attack underway in the dark of night. They attempted it anyway. Without the advantage of surprise, the enemy was able to repulse them.

We attempted to reconnoiter the enemy's posts this afternoon, but the weather prevented the enterprise.

Saturday, July 14, 1781 — Dobbs Ferry, New York

Upon a potential move below, I will leave Lord Stirling in command at this post. His attention must be paid primarily to camp order and the security of baggage and stores. No advanced pickets are needed. The camp guards are to be vigilant. No stragglers or plunder of the neighbors is allowed. The French and American soldiers who remain in this quarter must continue so in harmony with each other. Baron Viomenil will command the French line. He is superior in age of commission to Stirling, so Lord Stirling must act with deference toward him. I do not believe the enemy will make an attack on this camp. It has such a respectable force near the enemy's own lines.

In the meantime, I must keep the enemy concerned here in this quarter. We must be active to deceive the enemy from my true intent southward. Even so, if an opportunity presents itself here, how much better would our circumstance be in this war if we have a successful strike on New York. The enemy is being pushed southward. Pushing them in the north cannot help but force them to divide or decide. Either way, we are of the advantage.

Sunday, July 15, 1781 — Dobbs Ferry, New York

Richard Henry Lee flatters to think that if I were given dictatorial powers, I could rally the States, gain what we need, and defeat the enemy once-and-for-all. His unbounded confidence in me is an encouragement, but that is not necessary nor contemplatable. He is filled with anxiety as we all are. He writes that angels would weep to see this goodly force for freedom, after so many years of labor, struck down with one decisive blow. This would render all previous efforts moot. I have been trying to avoid that decisive defeat this whole war. I would rather minor defeats and retreats. I prefer the opportunity to fight another day, rather than to gamble it all and lose. The long approach has seemed best. The enemy plays it hoping we will give up. We play it hoping they will. At least we are on our home soil. I am writing Mr. Lee, as I have others, that I am fully persuaded the measures I am adopting at the present will give a more effectual relief to his State and this Nation. I am still advertising an attack on New York to divert the enemy from the south. In due time, my plans will be seen in execution. My wisdom or folly will be disclosed. We will need a naval superiority at one quarter or the other.

The Savage sloop of war of sixteen guns passed our post here at Dobbs Ferry. We were unable to oppose them. Colonel Sheldon was able to trouble three or four of their river vessels with four eighteen-pounders before they arrived at Tarrytown. The enemy was still able to capture one thousand rations of bread from one of our vessels.

Wednesday, July 18, 1781 — Dobbs Ferry, New York

Count de Rochambeau and I were able to pass the North river with the escort of one hundred and fifty men from the Jersey troops. We reconnoitered the enemy posts and encampments. An intimidating consideration is the enemy might take both of us captive. I cannot imagine what that would do to our cause. I shudder to think of it. I may need to communicate to Congress that if such an event occurs, they must necessarily let command fall to Greene on our end. The war must be prosecuted to its rightful conclusion. No such thing as a checkmate exists in this war. Capturing a commander should never end the war. This Nation's future is not based on the health or service of one man, but upon the American people alone. This is what distinguishes us from the enemy.

Thursday, July 19, 1781 — Dobbs Ferry, New York

The enemy shipping passed by our post at Dobbs Ferry. Our artillery on the Jersey side hit the masts and riggings of several of their vessels doing great damage and killing several of their men. They have now left the navigation of this river free for us once more.

Saturday, July 21, 1781 — Dobbs Ferry, New York

I have ordered about five thousand men to be ready to march at eight o'clock in the morning for the purpose of reconnoitering the enemy's posts at Kingsbridge and to cut off Delancey's corps.

At the time appointed, we marched four columns on different roads. General Parsons with the Connecticut troops and twenty-five of Sheldon's horses formed the right column with two field pieces on the North river road. The other two divisions of the army under General Lincoln and General Howe, along with the corps of Sappers and Miners with four field pieces, formed the next column. They marched on Sawmill river road. The right column consisted of the French troops with two field pieces and two twelve-pounders. General Waterbury with the mi-litia and State troops from Connecticut were to march on the East Chester road and be joined at that place by Colonel Sheldon's cavalry. Sheldon's infantry was to join Lauzun for the purpose of scouring Morrisania. They were to be covered by Colonel Scammell's light brigade. At Valentine's Hill, the left column of the American troops and the right of the French formed their junction. By mistake, the left of the French also met here instead of their intended spot of Williams' Bridge. The whole army then arrived at Kingsbridge about daylight. Lauzun and Waterbury proceeded to scout the Necks of Morrisania. The refugees of Delancey fled and by stealth got over to the Islands to the enemy's shipping which lay in the East river.

Sunday, July 22, 1781 — Dobbs Ferry, New York

The enemy did not appear to have even the least intelligence of our movements or know where we were until we were upon them. In our subsequent reconnoitering, it appears Fort Charles has small redoubts. To erect a battery thereon will be essential. I believe we could cross under Tippets Hill for a partisan stroke. Forts Tryon, Knyphausen, and Laurel Hill are formidable.

Congress has chosen Mr. Thomas McKean to be their new President of Congress. I am writing to congratulate him. I look forward to his support. I am in hopes he will increase communication to me. I feel in the dark ofttimes and am forced to make decisions with partial information. Providence has dealt bountifully with us. If we fail, the fault will be our own. God has given us all that we need for liberty, peace, and independence. We must commit ourselves to the effort.

I am writing Mr. Samuel Huntington who has been replaced by Mr. McKean. Huntington is returning home to Connecticut. Having been engaged in our needs from that position, he has a better idea of the complications we face. I am encouraging him to use that knowledge and his influence to impress upon his State this army's need for men and supplies.

Count de Barras has declined to move his squadron to the Chesapeake at this time. If he would have moved in that direction, I believe the measure would have brought valuable consequence. I must constantly show my appreciation for their efforts and decisions. They are here at our request. Their presence alone affords the enemy to act more cautiously, which buys us time.

Monday, July 30, 1781 — Dobbs Ferry, New York

Count de Barras writes more strongly his reasoning for staying in Newport as opposed to sailing for the Chesapeake. His desire is to await the arrival of Admiral de Grasse. He believes this would prevent the junction of the enemy's force at

New York, making it possible for him to block those in Virginia. He believes the West Indies fleet under de Grasse should arrive by the 10th of next month.

General Greene laments the arrival of reinforcements for the enemy Lord Rawdon. Even with this, I believe in time, Greene will be able to overcome this obstacle. Our efforts in New York seem to have caused Cornwallis to withdraw a considerable part of his troops from Virginia to assist the posts in this quarter. The Marquis will soon be at his side to provide succor. The enemy's operating force may be confined to South Carolina. This will leave the other States an opportunity to provide men and supplies for the southern army.

I am giving Greene a hint of our next operation (a hint which I have given the Marquis too) by requesting that he communicate with me at the earliest the most minute information of the present situation of the State of South Carolina — its strength, operative force, resources that can support this army, and places where we might be able to collect stores. I also want him to give me an assessment of the enemy's strength in that neighborhood. I am hoping he will infer a plan is under consideration to evacuate this quarter and make a major stroke in his sector.

Wednesday, August 1, 1781 — Dobbs Ferry, New York

General Schuyler sends good news that one hundred new vessels have been constructed in Albany for transport of our men. I am convinced more than ever that our move must be southward as the States have not provided the men for an attack on New York. We have the heavy ordinances we need. The stores from the Eastward have arrived.

Thursday, August 2, 1781 — Dobbs Ferry, New York

With the enemy reinforcing New York, I am attempting desperately to obtain the remaining number of boats we need to move our men. With de Grasse and the French providing naval superiority, the blow on the enemy to the south is practicable. I am writing Mr. Morris to ascertain the number of tons of shipping that can be procured in Philadelphia, Baltimore, and at the Chesapeake between this moment and the 20th. We need a few deep-waisted sloops and schooners proper to carry horses. The number of double-decked vessels of two hundred tons and upward should not exceed thirty. That the vessels on the move to this place be concealed is imperative so the enemy may not catch a glimpse of our plan and arrange to defeat it.

To see so many avenues working to make this next campaign successful is good. The States must do their part. I am writing New Hampshire President, Meshech Weare, to prod him for more men. At this late period, this army is little stronger than when we first moved out of quarters. I am informing every governor of our embarrassing situation. I had promised our allies our force would be considerable by this time. The requisition of Congress and the promises made by the States gave me reason to assure them. Instead, not more than half of what was requested has joined this army. We called for six thousand, two hundred to be with us by the 15th of last month. Only one hundred and seventy-six have come. Such a showing will give no small degree of triumph to our enemies. How can it not have a pernicious influence upon our friends? It would be a tragedy for the world to see this country's lack of energy toward securing its own freedom. At times, it would seem our allies want it more than we. Are our State governments content to have all this end with just an idle parade? I know our men would not be satisfied with this after all they have suffered. I continually encourage our allies with the hope this Nation will respond. Everything is falling to our favor. We just have to generate the resolve to grab freedom. The executives of the States must, with a degree of vigor, exercise the powers with which they have been vested. They must rise to enforce the laws lately passed.

As for me, I will act in faith that all will be tended to. I will request constant updates as I make my preparations. A cook cannot know what to prepare until he knows the ingredients available. I am hoping for an offensive dish as opposed to the tired-old defensive recipe. I cannot fathom the French so ready for action to leave our shores without a single attempt to remove the British. I will not countenance such a prospect. Even with the few men I have, we will act in concert with Greene, Rochambeau, and the French fleet to purchase our freedom or die trying. Our men deserve that.

Saturday, August 4, 1781 — Dobbs Ferry, New York

Fresh representations have come from the western frontiers. They are fearful of attacks on their homes and families. I had called for the militia to respond, but they report that few have answered. They request that I dissipate my small force for local defenses. This cannot be done. I am sending General Lincoln to the counties of Berkshire and Hampshire to enquire into the causes of these delays. He is to hasten the militia. I will suffer Cortlandt's Regiment to remain in that quarter until the militia comes in, but that time will be short. I refuse to be content to spend another inactive and injurious campaign at this critical moment.

Tuesday, August 7, 1781 — Dobbs Ferry, New York

I am urging Governor Greene of Rhode Island to keep the militia of his State in Newport. They are to give support to that post and to guard the shipping in the harbor. The enemy may enterprise to do something when Admiral Sir Rodney comes with the British fleet. He is expected in New York to junction with the troops from Virginia. Their intentions are uncertain at the present. That the enemy is focusing on New York for a potential attack from this army does give me comfort. Surprise and diversion are our greatest advantages. Both seem to be in our favor at this moment.

Wednesday, August 8, 1781 — Dobbs Ferry, New York

The American and British commissioners of prisoners have proposed a full exchange of Lieutenant-Brigadier Burgoyne and all the remaining officers of the convention for the remainder of our officers in this quarter and those taken lately southward. I do not believe I have liberty to accede to their proposal without the consent of Congress. Besides, I believe the British still owe the United States money for the subsistence of their troops. The court of Versailles has already directed the exchange of Burgoyne for the Honorable Mr. Laurens. I cannot help but think of Arnold. I wonder how much sleep he misses worrying a defeat might lead to his capture. He knows very well that if he is captured by this army, there will be no prisoner exchange for him. The gallows await his neck. How often does he look at the British serving under him and wonder how many of them would gladly hand him over to us for the right amount of money? If he should suffer a string of losses, will not the British leadership question if he has been working as a double-agent and kill him themselves? Arnold has placed himself in a sensitive position if I conceive it correctly. That is good. This man who betrayed all that is right and good should have no rest.

Back to the British, they are wanting an exchange of their officers for citizens of this Nation they have captured who have not been active in our military affairs. I have not joined in the game of capturing private citizens. I am going to warn the enemy that Loyalists are scattered throughout this country. I could secure any number of them if they wish to play that game.

The light company of the second York Regiment has joined this army under the command of Lieutenant-Colonel Alexander Hamilton and Major Fish. I am placing them under the orders of Colonel Scammell as part of his light troops.

Friday, August 10, 1781 — Dobbs Ferry, New York

Though it has taken longer than I expected, the invalids have arrived at West Point from Philadelphia and Boston. I am moving the first York regiment and Hazen's regiment to this place.

Saturday, August 11, 1781 — Dobbs Ferry, New York

A fleet of twenty sails has arrived at New York harbor with Hessian recruits from Europe to reinforce the enemy.

Help is also arriving from our allies. The Concorde frigate has arrived in Newport from de Grasse. We are expecting twenty-five to twenty-nine sail of the line and a considerable body of land force at Chesapeake any day. I am writing the Marquis to be looking for them in that quarter. Knowing the enemy may see them and retreat, I am directing the Marquis to cut off their path through North Carolina. If General Wayne has not left that area, I am asking that he be retained until we know more of what the enemy will do upon the French arrival. If General Wayne is already on the march to South Carolina, he should not be halted. I trust in Providence. Whatever movements that occur with or without my knowledge,

God is working it for our good. I need the Marquis and his men to do their best to conceal the expected arrival of Count de Grasse. If the enemy is not apprised of it, they will stay on board their transports in the Bay. This will be the luckiest circumstance in the world. He will need to open communications with the Count upon his arrival. Marquis can concert measures with him for making the best use of our joint forces. I am concerting plans too. I should be disposing myself and this army there soon.

Tuesday, August 14, 1781 — Dobbs Ferry, New York

Count de Barras sent a dispatch I received this morning. All things seem certain of de Grasse's arrival. As reported, he has with him twenty-five to twenty-nine sail, along with upwards of three thousand, two hundred land troops. They are due on the 3rd instant at the Chesapeake Bay. The Count is anxious we will have everything ready to commence operations the moment he arrives. I am exerting every effort. My sites are moving on the American army to the Head of Elk to be transported to Virginia.

Wednesday, August 15, 1781 — Dobbs Ferry, New York

The enemy made an attempt to capture General Schuyler. He was able to escape to his bedchamber where his arms were. He was successful in holding off the attack. The townspeople came at the sound of firing. The enemy escaped carrying off two of his men. I am grateful Schuyler was saved. I know many efforts are made to capture key officers. All of us must be on alert. I must order Cortlandt's regiment from Albany to join this army. I am asking General Clinton to leave a few men who are least capable of service to provide further guard for General Schuyler at that post.

Thursday, August 16, 1781 — Dobbs Ferry, New York

The Marquis writes Lord Cornwallis has taken possession of the towns of York and Gloucester. He has moved his army from Portsmouth and is fortifying these posts.

Friday, August 17, 1781 — Dobbs Ferry, New York

I am writing the Count de Grasse to ensure he is aware of our options and where we are turning our attention. We have given up New York, especially with the Hessian soldiers now there to reinforce that post. In response, we have moved the entire French army and a large detachment of the American army to the Chesapeake to meet the French fleet there. If the enemy employs the greater part of their force in Virginia, we ought to attack the enemy with our entire force. If the enemy leaves only a detachment in Virginia, we should reduce that enemy detachment and either move on Charleston or New York. If Charleston is not reduced, the enemy will have a strong position to regain the States of South Carolina and Georgia, along with valuable resources to supply their men. From Charleston, they will also have command of nearly four hundred miles of coast to restrain or block off trade. This would force the States to relinquish their hopes for liberty. If the British completely withdraw from Virginia, we should return to the enterprise upon New York.

I am sending General Duportail, commander of the corps of engineers, to give de Grasse a better idea on how to deal with Charleston should that avenue fall to us. Duportail was the engineer there during the last siege. He was also imprisoned there by the British for a considerable time. This gave him the opportunity for full observations. Duportail is fully acquainted with this army and our affairs in this quarter.

I am asking de Grasse to send all his frigates and transports up the Elk river at the head of the Chesapeake Bay for the conveyance of the French and American troops that have gone down to the bay.

I am writing Mr. Morris, our Superintendent of Finance, to deliver three hundred barrels of flour and as many salt-meat barrels as possible to the Head of Elk. We have no idea how many men will be drawn together there or what time they will be employed. He needs to work expeditiously. I am reemphasizing again that as many vessels as possible be procured in Baltimore and the upper parts of the bay be secured for our use. I am asking the quartermaster-general also to gather all small craft in the Delaware to transport troops from Trenton to Christiana. Further, we need at least one month pay in specie for our troops so that they will have no reason to distress.

Sunday, August 19, 1781 — Dobbs Ferry, New York

After a time of prayer, I feel a surge of excitement. The message this morning was "The Battle is the Lord's." How appropriate for this season!

As if conducting some musical with many instruments, I feel I am directing an orchestra, unfamiliar with each other. My task is to have them play a beautiful piece to overcome the noise we have heard so long on this continent. Though we are moving southward, I cannot leave the northern part of this country unprotected. Just as we have sought to divert the enemy, I know they may seek the same. If they believe an attack on New York is eminent, they may seek to take the first move to blunt it. I am leaving under General Heath's command two regiments of New Hampshire, ten of Massachusetts, five of the Connecticut's infantry, Sheldon's legion, a third regiment of artillery, State troops, and a corps of invalids. He must keep West Point secure as well as the posts in the Highlands. He is to dispossess his troops as circumstances require. I am beseeching him to keep the whole of the army together without many detachments. He should only send out corps to reconnoiter or to bring some harassment to the enemy. His rule of conduct is to be defensive unless a certain opportunity to strike a blow upon the enemy presents itself that has a reasonable chance of success. I wish him to keep the enemy in-check and to prevent their detaching to reinforce their southern army. He is to keep a large supply of salted provisions, have the fortifications perfected, and store up ample magazines of wood and forage against the approaching winter. The main of this army must move. I do not want to worry about what I leave behind.

We need horses. Without them, our march will be slow and disagreeable. Not only do we need to procure fresh horses; we must also better manage the ones we have. The detachments of this army are composed of the light infantry under Scammell, several light companies from New York and Connecticut, the remainder of the Jersey line, two regiments of New York, Hazen's regiment, and the regiment of Rhode Island. Lamb's regiment of artillery with cannon and other ordinances for the field and siege are in-tow.

I am throwing Hazen's regiment over at Dobbs Ferry with the Jersey troops to march between Springfield and Chatham. They can cover the French battery to veil our real movement and create apprehensions on Staten Island. I am mounting thirty boats on carriages with troops to give the appearance we are about to attack in that quarter. We are sending out dispatches to be purposely discovered so the enemy will be misled into thinking our intentions are on New York. I have ordered a siege camp be built on Staten Island. Workers are patching roads from Jersey to the Island. Huge ovens are being built in that area as if they will be needed to feed thousands of soldiers.

Monday, August 20, 1781 — King's Ferry, New York

I have marched American troops to King's Ferry. They have begun immediately to cross. My prayer is that the British are busy preparing for an attack on New York. They know we have the French fleet in port with more on the way. The enemy must expect a significant fight. They will get one. My hope is just that it will not be where they expect. Currently, even our own men are guessing.

Tuesday, August 21, 1781 — King's Ferry, New York

Count de Rochambeau has had a hard march. I am hoping their troubles will decrease as he proceeds. Our men arrived at the Ferry yesterday. We began to pass the river at ten o'clock.

We are now on the west side of the Hudson as of sunrise this day. I am hoping the French can cross with the same facility. I hope to meet Rochambeau by eight o'clock tomorrow. I gain a sense of satisfaction in how easily our men move under the most difficult of circumstances. This is a young army compared to our enemy and our allies. Yet, these men endure hardship better than any other. How I love being called with them — American.

I am writing the Marquis of our progress southward. I am also requesting that he do what he can to procure any watercraft in that country and send them to the Head of Elk by the 8th of September. This will facilitate the embarkation of the troops who will be there.

Mr. Morris and Mr. Peters are recommending the reduction of this army and its officers. I will candidly write my disagreement. The enemy has not reduced theirs. In fact, they rely on a confidence that success will come to them by our lack of exertions rather than by their military prowess. Such a reduction was attempted in 1777. The consequences were unfavorable. I know their concern is economy, but militia costs more than a standing army. Besides, does a price limit they are willing to set for freedom really exist? I will fight this because the outcome of this war is dependent upon it.

The enemy's brutality to our men on their prison ships is rising to greater severities. They are overcrowded on those ships. Men who die there are left in the prisons to distress those who survive. I am demanding that our commissary-general of prisoners be allowed on board these ships to see if the complaints are valid. If they are, the enemy needs to make different arrangements. We are powerless to force it except to reciprocate which is averse to all that is decent.

Count de Barras has taken a resolution to join de Grasse's fleet in the Chesapeake. He stated he would depart Newport on the 21st instant, today. Things are falling into place Providentially. I expect our march will arrive at the Head of Elk by the 8th of September.

Thursday, August 23, 1781 — West Point, New York

Rochambeau and I visited West Point today. I am delighted at how things are progressing.

Saturday, August 25, 1781 — King's Ferry, New York

The French army has been transported with its baggage and stores across the Hudson.

The American troops march in two columns. General Lincoln leads the light infantry and the first New York regiment pursuing the route by Paramus toward Springfield. Colonel Lamb with his regiment of artillery, baggage, and stores proceed to Chatham by way of Pompton and the two bridges. The legion of Laiuzun and the regiments of Bourbon and Deux-Ponts march from Parsippany.

Monday, August 27, 1781 — Chatham, New Jersey

Accounts brought by several vessels leave little doubt that de Grasse is near the Chesapeake. We must waste no time in preparing for our transportation from Trenton to Christian, and from the Head of Elk down to the Chesapeake. I have written Mr. Morris and Colonel Miles to gather all proper kinds of craft that can be found in Philadelphia and the creeks above and below it. Along with vessels from Baltimore, these are to come up to the Elk and assist us. The deposits of flour and salt must be delivered as soon as possible to the Head of Elk.

Tuesday, August 28, 1781 — Chatham, New Jersey

The American columns and the first division of the French army have arrived at their assigned destinations.

Wednesday, August 29, 1781 — Chatham, New Jersey

The second division of the French army has joined the first. The whole has halted. We have not heard of de Grasse's arrival and wish to remain here to prevent discovery by the enemy.

Thursday, August 30, 1781 — Chatham, New Jersey

I am marching some of our men to Sandy Hook to facilitate the entrance of the French fleet there to conceal our real object from the British.

Meanwhile, the entirety of the army was put in motion in three columns. The left consists of the light infantry, the first New York regiment, and the regiment of Rhode Island. The middle column consists of the Parke stores and baggage, Lamb's regiment of artillery, and Hazen's corps of sappers and miners. The right consists of the whole French army, baggage, and stores.

I have set out for Philadelphia to arrange for vessels of transportation.

Friday, August 31, 1781 — Philadelphia, Pennsylvania

I was unable to find adequate vessels for the purpose of transporting both troops and stores. Rochambeau and I have concluded it would be best for the troops to march by land to the Head of Elk. Only the second New York regiment would sail with the baggage in the batteaux.

Count de Rochambeau and his officers were received by the city with shouts and acclamation. They were treated like princes, and rightly so.

Sunday, September 2, 1781 — Philadelphia, Pennsylvania

The Marquis has written to inform me of the number of his regular force, along with militia he has called. With this and the French and American army on the march, I flatter myself we will not experience a want of men. General Knox is bringing heavy cannon, stores, and ammunition. He will be on hand to handle any need.

This turns my concern to our supplies. We have already suffered a lack of provisions. I have no idea how we will continue to be engaged in service without the necessary supplies. I have written the governors of the neighboring States on numerous occasions and will again — to provide for the needs of this army. I do wish the fifteen hundred barrels of salted provisions would have been ready before Count de Barras sailed. We will not gain any more articles of clothing, but we do have a full supply of shoes.

I am distressed beyond measure to know what has become of Count de Grasse's fleet. Added to that, I have heard nothing from the fleet of Count de Barras since they sailed from Rhode Island. I am determined still to persist as if all will work out in due time.

Wednesday, September 5, 1781 — Chester, Pennsylvania

I cannot contain myself. General Gist's letter found me. The Count de Grasse and his fleet have arrived at the Chesapeake with twenty-eight sail and three thousand men! They have made junction with Lafayette. I am overwhelmed. The

French army has reached Philadelphia. I rode back to inform Count de Rochambeau. When I got close, I took off my hat and waved it with joy to get his attention. I may have embarrassed myself. I was so elated that I literally hugged this man in a grip so tight, the French army seemed surprised. I pray they know what freedom means to this Nation. I pray they will grasp how long I have waited for a chance to secure our liberty. This means everything to us. I have risked my life for this, my estate of Mount Vernon, and even my family. This is what freedom means to me. I think before the French, they did not see a Commander-in-Chief in that moment, but simply a man who wants to live under my own vine and enjoy the domestic pleasures of life as I see fit. The war is not over, but we now have the means to make it so.

I am heading to the Head of Elk for the debarkation of supplies and men. I have written to gentlemen of influence to exert themselves in gathering every kind of vessel possible to answer our purpose. We are sending one thousand American troops and the grenadiers and chasseurs of the Bourbonne brigade with Lauzun's legion to be the first to embark. The remaining troops will continue their march toward Baltimore. They can proceed from there by land or by water.

I am asking the army in Virginia to gather materials for the siege. I am soon to head for the camp of the Marquis.

Thursday, September 6, 1781 — Head of Elk, Maryland

I am writing Count de Grasse to express this Nation's gratitude at his arrival. This is a happy event especially for me. We have two thousand men falling down the Chesapeake to form junction with Count de St. Simon and the Marquis to block Cornwallis in at the York river and prevent his escape by land.

Friday, September 7, 1781 — Head of Elk, Maryland

Everything has hitherto succeeded agreeably to my wishes. The want of sufficient vessels for the transport of our men could not be avoided. We will have enough to transport heavy cannon, necessary stores, and one thousand men each of the American and French armies. The rest of us will march as soon as possible to the theater of action.

Saturday, September 8, 1781 — Mount Vernon, Virginia

No better day to arrive at my home after a long time away than on the Sabbath. I am reminded to give thanks. I have and will continue. I have longed for home for six years. Every waking moment, I have wanted to be here. I never wanted to leave this place. The cause of our Nation begged me to sacrifice my wants for something higher. I have a peace that all is going to work out. I now have a taste today of why I have been engaged in this battle. The one thing that grieves me is that I have lost six years in this house, six years on these fields, and six years of fellowship with my wife, family, and friends. I have missed many events in six years. I pray that history will record, more than that Heaven will note, the sacrifices I have undertaken to see our Nation and its children independent and free. I have been able to sit by my fireside. I have been able to look down at the Potomac. This is a grandiose place. I often call it something less than that. Compared to many, it is small, but it is my home.

Monday, September 10, 1781 — Mount Vernon, Virginia

It has been my pleasure to host Rochambeau here as he has just arrived. I was delighted to show him my estate. So much has changed. I know my way around, but the landmarks, the trees, the roads, the fields have all changed. I long to get this war over. I may never leave this place again if I can ever get back to it.

Wednesday, September 12, 1781 — Mount Vernon, Virginia

We rode out today for Williamsburg. It was a sad parting. I told Mrs. Washington that I hope to be back soon. As we rode, I could not help but look back time-and-time again. I was embarrassed for others to see me. I let them ride ahead and pretended to attend to some fence issue. I have hoped to replace fences with some sort of a natural barrier. Maybe I can work on this when I return. Even so, riding behind the men, I kept looking back. As Mount Vernon faded in the distance, I felt a sadness, a want to return. To hand the war over to Greene and the Marquis and company would be so easy. But what kind of man places his hand on the plow and then looks back? The Lord says such a man is not worthy to be His servant. With that last impulse of conviction, I set myself not to look back, more determined than ever to get back.

Friday, September 14, 1781 — Williamsburg, Virginia

More familiar ground today as I arrive at the place where we once transacted government and business so long ago. My friend Mr. Wythe has opened his home on the Palace Green for my usage. His place is a beautiful brick home with a working town farm. The back of his home is my favorite place with a vegetable garden and a flower garden. There is also a shady brush arbor where I can spend time in the cool of the day. There is no time for that currently, we are preparing for our move on Cornwallis.

Saturday, September 15, 1781 — Williamsburg, Virginia

Good news has come to this place. Pleasing intelligence informs me Count de Grasse had put out to sea on the 5th in pursuit of the British fleet. He was successful in driving them from the coast. He has now returned to his former station at Cape Henry. He took two of their frigates and effected a junction with Count de Barras. I will have our troops proceed from the Head of Elk to the bay. I am writing de Grasse to congratulate him.

I am distressed our supplies are on too precarious a footing. We must take every measure possible to provide for these men.

I am writing General Lincoln to come with his troops to the College Landing on the James river. I have sent forward Count Fersen to hurry on his troops with all possible dispatch.

I am hoping the Count de Grasse can send transports to hasten the movement of our troops into position. Rochambeau and I would like an audience with him when he is able. We will need a fast-sailing cutter to receive us on board his ship.

No sooner did I write this, I have been informed that de Grasse anticipated our wish. He has provided transports up the bay for us.

I am directing Major St. Clair to forward immediately all recruits furnished by Pennsylvania. They are not to wait with some excuse that they need more of one article or another. The State should give them what they need. Whether they lack or not, they are to move forward. Our army has labored under lack of every necessity, yet our men serve valiantly. St. Clair needs to hurry them on to the Chesapeake embarking from Baltimore. They will debark in the James river, probably at College Landing.

Monday, September 17, 1781 — Ville de Paris

Rochambeau, Chevalier Chastellux, General Knox, General Duportail, and I set sail on the Queen Charlotte this morning. We have arrived on board de Grasse's ship the Ville de Paris. We settled most points for this engagement except for obtaining an assurance that he will send ships above York. I was gratified to find the French admiral disposed to give us all assistance within his power.

Saturday, September 22, 1781 — Williamsburg, Virginia

The 3rd Maryland regiment has arrived.

Intelligence informs us that the enemy Admiral Digby has landed in New York with reinforcements of six ships in the line. I am informing de Grasse of this immediately.

Sunday, September 23, 1781 — Williamsburg, Virginia

I attended worship services at the Church next to Mr. Wythe's home. It is called the Bruton Parish Church, an Anglican Church. The Reverend John Bracken has had sympathies for American freedom from before the start of the war. He has taken every effort to separate this parish from England and from the Church of England. As a result, I gladly maintain my pew in this Church. His sermons are based on Scripture as is the cause for these United States. To have a man who would stand for what is right even when it costs him members and money is refreshing.

Admiral de Barras has joined Count de Grasse with the squadron and transports from Rhode Island. They have sent some frigates to Baltimore to bring across the remainder of the French army.

Nothing is better than walking through Williamsburg — the streets, the shops, and the taverns. I did so today. I checked on the tenement house that Mrs. Washington inherited, and we managed for a number of years. To see so many familiar, friendly faces at the Market Place was great. I do not wish to live in a town, but if I did, Williamsburg would be the place. The town leaders have been able to maintain a very peaceful way of life. Though it was the seat of Virginia government for many years, it has maintained an air of the country. Sadly, at this instant, life has been interrupted for this community. The British have blocked trade. The war has brought hardships in this town and many others. The General Assembly and the governor have moved from here, slowing its prospects. Many have approached me expressing their longing for the war to end so they can return to normal. All I can tell them is that I am doing all I can to achieve their wishes.

Tuesday, September 25, 1781 — Williamsburg, Virginia

I feel as though I have been punched in the stomach. I informed de Grasse of Admiral Digby's arrival in New York. I did not expect the French response. The Count now believes the British fleet is on equal footing with the French fleet. He believes that where they sit in the Chesapeake makes them vulnerable. He plans to leave a few ships in the bay that currently blockade the James river, but sail the remainder out to sea with the hope of encountering the enemy on more favorable seas. He writes that he cannot sacrifice the troops under his command, that he may be unable to return to the Chesapeake at all. De Grasse inquires how I intend to proceed without the French fleet.

Oh Lord, what will I do? We need that naval superiority. If de Grasse moves out, then Cornwallis is no longer blocked. He will then have access to supplies and reinforcements from the bay. I am just sick.

I must write de Grasse immediately. There is no more certain a military operation than the one before us. We have the decisive superiority of strength. The surrender of this British garrison may prove the end of this war. This will benefit us both. This army has done all it could to get here with every expense sacrificed.

If we do not strike now, I do not believe this army can remain together. We have no supplies. If we pull away from this one encounter, the enemy will be indefatigable in strengthening their important maritime position. I believe in the naval talents of the French. I believe the size of Rigby's fleet is exaggerated and may be altogether a finesse. The British seldom enter conflict where the forces are of equal footing. This is why this war has lasted so long. Other than them waiting on our self-defeat, they have lacked the adequate superiority which they require to attack. Even a momentary absence of the French fleet will expose us to the loss of this garrison. It will allow Cornwallis to evacuate or worse. I am writing him now.

The letter of pleading has been sent. I have ridden out to the countryside outside of the city. The stars are out. The animals graze. There is no fear anywhere but within me. I am trembling. I am not one to cry, but I cannot help but want to weep bitterly. How close we are to victory. How close I am to being able to live and stay at Mount Vernon. Author of all, would You allow us to be this close and then lose? Have I done something wrong? Are my men in some rebellion against You of which I am unaware? I am praying this night. I cannot sleep. On my knees I cry out, Lord! The Psalmist put it best in the blessed chapter eighty-eight, "O Lord God of my salvation, I have cried day and night before Thee: Let my prayer come before Thee: incline Thine ear unto my cry. For my soul is full of troubles: and my life draweth nigh unto the grave. I am counted with them that go down into the pit: I am as a man that hath no strength." Please Lord, Please. Over and over on my knees I am praying. I get up, walk a few steps, and I fall on my face again. What will we do Lord? What will we do? Please Lord. Please. Hear my prayer. Answer my call. How can I go on?

Wednesday, September 26, 1781 — Williamsburg, Virginia

I am praying and fasting. I returned to the Church next to Mr. Wythe's. I caught Reverend Bracken as he was leaving. I asked him to pray with me over an unspoken request. I wanted to tell him everything, but I felt that would be unwise. It did not matter; he could tell by my countenance that much is wrong. He dared not to push the issue. Where two or more agree on anything in prayer according to His Will, the Lord said He would do it. I pray He will.

To conduct business when all may be lost is difficult. I cannot let our men know. We must proceed as if all is a go. I have run into a few French officers today. We do not speak of de Grasse's letter, but I cannot help but think they know. They look at me with pity, or so I think. My own officer family is excited at the prospects ahead. My fear is they have passed us by. So, I pray silently even more.

Thursday, September 27, 1781 — Williamsburg, Virginia

I must begin this entry with another passage from the Psalmist as recorded in chapter one hundred and sixteen, "I love the Lord, because He hath heard my voice and my supplications. Because He hath inclined his ear unto me, therefore will I call upon Him as long as I live. The sorrows of death compassed me, and the pains of hell gat hold upon me: I found trouble and sorrow. Then called I upon the name of the Lord; O Lord, I beseech Thee, deliver my soul. Gracious is the Lord, and righteous; yea, our God is merciful. The Lord preserveth the simple: I was brought low, and He helped me. Return unto thy rest, O my soul; for the Lord hath dealt bountifully with thee. For Thou hast delivered my soul from death, mine eyes from tears, and my feet from falling. I will walk before the Lord in the land of the living."

No better expression of my gratitude exists than what is recorded in the Holy Scriptures. Providence has heard my cry. He has answered my petition. Count de Grasse has written to follow through with our initial plan. He is going to leave a large part of his fleet anchored in York river. Four or five vessels will be stationed up and down the James river. He has asked that we erect a battery on Point Comfort so he can place cannons and mortars. I am so relieved. Today is a day of Thanksgiving. My family of officers here have no idea how close we came to losing this effort. As a result, they cannot comprehend why I feel so emboldened. Joy overflows. The Lord heard my prayer.

Count de Grasse has offered six-to-eight hundred of his men. He asks that I request no more. I will oblige with gratitude. He is going to help us. Praise the Lord oh my soul! Tomorrow we begin what I pray is the end.

Friday, September 28, 1781 — Camp near York, Virginia

I have debarked all troops with their baggage. We have marched and encamped in front of the city. We are having difficulty obtaining the horses and wagons sufficient to move our artillery and the necessary entrenching tools.

The French moved to the left to Murford's Bridge where they joined the militia. Rochambeau encountered some opposition. In response, he commanded some field-artillery toward them under the direction of Baron Viomenil. After giving a few shots, the enemy retired.

I am familiar with this part of the country. Having relatives in this area, I have visited here many times from childhood onward. As we rode in, the trees formed a canopy over our march. I had forgotten the distinct beauty of this area. It was almost as if we were walking under a vaulted cathedral for some Divine encounter. That is my prayer.

To look upon this delightful town where our friends and family have built their lives and now see the British have confiscated their peace and property grieves me. This is what they have done from the very beginning of this conflict. They intend to do it more if we do not put a stop to it.

We have dug in for the night. I have made a pallet under a beautiful tree overlooking the port below. Sleep may be difficult. I am anxious to move this thing forward. I wonder what recourse Lord Cornwallis is considering. He has had almost two months to prepare for such an event. The town is surrounded by a ditch and thick parapet. The batteries are lined with fascines.

Brigadier General Thomas Nelson who also is the governor of this State is laying just down the hill with his militia. To witness Virginia turn out so heartily is good.

Saturday, September 29, 1781 — Camp near York, Virginia

I moved the American troops to the right. We are encamped on the east side of Bever Dam creek. A few scattered shots came from a small work at Moore's Mill and a battery on the left of Pigeon Quarter. Our riflemen responded, trading fire with the enemy's Yagers. We are about cannon shot from the enemy's position. We are working on our plan of approach. Our hope is to secure a semicircle around them for attack, trapping them against the bay. The French have control of the water behind them. I have warned our officers over-and-over, leave a route of escape. I need to discover if Cornwallis has secured one for himself. I hope not.

Sunday, September 30, 1781 — Camp near York, Virginia

The enemy has abandoned their exterior works and the position they had taken outside the town. They retired to the interior works of defense in the course of the night. We now possess those outer works and are in near advance of their line. We have made the works to our left very serviceable. The heavy artillery and stores are being brought up. We are beginning two additional works on the right of Pigeon Hill near the ravine of Moore's Mill. When this is completed, we will commence fire.

Monday, October 1, 1781 — Camp near York, Virginia

The investment of the enemy is fully completed. We are drawn very near their lines. The one thing still at their disposal is the water communication above the town on the York river. Unless this is cut off, Cornwallis will have an outlet for his retreat. With a leading wind, he can move to West Point unmolested. I am requesting Count de Grasse to push a ship or two above the town to answer many valuable purposes. The main fleet is disposed in Lynnhaven Bay. Twenty-five miles beyond that, the enemy remains master of navigation. They are intercepting supplies, but they dare not get any closer to the French fleet.

We have left some men at the posts in Williamsburg and near the magazines to our rear. These will also keep the enemy from marching reinforcements to our left flank.

Saturday, October 6, 1781 — Camp near York, Virginia

As of early this morning, despite the rain, the trenches are in such a forwardness to cover the men from enemy fire. The work was executed in such a manner of secrecy and dispatch, I believe the enemy has been ignorant of the labor until the light of this morning. Our losses have been extremely inconsiderable. I had the privilege to grab a pickax and join the men in the digging. A unity was present between the rank-and-file, a feeling this may be the battle we have sought the entirety of the war.

The repairs on the enemy's works upon Pigeon Hill continue. We are constructing a new intermediate redoubt to give security to our forces as they make their approach. Fascines and gabions are being assiduously constructed.

Our heavy cannon, mortars, and stores are being transported from Trebell's Landing to this spot.

Our progress was slowed at first due to the heat and our lack of wagons and teams. That problem has been remedied. We will commence opening trenches.

General Greene has gained an important victory at Eutaw Springs, South Carolina. He was able to win a long hard victory over Lord Rawdon's replacement, Lieutenant-Colonel Stewart. Greene and his men inflicted heavy casualties on the enemy. We are all influenced by the same motive — love of our country, love for the cause in which we have embarked.

Sunday, October 7, 1781 — Camp near York, Virginia

The men are working on the first parallel. They are erecting batteries in advance of it.

Monday, October 8, 1781 — Camp near York, Virginia

We completed our parallel and finished the redoubts in them. We are establishing our batteries at the present.

Tuesday, October 9, 1781 — Camp near York, Virginia

At three o'clock p.m., I was honored by our men to issue Sir Cornwallis his first salutation. I lit the initial cannon shot at the enemy. A furious discharge of cannon and mortars followed.

The French opened a battery to our extreme left with four sixteen-pounders and six mortars and howitzers.

To our right at five o'clock p.m., the American battery of six eighteen-pounders and six twenty-four pounders along with two mortars and two howitzers began to play upon the enemy. All brought about good effects. Report is that they did great damage to the town. One particular shot directed at the enemy's embrasures injured them a great deal.

The enemy has withdrawn their pieces and moved back.

Wednesday, October 10, 1781 — Camp near York, Virginia

We began our second parallel within about three hundred yards of the enemy lines under the direction of Baron Steuben this morning. Their courage is great as they are being fired upon from two British redoubts against the York river.

All night the men worked. They were able to get it well-advanced to cover the men in the morning. Just one of our men was killed, three or four were wounded. Dr. Craik, my friend whom I have known since the French and Indian War, has set up our field hospital along with Dr. Thatcher near the Marquis's camp. These men are devoted to this cause. Our injured are in good hands.

Two French batteries, five eighteen and twenty-four pounders, six mortars and howitzers opened. Two more American batteries with one eighteen-pounder and two mortars began firing. Our fire was so excessively heavy that the enemy

Johnny Teague

withdrew their cannon from their embrasures. They have now placed them behind the merlins. The more we hit them, the farther the enemy moves back. With each retreat, our men work like beavers digging trenches and parallels where the enemy has vacated. General Knox works wonders keeping up. He has artillery firing from the first parallel, while moving other pieces forward as segments of the second parallel are being prepared.

We have fifty-two guns battering the enemy with a ceaseless roar. The enemy's response, their bombshells are meeting ours in the air. The effect of these shells is dreadful. They hit, whirl, and explode mangling men. I am grateful the enemy is on the receiving end of the vast majority.

The time is late afternoon. They scarcely have fired a shot in the last few hours. Ours continue to pound. The city is being destroyed. We can see spectators watching. Some are scurrying to help others find cover. To have to cannon our own town is heartbreaking, but the enemy is there. What else can we do?

The women who have followed this army are bringing meat and bread to the back of the line. Their help is indispensable. Such daring support allows the men to stay at the work.

This evening, the Charon frigate of forty-four guns was set on fire by a hot shot from the French battery. It was entirely destroyed. One deserter reported that our shells, which were thrown into the town, did much mischief in the course of the day.

Thursday, October 11, 1781 — Camp near York, Virginia

Two of the enemy's transports were hit by hot shot and burnt. They have moved their vessels as far over to the Gloucester shore as possible.

The second parallel is being worked on each night. It is stretching far in length. Looking back at the first parallel, it is encouraging to see the noose tightening on the enemy. However, the tighter the noose, the greater the cost. We have seven hundred and fifty men doing the work. Others are wandering up to watch out of curiosity. I have told these that if they are not working on the trenches and wish to gaze, they should do so on the enemy side of the trenches. I think they got my point.

Friday, October 12, 1781 — Camp near York, Virginia

I expect Lord Cornwallis to make some vigorous exertion this night or soon thereafter.

I cannot but acknowledge our obligations to Count de Rochambeau and the Marquis de St. Simon who commands the troops from the West Indies. The experience of these two men in the business before us is of great advantage in this present operation. I am delighted also that great harmony is present between these two armies. The French have said they wish to move out this month before winter hits. I feel the clock running. I pray we can get this done in short order.

I received a letter today from the Spanish government. They are willing to assist us against the common enemy. At the present, we are too engaged at Yorktown. I have no idea what circumstances will follow a successful venture here. I am asking them to continue to divert the enemy by pushing their arms against east Florida.

Saturday, October 13, 1781 — Camp at York, Virginia

The fire of the enemy cannon and royals this night became brisk. Their rebuttal was more injurious than it had been. Several of our men have been killed. Many were wounded in the trenches. Two redoubts on the left of the enemy line are raining down havoc on our progress. Our works were not retarded by it in the smallest degree because our men brave the fire even at great danger and loss. I am ordering a focused fire on these two. They must be neutralized.

At one point today, I was standing in one of the siege trenches about two hundred yards from the enemy studying their fortifications. The chaplain and a few engineers were with me. A cannonball exploded nearby. We could feel the concussion of the explosion. It scattered dirt all over us. The chaplain ran up to me with the widest eyes I have ever seen. I looked at him. Unable to blink, he took his hat off to show me how close that one ball got to us. I simply told him he ought to take that hat home and show his family. I told him while he was at it, rejoice that the Lord we pray to is watching over us as faithfully here as He does in our homes. The chaplain nodded with a smile. He quoted the verse, "Fear not for I am with thee." We both smiled in acknowledgment. This is what keeps me standing.

Our batteries were begun during the night. They should be a good deal advanced by morning. I am rotating our divisions on the siege lines every third day. We need them in prime condition for whatever it takes to finish this engagement.

Sunday, October 14, 1781 — Camp near York, Virginia

The fire from the enemy is so heavy that I dare think we can finish our works. The second parallel is near completion but has stalled. The engineers deemed the redoubts on the left of the enemy's line sufficiently injured by our shot. An assault on them is now practicable.

I am sending the American light infantry against these two redoubts. The right will be attacked by four hundred Americans under the command of the Marquis. The left will be attacked by the detachment of four hundred French grenadiers and chasseurs commanded by Baron Viomenil.

At about six o'clock this evening, both redoubts were carried. Our men were able to smash over the abatis and storm the parapets under heavy fire. Our men took the right redoubt, killed many and took seventeen prisoners. The Marquis writes that Colonel Alexander Hamilton led the advanced corps and performed gallantly as expected due his many talents. The French killed eighteen of the enemy and took forty-two prisoners in their attack to the left.

I have the pleasure to record that the attacks on the enemy redoubts were a complete success. Our soldiers advanced under fire without returning shot and effected by bayonet only. The bravery of our men is emulous. I am awestruck these men with unloaded muskets ran through a quarter mile of field into enemy fire. Engineers raced in front of them to remove the abatis so the soldiers behind could enter. Many engineers lost their lives. The soldiers then stormed the redoubts with bayonet. Four nations fighting in those two trenches — French, American, German, and British. Why did our men do it? Was it for a pension? Was it for a seat of honor? Was it because they were forced? No. These men love freedom. They want it so badly that they risk their lives to have it. How precious liberty truly is!

Monday, October 15, 1781 — Camp near York, Virginia

We have been busily employed getting the batteries in the second parallel completed. The men are also fixing new ones contiguous to the redoubts which were taken last night. Two howitzers were placed in each of the captured redoubts. Knox has overseen the repositioning of fifty-eight cannon. From these works, we should enfilade the enemy's whole line.

Our fire was opened upon the enemy at five o'clock this afternoon.

I have no idea what strategy Cornwallis wishes to employ. He has his back against the wall. For the first time, he is fighting from a defensive position with no means of escape. I am praying for his surrender, but I expect a vigorous exertion. Our men cannot become complacent. This thing is not over.

Tuesday, October 16, 1781 — Camp near York, Virginia

Just as I expected, at four o'clock this morning, the enemy made a sortie upon our second parallel. This is the biggest push by the enemy. This day may decide the war. The sound is deafening. I must go up.

The British fire is pouring heavily upon our position. Our men are warning me to get back, but I cannot. I will not. I love freedom as much as they. I will never let them be exposed while I remain safely back. We have come too far. I must see what is going on and direct accordingly.

My aide, Colonel David Cobb, has asked me to step a little back. I told him that he can step back if he is fearful. I am where I want to be. We must fight. Push forward. Heaven is our shield.

The enemy has spiked four French pieces of artillery and two of ours. The American guards are advancing on them regardless. How I love these men.

The British are on retreat from this sector. The spikes have been removed.

The British are making their sally upon that part of the parallel guarded by the French troops.

The French have pushed the enemy back. All is calm for the moment. The American losses — twenty-three killed, sixty-five wounded. The French losses — fifty-two killed, one hundred and thirty-four wounded. The enemy lost many more than that. I have seen firsthand what Rochambeau has stated concerning his grenadiers, "They charge like lions even if it costs them one-third of their men." America's debt to the French grows. For many, their life's journeys have ended here on the field of Yorktown. Why? Not for their freedom, but for ours.

At four o'clock this afternoon, the French have opened two batteries with two twenty-four pounders and four sixteen-pounders. Three pieces from our American guard battery are opened. The others are not ready.

Wednesday, October 17, 1781 — Camp near York, Virginia

Speaking of Heaven being our shield, the Marquis de Choisy has just sent an interesting report. Last night, Cornwallis and the British attempted to escape the siege of Yorktown. This is something I have done on numerous occasions for our survival. I am not surprised he made the attempt. He attacked Choisy's men, the French marines, and Virginia militia in the dark of night at Gloucester. The belief is as many as sixteen large boats were sent to ferry the British across the York river to safety. In the early morning hours, some of Cornwallis men broke through, but when they reached the river, a violent storm hit and washed every one of their boats down river. They were stranded. Cornwallis was able to get his men back to their fortifications of Yorktown this morning. Providence continues His Favor upon us.

The time is very early in the morning; now we will begin our fire from all redoubts.

From my vantage point, all I see are our bombs, howitzer shot, and cannon-balls raining down on them. Our movements have a purpose. For the first time, it is as though we are the true aggressors with every advantage. This is not some Hessian group at Trenton. This is the pride of their army. They are being domi-nated.

For the noise, I do not know what time, but at some point, this morning, the enemy has quit firing altogether.

The time is ten o'clock in the morning. Lord Cornwallis has beat a parley and sent a letter for me to consider. It reads, "I propose a cessation of hostilities for twenty-four hours, and that two officers may be appointed by each side, to meet at Mr. Moore's house, to settle terms for the surrender of the posts of York and Gloucester."

This is what we have been looking for. You should see the smile on the weary faces of our men. For all the suffering, for all the retreating, for all the doing without while the enemy danced and had balls in our meeting houses, this mo-ment is the sweetest we have seen. I am reminding them that this is a cessation request. I am hopeful for an enemy surrender. It could be a delay tactic, though I cannot see any chance for them to continue. I have responded that I must have Cornwallis's proposal in writing. I will only agree to a cessation for two hours.

I received his terms. Most of them are unacceptable. He is surrendering Yorktown and Gloucester. He wishes that all British and German troops be allowed to return to Europe. I will not accept this. They are prisoners of war. They are to be held on this continent for the time being. I will expand the cessation for the night and send my counter terms. Commissioners then can meet to digest them at the Moore House tomorrow. I am sending Lieutenant Colonel John Laurens and Second Colonel Viscount de Noailles to speak for us.

I am writing Count de Grasse to participate in the formation of terms. To welcome him on American shores and embrace him upon this occasion will be a pleasure. If he cannot for naval reasons, I am requesting he send one of his officers.

Thursday, October 18, 1781 — The Moore House, near York, Virginia

I wrote out our terms for the surrender of Yorktown and Gloucester. All his men are prisoners of war. Their arms and stores are to be handed over to this army. Only their officers may keep their small arms. Their shipping in the area is to be delivered to an officer of the French navy. They must surrender to the same terms they demanded of our army at Charleston.

The British commissioners are protracting the meeting, haggling over terms which we will not accept. An extension of the truce has been made for nine in the morning.

The time is midnight. The British have agreed to full surrender per our terms.

Friday, October 19, 1781 — Headquarters near York, Virginia

The treaty has been written. I have sent it to Cornwallis with the requirement that it be signed by eleven o'clock. Rochambeau and de Barras have signed. The British officers will be permitted to return to Europe or to any British-held American post on parole. Land troops will be considered prisoners of the United States. Naval troops are to be considered prisoners of the French. British soldiers will be kept in Virginia, Maryland, or Pennsylvania. They will be allowed the same provisions as are available to American soldiers.

I have ridden out to Augustine Moore's house now that the commissioners are gone. This is a beautiful two-story wood-framed house with a little porch jutting from the front door. Beautiful trees surround the house. The smell and breeze from the York river just in front are intoxicating. I have sent my Life Guards to the road to wait. I told them I needed time alone. They have been with me for the duration of the war. They appreciate my need for solitude. I can hardly ever kneel in prayer without hearing the rustle of one of them nearby keeping watch over me.

I have sat down on the porch and pulled out a piece of paper. No gun fire, no cannon, no barking orders, no confusion, and no commotion is present. All is quiet. Just me on this porch with the river sitting out past the front lawn. The water has such a peaceful influence on me, much like the Potomac in front of Mount Vernon. I believe this was the battle we have looked for since 1775. I entered this thing with hope. I continued to spur on Congress and my men. I am almost afraid to think that perhaps today, victory is within our grasp. British ships are still on the seas. Cornwallis is still held up in his position. Clinton still holds New York. Even with that being as it may, today is a defining day. Maybe we just had our Divine Encounter.

I am overjoyed to report that a definitive capitulation has been agreed to and signed by Cornwallis and Thomas Symonds. The reduction of the British army under Lord Cornwallis has been effected. At one o'clock, the two enemy redoubts in Gloucester are to be delivered to our men — one to a detachment of French, one to a detachment of Americans.

The garrison at Gloucester is to march out at three o'clock with shouldered arms and drums beating a British or German march. The enemy's cavalry is to ride out with their swords drawn, their colors cased. General de Choisy will direct at a post of his choosing, the enemy to ground their arms and return to their encampment.

The main of the British army is to march out at two o'clock here to formally surrender and ground their arms. Our army has lined up early. With our men standing side-by-side, the Americans on one side, the French on the other, we stretch almost a mile long. Citizens and spectators are crowding behind our men. Jubilation ensues. We wait.

The enemy is an hour late, but I have received word they are marching toward us. I hear the beat of their drums. The beat is slow as is their march. They are in their red coats; the Hessians are in their blue and green. Ours and the French lines have straightened and separated again to allow the enemy to march between. The French are on the west side in their stately uniforms. On the east side are my men. I have never felt prouder. At this moment, I realize what this army was able to do by Providence's Hand. Our men are poorly dressed for a fighting force. This United States army is in dirty clothes, ragged from wear, holes apparent, and many barefoot. Not one of our soldiers is dressed alike unless rags are considered the uniform of this Nation. We appear poor. Our weapons are various. We are men of all ages and many colors. It is as if our side of the line does not fit in with the French, British, and Hessian armies. We are the exception to the rule of a Nation. You could say this Nation is exceptional. We do not have the breeding, the education, nor the refinement. We only have one thing in common — a longing to be free, to set our own course, and to worship freely the One who has given us life and, yes, this victory.

Cornwallis has chosen not to attend. He claims some ailment. He has sent out his deputy, Brigadier-General O'Hara. With all the disrespect toward our men at Charleston, one would think he would be man enough to be as gracious in defeat as he was so ingracious in victory. All I can write is that he is consistent — ingracious to the end. He did not expect to lose this battle. I will accept his absence. The ritual continues.

O'Hara rode up to offer his sword to Rochambeau. That made sense, the British could accept more readily to be defeated by an international army than this ragtag one. Rochambeau refused it. He told them I am the commanding general of the allied forces. He then turned to me. I did not accept it. I am the commanding officer. The only sword I would accept was the one offered by Cornwallis. If he would not do us the respect to be here, then I would not return any respect to receive it from a lesser officer. I directed him to General Lincoln. It was General Lincoln and his men who were defeated at Charleston having been outnumbered. It was Lincoln and his men denied an honorable surrender. It was only fitting Lincoln be the one to accept the British's surrender. And Lincoln did. He accepted it with a smile and then handed it back. With that, the British grounded their arms in disgust, smashing them to the ground. The Germans were at least a little more gentlemanly laying theirs down neatly. They have surrendered twenty-seven flags and colors.

With the ceremony over, I heard the tune the British fife-and-drum played but did not recognize it. I was later told their song was "The World Turned Up-side Down." I suppose that is the case. I would rather say that it is turned right-side-up.

I invited Cornwallis to dine with our officers this evening. He declined due to health reasons. I guess he is still sick at his stomach. I wonder what Benedict Arnold is feeling right now? I would love to be a fly on the wall of his tent when he hears Cornwallis has surrendered. Maybe for once, he realizes he made the wrong choice. I do not doubt the opportunist in him fashions what his future would have been had he stayed with United States forces. Sadly, that traitor made his choice. Had Judas lived to see the Resurrection, I imagine he would have lamented with the same regret. My yearning still is to capture Arnold. He must pay for the lives he has taken and the lives he has exposed.

Our countrymen in these parts and beyond are rejoicing. They are dancing. They are laughing. They are weeping with joy.

Saturday, October 20, 1781 — Headquarters near York, Virginia

My morning orders of the day are no different from the others I have given over the last six years. This one though has a meaning that everyone can grasp and accede to without reservation. I am earnestly calling all troops not on duty to attend divine service with a serious deportment and gratitude of heart. We should give thanks to Providence for His merciful and gracious interpositions on our behalf. America stands for one reason — God. That was clearly seen in yesterday's surrender ceremony. No other way can describe the existence of this army, much less our victory had His Hand not been actively engaged. I am sharing with our men how the storm on the night of the 16th kept the enemy from escaping our clutches.

I do believe the victory of the past few days is a harbinger of what lies ahead, a conclusion in our favor. As for my part, I can honestly say the sacrifices and sufferings have been worth it. Every trial, every betrayal, every coup, every broken promise, and every misfortune is swallowed up with what has transpired as of yesterday. We cannot let up when freedom and liberty are so close at-hand. We must press on to the rightful conclusion. Nothing would be worse than to have this advantage and to somehow let it slip away due to our premature satisfaction.

An enemy still resides in New York. Enemy ships are still on the seas. I guess there will always be an enemy to freedom somewhere. So, we move out. I hope to retire to Mount Vernon someday soon. Retirement comes inevitably to everyone at some point. So, it will for me. I just hope others will take their turn in the fight for our faith, our families, and our freedom. With our eyes on Providence and our lives submitted to His Will, Heaven will always be our shield. I just pray our Nation never takes its victories as some attestation to our own goodness and efforts, ignoring the One who has brought us every one. The day we forget God will be the day our shield is removed. What then can become of our Nation? History testifies to the consequence.

HISTRIA
BOOKS

Addison & Highsmith

Other fine works of fiction available from Addison & Highsmith Publishers:

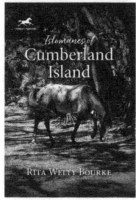

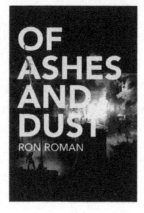

For these and many other great books visit
HistriaBooks.com